THE DEVASTATING COST OF WAR
THE PERILOUS PRICE OF DESIRE

For dashing young Union soldiers like Jimmy and Tom Chase and Richard Schuyler, the Civil War was a clarion call to arms, to defend their honor, fortunes, and country against the Southern rebels.

For daredevil reporter Cort Adams, it was a challenge that could not be denied, a chance to pit his wits against the enemy—until the risks became far too deadly; an opportunity to flirt with the lonely beauties whose men had gone off to battle—until he lost himself to the charms of a woman who could never be his.

For a young, independent New York woman like Miranda Chase, it was a time of fear, freedom, and testing. Fear for those who were fighting; freedom to assert herself in the masculine world of business; and a testing of her courage and spirit as she was forced to choose between loyalty to a hollow marriage and a few brief moments of ecstasy in another man's arms.

Here, from the first roar of the guns to the final resounding victory, is the tempestuous saga of a nation divided against itself—and of a courageous woman fighting to save her family's fortune and her own happiness from the ravages of a war that was destroying her whole world.

WHEN THE MUSIC CHANGED
"A WINNER . . . VIVID, EXCITING . . .
A POWERFUL LOVE STORY!"
—*Baton Rouge Sun*

SIGNET Bestsellers You'll Want to Read

- [ ] **I, JUDAS** by Taylor Caldwell and Jess Stearn.
  (#E9636—$2.75)
- [ ] **THE RAGING WINDS OF HEAVEN** by June Shiplett.
  (#E9439—$2.50)
- [ ] **BALLET!** by Tom Murphy. (#E8112—$2.25)
- [ ] **THE LADY SERENA** by Jeanne Duval. (#E8163—$2.25)*
- [ ] **LOVING STRANGERS** by Jack Mayfield. (#J8216—$1.95)*
- [ ] **TWO DOCTORS AND A GIRL** by Elizabeth Seifert.
  (#W8118—$1.50)
- [ ] **ROGUE'S MISTRESS** by Constance Gluyas. (#E9914—$2.95)
- [ ] **SAVAGE EDEN** by Constance Gluyas. (#E9285—$2.50)
- [ ] **WOMAN OF FURY** by Constance Gluyas. (#E8075—$2.25)*
- [ ] **TWINS** by Bari Wood and Jack Geasland. (#E9886—$3.50)
- [ ] **CLARENCE DARROW FOR THE DEFENSE** by Irving Stone.
  (#E8489—$2.95)
- [ ] **THE GREEK TREASURE** by Irving Stone. (#E8782—$2.50)
- [ ] **THE AGONY AND THE DEFENSE** by Irving Stone.
  (#E9284—$3.50)

*Price slightly higher in Canada

Buy them at your local bookstore or use this convenient coupon for ordering.

THE NEW AMERICAN LIBRARY, INC.,
P.O. Box 999, Bergenfield, New Jersey 07621

Please send me the SIGNET BOOKS I have checked above. I am enclosing
$_____(please add $1.00 to this order to cover postage and handling).
Send check or money order—no cash or C.O.D.'s. Prices and numbers are
subject to change without notice.

Name _____

Address _____

City _____ State _____ Zip Code _____

Allow 4-6 weeks for delivery.
This offer is subject to withdrawal without notice.

When the Music Changed

by

Marie R. Reno

A SIGNET BOOK
NEW AMERICAN LIBRARY
TIMES MIRROR

SIGNET, SIGNET CLASSICS, MENTOR, PLUME, MERIDIAN AND NAL
BOOKS are published by The New American Library, Inc.,
1633 Broadway, New York, New York 10019

First Signet Printing, August, 1981

1 2 3 4 5 6 7 8 9

PRINTED IN THE UNITED STATES OF AMERICA

PUBLISHER'S NOTE

For My Parents
John Linford and Marie Roth Reno

right after ; " He paused, as if considering whether to go

How your soft opera-music changed, and the drum and fife
    were heard in their stead,
How you led to the war (that shall serve for our prelude,
    songs of soldiers),
How Manhattan drum-taps led.

—WALT WHITMAN

Prologue

It was a small paid advertisement in *The New York Times* of Saturday, February 25, 1860:

> Hon. Abraham Lincoln of Illinois will speak at the Cooper Institute on Monday evening Feb. 27 to the Republicans of New York.

No one met him, this little-known lawyer from the prairie; no one met him that Saturday when his train pulled into the station at Jersey City or when his ferry docked at Cortlandt Street. He had left Springfield three days earlier, had stopped in Chicago overnight and shown a draft of his speech to the editors of the Chicago *Tribune*. Then he had boarded the train and—for the mixed blessing of company—he traveled with a Springfield neighbor and her little boy, all the way to Philadelphia. It was an uncomfortable journey, sitting up in the overheated day coach for two days and nights, sharing a lunch basket, taking on some of the burden of a fretful child, cooped up too long in a noisy, swaying railroad car.

It was a relief, finally, to leave the train and board the ferry in Jersey City for Manhattan.

The city stretched out before him, the skyline punctuated by church spires rising high over the five- and six- and even seven-story buildings of the burgeoning business district. New York, with its population of eight hundred thirteen thousand, was far and away the largest city in the country, dominant in wealth and power and influence. That, indeed, was why he was here.

Two years earlier, when he was running for the Senate against Stephen A. Douglas, his debates with the Little Giant had been widely reported, not only in Illinois but also in the eastern press. Douglas had been returned to the Senate by the gerrymandered Illinois legislature (even though he had trailed by four thousand in the popular vote), but Lincoln had emerged from the campaign with a greatly enhanced reputation. He was still unknown to the general public, but the leaders of opinion had heard of him, and they wanted a closer look.

The Republican party, only six years old and already reaping victories over the badly split Democrats, had no lack of candidates for high office. In fact, New York's own favorite son, Senator William Seward, was the odds-on favorite to be the party's candidate for President in this year's election. With four years as governor and twelve years in the United States Senate, Seward's experience far eclipsed that of the visiting Illinois lawyer, who had once served a single term in Congress and had later been defeated in a try for the Senate. Still, Lincoln had made a name as a good stump speaker, and there was a curiosity about him that could be satisfied only by seeing and hearing him on the lecture platform.

And thus an invitation was dispatched, promising two hundred dollars plus expenses, to address an audience in the Brooklyn church of the Reverend Henry Ward Beecher. Lincoln seized the opportunity, fully aware of its importance. There was, incidentally, the added bonus of being able to combine the speaking trip with a visit to his eldest son, Robert, enrolled as a student in a New England boys' school.

Leaving the ferry, carrying his carpetbag, he made his way to 4 Beekman Street and the office of Henry C. Bowen, owner and publisher of *The Independent*. It was from Bowen that Lincoln learned that the site of his speech had been changed from the church in Brooklyn to Mr. Peter Cooper's new building, which had the largest lecture hall in New York. The Young Men's Central Republican Union was now sponsoring the event—they had placed modest ads in the daily newspapers, and they had recruited the leading editors to occupy seats of honor on the platform the night of the speech. All in all, a promising beginning.

From Bowen's office, it was a short walk across City Hall Park to the Astor House, where Lincoln could, at last, stretch out on a bed and get a good night's sleep. Then there would be time to pull out the blue foolscap and go over the speech once more.

That was how Abraham Lincoln came to New York on Saturday, February 25, 1860.

When the Music Changed

BOOK ONE

Chapter 1

ON THIS LAST Saturday in February 1860, in a hotel one block north of the Astor House, Miranda Chase was having breakfast with her Aunt Sarah and, on specific instructions from her father, trying hard to be polite.

Sarah Chase Waltham had come to New York for her annual family visit—and her annual lecture on family shortcomings, most of them, apparently, concentrated in the startlingly attractive person of her only niece Miranda, just turned sixteen.

"Now, my dear," Sarah began calmly, "I have spoken to your father about your behavior yesterday, and he agreed that I should explain to you once again why you should not have talked back to Judge Daly."

Miranda spread a layer of plum jam on her muffin, affecting great concentration. "Just *listen* to her, Miranda," her father had told her. "She's worried about the way I brought you up, and maybe she is right. Growing up in a hotel *isn't* normal, and perhaps I was selfish to keep you and the boys with me after . . ." His voice had trailed off, and Miranda had impulsively rushed across the room to fling her arms around him. "Just be polite, Miranda." Will Chase coughed to cover the sudden huskiness in his voice. "Your Aunt Sarah is a good woman and she wants to help. Listen to her quietly and don't argue."

Miranda had found these instructions contradictory. If she listened, she would disagree, and if she disagreed, how could she not speak her mind? Her aunt called that talking back, but Miranda called it standing up for your principles. Since the goal was to soothe Aunt Sarah, the best way to handle the situation was to smile sweetly and think about something else.

In Miranda's opinion, the trouble with Judge Daly was all *his* fault. He had met them crossing City Hall Park, had bowed and offered the usual pleasantries. And then he had spied the journal Miranda was carrying and pretended to be horrified.

"*The Liberator?* Why Miranda, what are you doing with that miserable rag?"

"Reading it," she had replied sweetly. "I think Mr. William Lloyd Garrison is a courageous and noble man."

"Filthy abolitionist!" Judge Daly snorted. "Miranda, child, I don't think young girls should be defiled by anything so dangerous and unsuitable."

"I have *Godey's Lady's Book* back at the hotel," Sarah agreed quickly, putting a gentle hand on her niece's arm.

Miranda shrugged off the restraint, unheeding. "Judge Daly, I think you are wrong. On the question of slavery—"

"Miranda!" Aunt Sarah was clearly shocked. "Young ladies *never* tell gentlemen they are wrong. What is to become of you? Judge, I do apologize for her behavior. I can't imagine—"

"Now, Mrs. Waltham, I understand." Judge Daly pulled dignity around him like a mantle. "It's certainly not your fault. It's the modern times we live in. Young girls are so willful these days. But," his unexpected smile was almost lecherous, "when a girl is as pretty as Miranda," he reached out and pinched her cheek, unaware of her total revulsion, "I can forgive her almost anything."

"On the question of slavery," Miranda tried again, but Judge Daly just shook his head, winked at her, bowed to her aunt, and walked on, smiling.

Seething with rage, Miranda glared at his retreating figure.

"Such a kind and forgiving man," Sarah said approvingly.

"Rude and insulting," Miranda muttered under her breath.

"But you really behaved disgracefully, Miranda," Sarah went on, rebuke strong in her voice. "A proper girl does not . . ."

Miranda had heard it all before. She had heard it then, coming back to the hotel, and she was hearing it now, again, this morning over the breakfast table.

"Miranda," her aunt was saying it once more, "a proper girl does not contradict her elders. Are you listening to me?"

4

Miranda nodded, drinking the last of her tea.

"Now you have made a good beginning by not interrupting me once this morning." Sarah beamed at her. "I think that shows a contrite spirit, dear. I know it is hard to sit still and listen to a recital of your failings."

Miranda wondered what she had missed but decided it was just as well she hadn't paid attention.

"And it's no wonder you have had a hard time growing up," Sarah went on, returning to a well-worn theme. "I have told your father over and over again that a hotel is no place to bring up a family. And a hotel right in the middle of New York!"

Miranda stirred restlessly and fought back the familiar urge to contradict her elders.

Sarah went on, oblivious. "When your dear mother died, I offered to take you home with me. You were only five then and such a sweet child. I know your sister did her best, but she was just sixteen herself and—"

"Cordelia was perfect," Miranda said fiercely.

Sarah registered surprise at the interruption but continued as before. "I know she did her best, dear," she reiterated, "and we all admired the way she took over the household, but it was too much—all four of your brothers and you, too. When she died in that terrible fire—"

"I don't want to talk about it."

"No, of course not, dear. It's just that when that happened, you were only nine—"

"I was ten."

"Yes. The point is that you were still very young, and if you had come to me in Litchfield then, you could have grown up with my girls and it would have been easier for you to learn to be a proper young lady."

"I would never have left Papa and the boys."

"Yes, dear, I understand. I'm just explaining that in the long run it would have been better for you if you had grown up in a proper house instead of a hotel in New York. All those strangers about. Politicians lounging in the lobby at all hours of the day and night. Europeans just off the boat, filled with all sorts of queer, foreign notions. It could be very dangerous for a girl."

Sarah shuddered visibly and Miranda, by a great effort, kept silent. She concentrated on refolding her white linen napkin, tucking it with unnatural precision into its silver ring.

5

"When you compare the wholesome childhood you could have had in Litchfield," there was no stopping that relentless voice, "with the temptations of this wicked city, in a noisy hotel where—"

"I *love* it here in this hotel," Miranda finally exploded. "Don't you dare say a word against it. It was Papa's dream, and Mama's, too, and he got the best architect in the country to design it, and I wouldn't live anywhere else if you paid me. And if you try to compare Litchfield to New York—"

She stopped in mid-sentence, aware suddenly of her father standing in the doorway.

"I could hear you all the way up the stairs." Will Chase looked at his daughter reproachfully.

"I tried, Papa. Truly I did. But when she started saying bad things about the Stratford House—"

"Will, I certainly did not. I only said that it wasn't a suitable place to bring up a family. I've told you that and told you that, and the behavior of your daughter only confirms my worst fears. You have let her run free, Will, and that is the worst thing you can do with children, particularly with girls. How is she ever going to learn her place, grow up to be a dutiful wife and mother, submerge her spirit in—"

"I'm not *going* to submerge my spirit. Women have rights that—"

"Will, why do you let her talk such nonsense?"

Will placed a firm hand on Miranda's shoulder, and she looked up at him and sighed.

"I think you should apologize for upsetting your aunt, Miranda. And if you have finished your breakfast," he smiled at her and she nodded quickly, "you may esca— you may withdraw now."

"Yes, Papa." She suppressed the urge to wink at him and turned to her aunt, trying to sound regretful. "I am sorry I upset you, Aunt Sarah. I didn't mean to." And she hadn't meant to. It just happened. She hadn't meant to contradict Judge Daly yesterday, either. But when he was wrong . . .

She closed the door behind her and waited a moment, straining to hear, but her father's voice was so low that she couldn't make out the words. He was soothing her aunt, she supposed. He was very good at that—and he had had a lot of practice.

She allowed herself a smile and shrugged off the morning

unpleasantness, refusing to let it interfere with her shopping expedition.

First, though, she would stop at the front desk to see if anyone interesting had checked in. Imagine wanting to trade the bustling activity of the Stratford House for the dreary life of a parsonage in Litchfield, Connecticut. What a preposterous idea!

Behind closed doors Sarah had finished a litany of complaint, but after her departure Will lingered in the dining room, pulling out his pipe, giving himself up once more to memories of the past.

There was, first and foremost, his dear wife, Mary, always so tender and loving. His heart still turned over when he thought of her. And the fate that cut short that ardent life enraged him to this day. To die in childbirth . . . He blotted out the memory and concentrated on what had followed. He had held the family together, in spite of doubting relatives, and that was a triumph of sorts.

And then came the second tragedy, the fire that took the life of his oldest daughter, Cordelia. When Mary died, Cordelia had been sixteen, the oldest of six children—Cordelia, George, John, Tom, Jim, and little Miranda, only five years old then. He could still remember the child's shock, the wide gray eyes, unblinking, unnerving somehow until she finally broke into tears. But Cordelia had been there, a replica of Mary, old beyond her years, always there when the boys came home from school, always there to be a second mother to Miranda. Until five years later, fire swept away the house, and with Cordelia's death threatened to shatter the family again.

This time Miranda did not cry. She had willed back her emotions, refusing to acknowledge grief, insisting she was too grown-up for childish tears. Her determined spirit had triumphed, and Will had never seen Miranda cry again. She had grown up all fervent and flashing and quick, her enthusiasms bursting forth like so many skyrockets and Roman candles. Not even Will knew that under that sparkling surface she had locked away her deepest emotions and feelings. The two tragedies of her young life had convinced her that love was dangerous and could lead only to heartbreak.

All her youthful ardor and idealism were expended on the burning issues of the day, and it was a continuing frustration that hardly anyone took her seriously, just because she was pretty and sixteen and, worst of all, a girl.

Nevertheless, her commitments were solid, rooted in the past.

From the fire that had swept away her first life, she had salvaged one precious possession, her copy of *Uncle Tom's Cabin*, the last Christmas present from Cordelia. Inscribed in Cordelia's hand, it was a link to the past and an emotional bridge to the future. Miranda had found her first cause.

Will Chase had never bothered with causes, and as the only son in a family with four daughters, he had always been indulged. He had gone to Harvard, he had sailed to Europe for the grand tour—and he had declined to return to Litchfield after he had seen the world.

Boston lured him away. He paused there on his return from abroad, arriving by chance on the October day in 1829 when the elegant new Tremont House opened its doors. An old college friend had secured an extra ticket for the inaugural banquet, and the dollar that it cost Will was an investment that changed his life. It was not that he was impressed by the lavish menu or even by the exalted guests, among them Daniel Webster and Edward Everett. No, he was impressed by the hotel itself.

Will had traveled widely in Europe, staying in all manner of inns and coaching houses and taverns and *pensions* and hotels, none of them particularly comfortable and many of them quite unspeakable. But the new Tremont House was a revelation, so much so that he boldly introduced himself to its architect, Isaiah Rogers, and requested a complete tour of this new palace. And Rogers, at twenty-nine only six years older than this brash young stranger, was amused and flattered. More important, he arranged for the manager to serve as Will's guide the following afternoon.

Will arrived promptly, an eager apprentice, and by the end of the tour he had so ingratiated himself with Mr. Simeon Boyden that he had been hired as a general assistant, whatever that might be, and he had resolved to be proprietor himself one day.

The Tremont House quickly became the showplace of Boston, a handsome building three and a half stories high, built of Quincy granite blocks, with an impressive Doric entrance and four Greek columns. But the real wonders were inside:

the ten high-ceilinged public rooms with marble mosaic floors and the one hundred seventy rooms for guests, including private parlors and bed chambers with all possible conveniences. Every room had a patent lock, and every room was supplied with a bowl and pitcher and free yellow soap. There was running water in the basement for the kitchen, the laundry, the eight bathing rooms, and the eight water closets.

The Tremont House was the first hotel to have gaslight in the public rooms, with whale-oil lamps reserved for the guest rooms. It was the first hotel to have the ingenious annunciator system, so constructed that a guest could press a button in his room which sounded a buzzer in the office and dropped a metal disc indicating the room requiring service.

Off the imposing entrance hall were a separate baggage room and a separate bar, both innovations in hotel design. Another new idea was the reading room, stocked with magazines and a wide range of local and out-of-town newspapers. The room was free to hotel guests and open to visitors on payment of a fee.

The luxury extended to the furnishings—the carpeted floors, the carved walnut tables and chairs, the crystal chandeliers, the brocade hangings. No wonder the hotel cost three hundred thousand dollars. No wonder guests were willing to pay two dollars a day, all meals included.

Will Chase was in his element, and in three years he was indispensable.

And restless. He attributed that restlessness to a desire to move on, to buy into a small hotel somewhere—on his travels he faithfully inspected every hotel in every city—but there was something more basic troubling him: girls.

Will knew all about girls, the good ones and the bad ones, or at least he thought he did. And for a while he had half-heartedly courted a merchant's daughter in Lexington; but even she could see his lack of enthusiasm, and he was actually relieved when she declared her attachment to someone else.

Somewhere, though, there *must* be a girl for him. He lounged behind the reception desk, inventing a dream. She would be pretty, naturally, and well brought up, but open to new ideas and change. It would be an advantage if she had money, of course, because then he would have his hotel that much sooner. But if she were too wealthy, she might be demanding and imperious. Will had seen too many female guests at the Tremont who answered that description. She should have dark hair, he decided, and move with quiet grace . . . just like the girl who was even now coming through the front entrance with the distinguished older man who was obviously her father.

Will sprang to attention, remembering like the born hotelman he was that this was Judge George Leonard Schuyler from New York, here on his second visit. In his letter the judge had said he would be accompanied by his daughter Mary and would be staying three days. He had a speaking engagement at Harvard.

From behind the desk Will watched the girl—slight and sweetly pretty—watched her pause in the middle of the ornate entrance hall and gaze around in wonder. He caught her eye and smiled, and she smiled back, before she remembered that well brought up young ladies don't encourage strange young men.

Greeting Judge Schuyler with all the deference that gentleman expected, greeting his daughter with all the admiration she deserved, Will went out of his way to be helpful and agreeable. He was an alumnus of Harvard himself, he told the judge, and he would be delighted to arrange for transportation, sightseeing, shopping, the concert that night. Will himself was planning to attend the judge's lecture the next evening, he said, and he so looked forward to it.

Judge Schuyler looked at him shrewdly, and his daughter found it necessary to turn around and examine the entrance hall again. Will stood his ground, silently acknowledging all the judge's sudden suspicions. And the judge saw him for exactly what he was: an eager and ingratiating young man, with enough ambition and education to rise in the world. All he needed was an opportunity.

Six months later Mary Arden Schuyler became Mrs. William Augustus Chase.

They lived in Boston at first, and Cordelia and George were born there. But when Isaiah Rogers designed the elegant new Astor House in New York, Will went along with the Boydens, father and son, to become assistant manager.

The Astor House, which opened its doors in 1836, was even more impressive and more luxurious than the Tremont. Built on Broadway facing City Hall Park, it was at first considered to be rather far north of the business district, though the residential area had already expanded farther uptown, beyond Washington Square. Still, the city was growing so fast—two hundred two thousand in 1830, two hundred seventy thousand just five years later—that the Park location would soon be central.

In any event, the Astor House was a success from the start. Larger than the Tremont, it was five stories high, built around a hollow square. The public rooms were unsurpassed in size and luxury, and the modern conveniences for the paying guests were the most up to date imaginable: running water in the rooms, gas lighting throughout, water closets on every floor, and seventeen bathing rooms. Even New Yorkers were dazzled.

Will's hours were long, but his salary had increased, and there was also his wife's income, comfortably covering the expenses of an expanding family. Still, the dream of his own hotel kept receding beyond the horizon.

And then in 1843 three events coincided, giving him his chance—at a price.

His father died and he came into a small inheritance.

A suitable site for a hotel became available—on Broadway just a block north of the Astor House.

And suddenly widowed Judge Schuyler dangled the prospect of investing in the hotel business—if Will and Mary would sell their house and move in with him.

Mary succumbed easily to paternal pressure, but Will feared a loss of independence and refused. Judge Schuyler was not to be dissuaded, however. He was sixty-seven, and his wife's death had shocked him into a sense of his own mortality. And he was lonely. His two sons were dutiful but distant, caught up in expanding the prosperous Schuyler shipping business, leaving most of the ritual family obligations to their wives.

Will continued to hold back, convinced he could secure financial backing elsewhere. In the meantime, he approached Isaiah Rogers, who agreed to design this new hotel, smaller than the Astor House but even more modern. Bathing rooms on every floor. Steam heat in the public room. Hot water in every guest room. A more efficient kitchen. Will fell in love with his dream and was convinced it would be a success—until the expected mortgage money failed to materialize. He suspected that the judge had something to do with that, and he was right.

Mary, torn between husband and father, worked out a compromise that gave Will complete control of the hotel, in spite of minority ownership, conditional only on the move to the Schuyler family home. She sold the idea to her father with her oldest weapon: tears. And she got around Will by persuading him that his stubborn insistence on independence was robbing the children of their future financial security. It was a particularly effective argument because she was pregnant again.

One year after they drew up the papers, the Stratford House opened its doors. Mary had chosen the name, honoring a family legend of a distant connection with Shakespeare. All the relatives were on hand for the gala first-day celebration, and Miranda, eight months old, was already insisting on center stage.

When Judge Schuyler died three years later, he left his sons in full possession of the shipping business, but Mary and Will inherited the family house and the judge's share of the hotel. There was still a mortgage of a hundred thousand dollars, but even so, the Chases were wealthy now in their own right. They had two years to enjoy their riches before the first of the family tragedies.

Will came out of the fog of memory to see Sarah standing in the doorway, prepared for the February cold with bonnet and gloves and mantle.

"Have you seen Miranda, Will? We were to go shopping at Stewart's."

"I thought she said something about ice-skating in the Central Park this afternoon with her brothers."

"I didn't know that. If the girl had only told me—"

"It's all right, Aunt Sarah. I'm here." Miranda rushed in, breathless, then paused by the mirror to adjust her bonnet, its vivid blue ribbons exactly matching the braid on her new cloak.

"What a pretty picture you are, my dear." Sarah was more than willing to kiss and make up. "If you are going skating, though, I was just thinking that I'd like to go with you, to see how much progress they have made on the new park." She was unaware of Miranda's sudden dismay. "But probably this afternoon I'll be tired from shopping. It takes an hour to go all the way uptown, doesn't it?"

"Oh, sometimes even more," Miranda agreed promptly.

"Last week I was on a horsecar that jumped the rails, and we all had to transfer to an omnibus."

"Mercy. Was anyone hurt?"

"No. We ran into a dead mule, that's all. The cartmen hadn't cleared it away yet."

Sarah sniffed in distaste.

"I think it had *just* died," Miranda prostested.

"The streets are a disgrace," Sarah said. "Every time I come they have accumulated another layer of filth. New York is a *very* dirty city."

"Yes, you certainly must prefer Litchfield," Miranda agreed blandly.

Will chose that moment to tap out his pipe, and Miranda refrained from further comment.

"So you ladies are going to Stewart's." Will was always the peacemaker. "You were there only last Saturday, Miranda. What can possibly be new and different?"

"One of the girls at school said they had just brought in another shipment of silks and brocades from France. And you know I have that birthday money."

"Yes, and it's burning a hole in your pocket. All right, Miranda, just see if you can make it last out the week."

She smiled at him, blew him a kiss as he left, and then had a sudden mischievous grin for her aunt. "You should see the dress pattern I'm going to choose, Aunt Sarah." She paused for effect and then smiled at her own reflection in the mirror. "The bodice is cut way down to here." She drew a line across her bosom, indicating a décolletage that made Sarah gasp.

"No, not really." Miranda laughed and spun around to look at her aunt directly. "It's really very modest. I don't want to spend the whole evening wondering if any sudden movement will lead to disaster—with everyone else hoping for the worst. No one ever pays any attention to your conversation *that* way."

Sarah laughed then, too, a trifle unwillingly, not entirely sure that they were sharing the same joke.

Chapter 2

IT WAS AFTER one o'clock when they returned, Miranda bearing most of the accumulation of bundles and boxes and packages. In the lobby two of the men from the baggage room hurried to their assistance, and Miranda smiled her thanks.

The rotunda was churning with traffic, as usual, and Miranda saw three people waiting at the reception desk. Not pausing even to remove her bonnet, she crossed over quickly and joined her brother Tom behind the desk. He acknowledged her presence with a nod and went back to a detailed and patient explanation of a hotel bill to an irritated elderly gentleman whose companion was hard of hearing.

The third person was a stranger, a young man who had followed Miranda's progress across the lobby with great interest and was obviously astonished to see her take a place on the clerk's side of the big reception desk. He was tall and commanding in appearance, with an inbred self-assurance that comes from good looks and good family and old money.

Aunt Sarah had followed Miranda to the desk in a state of shock, but protest died on her lips. She couldn't make a scene right here in the lobby, even if her niece *had* overstepped the rules again. Miranda had already greeted this unknown young man. Sarah paused, then decided to retreat to the family quarters for a reviving cup of tea and, she hoped, a firm talk with Will. What would the girl decide to do next? Serve in the bar?

Miranda watched her aunt's departure with a barely concealed smile and turned her attention to the stranger again. "May I help you?" she repeated, disconcerted by his silence and by his appraising stare.

"Not unless you are Mr. Chase. Mr. Will Chase?" He surveyed her from head to toe and back again, his lingering examination missing nothing. "Mr. Will Chase?" he repeated blandly. "It doesn't seem probable."

"No," she agreed, feeling herself beginning to blush and completely missing the amusement in his eyes. "He isn't here at the moment. Do you wish to reserve a room, sir?"

"One thing at a time. I wish to speak to the proprietor, Mr. Chase. I thought I had made that clear."

"Very clear," she agreed. "And when he returns, I'll tell him you called, Mr. . . ."

"Mr. Adams. When will he be back?"

"I really don't know." The frost of February had entered her voice. "Now, Mr. Adams, if you—"

"Then ask someone and find out. You don't appear to be completely helpless."

"No. And I'm not completely rude, either."

"My dear young lady." He paused for another slow, sweeping inspection that made Miranda turn a deeper shade of pink. "I don't know why you are behind this desk, but it is obvious to me that you don't belong here. You arrived late, burdened with packages, far too grandly dressed, and you are still wearing bonnet and gloves and cloak. If you are, by some peculiar misfortune, suddenly forced to work for a living, you must learn how it is done. I doubt if you will keep *this* job very long."

"Indeed! Mr. Adams, you don't know who I am."

"No. Surely that is not relevant. Now I have asked for Mr. Chase, and I suggest that you find him. Otherwise," he paused for effect, "I'll tell you who you *will* be: A *former* employee of the Stratford House."

"You know Mr. Chase that well?"

"Since childhood."

"I see." Miranda allowed herself a slight smile. "And you could influence him to fire a poor working girl like me? Without a reference?"

"You're wasted behind a hotel desk." He deliberately looked her up and down again. "Cheeky enough, certainly. And pretty, too, though you rather overdo the maidenly blushes.'" He grinned suddenly, and there was calculated mischief in his next words. "Why don't you try out as a waiter-

15

girl in one of the saloons? I understand the tips are very good."

Caught completely by surprise, Miranda glared at him, for once in her life rendered speechless. And then, catching a glimpse of her father striding across the lobby, she choked back her rage and signaled him.

Beside her, her brother Tom, who had finally soothed the departing guest, moved to be helpful.

"Is everything all right, Miranda? Is there anything I can do for you, sir?"

Adams nodded briskly. "Yes. Find me Mr. Chase. Mr. Will Chase."

"Your servant, sir." Will was there, extending his hand, without recognition, and young Mr. Adams shook it vigorously.

"Mr. Adams claims he has known you since childhood," Miranda said, tasting easy triumph.

"Adams?" Will stared at the man and then beamed suddenly. "Bless me, it's Cort. Cort Adams. I didn't recognize you at first. How are you, my boy? And your brother and your dear mother?"

"Fine, sir. All fine." Cort gave Miranda a superior glance. "I stopped in Boston to see them on my way back from Europe. Mother is in excellent health and still a power to be reckoned with in local society. She sent particular greetings to you."

"Thank you, Cort. She's a true lady. I'm sorry I haven't been in touch with her, with the whole family, for so long. It must be ten years since I saw you last . . . at your father's funeral. You were only a boy."

"That's right, sir. It will be eleven years this summer, and I was sixteen."

"Yes, just Cordelia's age. I remember when you were born." Will turned to Tom and Miranda. "His parents were such dear friends in Boston in the old days." He paused, sighing. "But after my wife died, I didn't have much heart . . ." His voice trailed off and Cort nodded, understanding.

There was silence for a moment before Will went on. "So, you are in New York now, Cort. Will you be staying with us long? I hope you gave him a good room, Miranda."

"No, he insisted on waiting for you. The hired girl wasn't good enough for him."

"Hired girl?" Will caught the disdain in her voice.

"This young lady," Cort began stiffly, looking from Miranda to her father, and then realization made him pause. "We had a small misunderstanding," he said, recovering, "but I'm willing to forgive and forget."

"How very noble of you. And just as I was going to ask you about the future for waiter-girls. So they make good tips, you say. Are they permitted to talk back to an arrogant customer? Perhaps tip a bowl of hot soup in his lap?"

"It's not considered good form," Cort responded slowly, as if giving the matter serious thought. "Of course, if your father is the owner and lets you play house there—"

"Mr. Adams, I do not play—"

"I am an old friend of the family, Miranda. You may call me Cort."

"Well, now that you all know each other," Will broke in smoothly, "I'm sure you'll all be friends. What are your plans, Cort? Of course you are my guest here. I hope you can stay with us a long time."

"That's very kind of you, sir, but I wouldn't impose on you that way. And in any case, I'll be here only a week. You see," a touch of arrogance returned, "I have just been engaged as a special correspondent for *The New York Times,* and I will be living in Washington City."

"That's splendid, Cort."

"Yes, I was pleased. Some of my dispatches had appeared in the Boston papers, and I had a letter from Mr. Henry Jarvis Raymond, the publisher himself."

"We know him," Miranda said, unimpressed. "All the important editors and publishers—Mr. Greeley, Mr. Bryant, even Mr. Bennett—they come here frequently, and we know them all."

"The Stratford House is very convenient," Tom Chase spoke up eagerly. "All the newspapers are right across the park."

"I'm glad to know I'll be in good company." Cort smiled at him.

"Usually we don't get the reporters, though." Miranda would not be put off. "Except in the bar, of course. That's because reporters can't afford it here."

Will directed a sharp glance at his daughter, and she subsided—temporarily. "So you'll be with us a week, Cort." Will handed him a pen and indicated the register. "Just a formality."

Under Miranda's watchful eyes, Cort signed in with a flourish: Cortlandt Elliott Adams, Boston and Washington City.

"You took up half the page," Miranda accused him. "It's not as if you're signing the Declaration of Independence."

"No, that's true," Cort said, judiciously. "But it's not a declaration of abject surrender, either. I think we might call a truce, Miranda, and start all over again."

Conscious of her father's presence, Miranda made an effort to be brisk and professional, if not entirely sincere. "Welcome to the Stratford House, Mr. Adams. We do hope that you'll enjoy your stay here."

Chapter 3

THE STRATFORD HOUSE, which was almost as old as Miranda, was in the front rank of New York's smaller hotels. When it opened its doors in the fall of 1844, it shared with the Astor House the prime location in New York, and it was still convenient to Wall Street, City Hall, and Printing House Square. But the city was moving north relentlessly, commerce and industry overflowing into residential areas, the wealthy and the middle classes building their mansions and their brownstones ever farther uptown, forever pursued by shops and stores, hotels and theaters and restaurants.

From a city of two hundred and seventy thousand, when Will Chase had first arrived, New York had tripled in size by 1860. Immigrants, primarily from Ireland and Germany, were flocking through Castle Garden and establishing themselves in the spreading slums of Five Points on the Lower East Side, Klein Deutschland just to the north, and the festering tenements of the dock area.

The Bowery was the main commercial street for these newcomers, and it was lined with shops and saloons, beer gardens and theaters, factories and lofts and pawnshops and restaurants—bustling, crowded, dirty, noisy, colorful, exciting.

If the Bowery was plebeian, Broadway was patrician, and the wealth of the city was on lavish display, spilling over, always expanding farther uptown, to the north. From the Battery, the landscape was dominated by the spire of Trinity Church, rising high over the banking and commercial district, the proud substantial buildings—marble, brick, brownstone—marching up Broadway to City Hall Park. There at the southern point of the green triangle was Barnum's

19

Museum, just opposite St. Paul's Church. In the blocks north of the church were the Astor House and the Stratford House, facing the park and Printing House Square, where the major newspapers of the city were clustered. The brownstone headquarters of the *Times* had opened only two years before, the editorial offices on the upper floors, the newest of Hoe's lightning presses in the basement.

Just beyond City Hall was the major shopping area, beginning with the marble palace of A. T. Stewart. And there was no end of fine stores, shops, charitable institutions, hotels, and churches stretching up Broadway: the New York Hospital, Lord and Taylor's, Brooks Brothers Clothiers, the St. Nicholas Hotel and Prescott House at Spring Street, the Metropolitan Hotel a block farther north at Prince, Tiffany's and Ball, Black and Company for jewelry and fine silver. A little farther north and just off Broadway were the Astor Library and Cooper Union, and then Grace Church and the fashionable residences of Union Park, where Broadway crossed Fourth Avenue at Fourteenth Street.

And still the city spread north, to Gramercy Park, Madison Square, straight up Fifth Avenue. The Fifth Avenue Hotel at Twenty-third Street had opened only the year before, the first hotel to have a "perpendicular railway," the type of safety elevator demonstrated by Mr. Otis himself at the Crystal Palace earlier in the decade. It was, as the hotel brochure described it, for the convenience of those "desirous of sparing their ambulators any trouble."

Farther up Fifth Avenue the population and the buildings thinned out. There was the imposing Croton Reservoir at Forty-second Street (the Crystal Palace, which had been destroyed by fire, had been right behind it), and a block north was the Colored Orphans' Asylum. Up at Forty-ninth Street the foundation had been laid for the new St. Patrick's Cathedral, within sight of the recently relocated Columbia College on Madison Avenue.

And even farther north, starting at Fifty-ninth Street, was the vast park project designed by Olmsted and Vaux, under construction now for three years. It was characteristic of the optimism that pervaded the expanding city that these hundreds of acres so far to the north had been christened the Central Park.

From the time that the first water was piped into the lake, a mania for skating had swept the city. Now on every day from December to March when the ice was in good condition, a signal ball was hoisted on the arsenal building, the city horsecars broke out flags, and skaters converged on the park from all directions.

Even those who had not mastered this newly popular sport could participate, after a fashion, by hiring ice chairs with runners—and an attendant or a willing friend to push them.

Miranda had allowed herself to be pushed once or twice, too, but she much preferred to swoop across the ice under her own considerable power. On this February afternoon, hand in hand with her brother Jim, she set the pace, and they easily passed all the other couples on the ice.

The youngest and quietest of the boys, Jim was used to being bossed around, and, unlike his rebellious sister, he did not fight back. He had retreated into books, finding his niche as the only scholar in the family.

Miranda admired him wholeheartedly for winning all the prizes at school and at college, but she felt no urge to compete on that level, and, indeed, she was counting the days until she would be finished with classes forever. Finished with Miss Benson, the headmistress; the teachers, and the entire female seminary.

Miss Benson was counting the days, too.

Only last week she had called on Will Chase at the Stratford House to deliver an ultimatum: Apology and retraction from Miranda or abrupt and final dismissal.

Baffled by the vehemence of the usually sedate headmistress, Will had asked for particulars. Miranda, she informed him, had drafted a petition—a petition!—and was soliciting signatures from her fellow students! Who had ever heard of such a thing!

The New York legislature was considering a bill to give certain minimum rights to women—allow them to collect their own paychecks, let them sue in court, guarantee to a wife inheritance rights at her husband's death—and Miranda was enthusiastically in favor.

Miss Benson had no interest in the merits of the proposed legislation—she had never heard of it until the petition came to her attention—but she was infuriated by Miranda's actions. Nothing like that had ever happened at her school, and if the news got back to the other parents there would be an uproar. It could be as bad as the scandal seven years earlier when one of the teachers had advocated bloomers and been promptly dismissed for this heresy. The teacher hadn't actually *worn* bloomers, Miss Benson hastened to reassure Mr. Chase, who appeared bemused. She had only given it as her opinion that bloomers might be a practical alternative to crinolines on some occasions. Still, that was a foolish statement to make before impressionable young ladies—one of whom had gone home and told her father, who was properly outraged.

Equating petitions with bloomers, Miss Benson was clearly on the warpath, and it took all of Will's powers of persuasion to soothe her—and to extract the proper penitence from his daughter. The threat of expulsion bothered Miranda very little, but with Aunt Sarah expected in three days, the prospect of endless explanations made her pause. A suitable apology to Miss Benson had put an end to that particular crisis, but Miranda still brooded over the confiscated petition.

"I *know* I was right," Miranda said aloud, and beside her Jim slowed their pace to look at her, uncomprehending.

"Right about what?"

"Oh, well, right about everything, of course. I was just remembering . . . Never mind. There's George, at last." She waved at him across the ice, thinking, as always, that he was the strongest and handsomest of all her good-looking brothers and the one who was the most like Papa.

That was the family consensus, too. George was obviously going to follow in his father's footsteps, and he was already reveling in his responsibilities as assistant manager of the Stratford. Open, affable, easygoing, he nevertheless had a shrewd head for business and the sense to seize his opportunities. Through his Schuyler relatives—in the view of New York society, Schuylers always ranked much higher than Chases—George had been accepted into the crack Seventh Regiment, pride of New York. For this privilege, George, like all recruits, enlisted for seven years, bought his own uniform, paid dues to his company and special assessments for excursions, and showed up for drill once a week.

On this Saturday afternoon, coming straight from the Tompkins Street Armory, George brought with him two of his fellow soldiers. They had all, of course, shed their gray uniforms in favor of more appropriate skating attire, and this was a matter of some regret to Miranda—a regret shared by two of her classmates, Lucy Blaine and Diane Matthews, who appeared as if by magic as soon as George arrived.

When they paired off to resume skating, Miranda found herself, none too happily, with her stiff-necked cousin, Richard Schuyler. It was Richard who had pulled strings to get George into the Seventh Regiment with him, but otherwise Miranda found little in him to commend. She assumed that he disapproved of her—an attitude prevalent in the Schuyler family—and therefore she baited him at every opportunity.

"Your sister refused to sign my petition last week," Miranda challenged him, and he looked at her, surprised. Irene Schuyler was a fellow classmate at Miss Benson's, ordinarily a proper young lady, except on those increasingly rare occasions when she succumbed to Miranda's influence.

"What are you talking about? What petition? I don't know anything about it." From the tone of his voice, he obviously didn't *want* to know, either. Unconsciously, he skated faster.

And so did Miranda. "My petition for women's rights," she began, launching into a speech. "The New York state legislature . . ." It was a detailed explanation that Richard only half heard, though he was conscious that Miranda was working herself into a state of fury with her own vociferous arguments.

"And I say we have a constitutional *right* to petition," her voice rose as she reached the finale, "and it's probably *illegal* for Miss Benson to expel me."

That caught his attention at last. "Oh, Lord, Miranda, don't get yourself thrown out of that school. The family will never—"

"Family? What's that got to do with it?" She skidded to an abrupt stop, and he kept his balance with difficulty. "All you ever worry about is your precious family. Schuylers and Brevoorts and Beekmans."

"And Chases," he reminded her.

"And Chases," she agreed. "But only because you're afraid we'll disgrace you."

He drew himself up to his full height and looked down at her. "Don't be so touchy, little cousin. Eventually, I know, you'll reach the age of discretion." He was teasing her, she knew, but it was the kind of teasing that struck too close to the bone. "Unfortunately, it *does* seem to be taking a very long time."

She glared at him. "I wouldn't wait, if I were you. It might take years. Of course," inspiration seized her, "you could go away until then. To England, perhaps." It was a barbed

23

comment, and meant to be. Her brother John was living in England, embarked on a career with the Schuyler Shipping Company. Miranda regarded his absence as a terrible breach in family solidarity, almost a betrayal of loyalty. Will had been more philosophic and accepting. After all, as he had said on more than one occasion, John is more Schuyler than Chase. Miranda, however, remained unconvinced.

"John is doing very well in England," Richard said calmly, starting to skate again, holding her hand as if nothing had happened. "We heard from him only yesterday, and he had just secured a new contract from a mill in Manchester. Papa is very pleased with him."

"I'm glad that Uncle Paul is happy." The tone of her voice belied her words. "But I wish John would come *home*."

In the cold clear air of Central Park, the winter afternoon passed quickly, and it was after dark when they returned to the hotel—Miranda and her brothers and her cousin Richard and his friend Damon McMasters and two of her classmates from Miss Benson's female seminary.

They burst into the lobby, laughing and red with cold, heading for the library with its roaring fire. Two waiters followed immediately to take orders for food and drink, and a half hour later Cort Adams sauntered in, drawn by a familiar voice raised in anger.

He stood in the doorway unobserved, watching Miranda tick off points to a rigidly controlled young man whose responses were goading her to fury.

"But you aren't being logical, Richard. You admit that slavery is wrong, and you agree it should not be extended, but then you won't *do* anything about it. Now when John Brown was in Kansas—"

"Don't start that again, Miranda. When they finally hanged that old fire-eater two months ago, I thought we'd be rid of him at last. He was a traitor, and that's all there is to it. Don't turn him ino a martyr. You're getting to be as fanatic as old Beecher."

"Well, *he* does things. He sent rifles to Kansas and—"

"Beecher Bibles," Richard scoffed. "A minister of the gospel preaching sedition."

"It's not sedition. It's a moral crusade. When I actually saw what a slave auction was like—"

"You *saw* a slave auction?" Cort could restrain himself no longer.

"She means one of Beecher's Sunday morning melodramas," Richard said impatiently, looking at Miranda for an explanation of this stranger's presence. She performed the introductions hastily, eager to resume the argument, but Richard pulled away, having heard it all before.

"Tell me about this slave auction, Miranda." Cort's amusement showed through, and he made no effort to hide it.

"This is not a laughing matter, Mr. Adams," Miranda said frostily, turning away in impatience.

"I told you to call me Cort." He reached for her hand, and she spun around angrily.

"And please don't touch me."

"Ah, the ice maiden," Cort said. "The ice maiden who blushes. Now, Miranda, I am not going to attack you, I am not going to insult you—"

"No, you've done that already. Waiter-girl!"

"So that pricked you. Strange. I had a brief conversation with your Aunt Sarah a little while ago, and she led me to believe that you enjoyed the give-and-take of free discussion—perhaps even to excess. What a pity she misread you so completely." He was challenging her, and she rose to the bait in spite of herself.

"Here, when you finally meet an old friend of the family," Cort went on, "one who is actually eager to listen to your views on slave auctions and abolition and Henry Ward Beecher, all you can do is turn your back on him."

His voice was serious, and even though she knew there was laughter lurking there, she wavered.

He smiled and seized the moment to lead her to the alcove window seat overlooking the park, across the room from the fireplace that was the mecca for the rest of the party.

"What else did Aunt Sarah have to say?" Miranda was still dubious about this conversation.

"She filled me in on some of the family history, and then she quizzed he thoroughly on my plans and prospects and was quite properly shocked."

"Shocked?"

"Yes. I told her I would only marry an heiress, and that upset her. I don't see why. She is shopping for a husband for her youngest daughter—and, incidentally, for you—and financial considerations are certainly important to *her*."

"But you *have* money. Don't you?"

"What a question for a young lady to ask! Aunt Sarah was

25

right after all." He paused, as if considering whether to go on, then shrugged. "There's no point in misrepresenting the situation. As a matter of fact, Miranda, the panic of 1857 played havoc with the family fortune, and my brother does not quite have the Midas touch of our late lamented father. Oh, there is enough to maintain my mother in the style to which she is accustomed, and I doubt if I will ever go hungry, but on the other hand," he grinned at her suddenly, "I would not choose a bride who blithely buys out Stewart's on a Saturday morning shopping expedition, even if she *is* willing to work behind a hotel reception desk. And with four brothers to split the inheritance . . . Aunt Sarah told me everything, you see." He shook his head. "And so, Miranda, you can rule me out of your future calculations."

"You were never in them."

"Good. That's settled. Now—"

"But if you are so interested in making money, why are you a newspaper reporter?"

"Special correspondent," he corrected her. "But you miss the point, my dear. I'm not interested in *making* money. What a grubby way to spend a life. I'm only interested in *having* money." He took on a mock professorial air, ready to conduct a seminar for a bright if wayward pupil. "Now, there are three ways—three honest or at least nominally honest ways—to be rich. The first and simplest is inheritance. The second is marriage. And the third is work, combined, of course, with luck. The three are not mutually exclusive, by any means. In fact, they frequently build on each other. If I were completely penniless, for instance, I doubt if I would have a rich bride."

"I think you are a heartless monster."

"Not a bit of it. I have frequently heard it said that a girl can fall in love with a rich man just as easily as a poor man. Why shouldn't it work the other way around?"

It was a new idea to Miranda, and she paused to examine it from all sides. "But . . . how could a girl trust you, respect you? Or wouldn't you tell her?"

"I *have* told her. And she respects my honesty."

"You mean you have actually found some poor girl who—"

"No, not a poor girl. A very *rich* girl. You haven't been listening."

"What's the matter with her?"

26

He choked back his laughter. "Miranda, how little respect you have for my charms. There is nothing the matter with Susanne. She is beautiful and cultivated and agreeable and much sought after. Would you like to see her picture?" From an inside pocket Cort extracted a small leather case and opened it with pride.

Miranda examined the photograph showing a serious but undoubtedly attractive young woman, eyes staring straight into the camera, a touch of aristocracy in the high cheekbones, the firm line of the jaw.

Cort peered over her shoulder. "The photographer intimidated her a little, the way he adjusted that iron clamp of an immobilizer. He insisted that she maintain that rigid pose. And she really has the most enchanting smile . . ."

Miranda nodded doubtfully and then looked more closely at the photographer's identification in tiny lettering under the picture. "But this was taken in Paris."

"Yes, five weeks ago. Just before I sailed for home."

"You mean she's French?"

"No, not at all, though she *does* have a delightful accent." He smiled at the recollection. "She was traveling with her parents and sister. I met them all in the south of France. Charming family. The Robillards. Susanne Robillard."

"Yes. Well, I hope you'll all be very happy." Miranda handed back the picture and watched Cort tuck it away carefully. "And you're getting married soon?"

"In the fall, probably. If we are to be living in Washington City, I must find a suitable house."

"I don't see why you want to live there and just be a reporter."

"Special correspondent," he corrected her again. "But you meet such interesting people—senators and congressmen, Cabinet officers, ambassadors, visiting royalty—though in point of fact *they* can be fairly boring. And if you persist in worrying about my finances, Miranda, remember that I'll be in the best possible position to know what is happening, where it is wise to invest and when it is important to pull back. In five years I expect to be able to buy my own newspaper, if I'm still interested in journalism by then. Perhaps I'll go into politics instead."

"You have it all planned out, cold-bloodedly. But it won't happen that way. What will you do if there's a war?"

"I devoutly hope we can avoid that."

"Mr. Seward says we're going to have an 'irrepressible conflict.' "

"An unfortunate phrase, and one that terrifies me."

"But it's true just the same, and the fighting in Kansas was just a beginning." By force of habit Miranda embarked on another speech. "Slavery is wicked, and until we abolish—"

"We can't abolish all evil from the world, Miranda." Cort's interruption was stated mildly and had no effect at all.

"We can try. It's our duty to try. When I saw that slave auction—"

"Yes, you were going to tell me about that. Just last week, was it?"

She was too intent in her zeal to see the gleam of amusement in his eyes. "Three weeks ago. And it was like a real auction—for a little girl. She was only nine years old. Imagine! So far from home and a slave!"

She paused for Cort's reaction, but he merely sighed.

"I'll start from the beginning," she said, warming to her narrative. "When I heard that Mr. Beecher was going to have an auction, I asked Papa and he took me over to the church in Brooklyn to see it. Ordinarily we go to St. Paul's," she tucked in parenthetically. "We're really Episcopalians, not Congregationalists, and our church is just two blocks away, right across from Barnum's Museum."

"A convenient reference point," Cort noted solemnly. "But you went to Brooklyn," he prompted.

"Yes. You take the Fulton Street ferry. Beecher's ferry, they call it on Sunday morning because everybody is going to his church. It's very crowded."

"And so the receipts are good. For the slave auction, I mean."

She looked at him sharply. "Yes, for the slave auction."

"And this slave, this little girl . . . She had light skin, I suppose."

"Why, yes. She did. How did you know? She was such a pretty child. Intelligent, too. Named Pink. Isn't that a strange name?"

"Passing strange. All of it. So you paid your money and saved her from a fate worse than death."

"Yes," Miranda agreed. "That's exactly what we did. It was thrilling! We needed seven hundred dollars, Mr. Beecher said. Pink cost nine hundred dollars, and her grandmother had already contributed two hundred—all she had. Oh, you should have heard Mr. Beecher tell about it! He was wonderful—and so dramatic. I was impressed."

"Yes," Cort said. "I can see that. So Mr. Beecher raised the seven hundred dollars."

"Even more!" Miranda's eyes were shining. "Everybody gave—more than a thousand dollars. Enough to buy Pink her freedom and get her some proper clothes and send her to her grandmother in Washington City. It was wonderful. People cried."

"Very touching, I'm sure." Cort paused. "But was it necessary? If the child was here, in a free state, surrounded by friends, why did you have to send all that money to some slave dealer in the South? Why not just slip her over the border to Canada and not make all this fuss?"

"Why, why . . . I don't know," Miranda floundered. "The slave dealer was owed the money, I think, and someone had to pay."

"So Mr. Beecher obliged with a dramatic show and a little hysteria."

"You're getting it all twisted. What matters is that Pink is *free* now, and she has the papers to prove it. She doesn't have to go to Canada; she can live with her grandmother in Washington. Both of them. *Free.*"

She looked at Cort, still refusing to believe that he wasn't caught up in the drama of her story, but he remained impassive. She shook her head and faced the reality of the situation. "Well, we saved Pink, but slavery goes on. When you think of all the others, forced to submit to . . . It is *evil*, Cort. I don't see how you can deny that."

"I don't deny it. I don't deny it at all. I'm just not sure that a travesty of a slave auction is the way to accomplish anything. It just stirs people up and makes compromise that much more difficult."

It was Miranda's turn to sigh. "There *is* no compromise. Mr. Seward was right: it's an irrepressible conflict."

"Irrepressible conflict," Cort repeated. "What does that mean to you?"

"If he is elected President, there will probably be a war." She perched on the edge of the window seat and looked at him intently, her wide gray eyes innocent. War was a word that conjured up drums and bugles and the gray-clad Seventh Regiment marching down Broadway, off to a quick and easy victory.

29

"And do you want a war, Miranda?"

"I don't *want* it. I just think it's probably going to happen, and it won't be as bad as letting slavery go on and on and on."

"Perhaps." Cort's mood had darkened, and he looked older. "But I have seen a war, Miranda, and I'm not sure that anything is worse than that."

"A war," she echoed, impressed. "Where were you?"

"The Crimea."

"As a soldier?"

"No, as a spectator at first. It was my post-graduate education, you might say. Somehow I had wandered rather far away from the usual itinerary of the Grand Tour. Rather far away," he repeated heavily. "And then later I filed a few dispatches and suddenly I was working for a newspaper."

"So that's how you started," Miranda said. "With a war. Did you see the Charge of the Light Brigade?"

"No, I missed that bit of foolishness. But I saw men dying. I'm not sure if there is ever anything glorious about death on the battlefield—probably not. But I know damn well there is nothing glorious about typhus and cholera and filth and misery, and that is how most soldiers die in a war. It is a form of evil not dreamed of by your preachers, Miranda, and I don't want to see it brought home, here in America."

His outburst surprised her, and she thought that perhaps it surprised him, too. The thoughts of war certainly seemed to arouse him to more passion than did the photograph of the aristocratic Miss Robillard.

He fell silent, withdrawing from her, and Miranda studied him with renewed interest. In the alcove with the gaslight turned low his face was lost in shadow, his dark good looks merging with the gloom. There was something alarming about him, almost frightening, something more than his calculating approach to marriage, his bleak view of war; his very presence triggered an inner warning signal and made her wary.

Miranda stirred uneasily, suddenly uncomfortable with this brooding stranger, so different from the cheerful young people gathered around the blazing fire.

A burst of laughter from across the room broke the tension, and Cort looked up, startled, aware again of where he was, aware of her existence. He forced a smile. "So, you were telling me about what would happen if we elect the admirable Senator Seward the next President of these United States."

"He *is* admirable." She rose to the bait automatically. "Even if he isn't an abolitionist, at least he's anti-slavery. And he's not wishy-washy like President Buchanan."

"That's true enough," Cort agreed. "But Seward is never going to unify the country with all that talk about 'irrepressible conflict.' " He held up a hand to ward off her reaction. "I know you're itching for a war, but there are some of us who are still looking for a way out. With the right man . . ."

"Right man? The Republicans won't run Frémont again, and Douglas and the Democrats are impossible. Who else is there?"

"I'm not sure. Mr. Raymond and I were talking about it this afternoon. He suggested that I go to Cooper Union on Monday to look over that lawyer from Illinois, Abraham Lincoln. I was out of the country two years ago when he was debating Douglas for the Senate, but I understand he made a big impression."

"He lost."

"He lost in the legislature, but he won the popular vote."

"That doesn't count." Miranda dismissed Mr. Lincoln with a wave of her hand.

"You ought to come hear him, Miranda," Cort persisted. "I wouldn't be surprised if he runs with Seward—a balanced ticket, New York and Illinois, Seward and Lincoln. Don't you want to see the next Vice President of the United States?"

She wavered. "If you're inviting me to come with you, I have to ask Papa first."

He shook his head. "I'm sorry, Miranda. I can hardly arrive at my first assignment bringing a pretty girl. Mr. Raymond might think I'm not serious about this job." He saw her disappointment and moved to make amends. "I'm sure I can get you tickets, though. You and your father and any of your brothers . . . Your aunt, perhaps?"

Miranda laughed. "No, she wouldn't be interested. But I'll ask Papa, and maybe Tom. He might go into politics himself, though I know more about it than he does."

Cort raised an eyebrow.

"Well, I do. All Tom does is lounge around the lobby with those Tammany Hall Democrats," she spit out the words, "but *I* read the papers and follow the issues. I've even been to Cooper Union before."

He caught the challenge in her voice and smiled.

"Aren't you going to ask me who was on the program?"

"I think you are going to tell me anyway."

"You're right. I am. It was Lucy Stone."

If she had hoped to stump him, she did not succeed.

"The lady who wouldn't take her husband's name after she got married. Trivial, Miranda. Not in the same class with abolition at all."

"But it's a symbol, you see, of something basic. The whole patriarchal society that—"

Cort held up his hand. "One war at a time. Don't you think you ought to save us all from slavery first?"

"Perhaps. But when there are so many evils in this world . . ."

"And you must battle them all. How very exhausted you are going to be. Abolition, women's rights . . . What else is there? Are you part of the temperance movement, too? Will you ask me to sign the pledge? There I absolutely draw the line. I'll promise never to buy a slave at auction—except from Mr. Beecher—but I cherish my glass of brandy, and—"

"Oh, don't talk nonsense. And of course I'm not asking you or anyone else to sign the pledge. I've seen the hotel books and I know what the bar receipts are. Papa says that's what paid off the mortgage in record time."

Cort laughed, unrestrainedly this time. "There's hope for you, Miranda. That practical streak may save you in spite of yourself." He consulted his pocket watch and stood up to leave. "It's late, and I have kept you from your friends too long." He nodded toward the group by the fireplace and she followed his gaze. One of the girls—it was Lucy Blaine—stared at him with interest, and he deliberately winked at her.

Miranda stood up then, too, reluctantly, wondering where he was going, sensing it would do no good to ask.

He bowed over her hand, all sudden gallantry, and was gone.

"Miranda, *who* was that handsome man?" Lucy's voice was piercing, and Miranda was sure that Cort could hear her all the way to the lobby.

"Not so loud." She found a place on the ottoman near the hearth, and Jim moved over to give her more room. "He's just a newspaper reporter, Lucy, and an old friend of the family, too old to interest you." Lucy was one month younger than Miranda. "Why, he is even older than my brother George."

George reached out to cuff her affectionately and then ducked as she swung back.

Diane Matthews stepped between them and held on to George's arm. She had been looking for an excuse to do that for the past hour.

George smiled, but as unobtrusively as possible he detached himself from her grasp.

Lucy observed this with interest, but she was not to be diverted. "Tell me who that man is, Miranda. He looks just like Edwin Booth, only taller and handsomer. And I've never seen you show this much interest in anyone before," she added shrewdly.

Beside her, Damon McMasters stirred unhappily. He had been in quiet pursuit of Miranda for three months now and had even challenged her to a race today, his second time on ice, just to have another excuse to talk to her. She had beaten him by five yards, and now he'd have to practice and challenge her again. He hated iceskating.

"I was interested in that man, Cort Adams," Miranda said, choosing her words carefully, "because he was willing to sit and talk about important subjects, like politics and abolition. He's not like *some* people I know," she turned her attention to her cousin, "who get up and walk away whenever a girl says something intelligent."

Richard Schuyler gave an exaggerated groan. "I have heard everything you've had to say twenty times over, and I don't want to hear it again. I think it's a pity this Adams is going away. To Washington City, George says. Why, he could have been a whole new audience for you and given the rest of us some peace for a change." A sudden thought struck him, and he grinned at her wickedly. "I have the perfect solution. You can marry him and go to Washington and lecture President Buchanan on how to run the country."

"He's already engaged," Miranda said flatly.

Diane Matthews, still feeling bereft by George's lack of interest, had let her attention wander, but the last few words had penetrated. "I didn't know that," she said, puzzled. "Was it in the papers today?"

"Was what in the papers today?" Miranda had always found Diane mindless and exasperating.

"Why, that President Buchanan was engaged to be married. I think that's wonderful. Every man should be married." She was quite hurt by the sudden laughter that followed this statement, but she allowed herself to be mollified by Damon's gentle explanation.

Miranda breathed a silent prayer of relief. The conversation had shifted away from Cort, and Diane now had a firm grasp on Damon. If Diane would just forget about George and Damon would turn his calflike adoration toward Diane, it would solve two minor but vexing problems.

And then Richard suggested that they all play charades, and Miranda agreed enthusiastically. Richard could be as haughty and rigid and stiff-necked as all her other Schuyler relatives, but there were occasions when he unbent and was even fun to be with; and they were always an unbeatable team in these silly pantomines. She had decided months ago that it was because they were so good together at party games that he ever paid any attention to her at all.

Miranda could be singularly obtuse about people.

Chapter 4

Aт BREAKFAST SUNDAY morning Tom Chase appeared late, showing the aftereffects of the night before. Will looked at him disapprovingly but said nothing, finished his coffee quickly, and departed. Aunt Sarah and the other boys had already come and gone, but Miranda lingered, curious to know what had prompted this fall from grace. Tom's first since New Year's Day.

"What happened?" she asked him eagerly. Tom may not have been the only one of her brothers to sow a few wild oats, but he was the only one who ever told her anything at all—not that he ever revealed as much as she wanted to know.

Tom shook his head, thought better of the action, and stopped abruptly. "I don't know why I got out of bed. Is Cort up yet?"

"Cort?" Miranda looked at him, surprised. "Why do you ask? Was he with you, Tom? Where did you go?"

"Every saloon west of Broadway, I think. I don't know. Ask Cort. He was telling me about some waiter-girl and how pretty she was. I don't remember. Looked like you, he said, and he wanted to find her again. She came from Boston and she was supposed to be here in New York now. Damn fool wild-goose chase."

"And did you find her?"

"No. That is . . . I don't know. I think I must have passed out."

"And Cort?"

"I don't know. He brought me home, I think. And there was this girl with us. An actress she was."

"He brought her here? To the Stratford House? That's terrible. If Papa ever found out that—"

"No, he was alone when he brought me into the lobby, and then he went back to the carriage."

Miranda sighed her relief. No one should *ever* be permitted to ruin the solid respectable reputation of the Stratford House.

Miranda's innocence went hand in hand with an avid curiosity—which had recently been stimulated when she came across a small privately printed guidebook to New York's "better seraglios." (She had to look up the word.) With Lucy Blaine as her giggling confidante, she had set out on an afternoon walking tour of Mercer and Greene streets, noting each "quiet discreet house of assignation," and every "fashionable elegant parlor house," where, the guidebook said, a gentleman was offered the best imported wines and had his choice of the pretty young lady boarders.

The two girls had failed to spot a single "boarder," though they peered hopefully at the heavily draped windows. And they were so intent on their mission that Lucy walked straight into the arms of a policeman and then backed off immediately, apologizing profusely. He looked at her curiously, and both girls fled in sudden alarm, back to the safety of Broadway.

But Miranda's worldly wisdom had been enhanced to some degree. If Cort had found an actress, then the place to take her was a house of assignation—unless she had rooms of her own somewhere. It was all very mysterious and no doubt sinful, but for some reason not nearly as sinful for Cort or her brothers as it would be for her.

"You'll never guess who was there at the first saloon." Tom had poured himself another cup of coffee and was trying to assure himself he was feeling better.

Miranda looked at him, expectant.

"Marty Schuyler."

"That miserable wretch." She made a face.

Martin Schuyler was their cousin, the only son of their mother's younger brother and, like his cousins Richard Schuyler and John Chase, he was working in the family shipping business. He had been a nasty little boy, rude and selfish and indulged by his sickly mother, and, now that she was dead and he was grown up, he was a nasty young man, still rude and selfish, though he had become more adept at disguising his true nature, at least in the presence of the older generation of the family. Miranda had never liked him, and since last Christmas, when he had caught her under the mistletoe, she positively loathed him. She still shuddered when she remembered his hands, pawing her clumsily, and his wet mouth coming down on hers. He had been into the punch bowl, of course, but that was no excuse.

"Marty saw me," Tom went on, "and he waved us over, but Cort didn't like him either, so we didn't stay."

"I don't see how anyone can bear him," Miranda agreed.

Tom nodded and then, because he was still feeling terrible, he spoke without thinking. "Marty told Cort he didn't see why he was out looking for waiter-girls when he had a little cousin lying abed back at the Stratford House just yearning for the day when she—" Tom stopped abruptly, hearing what he had said. "So I stood up and knocked the table over on him," Tom went on matter-of-factly, "and Cort delivered one beautiful knockout punch. And it was afterward that I got drunk. And I'm sorry I told you."

"That's horrible." Miranda was appalled. Marty was a thorough bounder, but it had never occurred to her that he might still be thinking about her, talking about her, perhaps planning some new deviltry.

That he would come to see her that very afternoon was a complete shock. The family had gathered for tea in the parlor, and Cort joined them, quiet and polite, showing no effects of the previous night. He had been to Plymouth Church that morning, he informed them, taking the ferry to Brooklyn to hear the Reverend Henry Ward Beecher. And very interesting it was, too, even without the slave auctions he had been hearing so much about. He caught Miranda's eye and winked. Why, the whole experience was almost as fascinating as his trip to Barnum's Museum. And as he left church, the editor of *The Independent* introduced him to his guest, Abraham Lincoln. Wasn't that a coincidence? Now they must be sure to hear the speech at Cooper Union the next day. Miranda found herself agreeing to go, together with her father and her brother Tom.

Just as they had made that decision, Marty Schuyler burst in, accompanied by his sister Caroline. Caroline was subdued and quiet, as usual, always in the shadow of her red-haired older brother.

Marty's left eye was slightly puffy, but otherwise he

showed no signs of what Tom had called Cort's beautiful knockout punch. Indeed, he showed no signs of ever having met Cort at all, and he extended his hand in greeting when Will made the introductions. Cort shook hands reluctantly after bowing to Caroline and then moved to withdraw. At the door he paused and smiled suddenly at Miranda. "Didn't you say you were going to find me that magazine article on John Brown?"

She looked at him blankly, and then she grasped the opportunity to escape. "Of course, Cort. I'll be glad to." Aunt Sarah looked puzzled and Tom grinned, but Miranda was simply glad to make her dash for freedom.

Cort closed the door behind them and followed Miranda to the library.

"That was very clever of you, Cort. I can't stand Marty Schuyler."

"Yes, he's a bit uncouth," Cort agreed. "I can hardly fault him in his taste for pretty girls, though, even if his tactics leave something to be desired." He had drawn her closer to the light, and he continued to hold her hand as he gazed at her in frank admiration.

"Yes. Well . . ." Miranda felt herself beginning to blush and wasn't quite sure how to handle the situation. After all, he was an old friend of the family, as he kept saying, and he was engaged to marry another girl, so it was foolish to be conscious of her pounding heart and to be absolutely at a loss for words. A magazine article, he had said, but why was he still looking at her that way? "John Brown," she said aloud, and her voice didn't sound quite normal, even in her own ears. She made an effort and pulled her hand free. "You said something about an article . . ."

"An excuse," Cort said. "You wanted to get out of there, and I—" He stopped in mid-sentence as the library door opened and Marty Schuyler stared at them suspiciously.

"I remember you now." Anger had turned his freckled complexion bright red. "Last night, for no reason at all . . . And she's *my* cousin."

"Your cousin," Cort acknowledged. "For whom you have only the purest of family feelings, of course. So, Miranda," he deliberately turned his back on Martin Schuyler, "you were telling me about an article—"

Marty caught him as he turned, a well-directed right punch to the jaw that staggered him. Miranda screamed and blundered into Cort's way, and a second blow had him on his knees. Marty was prepared to finish him off when Miranda scrambled between them and Marty fell on her. Finding this kind of wrestling to his taste, he pinned her easily, the whole weight of his body on hers as she struggled to escape.

Cort wasted no time on the niceties. He kicked Marty once in the back of the head and rolled him off Miranda. "Are you all right?" he asked, helping her to her feet. "No bones broken? Virtue still intact?"

She nodded, a little shakily. "I'm all right, I think. But what about you? Your chin." She reached out and touched him tentatively, tracing the line of his jaw.

He grinned at her and caught her hand and kissed it. "For that, it's almost worth a silly fight."

"Oh." She felt herself blushing again and retreated a step, almost falling over the prostrate Marty Schuyler, who was now stirring feebly.

Cort bent over him and pulled him to a half reclining position against an ottoman. "He'll be all right, though I don't think there's any more fight left in him this afternoon."

Marty glared at them and held his head with both hands. "There will be another day, Cort Adams. I will remember you. I will—"

The door opened and Marty stopped abruptly. His sister Caroline, looking embarassed, as usual, paused on the threshold, with Tom Chase standing beside her. "We w-wondered what happened to you, Marty." Caroline always sounded apologetic.

"Aunt Sarah sent us to find all of you," Tom explained. "She particularly wanted you, Miranda, to help her with the tea things."

Reluctantly, Miranda allowed herself to be escorted back to the family parlor. Cort, she noted, was under no such obligation. She wondered if he would go looking for that actress again.

For the Monday night appearance of Abraham Lincoln at the Cooper Union, the Young Men's Central Republican Union had made a strong effort to fill the auditorium. Still, it was uncertain how many of the two thousand seats would be occupied, partly because it was unusual to levy an admission charge (twenty-five cents) for a political speech.

The competition of other events that night was formidable:

Adelina Patti singing in *Martha* at the Academy of Music, the Cook's Royal Amphitheater Equestrian Troupe at Niblo's Garden, *The Governor's Wife* at the Winter Garden, *The Romance of a Poor Young Man* at Wallack's Theatre, *The Octoroon* at Barnum's Museum, and George Christy's Minstrels at Niblo's Saloon.

But the most severe competition, as things worked out, was the weather. It was a miserable evening, snowy and slushy, and Miranda had second thoughts about going.

"The next Vice President," Cort had challenged her, and her father nodded in agreement. He and Tom had already summoned a carriage, and Miranda decided it was too late to turn back.

In spite of the weather, some fifteen hundred New Yorkers, most of them men, had made their way to the Great Hall of the Cooper Union. The auditorium, which had opened in November, less than four months before, was already becoming a significant platform for politicians and preachers and spokesmen of all causes, and the press paid attention to what went on there. That very afternoon Lincoln had given his handwritten copy of his speech to the *Tribune*, which arranged to forward proof slips to the other New York papers in time for the next morning's editions.

Miranda, who had been to the hall before, led the way to the red leather seats in the second row. The gaslight was sizzling in the twenty-eight chandeliers, reflected endlessly by the wall mirrors, and the crowd had that expectant hum that precedes a theatrical performance.

At eight o'clock Mr. Lincoln was escorted to the platform by David Dudley Field, a lawyer and the brother of the inventor Cyrus Field, and by William Cullen Bryant, poet and editor of the New York *Post*. Among the other editors and distinguished New Yorkers on the platform, Cort Adams had managed to secure a place. He winked at Miranda, who was gazing in some surprise at the gangling figure of the principal speaker, now waiting to be introduced by Mr. Bryant.

Mr. Lincoln was badly dressed, she decided. The frock coat might be new, but it was too short in the arms, and his shirt gaped at the neck, leaving his long throat exposed. And his suit was wrinkled, still bearing the marks of its confinement in his trunk. All in all, decidedly unprepossessing. Senator Seward would have nothing to fear.

She settled back to listen to the speech, delivered in a

high-pitched voice with an unfamiliar Midwest accent. Though Lincoln made a shaky start, he quickly drew the audience into his grip with a tightly reasoned analysis of the attitudes of the founding fathers toward the institution of slavery. Slavery was wrong, he insisted, and men of conscience must proclaim that fact. Moreover, Congress could and should prohibit the spread of the "peculiar institution" to the new territories; but where slavery already existed in the states, he, Lincoln, would do nothing.

Miranda stirred uneasily at what she regarded as weakness.

"Wrong as we think slavery is," Lincoln said, "we can yet afford to let it alone where it is . . . an evil not to be extended, but to be tolerated and protected only because of and so far as its actual presence among us makes that toleration and protection a necessity."

This was a position that abolitionists found completely inadequate, and Miranda shook her head in disapproval. Nevertheless, she joined in the hearty applause and cheering that greeted Mr. Lincoln's conclusion:

"Let us have faith that right makes might, and in that faith let us to the end dare to do our duty as we understand it."

"It's not duty the way *I* understand it," she said later to Tom and her father in the carriage going home. "If slavery is wrong, it's wrong. In the terrritories *and* in the states."

"There is a question of what is feasible." Will was thinking aloud. "Lincoln is looking for a middle ground, to hold the party together, to hold the country together. Then perhaps, with time, slavery will wither away. After all, it's been only a generation since it was completely abolished here in New York."

"Wither away," Miranda scoffed. "Papa, you're a dreamer."

"All the same, that was a rousing speech tonight," Tom said. "It was good of Cort to get tickets for us, and I must thank him again in the morning before he leaves."

"Leaves? Is he leaving? I thought he was going to stay for a whole week." Miranda did not bother to conceal her disappointment.

"He changed his plans after he spoke to Mr. Lincoln again this afternoon," Will explained. "Mr. Raymond had given him a letter of introduction, and Cort called at the Astor

House, went along with Mr. Lincoln to Mathew Brady's portrait studio and had a long conversation afterward."

"So Cort is going back to Illinois with him?"

"No, not Illinois. Mr. Lincoln is going to New England. He has a son in school there, I believe, and he is planning to visit him. But now he is being pressed to give additional speeches, and I think Cort is interested in learning how the New England politicians size him up."

"A man to watch," Tom asserted. "Perhaps our next Vice President."

Chapter 5

Aunt Sarah prolonged her visit into March without creating any visible reforms in her brother Will's family. The boys were doing reasonably well, she decided, and that left only Miranda to worry about.

George was obviously going to follow in his father's footsteps at the hotel. John wrote frequently from London, dwelling on his triumphs with the Schuyler Shipping Company. Tom was reading law in desultory fashion, having squeaked through Columbia College. Sarah found it unfortunate that he was spending more time talking politics than reading Blackstone, but he paid little attention to her criticisms. Jim, by contrast, had delighted his aunt by deciding to enter theological seminary in the fall. Sarah would have preferred him to be a Congregationalist minister, but she allowed that Episcopalian priests were Christians, too.

Sarah had not quite given up on her niece, who had seemed remarkably subdued of late. Miranda had even agreed to accompany Sarah to Brooklyn that last Sunday, first to Mr. Beecher's church (Mr. Beecher was from Litchfield originally, Sarah reminded her for the twentieth time), and then to the Greenwood Cemetery to place flowers on the graves of Mary and Cordelia Chase.

Miranda went along reluctantly on the second part of this expedition, unwilling to relive the first tragedies of her young life. But her cousin Richard had unexpectedly offered to escort them, and afterward he had insisted that they return with him for tea with his parents and sisters on Washington Square.

Miranda had never cared much for her Uncle Paul

Schuyler, and Aunt Faith, née Beekman, was even worse. She had been straitlaced and disapproving from the time Miranda could first remember her (even bending over her crib, Miranda had once declared to her father). And so, even though they were family, Miranda and her aunt would have been perfectly willing to reduce their social obligations to the minimum of formal calls. Or, better still, the arid exchange of calling cards.

Several barriers stood in the way of that. To begin with, Aunt Faith's daughters, Ann and Irene, were singularly unattractive girls. Although Faith did not covet any of Will Chase's boys as prospective sons-in-law (she had a horror of cousin marriages in any case), they were undoubtedly good-looking and personable young men, and they were a convenient asset at parties, teas, and formal dinners. Inviting the boys, she could not exclude Miranda, and thus Faith saw more of her niece than she would have preferred.

Her daughter Ann, who was five years older than Miranda, had no use for her cousin at all, but Irene, the baby of the family at sixteen, had gone through phases of declaring that Miranda was her very best friend. These periods, usually limited to no more than two or three weeks a year, were times of trial in the Schuyler household, and Faith declared that they left scars.

However, this spring Faith had a more nagging worry. Her son Richard was obviously paying too much attention to the girl, and when he suggested bringing her back for tea, together with her Aunt Sarah, Faith had difficulty concealing her true reaction.

So now they were all seated in the formal front parlor of the house on Washington Square, Sarah chatting easily with Paul Schuyler, learning with delight that her nephew John in London was devoting himself to becoming a solid businessman, an asset to the shipping company, a young man who was going to make his mark on the world.

Faith listened with growing impatience to this recital of the virtues of John Chase. "I am sure he will be a very helpful assistant to our Richard one day," she observed, making clear who would be in real control of Schuyler Shipping eventually.

Miranda stirred uncomfortably, but she was still subdued from the expedition to the cemetery, and she had no heart for argument.

Richard provided unexpected balm. "More than that,

Mother. We'll certainly be expanding in the future and needing more partners. It's too hard on Papa, working so hard now that Uncle Martin is dead. Cousin Marty is useless, and—"

"Don't be so hard on the boy," Paul Schuyler said. "He's still young, and I think he'll work out."

"Of course," Faith agreed. "But I don't think we should be talking business on a fine Sunday afternoon." She changed the subject. "Won't you have some more ginger cookies, Mrs. Waltham? And do tell me about your visit to New York. Richard says you are returning to Litchfield this week, but I'd like to hear all about your time here."

Sarah responded dutifully, and Miranda drank her tea in silent boredom. Ann and Irene started a low-keyed conversation about summer plans, and Miranda finally replied to a direct question.

"No, Papa says we can't go to Europe this year. I wish—"

"Why don't you come to Saratoga with us?" Richard suggested.

"That's a splendid idea," Irene chimed in. "Saratoga gets boring after a while, but you always stir things up when you come along."

Ann looked daggers at her sister, but Irene only laughed.

"That's kind of you," Miranda responded, stalling for time, "but I'll have to ask Papa."

Ann heard the reluctance in Miranda's voice and moved to reinforce it. "I know you really prefer the seashore, and we're probably too dull for you. Richard only wants to go back to see those Southern girls again. He'll be quite invisible once they appear."

Miranda looked at her, puzzled. If Richard were eagerly chasing after other girls, it wouldn't matter to her at all. He was always such a dutiful and available escort, almost like another brother, that at times he simply got in the way. Perhaps if he were diverted to someone else, Saratoga would be worth trying again. She had really been too young for the perpetual round of dances when she had been there before, but now that she was grown up, it might be worth seeing again. In any case, Richard deserved to be teased about his Southern belles.

"So your true love is a Southern girl," Miranda began. "No wonder you are so wishy-washy in your politics these days. Is she so beautiful in the moonlight that—"

"Don't talk nonsense, Miranda. Ann is exaggerating a mild flirtation."

"You asked them if they'd be back this summer," Ann contradicted him. "I was on the veranda and I heard you. You were terribly sorry to be leaving just a week after they arrived, and you made sure to find out that they always come for the whole month of August every year. And that," she explained to Miranda, "is why we'll be there for all of August ourselves. Just so that Richard can pay court to the Robillard sisters."

"Robillard sisters," Miranda echoed. The name rang a bell. "I think I have heard about them. Is one of them named Susanne by any chance?"

"You must have second sight!" Irene exclaimed. "I always knew there was something about you that—"

"Susanne Robillard," Miranda repeated, remembering that conversation with Cort. "He *said* she had an accent." She caught the look of astonishment on Irene's face and realized that she had spoken aloud. A Southern accent. Why—she probably owned *slaves*. She and her whole family, traveling around Europe on their ill-gotten gains. And Cort was going to marry her? For her money, of course. Cort, with all his fine lectures on honest ways to acquire a fortune. How unprincipled men were. There was Cort, inventing horror stories about war, when all the time he was going to marry into a family that bought and sold human beings like chattel. He had actually laughed at her when she told him about the slave auction at Mr. Beecher's church. And now Richard was running after the family, too. Completely unprincipled. Two sisters. Did he want to marry them both? That would be bigamy, and they'd have to go off to Utah and live with the Mormons. There was no end of stupidity in this world.

She looked up to see Richard smiling at her, a complacent and self-satisfied smile that brought all her anger to the surface.

"Are you really courting *two* sisters? That's disgraceful! Why, it's almost bigamy!" She gave him her most haughty look of disdain. "And after all your talk about protecting the family reputation. Now it's my turn to lecture *you*. Yes, and to save you, too. You see," there was triumph in her voice, "I have it on the best authority that Susanne Robillard is already engaged to be married."

"That's all right." His smile broadened. "Danielle is prettier anyway."

Paul Schuyler moved his chair closer, to join the conversation. "I didn't catch that, Richard. You were saying . . ."

"I just said that Danielle Robillard is a pretty girl. Remember her from Saratoga last summer?"

"Oh, yes. Magnolias in her voice, I believe you told me. Sweet little thing. But our Miranda is prettier, I think. I was watching you, my dear, and with the light on your hair like that, for a moment you looked exactly like our dear Mary."

Richard seized the moment, while his father was vulnerable and his mother still occupied. "I have just invited Miranda to come to Saratoga with us in August." He looked inquiringly at his father, as if asking for his consent.

"Of course, Richard. A capital idea. Faith," he interrupted his wife, still engaged in conversation with Sarah. "Miranda is coming to the Springs with us in August. Isn't that splendid?"

An hour later, after Miranda and Sarah had departed, Richard was still rejoicing. "That was brilliant, Ann."

Ann looked at her brother in surprise. "I don't know what you're talking about."

"Why—bringing up the subject of the Robillard girls. It made all the difference. I could tell. Miranda wasn't the least bit interested in coming to the Springs until you mentioned them. And now she's jealous!" He laughed and went so far as to blow a kiss to his sister. "Simply brilliant!"

Ann acknowledged defeat. "A whole month. And without any of her brothers, either."

"Cheer up." Richard was willing to share his high spirits. "I'll bring John home from England for you."

Chapter 6

By THE TIME the Schuylers arrived in Saratoga in August with Miranda, she was already regretting her decision to come. A whole month, even with her brother John expected next week, loomed like an eternity. Richard was always there, like an unwelcome chaperone, and she was counting on the unknown Robillard sisters to distract him. That is—if they decided to come after all.

Many Southerners, uncomfortable with the rising sectional antagonism, had canceled their usual vacation plans. There was increasing talk of secession, and the first major political break had already occurred.

The Democratic party, meeting in Charleston in April, had split apart; and after the Southern delegates walked out, it was impossible to choose a Presidential candidate. Stephen Douglas led the field, but without the Southerners, no one could win a two-thirds majority, and the convention adjourned in considerable confusion.

In early May the Constitutional Union party, made up of remnants of the Whigs and the Know-Nothings, met in Baltimore and chose John Bell of Tennessee as their candidate for President and Edward Everett of Massachusetts for Vice President. They couldn't win, but they could further fragment the weakening political union.

The confident Republicans, scenting victory, assembled in Chicago later in May in their specially constructed "Wigwam." New York's Senator Seward led by a wide margin on the first ballot, as expected, but he was still haunted by his "irrepressible conflict" speech, and thus was viewed as a radical on the slavery issue. The more moderate Abraham Lincoln, who had made such a favorable impression with his Cooper Union speech, emerged as a possible compromise candidate. He had stayed in Springfield, of course (it was unbecoming of a candidate to be present), but he had all the advantages of the convention's meeting in his home state. The Chicago newspapers were fervent in his support, and his backers—possibly with the help of counterfeit tickets—had packed the Wigwam. When Lincoln drew nearly even with Seward on the second ballot, his victory on the third was assured, thus shattering all the preconvention predictions. Hannibal Hamlin of Maine was nominated for Vice President.

In June the Democrats tried again, this time in Baltimore, and again they split. The nomination, which finally went to Douglas, was of dubious value without the Southern wing of the party. And the Southerners, meeting in rump convention, chose their own candidate, John Breckinridge of Tennessee.

Inexorably, the political divisiveness was permeating the whole fabric of society.

On their fourth day in Saratoga, the Schuylers and Miranda returned late from their afternoon drive and found the vast lobby of the United States Hotel a confusion of newly arrived visitors, their servants, and small mountains of luggage. Viewing the disorganization with a professional eye, Miranda gave low marks to the management and decided that what was needed was a Chase at the reception desk. And then she looked again and blinked, because there *was* a Chase there—on the visitors' side. She rushed through the crowd and threw her arms around her brother John.

"You weren't coming until tomorrow. What happened? I'm so *glad* to see you."

John disentangled her arms from around his neck and stepped back, clearly embarrassed by her lack of restraint.

Miranda sighed. She had noticed it in New York and it was even more evident here: The year in England had ruined him. The rigidity of his manner—always more Schuyler than Chase—was more pronounced than ever, and he looked with distaste on her American exuberance.

"My sister Miranda," he explained to the courtly gentleman on his right. "Miranda," there was a chilling formality in John's manner that put her on guard. "Miranda, may I present Mr. Douglas Robillard. The Robillards have been our guests at the Stratford for the past three days, and we traveled here together."

For the first time she became aware of the strangers with John, the two attractive girls, their handsome parents, two Negro servants—slaves?—hovering in the background with a collection of trunks. And then the Schuylers were with them, and Richard was laughing with Danielle, and Faith Schuyler relaxed for the first time in four days, while Miranda fixed her attention on the slight figure and undoubtedly pretty face of Susanne Robillard.

"Cort told me all about you and your family." In Susanne's soft accent, the r's were almost inaudible and for a moment Miranda looked at her baffled; and then recognition broke through.

"Oh, you mean Cort. Cort Adams. He told you about us? What ever for?"

Susanne looked surprised. "Why, he told us to stay at the Stratford, told us we would be very welcome. We were a little worried about coming North, you know. But this has been such a hot summer in Georgia, and we *do* enjoy the Springs so much." Susanne smiled fondly at her sister, Danielle, now in animated conversation with Richard and Ann. "And after we heard from Mrs. Schuyler, saying how much the family was hoping to see us, we just couldn't stay home."

At the dance that evening there was an excess of attractive girls over eligible young men, and for once even Miranda's dance card was slow to be filled. Richard and John were paying altogether too much attention to Susanne and Danielle, in Miranda's opinion, though the boys had dutifully added their signatures to the cards of all the women in both families. Miranda had allowed herself to be led through the paces of a quadrille by Uncle Paul, but she was grateful beyond words when Mr. Robillard announced he had long since given up dancing—the terpsichorean art, he called it. Susanne and Danielle giggled dutifully at what seemed to be a rather feeble family joke.

Miranda's smile became a trifle more glazed, and she retreated into numb boredom. Eyes half closed, she was completely unaware of the approach of Damon McMasters until he stood directly in front of her and called her by name.

Damon had never been a particular favorite of hers in New York, but here in Saratoga he took on the guise of a knight riding to the rescue, and the smile that she gave him was positively dazzling. He blushed with delight, and with some difficulty remembered his manners long enough to greet the Schuylers and acknowledge an introduction to the Robillards. And then he turned his full attention back to Miranda, who had never been so welcoming. He filled in the rest of her dance card, and they whirled off in a galop, unconscious of the varied reactions they had left behind.

Damon's conversation might have left something to be desired, but he did dance divinely, as Miranda assured him repeatedly throughout the evening, consciously mimicking the accent and the sugar-sweetness of Susanne Robillard. And Damon, who had dutifully danced once with Susanne, smiled his appreciation, conscious that Miranda was sharing a joke with him, that she was paying attention to him, that she was making this altogether the most wonderful evening he had ever had. It was with reluctance that he allowed Richard Schuyler to claim her for the last waltz.

"You don't have to," Miranda said as Richard led her back to the dance floor. "Danielle is free, and I can certainly sit this one out. That last polka was truly exhausting."

He chose to ignore the remark about Danielle, but he was willing enough to leave the dance floor for the cooler air of the balcony.

A fresh breeze stirred the trees and ruffled her hair, and she welcomed the respite from the crowded ballroom. She would have welcomed a respite from Richard's conversation, too, but he reverted immediately to his one theme of the evening.

"They are attractive girls, the Robillard sisters. Don't you think so, Miranda?"

"If you like the type, perhaps." She refused to be baited, and her voice was deliberately cool. This was the third time he had broached the subject, looking at her expectantly, as if he wanted her to react and make a scene. It made no sense: This was her rigid cousin, always lecturing her on the proprieties, now deliberately trying to provoke her. She was being ladylike and controlling her temper and staying out of his way, and he was perversely being difficult.

The silence lengthened, and he was the first to break it.

"You seem to be getting along remarkably with Damon tonight."

"He dances very well," she acknowledged.

"And that's all there is to it?"

"What a strange question!"

"Very natural, I think. When you spend an entire evening flirting with—"

"Are you my chaperone, Richard?" Her restraint was crumbling at last. "You and John—you're both impossible. You go chasing after those silly Southern accents, and you both worry that I am going to do something irresponsible. You know as well as I do that Damon McMasters is the solidest, dullest, most conventional young man in all Christendom, and when he came to rescue me from being a wallflower—"

"You? A wallflower? Don't be absurd!"

"Came to rescue me," Miranda repeated doggedly. "And now you carry on as if I am going to run off and marry him."

"And you're not?"

She laughed and shook her head.

"Poor Damon," Richard said. "But don't lead him on and break his heart."

"I don't need lessons from you."

"Oh, you think I am about to break someone's heart?"

"Not at all. You can go right ahead and get married and live happily ever after—if you have a taste for all that sugar."

He laughed and said something about his sweet tooth, and Miranda let it pass.

In the silence between them, the orchestra was faintly audible, and she strained to hear. The last notes of the waltz had barely faded away when Damon appeared on the balcony with Susanne Robillard.

"Danielle *said* you were out here." Susanne's voice was lightly accusing, Miranda thought, and almost possessive. If Susanne had Cort, why did she want Richard, too? But perhaps it was just her Southern-belle technique, so ingrained that she automatically flirted with any man, even her sister's new beau.

Miranda and Damon exchanged knowing glances, which Richard chose to ignore.

"I was just telling my *cousin* Miranda," Richard emphasized the relationship for Susanne's benefit, "how very attractive you and Danielle are." He looked at Miranda for confirmation, and she was only too willing to agree.

"Yes, dear *cousin* Richard can talk of nothing else. In fact, he's becoming quite a bore on the subject. He goes on and on and on—"

"I believe this is our dance," Richard cut in hastily, offering his arm to Susanne.

Miranda followed their departure with unconcealed amusement—and undivided attention. She was unaware of Damon, moving closer to her on the shadowed balcony. And when she turned to him to comment on Susanne, she was startled to find his arms around her. And he was, undoubtedly, trying to kiss her.

Surprised by his clumsy embrace—the kiss had grazed her nose and landed on her cheek—she broke away quickly and backed off, staring at him with reproach.

He was flustered and apologized immediately. "I don't know what came over me, Miranda. You are so beautiful, and I . . . It was unforgivable, I know. We aren't even engaged, and I haven't spoken to your father or asked—"

"Stop. Stop right there. Please don't say any more, Damon. I don't want to hear." She covered her ears to shut off his declaration, and he retreated a step, consciously giving her more room.

Feeling a little foolish, Miranda lowered her hands, looked around to make sure they were unobserved, and then smiled tentatively. "Let's just pretend it never happened. We'll go back in and finish this dance and say no more about it."

"But Miranda—"

"I know. You're sorry. And I'm sorry. I had no idea . . ." And to think she had scoffed when Richard warned her about leading him on.

"It was all my fault." Damon looked at her with misery in his eyes. "I was so happy to be with you, and now I've ruined—"

"Please. Let's just forget it."

It was the last dance of the evening, and their absence from the ballroom, like their reappearance, did not go unremarked. If Miranda's color was a little higher than usual, there was always the cool breeze on the balcony to be blamed.

But not even her Uncle Paul could quiet swallow that explanation. "A devilishly pretty girl," he said to Richard while the musicians were packing up their instruments. "Damon is a lucky young man."

Richard said nothing, watching Miranda follow Damon to the door to say good night.

"I invited him to come along to the picnic tomorrow," Paul Schuyler continued. "And if Susanne's beau arrives in time, he'll join us. What's his name again?"

Richard didn't hear, his attention still on Damon, who was bowing formally to Miranda. Too formally, Richard decided, the stiff manners in violent conflict with his real emotions.

"What's his name again?" Paul Schuyler repeated.

"Damon," Richard said, finally conscious of his father's voice. "Damon McMasters. You've known him for years. You know his father."

"Of course I know Damon. And his father. What's the matter with you, boy? I asked you for the name of that beau of Susanne's."

Irene Schuyler moved to her brother's rescue. "It's Cort Adams, Papa. He's a reporter for *The New York Times*."

Miranda, returning to pick up her reticule, caught the name and looked inquiringly at her uncle.

"Adams," he repeated. "Susanne's fiancé. I was just saying that he would join us at the picnic tomorrow—if he arrives on the morning train."

Chapter 7

SHORTLY BEFORE NOON the next day Miranda was crossing the lobby when she spotted Cort Adams waiting to register. Succumbing to a spirit of mischief—five days with the Schuylers was a *very* long time—she whipped around to the clerks' side of the reception desk while Cort was distracted by an insistent newsboy.

The elderly clerk looked at her in surprise, and he was clearly unsettled when she winked at him; he turned back to his newly arrived guests in some confusion.

"May I help you, Mr. Adams?" Miranda had put on her brisk, professional voice, and she caught him completely off guard.

"Good Lord, Miranda. What are *you* doing there?" Cort surveyed her from head to toe and shook his head, smiling. "You'll never get the hang of it, my dear. Still dressed to the nines."

"And cheeky, too?"

"More than ever. What are you doing there? And don't tell me that your father owns *this* hotel, too." He gazed around the vast reception area of the States, taking in the ornate chandeliers, the marble tables, the heavy walnut furniture—and the vast throng of prosperous guests. "I'll have to revise my opinion about how much of an heiress you really are."

"Why Cort! Are you still fortune hunting?" She had borrowed Susanne's accent and then dropped it when he laughed. "You see—you hear—I've met your Miss Robillard. I've even admired her engagement ring."

"She's here then. Good. And everything is all right?"

Miranda nodded. And then had second thoughts. "Every-

55

thing is all right unless you're going to take back the ring and look for somebody richer."

"Why Miranda!" He echoed her earlier exclamation. "What put such a thought in your head? Do you mean to say you have come into an inheritance and *you* are now available?" He grinned at her, and she felt her color rise.

"You are the most conceited man I've ever met. Thank God Papa *doesn't* own the States. I'd hate to think I was rich enough to interest you."

"Look at it this way, Miranda. You interest me for yourself alone. If I choose to flirt with you, it's purely for the pleasure of the experience." He lounged against the desk and watched her think that through, taking an almost scientific interest in her reactions.

Miranda opened her mouth to protest, thought better of it, and then breathed a sigh of relief to be interrupted by the elderly clerk, ready at last to deal with Cort's reservation. She still hadn't thought of a properly withering response, and it was too late; the Robillards descended on Cort *en masse* and swept him away in a confusion of greetings and handshakes and bows and one token kiss on the cheek from his fiancée. Susanne clutched his arm as if she would never let go, and Cort smiled down at her. But when he caught Miranda's eye, there was the faintest suggestion of a wink.

Two carriages took them to the lake for the afternoon picnic, the Robillards with Cort Adams and John Chase in the first, the Schuylers with Miranda and Damon in the second. Under Richard's watchful eye, Miranda had been polite but formal with Damon. Truth to tell, she wanted no repetition of Damon's advances, and she made it clearly understood that she was not leading him on. Damon responded with more whispered apologies, and he hovered at her side for the rest of the afternoon.

John had brought a croquet set with him from England, and he took great delight in instructing them all in the intricacies of this new game. Danielle had to be shown repeatedly just how to hold her mallet, and John was most obliging in his demonstrations, standing right behind her, his arms around her and his hands over hers on the handle. And when Ann Schuyler needed similar help, he was equally patient with her. Then it was Danielle's turn to be instructed by Richard, more than once.

Miranda raised an eyebrow, but both John and Richard refused to look in her direction. Observing from the sidelines, Cort grinned and sauntered over.

"Would you like some instructions, too, Miranda?"

"There's nothing to it," she said, taking a vicious cut at her ball and sending it through the next hoop. She was far ahead of the others, perhaps because she was the only one with her mind on the game. Damon was too polite to hit anyone else's ball, and Richard and John lagged behind, playing their own games with Danielle and Ann.

"The thing is," Miranda took her bonus stroke and watched the ball take a bad bounce on the uneven ground, "it might even be a good game if they would only play it properly."

"I'll challenge you for the next round," Cort volunteered.

"But Susanne—"

"Is impressing me with her domestic traits." Under the trees Susanne and her mother and Mrs. Schuyler and Irene were busily laying out the picnic fare. Cort waved, and Susanne blew him a kiss.

"I think Irene should play, too."

"By all means," Cort agreed. "She's eager to flirt with Damon."

"But Damon is my—"

"Come, come, Miranda. Be generous. It's obvious that you don't want him, and I think Irene does. And look how happy you would make your Aunt Faith."

"Why would I want to do that?"

"A good point. Still, you *are* her guest here, and a most exemplary one so far, I understand. You have stayed out of Richard's way in his pursuit of Danielle, your admirable brother John—he's not much like you, is he?—John seems to be living up to his escort duties with Ann, and that leaves only Irene to worry about. And see what you can do for her! Why, now that you have enticed the eligible Damon McMasters into the family circle, you can bestow him on Irene, and all the Schuylers will live happily every after."

Miranda laughed in spite of herself. "What silly fairy tales you invent. Where did you get all that?"

"You mean it's not true?" He looked at her in mock surprise. "And to think I pride myself on being such a good reporter. Two hours in your company," his gesture took in the whole group, "and I can write a definitive analysis of all your prospects."

"No wonder Papa says not to believe everything you read in the papers. If all reporters are as mixed up as you are—"

"You mean I didn't sum up the situation correctly?"

"Not at all."

He gave an exaggerated sigh and watched her stroke the ball toward the last pair of hoops. One more turn and she'd win the game.

"I didn't think I had it right," Cort went on. "But I thought I'd try out the story on you. All of that was wishful thinking from your Aunt Faith. Just be prepared for her reaction when it doesn't turn out that way."

"It won't be *my* fault. If my behavior has been so exemplary—"

"It must be a terrible strain for you."

She glared at him, swung the mallet dangerously close to his feet, and had the satisfaction of seeing him jump back hastily.

"I see the strain is beginning to tell," Cort said.

"Must you always say exactly what you think?"

"I find it refreshing. And when you aren't trying so hard to be proper," he leaned forward confidentially, "I think you rather like it."

"It's your turn, Miranda." Damon sounded plaintive, and she realized he was watching her—they were all watching her. "If Mr. Adams is explaining the game to you . . ."

"No, nothing like that." She took her last turn, and the ball hit the post with a satisfying thump. "You see, I can win without him."

They played once more, and this time Cort edged her out at the last minute, sending her ball flying all the way to the trees, where Susanne stopped it from rolling onto the picnic cloth.

"You poor darling," Susanne clucked over Miranda. "I don't think that was fair of him at all. He took advantage of you, just to win that silly game. And if he insists on using brute strength . . ."

Miranda let her rattle on, wondering if there was a real person under all that chatter.

Later that afternoon, much later, she had a chance to find out.

After all the picnic hampers had been packed away, after

Uncle Paul had tipped his hat over his forehead and quietly dozed off, and Mrs. Robillard was nodding, and a general air of somnolence had overtaken the company, Miranda wandered off alone to the edge of the lake. She was surprised to be joined there by Susanne, a quiet and reflective Susanne. Only the plummy accent stayed the same, setting Miranda's teeth on edge.

They sat on the grass, gazing across the lake at the distant hills.

"I wonder if we'll all be here together next year." Susanne was thinking aloud, hardly expecting an answer.

"*We* won't be here." Miranda sighed and stretched out, closing her eyes. "Papa has been promising me a trip to Europe for three years, and *next* summer . . ." He could never seem to tear himself away from the Stratford for more than a week at a time, but surely by next year George could handle things. The Grand Tour, she thought sleepily. London. And Paris. And Rome.

"You'll like England," Susanne's voice seemed to come from far away. "And France. That's where we met Cort, you know."

"Mmm." Miranda was barely paying attention.

"I'd like to go there again on our honeymoon," Susanne said dreamily, "before we settle down in Savannah."

"Savannah?" Miranda who had been ready to doze off, came alert at once. "Did you say Savannah?" She propped herself up on one elbow and stared at Susanne. "But Cort is in Washington City—that is, when he isn't wandering all over the country talking to obscure politicians."

Susanne had a tinkly laugh, and she was not reluctant to use it. "Oh, honey, that's just for now, while he's single. And maybe for a year or two after we get married. I wouldn't mind living away from home at the beginning, though Washington City is awfully dull. But after we have responsibilities . . ." She colored under Miranda's steady gaze. "I mean, we'd have to build a house and all, and that will take time."

"I see." Miranda was frankly staring at her, suddenly glimpsing a hard core of determination under all that melting sugar. "And what will Cort be doing in Savannah?"

"Why, he will go into the bank with Papa, of course. Papa thinks he's wonderful. And with all the important people Cort knows from all over the country . . . I know some of our friends think he has a Yankee accent and won't fit in, but that's silly. Cort lived in England so long he really sounds British most of the time. And I *do* like his voice." Susanne looked at Miranda expectantly. "Isn't that right? Don't you like his voice, too?"

"I hadn't thought about it," she replied in all honesty. "And what does Cort say about the bank?"

"Why," the little laugh tinkled again, "he says that will take some getting used to, and we'll think about it in Washington City."

"It seems to me," Miranda paused to choose her words, "it seems to me that Cort usually get exactly what he wants. You may be living away from Savannah for years and years."

"We'll work it out," Susanne said confidently. "He wants me to be happy and—"

"And you want him to be happy, too," Miranda cut in brightly, an innocent comment, concealing barbs.

For the first time she had dented Susanne's supreme confidence.

"Why, why, of course I want him to be happy." Susanne eyed Miranda with the early stirrings of doubt, and she groped to justify herself. "Cort is so clever," she said. "He could take over the bank and do something else, too. Anything he wanted. Why, he could run a newspaper," she said with sudden inspiration. "That's it. Papa so looks forward to having him in the bank, but we can buy a newspaper, too. I'll ask Papa about it tonight."

"I'd ask Cort, too," Miranda said dryly, but Susanne hardly heard her, too busy rearranging the future to suit herself.

Southerners! Miranda raged silently. They're so used to buying and selling slaves they're now in the business of buying husbands, too. It would be fascinating to see if they actually succeeded in shackling Cort. Not that he didn't deserve it, of course. She smiled with satisfaction and relaxed once again, ready to drift into sleep.

Back at the hotel John surprised her by suggesting a stroll on the piazza, away from the others. It was the first chance she had had to say two words to him all day, and she was delighted. Maybe the Schuyler influence was subsiding after all.

They paced the length of the veranda, beyond the last of the rocking chairs and the last of the people, and then John came right to the point: "Damon thinks he's in love with you."

That wasn't what she wanted to hear at all, and Miranda allowed her irritation to show. "Did he tell you that? Why would he go to you and—"

"He didn't come to me—I went to him. I asked him what his intentions are."

Miranda was appalled. "John, you didn't! What right do you have to—"

"But I'm your brother, Miranda. Your older brother. And since Papa isn't here, I'm responsible for you. When Richard told me—"

"Richard! You mean to say that the two of you took time out from . . . from *croquet* lessons long enough to gossip about me? Just like a couple of old-maid aunts!" Her voice had risen and John tried to shush her.

"Don't make a fuss, Miranda. I meant it for your own good."

She glared at him and he tried to explain. "It wasn't just my opinion. Richard suggested that—"

"Stupid idiot! I should have guessed. So he's the one who put you up to it."

"Not exactly." John looked increasingly uncomfortable. "I've been away, Miranda, and you have changed so much, and . . . I just thought you ought to know."

"Know what?"

"I *told* you. Know that Damon loves you and his intentions are honorable. And," he added as an afterthought, "I approve."

She stared at him in disbelief. "I think the sun had addled your wits. The sun and those Southern accents."

He started to protest, but she cut him off.

"Listen to me. I will explain it so that even *you* can understand.

"One, I know perfectly well what Damon thinks about me. And I didn't need you or Richard Schuyler to tell me, either.

"Two, I know Damon's intentions are honorable.

"Three, I don't care whether you approve or not.

"Because, four, I don't love him, and I have no intention of loving him, and I am not going to marry him or anybody else. And if I should ever change my mind, which I doubt very much, I will not come to you for persmission first. Is that clear?"

"Oh, it's clear enough. But I wish you'd keep your voice down." John looked around anxiously to see if they had been overheard, but they were at the deserted end of the veranda.

"All right, then," Miranda said, obligingly lowering her voice, "now it's my turn."

John looked at her blankly.

"You've been prying into my affairs, so I can at least comment on yours. Yours and Richard's."

"I'm not sure that—"

"Oh, for heaven's sake, John, let me tell you what I found out." She perched on the railing, and he looked at her dubiously.

"This is about Susanne," she said confidentially, "but it probably applies to Danielle, too, so I think you ought to warn Richard."

"Warn Richard?" An odd expression flickered over John's face, but Miranda was oblivious.

"Yes. Warn him. The Robillards expect Cort and Susanne to live in Savannah, and I think they probably want Danielle and *her* future husband to live there, too. Wouldn't that be awful? So far from New York! And in a *slave* state."

"Are you still on that?" He was relieved to get her off the subject of the Robillards, even if it led to another kind of argument. "I know you were an abolitionist before I left, but I thought you'd grown out of that by now."

"Grown *out* of it? When Southerners allow slavery—"

"Yes, yes, yes. I know. But if we don't bother them about it, they won't bother us."

"I think that attitude is immoral."

He refused to respond, but she would not let go.

"What do the Robillards think?"

"I have been polite enough not to ask them. And I fervently hope that you will not raise the subject."

"I've just been waiting for the right moment."

"*Please*, Miranda. I admire your restraint up to now." John was trying hard to mollify her. "You really *are* learning to be grown up."

"I'm learning to be a hyprocrite, if that's what you mean, and I don't like it one bit. It's too high a price to pay for peace." She sighed and reverted to the subject that had interested her all along. "Those Negro servants with the Robillards—they *are* slaves, aren't they? Why don't they run away? We're not far from Canada, and the underground railroad—"

"They wouldn't run away, Miranda. They're *house* servants. Part of the family."

"Is that what Danielle told you?"

"Yes. And Mrs. Robillard, too."

"I think there's more to it than that. Most Southerners don't *dare* bring their slaves into free states any more. Anyone would help them get away."

"The fugitive slave law—"

"Nobody pays any attention to that. It would be so easy. If I just spoke to them about—"

"Miranda!"

"But they could be free!"

"They have family back in Savannah, Miranda."

"So that's it. Hostages! I knew there was something holding them back."

"Don't be so dramatic. It's not as if the Robillards have a big plantation, you know, with vast *numbers* of slaves." John was trying to put a good face on it.

"Just ten or fifteen around the house and yard, is that it? Does that make it all right? What is the permissible number of human beings you can buy and sell? Did the Robillards tell you that?"

"Not so loud." John looked around uneasily. "I don't want to fight with you about this, Miranda. And it's not as if I am defending the system exactly."

"A pretty feeble case you're making."

He tried to ignore that. "Maybe in England I learned to look at it from a different perspective. If we give it time—"

"It will just go away? I don't believe it. The whole economy of the Southern states—"

"Is greatly misunderstood." Cort had rounded the corner from the side porch and jumped into the argument as if he belonged there.

"It's not worth fighting about," John said uneasily, eying Cort, unsure how much he had heard.

"I disagree with you about that." Cort pulled out a cigar and took his time about lighting it. "A good fight can clear the air," he said, drawing on the cigar and preparing to propound a favorite thesis. "I don't mean to encourage an ugly war of words, you understand. No hurt feelings. No recriminations. But a healthy, arm-waving argument that puts a sparkle in the eye and a flush in the cheek—that's a pleasure. It's al-

63

ways worth fighting with Miranda, for instance. It's positively exhilarating, in fact. Better than croquet."

"Mr. Adams," John began stiffly.

"Call me Cort."

"Mr. Adams," John repeated, "my sister—"

"Is perfectly capable of speaking for herself." Miranda was exasperated with both of them. "You keep getting off the subject. Now the reason abolition is necessary—"

"I have a theory about Miranda," Cort went on imperturbably. "She has all this passion bottled up inside, and for some reason it's all directed at causes, not at people. And so when the passion emerges, it takes the form of rage. And the longer she keeps it pent up, the louder the explosion when it comes."

"You make me sound like a steam engine." Miranda gave him a withering look.

"Not a bad comparison," Cort agreed. "And here I am, ready to be a safety valve. How many days has it been since you've had a good rousing fight? You must need me."

"If you would stop making personal remarks," Miranda struggled to preserve her equanimity, "half the reasons for fighting would go away, and we might talk sensibly for once."

"Behold, the peacemaker." Cort flicked ash from his cigar and looked at her expectantly. "You were going to tell us all about the slave economy in the Southern states. You have been there I assume?"

"No, but that doesn't mean—"

"Ah. Your knowledge comes from other sources, perhaps. A comparison study. You have looked into conditions at the mills in Massachusetts, I suppose, where the girls go to work at six in the morning and . . . You haven't seen that? Your research is closer to home, then. And certainly the problems in New York would be enough to keep you occupied. There is probably more concentrated misery in the slums around Five Points than anywhere else in the country. When were you there last? It's not more than ten blocks from the Stratford, I believe."

"You never stick to the subject," Miranda protested. "I'm not saying slavery is the only thing wrong with the world. I'm just saying it's the worst. And I don't see how you can even consider living in Savannah as long as—"

"Where did you ever get such an idea? Washington City—"

"Where slavery is *still* in force," she interrupted.

"Miranda never gives up," John observed, rather glad to be

out of her line of fire. "I don't think you are going to change her, Mr. Adams. Cort," he amended. "Look at it this way, Miranda. Cort has the right idea. If enough of us Yankees marry Southern girls and rescue them from being slave owners, the whole problem will solve itself in a generation. The entire slave-owning class will die out. I keep telling you that it's just a matter of time."

"Peace through intermarriage," Cort mused. "A fascinating idea—one that the politicians haven't thought of yet. I compliment you, John. Have you considered running for President? You have as good a party platform as any I've read."

John laughed and seized the opportunity to ask Cort about the progress of the political campaign, and Cort was ready enough to be diverted. Even Miranda held her peace.

Thus far there had been little to report, he said. Of the four candidates, only Douglas was actually traveling around the country making speeches, something most people regarded as demeaning and undignified in a Presidential election. Douglas had been at the Springs, at this very hotel, only two weeks earlier, welcomed with a hundred-gun salute and a band playing "Hail the Conquering Hero Comes." After his swing through the North, he was contemplating a trip to Virginia and perhaps even farther south. There were frantic attempts behind the scenes to patch up some kind of unity in the Democratic party to make an alliance that would stop Lincoln.

Lincoln was not campaigning at all. And he repeatedly refused all the persistent demands that he express himself on the issues of the day, referring all questioners to the Republican party platform and to his own past speeches. Like other reporters, Cort had traveled to Springfield and had been granted an interview. Lincoln had greeted him cordially and told him a funny story or two, but he had not said anything at all relevant to the course of the campaign or the election.

No one knew what would happen if the Southern states attempted to secede, as some hotheads were threatening. But of course such threats had been made before . . .

John weighed the possibilities. "Under the circumstances," he said, "I'm glad to be living in England."

"England?" Miranda was immediately diverted from politics to more immediate family concerns. "You mean you're going back? Uncle Paul said it would be just for a year, and I don't think it's fair—"

"I want to go back," John interrupted. "I've asked to stay on, and he has agreed. We're building up a flourishing business abroad, and I—"

"What did Papa say?"

"He said he was glad I'd found my niche and he'd be over to see me next year. Maybe he'll bring you if you're good— and not married to Damon yet."

She made a face at him and he laughed.

"Everyone is traveling these days, Miranda. Even the Prince of Wales is crossing the ocean."

"And I'm not going to marry *him*, either. England is too far away to live."

"It's getting closer every year. The *Great Eastern* made the crossing in ten days, and that's faster than overland to California."

"I wouldn't want you living out there, either."

"You want us all at the Stratford forever?"

"It's big enough," she insisted stubbornly.

"Don't you ever want to move away?" Cort asked, obviously surprised.

"No. Why should I? Everything is right there, with Broadway on the doorstep."

"But don't you want a house of your own someday—a husband and children?" For once Cort sounded just as conventional—and stuffy—as Richard Schuyler.

"I don't think so. Maybe it will happen—everyone seems to expect it—but I'd rather do something different. Manage the hotel, perhaps, with Papa and George." She brooded about that and then shook her head. "I don't know. I don't like to worry about things like that. All I know is that I don't want to make any changes. I want everything to go on exactly the same."

"Stop time dead in its tracks and be sixteen forever?"

"Well, maybe seventeen is all right, too." She made a joke of it, but she was half serious.

"I'm not sure I have this straight." Cort looked at her for enlightenment. "On the one hand you want everything in your life to stay the same."

She nodded vigorously.

"But you're willing to crusade for vast changes for everyone else—abolition, women's rights, all those noble causes."

"That's right."

"And you don't see a contradiction there?"

She paused to weigh her answer, putting into words what she had never thought through before. "I know I can't freeze everything in place just for me, if that's what you mean. And there is no way to stop the clock, so that means there will be change." She looked at Cort for confirmation, and he nodded gravely. "But we have to work for the right *kind* of change," Miranda went on. "If we don't do that, then what are we here for?"

Cort drew on his cigar again and released a fragrant cloud of smoke, the haze lingering in the air almost as long as Miranda's question. "I wasn't prepared for a philosophical discussion," he said at last. "You're full of surprises, Miranda. Just when I think you are cornered and pinned down, you spin off in another direction. I'm not quite sure whether we're playing croquet or chess."

"I don't play chess," Miranda said, choosing to take him literally. "That is, Jimmy taught me the moves once, but he's so smart he always beats me, and that's no fun. I don't like trying to plan everything six moves ahead."

And Cort did, of course. Marriage, money, family, future. Shrewd player that he was, he was bound to make the game come out in his favor. Susanne Robillard's tactics were going to be no match for his grand strategy. Unless the rules changed, of course, and the game turned out to be considerably more complicated than anyone thought.

Chapter 8

THE NEXT WEEK passed in a continuing round of picnics and dances, band concerts and carriage rides, and, always, the obligatory strolls on the piazza. Damon returned to New York, having made no discernible progress with Miranda. Two brothers from Philadelphia had met the Schuyler girls and were dividing their time between them and two Southern belles at the Clarendon; Irene and Ann were alternately floating on a cloud or plunged into the depths.

Will Chase arrived for a week's vacation but spent most of his time talking shop with all the hotel proprietors, and Miranda wasn't really surprised when he cut short his visit after five days and went back to the Stratford. He would have left a day earlier, but there were no trains on Sunday, and so he had dutifully attended church with everyone else. They were serious about such rituals in Saratoga. That Sunday night the whole family went to hear Millard Fillmore preside at a meeting to discuss keeping the Sabbath.

"I'd rather hear Lincoln tell a funny story," Cort said afterward, out of earshot of the Robillards. But that was the only provocative comment he had made in a week. He was being scrupulously attentive to Susanne, and in his presence she gazed at him with frank adoration, and in his absence she talked about him constantly.

Miranda found this so irritating she could hardly bear it. And she found Cort's attitude incomprehensible. On the rare occasions when Miranda was alone with him, he flirted with her outrageously, daring her to respond in kind. But how could she, when she knew he was going to marry Susanne? It was all very bewildering and unsettling, particularly because, as she assured herself over and over again, she wasn't interested in him. She didn't *want* to be interested in him. If he insisted on marrying Susanne for her money, then that was the end of it. She should just forget about him. She would put him out of her mind. It was foolish to spend any more time wondering why it was so disturbing when he looked her up and down or why he held her so closely when he claimed her for a single dance every night. It didn't make any sense. And she wasn't going to lie awake again tonight worrying about it. She punched her pillow and turned over to the other side and for the hundredth time assured herself she wouldn't think about Cort Adams any more at all.

A distraction arrived the next day on the morning train, a distraction in the form of her cousin Marty Schuyler. Miranda had carefully avoided him for months—and he had made no effort to see her—but there was no escape when the whole family was under the same roof.

That first day Marty was on his best behavior, and he made a particular effort to be charming to the Robillard girls. Susanne, out of some misguided attempt to tease Cort, chose to wander outside on the terrace with Marty between dances and found herself in an unforeseen wrestling match. She was rescued by Richard and promptly fled to her mother, feeling considerably subdued. Marty just grinned and turned his attention to Miranda. She had refused his invitation to dance and was about to plead a sudden headache when Cort appeared at her side. She followed him to the terrace gratefully, with Marty in unexpected pursuit.

"I was here earlier this evening," Marty noted, with a wolfish grin for both of them. "You really should keep better track of Susanne, Mr. Adams, although I realize you have so many *other* interests that one fiancée, more or less, can easily get lost in the shuffle."

"Ignore him, Cort." Miranda put a placating hand on his arm, and she could feel the tension coiled there, through all the layers of clothing. "Just because he insists on acting like a boor—"

"I don't know what hold he has over you, Miranda," there was a thread of jealousy in Marty's voice, "but if you really want to wait in line behind the misguided Miss Robillard and the woman in England and that scandalous actress in New York and God knows how many—"

"I see you are all enjoying a beautiful evening." Richard sauntered out of the shadows. "Susanne was looking for you," he said to Cort. "I think she is suffering from a mild indisposition and wishes to say good night."

Cort looked at him doubtfully but seized the opportunity to take his departure, bowing to Miranda and giving Marty a mock salute.

Marty sighed. "I wish you would stop interfering, Richard. I wanted to talk to him. You know we were dead right about his past."

Miranda looked from one to the other, shocked. "What do you mean? Are you spying on Cort? And are you in on it, Richard? What's the matter with you?"

"Marty, you never know when to keep your mouth shut." Richard's voice was so controlled that Miranda knew he was struggling to contain his anger.

Marty shrugged. "Well, what's the point of investigating him if we—"

"That's enough. This is not the time or the place to go into all that." Richard spoke with authority, and Marty glared at him.

"You needn't be so high and mighty all the time. You thought it was a good idea when I suggested—"

"Marty!"

"Oh, all right. Though I still think Miranda ought to know—put her on her guard."

Richard shook his head, and Marty departed, still muttering under his breath.

"And what was that all about?" Miranda looked at Richard with distaste.

Richard sighed. "I'm sorry you had to find out this way."

"Find out what? That you have been spying on Cort? That's an utterly despicable thing to do, and what possible reason could you have?"

"The man is a fortune hunter."

"I know that. What business is it of yours? Susanne knows his family lost most of their money in the last panic. If it doesn't bother her, why should it bother you?"

"You knew about it all along?"

"Of course. Cort told me practically the first time I met him."

"And you weren't shocked to know he had cold-bloodedly set out to marry money?"

"Well, yes, at first. But after all," she was rather proud of how worldly she was becoming, "it's not *my* fortune he's marrying." Realization struck her. "No, it's the Robillard fortune he's after. So that's what is bothering you. You hypocrite, Richard. You're afraid that—"

"Miranda, you've got it all wrong. As usual. Marty had a disagreeable encounter with Cort last February, and they actually came to blows."

"Oh, you don't understand a thing about it. Cort was defending me."

Richard eyed her skeptically. "In any case, we took advantage of an unexpected opportunity. Marty and I were dealing with the Pinkertons at the time—there were some labor agitators trying to stir up the dockworkers—and one of the agents said he'd be glad to look into the background of this Cort Adams. He didn't trust newspaper reporters, and there was bound to be something fishy about him. I was a little hesitant at first, but when the agent discovered Cort's connection to the Robillards—not to mention the actress and a few other matters . . ."

"And now that you think you've discovered something, what are you going to do about it?" Miranda was still belligerent.

Richard studied her, and whatever he had planned to tell her remained unsaid. "I don't see why you are defending him. But let's just pretend he has reformed completely, and now he has earned his just reward. He can marry Susanne and both of them can disappear to Savannah forever. I think that might be the best solution after all. What do you think?"

"I think you have behaved disgracefully. And what's more, you're probably hiding something from me."

Richard laughed. "You disapprove thoroughly of the investigation, but you want to know what we found out just the same."

Miranda refused to acknowledge the contradiction, and she glared at him.

"Ah, well. One further tidbit, and that's all. The actress, Susan Jefferson, has a touch of the tarbrush. Her grandmother was a slave in Virginia. What do you think of that?"

"I think . . . I think . . ." Miranda was struggling to mas-

71

ter her confused reactions. "I think it just proves again how dreadful slavery really is. That poor woman."

"The actress?"

"No. Her grandmother. At the mercy of her white owner. I don't see how anyone can look at the evils of slavery and not be an abolitionist."

Richard sighed and shook his head. "Ah, Miranda, your devotion to your cause is truly remarkable. But if you would only open your eyes to what is going on closer to home—"

"You sound like Cort. The mill girls in Massachusetts and the slums of Five Points."

"No, I meant what is happening right under your nose. The people who really love you and pay attention to you and protect you from your own youth and impetuousness."

Miranda lay awake that night for a restless hour, wondering what in the world those Pinkerton agents had dug up about Cort. Richard was holding something back. She just knew it.

She was not at all surprised the next morning when Richard told them that Marty had been called back abruptly to New York.

It was two days later when Miranda strolled out onto the terrace in the late afternoon and saw Cort kissing Susanne—more than kissing: Susanne was clinging to him, and he was holding her, touching her, his hands moving over her in a way that made Miranda conscious of the flesh under all those prim layers of hoops and skirts and petticoats. She retreated hastily, aware suddenly of her own body, her own heart pounding, her own face flushed.

In the parlor Richard looked at her curiously. He was hovering over Danielle at the tea table, and Miranda joined them.

"The tea is all gone, I'm afraid," Danielle said. "But I am sure that the waiter—"

"No, thanks." Miranda sat down and smiled at them tentatively. She wondered if Richard and Danielle embraced like that, and somehow she couldn't picture it.

"We're waiting for John," Richard explained, "and then we're going for a stroll in the gardens. Why don't you join us?"

"Oh, I don't think—"

"Please come," Danielle insisted. "I want to ride on the circular railroad, and we really need two couples for that."

With that enticement, Miranda succumbed immediately.

The circular railroad still filled her with childish delight, and she would willingly have ridden it every day. It was something like a merry-go-round, with two light cars moving on two concentric tracks. The cars were propelled by foot pedals, providing an energetic workout for a gentleman escort while his lady passenger clutched at her bonnet and encouraged him to greater efforts as they whirled around the circle, waving to the couple whizzing by in the opposite direction.

"I'll need my hat," Miranda said, rising.

"I'll get it for you." Richard was halfway to the door. "Irene is in the room primping, and she can find it. The blue one?"

Miranda nodded, sitting down again. "Richard is being very cooperative," she said to Danielle.

"Yes, he's a dear. Like the whole family. So warm and hospitable. We *do* love it here."

"Yes, it's fine for a vacation," Miranda agreed. "But I suppose you'll be glad to get home to Savannah."

Danielle shrugged. "Susanne will be glad. After Cort leaves tomorrow—"

Miranda looked at her in surprise.

"Yes, he's decided he has to follow Senator Douglas to Virginia. I think he got a telegram this morning from the *Times*."

"So he is saying good-by to Susanne," she said, half to herself.

"I suppose so." Danielle was matter-of-fact. "All Susanne wants to do now is to go home and get ready for the wedding."

"When will that be?"

"In November, probably. After the election. I don't see what that has to do with it, but that's what Cort says."

"You'll be in the wedding, I suppose, as maid of honor."

There was the slightest of pauses, but when Miranda glanced over at Danielle, she nodded in sudden agreement. "Maid of honor. Yes."

"And then they'll be living in Washington City?"

"For a while, I think. I'm not sure."

"But of course you'll want to stay in Savannah," Miranda went on, probing relentlessly.

"Not necessarily." A note of caution had entered Danielle's voice. "I like to travel, and I think I could live anywhere."

"I see. And your parents wouldn't object?"

An odd little smile flickered briefly and was replaced by a carefully neutral expression before she answered. "We'll work something out."

That sounded pretty definite, Miranda thought, and she couldn't resist one more question. "Does that mean you'll be announcing your engagement soon? You and Richard?"

Danielle's face was a study in conflicting reactions, and this time the silence went on so long that finally Miranda was conscious of it.

But whatever Danielle might have chosen to say was cut off by the return of John and Richard, Richard carrying Miranda's bonnet and presenting it with a flourish.

"Miranda was just asking me," Danielle looked meaningfully at Richard, "whether you and I would be announcing our engagement soon."

"I think you should keep it a secret," John cut in quickly.

"That's right," Richard agreed emphatically. "We don't want anyone to know."

"But since your parents approve . . ." Miranda felt she was missing something.

"Think about Susanne," John said with sudden inspiration. "This is *her* time to be the center of the stage. Dany doesn't want to interfere."

Miranda looked at him doubtfully, but Danielle agreed with a smile.

"That's right. Susanne is all wrapped up in Cort and the preparations for the wedding. We just want to take care of one thing at a time."

Miranda was conscious of an odd undercurrent, but John looked at her pleadingly, and she let it pass. Pausing at the mirror to adjust her bonnet, she saw Richard give a thumbs-up signal to John, and she stared at his reflection in the glass. Richard grinned at her then, and she motioned to him.

"You're right, you know," Miranda whispered when he was close enough to hear. "She *is* willing to move to New York or anywhere else."

"Yes," he agreed. "I know." He was obviously in high good humor, and his mood was catching. John and Danielle were bubbling with suppressed glee, and Miranda cast off any lingering suspicions.

Hand in hand, laughing, the four of them headed for the park. And at the circular railroad, John yielded to Miranda's pleas and let *her* work the foot pedals before they switched partners.

"I think I like Danielle better than Susanne," Miranda confided to Richard. "If you get her away from Savannah, you might even be doing her a favor."

Richard laughed and pedaled faster, but in the race back to the starting place, John and Danielle won.

Cort was to leave next day, in the late afternoon, and as a farewell they had planned an all-day picnic at the lake. John, who was making preparations to return to England, said he would join them later. And Danielle, who thought she was coming down with a chill, begged off at the last minute, too. Richard professed great concern but was persuaded to go on the picnic just the same.

Ann and Irene were happily paired off with the boys from Philadelphia, Susanne clung to Cort all day, and Miranda found herself with an oddly exuberant Richard, who proceeded to take over the picnic. He organized the games, rented the rowboats, proposed the toasts, and even led the singing, which he prolonged until they exhausted their repertory. By then it was so late that Cort and the Robillards had to rush their departure to make sure he could catch his train. Miranda went with them in the first carriage, impatient to lay to rest a small, nagging suspicion. John had not put in an appearance all day, and when she commented on his absence to Richard, he had brushed off her concern with a smile and a joke and another glass of champagne.

It was even worse than she had feared: John and Danielle had eloped.

Mrs. Robillard discovered it first, hurrying to Danielle's room to see if she had recovered from her chill. The room had been swept clean of her belongings, and there were notes for all the family—and for Miranda, too.

Mrs. Robillard burst into tears, and her husband raged, but they seemed singularly incapable of taking action.

"Send a telegram!" Miranda burst out. "Stop them!"

"They must be in New York by now," Cort said, consulting his pocket watch. "With that long head start . . ."

The frightened servants had confirmed that Miss Dany and

Mr. John had caught the morning train for the seven-hour trip to the city.

"*Do* something," Miranda appealed to Cort.

"I'll check as soon as I get there, of course." He was supervising the loading of his trunks in the carriage, and all the family had gathered on the front steps, looking to him for guidance. "The problem is that I'm taking the night boat from Albany, and it will be morning before I arrive."

"My poor lamb," Mrs. Robillard sobbed. "All *night*. Her reputation!"

"I'll take a shotgun to that boy!" Douglas Robillard raged.

"I don't understand," Mrs. Robillard wailed. "We liked John. If he had just come to us and asked permission to court Dany, we would have agreed. We would have given them time to get to know each other, invited him to Savannah . . ."

It was Susanne who had the obvious answer for that. "Why, they must have decided they didn't want to wait!"

Mrs. Robillard turned to her husband and began to sob again.

Cort patted her arm, shook hands with Mr. Robillard, and kissed Susanne hastily before springing into the waiting carriage. "Miranda," he called out as the carriage began to move, "since John and I are marrying sisters, does that mean I'll be your brother-in-law?"

Her face reflected her confusion, and he blew her a kiss, a brotherly kiss, and waved a last good-by.

Susanne threw her arms around Miranda and kissed her, too. "He's right, you know. We will be sisters now. Why, if Dany is in England in November, you can come to Savannah and be my maid of honor."

Miranda looked at her, horrified, and was spared from answering by the arrival of the Schuyler carriage.

Richard took one look at the distraught family and knew the secret was out.

"It's all your fault, young man!" Douglas Robillard accused him.

"We'll talk about it inside," Richard said, helping his mother and sisters alight. They had stopped at the Clarendon first and dropped off the two Philadelphia boys.

"Talk about what?" Faith Schuyler was suddenly alert.

"Didn't Cort get away?" Paul Schuyler had handed over the reins to a stableboy and joined them on the steps. "Is that what the problem is? If he was too late to catch the train—"

"No," Miranda burst out. "The problem isn't Cort. It's John and Danielle. They've eloped! And you knew it all along," she accused Richard.

"Not so loud," Richard protested. "Do you want the whole world to know?"

For the first time, Miranda became aware that they were giving a public performance. The rocking chairs were motionless, the strollers had ceased their promenades, and the expectant audience on the piazza was waiting for the next act of the drama.

Faith Schuyler reacted with calm dignity, hauteur masking the horror of being a public spectacle. "We will go to our suite," she announced. "All of us." And with that she swept into the hotel, regally sure that she would be followed—and in silence.

In the Schuyler suite she was still in command, and she listened to Douglas Robillard's recital of events with surface calm, inwardly seething.

"And you knew about all this?" she accused Richard. "You let John Chase run off with the girl you loved?"

"No, Mother. You have it all wrong. I was never in love with Dany. I like her, of course, but she isn't—"

"So you knew about it all along," Douglas Robillard confronted Richard. "And you conspired to help them instead of coming to tell me. An honorable man would have—"

"Come, sir." Paul Schuyler moved to defend his son. "He could hardly betray a confidence. If John Chase—"

"Exactly," Faith Schuyler agreed, finding a target that suited her. "It's all John's fault. I knew it was a mistake to—"

"I wouldn't be so hard on John," Paul Schuyler contradicted her. "He's a good lad, and he's going far. The courtship may have been a trifle precipitous, but you can't really quarrel with success. And if Danielle loves him, I don't think there's anything we should do but wish them good fortune and happiness."

"That's right," Susanne agreed emphatically. "I think it's very romantic, and I like John. And besides, now that Dany is gone, we can go right home to Savannah, and I can start getting ready for my own wedding."

"In any case," Douglas Robillard was in partial agreement, "I think we should leave for New York on the morning train. We'll find out what has happened, and perhaps we'll be in time to confront them before they leave."

"They were planning to take a ship for England tomorrow afternoon," Richard volunteered. "Dany thought it would be romantic to be married by the captain, but John is sure that our rector will marry them without waiting for the banns."

Mrs. Robillard sighed. "It isn't at all what we had planned for her. My dear Dany, going to live so far away." Just saying the words aloud convinced her it was a *fait accompli*. And she burst into tears again. Susanne put her arms around her mother, rather enjoying the drama of it all, and the sobs subsided gradually. Mrs. Robillard wiped her eyes and held on to her younger daughter. "My baby, you'll be different. We'll go right home to Savannah and stay there. I think we should start packing right away. Find out when the first train leaves for New York."

"I'm going on that train, too," Miranda said decisively.

"There's not a thing you can do to stop John," Richard protested. "You might as well stay in Saratoga for the last week and we'll all go back together."

"No, I want to be in New York. I can travel with the Robillards. After all," her smile was wry, "we're practically related now."

Back at the Stratford, Miranda discovered she had missed all the excitement.

"I gave them the bridal suite," Will Chase said. "They were already married by the time they arrived here—and it was two hours after that when your telegram was delivered. It's so unlike John, moving with such reckless speed, but he and Dany seem very happy together, so it may all work out for the best."

"And is Cort still here?" Susanne asked impatiently.

"No, he's halfway to Virginia by now. We all went to the ship together to see the newlyweds off to England, and then Cort took the ferry over to Jersey City to catch the train."

"So they are all gone." Miranda was feeling forlorn. "And I missed everything."

"Cheer up, Sis." George smiled at her. "Damon McMasters came by the hotel today and asked when you'd be back. He has the most wonderful surprise, and he can hardly wait to tell you. Or ask you, perhaps I should say."

Miranda's gloom deepened. "If you are going to start acting like John, passing judgment on Damon and telling me how much you approve, I might as well turn right around and go back to Saratoga. What did John *say* to you?"

George looked at her, surprised. "I don't believe he once mentioned your name, though Dany did. She said she had wanted to confide in you, but John persuaded her not to. The subject of Damon McMasters did not come up at all. Is there some reason it should?"

Miranda sighed, but Susanne was eager to answer. "I thought you knew. Damon followed her around like a little puppy dog for a whole week. I think *I* know what he wants to ask her."

Miranda restrained herself with difficulty. "There are *some* people who don't spend every waking minute thinking about matchmaking and marriage, and I am one of them."

"Good," George interjected, "and in this case, Damon is another. He has an invitation, not a proposal of marriage. But I shouldn't say another word or I'll ruin the surprise."

Miranda shrugged, her indifference all too evident.

Chapter 9

BY THE FOLLOWING evening, when Damon arrived at the hotel, Miranda had already forgotten the conversation. The Robillards had departed that day in a flurry of trunks and boxes and barely coherent instructions about a delivery of silks and fine cambric for Susanne's trousseau. Miranda had steadfastly refused to participate in the wedding, and the more the Robillards entreated, the more she sympathized with Dany's elopement. No wonder the poor girl had wanted to get away. They could be positively stifling, and she had a sudden vision of Cort enmeshed in their toils.

She was in the family parlor browsing through all the magazines she had missed in Saratoga, and she looked up from a stack of *Frank Leslie's* and *Harper's Weekly*s to see Damon arriving with George.

They exchanged the proper greetings, Miranda trying hard to be politely friendly and no more, but Damon was oblivious.

"Have you guessed yet, Miranda?" He looked at her expectantly, rejoicing in his secret, in his sheer delight at seeing her again.

Susanne's comment came back to haunt her. He *is* like a puppy dog, she thought. He sits there looking at me with those big spaniel eyes, and if I reached out to pat him, he'd wag his tail in a paroxysm of joy.

"But of course you just got back yesterday," Damon answered his own question, "so maybe you don't know."

"No," she agreed, looking from him to George. "I have no idea at all what you are talking about."

"The Prince of Wales!" Damon said triumphantly. "He's coming to New York!"

"Oh, yes, I guess I did hear something about that." She was baffled by his excitement.

"But, Miranda, it's the most important thing that ever happened. The Prince of Wales! Queen Victoria's oldest son!" Damon insisted on explaining the obvious. "He's going to be King of England someday. Albert Edward. King Albert I."

"Or Edward VII," George suggested. "I think they can choose whatever name they want. He's got a long time to think about that—he's only eighteen and he might not be king for years and years."

Damon brushed that aside. "He's coming in October, Miranda, and you just don't understand how important it is. It will make the visit of the Japanese ambassadors look like nothing at all."

Miranda, who had flipped through all the recent copies of *Leslie's* and *Harper's*, contradicted him immediately. "That's impossible. Why, the Japanese have crowded out all the other news. I can't find out a thing about the political campaign."

"Just wait until you see what it will be like when the Prince arrives," Damon said confidently. "And, Miranda, there's going to be a ball, the most wonderful ball we've ever had!"

A glimmer of his excitement reached her at last, lighting her eyes with sudden sparkle. "Damon, that's why you're here. To invite me—"

"Will you come?"

"Oh, yes! What a wonderful idea!"

"It will be truly splendid," Damon promised. "Invitations are very hard to get, but Papa knows Mr. Strong—he's on the committee—and we are getting up a party. George is coming, too."

"I'm taking Damon's cousin," George explained. "Emily Bradley."

"She's from Brooklyn," Damon said. "I don't think you know her."

"No," Miranda agreed. "I don't know her." She doubted if George did either, but that hardly mattered. They were used to having the older generation arrange their social engagements, and Miranda was quite sure that her own invitation from Damon had first been discussed with his parents, particularly since Mr. McMasters was organizing the party and providing the tickets. And very expensive the tickets turned out to be—ten dollars each, more than a workingman's weekly wages. Still, as the weeks went by and the excitement built, invitations to the Prince's ball were more coveted than rubies, and members of the committee—Peter Cooper, General Winfield Scott, William B. Astor, George Templeton Strong—were besieged with requests.

The Prince's progress through Canada and the United States was chronicled at enormous length, the illustrated weeklies as well as the daily newspapers devoting far more space to the peregrinations of Baron Renfrew, as he was sometimes styled, than to the entire Presidential campaign.

Perhaps that was because by October 11, the date of the Prince's arrival in New York, the election of Abraham Lincoln appeared certain. Frantic attempts to patch up some kind of alliance between the Constitutional Union party and the divided Democrats had come to nothing, and Senator Douglas found himself in the curious position of being the only truly national leader, running against Lincoln in the North and against Breckinridge in the South, two sectional candidates who weren't even on the ballot in most states outside their own regions. But the hard fact was that the North had the electoral votes to win, and by mid-October, when local contests in Maine and Vermont and Indiana and Ohio and Pennsylvania resulted in Republican victories, the outcome of the November Presidential election was no longer in doubt. What the South would do then was a matter of some concern—the stock market was dropping every day. But since compromise had always been found in the past, there was still hope. In any case, few people were worrying yet.

The major news, dominating all else, was the arrival of Prince Albert Edward in New York on a bright blue October day, debarking from the *Harriet Lane* at the Battery to review the troops and receive the official city welcome. Handsome in his scarlet uniform of colonel, the Prince was greeted by an ocean roar of cheers as his open carriage rolled up Broadway to City Hall for more ceremonies. From there he proceeded to his suite at the Fifth Avenue Hotel through streets still thronged with people, the greatest turnout in New York history. Even the Irish were caught up in the spirit of the day. Everywhere there were flags and uniforms, marching bands and thunderous salutes—a high tide of enthusiasm and good will.

From the library windows of the Stratford, Miranda had an excellent view of the procession on Broadway, though Irene Schuyler held on to the field glasses so long that Miranda saw the Prince as little more than a distant red speck. Still, she could hardly begrudge Irene that much, Irene who was missing the ball. When Richard Schuyler secured two invitations, his mother had decreed that he must take one of his sisters, and since Ann was the older . . . Irene had moped for weeks, convinced that all that stood between her and the throne of England was an opportunity to waltz with the Prince.

"If only I could meet him tomorrow," Irene sighed, finally passing the field glasses to her sister.

"His itinerary is in the papers," Miranda said helpfully, and Irene took time out to scan the endless columns about the life and times of Lord Renfrew.

"It says he's going to the Woman's Library." Irene lost herself in a daydream. "I could be there holding a book, and he would come in and see me . . ."

"New York University, Astor Library, Cooper Institute, Free Academy," Tom Chase read over her shoulder. "Central Park. Lunch with Mayor Wood at his residence on the Bloomingdale Road."

"That's a possibility." Irene considered it. "Papa met the mayor once, and if we called on him—"

"Here it is!" Tom exclaimed. "The very thing. " 'After lunch with the mayor, Lord Renfrew will visit the Deaf and Dumb Institute at Fort Washington.' Why don't you show up there, Irene? You wouldn't have any competition, and—"

"I think you're hateful." She snatched the paper from him. "Ann and Miranda are going to the ball tomorrow, and I'll be just like Cinderella. At home in the ashes. I don't see why I can't go, too. I want to dance with the Prince."

"Irene, you know that's impossible," Ann finally surrendered the field glasses to Miranda, but only the Seventh Regiment was visible. "And anyway, they aren't allowing him to choose his own partners. He's going to be paired off with all those old ladies. The wife of the governor. Middle-aged matrons. Mothers. I think it's terrible."

"You mean you won't be able to dance with him either?" Irene cheered up—just for an instant. "But, oh, I wish I could go. Are you sure you're feeling all right, Ann? Not feverish or anything?"

"I've never felt better," Ann proclaimed. "And I'd drag myself to that dance even if I were on my deathbed."

Irene sighed and consulted the newspaper again. "Central Park. I could be riding there, and his carriage would come along . . ."

The ball was at the Academy of Music on Fourteenth Street, the building transformed for the occasion from opera house to royal pleasure dome. A dance floor had been laid down over the orchestra seats, the boxes were decorated with the flags of the United States and England entwined with ostrich plumes, and floor-to-ceiling mirrors reflected the hundreds of bouquets that had emptied all the florist shops for miles around.

Next door, on the land between the Academy and the Medical University, the ball committee had had constructed a special supper room to accommodate the thousand of guests. Inside the wooden structure was a tent of silk, and again there were flowers and mirrors, brightly illuminated by twenty brass chandeliers. Under direction of the Delmonico staff, waiters scurried through their last-minute preparations.

Prince Albert Edward was due to arrive at ten o'clock, but invited guests started coming as early as seven-thirty, and they were in full flood an hour later. They made their way through the blazing glare of calcium lights to the Irving Place entrance, the police holding back the crowds of gaping bystanders.

All New York had turned out for this most glittering and magnificent party in the city's history, surpassing even the reception for Lafayette a generation before.

Irene Schuyler was sick with envy watching Richard depart with Ann, resplendent in pale green taffeta, flounced skirt over wide crinolines, an off-the-shoulder ruffled bertha of creamiest Chantilly lace, and the pearl necklace that had once belonged to Grandma Beekman. There had been a shocking fight over the jewelry for the ball, Ann demanding the family diamonds and her mother equally insistent that diamonds were not appropriate for young unmarried daughters, no matter what the occasion. Ann lost, but by the time she arrived at the Academy of Music, she had forgotten all about that. The crowds, the blazing lights, the cheers had driven it from her mind, and she was intoxicated by excitement.

Carriage after carriage drew up to the entrance, discharg-

a reverse that almost caught her off guard and left her breathless. He smiled and then steered her into a distant corner where they could talk more easily, "What do you hear from John?"

"Not much. They are happy, I guess, but he writes to Richard more than he does to us—business letters, mostly. I don't pay attention to all that. I think the stock market is going down and they worry about it, but nobody can do anything. They seem to blame it all on the fact that Lincoln will be elected." She looked at him for confirmation.

"Yes, if that happens, the Southern states will probably secede."

"I don't see why. Lincoln isn't going to interfere with slavery—he's said so. I think they are just a lot of spoilsports down there. As long as their candidates won, they were willing to stay in the Union. The first time they lose, they want to pick up their marbles and leave. Like little boys."

"And you would spank them and keep them at home, is that it?"

The waltz ended before she could reply, and he stood waiting for her response.

"Spank them," she repeated vaguely. "Yes, I suppose so." She consulted her dance card. "Richard will be looking for me—across the floor, with Mr. and Mrs. McMasters." She expected to be escorted there.

"Let him look."

"But it's his dance . . . And didn't you come with a party? Aren't you supposed to—"

"A member of the press can always get in anywhere."

"You mean you don't have a ticket? You don't belong here?"

"I wouldn't say that." Cort contrived to look injured. "Surely I belong wherever there might be news, and when the floor crashed, that made me legitimate."

Miranda looked doubtful, but he grinned at her, and when the orchestra struck up the music for a polka, she automatically moved into his arms.

"Did you know, Miranda, that when the carpenters had nearly finished their repairs, they discovered they had nailed up one of their comrades under the floor, and they had to undo their handiwork and start all over again."

"Really?"

"Really and truly. There was some sentiment for letting the

poor fellow stay there all night, but I was among the wiser heads who insisted he be pulled out immediately."

"That was good of you."

"And practical, too. He had a hammer with him and might very well have attracted enough attention to spoil the dancing for the rest of the evening. Or even pulled the floor down around him again. One catastrophe is enough."

She laughed and Cort smiled at her; Richard Schuyler was forgotten. They circled the Prince of Wales once, and Miranda looked at him longingly.

"If you got in here without an invitation, Cort, you ought to be able to arrange an introduction for me."

"I don't quite follow your logic, but I'll see what I can do." He scanned the dignitaries clustered near the Prince's reception room, considering the possibilities. "You *really* want to meet him?"

She nodded vigorously, and he directed their steps toward an elderly man in uniform.

"I'll introduce you to General Scott," he whispered in her ear. "He doesn't remember me, I'm sure, but I met him two months ago. Anyway, he'll find you so dazzling it doesn't matter. And then," he explained, "*he* can introduce you to the Prince."

General Scott pretended recognition of Cort, but there was no pretense at all about his enthusiasm for Miranda. There was nothing he could do about the Prince's dance card, he said regretfully, but an introduction was certainly possible. And then Cort had an inspiration: If, when they took their places for the lancers, General Scott could arrange for them to be in the same quadrille pattern with the Prince . . .

Miranda waited impatiently for the polka to end and the Prince to return, but Richard Schuyler found her before Albert Edward arrived.

"I believe this was my dance," he informed Cort, his voice cold. Miranda, I have been looking for you since—"

"Not now, Richard, I'm waiting for the Prince."

"Don't be ridiculous. This was supposed to be my dance. And the next one is George's, but he said that if I found you, I could take his place. He grasped her firmly and tried to lead her away.

"No."

"No? Miranda, it was very rude of you to go off with Cort,

but I was willing to overlook one lapse. It's not as if he . . . I mean, he *is* getting married next month."

"Richard, you're embarrassing me." She tried in vain to break his hold on her. "I am going to meet the Prince," she said again. "Cort introduced me to General Scott, and he—"

For the first time Richard became aware of the beribboned officer standing three feet away, and if he didn't quite snap to attention, he at least loosened his grasp on Miranda, and she was able to disengage and massage her arm. She was wearing long gloves, and she didn't bruise easily, but in any case she wasn't going to let Richard Schuyler leave his mark on *her*.

"Now do you believe me?"

He was tense with anger, six feet of thunder cloud. "All right. An introduction to His Royal Highness will take less than two minutes, and I'll wait. And then it's my dance."

"What a gracious invitation. But the answer is no. Cort and I—"

Richard looked at them both, barely controlling his fury. "If you—"

"The lady says no," Cort repeated, not bothering to conceal a smile.

Richard turned on his heel and stalked away, blind to the arrival of Prince Albert Edward and the twittering ladies in his wake.

General Scott stepped forward to perform the introductions, and Miranda curtsied gracefully. The Prince looked hopefully at the distinguished nobleman in charge of his entourage—who shook his head and indicated the next matron to be his partner. Albert Edward sighed and acknowledged his duty, but he enthusiastically endorsed General Scott's arrangements for the lancers. Miranda counted that as at least half a dance with royalty, and she whirled through the steps as if possessed. Richard Schuyler glowered from the sidelines, but she didn't see him at all. And Cort, who had engineered it all, smiled at her indulgently and swept her into his arms for the last figure of the dance. And he kissed her. She was hardly aware of it, still gliding on some spectral cloud with a fairy-tale prince who had no more substance than a dream. Even when Damon claimed her for the galop, she was still floating in another world, and he was content to be silent, or perhaps merely tongue-tied, waiting for her to come back to earth.

Cort was making himself agreeable to Mrs. McMasters,

and he dutifully danced twice with Ann Schuyler and once with Damon's cousin, the shyly attractive Emily Bradley. George Chase, who had missed the earlier contretemps over Miranda's choice of partners, willingly agreed to let Cort take his place with Miranda in the next waltz. This time she was aware of Richard's glowers and Damon's wistful sighs, but she was even more aware of Cort's arms around her and the seductive music of the waltz.

They danced in silence, and she followed him easily, very conscious of the pressure of his arm around her waist, of the warmth of his gloved hands, of his face too close to her.

She tried to open up a space between them, but he held her in an iron lock, seemingly oblivious. "Cort, you're holding me too tightly," she protested. "Everyone is looking."

"Green with envy, no doubt." He made no move to free her, and she could hardly wrestle with him in the middle of the dance floor. Besides, she would undoubtedly lose.

"All I have to do is signal Richard," she said with sudden inspiration, "and he'll rescue me."

The space between them widened magically, and she smiled with satisfaction.

"A minor victory," Cort acknowledged. "But I'm sorry to find you so conventional."

"This is much better," Miranda said. "You were making me breathless, holding me like that."

"Breathless," Cort echoed, examing the word. "What a pity we don't have more time. I think I might draw out a more interesting reaction than that."

"*You* are getting married next month," she reminded him.

"And I expect to live happily ever after," he confirmed. "But you are a deucedly attractive girl, Miranda, and it would be an interesting project—setting out to win you. If you ever turn loose all that passion on a man instead of a cause . . ."

"It won't happen," she said confidently. "Love is too risky, and I don't believe in all that nonsense."

"One day you will eat those words," Cort predicted solemnly, brushing aside her objections. "I will come to your wedding, and you will be looking up at your husband, all worshipful and starry eyed, and I will waltz you around the floor once and whisper in your ear those wonderfully satisfying words: I told you so."

"Never." She shook her head. "Never, never. Oh, you can

come dance at my wedding, if you like, but you won't see me turn into some weak quivering bowl of mush, wagging my tail—"

"That's a horrible mixture of images."

"Well, you know what I mean. If ever I get married, it will be because I have looked at the situation clearly and dispassionately and it seemed like the logical thing to do. I shouldn't have to explain that to *you*."

"But you must add in a *soupçon* of romance or it won't work." He looked at her dubiously. "And the way you throw yourself into things, I'm not sure you are capable of measuring out something as delicate as a *soupçon*." He sighed. "If I weren't otherwise occupied with Susanne, I would be delighted to stay on for a few months and give you private lessons. However . . ."

"However, this dance is over, and now I really must find Richard and soothe him." She consulted her dance card. "Yes, it's Richard. If he's still speaking to me."

He was, barely. He bowed to her formally, and she tried to look contrite, but a smile kept breaking through. Richard was the first to break the silence.

"How long is Cort going to be in New York?"

"I don't know," Miranda said, surprised. "I didn't think to inquire."

"Shouldn't he be going to Savannah soon? I trust the marriage is still on."

"Of course."

"He doesn't behave much like an engaged man," Richard observed. "And I don't mean just because of his conduct with you, although that has certainly been disgraceful enough."

"Will you stop that! I wanted to meet the Prince, and he—"

"Yes, yes, I know. The ever resourceful Mr. Adams brought off his little miracle and proceeded to collect his reward."

She colored under his disapproving stare and said nothing.

"But I am sure you can take care of yourself," Richard went on. "It's Ann I'm worried about."

"Ann! What's she got to do with Cort?"

"Nothing at all, I assure you. But he danced with her twice and God knows what he said to her, and she has been mooning over him ever since."

"That's silly."

"I agree. It's silly. But it's also irresponsible of Mr. Cortlandt Elliott Adams, and I am fed to the teeth with that man. I have told Ann that she is to have nothing more to do with him, and we will leave immediately if she—"

"He's with her now. Right over there." Miranda registered amazement.

Richard stopped dead on the dance floor. "Where are they? Never mind. I see." He was there in three strides, tapping Cort on the shoulder. Cort surrendered at once, smiling broadly, but Ann was furious.

"Richard Schuyler," she hissed. "What possesses you?"

"I warned you, Ann." He gripped her arm and steered her directly toward an exit, providing an odd diversion for the nearby guests.

"Shall we dance, Miranda?" Cort bowed to her formally, manners impeccable, and she agreed, laughing in spite of herself.

"You did that on purpose," she accused him.

"I? Surely it was the honorable Richard Schuyler who almost caused a scene, spoiled the decorum, abandoned you in the middle of the dance floor. *I* have behaved like a perfect gentleman. I was politely dancing with his sister," he savored the scene, "and she was remarkably glad to be with me, I might add."

"Yes. Richard said you turned her head. That wasn't a very nice thing to do. You're getting *married* next month."

"I am aware of that. You are aware of that. Miss Schuyler is aware of that. I believe that we have exhausted the subject of my marriage as a topic for further conversation."

Miranda considered that and then voiced her thoughts. "I wouldn't be Susanne Robillard Adams for all the tea in China."

"Now why do you put it that way?" Cort asked her seriously. "All the tea in China. It's a trite phrase, a vile phrase, hardly apt for the situation. It would be much more arresting to say 'for all the cotton in the South.' "

Miranda had an irrepressible urge to giggle.

"And then we could discuss the dollar value of the cotton crop, and what it means to the economy of the mills in Manchester, and whether Schuyler Shipping is profiting indirectly from slave labor. And you would work yourself into a passionate rage, and I could admire your rising color and the effect of rapid breathing on your enticing . . . figure."

"I think you—" She stopped abruptly, aware she was starting to blush and suddenly self-conscious about breathing, too.

His smile was bland, and she studied him in silence.

"How do you do that?" she asked finally.

He shook his head, all innocence.

"How do you turn everything upside down? Make *me* look guilty when it's really you? Force Richard out of his rigid mold and make him seem boorish when *you* are the one to blame?"

"It's a gift," he said solemnly. "When the good fairies hovered over my cradle—"

"Not the *good* ones, surely."

"Good, bad, ambivalent—I find it hard to judge. You're always so sure of yourself on the great moral issues—"

He was interrupted by Richard, returning to claim Miranda for the final measures of the dance. Cort shrugged and departed with one last exaggerated bow.

"I thought you had left," Miranda said, her voice cold.

"It was all a mistake," Richard replied stiffly. The music stopped and he escorted her off the floor. "It was not Ann's fault that Cort behaved badly, and I . . . I lost my head." It was obviously a wrenching admission for him. "I apologize, Miranda. I spoiled our dance, and I am truly sorry."

"Don't worry about it. It was all right because Cort was right there and . . ." She backed away from that subject and then recovered. "I'm sorry, too, Richard. And before, when I was rude, I didn't mean it. It was just that the Prince . . ."

"Yes. Well, once he's safely back in England, and the other one is mired in Savannah . . ." Richard summoned a rather wintry smile. "There will be other evenings, other dances."

But none like this, Miranda thought, gazing around the ballroom, still a fairy-tale palace of light and color, though a few of the flowers had started to droop. Some of the guests were wilting, too, and George had already confessed that he could hardly wait to get out of his new patent leather pumps.

She had the last dance with Damon, and he beamed at her. "I told you it was going to be splendid," he reminded her.

"And it has been, Damon. Every minute. I thank you very much for inviting me."

Behind him she saw Cort, standing alone near an exit. He looked at her questioningly, ready to rescue her, but she smiled and shook her head.

"My father likes you," Damon said shyly.

"That's nice. What about your mother?"

"She wants to know you better."

Miranda laughed. "How diplomatic of her."

"No, you don't understand." The spaniel eyes were completely innocent. "She is going to invite you to tea. You'll like her, Miranda. And she will adore you."

Miranda pulled back from him, and he missed a step.

"I don't think we should rush things," Miranda said, looking for a polite excuse.

"Oh, no, of course not." The worship was still in his eyes. "I just want my family to know you, Miranda, and love you, because—"

"Please, Damon." This time, if she had spotted Cort, she would have beckoned, but he had disappeared.

"Are you still angry about last summer? Because if you are—"

"I told you to forget that. I'm just not ready to think about . . . about anything serious. And I don't believe it would be a good idea to have tea with your mother, Damon. Truly, I don't." Miranda was decisive.

Damon gave up on that invitation. "But I will see you again very soon," he persisted. "Tomorrow? Where will the Prince be tomorrow? When he goes to Barnum's Museum—"

"No, I don't think so, Damon."

"The firemen's procession tomorrow night? Torchlights and music and—"

"But there have been so *many* parades—for the Prince yesterday, and then all the political parties all the time. If the Wide-Awakes march once more—"

"Yes, I see what you mean." He cast about for some better idea. "We could take a carriage ride in the park . . ."

"I think I will want to sleep very late tomorrow after this wonderful ball. Thank you again, but—"

"Sunday," Damon persisted. "The next day is Sunday. If the Prince goes to morning service at Trinity—"

"It will be mobbed. No, we'll go to St. Paul's as usual and—"

"I'll go with you," Damon announced.

Miranda sighed, defeated, and Damon misunderstood.

"Yes," he said, "I am very happy, too. You have made this the most wonderful night of my life." And *his* sigh was pure bliss.

* * *

Cort was staying at the Stratford, but Miranda saw very little of him. Like half the *Times* staff, he had been pressed into writing stories about the Prince, and he was increasingly impatient with that dutiful young man. "If he ever cuts loose, there will be an explosion," Cort muttered, "but until then . . ."

He had one more encounter with the Schuylers that left both Ann and Irene atwitter.

As a consolation for missing the ball—and to celebrate her seventeenth birthday—Irene had been promised coral earrings and a necklace. And so, late Saturday afternoon, with her mother and sister in tow, she was at Ball, Black and Company, poring over the selection of jewelry, lingering over the trays, asking endless questions of the dutifully patient clerks. Closing time arrived and they were the last ones in the store, and an apologetic manager hurried over to speed them on their way. The reason for the rush, he explained, was the expected arrival of the Prince of Wales.

Irene had a lightning fantasy of a diamond ring slipped over a willing finger, but she was practical enough to point to the necklace and earrings she had already chosen, and the purchase was hastily executed.

They slipped out of the door just as the Prince and his entourage arrived. Cort was talking earnestly to one of the young men in the party, but he spotted the Schuylers and hailed them. Surprised but eager, they paused to be introduced to the baffled young equerry, the five of them effectively blocking the sidewalk entrance to the store. Prince Albert Edward was forced to pause, and Irene had a long close-up view of her idol.

"He nodded to me," she reported excitedly an hour later—she had insisted on going to the Stratford immediately to report this earthshaking news to Miranda. "The Prince looked at me and he almost smiled, and if that equerry hadn't shoved me out of his way, I think he would have *talked* to me." She was in a state of bliss that had nothing to do with a new coral necklace and matching earrings.

"And Cort arranged it all," Ann Schuyler sighed. "What a perfect gentleman he is. I don't see what Richard has against him. And if he weren't marrying that silly little Southern girl next month . . . What in the world do you suppose he sees in her?"

"She's very pretty," Irene offered.

"And rich," Miranda added, *sotto voce*.

"But the way she was clinging to him," Ann protested.

"I didn't see Cort objecting," Irene said. "And I saw him looking at her—that last day at the lake—looking at her as if he couldn't wait to get his hands on her. If a man looked at me that way, I'd cling to him, too. I'd follow him anywhere."

"Yes," Miranda said, thinking out loud. "I suppose that explains it. She'll do anything he says, and as soon as he gets her away from her family . . ."

"Now let me tell you what the Prince was wearing," Irene said, impatient to return to Topic One. "When he nodded at me and I stared deeply into his eyes . . ."

Miranda smiled and gave herself up to Irene's romantic fantasies.

Cort left Monday morning, boarding the *Harriet Lane* with the Prince for the cruise up the Hudson to West Point. Miranda overslept and almost missed breakfast with him and her father. The boys had long since departed, but Will Chase still lingered over his coffee.

Cort was grumpy and out of sorts. "Lord Renfrew. Lord Froufrou. Who cares? I have to follow him all the way to Boston. And do you know why? Because Mr. Raymond was so intrigued by my account of the ball Friday night! I wasn't even supposed to be there, and I just wrote it up as a lark, and *then* he cut out the best parts. But even so, now I have to go to the ball in Boston, too."

"You mean you'll go legally this time?" Miranda asked.

Cort's response was a glum nod.

"But you must know a lot of people in Boston," Miranda protested.

"Yes," Will Chase agreed. "Do give my greetings to your dear mother. Will she be going to the ball?"

"I suppose so," Cort responded. "And my brother Warren and his wife and all their friends. And they'll all want to meet Albert Edward and swoon."

"You'll be very popular," Miranda said. "You can arrange it all."

"Perhaps. But unfortunately I can't count on the floor collapsing again. No, the only good thing about all this is that I may have a chance to become better acquainted with General Scott. Once we're embarked for West Point and everyone else is training a beady eye on His Royal Highness, I will corner the general. If nothing else, he will remember me the next time we meet."

"Well, of course he's a nice old man," Miranda began, "and I think that calling him 'Old Fuss and Feathers' is cruel, but—"

"He is still commander in chief of the army," Cort interrupted, "and it's always useful to be on good terms with a commanding general." His tone turned grim. "You never know when we might need him."

"Surely it won't come to that," Will protested. "You shouldn't let those Southern hotheads worry you. We have always managed to find a compromise. When you are in Georgia for your wedding—"

"Yes, let's talk of happier things," Cort agreed. "I hope the Chase family will be represented in Savannah." He looked expectantly at Will and Miranda. "Susanne is so disappointed that John and Dany can't return from England for the occasion, but if you—"

"I wouldn't set foot—" Miranda began, and then stopped abruptly when Cort grinned at her. "Will your family be there?" she asked, recovering.

"Mother will certainly make the trip, but I don't know about Warren and Abby—my brother and his wife. That's what I'll find out in Boston." Cort consulted his watch and then excused himself hastily. "But I won't even get to Massachusetts if I don't catch the *Harriet Lane* first."

"Let us know your plans, my boy." Will clapped him on the shoulder. "And perhaps I'll get to Savannah myself."

Miranda stared at him in surprise.

"I haven't inspected the hotels in our Southern states for years," Will said by way of explanation.

"But Papa—"

"And I'd be interested in discovering for myself exactly how tense the situation is down there. All this secession talk."

Miranda continued to stare at him dubiously.

"And after all, I've known Cort all his life." Will had no end of reasons for the trip. "And I'd like to see his family again, too," he added as an afterthought.

Miranda shook her head, dismissed the whole idea as an aberration, and finished her tea.

"And now I have to go over the accounts with George." Will departed with a final handshake, and Cort looked after him thoughtfully.

"You said you were in a hurry," Miranda reminded him. "You've seen to your trunks?"

"All taken care of." He came out of his trance. "And if you have a farewell kiss for the bridegroom . . ."

Miranda smiled and offered her cheek, but he shook his head and then reached out to pull her into his arms. She was startled when his mouth came down on hers, insistent and demanding, and for one brief moment she yielded, betrayed by some passion struggling to be born. And then, shocked by her reaction, she fought free and slapped him.

"How conventional of you." Cort collected his hat and cane while Miranda glared, still speechless with fury.

"Yes, I know." He grinned at her. "You're only breathless. And you want to remind me again that I'm getting married next month. And you're glad you're not Susanne." He paused in the doorway and blew her a kiss. "But I still wish we had more time."

"Impossible!" Miranda finally recovered her voice. "You're impossible. And I never want to see you again," she called after him, but he was already racing down the stairs.

Chapter 10

THE POLITICAL EXPERTS who had been so sure that Seward would win the nomination were now equally sure that Lincoln would win the election, and this time they were right. It is true that Lincoln polled less than 40 percent of the popular vote, but he led his three rivals by a wide margin; and in the electoral college, where it really counted, he had a decisive majority. By all the terms of the Constitution, there was no doubt that he had been elected President. Consequently, the experts—and the public at large in the Northern states—were completely unprepared when the South reacted with outrage.

Will Chase, who had gone to Savannah two weeks after the election and had planned a leisurely journey through Georgia and the Carolinas, left abruptly, the day after Susanne and Cort's wedding.

"It was dangerous," Will asserted, still astonished by the abuse and hostility he had found on all sides. The flurry of greetings over, the family had gathered in the library, eager to see the traveler so unexpectedly returned. Miranda perched on the arm of his chair, touching him periodically to make sure he was really there.

"Dangerous," he repeated. "Even frightening. At the hotel bar I was almost attacked."

Miranda gasped and the boys were outraged.

"If Cort hadn't been there—he passed himself off as an Englishman instead of a Yankee—I don't know what would have happened. One young hothead brandished a cane and threatened me with a beating."

"Oh, Papa, I'm so glad you're home again." Miranda kissed him impulsively and touched his cheek.

"What happened?" George asked. "What did they say?"

Will pulled out his pipe and tobacco and paused to reconstruct the scene. "It all started as a peaceful discussion. The usual pleasantries. Toasts. The weather. Some talk about local politics. They were aware I wasn't a Southerner, of course. And then they asked me what I thought of Lincoln. I didn't introduce the subject. *They* asked me," Will emphasized. "I said I had heard him speak once and he seemed to be a reasonable man. That was all it took. The shouts! The threats! The madman with a cane! I tell you if Cort hadn't stepped in front of me and given them a long speech about Southern hospitality and innocent strangers in their midst and the beauties of the countryside and the charm of their pretty girls, I'm not sure what would have happened."

"And the Robillards?" Jim asked. "What was their attitude?"

"They were gracious, as always. I didn't mention the rudeness I encountered in the city. And they asked about you, Miranda. Cort told them all about the Prince's ball, and Susanne was almost jealous when he said you were the most radiantly beautiful girl there."

Miranda sniffed. "He's impossible."

Will glanced at her, puzzled, but resumed his narrative. "It was a beautiful wedding, but don't ask me to describe all the dresses." Miranda had had no intention of making such a request, and the boys looked at each other and laughed.

"Susanne is a pretty little thing," Will went on, "though I think Constance—Mrs. Adams—was a little surprised when she met her. Cort had been engaged to be married once before, to a Boston girl, and I understand she was quite different. More spirited."

"What happened to her?" Miranda asked.

"She married someone else, I believe."

"And broke his heart?" Miranda looked at her father hopefully.

"No, I think he had gone to England by then and didn't really care one way or the other."

Miranda subsided, disappointed.

"You mentioned Mrs. Adams," George said tentatively. He and Jim had speculated about their father's sudden interest in attending this wedding, but they had kept their suspicions to themselves.

"A charming lady," Will said. "But more strong-minded

than I remembered. A bit like Miranda, though Constance conceals it better."

"What do you mean?" Miranda was indignant—and conscious of a criticism, though her father had smiled and patted her on the arm.

"It's all right, Pet. I just meant that she's a New England Puritan through and through. The Southern way of life—particularly slavery—repelled her, and she left Savannah the day after the wedding. Warren was eager to get home to his wife. I understand that Abby is expecting their first child in January." Will drew on his pipe and sighed. "Constance a grandmother! It's hard to believe."

Tom Chase had had enough of weddings and babies and grandmothers, and he circled the room restlessly, pausing to poke at the fire and add more coal to the blaze. "Nothing has been happening around here," he complained. "Except we almost didn't have Thanksgiving."

"Tom!" Miranda warned him. "We weren't going to bother Papa with all that."

Jim put a placating hand on her arm, and Will looked at him inquiringly.

"I'd like to hear about it."

George was resolutely gazing into the fire, Miranda glaring alternately at him and at Tom for raising the issue.

"You weren't here," Jim began tentatively, and Will nodded encouragingly. "And George was invited to Brooklyn to have dinner with the Bradleys. Emily is really a very nice girl," he added for George's benefit, but George refused to look at him. "Miranda wanted us all to be together."

"We've *always* been together," Miranda insisted. "But now John is married and you were away, Papa, and I didn't think it was fair for George—"

"You were invited by Damon McMasters—" George interrupted.

"And you put him up to it!"

"I did not. I only told him that I would be in Brooklyn and—"

"There, you see!" Miranda's anger returned full-blown. "And I made the mistake of saying something to Irene, and Uncle Paul heard me and invited all of us without telling Aunt Faith. And I said no and I kept saying no, but it didn't do any good because Richard insisted, and by then Aunt

Faith had rearranged her whole guest list." Miranda relived her defeat, and it still rankled.

"So you all went to the Schuylers?" Will asked.

"Except George." Miranda glared at him again. "And it was all his fault!"

"It wasn't so bad," Jim said in mild protest.

"Oh, yes it was," Miranda contradicted him. "You didn't have to sit there and listen to Ann Schuyler mooning after Cort Adams on the very day before his wedding. Stupid girl. At least when Irene falls in love with someone impossible, she chooses the future king of England."

"My girl is more sensible than that." Will smiled at Miranda, trying to soothe her. "You'll stay close to home, I hope. I don't see how the Robillards are going to manage, losing both Dany and Susanne."

"So Cort got his way." Miranda wasn't really surprised, but she hadn't expected the decision to be made so quickly. "When do they go to Washington City?"

"I don't think it has been settled yet." Will paused and drew on his pipe. "You can keep a secret, I trust."

They looked at their father, mystified, but agreed to be silent.

"Well, then. After their honeymoon Susanne will stay in Savannah for a month or two because Cort is going to undertake a secret reporting job for the *Times*. I can still hardly believe it." Will looked at them all and sighed. "To resort to such a thing in your own country."

"He's going to be a spy?" Tom perked up immediately.

"That's a little melodramatic," Will hedged. "No, he's just going to report what he sees on his travels through the South. He'll talk to local citizens, find out how popular secession is, look for any sings of war fever, and send back dispatches to the *Times*. And after what we saw in Savannah, he thought it would be wise to pass himself off as an English businessman. Yankees simply aren't welcome. And a Yankee reporter . . . It could be dangerous for him."

Miranda scoffed. "The worst that would happen would be a little tar and feathers. Might do him good."

Will was not amused. "No, Miranda. It is worse than that. I was there, and I saw the rage. Some of those hotheads are spoiling for a fight. Anything could happen."

Lincoln had been elected November 6, but he was not to

be inaugurated until March 4, and in those four months the chasm between North and South was steadily widening. South Carolina seceded in December, followed quickly by six more states. Their seizure of Federal property presented an immediate problem to the lame-duck Buchanan Administration, which was as divided as the country itself.

There were still voices of calm in the South, but they were being drowned out in the rising clamor for secession. And sentiment for secession was not confined to that one region. The *Tribune*'s publisher, Horace Greeley, was widely quoted for his editorial, "Let the erring sisters go in peace." General Winfield Scott offered a plan to split the country into four separate nations. And New York's mayor, Fernando Wood, went so far as to propose that the city should secede from the whole country and be independent, a free port, trading with North and South alike. Virtually everyone scoffed at that idea and Lincoln referred to it as the front door wanting to set up housekeeping on its own.

Looking for a compromise, Congress considered a proposal that would have opened some of the territories to slavery, but this legislation failed when Lincoln insisted, logically enough, that the Republican party platform was firmly opposed to *any* extension of slavery, and the voters had spoken on this issue by electing him.

In the South, representatives of the seven seceding states met in Alabama in February to draw up a constitution, and they selected Jefferson Davis as President. By curious coincidence, on February 11, when Davis was leaving his Mississippi plantation for the new capital in Montgomery, Lincoln was leaving Springfield for *his* capital in Washington City.

Lincoln's journey was in marked contrast to his trip east less than a year before. Instead of a seat in a crowded day coach, he had a private train, decorated in the height of Victorian elegance: tapestry carpet, crimson plush walls, festoons of heavy blue silk studded with thirty-four stars, and dark-panelled furnishings, every last inch decorated with carving, scrolls, and tassels. And everywhere along the way there were crowds hoping for a glimpse of the President elect and his wife and sons (the eldest had been dubbed the Prince of Rails).

Pausing frequently for impromptu speeches, stopping overnight at state capitals and principal cities, Lincoln and his entourage made such slow progress that by February

18, when they reached New York, Jefferson Davis had already been inaugurated in Montgomery and was forming his cabinet.

New York's reception of Lincoln the President-elect bore no resemblance to the quiet arrival of Lincoln the obscure lawyer coming to deliver a speech at Cooper Union. When the Presidential party arrived from Albany at the new Hudson terminal at Thirtieth Street, police had to hold back the throngs. There were the usual receptions and speeches, greetings from the mayor, and even a visit to Barnum's Museum. The President-elect was also greeted warmly at the Academy of Music, where he attended a performance of the new Verdi opera, *Un Ballo in Maschera*. At this ball no floors collapsed, but it was widely noted—there had to be *some* scandal—that Mr. Lincoln was the only gentleman present whose kid gloves were black. All the fashionable world knew that the only proper gloves at the opera were white.

"It doesn't *matter*," Miranda defended him the next day.
"It's just another sign that he's no gentleman," Ann Schuyler contradicted her. "What does a rail-splitter know about anything?" Ann had stopped at the Stratford, ostensibly to find out if Miranda would be ice-skating Saturday but actually to see if there had been any word from Cort. Ann's interest in politics, like her interest in ice-skating, was minimal, but she had read all of Cort's anonymous and increasingly pessimistic dispatches to the *Times,* and they left her confused and uncertain.

She was not alone in that reaction.

The secession of the seven Southern states had bewildered and shocked the entire North. The breakup of the Union was everywhere deplored, and there was widespread fury about the takeover of Federal buildings and military installations by the Confederate states.

For the most part these properties had been undefended, and local authorities had simply moved in. But attention was increasingly focused on one fort still garrisoned by Federal troops, occupying one small island in the harbor at Charleston. There at Fort Sumter the United States flag was still flying, a symbol of Federal authority and an affront to the South Carolina citizens who had led the movement to secede.

One attempt to supply the fort had already been turned back, but it was increasingly apparent that something would

106

have to be done or Major Robert Anderson and his small garrison could no longer hold out. The problem was that the use of Federal force might well save the fort but at the same time provoke additional states into leaving the Union. In Virginia the legislature had already voted against secession once, by a narrow margin, but one wrong move in Washington could tip the balance.

In a further attempt to placate the South, on March 2 the Congress—even without the representatives of the seceding states—passed a Constitutional amendment guaranteeing no interference with slavery where it already existed. And Lincoln backed this pro-slavery amendment in his inaugural address two days later. But events had long since overtaken that issue. The question now was secession, and Lincoln met it head-on, declaring the breakup of the Union illegal, promising to use his constitutional power "to hold, occupy, and possess the property and places belonging to the government." There was no doubt that this included Fort Sumter, now more than ever the focus of all attention.

Still posing as an Englishman, Cort Adams arrived in Charleston, lingering there through March and into April, measuring the rising war fever and sending his dispatches to the *Times*. It was perhaps inevitable that he was finally recognized, but it was unfortunate that the challenge to his identity came at the reception desk of the hotel where he was staying. The proprietor gave him half an hour to clear out all his belongings and leave the city, assuring Cort he would be equally unwelcome at every other establishment in Charleston. Cort took one look at the menacing crowd beginning to assemble, agreed that it would be wiser to depart, and left on the next train. The telegram giving his destination—as usual he sent it to the Stratford, message to be forwarded to the *Times*—never reached New York.

When they didn't hear from him on schedule, the *Times* publisher became alarmed, and at Henry Raymond's request, Will Chase wired the hotel at Charleston. There was no response.

Twenty-four hours later, when they had still heard nothing, Will paced the family parlor listening to the conflicting suggestions of his sons and the peculiar comments of his daughter, and the situation was still unresolved.

"Mr. Raymond telegraphed a reporter in Washington City,

directing him to go to Charleston immediately," Will said. "So we should get some kind of information by Friday."

"All this fuss about nothing," Miranda protested. "I don't see why."

"I wonder if I should telegraph his mother." Will was thinking out loud. "I don't want to alarm her without cause, but she should know."

"And the Robillards," George added. "We should tell them, too."

"I don't think we should be upsetting Susanne." Will was even more uncertain. "She's such a delicate child, and with the baby . . ." The news of Susanne's pregnancy had reached them only the week before in a letter from Dany in England.

"You could notify Mr. Robillard," George suggested.

"That's it," Will agreed. "That's what I'll do. Douglas Robillard can go to Charleston himself and make inquiries. Surely he can discover what happened."

Will's telegram drew an immediate response—from Cort, who was in Savannah.

"Of course I came here to see Susanne," he wrote in a follow-up letter. "I'm sorry that my message from Charleston went astray, but I'm even sorrier that I wasn't there yesterday, on the scene when General Beauregard gave the order to fire at Fort Sumter. You have no idea the astonishing effect this news has had on the populace here. Perhaps war was always inevitable, but this has triggered it, certainly. I will be returning to Washington City, but Susanne is reluctant to travel now, and I have agreed that it is best that she stay here for the present. Everyone in Savannah expects the war to be over with the first battle, and all the young men are in a fever to participate and share in the victory celebrations. Their only worry is that the Yankees will sue for peace before they get a chance to fight at all. It is useless to attempt to disillusion them, and I fear this coming conflict and what it will mean to all of us."

The attack on Fort Sumter galvanized the South, but it had an even more electrifying effect on the North, unifying all factions immediately.

Miranda, who had long thought that the destruction of slavery was worth a war, was stunned by the sudden outpouring of patriotic emotion and war fever. And slavery seemed to have nothing to do with it.

"But they fired at the *flag!*" Richard Schuyler exclaimed for the fourth time. He was in full uniform, having stopped at the Stratford after being photographed at Brady's Gallery. "Of course that means war. We have to protect the Union."

Miranda shook her head, still bewildered. "I don't understand you at all. Back in January you were still echoing that fool editorial about letting the erring sisters go in peace. Now you're ready to shoot to keep them in the Union."

"But they fired at the *flag!*" Richard repeated in exasperation. "If they want a war, we'll give them a war. They don't have anything like our Seventh Regiment. One battle and all those Southerners will come crawling back."

"With all their slaves?"

"Why not? Abolition has nothing to do with it. The Union must be preserved."

"I think you have all gone mad. Just because they fired at Fort Sumter? Suppose that idiot Beauregard had held off and just starved Major Anderson into surrender. Suppose he hadn't fired a shot. Would you all be rallying around the flag just the same, shouting about preserving the Union?"

"I think so," Richard said. "It would still have been force." He paused to consider. "Perhaps it was inevitable that we should clash—if not at Fort Sumter, then somewhere else. In a way we may be lucky that they fired first. Nothing else would have pulled us all together so quickly. All those men flocking to enlist when Lincoln called for seventy-five thousand volunteers . . ."

Miranda nodded, willing to be convinced. "And you think we can beat them in a single battle? Cort says—"

"What does *he* know?"

"I don't like him either, but he usually knows what he's talking about. In his letter to Papa—"

"Why don't you like him?" Richard seized on her comment with peculiar interest. "I thought that you and Ann . . . But Ann has finally seen the light. Now that she has met Madison Bradley—"

"Madison? You mean Emily's brother?"

"Yes. Do you know him? Nice chap. Mother is so relieved."

"I think he's boring." Miranda was always quick to judge.

"He came here once . . . But why are we talking about him? I was going to tell you what Cort said."

"Yes. Cort. Why don't you like him?" Richard repeated.

"What difference does it make? Do you want to hear what he wrote to Papa or not?"

"Since you insist on telling me."

"Well, then. He says that in Georgia they think they can beat *us* with one battle, and then we'll sue for peace."

"Impossible! I'm surprised at him. Cort has traveled around the country, supposedly with a reporter's eye. Anyone with even the most superficial knowledge knows that the North has the shipping and the railroads and the industry and the men to fight—"

"Richard, you don't listen. Cort doesn't say the South will win with one battle. He says that's what the Southerners believe. Just the way you believe we'll beat them immediately."

Richard shrugged. "If they are so stupid that they have to be beaten a second time or even a third or a fourth before they know who has won, so be it. Which side is Cort Adams on?"

"Why . . . I don't know," Miranda stopped short. "Isn't that strange? All the argu—discussions I've had with him, and I still don't know." She tried to remember if he had ever committed himself to anything except the perverse pleasure of infuriating her, and she groped for one single moment of sincerity. "He's against war," she said finally. "That's the only thing I ever heard him say about his beliefs."

"Brilliant," Richard scoffed. "Everyone is against war, but when it comes, you must take a stand. Is he going to hide behind Susanne's skirts down there in Savannah? All that skylarking around the Confederacy writing for the *Times*, pretending it was dangerous."

"But Papa says it *was* dangerous." For Miranda it was almost a reflex action to argue with Richard, but she hadn't planned to defend Cort in the process. "Oh, why are we talking about him?" She stood up impatiently as if to dismiss the subject. "To think that we are in a war at last!" Patriotic fervor had merged completely with her devotion to the cause of abolition. No matter what Richard said, she was sure that war would free the slaves and also bring glory to all the brave young men marching off to battle. Glory and honor and fame. They were heroes, all of them. That included

Richard, too, standing tall in his gray uniform, white crossbelts immaculate.

"I'm so glad that General Scott asked for the Seventh Regiment," she said. "You *do* look handsome in that uniform, Richard. All of you. George had *his* picture taken this morning, too."

"And Damon McMasters was at Brady's waiting for his sitting just as I was leaving. We will be the most photographed soldiers ever."

"I think you are all wonderful." Miranda had a possessive pride in the whole regiment. "I saw the Sixth Massachusetts this morning—did you know they all had breakfast at the Astor House?—and they looked handsome, too; but there is nothing like our Seventh Regiment."

"Nothing at all," Richard agreed wholeheartedly. "Will you miss us while we are gone?"

"We'll miss George," Miranda said, completely unconscious of where that statement left Richard. "Papa was just starting to rely on him. But George says the regiment will be gone for just thirty days. Does General Scott really think you can save Washington City in only a month?"

Richard suppressed a sigh, and his answer was matter-of-fact. "We'll just hold the line until the raw recruits get a little training. The Confederacy doesn't have an army yet, either. I don't suppose the Virginians will really swarm across the Potomac immediately. They just seceded yesterday."

"You could invade *them*," Miranda suggested.

"It's a good possibility," Richard agreed. "But first we have to protect Washington. If the secessionists get the upper hand in Maryland, too, the capital will be cut off completely."

"You won't let that happen," Miranda said confidently. "Anyway, you leave tomorrow, and they can't do anything that fast. Are you all ready?"

"Mother is fussing about, but if I paid any attention to what she thinks I should take, I'd have to hire two porters just to carry my luggage."

Miranda laughed. "George says that you need just your basic kit and one day's rations."

Richard agreed. "And Delmonico's is catering the first day's sandwiches."

"It will be like a picnic," Miranda said eagerly. "A traveling picnic. I wish I could go along. I'll watch you march away and wave my handkerchief, but it would be so exciting to take the train with you all the way to Washington City."

"I doubt if Colonel Lefferts would approve of that." Richard allowed himself a smile. "But if you were to take a vote of the men in my company . . ."

There was a knock at the open door, and they looked up to see Damon McMasters standing there, hesitating. "I just had my picture taken," Damon began, "and since the studio is so close . . ."

"Of course, Damon." Miranda directed a look at Richard that plainly begged him to help her get rid of this persistent suitor. "We were just talking about the regiment. You are all going to be heroes."

Damon blushed under her praise. "We'll do our best," he said simply. "For as long as our country needs us."

His evident sincerity reached her, and she responded with more warmth than she intended. "That's wonderful, Damon. I am so proud of all of you."

"Are you, Miranda?" His spaniel eyes were all devotion. "I hope . . . I hope you will write to me. I would cherish your letters and carry them with me next to—"

"I'll write to all of you," Miranda interrupted him. "You and Richard and George and all the rest of the company, if you think it would help."

"Oh, yes!" Damon agreed eagerly. "And I'll write to you. Every day if I can. And Miranda . . ." He hesitated and then looked at Richard, obviously hoping he would leave.

Richard ignored the unspoken request, though he retreated a few paces and pretended to examine the books on the nearest shelf.

"Miranda," Damon lowered his voice, "I made arrangements with the photographer. Mama wanted a picture of me in uniform, and of course I'll give her one. But I want *you* to have a picture, too, and Mr. Brady's assistant said he'd deliver it to you himself next week. Wasn't that nice of him? And if you would go to the studio, he will take *your* picture, too. I wish you would, Miranda. It would mean so much to me." He looked at her hopefully, without guile, and said the only possible words that would convince her. "Now that I am going off to war . . ."

"Oh, Damon, what can I say?" She looked to Richard for assistance, and he shrugged.

"Say yes," Richard advised. "Have pictures made for all of

us. Why not? It will give us something cheerful to look at before the bullets start to fly."

"Bullets," Miranda echoed, trying to conjure up a vision of battle. Gallant soldiers on galloping horses. The Charge of the Light Brigade. Into the valley of death . . . No, that was all wrong. A terrible blunder—the poem said so. But if wars weren't fought like that, then how? She looked uncertainly at Richard and Damon, off tomorrow on this great adventure. Modern knights ready to sacrifice all. Surely they deserved any tokens she could give them.

"Of course you may have my picture, Damon. I'll make an appointment with the photographer right away."

"Oh, Miranda!" Damon's eyes were shining. "I will treasure it. More than you can ever know. When I come back—"

"We'll be gone only a month," Richard interrupted.

"Yes, that's right." Miranda was glad to be called back to reality. "I'll watch you parade tomorrow and cheer you all the way."

"Will you, Miranda?" Damon was taking every word to heart. "That will mean so much to—"

"Major Anderson will be in the reviewing stand," Richard cut in again, and Miranda was transparently grateful for the interruption.

"Our first hero," she said. "I can hardly wait to see him."

The library clock chimed the half hour, and Damon stood up reluctantly. "My mother is expecting me for tea," he explained.

"And you don't want to be late," Richard agreed swiftly. "I was about to leave, too. We can share a hack."

Miranda followed them to the door for a farewell handshake, and she allowed Damon to kiss her cheek. She was surprised when Richard claimed the same privilege, but then she gave him a conspiratorial smile. Of course! Damon must not think he had progressed beyond the bounds of a cousin's dutiful farewell. Richard could be remarkably understanding. She'd certainly send *him* her photograph, too.

Chapter 11

EVEN AS NEW YORK'S Seventh Regiment was departing the next day, Friday, the Sixth Massachusetts was encountering secessionist mobs in Baltimore. Changing trains—which meant marching through the city streets to another railroad station—the Massachusetts troops were forced to fight their way through the hostile crowds. Stones, bricks, and pistols in the hands of Southern sympathizers were answered with rifle bullets, and by the end of the day twelve civilians and four soldiers lay dead.

In an effort to prevent further bloodshed—and further transit of Federal troops—the state and local authorities disabled the railroad bridges leading into Baltimore. And then sucessionist mobs tore up the tracks, occupied the telegraph offices, and cut the wires to the north.

This meant that Washington City, the nation's capital, was effectively isolated, cut off from normal communication with the loyal states to the north and west. The city was protected only by the Massachusetts Sixth Regiment, which had come through on the last train, and by a few companies—five hundred fifty-two men—from Pennsylvania. Surrounded by the slave states of Virginia and Maryland, the city was a Federal island—and a ripe prize for whichever army arrived first.

Days passed, and the government knew nothing of the progress of any troops, friendly or hostile. Guards were posted on the Potomac bridges leading to Virginia, and there were rumors that Beauregard was coming with ten thousand soldiers. In vain the President looked at the empty train tracks leading north, through the avowedly neutral but slaveholding border state of Maryland.

And five days passed. Where were all the rescue forces, the vanguard of the seventy-five thousand volunteers?

In its isolation, Washington seethed with rumors. No trains, no troops, no supplies. Congress was not in session, and the city was half deserted. Willard's Hotel, which had sometimes been jammed with as many as a thousand guests, had only forty customers. In a city full of Southern sympathizers, many residents were packing to flee, and more and more carts and wagons piled high with possessions lurched through the cobblestone streets as families sought greater security outside the district.

In the best of times Washington City was just a provincial capital, sixty thousand people and a scattering of half-finished marble buildings—little more than a promissory payment on L'Enfant's exalted dream. Ambitious plans to enlarge the Capitol building were proceeding at a desultory pace, with only a wooden derrick to mark the place where the landmark dome would rise again. Funds had run out during construction of the Washington Monument, and it was already weathering into a jagged marble stump.

The very phrase, "city of magnificent distances," was something of a joke. The reality was a cluster of unimpressive buildings in the business district, a small and scattered residential area, a festering Negro slum, and then muddy streets, overgrown fields, and vacant lots. The hotels and boardinghouses stood half empty most of the year, becoming filled to overflowing only when Congress was in session.

Muggy and hot in the summer, damp and cold and gray in the winter, Washington showed its promise only fleetingly in the spring and fall.

But not this spring. The April days ticked by, and the isolated city was still cut off.

Where were all the troops?

On Wednesday, April 24, Lincoln spoke to the Sixth Massachusetts. "I don't believe there is any North!" he said, only half in jest. "The Seventh Regiment is a myth! . . . *You* are the only Northern realities!"

The Seventh Regiment had departed on schedule, Friday afternoon, April 19, parading down Broadway through solid walls of cheering crowds. Then the troops boarded the ferry to Jersey City and a train to Philadelphia, only hours behind the Eighth Massachusetts, which had passed through New York that morning.

The Seventh reached Philadelphia in the middle of the night, and it was there that they heard they must detour around Baltimore. While arrangements were made to charter a steamer, the troops were told to scavenge three days' rations.

Then they crowded on board the *Boston* for the brief cruise that brought them to Annapolis by dawn Monday. The Eighth Massachusetts was already there, their ship having run aground. While the commanders of the two regiments argued about the best way to proceed to Washington City through possibly hostile territory, the soldiers fraternized, the hungry Massachusetts troops gratefully accepting rations from the well-supplied New Yorkers.

Finally it was decided to proceed overland, repairing the railroad as they went—laying track, rebuilding a bridge, marching through the 90-degree heat and then through a drenching rain and, finally, showing signs of fatigue, trudging endlessly all one long and weary moonlit night. It was dawn on Thursday, April 25, when the two regiments reached Annapolis Junction and were able to board a train for Washington City, thus reopening communications with the rest of the country.

That afternoon they marched up Pennsylvania Avenue to the White House to the city's cheers. The President himself reviewed the troops, and Mrs. Lincoln presented them with a bouquet from the White House conservatory.

And then, splitting up into companies, they were given hot meals at the local hotels and were quartered, temporarily, in the Hall of Representatives in the domeless Capitol. It was a week before the Seventh could move out, establishing Camp Cameron on Meridian Hill, two miles north of the center of the city.

Almost immediately their evening dress parade became a prime tourist attraction, drawing local residents as well as the travelers that came pouring into Washington once the lines were secured. Fashionable carriages rolled out Fourteenth Street to the camp every afternoon, twice bringing the President himself. And in early May, after Lincoln called for three hundred thousand more soldiers, Army recruiters came, too, offering commissions even to privates, if only they would volunteer for three years in one of the many new regiments being organized. The Seventh Regiment, ran a familiar joke, was really the country's second West Point.

George Chase, a corporal in the Seventh, was offered the rank of captain, and, as he wrote to his father, it was a powerful temptation—not just the rank but the opportunity to stay in the army and see some real fighting. The Seventh was going to be mustered out in early June, and George, having tasted this much of military life, had virtually made up his mind to volunteer.

In New York Will Chase read this letter with mixed emotions, and it took very little urging from Miranda to decide to take the train the next day for Washington. With some misgivings he left Tom in charge of the Stratford, but Miranda and Jim insisted on coming with him.

In Washington Willard's was full to capacity, and only a hotelman would know with what legerdemain a room was conjured out of nowhere for the proprietor of the Stratford and his son and daughter. It was not a large room, to be sure, and Miranda looked with distaste at the three beds overcrowding the cramped space, but it was a small miracle that they were accommodated at all.

Washington was swarming with new arrivals. With communications and transportation through Maryland secured, volunteer regiments had poured into the city and its environs, followed by hordes of civilian relatives, job-seekers, speculators, tradesmen, merchants, and businessmen in search of government contracts. No one knew if the war would be long or short, but it was obvious there was money to be made, and Washington was the mecca for profiteers as well as patriots.

Once unpacked, Miranda was impatient to leave the hotel, to find a carriage, to join the hundreds driving out to Meridian Hill for the Seventh Regiment's dress parade.

Appropriately enough, the band was playing "The Girl I Left Behind Me," as they arrived, and Miranda alighted from the carriage feeling the music was for her alone. She bestowed a dazzling smile on the band leader, who gave her a half salute; and in one sweeping glance she took in the ranks of assembled soldiers, picking out George and waving to him enthusiastically.

When the band concert and parade had ended, George pushed his way through the crowds to greet them, with Richard and Damon hard on his heels.

"You must have caught the first train!" George exclaimed.

"Oh, I am glad to see you!" He embraced them all, holding on to Miranda, with the result that Richard and Damon could only nod their greetings.

"But you are too late," George continued, talking directly to his father. "I have decided. I'm volunteering for three years—as a captain."

"Oh, George, that's wonderful." Miranda kissed him impulsively. "We'll miss you dreadfully, but it's the right thing to do. Right and noble."

George hugged her, but he looked at his father for reassurance.

Will suppressed a sigh and clapped him on the shoulder. "My dear boy. I had hoped you wouldn't be impulsive . . . but I'm proud of your decision. Proud of you!"

Jim echoed his approval, and George basked in the warmth of family affection.

Damon stood silent, watching Miranda glow with pride in her brother's commitment. Pride and love. Whatever doubts he may have harbored vanished, and his mind was made up. "I am volunteering, too," he said. "I've been offered a lieutenant's commission, and I'm going to take it. Three years." He looked at her for approval, and she beamed at him.

"Oh, Damon, that's wonderful. To serve your country when duty—" She broke off and looked expectantly at Richard Schuyler.

"No, Miranda." He shook his head. "Some of us see our duty differently. I am not volunteering. I was willing to drop everything to go with the Seventh, and I will go again if we are called back. But Father needs me. Even if Marty hadn't enlisted, I couldn't have gone. The shipping business—"

Miranda looked at him with disdain.

"But we have to carry on trade, Miranda," Richard tried to explain. "Now that all the Southern planters and merchants have refused to pay their just debts—"

"Debts!" Miranda was shocked. "You talk of debts? Here we are at war, and *you* are worrying about collecting money!"

"But it's not just the money," Richard protested. "They reneged on their pledged word. In commerce, when a gentleman makes an agreement . . . But that's beside the point. Shipping is as vital to the Union as soldiers in the field, and . . ." He trailed off, aware that she would not be convinced.

Will Chase came to his rescue. "Of course you must do what you think best, my boy. And ships *are* important."

Miranda sighed, disbelieving, and Will changed the subject. "Now I understand you will all have a few hours off tomorrow. Why don't you meet us at Willard's," he included all three boys in his invitation, "and we'll have dinner together. Perhaps explore the city. It's been three years since I was here last."

In the carriage returning to the hotel, Miranda chattered eagerly about the war, the army, the Seventh Regiment, and the excitement of being in Washington City, small and provincial and unfinished though it was.

Will smiled at her enthusiasm and joked about how she would look in a uniform, if only girls could enlist in the army, too.

Miranda would happily have abandoned crinolines for Seventh Regiment gray, but she agreed, eyes sparkling, that she would be very unconvincing as a soldier boy. She looked at Jimmy for confirmation, but he was off in another world, dreaming as usual. She actually had to prod him with her parasol to get his attention, and he came to with a start.

"I have decided," he said, the usual tentative quality gone from his voice. He looked directly at his father. "I am enlisting, too."

"Oh, Jimmy!" Miranda hugged. "What a wonderful idea! Another hero in the family."

"Now, Jim," Will began. "Don't be hasty. I know you are as patriotic as your brother, but you're a scholar, and for you the life of a soldier—"

"I have decided," Jim repeated, each word firm and clear. "With George gone, Tom can help you at the Stratford, better than I ever could. John is in England, and he has a wife. Besides, Richard is right: Shipping *is* important, and John will be useful, even over there. But there is no reason at all that *I* can't be a soldier. Lincoln needs three hundred thousand men, and I—"

"My dear boy—"

"I'll be twenty next month. I am a man."

Will looked at him and sighed. "You are a man," he acknowledged. "But you will always be my dear boy. I am only asking you to think this through. Perhaps if we had not come to Washington to see George—"

"I would have enlisted just the same," Jim said. "It was simply a question of whether I would finish the school term or not. But I was worried that Tom would go first. This is a perfect opportunity. I am here, and I have thought it all through. It's better for me to go. You can convince Tom to stay with you. I'll enlist with Damon."

"But if you went with George . . ." Miranda began.

"No," Jim contradicted her. "George will be a captain. If I were in his company, he'd always think of me as his little brother, and that wouldn't work at all. No, I am enlisting tomorrow. That's all there is to it. This is the greatest adventure of my generation, and I won't be left out." And he could not be budged from his decision.

They were finishing a late supper, still working out the problems entailed in Jim's sudden announcement, when Miranda, looking over her father's shoulder, recognized a familiar figure looming in the doorway. Why was *he* here, and how could she avoid him? She still cringed when she thought of that parting embrace. Whatever Cort Adams was doing in Washington, Miranda was firm in her resolution: She never wanted to see him again. Luckily he had not noticed her, and she averted her eyes and slid down in her chair, the better to remain undetected. But she had stopped in mid-sentence, and Will turned around to discover what had distracted her.

He hailed Cort, who joined them with alacrity, shaking hands with Will and Jim, bowing formally to Miranda before sliding into the empty chair next to hers. He kissed her cheek before she could protest, smiled at her confusion, and proceeded to order his supper as if nothing had happened.

She glared at him and edged her chair as far away as it would go—only three inches and right up against the wall.

Cort was full of news, having arrived in Washington only the night before, coming from Savannah by way of Montgomery and Richmond to see both the old and the new capitals of the Confederacy. "They are still disorganized, too," he said, tucking into his fried ham with gusto. "I haven't eaten since breakfast," he explained parenthetically. "I called on General Scott this morning, and he wanted me to meet Mr. Cameron, and then, much to my surprise, I was even taken to see President Lincoln."

Miranda sighed, feeling trapped. He was still absolutely infuriating, and she would have cut him dead if it hadn't been too awkward to explain the reasons. And right now, this very minute, she would get up to leave, but his chair was blocking hers. But the awful thing was that she knew she couldn't tear herself away—she wanted to hear everything he had to say about the state of affairs in the Confederacy and all his travels and adventures and his subterfuge in crossing the lines and, most of all, the reactions of General Scott and President Lincoln.

Perhaps if she just sat silent, refusing to say a word . . .

That resolution lasted barely five minutes.

"You know that British reporter, William Russell?" Cort looked at them expectantly, and, in spite of herself, Miranda spoke up, as if to prove her knowledge.

"From the *Times* of London," she said. "He had dinner once at the Stratford." She looked directly at Cort for the first time. "And I thought he was very polite. A true gentleman." She paused for effect. "Not like a reporter at all."

"You always put things on such a personal level," Cort said. "But then, so do I. The last time I saw you—"

"You were going to tell us about Mr. Russell," Miranda reminded him hastily, feeling herself beginning to blush.

Cort grinned at her, and this time she refused to meet his eyes. "Russell," he repeated, resuming his narrative. "Yes, I had met him years ago in the Crimea, and I ran into him again on the train when I left Savannah. We joined forces, and he introduced me everywhere as a colleague from the *Times*. He even took me along when he met Jeff Davis himself! They thought I was British, too. If only they had known that *my Times* is in New York!"

"What a chance you were taking," Jim said in admiration.

"Oh, well." Cort drained the last of his coffee and signaled the waiter for more. "And a brandy, too," he added as an afterthought. "Probably the worst that would have happened is that they would have thrown me out, given me half an hour to leave town, the way they did in Charleston." He gave them more details about that and then told them about Susanne and the Robillards. "They are all convinced that the Confederacy will win the first battle and that will end the war."

"But we have the industry," Jim began, "and our population—"

"I know," Cort agreed. "But they can't believe that the North really wants to fight to preserve the Union. They truly think that they will win the first battle and then the North will come to terms."

"Nonsense," Miranda snapped. And then, remembering Richard's question, she asked Cort pointblank which side he was on.

"The side of peace," he answered promptly.

"But there *is* no peace," she contradicted him. "You have to choose. Jimmy is enlisting tomorrow, and George is going to be a captain, and Damon has a commission, too. They are all volunteering for three years."

"Pray God it won't take that long," Will interjected.

"Amen," Cort agreed. It had been a long day, but food had revived him, the brandy was warming, and here was Miranda beside him, all fervent ardor, challenging him again.

"Which side are you on?" she reiterated, impatient for an answer. "In a war you must dedicate yourself to—"

"Could I be a dedicated bystander?" he baited her. "I don't fancy myself in uniform, and as a firm believer in peace—"

"You aren't a firm believer in anything!" Miranda slammed down her fist so hard it hurt. "This is a *war*, but all you can think about is yourself. When brave men are going off to fight and die, you sit there like a coward and make jokes about—"

"Miranda!" This time it was Jim who cut in. "You are being very unfair. Cort has been taking enormous risks, traveling all through the South. Who knows what kind of information he brought back? If General Scott thought that even President Lincoln should see him . . ."

Miranda set her jaw stubbornly, and Cort grinned.

"Miranda," he said, "you have enough fighting spirit for a whole regiment. Did you, perhaps, inspire all those enlistments you were telling me about?"

"Not mine," Jim said firmly. "I decided myself. And so did George. Both of us. I'm not sure about Damon," he added as an afterthought.

Miranda wasn't sure, either.

Cort eyed her quizzically. "So, Damon may have enlisted because of you. Do you claim him as your responsibility? It's a serious matter, Miranda. It may be his life or death."

"Now, Cort," Will protested. "You can't charge her with such a burden. Surely the lad could make up his own mind."

"I thought perhaps she provided the inspiration," Cort said, "and I wanted to make sure she understood the gravity—"

"I understand," Miranda interrupted impatiently, not at all sure what he was talking about but unwilling to be patronized any longer. "I admire Damon for enlisting. If I inspired him, I'm proud I did. I'll tell him so tomorrow," she rushed on, "when I give him my photograph."

Her father looked at her in surprise.

"You knew I was having copies made," she said in explanation. "I was going to give one to Richard, too, but now that he is refusing to enlist . . ."

"Ah, another bystander," Cort observed. "I thought he would be hell-bent on preserving the Union—for business as well as patriotic reasons."

"He's bent on preserving the family fortune," Miranda snapped, "though *he* says he's only staying home because shipping is so important."

"Perhaps there's some truth in that," Cort agreed, pausing to consider the matter. "Certainly the South is going to be dependent on trade, and if the blockade is effective . . ." He sighed. "I hope to God that I've persuaded Mr. Robillard to transfer more of his investments abroad."

"I suppose Susanne wants him to sink everything in Confederate bonds." Miranda did not conceal the disdain in her voice, but whether it was directed at Susanne or at the Confederacy was unclear.

Cort registered surprise, but he held on to his temper. "Susanne does not concern herself with financial affairs," he said evenly. "*She* wisely leaves all of that to her father and to me."

There was an awkward pause, and Miranda seethed at his reproof. He was always so smug, so sure of himself; and she always came in second best. Why did he upset her so much? She was furious with him—and with herself. She should have stayed with her first resolve and never spoken to him again. She listened in silence when the conversation resumed, and she held fast to her determination not to say another word, even when Will invited Cort to join them for dinner the next day. Luckily he begged off, pleading appointments, and Miranda breathed an audible sigh of relief.

When they rose to leave, Cort moved so unexpectedly slowly that Miranda bumped into him. His arms went around her protectively, ostensibly to keep her from falling, and he held her a moment longer than was strictly necessary.

"Are you all right, Miranda?" He was all mock gravity,

and his arm still circled her waist, holding her so tightly that she had to struggle to free herself.

"Perfectly all right, thank you." She was breathing rapidly—from the exertion, of course—and she glared at him.

"Perhaps a little breathless?" He eyed her quizzically. "I seem to remember that you get breathless—"

"I am perfectly all right," she repeated, feeling her color rise. Breathless indeed! He was impossible. No doubt about it. Even now that he was safely married, he felt free to take advantage of her. From the very beginning he had been like that. Treating her like a waiter-girl! And no one ever noticed. Not her own father or her brothers or . . . Her cousin noticed. How strange that Richard Schuyler could be so shrewdly observant. It was tiresome, of course, but he was always so stiff and proper that he was promptly aware of any deviation from his own strict standards. But now that he was refusing to enlist, he was in her black books, too. Suddenly the thought of Damon McMasters attaching himself to her tomorrow was almost welcome. Just one day. And then it was back to the safety of the Stratford, where she could escape them all.

The skies were gray and threatening rain when Richard Schuyler and Damon McMasters arrived next morning in a hired carriage. George, they explained, had been asked to call at the war department—some formality about his new commission. He hoped to join them later for dinner.

Miranda was openly disappointed, and Damon tried to reassure her.

"He'll come as soon as he can, Miranda. He's sorry, too. But he's a soldier, after all, and now that we are at war—"

"Of course, Damon," she agreed, cutting him off impatiently. "I had just hoped . . ." And then, aware of the obvious hurt in his eyes, she smiled—a little too warmly—and asked to hear more about his new regiment.

He responded immediately, blossoming under her apparent interest, and Jim joined in with enthusiasm. Richard sighed and consulted his guidebook, and Will eyed the threatening skies and was the first to suggest that they head back to Willard's as soon as they circled the President's mansion. They reached the hotel only minutes before the rain gushed down, and they were still congratulating themselves on their timing when the waiter brought the menus for midday dinner.

George arrived half an hour later, wet and bedraggled and miserable, but his grim mood had nothing to do with the weather.

"A staff job!" he said disconsolately, joining them at the table. "I've been ordered to take a staff job! I have to stay right here in Washington to buy supplies!" His outrage was almost palpable. "Somehow my new colonel discovered my hotel background, and he recommended me to the war department. I think it's criminal!" He brushed aside the proffered menu and ordered whiskey.

"And there's nothing I can do about it," he went on. He downed the whiskey and ordered another. "Like an idiot I answered all their damn-fool questions, and they declared I was needed right here. To order supplies! Dear God, I should have stayed at the Stratford. At least I was buying something more imaginative than salt pork and flour and molasses." He shuddered and took another gulp of whiskey, coughing this time and staring at them all morosely.

Jim and Damon were all sympathy. Richard shrugged and said something about the necessity of feeding the army—and maintaining the ships, too, of course. He tried to catch Miranda's eye, but she refused to acknowledge the argument.

"But, George, if they know you are willing to fight, won't they give you a chance?"

"No," he said bleakly. "I am under orders. For three years ..." He finished his second whiskey and ordered a third.

Will caught the waiter's attention, pointed significantly to his own plate, and was relieved when George's next drink arrived accompanied by roast beef, potatoes, and vegetable. George looked at the dish, puzzled, but automatically began to eat.

"You'll still get to wear a uniform, won't you, George?" That loomed large in Miranda's eyes, the difference between patriotism and cowardice.

George shrugged. "I'll have my captain's bars. But I might as well be wearing the green eyeshade of a clerk. I won't feel like a soldier at all. I wouldn't have given up the Seventh if I had known. And what will Emily think?"

"Emily?" Miranda was honestly puzzled. "What does Emily have to do with it?"

"But she writes to George every day!" Damon exclaimed. "I thought you knew. Why, after I introduced them—"

"But George doesn't care about . . ." Miranda began her

objection and then trailed off, aware suddenly that George *did* seem to care. About Emily Bradley, of all people. That quiet, retiring girl. It's true that George had gone to Brooklyn with increasing frequency in recent months, but Miranda had simply teased him about running away from all the eager girls at Miss Benson's Female Seminary. It had never occurred to her that George might be running *toward* someone else. So he was really interested in Emily Bradley. Well, thank heaven, then, that he would be in Washington now, too far away to see her and court her. Miranda knew in a vague sort of way that all her brothers might marry eventually and move away, but she wanted to postpone that evil day as long as possible. She sighed, looking woebegone, and Damon found the courage to pat her hand.

"Don't worry, Miranda. It's disappointing for George, but he is a true soldier just the same. And Emily will understand. I know she will. I'm not supposed to tell you," he looked from Miranda to George, "but she cried when we marched away. She cried for *you*, George."

"She did?" For the first time George allowed himself the trace of a smile. "The dear, sweet girl." He fumbled for his leather case and pulled out her picture. "How very much I miss her." He displayed the photograph to be admired, and Miranda murmured a dutiful compliment.

"And where is mine?" Damon was emboldened to ask. "You promised me a picture, Miranda, and I—"

"Oh, I forgot. Upstairs in my satchel." She made a move to rise, but beside her Jim was already on his feet.

"I'll get them," he said. "I'll just run up to the room while you all finish."

He had no sooner disappeared than Cort arrived, dripping with rain but in high good humor.

"I've bought a house!" he exclaimed, dropping into Jim's chair. "A house and all its furnishings and two servants to go with it!"

"You *bought* two servants?" Miranda was outraged. "When we are going to war to free—"

"Whoa, there, my girl. Easy. Don't take me so literally." He laughed and put a placating hand on her arm.

Miranda pulled away, brushing off his lingering touch, very conscious of his physical presence.

"Did I get you wet, Miranda?" Cort was all innocent concern. "I didn't mean to bring the rain in with me." He pulled out a monogrammed handkerchief, ready to use it as a makeshift towel, and she snatched it away from him, glaring.

"I'm all right," she said through clenched teeth, dabbing at the nonexistent raindrops.

"Of course you are," he agreed blithely. "Now, as I was saying . . . There are two servants—servants, not slaves—free to stay or go. Happily for me they prefer to stay. And I'm lucky to have them. And the house! You should see it! Near the top of a hill, with its own grove of trees."

"I didn't know you were looking for a house," Will said. "At least, not immediately."

"I wasn't," Cort agreed. "But I was talking to a lawyer who had been left with this property to sell, and it was such a giveaway price . . ." He summoned a waiter to place his order and then settled back to describe his purchase. A handsome red brick on Massachusetts Avenue, he said, with fourteen rooms. And a carriage house in back. No, he hadn't bought the carriage or the horses. The previous owner and his family had made use of them six weeks earlier when they fled to Richmond, taking only their clothes and the family silver and a few portraits.

"A Rebel's house," Miranda sniffed.

"Yes," Cort confirmed, "and practically a steal. Property values are going to skyrocket the way Washington City is starting to grow. The Southerners were virtually dumping their property on the market in their hurry to get away, but now . . ."

"Very shrewd of you, Cort," Will observed. "It would be a good time to buy into a hotel, too." He was thinking out loud. "All living space is going to be at a premium, and when Congress comes back in July . . ." He contemplated the prospect and looked at George with real regret. "If you were free to take on the management, I'd be tempted to take a flyer right now."

"It's too late to think of that now," George gloomed. "I'm going to be trapped in some horrible little office, all tangled up in red tape, and at the end of the day I'll go back to some miserable little room in a second-rate boardinghouse, and the war will pass me right by."

Cort looked at him, puzzled, and George explained.

Cort offered no sympathy on missing the war, but he had an immediate solution for George's living quarters. "You'll move in with me," he declared. "There's plenty of space. I'll be rattling around in my fourteen rooms."

"Oh, I couldn't do that." George's response was automatic. "With you and Susanne and the baby . . ."

"I insist." Cort seized the idea and examined it from all sides. "It will be October before Susanne can travel, and you can stay at least that long. You'd be invaluable. Why," his growing enthusiasm would brook no objection, "if you move in, you can run the place—servants and provisions and everything."

"I don't know . . ." George was obviously weakening.

"You'd be doing me an enormous favor." Cort drove the point home. "I'll be traveling a lot, and I'd want someone reliable to be living there."

"Well, when you put it that way." George allowed himself to be convinced. "We could try it out and see how we get along."

"Capital!" Cort raised his glass in salute. "When can you move in?"

George laughed. "I haven't been mustered out of the Seventh Regiment yet, and then I'll want to wind up my affairs in New York. And see Emily, of course."

Cort eyed him speculatively. "There is plenty of room," he reiterated. "And while you live there, it will be your house as much as it is mine. The whole family will be welcome." He made a broad gesture that included Richard Schuyler and Damon McMasters as well as all the Chases in his invitation. "No need for any of you to stay in a hotel in Washington ever again. In fact, why don't you move in today?" He directed his question to Will, but he spared a glance for Miranda, noting her shock.

"That's very good of you, Cort," Will responded, "but we'll be going back to New York tomorrow, and I don't think we'll make the change for just one night. But now if the rain has stopped," he peered across the room at the distant windows, "we'll certainly want to inspect your new estate."

They were crossing the lobby when Jim finally reappeared. "It took me forever to find the pictures, Miranda. But here they are." And before she could protest, he had handed out copies to all of them—Damon and Richard and George and Cort. "I'll keep one, too," Jim went on, "and Papa already has his back in New York. It's lucky you brought so many."

Miranda opened her mouth to protest, knew it was too

late, and tried to put the best possible face on the matter. This way, at least, the gift was so diluted that Damon couldn't read anything special into being included.

"The sweetheart of the regiment," Cort observed, *sotto voce*, while they waited in the entrance hall. "Nevertheless, I am pleased to be included among the many recipients of your favors."

She spared him a withering glance.

"And I do so look forward to your next visit to Washington," he went on, unheeding, "when I will try to repay your gracious gift with my own brand of hospitality."

"I would come only to see George," Miranda said firmly. "Perferably when you are away. When you are away visiting *Susanne*," she emphasized. "What kind of marriage can you have when you are separated by hundreds of miles and a battle line?"

"The reunions are very pleasant," Cort responded with a broad smile, "and we make the most of them. And the rest of the time . . . Well, at least she is safe. And I am free to pursue my job and other . . . interests."

"She ought to be here to keep an eye on you," Miranda observed tartly.

Cort shrugged. "She has made her choice, and I have made mine. Once the baby is born and she comes to Washington, we will be a proper family again."

"But the war—"

"If it's over by October, there will be no problem. If it isn't, I can pull a few strings. It won't be all that hard to get a pass through the lines for a woman and child. But until she comes, I consider myself free to take advantage of—"

He was interrupted by the announcement that their carriage was ready, and Miranda was spared any further revelations of Cort's singularly candid and self-serving interpretation of his marriage vows.

When they pulled up in front of the red brick house on Massachusetts Avenue, Cort transformed himself into lord of the manor, eager to show off his estate. The parlor, the music room, the library, the dining room, the kitchen.

"And you may have your choice of bedrooms," he said to George when they reached the second floor.

"But you'll want this master suite, surely," George objected. There was already wood laid in the fireplace, just waiting for a match to set it ablaze. "I think the servants are getting it ready for you."

"And this door opens directly to the little room next door." Will was exploring. "It's very similar to our old house in New York." He was half talking to himself. "We always used it as the nursery for the new baby," he explained to Cort. "So convenient. The room opens off the hall, too, of course, but we always left this connecting door open." He trailed off and looked at Miranda and sighed. She had been the last baby. "I envy you, Cort. All the early years of marriage. It will be a wonderful house to bring up a large family."

"But there's another corner bedroom, just as big," Cort said, leading the way, "and I think it gets the morning light."

"Well, of course if *you* prefer this one . . ." George clearly did not.

"I do." Cort laughed. "And besides, George, I think you can already see yourself moved in over there, with your own first child asleep beyond the door."

"The thought occurred to me," George admitted. "But you invited *me*, not a whole family."

"You and yours," Cort corrected him. "We could use a woman's touch, but I didn't realize you were so close to marriage."

"Neither did I." Miranda was appalled by this turn of events.

"We have an understanding," George explained, "but I thought the war would delay a formal engagement. Now, thanks to you, perhaps . . ." The morning gloom faded completely, and George explored the rest of the house with new enthusiasm.

In the carriage house he met Jeff and Hattie, the young Negro couple engaged as servants. They were free, Jeff explained with pride. He had been given his freedom three years ago by the old master just before he died, and then Jeff had worked and saved to buy Hattie's freedom, too. He hadn't quite earned her full purchase price when the young master fled last month to Richmond, but as a parting gift the rest of the debt had been canceled. Jeff had promptly left his hovel in the flats and moved to the comparative luxury of the carriage house, where a honeymoon was obviously in progress.

Both Jeff and Hattie were delighted to be able to stay on as paid servants. There had been a staff of six before, but if there were only two young gentlemen to take care of, they were sure they could manage. They should hire someone to do the yard work, but otherwise . . . Hattie nodded in vigorous assent, and George agreed that, yes indeed, he had found the big house in very good condition. He would leave them a list of instructions—Jeff had already announced proudly that he could read—and he would check the pantry and kitchen and linen closet for supplies.

Cort looked on in admiration as George took charge, and Miranda wandered off disconsolately to the music room. Richard Schuyler and Damon McMasters followed her.

"It's all working out splendidly, isn't it, Miranda?" Damon looked at her hopefully.

"Splendidly for Cort," Miranda agreed. "He's got George to run things for him while he comes and goes as he pleases."

"But it's a wonderful house," Damon insisted. "Emily will love it. Even the wallpaper in the bedroom. That shade of blue is her favorite."

Miranda sat down at the piano and struck a few discordant notes.

"It needs tuning," Richard observed.

Miranda agreed, and her comment was sour. "I have no doubt that George will take care of it."

Richard laughed. "Always the organizer. But he's good at all this, and he likes it. What's more, I think the war department is right for once—putting his skills to use where they belong. We should all work where our talents will do the most good," Richard said, warming to his subject. "For some of us, that means being stationed in Washington, but for others—"

"I've heard all about your ships," Miranda broke in impatiently. "Why must you everlastingly harp on the subject? I know you don't care a rap about what *I* think, so why do you go on and on?"

"I care about what you think, Miranda." Damon's voice was soft at her side.

He always took everything so literally, and Miranda found it hard to conceal her exasperation.

"I knew you wanted me to enlist," he went on, speaking louder. "You inspired me, Miranda."

She struck a minor chord and sighed.

"Miranda is an inspiration to all of us." Cort lounged in

the doorway, taking in the scene. "Why, she even inspired me to buy this house."

Miranda looked at him, startled and disbelieving.

"Yes, she worries so about my separation from Susanne that I thought it necessary to find a house for us as soon as possible. And now that I have it," his gesture, like his mood, was expansive, "you may all come to stay whenever you like. Why, once George is married, we'll even be properly chaperoned, whether Susanne's arrival is delayed or not. A nice long visit. Won't that be splendid?" He looked at each of them in turn.

Damon nodded in happy agreement, but Richard and Miranda maintained a frigid silence.

Chapter 12

WITHIN THE MONTH, Emily Clara Bradley, radiant in antique ivory satin, walked down the aisle of the Church of the Holy Trinity in Brooklyn to become the bride of George Washington Chase, beaming and proud in his brand-new captain's uniform.

For once Miranda was outshone, a sad-eyed maid of honor in pink organdy who looked on this marriage as another kind of attack on her once close-knit family. She couldn't even bring herself to flirt with the best man, Madison Bradley, though he was doing his best to make an impression on her. As far as she was concerned, though, even Damon was preferable—at least he was in the regular army. Miranda no longer considered the Seventh Regiment the place of true patriots.

Discouraged, Madison turned his attention back to Ann Schuyler, who had been looking daggers at Miranda all through the wedding reception, not that Miranda was conscious of that. She was aware only that her tight little world was breaking up, and there seemed to be no place for her now.

She was seventeen, and school was over at last and forever, but there was nothing useful for her to do at all. Her father was singularly unresponsive to her hints and then urgings and finally pleas that she be entrusted with some part of the running of the Stratford.

"But now that George is gone, Papa . . ."

"Tom is working out splendidly, Pet. I never realized he had it in him. His idea about remodeling the hotel is first-rate." Will resumed his study of the blueprints spread out on the desk and went on, half talking to himself. "Now with the main dining room opening off the hall, we can expand the bar by cutting through this partition here . . ." The Stratford's architect, Isaiah Rogers, disappointed that the war had delayed the opening of his newest hotel, the Maxwell House in Nashville, had made a brief stop in New York, and Will had prevailed upon him to supervise this renovation of the Stratford.

"But, Papa, I know I could learn to do the accounts. You always said I had a good head for figures and—"

"Now, Miranda, love, don't bother me with all that. Don't you have something else to do? Letters to write?" Will glanced up briefly. "When your Aunt Sarah was here for George's wedding, she said you had been neglecting her. Why don't you just run along and tend to your correspondence?" He bent his head over the blueprints once more, and Miranda wandered off, feeling sorry for herself.

It was summer—hot and humid and uncomfortable—and everyone she knew was away or in the army or unavailable for some reason or other. Lucy Blaine was in Europe with her family, and Miranda had seen her off, only mildly envious. This was the summer *she* was supposed to travel abroad, but of course Papa could never get away now; and with the war on, Miranda would have felt positively unpatriotic if she had left.

George was in Washington City, and Jimmy, too, and John seemed to be stranded in England forever. He and Dany, to their mutual surprise, had discovered themselves on opposite sides of the war raging at home, and they were thankful to be in London and far away from the conflict. Tom was so engrossed in helping to run the hotel that he had almost forgotten his initial disappointment when Jim had enlisted and Papa had so persuasively argued that he, Tom, must stay home. Richard Schuyler had assuaged Tom's feelings somewhat by pulling strings so that he could join the Seventh Regiment, a move that Miranda greeted with mixed reactions. On the one hand, she was glad to have one brother still at home, but then again she thought that every young man should be on active duty, the better to crush this rebellion as soon as possible.

She was in fervent sympathy with "The Nation's War Cry," as reiterated every day in Mr. Horace Greeley's *Tribune:* "On to Richmond! On to Richmond!" So when the first massive Federal thrust into Virginia led to the disaster of Bull Run, she was shocked and horrified. Unlike Mr. Greeley, however, she was not ready to sue for immediate peace. The realization had come to her, as it came to many others, that it might take more than one battle or even more than one campaign before the Confederacy would acknowledge what was the obvious truth for her: The Union would win.

There was still no general sentiment for the abolition of slavery; indeed, the very day after the defeat at Bull Run the House of Representatives passed a resolution announcing that the war was being fought to preserve the Union and the Constitution and not to interfere with slavery.

Still, slavery *was* being interfered with.

Wherever Federal troops advanced—and in Missouri and Maryland and the loyal counties of western Virginia they were making progress—wherever that happened, fugitive slaves were entering the lines and claiming the protection of Union soldiers. "Contraband," General Benjamin Butler proclaimed them, and the term came into common use almost immediately. In the absence of firm directives from Washington about what to do with these fugitives (surely returning them to the enemy was unthinkable), the contrabands became, *de facto*, free men and women, dependent, perhaps, on the uncertain largesse of the nearest army commanders, but slaves no longer.

The first limited steps had been taken on the road to freedom, and there was no turning back.

Miranda felt increasingly frustrated in her search for something useful to do, either at the Stratford or in the aid of the Union cause. Her wishful dream of being an American Florence Nightingale faded in the hard light of reality and government policy.

In Washington City, over the opposition of the fossilized army medical bureau, Dorothea Dix's offer to establish hospitals for the sick and wounded had been accepted, and eventually orders were issued allotting nurses a wage of forty cents a day and army rations. But Miss Dix, aware of the hostile reactions of army doctors, had ideas of her own about what kind of nurses could best adjust to the difficulties of working where they would be so coldly received. Nurses, she proclaimed, must be strong women, plain in appearance, and over the age of thirty. And no hoop skirts would be permitted. Although this age barrier was eventually to fall, in the beginning it effectively discouraged the young and untrained girls, like Miranda, who would otherwise have volunteered.

Battle casualties were, as yet, relatively light, but the sick rate and the mortality rate were mounting alarmingly just the same. In the hastily built camps and fortifications circling Washington, sanitary conditions were deplorable, and diarrhea and dysentery and various ill-defined camp fevers—typhoid, typhus, malaria—were taking a heavy toll.

It took pressure from the United States Sanitary Commission, a largely volunteer organization, to force the first improvements.

The Commission had its beginnings in New York. In the first surge of patriotic fervor after Fort Sumter, there was a mass meeting at Cooper Union to organize the Women's Central Association of Relief. And, being proper as well as patriotic, the ladies were pleased to have a number of eminent gentlemen serve as their principal executive officers.

The well-known Unitarian clergyman Henry W. Bellows became president, with Frederick Law Olmsted, architect of Central Park, as executive secretary. They moved to coordinate the efforts of the volunteer aid societies that had sprung up spontaneously all over the country, modeling their organization on the British Sanitary Commission that had done such effective work during the Crimean War.

Somewhat reluctantly, referring to it as "the fifth wheel of the coach," President Lincoln signed the Commission into law in June, but the bounds of its authority were never clearly defined. The Sanitary Commission could inspect the soldiers' camps and recommend that they be cleaned up, but the commanding officers had to issue orders. The Commission could send volunteers into the shockingly mismanaged hospitals, but the surgeons in charge could decide whether or not to accept them—as well as the money they raised, the medicines and supplies they provided, and the vegetables and fruits they offered to supplement the standard army diet of salt pork and beans and hard tack and coffee. The Commission's one recourse was the power of an aroused public opinion when its efforts were thwarted.

War fever raged in New York. City Hall Park was a mass of temporary wooden structures—recruiting offices and barracks—and sometimes it seemed that all of lower Manhattan was one vast staging area.

Across the park the newspapers were booming as never before, putting out Sunday editions for the first time as well as extras at any hour of the day or night. An army of ragged newsboys hawked the latest bulletins on every street corner, and Miranda rarely came back from any expedition without succumbing to their pleas to purchase at least one of their offerings.

For New York's "secessionist" newspapers—the *Daily News*, the *Journal of Commerce*, the Brooklyn *Eagle*—she had great disdain, and when they were hauled into the United States Circuit Court on charges of disloyalty and the Federal government refused to carry them in the mail, it bothered her not at all. If this interference with a free press violated the Constitution, avid patriots were willing to look the other way. Indeed, it seemed to most people that the press was almost too free—it was routine for even the most staunchly loyal newspapers to publish detailed information about troop movements and battle plans. Attempts at censorship were erratic and inconsistent, and the result was that individual officers in the field made their own policies, arbitrary and frequently contradictory.

In this first war to be covered by a self-styled "Bohemian brigade" of reporters in telegraphic communication with newspapers of mass circulation, a whole new code of journalistic conduct was evolving, best summed up by the statement of aims of the Chicago *Times:*

"It is a newspaper's duty to print the news and raise hell."

Cort Adams couldn't have put it better himself.

This was a point of view that sometimes brought him into conflict with the solidly loyal *New York Times,* and he and his publisher differed sharply on matters of policy and procedure. Cort was furious when he was left behind because Henry Raymond himself insisted on covering the first major battle of the war. And when the first published reports of the battle of Bull Run were completely wrong, Cort could hardly conceal his glee. It wasn't that Mr. Raymond's account of the defeat was at fault—it's just that his story, like the stories of all the other reporters on the scene, had been delayed in transmission on General Scott's orders. And this early misguided attempt at censorship resulted in the publication of false and garbled news of victory. The letdown that followed when the true story was printed made the disaster of Bull Run seem even worse than it was. Cort Adams always maintained that if *he* had been there, he would have avoided the censorship by getting his copy to the telegraph office in Baltimore, beyond the reach of General Scott's orders. Mr. Raymond raised a skeptical eyebrow, but after that Cort virtually created his own assignments.

In September he disappeared completely, passing through the lines and taking a train to Savannah to be with Susanne when the baby was born. His timing was two days off, but he was delighted to find mother and son doing well, and he began pressing immediately for them to return with him. It was still relatively easy to run the blockade, and Cort was eager to take ship to Nassau as soon as Susanne could travel. From there they could find a packet to New York or Philadelphia, and thence by train to Washington.

Much to Cort's surprise, Susanne was adamant in her refusal. She wouldn't go north and live with the enemy, right in the same house with a Union army officer. And she didn't care whether Captain George Chase was her brother-in-law or not—she wouldn't go. And besides, if Cort was still traveling—and he acknowledged he was in Washington less than half the time—it was silly for her to tear herself away from parents and family and all she held dear to go live among strangers. *Enemy* strangers. And anyway, the Confederacy had won the first major battle, and surely the Yankees would give up pretty soon and let them have their own country. *Then* they would decide where to live. In the meantime, she had the baby to take care of, and didn't Cort think that Robert E. Lee Adams would be a wonderful name for their firstborn. "Little Bobby," she crooned, kissing the child and trying to tease Cort out of his foul mood.

He was not amused. He stayed only long enough for the christening (they agreed on Cortlandt Robillard Adams for the baby's name—and Susanne could still call him Bobby), and then Cort boarded a Confederate merchantman bound for England.

His anonymous page-one stories in *The New York Times* about his voyage with a blockade-runner were avidly read, but when Cort passed through New York in November on his way back to Washington City, he was obviously depressed. Tom and Will plied him with questions, and he answered dutifully enough, but something was missing. Miranda was cool and barely polite, and he made no effort to strike any sparks or shock her at all. She told herself that she was relieved to be spared any of his unwelcome advances, but she couldn't shake off a sense of disappointment. Without even knowing what was bothering her, she missed some edge of excitement, some hint of reckless danger.

About Susanne Cort had little to say, and he reserved his only enthusiasm for his son. Bobby was a paragon of newborn babies, and he challenged anyone to deny that. Will clapped him on the back affectionately and confided that all newborn babies are paragons, and in a few months Cort would be able to judge for himself. George had written from Washington that Emily was expecting a child in April, and Will was delighted at the prospect of becoming a grandfather.

The renovation of the Stratford had been completed and the hotel was more crowded than ever. Over Miranda's protests, Will had hired a new assistant manager, Guy Dawson. Miranda had no objection to Mr. Dawson himself, who was a pleasant enough middle-aged man from New Bedford, but she still desperately wanted to work at the Stratford herself, and she was crushed when her father brought in a stranger and continued to ignore her pleas.

"Miranda, my dear child, I need a man who has had experience as a manager, someone who can deal with the staff and contract for supplies and balance the books."

She stared at him rebelliously, and he sighed.

"You know I'm right, Pet, and this is just one of your passing enthusiasms, like being a missionary to Africa or an American Florence Nightingale. It isn't sensible for you to think about—"

"Papa, I'm grown up now. I'm just as smart as any of the boys—except Jimmy—and you let all of *them* go to work in the office. I don't see why you won't let me."

"You're a young lady, Miranda. You know perfectly well that—"

"I know perfectly well that no one wants me. No one wants me anywhere." She looked at him dolefully. "Not even you, Papa."

"Oh, my dear girl, you know that's not true. You are dearer to me than life itself, and I would give you the moon if I thought it would make you happy, but—"

"You would give me the moon," Miranda said bitterly, "but you won't let me earn even a little piece of the Stratford. It's not fair. It's just not fair at all." She set her jaw stubbornly, and Will remarked on the uncanny resemblance to her grandfather, the late Judge Schuyler.

If that was the problem, Miranda knew exactly what to do. She crossed the room and posed deliberately in front of the portrait of her mother, and then she gave her most dazzling smile.

Will laughed—it was such a transparent tactic—and he felt himself weakening. "Well, Pet, perhaps it wouldn't do any harm if you spent a few mornings a week in the office helping with the correspondence. You may find it boring, but it's a way to learn."

"Oh, Papa!" She beamed at him.

"I wouldn't want you to consider it as a job, you understand," he added hastily. "I think you should continue your volunteer work with the Women's Relief Association. After all, the war comes first. But if you have all this extra energy and enthusiasm . . ."

"Those women don't need me up there," Miranda said candidly. "I'm just another pair of hands, and anyone can roll bandages and scrape lint and pack boxes. If I were doing something really important, with the soldiers . . . I suppose I can still go in one day a week—Aunt Faith would scalp me if I didn't. But I'd rather work for you, Papa. You'll be glad I'm here, I promise you."

And she threw herself into her apprenticeship with such fervor that even Will was startled. As for Guy Dawson, he went home every night the first week singing her praises—until his wife began muttering, with her first attack of jealousy in twenty-seven years of marriage. After that he maintained a tactful silence at home, but he was unrestrained in his enthusiasm at work, looking on Miranda as the daughter he had never had.

He said as much to her one day, and she was startled and enormously pleased.

"And do you really think I'm doing a good job, Mr. Dawson? Will you tell Papa?"

"He already knows, Miss Chase."

"Well, then." She gave a sigh of satisfaction. "You're sure he knows? And Tom, too?"

"Both of them," he assured her. "Even my wife," he added, smiling. "And my son Andy."

"Andy? But he's the one in the navy, isn't he? How does *he* know?"

"I wrote to him, Miss Chase. I've told him all about you, and he's looking forward to meeting you when he comes home on his next leave."

She was surprised.

"That's all right, isn't it?" Mr. Dawson looked at her for reassurance. "He's a fine young man—but of course you must allow for a father's pride. He's only twenty-four, but he's been all over the world these last ten years, even to China."

Miranda was properly impressed. Mr. Dawson had talked about Andy before, and she knew he was a lieutenant in the navy, but she hadn't realized he had spent so much time at sea.

"He must have started as a cabin boy!"

"He ran away on a whaler," Mr. Dawson explained. "That nearly broke his mother's heart—though it was her own brother who encouraged the boy. Still, she's reconciled finally. He was gone two years on that first voyage and he had enough of whaling to last him a lifetime, but he learned to love the sea. He was second officer on the *Flying Cloud* when the war started, and he decided the navy needed him."

"And now?" Miranda asked.

"Now he's on one of the picket ships blockading Savannah, and I think he finds it a little tame. But he'll tell us about it when he gets his next leave."

Lieutenant Dawson's homecoming coincided with Christmas, the first Christmas of the war and a time of family reunions all over the country. Although Captain George Chase and his expectant wife, Emily, had decided to stay in Washington, Lieutenant Damon McMasters and Private James Madison Chase got furloughs and took the first available train to New York.

There were three straight days of celebrations, and after Christmas Will gave a party for Jimmy. Originally it was going to be a small family gathering, but somehow it expanded to fill the entire new ballroom of the Stratford. Tom invited half his company from the Seventh Regiment, together with their wives and girl friends, and Miranda declared halfway through the evening that this was the most gala affair she had attended since the Prince's ball—but the guest of honor was nicer. Jimmy acknowledged the compliment, but he confided that he wanted a breather, and he thought he'd retreat to the family parlor for a little peace and quiet.

Miranda followed, unwilling to let him out of her sight. "Aren't you enjoying it, Jimmy? We planned it all for you."

Away from the throng and in the flickering light from the fire he looked younger, more boyish again. Miranda had been shocked by his appearance when he descended from the train five days earlier, finding him unrecognizable, this excessively lean young man, harder and more sinewy than when he went away, with a disquieting, haunted look in his dark brown eyes.

"It's a fine party, Miranda." His smile didn't quite reach his eyes. "It's just that I've been living in the middle of so many people for so many months, and I'm glad to get away now and then." He poked at the dying fire and added a log and seemed content to sit and watch it blaze without saying a word.

Miranda stirred, a little restless, conscious that the party was going on without her but unwilling to give up these few quiet minutes with Jimmy. He had changed, and she wasn't quite sure how. He had always been quiet and withdrawn, and she had attributed that to shyness. But there was a different intensity to his silence now, as if he had glimpsed the horrors of the world, and now he needed an inner refuge. On the first night home, with Damon and his parents present, Jim had made an effort to entertain them with stories of camp life—daily drill and dress parades, songs around the campfire and raucous roughhousing, and wry jokes about the consistently woeful rations. Damon echoed his jokes and talked almost volubly, but Miranda saw the look that passed between them, and she knew they were leaving something out. Jimmy remained inaccessible, but Miranda eventually pried one aspect of the truth from Damon the next day.

"What's the matter?"

Damon looked at her blankly. He had called to deliver his Christmas present, a small bottle of her favorite French perfume, and she had thanked him dutifully and given him a muffler she had knitted herself, but her mind was on other things.

"What's the matter?" she repeated. "What aren't you telling

us? Is Jimmy really all right? Not sick or anything? He looks . . . he looks as if he's seen a ghost."

Damon shifted uncomfortably. "Jim's all right. He's just learning to be a soldier, that's all. We are all learning that."

Miranda looked at him expectantly, and Damon felt forced to continue.

"We haven't been in any real battles yet—General McClellan is going to make sure we're ready, and he's right—but that doesn't mean that we haven't had casualties."

She nodded, feeling as if she were pulling the words out of him, one by one.

Damon sighed and looked away, but he went on. "Last week, on picket duty, the corporal sent to relieve Jimmy was shot and killed. And then . . ." he trailed off.

"And then?" Miranda prompted him.

"And then the second soldier, a private, was shot, too. Jimmy carried him back to the lines, but the boy died on the operating table."

"I see." She tried to imagine it, Jimmy and the dying soldiers, but her mind rejected the picture.

"Captain Marshall is going to insist that Jim accept corporal's stripes now," Damon said. "I don't know why he's so reluctant."

"I didn't understand why he went in as a private in the first place." Miranda shook her head. "I *know* George could have managed to get him a commission."

"He doesn't want that, Miranda. He wants to earn anything he gets."

"Yes." She nodded. "But I think he deserves it anyway, just by being himself."

The log in the fireplace settled, throwing off sparks, and Jimmy stood up to adjust the screen. "You probably ought to be getting back to the party," he said. "Damon will be looking for you. And all those boys in the Seventh Regiment. And that navy lieutenant. What's his name again?"

"Andy Dawson. He's the son of the assistant manager."

"So that's the connection. I was wondering where he came from. He seems to be very much interested in you, but I thought . . ."

"You thought what?"

"I was sort of hoping that Damon had the inside track."

She shook her head. "No one has the inside track. I have other things to think about."

"Yes," Jimmy agreed. "You always do. Tom says you hardly have a minute any more—between the hotel and the Sanitary Commission. But one of these days," he looked at her fondly, "when we have won the war for you and emancipated all the slaves and settled down to think about peace again, *then* what will you do?"

"Why then," she made up the most shocking thing she could think of, "then I'll lead a parade up Broadway for women's rights. What would you think of that? Will you join the march, Jimmy?"

"I think I will have had my fill of marching by then," he said wryly, "but I might preach a sermon or two on the place of women in our society."

"And where is that?" She looked at him expectantly, rising to his bait.

"Why, a woman's place is one step behind a man—to prod him forward. I always thought you knew that."

She threw a pillow at him and he ducked, and the pillow sailed over his head, to be caught easily by Lieutenant Andrew Dawson. Andy and Richard Schuyler, seeking a place for quiet conversation, had wandered away from the party, too, but Andy seemed willing enough to suspend their discussion of ships and commerce now that he had accidentally found Miranda again.

"Miranda doesn't want to hear about the blockade," he said to Richard.

"Oh, but I do," she contradicted him. "I want to know how Cort got through so easily."

Andy looked at her blankly. "Cort?"

"A newspaper reporter for the *Times*," Richard said with marked distaste. "It was some sort of stunt—he was on a Confederate ship out of Savannah."

"Oh, yes," Andy responded with enthusiasm. "I read those articles—we all read them with great interest. Very useful they were. That reporter fellow managed to confirm our estimates—the blockade has already cut shipping in and out of Savannah to less than a fifth of what it was last year."

"But *he* got through," Miranda protested.

"It's a long coastline, and we can't be everywhere at the beginning. But by next year, I'd like to see him try it again. When Mr. Ericcson builds us his ironclads—"

Chase hurried toward to apologize to the guests, and he signaled the band leader to resume playing while Richard and Damon carried Marty to the library.

Caroline followed, Miranda and Andy in her wake.

"I d-don't know why he always gets so b-belligerent," Caroline apologized. "And it was very rude of him to criticize the Seventh Regiment and General McClellan and everyone."

"It was very rude of him to criticize *you*," Miranda said. "That's more to the point. Why did he call you a nigger-lover?"

"Oh, M-Marty doesn't mean it. He just gets upset. I've been teaching sewing at the C-Colored Orphans' Asylum and . . . But I think he's stirring a little now."

Richard and Damon had stretched him out on the leather couch in the library, and Andy was preparing to dash a pitcher of water on him until Caroline grabbed his arm.

Andy yielded to her pleas, but he protested. "Direct action. That's the best way. Knock him out, bring him to. I've dealt with enough sailors to know."

Caroline shook her head and dipped her handkerchief in the water, making a cold compress for Marty's head. "He's always been excitable—that's the problem. And he really *is* a hero, you know. And it bothers him that the war is going so slowly."

"As for that," Andy said, "it bothers me, too. I don't even disagree with him. God knows what Little Mac is doing with the army—just watching it grow. Why doesn't he use it for a change and fight?" He didn't wait for an answer, though Damon was shaking his head in protest. "He wasted all the autumn reviewing the troops, and now they're all going to be in winter quarters and it will be spring before he moves at all. If he ever does."

"Damn right." Marty was struggling to sit up, clutching the compress to his head. He hadn't met Andy—or spotted him as his assailant—but he thought he recognized an ally. "All our lily-livered generals. All those pasty-faced politicians in Washington, ready to give up what's ours." He turned on Richard. "Afraid to stand up for our rights. Afraid England will—"

"Marty, you don't know the first thing about it." Richard refused to take him seriously. They had had a long argument earlier in the evening about the so-called *Trent* affair, and Richard had found Marty still stupidly belligerent on the whole subject.

In November, acting on his own, the commander of a United States warship had stopped a British mail packet, the *Trent*, and had seized two Confederate commissioners, James Mason and John Slidell. The capture of these two men from an unarmed ship of a neutral country provoked an international incident that could have brought dire consequences. Faced with an ultimatum from the British to surrender the commissioners or face the possibility of war and the probable recognition of the Confederacy as an independent state, Lincoln had yielded. The news had been in the New York papers that morning, and although most people breathed a sigh of relief that the incident was closed, Marty Schuyler was not alone in regretting what was, in his eyes, an abject surrender.

"If we would just *fight*," Marty repeated. "McClellan doesn't know—"

"McClellan knows enough not to send us into another Bull Run," Damon defended his general. "We'll move just as soon as we're strong enough, and he'll make sure we win. Why, he's even got the Pinkertons working for us."

"Pinkertons," Marty repeated, not hearing the rest of Damon's defense. He looked at Miranda for the first time, and a memory stirred. "Pinkertons," he said again. "What ever happened to that Cort Adams investigation, Richard? Did you hear any more from England? It *was* bigamy, wasn't it? Could they prove it?"

"Bigamy!" Miranda's eyes were wide with shock.

"Marty, you're a damn fool." Richard glared at him.

"Bigamy!" Miranda repeated. "Do you mean Cort? Is it true?"

Richard sighed. "Probably not, but I saw no reason to pursue the matter. I thought Cort was safely out of our hair once he was settled down with Susanne. I didn't know he would keep turning up, like a bad penny."

"But . . ." Miranda had still not quite taken it in. "If you mean he was married before . . . There's a baby now. He and Susanne have a little boy."

"A little bastard," Marty corrected her, and he was amused by her shock. "Like father, like son."

"That's enough, Marty." Richard sounded almost threatening.

"I could hit him again," Andy offered.

"Richard, if you knew that Cort already had a wife," Miranda's voice dripped icicles when she turned on him, "I don't see how you could let Susanne marry him. You should have told Mr. Robillard at once."

"I seem to remember," Richard's voice was equally cold, "that you were the one who objected most fiercely to the Pinkerton investigation in the first place."

"I did," Miranda acknowledged. "But if you could really prove he was married before—"

"We had no proof," Richard said. "It was supposed to have happened in England, and there was a child, a little boy. The woman called herself Mrs. Adams, but that means nothing, and there's not even any proof that the child was his. She had a number of . . . protectors, and I think she tried to get money from all of them. And in any case, the woman has since died—just this past summer—and the child disappeared. I am sorry to be telling you all this. It is not a fit topic of conversation for either of you." He looked from Miranda to Caroline. "And I think we should close the subject now, once and for all."

Caroline looked properly abashed, but Miranda was mutinous. And fascinated. "But if he *was* married to her, then Susanne isn't legally his wife now, and he must be single again! Isn't that so?"

Richard refused to answer, and Marty laughed. "You see him as an eligible bachelor, Miranda? Is that it? I suppose you want to add him to your list of conquests. Our chaste little Joan of Arc, counting her scalps. Why waste your time on him? He eats little girls like you for breakfast. But closer to home—"

"Damon, why don't you take Miranda back to the party!" Richard made it a command rather than a question. "And Caroline and I will take Marty home."

Miranda allowed herself to be led away, but she could see that Richard was going to have his hands full with Marty, and it was a good thing Andy stayed with him to help.

"I don't believe any of that," Damon said on the way back to the ballroom. "Of *course* Cort is truly married to Susanne. He's a gentleman. Why, you should hear my cousin Emily talk about him. Just a week ago in Washington Jimmy and I were there for dinner, and Cort couldn't have been nicer. Emily is . . ." He fumbled for a delicate way to explain her condition. "That is, she and George are . . ."

"I know." Miranda came to his rescue. "Emily is going to have a baby in April."

"Yes," Damon said, relieved that he hadn't had to say the words. "Well, you should see how protective Cort is of her. And you should listen to him talk about his own little boy, Bobby. He misses him so much. I just don't believe that a man like that would have abandoned a wife and child in England, just gone off and left them."

And yet, Miranda was thinking, Cort was equally separated from Susanne and Bobby, and it *could* be a pattern repeating itself.

Chapter 13

WITH THE CHRISTMAS season over and the soldiers back in camp, life returned to normal, or what passed for normal in the early months of 1862. The Army of the Potomac settled into winter quarters in northern Virginia, and General McClellan resisted all of President Lincoln's repeated requests for action. There was brighter news from Kentucky and Tennessee where General Grant was advancing, and on the Carolina coast where General Burnside's men took Roanoke Island and established an effective base for the tightening naval blockade.

But the most dramatic news was the duel of the ironclads, the *Monitor* and the *Merrimack*. The year before, when the Federals had cleared out of Norfolk, the U.S.S. *Merrimack* had been burned and sunk and abandoned to the enemy. The Confederates had raised the ship, converted her into an ironclad, and rechristened her C.S.S. *Virginia*. In early March, awkward and sluggish but seemingly invincible, she steamed out of Norfolk harbor and wreaked havoc among the wooden ships of the United States fleet in Hampton Roads. The timely arrival next day of the U.S.S. *Monitor* restored the balance, and the battle between the two clumsy ironclads resulted in a draw. Neither vessel was seriously damaged, but the *Merrimack*, handicapped by poor engines and a heavy draft, withdrew to Norfolk for repairs; and from then on she was virtually imprisoned in Hampton Roads. With the *Monitor* standing guard, the wooden vessels of the Federal fleet were freed from immediate danger.

Through peace and war, New York went right on growing. The rush of immigrants through Castle Garden continued unabated, crowding the slums and tenements, overflowing into the shanties that dotted the upper reaches of Manhattan and still speckled parts of the Central Park. But there were plentiful jobs, however ill-paid—on the docks, in the warehouses, in the loft factories and the booming shipyards and the counting houses and the ever expanding shops and stores and restaurants and hotels.

And New York was still moving north. Mr. Stewart would be employing two thousand clerks in his elegant new store uptown at Broadway and Ninth Street—Miranda was appalled at the thought that his marble palace just three blocks from the Stratford would be converted to a wholesale operation. Delmonico's had announced plans to move up to Fourteenth Street, and only the Astor and the Stratford remained as the last major hotels as far downtown as City Hall. Miranda knew scarcely anyone who lived south of Lafayette Place or Washington Square any more. It was all business and commerce and traffic now.

And war fever.

Miranda had continued her volunteer work with the Women's Central Association of Relief, and one day a week she reported faithfully to the Cooper Institute to pack boxes of supplies for the Sanitary Commission. Medicines and blankets, soap and socks, onions and potatoes and dried fruit and fresh oranges and homemade cookies, needles and thread and buttons, and farina and condensed milk and crackers and tea and sugar and a thousand things a soldier might need but a hard-pressed government rarely supplied. She found the job tiring and agreed it was necessary, but it wasn't much fun. Aunt Faith had thrown herself into the work of the association with all of her considerable executive skill, but Miranda did not take kindly to her tyranny.

Miranda was no longer enchanted with handling the routine correspondence at the Stratford, either. Mr. Dawson was still full of compliments, but he was adamant in his refusal to let her help Tom with the books or deal with the suppliers or solve any of the day-to-day problems in running a busy hotel.

And Will sided with Mr. Dawson. "I know you are capable, Miranda, but be patient. You're doing a fine job where you are, and I don't think you should turn yourself into a drudge. Why, you haven't been skating for three weeks. If you would just see more of your friends . . ."

But her best friend, Lucy Blaine, was engaged to be married and was all wrapped up in wedding plans, and all the interesting boys were in the army.

Feeling restless and deflated, Miranda wandered off to write a letter to Jimmy.

When Richard called later that day, she was almost glad to see him. And when she learned he had secured tickets to the Gottschalk concert at Niblo's Garden, she was delighted to accept his invitation. Irene would go with them—Irene thought Gottschalk was almost as fascinating as the Prince of Wales.

Louis Moreau Gottschalk was the first American-born pianist to achieve an international reputation, and there was great excitement about his return to New York after a six-year absence abroad. He was handsome and young and undoubtedly gifted, and he brought a passionate, romantic intensity to the keyboard that Miranda found enthralling. Richard smiled at her enthusiasm and promptly bought tickets for the next concert. And perhaps she would be interested in seeing *Martha* at the Academy of Music, too.

After that their excursions fell into a set pattern, always with at least one other person, the tickets usually for performances she really wanted to see. He was thoughtful that way, and she found herself spending more time with him than ever before.

Still, the most lasting solution to Miranda's restlessness came from a completely unexpected source: Her cousin Caroline. Miranda had carefully avoided seeing Marty Schuyler again after Jimmy's party, and she was relieved when his furlough was over and he had safely vanished back into the army. But she didn't really think it was necessary for Caroline to make a formal call, just to apologize for her brother's behavior.

With her father at her side, Miranda dutifully returned the visit, expecting to find the afternoon depressing. The brownstone on West Ninth Street had always been dark and cheerless, and now that Caroline was living there alone with her maternal grandmother, it would surely be worse.

Strangely enough, it wasn't. The long shadow of gloom that had been cast by the protracted last illness of Aunt Josephine, followed so quickly by the unexpected death of Uncle Martin, seemed to have faded away. And with Marty gone, too, there was nothing to weigh down the spirits of the two unexpectedly cheerful ladies who greeted Miranda and her father on that wintry Sunday.

Miranda barely knew Mrs. Cantrell, who had moved in with Caroline only the year before. She proved to be a voluble Quaker lady from Philadelphia and, much to Miranda's delight, a staunch abolitionist. Her influence on her granddaughter was pronounced, and in Miranda's judgment all to the good. In Marty's absence, Caroline showed every sign of blossoming on her own, and in her dark green dress she looked slimmer, prettier, positively demure. She even moved less awkwardly, and her stammer was starting to fade.

Caroline knitted while they talked, a man's dark shawl taking shape and growing as her needles clicked rapidly through the gray wool. She had always been good with her hands, Miranda remembered, making samplers, embroidering, sewing, crocheting—it was a way to pass the endless hours in the company of her invalid mother. Now Caroline was putting her talents to use and, her grandmother declared proudly, she had supplied half a regiment with socks and shirts and mufflers. She was making children's clothes, too, as part of the war relief project of the Sanitary Commission. But what she liked most of all, and Caroline's eyes glowed as she talked, was giving sewing lessons and teaching all kinds of needlework to the little girls at the Colored Orphans' Asylum, way uptown at Fifth Avenue and Forty-third Street. Miranda knew where the building was, having passed it frequently on her way to the Central Park, but she had never stopped to go inside.

"Then you must come," Mrs. Cantrell said firmly.

"Yes," Caroline agreed. "I'm there every Monday afternoon, after the children have finished their regular classes, and I enjoy it so much."

Will cleared his throat and prepared to make a polite objection. "In this cold weather, Miranda, I'm not sure that it would be wise to visit. The possibility of contagious disease—"

"Mr. Chase, I must contradict you." Mrs. Cantrell spoke mildly, but she was strong in her protest. "Our children are healthy and well cared for. You must not confuse our orphanage with those city institutions on Blackwell's Island. *We* have no former convicts tyrannizing the children, no abandoned women acting as matrons. And liquor is absolutely forbidden on the premises. As for illness and disease, we make every effort to shield our children from epidemic. We are not always successful—who is?—but we have our own hospital with an isolation ward, and I assure you that Miranda would be in no more danger than in any respectable building in the city."

"I certainly meant no insult," Will assured her. "But Miranda is so busy with the hotel and her work for the Relief Association that—"

"I want to go," Miranda cut in. "I have tomorrow afternoon free, Mrs. Cantrell, and if I can go with you and Caroline . . ."

Will sighed and acknowledged defeat. "In that case, I will come and see for myself. If it is truly such a well-run institution," he gave Mrs. Cantrell a wry smile, "perhaps I will learn something useful to take back to the Stratford."

"I'm not sure about that, Mr. Chase, but we would be delighted to have you come. And I am sure you can teach *us* a great deal."

The Association for the Benefit of Colored Orphans had been founded in 1836, and it was the first and still the only organization in the city that provided continuing care for Negro children. The Quaker ladies who started it had great difficulty at first in raising money and getting support; and even locating a neighborhood where such an orphanage would be tolerated was a major problem. But they persisted, and the city came to the rescue by giving them building lots on the west side of Fifth Avenue, so far north at Forty-third Street that there were no neighbors nearby to protest. In 1843 they opened their new building, a three-story red brick, set well back from the street, with trees and shrubs in the large fenced-in yard. Other buildings were added later—the hospital, a house for the superintendent, several workshops—and now there were more than two hundred children living there, most of them between the ages of four and twelve. They had their own school on the grounds where they were all taught to read and write and cipher, with a heavy dose of religion permeating their studies. The day began with a chapter from the Bible and ended the same way, and every child received a Bible as a parting gift on leaving, usually at the age of twelve. That was the age when most working-class children were apprenticed or indentured, customarily for a term of seven years. The Board of Managers made an effort to keep in touch with graduates during this period, to make sure that the contractual terms of the apprenticeship were being carried out. The policy may not have been ideal, but, in the context of the times, it was considered enlightened.

In the asylum itself, the food was plain and the clothing utilitarian, but medical care and education were provided and, compared to the urchins in the streets, these children were getting some kind of chance. There were even such conveniences as running water, a bathing room, and hot-water heating.

On an informal tour the next day, Will inspected the buildings with growing interest, and before he got away, Mrs. Cantrell had persuaded him to become a patron of the Association by making a contribution of fifty dollars. When he returned to the front parlor to collect Miranda, he found her at the piano, surrounded by a crowd of children, their voices raised in a rousing chorus of "John Brown's Body." Miranda broke off hastily, but Mrs. Cantrell did not seem to be disturbed.

"I'm not very good at helping Caroline with the sewing," Miranda apologized, "but I saw the piano . . ."

"It's sadly out of tune," Mrs. Cantrell said regretfully. "Someone discarded it years ago, and I'm afraid we'll never be able to afford a better one. But if you can get any music out of it at all, you're welcome to use it."

"There's an extra piano at the Stratford," Miranda looked at her father hopefully. "After the renovation, Papa, when you bought the new Steinway for the ladies' parlor, you were going to get rid of the old one, weren't you?"

"It's still in the storage room," Will acknowledged. "I was going to sell—" He broke off and looked at the expectation shining in her clear gray eyes. "Of course you can have it here, Pet."

"Papa, you're wonderful." She threw her arms around him, and he looked at Mrs. Cantrell with a rueful smile.

"If I had known this was going to be such an expensive afternoon, I'm not sure I would have come."

Miranda's weekly visits to the orphanage provoked varying comments from the family, ranging from Jimmy's wholehearted approval to Aunt Faith's unconcealed disdain.

Richard defended her conduct, though he thought she was working too hard and suggested she cut back her time at the Stratford.

"I can't do that," she protested. "It's hard enough to convince Papa and Mr. Dawson that I'm serious."

Richard had stopped off to see her on Sunday afternoon—it was becoming a habit with him, she noticed, but then he was a creature of habit. And she was surprised to find herself looking forward to seeing him, even though they disagreed on practically everything and frequently parted in anger. Still, he kept coming back, and he was, if nothing else, reliable. Reliable in his reactions, too. She just knew he would be against her ambitions, but that didn't stop her from voicing them.

"If I truly want to manage the hotel one day—"

"Now, Miranda, you know that is out of the question. When the war is finally over and this exaggerated need for women to—"

"The war would be over much faster," she said, biting off the words, "if all the trained officers would go off and fight the Rebels instead of sitting around in their comfortable New York shipping offices."

"Damn it, Miranda, let's not start that again." He paced the library restlessly and came to a temporary stop by the fireplace, confronting her. "Do you think I *want* to stay home? Do you think I enjoy listening to Marty brag about his exploits? He thinks he's taken the Carolina coast single-handed, but *some*one had to get those ships there. If you knew the problems in converting merchant vessels to navy gunboats . . ." With an effort of will he forced himself to stop. He took a deep breath and she could almost hear him counting to ten. "Let's not quarrel, Miranda. You'll understand one day." He managed a smile. "Or maybe the war will go on long enough for me to get into it after all. McClellan seems to be in no hurry to fight."

"Jimmy thinks he's wonderful."

"Yes. Well, I devoutly hope he is right." Richard resumed his restless pacing, pausing at the window to look down at the traffic on Broadway. "Did you say Caroline was coming?"

Miranda nodded. "With Mrs. Cantrell."

"I see them," Richard said, "and I don't think I'll stay. The last time that woman came here, she pried another donation for that orphanage out of me. Incredible! If she were a man, she'd be running the Treasury Department."

Miranda laughed. "Papa avoids her, too. Last week she wanted to see the hotel kitchen, and he was afraid she'd make off with all the kettles and pots and pans. I like her, though, and she's done wonders for Caroline. Why, Caroline even has a beau now!"

Richard looked at her, astonished.

"And very presentable he is, too. He's an army lieutenant from Boston, and he stopped to see her last week on his way home, and I was introduced to him then. You'll never guess how she met him."

"I'll never guess," Richard agreed.

"Well, you know she's always sewing and knitting and sending things off to the Sanitary Commission. Mrs. Cantrell told her to attach little notes to all those shawls and shirts and socks, and maybe the soldiers would write and thank her. And some of them do. And Lieutenant Lorimer stopped off last week—he's convalescing from a shoulder wound—and I think he fell in love with her at first sight."

"*You* were there and he fell in love with Caroline?"

"Why, Richard, what a pretty speech!" She laughed and dismissed the compliment. "Anyway, he was already there talking to her when I came in, and he hardly paid any attention to me until I asked him if he knew Cort Adams."

"Now why would you ask him that?"

"Well, why not? They're both from Boston and it seemed like a logical question. And he *does* know him. So there! I was going to ask him about that bigamy story—"

"You didn't! Damn Marty and his loose tongue."

"No, I didn't," she reassured him. "I'll probably see Cort in April, after Emily's baby is born, and I thought I'd ask him myself."

"As if he would tell you!"

"I'll be subtle," Miranda promised, and Richard laughed.

"The day you are subtle the moon will turn to green cheese."

Unwillingly, she laughed, too, and neither of them heard Mrs. Cantrell's knock at the open door.

"Well, you two seem to be having a good time." She glided into the room, a cheerful little woman in Quaker gray, but she dominated the scene as truly as if she were an ironclad battleship. "I was just saying to Caroline that I hoped to be seeing you again, Richard. You still haven't paid a visit to the orphanage, but I know if you could see the good work we are doing there . . ."

Richard acknowledged one of his rare defeats and reached for his wallet, and Miranda did not bother to conceal a smile.

Chapter 14

Emily's baby was born in April, and Will and Miranda went to Washington for the christening. The child was named Mary Theodora for her two grandmothers, and Will was overcome with emotion: pride, gratitude, love—and an aching sense of loss that Mary wasn't here to see their first grandchild.

Miranda was oddly touched by the occasion, too. She had been surprised and enormously pleased when George and Emily had asked her to be the child's godmother, and she accepted with alacrity. And then she was surprised and considerably less pleased when she learned that Cort was to be godfather. Still, he was on his best behavior all through the ceremony, and he seemed almost wistful when he returned Mary Theodora to her mother's arms.

"You've had a lot of practice with christenings, haven't you, Cort?" Miranda asked him afterward in her most artless and guileless manner.

It was a balmy spring afternoon, and they were sitting on the front porch of his house on Massachusetts Avenue, admiring the view. The forsythia had passed its peak, but the dogwood and magnolia and lilac were in bloom, and the air was delicately scented with their fragrance.

Miranda occupied the porch swing, looking almost flower-like herself in a yellow-sprigged organdy dress, sashed in leaf green. The late afternoon sun caught the glints of copper in her dark hair and cast a warm tawny glow on her animated face.

"Christenings," she prompted him, conscious of his eyes on her, finding his gaze disturbing. This was the first time she must be so. I didn't know you were such an accomplished musician."

"Oh, I'm not," she said frankly. "Compared to my sister Cordelia . . . But she made me take lessons, and I learned to play after a fashion, and now that I am supposed to be a teacher, I've started practicing again. Jimmy will be so pleased." She sighed. "I was hoping he'd be here, but I suppose his regiment was sent to the Peninsula, too." She looked at Cort questioningly, assuming he had some special source of information.

He shrugged. "Probably. McClellan keeps demanding more troops, though I think he already has enough men to take Richmond three times over. If he doesn't watch out, Washington will be left defenseless, and then Stonewall Jackson will swoop down on us while Little Mac is still stuck in the mud at Yorktown."

"Do you really think so, Cort?" Her eyes widened with alarm.

"Let's hope not. It's just one of my blacker fantasies. But if Lincoln doesn't get rid of incompetents like McClellan—"

"Damon and Jimmy think he's wonderful," she protested. "And they are *soldiers*. They know."

"And I, of course, am just an ignorant civilian observer. Like you. But you asked for my opinion, and if it were up to me, I'd get that boy wonder out of there. And the Pinkertons, too," he added as an afterthought. He grinned at her, and he watched the play of emotions on her face as she determined to find out how much of the story about him was true.

"If you weren't married in England," she began cautiously, "did you at least know that woman who called herself Mrs. Adams?"

"Would you like to define your terms, Miranda? I was acquainted with her, if that's what you mean. If you are asking me if I *knew* her in the Biblical sense of the word . . ."

She blushed scarlet, and he laughed. "It must be very puzzling for a virtuous young lady like you—one with a reasonably healthy curiosity and a certain practical turn of mind. It must have occurred to you that with all the . . . I believe that Cyprians is the approved euphemism. Yes, with all the Cyprians in the world, there must be an astounding number of seemingly upright men who seek them out. Men that *you* know, Miranda. Husbands and brothers and fathers and cousins and soldiers and perhaps even newspaper correspon-

164

had spoken to him alone, and she was determined to find out the truth behind those rumors of a marriage in England.

"Christenings," Cort repeated. "Yes, I've participated in three in little more than a year."

"Three?"

"Certainly. Mary Theodora, Bobby, and Elliott, my brother's child."

"Oh, I forgot about him." Miranda was plainly disappointed, and Cort laughed.

"I do believe you thought you were setting some kind of trap for me."

"A trap? Why, Cort," her laugh wasn't quite genuine, "what in the world do you mean?"

"What a miserable actress you are, Miranda. It's one of your charms, you know. You are usually so open and so direct that you don't know the first thing about how to be devious. I don't think you could deceive me if you tried. Your face is such a perfect mirror of all you are thinking and feeling—it's pure pleasure to watch you."

She sighed. "Why must you always talk like that? Make such personal remarks?"

"It keeps you off balance," he answered promptly, "and it makes you think about me. Admit it, Miranda. You *do* think about me. A lot."

She felt herself starting to blush. "I think . . ." If she couldn't deceive him, perhaps she could squelch him. "I think you are probably the most conceited man I've ever met. And the most wicked! If you *knew* the scandalous stories I've heard about you!"

"Yes, I thought you were leading up to that. My alleged marriage in England—that's what you mean?"

"You admit it?" She stopped the swing abruptly, both feet flat on the floor. Surely the fact that he had brought up the subject was tantamount to confession.

"There's nothing to admit."

"Then how did you know that's what I meant?" She felt triumphant, convinced she had him cornered.

He smiled. "You forget that Damon comes here at least once a week to see Emily—and to get a decent meal—and he told me about that little episode at the party in New York. Very shocking, I must say." His eyes gleamed with amusement.

"Shocking! It certainly was. When I heard that you—"

161

"No, not about me. The shocking part was employing the Pinkertons to discover my past. They'd be the last ones to know—always seeing things in the dark. Why, they count all the shadows of all the trees in Virginia as Lee's soldiers, and General McClellan believes their reports like true gospel. That's why he never fights. But I gave *you* credit for more common sense."

Miranda swallowed the compliment whole and allowed herself to be diverted into talking about the war. It was true that everyone but McClellan's own troops knew the little general was moving too slowly. When he finally took the army out of winter quarters, preparing to attack, he discovered that Lee had already pulled back his soldiers. It was gratifying for the Federals to be able to occupy Leesburg and Manassas and Winchester, of course, but the Confederate army had escaped without a casualty, so McClellan could hardly claim a victory. Now, however, there had been massive troop movements, and the bulk of the Army of the Potomac had been spirited away by transports, supposedly in secret, though everyone knew immediately that the target was Richmond again. The attack this time was from the peninsula, but it had stalled near Yorktown, with both sides digging in.

Still, the war did seem to be going well at last. There were convincing victories in Tennessee and Florida and strong bases in North and South Carolina, and if McClellan could just advance those few miles into Richmond, the war might be over by summer.

Cort did not prick her bubble of optimism, but he sighed, and she looked at him, puzzled.

"But they are retreating everywhere, Cort. Aren't you pleased?" She didn't wait for an answer and she resumed swinging with a little skip of pure joy. "*I* think it's wonderful. And with all the talk about emancipation, we'll just *have* to end slavery. Everywhere!" Lincoln had just signed into law the congressional bill that abolished slavery in the District of Columbia, and there was good reason for her optimism.

"In another minute, Miranda, you are going to tell me that you have been right all along."

"And what is the matter with that?" she challenged him.

"It's just a rather dangerous form of pride, that's all. Hubris. The gods will be lying in wait to strike you down. A little humility is more becoming."

"*You* talk about humility?" She laughed, and he smiled.

"Well, perhaps you're right. I'm not very good humble. Cautious, though—that you will have to adm

"How cautious was it to go up in a balloon?"

He had made the ascent with a photographer and army officers in one of the first attempts at aerial reconna sance, but a sudden shift in the wind had almost sent them behind enemy lines, and it was only by extraordinary good luck that they bumped back to earth in the cornfield of a friendly farmer.

"I was scared stiff the whole time," he told her, feigning exaggerated fright. "And you'll notice that I have not gone up again."

"What I noticed was that you managed to get three stories out of it for the *Times*."

"To think that you are such a faithful reader that you recognize my handiwork."

"I read *all* the war news," she said with dignity.

"Since it is all attributed to 'Our Own Correspondent,' how do you know when that means me?"

"If it's crazy enough, then it's you."

"And then you ask Mr. Raymond," he corrected her. "Your father was telling me this morning. He is very proud of you, Miranda. Oh, not for being able to recognize my articles in the *Times*—he just said that in passing when he was talking about your all-consuming interest in the progress of the war. No, he meant your work with the Sanitary Commission, and all the hotel correspondence you have taken over, and all the letters you write to soldiers. And now I understand you have become interested in an orphanage for colored children."

"That's the most fun of all," she said, her eyes sparkling with enthusiasm. "And to think it was Caroline, of all people, who got me to come!"

He looked at her inquiringly, and she explained. "You met Caroline once—Marty's sister. The day you had the fight with Marty in the library."

He nodded. "The awkward little redhead."

"She's not so awkward any more. You'd be surprised! Anyway, I go to the orphanage with her every Monday afternoon, and they are letting me give some of the children piano lessons. Isn't that wonderful?"

"If you think it's wonderful, Miranda, then obviously it

dents. If you really want to sweep away the veil of hypocrisy that prevails in polite society—"

"Oh, no," she cut in hastily. "Don't tell me about it. I don't want to know about anyone else."

"Just about me?" He raised an eyebrow. "How very flattering."

"No, that's not what I meant at all. I wish you wouldn't . . . Oh, how do you always manage to twist things around and confuse everything?"

"*I* am not the least bit confused."

She glared at him, and he laughed. "All right, Miranda. For being so marvelously transparent and curious, I will tell you as much of the truth as your delicate ears can bear to hear. I was not married before. To the best of my knowledge, Bobby is my one and only child. I *did* know the British Mrs. Adams, but an accurate reading of the calendar would eliminate me as the father of her child. However, I gave her some money at the time—she was in rather desperate straits—and I went so far as to look her up when I was in England last fall. I found out that she had died in June, probably of cholera, and the boy is being brought up by the grandmother. Does that answer all your questions?"

She nodded, too embarrassed to look at him.

"Because if there is anything else you want to know about the wicked ways of the world, I would be only too happy to enlighten you. Men have all the best of it, you know. We are permitted to roam the world, seeking pleasure where we will, confident that at home, waiting patiently, is a true and faithful woman, always willing to forgive and forget."

He had shocked her again. "Do you really believe that?"

"No. But there are enough women who do to make the world go around very comfortably in all its old familiar patterns."

"Well, I don't think it's fair!"

"You're right. It isn't fair. But what are you planning to do about it? No, don't give me your speeches about women's rights and voting and all those high-flown political arguments. I want to know what *you* are going to do about it. Are you going to be willing to sit at home to be taken care of by your father and your brothers and perhaps one day by a husband? Or are you going to venture out on your own and taste whatever life has to offer, its risks as well as its joys. And there *are* joys, Miranda."

He reached for her hand, and she drew back, startled.

He smiled and watched the color rise in her cheeks. "You are an extraordinary beauty, my dear. No wonder Damon is in love with you."

"Damon! What are you talking about him for?"

"Well, I can hardly speak for myself, can I? I am a properly married man, as we both know, and you would undoubtedly be shocked if I presented myself as a devoted Romeo. But since Damon isn't here, perhaps, a proxy courtship—"

"Did *he* put you up to this nonsense?"

"No, alas. He doesn't have the imagination. It was a spur-of-the-moment decision on my part. If you remember John Alden with Priscilla—"

They were interrupted, much to Miranda's relief, when the front door opened and Emily joined them, followed almost immediately by George and Will.

"So this is where you are." Emily sank gratefully into the nearest chair. "I didn't think the baby was ever going to fall asleep."

"Such a pretty child," Will said. Miranda moved over to make room for him on the swing. "Like you were at her age, Pet."

"And just as demanding," George agreed. "But worth it all."

"I should hope so," Miranda smiled. "My niece. My very own godchild. Mary Theodora Bradley Chase."

"Polly," Emily corrected her.

Miranda looked at her blankly.

"You missed all the discussion just now about her name, but we decided that Mary Theodora was just too long and impressive a title for such a little mite of a baby girl—so she's Polly until she grows up and chooses for herself."

"Polly," Cort said, trying out the name. "I think I approve. That was the name of my very first girl friend, when we were both six years old. I remember I climbed a tree, showing off to impress her, and I fell from the first branch."

"And you have been falling for girls ever since," George laughed.

"Were you hurt?" Emily sounded like a mother already.

"No. But I think Polly had a few bruises—she tried to catch me. There's probably a moral there somewhere, but I wouldn't search too long for it."

truly. But . . . marriage is such a big step, and I don't really think I love you the way I should to consider—"

"I love you enough for both of us," he said, and he kissed her.

She didn't resist, but she remained passive in his arms, and he sighed and released her. "What is it, Miranda? What can I do that will make you change your mind about me?"

"I don't know. But it's not as if there is someone else," she assured him. "Maybe I am just not ready. Not grown up enough, even at eighteen." She smiled at him, but he was not cheered. "I wish I had a better answer for you . . ."

He gazed at her wistfully, and in silence they returned to the ballroom.

She made a particular effort to be friendly and agreeable for the rest of the evening—and attentive to his parents, too. He responded with gratitude and perhaps with renewed hope. At midnight as the orchestra played "When This Cruel War Is Over," he looked at her meaningfully, and she sighed and let him kiss her again when the dance was over. He was going off to fight her battles, and how could she deny him his dreams?

By mid-November, under General Burnside, the Army of the Potomac was on the move again. The ultimate target, as always, was Richmond, but this time the troops were to march overland, by the direct route through Fredericksburg.

McClellan had had the bulk of his forces poised near Warrentown and Culpepper, preparing for a wide swing south, so it was necessary to reposition the army as quickly as possible, before Lee could transfer his troops to meet the Federal advance.

At Fredericksburg the Rappahannock River flows almost due south, with the town occupying an open plain on the west bank, surrounded by a curving range of hills. The whole area was one vast amphitheater—and unexcelled terrain for defense.

The Federal forces began to arrive on the east bank of the river as early as November 17, but the pontoon bridges that were necessary for the crossing were delayed, and then delayed again. And as the days passed, and the weeks passed, all hope vanished for the element of surprise in the attack.

Confederate troops occupied Fredericksburg in force and

dug in on the hills, with batteries of guns in place ready to rake the attacking forces in a withering hail of crossfire.

It was Thursday, December 11, and a foggy winter morning when the Federals began constructing their five pontoon bridges across the Rappahannock, and on the same day the troops successfully fought their way into the town of Fredericksburg, into the trap of Fredericksburg. For two days the Army of the Potomac poured over the bridges, and on Saturday the soldiers began their assault on the heights. The morning fog shielded their advance, but about eleven o'clock, like the rising of a curtain, the fog vanished, and the bright sun, stronger than any spotlights, illuminated the advancing columns of Union troops. And, louder than any applause, the guns boomed out. The drama—a tragedy—would be written in blood.

Again and again, in frontal assault, the Federal troops charged forward to the low range of hills called Marye's Heights. Forward to be slaughtered. If they survived the dash across the wide fields, raked by artillery and strewn with the bodies of the wounded and the dying, they ran into the deadly rifles at the stone wall, where the Confederate infantry, enjoying almost perfect protection, could fire and fire and fire again. By the end of the day, not a single Union soldier had come within a hundred feet of that wall.

That night, on the bitterly cold battlefield, while the stretcher-bearers groped their way through the fog to bring out the wounded, the ill-supplied Confederates ventured out to strip the Union dead of uniforms and boots. And the sun rose next morning on a grotesque and grisly scene—hundreds of frozen, naked corpses, stark and stiff, the troupers and spear carriers in a vast drama, denied even the grace of a dignified farewell exit.

Stubborn, rash, impetuous, Burnside wanted to renew the attack, leading at himself, but his officers persuaded him to pull back; and by Tuesday morning the Army of the Potomac, somber and heavy with defeat, had withdrawn to the east side of the Rappahannock.

Reports of the disaster had already reached Washington, casting a pall of gloom over the city. From the makeshift medical stations near the battlefield, the wounded were starting to flood the crowded and inadequate hospitals in Washington and nearby Georgetown, overflowing into schools and churches and warehouses and factories, straining the resources and provisions stockpiled by the Sanitary Commission. Volunteer aides were welcome as never before, and Miranda found herself pressed into service as soon as she arrived for her Christmas visit.

George had met her at the train, a tired and drawn and overworked George, ashen with the news he had received that morning: Jimmy had been at Fredericksburg, and he was missing. The report was unofficial—George had it from a wounded officer—but it sounded definite: After the assault on Marye's Heights, Jim had not been seen again.

Miranda went white, but she stayed calm and controlled, and when George told her that he could get her a temporary billet as a nurse, she wasted little time reporting for duty.

The Potomac Inn Hospital was a dismal place, a seedy, second-class hotel that had been hastily converted for medical use. The shabby rooms were ill-equipped to shelter a crush of wounded soldiers, the food was abominable, and the nursing staff consisted of twenty-seven convalescent soldiers who belonged in bed themselves and a dozen women who were, for the most part, as untrained as Miranda herself. Luckily the matron who had just been put in charge was briskly efficient, and she had taken it upon herself to hire some of the contrabands flocking into the city looking for day labor. With their help the worst of the dirt and grime had been washed away, and one of the former slaves turned out to be adept at repairing plumbing and was immediately hired full time—the most valuable man on the staff. More valuable than the doctors, Miranda had decided by the end of the first day. The chief surgeon appeared to be interested in nothing but amputation, and his second in command was overly fond of the whiskey bottle. Only the youngest, Dr. Hamilton, seemed concerned about the welfare of his soldier patients, making his rounds faithfully, dispensing his drugs, instructing the volunteer nurses, and even taking an interest in the meals prepared for the patients and staff.

The usual army field ration—salt pork and beans and hard tack and coffee—was so inadequate that many of the soldiers arrived suffering from scurvy as well as battle wounds. And diarrhea was so common as to be endemic. Even the standard hospital diet was little better, with the addition of bread and butter, boiled potatoes, soup, farina gruel, tea with milk, and bread pudding. Dr. Hamilton paid a visit to the Sanitary Commission and brought back a supply of onions and apples

173

and stewed blackberries, and Miranda prevailed on George to search for a bushel of oranges to be dispensed next week as a special Christmas treat.

Miranda's mornings were spent in a ceaseless round of feeding patients, dressing wounds, changing beds, and running for supplies. The afternoons were a little calmer, and there was time to write letters for the soldiers and talk to them and brew a pot of tea for the more active convalescents. But afternoons could be hectic, too, with ambulance wagons drawing up to the door to discharge their loads of mud-caked patients, not all of whom had survived the rough and hazardous journey from battlefield to medical station, from station to field hospital, from stretcher to ambulance wagon to railroad boxcar to wagon again. Jumbled together, the diseased and the dying mixed indiscriminately with the wounded still nursing the stumps from bloody amputations, they arrived at the ill-equipped hospitals and were bedded down wherever there was space. Typhoid and pneumonia side by side with cholera and festering stomach wounds, the stench of death mingling with the fetid odors emanating from unwashed bodies and gangrenous flesh. Even with all the windows open and the cold December winds blowing a gale, there was no relief from that all-pervasive smell.

Miranda made her escape every afternoon, arriving at the brick house on Massachusetts Avenue yearning for the welcome balm of a hot bath and the restorative powers of Hattie's good cooking.

On the fifth day, George tried to call a halt.

"You're overdoing it, Miranda, as always, and you're wearing yourself out. It won't do those soldiers any good if you collapse. And God knows what diseases you might bring back to the baby."

"I'm all right, George. Truly. And if I felt the least bit feverish, I would stay away from Polly." The baby was sitting on her lap, fascinated by the bright ribbon in Miranda's hair and finally wailing her frustration when she couldn't reach it.

"Let me take her. I think she's ready for bed now." Emily calmed the child and tried for peace between brother and sister, too. "Miranda *is* being careful, George, and I think that the least we can do is make things easier for her when she comes home at night. I long to be at the hospital myself, and just as soon as—"

"*Not* while you're nursing the baby," George decreed.

"Dearest, I am not arguing with you about that. And I am sure that Miranda will take a day of rest, for my sake as well as hers. Why," she turned to Miranda, "I've hardly had a chance to talk to you since you've come. Now it's Christmas Eve tomorrow, and if you ask the matron—"

"I'll try to leave early," Miranda promised. "And I have Christmas morning off—unless there are more ambulance wagons coming in."

"Surely all the wounded from Fredericksburg have been brought here by now." Emily looked at George for confirmation, but he sighed.

"They're still coming in from the field hospitals. And the Sanitary Commission is working overtime to identify all the survivors. As for the unmarked graves . . ."

No one spoke for a long moment, and then Miranda shook her head, rejecting the idea of death. "Jimmy *must* be alive," she insisted. "In a field hospital somewhere. And they will bring him to Washington and I will make him well again. It has to happen that way. It just *has* to."

"I've been making inquiries, Miranda. And I've told Cort, and he—"

"You've seen Cort?" Miranda was astonished.

"You didn't know he was back?" George looked at her, surprised, and Emily explained.

"It must have been midnight when he got in last night, and Miranda left for the hospital very early this morning, and I guess the servants didn't think to tell her."

"He's back," George confirmed, "and he should be here for supper any minute."

Emily departed to tuck Polly into bed, and Miranda tried to adjust to the news that Cort was in Washington. He had filed dispatches from Fredericksburg, she knew, but she had some hazy idea that he had gone off to see the war in the west, to interview General Grant, perhaps. Well, maybe he wouldn't stay long. And in any case she was so busy with the hospital and so worried about Jimmy that she couldn't spare a minute to be disturbed by him. Not this time. She would be polite but distant, and he would certainly disappear from her life again.

Cort joined them at the supper table, looking grave, and Miranda knew he was bringing bad news.

"Jimmy?" It was more a plea than a question.

Cort nodded. "Seriously wounded," he said, "but still alive. He's at Aquia Creek, and they are bringing him to Washington. I hope to God the doctors know what they are doing, moving him in his condition."

Miranda found it difficult to swallow, and it was George who asked what had happened.

Jim had been found more dead than alive on the field before Marye's Heights, his right arm shattered, unconscious from loss of blood, and stripped of his boots and all identification.

"It was a miracle the stretcher-bearers even bothered to bring him out," Cort said. "I saw that field on the morning after the battle . . ." His expression was grim and no one pressed him to continue.

"As to how I found out about Jim," he went on in answer to another question from George, "it was pure chance. I alerted everyone I could think of, including a chaplain I saw this morning on his way to the field hospital in Aquia Creek. And he sent word back with one of the inspectors from the Sanitary Commission, who just happened to be returning to Washington late this afternoon. It was a miracle of timing."

"A miracle," Miranda agreed. "I prayed for him. Dear Jimmy. I just knew he was alive. And he's coming to Washington?"

"That's what the inspector said," Cort repeated.

"When? And will they bring him to me?"

"I'll make sure they do." George pushed his plate away, the food still untasted, and stood up. "I'm going back to the office to issue a few orders. And if they don't pay any attention to an army captain, I'll forge the signature of the President himself."

It was noon on Christmas day when they got word that Jimmy had arrived at the Potomac Inn Hospital, and George and Miranda hurried there immediately. They found him lying on a straw pallet in the hall where the stretcher-bearers had left him, bleeding again from the stump of his right arm. George was horrified and rushed to find a doctor, but Miranda reacted with a competence painfully acquired from meeting too many ambulance wagons. She grabbed a sheet from the pile of clean linen on the table and staunched the bleeding, and she raged again at a system that allowed a dozen wounded soldiers to be crammed into a jouncing ambulance and left to the mercy of a callous, drunken wagon driver. The soldier on the next pallet had not survived this journey, and two of the contrabands were already there to carry his body to the dead house.

Jim returned to consciousness with Miranda hovering over him and George springing to attention at the foot of the bed. He blinked as if seeing a vision, and shut his eyes, and then opened them again slowly, testing whether the dream was real.

"We're here, Jimmy." Miranda touched his cheek and leaned over to kiss him. "You're in a hospital in Washington City, safe with us, and I'm going to stay with you every minute until you're well enough to come home."

He breathed a sigh and she helped him drink some water, and then he slept.

"Shouldn't you get some food into him?" George asked. "A bowl of soup or some meat or something?"

"When he wakes up," she agreed. "But that might not be for hours. Why don't you go home now, George, and have Emily pack a satchel for me. I'll be staying here for a few days, and I'll need a change of clothes." She was still dressed for the Christmas dinner they hadn't had time to eat, and her stomach growled suddenly, reminding her she was hungry. "Bring back some turkey, too. We'll have a celebration feast when he wakes up."

She was peeling an orange when Jimmy stirred again, and they smiled at each other, and she offered him the fruit as if she were giving him the world. "Merry Christmas, Jimmy."

He struggled to sit up, wincing with pain, and she propped an extra pillow behind his back and then fed him the orange, one section at a time. George returned before she had finished, bringing her clothes and a picnic hamper loaded with enough food to supply all the patients in the room.

"Emily wants a list of everything you might need," George said. "*Everything*. And just as soon as you can be moved safely again, we'll bring you home."

Jim nodded and blinked back his tears. "I forgot it was Christmas. If only I had brought *you* a present, too."

"You did, Jimmy." Miranda kissed him. "You're our present. We didn't know what had happened to you." She couldn't resist touching him again, brushing back a lock of hair from his forehead. "Those wicked Rebels, leaving you for dead on the battlefield and stripping your body."

"Just my boots," Jimmy corrected her. "And I gave them away when he saved my life. It seemed to be a good trade."

"Who? Who saved your life?"

"I don't know his name. Some poor farm boy from Alabama." He sighed and refused her offer to feed him, struggling to do it himself. "It's strange, isn't it? He spent all day shooting at us from behind that stone wall, aiming to kill, and that night he saved my life. Not that he planned to, I suppose, but it happened that way." Jim paused to take a spoonful of soup, managing it awkwardly with his left hand.

Miranda looked away, choking back her emotions, and she concentrated on buttering him a roll.

"He saved you?" George prompted him.

"Yes. He thought I was dead at first, but I was just unconscious. And I came to only because he was jerking off my boots and the sudden movement . . . God, the pain in that arm. And when I groaned he thought I was a ghost. But then he realized I was still alive, and he gave me some water from his canteen. And he spotted the stretcher-bearers and called them over—they would never have seen me otherwise, and I would have frozen to death if he hadn't yelled at them. So you see, the least I could do was give him my boots."

Miranda nodded, finding it hard to swallow again.

"But why didn't you have any identification?" George asked him. "It took us so long to find you. What happened?"

"I don't know. I was unconscious or knocked out with drugs so much of the time. Somewhere along the line everything was stolen. The stretcher-bearers, the drivers, other soldiers. What does it matter now? I'm here."

"And we will make you well again," Miranda vowed.

"Yes, I believe you will," Jim smiled at her. "You are so determined, Miranda. Do you like being Florence Nightingale?"

"No," she said frankly. "I hate it. I hate the dirt and the smell and the blood and the death. And the death," she repeated. "That's the worst of all."

Jim nodded. "I will never get used to it, either. That day at Fredericksburg . . ." He trailed off and waited while Miranda cut his turkey into bite-size pieces. "And it was all so useless. McClellan would never have sent us charging up those hills. I was talking to Damon about it yesterday—"

"Yesterday? In the hospital? We didn't know he was wounded, too!" Miranda looked at George accusingly, as if he had been holding something back.

"I didn't know," George defended himself, puzzled. "Emily had a letter from him three days ago—you saw it. He didn't say a word about himself. He knew you were missing, Jim, and he said he was searching for you. Nothing at all about himself. What happened?"

"Well, it wasn't serious, luckily. Just a nick on the cheekbone—he'll have an elegant scar, as if he had been dueling at Heidelberg."

Miranda gave him a skeptical look.

"No, really," Jim insisted. "He probably bled a lot, but Damon says that the worst casualty was his handsome beard and mustache. He thought the doctor had rather mangled it, getting through all that hair to dress the wound, so two days later Damon made the sacrifice and shaved it all off." Jim laughed for the first time. "I must warn you that he looks a little strange—his forehead and nose all tanned and dark and his cheeks and chin as pale as a girl's."

"Is that why he is still in the field hospital at Aquia Creek?" Miranda was still suspicious.

"No, they pressed him into service as a nurse afterward. All the walking wounded were drafted that way. Why don't you send for him to help you here? You could pull a few strings, couldn't you, George?"

"I can try," George agreed. "Mr. Stanton didn't object when I used his name to get *you* here. Not that he knew, of course."

"I thought you were going to sign the President's name." Miranda looked disappointed.

"I was holding that in reserve," George smiled at her. "I thought the Secretary of War would be pressure enough. No point in bringing up all your big guns at once."

"What kind of strategy is that?" Miranda objected. "Now, if McClellan had just used *all* his men and guns—"

"No, if Burnside—" Jim interrupted.

"Or if the pontoon bridges had only arrived in time." George cut in.

Reducing war to a strategic game of chess. It was one way to distance it, to forget for a while the bloody horror of it all—the mangled bodies of the dead, and the mangled bodies of the living, too.

Miranda checked on Jimmy frequently that night, and in the early morning hours he began to shake with fever.

"Quinine pills," he told her, his teeth chattering, and she rushed off to the dispensary to commandeer a supply.

"You haven't been taking these regularly," she accused him, holding a glass of water to his lips; and then she apologized for being so stupid. How could he have dosed himself these last two weeks when he was barely conscious most of the time?

He seemed a little better when the surgeons made their rounds later that day, but Dr. Hamilton looked grave and drew Miranda aside afterward.

"I don't know if he is going to make it," he said bluntly. "It's a miracle to me that he survived that wretched amputation in the first place. And with malaria weakening him further . . . I just want you to be prepared for the worst."

"I am going to make him well," she insisted fiercely.

But when George came by at the end of the day, he was shocked by Jimmy's appearance. Reluctantly, Miranda passed along the doctor's warning.

"I am going to send a telegram to Papa," George decided.

"Didn't you do that last night?" Miranda was shocked. "You know how worried he's been about Jimmy."

"Of course I did," George soothed her. "But now I'm going to ask him to come right away. If there is any danger that Jimmy might—"

"Don't say it. We aren't going to let it happen."

"We aren't going to let it happen," George agreed, patting her shoulder. "But it will be better if Papa is here just the same. You'll see."

Will arrived the next night, and by then only Miranda was refusing to acknowledge that Jimmy was fading rapidly. He was dying, and he knew it, and he accepted it with the same puzzled courage that had sent him charging up Marye's Heights. Surely somewhere there was a reason for this madness, and if only he were older and wiser he would understand. All his young life he had been running to catch up to older, stronger brothers, to a benevolent and protective father, and his trust in them carried over to a religious faith that sustained him now.

It was left to Miranda to rage at the unfairness of it all, a silent rage that rejected the pain of his approaching death and drove her to a feverish denial that there was anything wrong at all. She stayed with him around the clock, and she smiled and talked and fed him and dressed his wound and changed the sheets and forgot to eat herself until her father threatened to send her home unless she started to take better care of herself—right now, this very minute.

Unwillingly, Miranda submitted to his ultimatum, and Will dug through the hamper of food beside Jimmy's bed and presented her with cold roast chicken and a buttered roll and a small jar of stewed fruit. She had barely choked down the first bite when one of the new nurses paused in the doorway and looked at her inquiringly.

"Miss Chase?"

Miranda nodded.

"There's another ambulance wagon here."

"But I can't leave Jimmy now. Aren't there enough nurses downstairs?"

"Yes, we can take care of everything. But there's a soldier who keeps asking for you—and he's very sick. I think you should come for a minute to see him."

"A soldier?" She stood up, brushing off the crumbs, wondering if she could leave Jimmy while he slept. "Who is it?"

"I think he said his name is McMasters. David McMasters?"

"Damon! But Jimmy said . . ."

"Go see how he is, Miranda." Will looked at her with compassion. "I'll watch over Jimmy."

Damon was lying on a straw pallet in the entrance hall, in the same place where she had found Jimmy four days earlier. He was pale and dirty and soaked to the skin—it had been raining all day—but when she put a hand on his forehead, he was hot to the touch.

He opened his eyes and smiled at her, and his voice was so raspy and soft she could barely distinguish the words. "Miranda? Is it really you?" He clutched her hand. "Stay with me. Stay as long as I need you."

They found a place for him in the room across the hall from Jimmy, and she had barely seen him settled in bed when Will appeared in the doorway and nodded once in silent confirmation. She excused herself to Damon calmly and crossed the hall.

"He slept away, Pet. There was nothing more we could do."

She pulled the sheet away from his face and gazed at him. "He looks so young. Dear Jimmy." She touched his forehead, smoothing back his hair, and kissed him one last time. This isn't happening, she told herself. This is some terrible nightmare, and if I just stay calm, I won't cry, and then Papa will hold back his tears, and George will come and take care of everything, all the details, all the terrible, final details of death. George always managed things right. If I just take care of Damon, God will take care of Jimmy, and somehow we will all keep going. If I can just not cry.

"I have to stay here, Papa." Her voice cracked, but she went on. "Damon is all alone and he needs me. You must send a telegram to his parents and have them come right away."

Will looked at her doubtfully. "We'll certainly send for his parents. But you, Pet, you're exhausted, and I think you should come home with us."

"I'm all right." She tried to smile, but her muscles wouldn't cooperate. "I'm all right," she repeated stubbornly, and she fled from the grief in his eyes.

Dr. Hamilton was with Damon, examining him, tapping his chest, listening through his stethoscope, and looking grave. "Pneumonia," he said aloud, answering Damon's question. He peeled the dirty wet bandage from Damon's cheek and examined the healing wound. "No problems here," he said, forcing a smile. "If they hadn't kept you in that field hospital to nurse the other soldiers, you'd be all right now, and I'd be sending you back to your regiment."

Damon nodded, responding to the doctor's forced optimism. "I just wanted a good excuse to be with Miranda again."

She reached for his hand, willing herself to forget what was happening across the hall. "I'll take care of you now."

Damon was asleep by the time George came, and he slept straight through while Jimmy's body was taken away, while Will agreed, reluctantly, that Miranda should stay in the hospital until Mr. and Mrs. McMasters arrived.

"Papa and I will take Jimmy home to New York," George said, "to bury him next to Mama and Cordelia."

Miranda nodded.

"And you can come home as soon as you feel ready to

travel. Let *Emily* decide that," George insisted. "You never know when to stop. I'll come back right after the funeral. Emily is going to have her hands full with her aunt and uncle. And you. And the baby. So for heaven's sake, take *care* of yourself. Just as soon as the McMasters arrive, you must let Aunt Julia take over the nursing."

"Yes, George. But I promised to stay with Damon as long as he needs me."

"That may not be long, Miranda." Will put his arm around her protectively. "I spoke to Dr. Hamilton, and he isn't sure that Damon will survive, even until his parents get here. I wasn't going to tell you, but I don't want you to blame yourself if he doesn't pull through."

She was beyond shock. "I'll do the best I can, Papa."

Will hugged her and looked doubtfully at George. "Perhaps if we stayed another twenty-four hours, just until his parents arrive . . ."

"I don't think so, Papa. Miranda insists on staying at the hospital anyway, and I don't think it would do any good for us to delay Jimmy's funeral. Besides, maybe Dr. Hamilton is wrong. Maybe Damon *will* survive—a day, a week, indefinitely. No. We should go ahead with our plans. I'll have Cort look in on her tonight and again tomorrow. And by then Aunt Julia and Uncle Ralph will be here."

They left it that way and, like a sleepwalker, Miranda returned to Damon.

He was feverish in the night, and she held him in her arms and soothed him and gave him more water to drink and listened while he spun out his dreams of marriage and children and the rich, full life they would have. And she agreed with everything he had to say and kissed him. And when he finally fell into an exhausted troubled sleep, she stretched out on the floor beside his bed and slept, too. She woke up, stiff and still tired, and hungry enough to eat the breakfast that Damon pushed away.

Cort looked in on her that morning, and she saw the alarm in his eyes. And he brought Emily with him in the afternoon.

"You aren't supposed to be here," Miranda protested. "The baby . . ."

"We are worried about *you*," Emily said. "And you can't have Damon all to yourself." Her smile was forced and fleeting. "After all, he's *my* cousin." She took his hand, but he was barely conscious and he stirred, restless, and murmured Miranda's name.

Emily sighed and relinquished her place, and Miranda sat down beside him again, holding his hand. The minutes ticked by and time had no meaning. Miranda stared at Damon, unseeing, and he merged with Jimmy in her mind and then separated and merged again.

Afterward not one of them could be sure exactly when Damon stopped breathing. Cort summoned the doctor just minutes before Mr. and Mrs. McMasters arrived, and Miranda turned to Emily in sudden panic.

"You tell them," she said. "I can't . . . I can't hold on any longer."

And then blackness descended, and she fainted.

Chapter 16

MIRANDA CAME TO in a carriage with Cort's arms around her, cradling her like a baby, holding her gently, her head on his shoulder. She stirred slightly, only vaguely aware of the soothing murmur of his voice, of his hand brushing back a wisp of curl from her forehead. And then she slept.

It was dark outside when she woke up, the only light coming from the fire blazing on the hearth. Somewhere a clock chimed six, but whether that was morning or evening she had no idea. And then Hattie was there, hovering over her, and full consciousness returned with a rush. She was in Cort's house, in the yellow bedroom, waking from that hospital nightmare, clean and fresh, in her best cotton nightgown.

"Lord, Miss Miranda, you had us scared." Hattie touched her hand for reassurance. "You slept the clock around. I'll just go tell Mr. Cort you's awake now."

"No, wait." Miranda clutched her hand. "What happened? How did I get here?"

"Why, Miss Miranda, don't you remember? You done collapsed in that hospital, and Mr. Cort brought you home. He carried you up here, calling for me, and I been taking care of you ever since. I undressed you like a little baby and put you to bed."

"And Cort?"

"He's right here. Right downstairs. You just let me call him. And I'll go get you something to eat. Lord, you must be starved."

Cort loomed in the doorway, and Miranda gave him a shaky smile, pulling up the covers as if for protection.

He handed her a robe and obligingly turned his back while she slipped it on.

"I hate to tell you this, my dear," he was obviously relishing every word, "but your attack of modesty is a little late. Who do you think helped Hattie put you to bed?"

She blushed scarlet, and he extended his hand to feel her forehead.

"A trifle feverish, no doubt to be followed by a slight attack of breathlessness. Otherwise, completely recovered."

She changed the subject abruptly. "Where is everyone? George and Emily and the baby?"

He sobered immediately. "You don't remember?"

"No. I was in the hospital talking to Jimmy and . . ." A chasm opened at her feet, and she looked at Cort in sudden terror. "Jimmy! He's dying, Cort." She scrambled out of bed, and the sudden movement made her dizzy. She stood swaying a moment, and he reached out to steady her.

A vision of the hospital rose before her, grim and crowded, reeking with the stench of death and the corruption of gangrenous flesh. In that nightmare world Jimmy was dying.

No. In that nightmare world, Jimmy was dead.

"I must go to him, Cort. How could you take me away when his body—"

"My dear child." He held her gently for a moment and then sat her down in the big chair by the fireplace. "I don't wonder that you are confused. You were with him for four days and four nights. And just as he was dying, they brought in Damon McMasters."

It all came back to her in a rush.

"I held him in my arms," she whispered.

He nodded.

"Damon was dying, and I held him in my arms. His parents came too late. Where is he, Cort? What has happened? The funeral. Someone must—"

"It's all being taken care of, Miranda."

She stared at him, groping for reality.

"Your father was here, too. Don't you remember? He and George. They took Jimmy with them, back to New York."

"They took him?"

"The funeral was to be today, Miranda. Burial in Greenwood Cemetery, next to your mother and sister."

She struggled out of the chair again. "Without me? I

should be there, Cort. Why didn't they take me? My own brother—"

"Miranda! You were in no condition to travel. And besides, you insisted on staying with Damon. God knows where you found the strength. Four days with Jim, and then another day and a night with Damon. That's when I found you, exhausted and drained."

Hattie arrived with a tray, but Miranda waved her away.

"Don't be foolish." Cort took the tray and forced it into her lap. "I am going to sit right here and watch you eat every bite. How else are you going to regain your strength so that you can go out and nurse more gallant recruits in this miserable war?"

She glared at him, but she took a spoonful of soup and sampled one of Hattie's biscuits. Hattie departed, grinning, and Cort goaded Miranda into eating the entire meal.

"Do you know what day it is, Miranda?"

She stared at him, puzzled, stirring her coffee.

"It's New Year's Eve. Wednesday, December 31, 1862. Do you think we should celebrate?"

"Celebrate!" Her voice was stronger now and touched with outrage.

"Celebrate," he repeated firmly. "Tomorrow the Emancipation Proclamation goes into effect. All your hopes and dreams, Miranda." He paused to consider. "Well, perhaps not quite all. The emancipation extends only to the slaves whose owners are still in rebellion, so there's no way to enforce it. And in the loyal states, where it could have had an effect, it doesn't apply. A paradox, surely. Still, why should we quibble? Somewhere, somehow, somebody will be emancipated, and we should celebrate. It may not be a victory, but it's a milestone of sorts."

She was reviving, there was no doubt about that, but she was still too dazed to argue coherently. "But we will win," she said, repeating it like a litany. "We will win. We *have* to win. And then we will abolish *all* slavery." She looked at him and tried to still a nagging doubt. "We *will* win, won't we, Cort?"

"And will it be worth it, Miranda? Worth all the sacrifice? All the lives disrupted. All the lives lost."

"Yes." She nodded her head vigorously, anxious to convince herself. "Yes. It's worth it. It *must* be worth it all."

He looked at her and sighed. "Well, then. I suppose we

187

should drink a toast to victory." He took the tray from her lap and extended a hand to help her rise. "We'll go downstairs. You are feeling better, I think, and a change of scene will do you good."

Another fire was blazing in the music room, and Cort summoned Jeff, who brought a bottle of champagne from the cellar.

"Will that be all, Mr. Cort? Now that Miss Miranda is better, you won't be needing Hattie to sit up with her any more."

"You're right, Jeff. Take some time for yourself. It's New Year's Eve. Celebrate."

Jeff withdrew, smiling, and Miranda looked after him, a sudden shiver of doubt overtaking her. It wasn't right for her to be alone in this big house with Cort. All her life she had been lectured on the proprieties, and the need for a chaperone had never been more clear. What could she do if he tried to take liberties? Her hand trembled when she accepted the proffered glass of champagne, and he noticed it. He always noticed everything.

"To your health," he saluted her, and his eyes gleamed in the firelight.

She pulled back and found security in the little sidechair by the hearth while he stood watching her.

"You never cry," he said suddenly, unexpectedly. "Why is that?"

"I'm too grown up."

"Or perhaps not grown up enough. Yes, I think that's it. Tears are nothing to be ashamed of, Miranda. Emotions, feelings—they are a part of living. I know you cared deeply about Jimmy. And Damon . . . well, perhaps not the same way. Still, he was a brave young man, and he died clutching your hand. You must have felt some emotion."

She nodded, surprised and relieved at the way the conversation was going. She had misjudged him. He was kind and concerned and gentle. Why, he had been the one who found Jimmy in the first place. Disarmed, she relaxed and sipped her champagne. The firelight turned her hair to burnished copper, and he reached out to touch it. She glanced at him, surprised, but she did not withdraw.

"I haven't cried since I was a child," she said, remembering.

"Go on." He nodded encouragingly and refilled her glass.

"It was all so long ago. When my sister, Cordelia, died, five years after Mama, I knew that was the very worst thing that could ever happen to me." She looked at him over her glass and drank quickly. "And I just decided then that if I could hold back my tears that one time, I would never cry again." She lifted her head proudly. "And I haven't. I just knew that I would never be hurt that much again. And so now, when Jimmy . . ." She held out her glass for more champagne and swallowed to cover the sudden huskiness in her voice. She even managed a weak smile. "You see, it doesn't hurt so much this way."

"My poor child. It's a hurt that goes all through you." He contemplated her in silence and resolved a lingering doubt. "How will you ever wash it out unless you cry?" He took the glass from her hand and pulled her to her feet. "But since you insist on being so foolishly brave . . ." He pointed to the piano and asked her to play for him. "Something simple," he said. "Simple and sentimental. Whatever has meaning for you."

He spread out the sheet music of the popular songs of the day, and she played them, one after the other: "We Are Coming, Father Abraham," "The Girl I Left Behind Me," "Just Before the Battle, Mother," and "When This Cruel War Is Over." She stumbled over the final notes in the last song, remembering her last dance with Damon, and, as if to exorcise the memory, she insisted on playing it all the way through again.

"Sing it," Cort commanded, standing over her, watching her so closely that she became self-conscious.

Obediently, though, she picked up the verse midway through:

> Oh, how proud you stood before me,
> In your suit of blue,
> When you vowed to me and country
> Ever to be true.
>
> Weeping sad and lonely,
> Hopes and fears how vain!
> Yet praying, when this cruel war is over,
> Praying that we meet again!

Her voice cracked over the last word. She would never meet them again. Not even when this cruel war was over.

Not in this world. Not Damon or Jimmy or Cordelia or Mama . . . And the tears, so long repressed, welled in her eyes. She groped for her handkerchief and tried to clench her jaw.

"It's all right," Cort said softly.

She turned to him blindly, and his arms went around her.

"It's all right to cry, Miranda. You should give way to your feelings. It's better for you." He stroked her hair. "Weep for the dead, my dearest girl. They deserve your tears. Weep for Jimmy and Damon and all the brave young soldiers marching off to this cruel war." His voice was gentle, soothing, gliding over the barriers she had worked so hard to raise. "Weep for them all, Miranda, all the lost joys of all their lives."

She clung to him then, sobbing uncontrollably, crying all the tears of childhood, crying as if she would never stop.

His arms around her were comforting, and he held her quietly, brushing back stray tendrils of hair, whispering soothing endearments, calming the final sobs, wiping away her tears. They were sitting on the couch by, then, watching the dying fire, his arms still around her.

It was only gradually that she became aware of a subtle shift in the tension of his embrace, and when she looked up at him finally, dry-eyed now, she was not really surprised when he kissed her, a long, increasingly passionate kiss, forcing her mouth open under his. She yielded then, clinging to him, the only solid force in this shaky, bewildering world.

"I think you are breathless again," he murmured in her ear, and she could not restrain an urge to giggle. She felt light-headed: Too much champagne, perhaps, and this violent spin from tears to laughter—and most of all her awareness of Cort and his dominating physical presence.

"I do believe you are waking up to the world." He held her at arm's length for a moment and watched the color rise in her cheeks. "Yes, all the emotions so close to the surface now." He traced the outline of her lips. "How beautiful you are," he said, and he kissed her again. "And how much I want you. How much I have always wanted you." He opened her robe, and his hands were warm through the thin cotton of her nightgown, warm on her back, warm cupping her breasts, stroking her gently.

"No, Cort. Please. You shouldn't." Her voice was barely

audible, even in her own ears, and he stilled it, kissing her again.

She raised a protective hand to the row of little buttons on her gown, but he brushed aside the restraint, unheeding, and a moment later he was kissing her throat, kissing the soft swell of her breasts, his tongue lingering on her hardening nipples. She was naked to the waist, and he drew back to admire her. "Beautiful," he murmured again, and he pulled her to her feet. She stood there, swaying for a moment, and then he opened his arms and she stepped into his embrace as if he had willed it. There was nothing in her world but Cort, nothing but his arms around her, his mouth hard on hers, his whole body thrusting forward to claim her.

And then, deliberately, he detached himself from her and walked away, five long steps away, too far away to touch her at all. She looked at him, bewildered, unaware of how the light from the fire outlined her body in her gaping nightdress.

"I want you to be very sure, Miranda." His voice was low and she strained to hear him through the roaring in her ears. "I want you to know and remember that I . . . I didn't overpower you. Do you understand me?"

"Yes, Cort."

"I want you to remember that *you* are making this choice. If you tell me to go away right now, I will. I want you very much, but I want you to come to me freely. Do you understand me?"

"Yes, Cort."

"Then tell me. Tell me in your own words, so that you will remember this decision for the rest of your life. The rest of both our lives."

"Yes, Cort." She had no more power to refuse than a puppet on strings. "I'll remember. I want you," she echoed him. "I want you to hold me in your arms and love me." She realized suddenly that it was true. "I want you to shut out the world and make me forget—"

There was triumph in his kiss, and in his hands exploring her yielding body. And then he carried her upstairs.

His room was dark, and he lit the gaslight and kindled a fire in the grate. "I want to see you clearly, Miranda." He stripped off his coat and waistcoat and shirt, watching her all the while. "I want to see the passion glow in your eyes, and I want you tō love me with all the emotions you have been storing up for all those years."

She stood silent, uncertain, her arms crossed over her breasts, clutching the high neck of her nightgown.

"Let me help you with that." He moved toward her and pulled gently at her gown, easing it down over her shoulders. "You are so lovely," he said, bending to kiss her again—her throat, her shoulders, her breasts. "Lovelier than anything you could ever wear." His hands moved down over her body, and the gown fell in a little heap on the floor. She hesitated then, but she stepped over it, into his outstretched arms. The feel of his flesh on hers had started the blood roaring in her ears again, and his hands exploring her body were setting off waves of emotion that swept away her last anchors to reality.

She clung to him, drowning, floating, surging with a tide too strong to resist, and she abandoned herself to a rush of joy and pain and elation and astonishment, acutely aware of the hungers of her body—and of his.

Afterward he smiled at her, caressing her breasts, kissing her lightly on the forehead. "You are wonderful, darling. I always knew you would be wonderful." His hands played over her body. "From the first time I saw you, behind the desk of the Stratford, looking like a saucy waiter-girl, I knew even then."

She stared at him in surprise.

"Oh, Miranda, my love. Don't be shocked. You have a talent for passion, and you should not be ashamed. There is no greater gift."

"But Cort—"

He kissed her. "You have made me very happy, darling. And I can see my own joy reflected in your eyes. Isn't that true? Tell me that it's true." He traced a line straight down her body, and she shivered. "Tell me what you are thinking right now."

"When you hold me, Cort, when you touch me like that, I . . . I can't think any more. All I can do is feel. All I want—" She gasped as his hands moved over her. "Oh, darling, *you* are all I want." She kissed him once more and nestled into the crook of his arm, her head on his shoulder, and there was no past and no future, only this drowsy delicious present where time stopped and feelings blotted out all thought.

From somewhere beyond the haven of this room, this bed, this shared moment, there came the sound of church bells, and then an almighty clamor of guns and cannon and firecrackers.

She looked at him, startled, and clutched his arm. "What is it?"

"What is it?" He smiled at her lazily. "Why, it's New Year's Eve. Have you forgotten? The whole world is celebrating." He followed her to the window, wrapping her in a quilt, but there was nothing to see—only a few stars and the moon rising in the distance. The fire in the grate had died down, and she shivered suddenly, uncontrollably, and scrambled back to the comfort of bed.

"Hold me, Cort." She burrowed into his arms. "Make me warm again."

The bells and guns faded into a distant clamor, blotted out by the rising passion that gripped them both.

It was broad daylight when Miranda woke up. She stretched lazily and opened her eyes, and for one bewildering moment she didn't recognize her surroundings. And then she sat up abruptly, alone in the big double bed, and the sheets and blankets fell away from her naked body, and she remembered. She remembered it all, and she blushed with shame. What had come over her last night? What had Cort done to her, forcing her into his bed, taking advantage of his power . . . And she had wanted him. She remembered now. He had given her a chance to say no, and she . . . She had to get away. She could never face him again. She must go home immediately, back to the safety of the Stratford and her father and . . . And Jimmy was dead. They had buried him yesterday, Cort said. They buried him on a cold and wintry day, and that very night she had thrown herself into the arms of this man who . . .

She pulled a blanket around her and tiptoed to the door, peering out to make sure she was unobserved, and then she scurried to her own room. She would get dressed immediately and leave this house. This unchaperoned house. What could her father have been thinking of, and George, too, going off and leaving her to the mercies of this man? But of course they thought that with Emily here, and the baby . . . She tried to sort it all out as she haphazardly threw her belongings into a satchel. She could never manage her trunk, but afterward George could arrange to have it sent. Emily must have decided to go back to New York when Damon died. She had some dim memory of her at the hospital, the loving niece, soothing Damon's parents. It would never have occurred to her that Cort was lying in wait to swoop down . . .

Miranda heard his footsteps pass on the way to his bedroom, pause, and turn back. A moment later he was standing in her doorway, breakfast tray in hand. He took in the scene at a glance, the half-packed satchel, the half-dressed girl, the sudden fear mixed with defiance in her eyes.

He closed the door abruptly and set down the tray.

"Listen to me, Miranda."

She retreated a step, but she had no choice but to listen.

"I will not try to stop you. If you insist on going, I will escort you to the depot myself. But we must talk about it first, and you must have breakfast. I don't want you fainting on the train." His eyes gleamed suddenly. "Who knows what stranger might take advantage of you, a beautiful young woman traveling on her own."

"Go away. I don't want to see you, ever again."

"That's not what you said to me last night: 'Hold me, Cort. Make me warm again.'"

She blushed furiously. "I was not myself last night."

"You were completely yourself, stripped of all these silly social conventions. Beautiful. Passionate. Wanton."

She glared at him.

"At least eat your breakfast. After Hattie took such special care . . ."

"Hattie? Why did . . . Dear God, that's unforgivable, Cort, telling the servants."

"My dear, they knew without my saying a word. Even if you hadn't dropped your paisley robe where they could find it, right by the fireplace in the music room . . ."

She sat down heavily.

"Oh, Cort, what will I do? What if anyone else finds out?" For the first time she looked at him for support. "Do I seem different?" She peered at herself anxiously in the mirror. "Do you think anyone can tell?"

"Not unless you go around with a scarlet letter A."

"I don't think that's a bit funny." She moved away from him and searched through the wardrobe for a suitable dress. She had nothing black, but she should be in mourning for

Jimmy. And then she was seized by another thought. "I might have a baby!"

"I think that is highly unlikely."

"That's easy for you to say. *You* don't have to worry."

He shrugged. "I see no point in worrying about a hypothetical problem."

"But what would I *do?*"

"Are you afraid to have a baby, Miranda?"

"No, but . . . That is, in this situation, without a husband, yes, I would be afraid."

"Well, then, in the unlikely event that you are truly pregnant, we will find you a husband. God knows you are ripe for marriage." He looked at the misery in her eyes and his flip tone vanished. "I would marry you, Miranda, if I were free. You are a rare prize, and you must not feel . . . guilty or unhappy about what happened last night. I took advantage of the situation. I even created the situation," he acknowledged. "And if you were to stay here, I would do it again. So you see," in a theatrical gesture he knelt at her feet, "I confess. But 'Your beauty was the cause . . . So I might live one hour in your sweet bosom.' That's *Richard III*," he added parenthetically.

"I know." The laughter came unbidden. "Edwin Booth does it better."

He smiled at her. "Eat your breakfast. And there's a plate for me, too."

She discovered she was ravenous, and he was, too. The split the last muffin, and she buttered his half and fed it to him, bite by bite. He kissed her fingers then, and the palm of her hand, and the pulse beating rapidly at her wrist, and she was in his arms again.

"In the daytime?" She looked at him, shocked.

"Do you really want to wait until night? You would miss your train." He was already loosening her chemise.

"I might miss it anyway," she sighed, succumbing to the new waves of desire he was evoking.

"There will be other trains," he murmured. "Later in the day. Tonight. Tomorrow . . ."

"Oh, Cort." She surrendered completely as his body pressed against hers. "How can I be so wicked?"

Sunlight streamed into the yellow bedroom, casting a golden glow on her warm flesh, and he kissed away her lingering doubts. Through half-open eyes she saw him looming over her, a halo of light endowing him with the magic of a god. For a long moment he hovered there, skimming the waves of emotion that threatened to engulf her, rousing in her such a flood tide of passion that she cried out, wanting him desperately. And he answered her cry and took her with him to that sensual new world he had opened for her, for them both.

Later, much later, he lounged back against the pillows and watched her dress.

"There's no need for you to go today," he said, all calm and reason in his voice.

"They'll worry about me," Miranda insisted. "Papa is probably already regretting leaving me here, and when he sees Emily and realizes that I am alone—"

"Not alone." Cort smiled. "How can you forget that I am here?"

"That's just the trouble, and you know it." She had secured the last button on her gray dress, and she sat down in front of the mirrored vanity to brush her tangled hair.

"Now let's think this through reasonably," Cort said. "Emily probably reached New York yesterday with Damon's parents, wouldn't you say?"

"*I* don't know, Cort. I didn't see them off. I was in no condition to keep track of them."

"Precisely. You were in no condition to travel yourself, so no one can blame you for being here. I am just trying to work it out so that you can stay with me for another day, or two, or three. Until George and Emily come back. Wouldn't you like that, darling? You *know* you would like that."

His eyes caught hers in the mirror and held her for a moment, transfixed. And then she shook her head stubbornly and resumed brushing her hair.

He went on confidently, as if he had secured her assent. "All right, let's assume they arrived yesterday. Today is New Year's, and they will probably have some difficulty making immediate funeral arrangements for Damon."

"George will find a way," Miranda said, with assurance born of experience.

"Yes, you may be right. Still, at the earliest, they can't have the funeral before tomorrow, and it would certainly be late afternoon before they could start back. That gives us today and tonight and all day tomorrow and tomorrow night

. . . A little lifetime of happiness to seize and enjoy. And God knows, Miranda, you deserve a little joy."

"But Papa will worry and wonder what is keeping me. And he'll suspect—"

"He trusts you completely, and he thinks I am a safely married man."

"All the more reason for me not to deceive him."

Cort shook his head and smiled at her reflection. "You are deceiving him already. You know damn well you aren't going to tell him about us. Twenty-four hours, forty-eight hours, will it make any difference to him? For us it's a lifetime."

"But if I don't go today . . ."

She was wavering, and he moved to secure his victory.

"We'll send him a telegram," he said. "I've thought it all out. 'Miranda recovering from slight indisposition. Will return Saturday.' That explains and reassures all at once."

" 'Slight indisposition'? What does that mean?"

"Anything you like. Probably some unmentionable female complaint. No one will question you, I'm sure. You forget, Miranda, you were something of a heroine in that miserable hospital. You have a right to a mysterious indisposition. It makes you sound very proper and ladylike."

She nodded in doubtful agreement. "Proper and ladylike," she echoed.

He grinned at her. "We know better, don't we? Wild and abandoned is more like it. My precious little tiger. How can I let you go? I'll have to think up many reasons to pay discreet visits to New York."

"Oh, Cort, it would never work. There's my whole family there. And even here in Washington in this house, if George—"

"No, not here," Cort agreed. "If your brother thought I was dishonoring his sister under the family roof, he'd throw me out. And quite right, too."

"He couldn't throw you out," Miranda objected. "It's *your* house."

"Yes. Well, it would be deuced awkward all the same. He'd move out, then, in righteous indignation, and that would be very upsetting."

"For you or for him?" Miranda said bitingly. "I don't think you're a bit worried about George's peace of mind. You have a nice, cozy situation here, and you can come and go as you please. All the advantages and none of the responsibilities."

"We have worked it out to our mutual satisfaction," Cort said calmly. "I will not risk making any changes. You forget that I am trying to protect *your* reputation, too."

She rolled her eyes in disbelief, and he laughed. "I'll get dressed and we'll go out for a walk. We should send off that telegram right away to forestall the dispatch of a rescue party." He donned his dressing gown and paused at the door. "I'll give Jeff and Hattie the rest of the day off. Incidentally, they are the only ones who know. Yesterday I told everyone else to take three days off to celebrate the emancipation jubilee. We'll go out for dinner later."

"But won't there be callers, Cort? It's New Year's Day and—"

"You forget. We're in mourning. There's a black wreath on the door. And no one would expect you to receive guests—even if they knew you were here."

She looked after him, a faint shadow of doubt clouding her day. He overrode all her objections with words, but there would be a time of retribution. She knew it. Anxiously, she studied her reflection in the glass. Did she look like a fallen woman? In the golden light her skin glowed, her eyes sparkled, and she couldn't help smiling at herself, a secret, knowing smile that almost accepted this transformation in her life, at least for today and tomorrow. She didn't want to think beyond that.

When she woke up in his bed the next morning, it seemed almost natural. He was gone, and she hurried into her clothes and raced down to the dining room. She was dismayed to find he wasn't there, but she concealed her disappointment from Jeff and accepted the breakfast he brought her.

Cort came in moments later, bearing a vast armload of roses, and he stopped short when he saw her. "Oh, what a pity—you've ruined my surprise." His smile was rueful. "I'm too late, or you're awake too early. I was going to spread these out on the bed, just for the pleasure of watching you wake up in a sea of flowers."

He bent to kiss her upturned face. "And you, the fairest of them all." He tucked one rose in her hair and touched her cheek.

"Oh, Cort." She kissed the palm of his hand. "I missed you so."

He smiled and sat down to pour himself a cup of coffee. "I was gone for only half an hour."

"Yes, but I didn't know how long you would be."

"And when you leave tomorrow," he studied her over the rim of his cup, "neither of us will know how long it will be."

She sighed, and he reached out to take her hand. "I can come to New York, Miranda. I *will* come, you know. This will not be our last day. Our last night."

She shivered. "It's all so complicated. If only we really could ... But I don't want to talk about it now."

Only twenty-four hours earlier she had refused pointblank even to consider seeing him in New York. He kissed her hand and, for the moment, obediently dropped the subject.

"What do you want to do today, darling?" He looked at her expectantly. "I have to call at the war department and then spend a few hours working, but I want to buy you something extravagant. What would you like?"

"Oh, Cort, you can't do that. I could never explain an expensive gift."

"You must want something. A new dress?"

"I can't let you do that, darling. And anyway, what I need is a mourning dress, and I can't possibly have that made by tomorrow. I'll have to check with Hattie and see if we can dye—"

"No. I'll get you a dressmaker. Two dressmakers. And a bolt of silk and all the trimmings. And a new bonnet." He grinned at her. "You will be the very picture of propriety."

"But Cort ..."

He would not be denied, and an hour later she was in a Washington shop, choosing a pattern and finding the proper fabric—a wildly expensive black moiré with a handsome dull sheen. By the time she returned to the house, two dressmakers had appeared as if by magic. They were all sympathy at her tragic loss, and they willingly went to work, cutting, basting, fitting, stitching, sewing on the tiny buttons of the bodice, working painstakingly to finish the buttonholes as the daylight faded and the gaslight was turned up full force.

Cort arrived as she preened in front of the mirror, admiring their handiwork, and he smiled and thanked them and paid them twice what he had promised.

Miranda saw the money change hands, and doubt returned.

"It's too much, Cort," she protested after they had left. "I can't possibly explain—"

"Don't be foolish. There's nothing to explain. Who will know?"

"But when Papa sees me—"

"Do you really think he remembers all your dresses, Miranda? If you were to arrive tomorrow in an old frock that you had just dyed black, would he know the difference?"

"Well, no. But it's a *new* dress, Cort, and any woman seeing it would know—"

"Any woman seeing it would know you had a new dress. That's all. Why should anyone suspect anything? You can't tell me you haven't had new dresses before." He grinned at her. "Why, the very first time I saw you, you were completely laden with bundles from Stewart's, and it never occurred to *me* that they might be paid for by your secret lover."

She looked at him ruefully. "Yes, that's what you are. My secret lover."

"Your generous secret lover," he corrected her.

"That's true." She pondered the change in his fortune and asked him a direct question. "Are you rich now, Cort? When you married Susanne for her money—"

"We will not talk about my wife," he interrupted her.

"But she—"

"She is in Savannah and we are here." He kissed her, as if to remind her of that fact. "Now," he smiled at her, "you asked if I were rich, and I am glad to say that I am rapidly approaching that state. There's a fortune to be made from this war. With the capital that I persuaded Mr. Robillard to get out of the Confederacy, I have done quite well—for all of us. If the South goes down to defeat, as it very well may, I will have salvaged most of his fortune—for him as well as for me. You see—from a strictly financial point of view, it was a good bargain all around."

"But Susanne—"

"She is the mother of my son. And we will not talk about her any more."

"And after the war?" Miranda persisted.

"That's too far away to think about." He dismissed the subject. "We still have tonight, Miranda. I just want to look at you and admire you. Why don't you put on your new bonnet, and we'll go out for a late supper."

She agreed willingly, eager suddenly to get out of this

house, wanting to forget this disquieting conversation. The words were still unspoken, but she could hear them just the same. Susanne was his wife. And, though he hadn't said it, she, Miranda, was his mistress. He wanted to give her expensive presents and visit her in New York and . . . Why, he had never even said he loved her! Dear God, how did she ever get into this situation? Jimmy was dead, and Damon, too, and instead of mourning for them both, she had flung herself headlong into Cort's arms. It was madness, wicked madness, and she would pay for it.

And tonight, when they returned, Cort would expect to take her to bed again. And how could she refuse him now? He would laugh at her, at this sudden yearning for lost innocence, and he would delight in riding roughshod over all her defenses. And, what was worse, some newly discovered part of her would delight in it, too.

She was quiet at supper, too quiet, and he probed for the cause.

"Something is worrying you, my dear. What is it?"

She refused to answer and made only a pretense of eating.

"It must be very serious if you won't tell me. Are you worried that I won't follow you to New York, Miranda? You should know by now that—" He broke off and studied her reaction. "No, by God, it's just the opposite. You're afraid I *will* come." He reached out and took her hand. "Would that be so terrible? If I see you now and again and hold you . . ." He kissed her palm and she snatched her hand away.

"Oh, Cort, where will it all end? I must leave you and forget you. There is no future in this for me at all."

He shook his head. "I think you are wrong. But, just as a matter of curiosity, what kind of future do you see without me?"

"Why," she floundered for a moment, "I'm not sure. Something for the war. With all the brave young men going off to fight and die . . ."

"Another tour of duty in a hospital? You have an excessive taste for martyrdom. How many dying soldiers do you want to comfort? Why not think for once of the living?"

"Yes, that's right. That's what Damon said before he died."

Cort looked at her, puzzled.

"He wanted to marry me. It's what he regretted most as he lay dying—that he hadn't married me and given me a child,

201

something for us both to live for." She nodded, convincing herself. "He was right. I will marry a soldier and have a baby right away."

"Is there anyone in particular you have in mind?"

She saw the glint of laughter in his eyes, and she set her jaw stubbornly. "Just because *you* can't marry me, that doesn't mean I can't find a husband."

"You are absolutely right! Shall I give you a written recommendation?"

"Oh, you are unspeakable!" She groped for her mantle, and a hovering waiter placed it on her shoulders.

"The lady is cold?" he said questioningly.

"Not usually," Cort murmured, grinning, and he put a restraining hand on her arm.

Miranda had half risen from her chair, and the nearby diners glanced at her curiously.

"It's all right," Cort said to the waiter. "Perfectly all right. I think her cloak had just fallen on the floor."

She glowered at him, but she subsided. The last thing she wanted to do was make a scene.

"I apologize," Cort said. "That was unforgivable. It's just that you took me by surprise and I . . . I will miss you very much."

Her silence was icy, and he tried to break it.

"So, you will find a worthy man and make him happy. And when he departs for the war—"

"*I* will be faithful to my marriage vows."

"While he—"

"Is faithful, too. I don't know what kind of arrangement you have with Susanne, but if she is taking lovers with the same abandon that you—"

"That's enough." He glowered at her. "I said we would not discuss my wife." It was a command, not to be challenged. He summoned the waiter and settled the bill and stalked from the restaurant, Miranda following in his wake. He handed her silently into a waiting carriage, paid the driver, and instructed him to take her home.

"But, Cort, where are you—"

He turned on his heel and walked off into the night.

She reconstructed the conversation over and over again all the way home, and by the time she arrived, she had worked herself into a towering rage. In her bedroom she stripped off the new dress and threw it on the floor. On second thought, she picked it up, crossed the hall, and threw it on Cort's floor. And then, taking a firm grip on herself, she went back to her room, locked the door, pulled out her trunk, and began to pack. She moved silently, alert to any sound that might signal his return, and she was nearly finished when she heard his step on the stairs. She froze at once, but he walked by to his own room. On tiptoe she crossed to the light and extinguished it. When he knocked at her door a moment later, she made no response.

"Miranda, I know you're awake. I saw your light as I came up the drive."

She said nothing.

"Don't be foolish." He tried the door and found it locked, and then she heard him laugh. His steps retreated, returned, and there was the sound of a key turning in the lock. He stood silhouetted in the doorframe, holding the dress. "Did you really think you could keep me away if I wanted to come in?"

She retreated behind the trunk, but he made no attempt to follow her. Instead, he struck a match to the gaslight, draped the dress carefully over the big chair, relocked the door, pocketed the key, and sat down on her bed.

She eyed him warily, judging the distance to the door, the windows, any way out.

"It's a long way to the ground," he said, following the direction of her glance, "and you might have a nasty fall. What if you broke your ankle and had to stay here for weeks and weeks?"

"You miserable cad, taking advantage of me this way."

He inclined his head. "*I* am a miserable cad, and *you* are my willful, passionate mistress"—she cringed at his use of the word—"and I see no reason for us to waste this last night together."

"And you aren't giving me even the pretense of a choice."

"No." He lounged back against the pillows, but his eyes were on her like a hawk, and she shivered.

Was there really no way out? He had lured her into this strange new world, and now she was trapped. Unbidden, the tears welled in her eyes and overflowed, and she had no will to stop them. She curled up on the carpet and gave way to her misery.

He stared at her uneasily, but the sobs persisted, and he moved to comfort her.

"Don't you dare touch me!"

He hovered over her, uncertain, but she rejected even his offer of a handkerchief. "I'm sorry, Miranda. I said some unforgivable things to you, and I didn't mean to." He knelt beside her and tried again. "We have lived a beautiful idyll, darling, and it was a tragic mistake to let anything from the outside world spoil it."

She made no response, and she shook off his tentative hand on her shoulder.

He sighed. "It's ironic. The whole key to winning you was to teach you how to cry again, and now you have found the one weapon to fend me off."

She looked up at him in surprise, instantly aware that he was right. She was so astonished by this revelation of the power of her tears that for a minute she stopped crying. He looked at her curiously, and she dropped her eyes hastily and resumed her sobbing, though with conscious effort now.

She felt his hand on her shoulder. "Miranda, look at me."

She kept her head down and dabbed at her eyes.

"Miranda." He put one finger under her chin and tilted her head back. He smiled at her. "What a terrible actress you are!"

"But I *was* crying," she protested. "Really and truly."

"Yes, I know." He pulled her to her feet and embraced her, kissing her eyes, her tear-stained cheeks, the tips of her ears. "Why were you crying?" he whispered. He was holding her so tightly that she had difficulty breathing.

"I don't know. That is, I thought . . . I thought you didn't . . . Oh, darling, you mix me up so much I don't know what I'm saying or thinking."

He kissed her again, his mouth insistent on hers, and she yielded, clinging to him, wanting him in spite of herself. He held her away from him and looked at her questioningly before he pulled at the cord of her robe. She sighed her surrender and began unfastening the buttons of his frock coat.

And then she stopped suddenly. "Cort, where did you go tonight, after you put me in that carriage?"

He looked at her and his smile was rueful. "I walked around in circles, cursing myself for being such a clumsy fool. And I thought of you, coming back to this empty house, and I knew there was nowhere else in the world that I wanted to be. Only here. With you."

Chapter 17

IT WAS LATE the next night when Miranda arrived back at the Stratford. There was a new clerk at the desk who didn't recognize her, but one of the porters hurried forward for her trunk, and she smiled her thanks and paid off the cabby.

"Mr. Chase is in the library, ma'am." The porter lingered for a moment, hitching at the trunk to get a better grip on it. "We were all mighty sorry to hear about Corporal Jimmy."

"Thank you, Mike. He was a brave soldier."

Mike nodded his agreement and bore away his burden. Miranda looked after him thoughtfully. He had never called her ma'am before. Was there really something different about her? Self-consciously, she blushed, remembering last night, and the night before, and the night before that. Surely no one could tell. No, it had to be the effect of the black dress and the solemn aura of death. Dear Jimmy. She would mourn for him properly now that Cort was not here to distract her.

She had worked it all out on the train, letting the effect of time and distance lend perspective to those three days. An idyll, Cort had called it. And that was what it had been, a dream far removed from the realities of everyday life. He had fed her on passion, and she had found it intoxicating. But now she was waking up—and she only hoped that her head would clear again. And her heart too.

The library was faintly illuminated by the light of a dying fire, and her father was slumped in his leather chair, asleep, she thought, as she tiptoed closer. How white his hair had become, just in the last year, and there were lines in his face, etched more deeply than she remembered. He opened his eyes as she hovered over him uncertainly, and he reached out a hand to her.

"Oh, Papa!" She threw her arms around him. "I am so glad to be home."

"My dear child, are you really here?" He gripped her arm, peering at her in the dim light. "We were so worried about you. Are you all right now?" He touched her cheek. "A fever, was it? You are still a little flushed."

"A fever. Yes, I think you could call it that."

"And the doctor? What did the doctor say?"

"Papa, it wasn't that serious, really."

"No doctor? Cort didn't call one for you? That was irresponsible of him. We should never have gone off and left you, but I thought that Emily . . ."

"It's all right, Papa. Really. Hattie was there, remember, and she is very capable."

"Yes, of course." He patted her hand, but he still looked troubled.

"I am sorry I missed Jimmy's funeral, Papa."

"The dear, gentle boy. All that promise . . ." He sighed heavily. "Three of them gone. Three graves together. Mary. Cordelia. James." His eyes welled with tears. "I hope I am next, Miranda. I couldn't bear going through this again."

"Oh, Papa!" Her voice caught in sudden emotion. "Don't say that. Don't ever say that. I love you so." She gave way to tears and sobbed against his shoulder.

He patted her gently. "Why, Miranda, is this my brave girl? My little heroine who never cries?" With an effort he was pulling himself together. "I was so proud of you in the hospital, easing Jimmy through his last struggles. Contriving somehow to look bright and cheerful. You were an inspiration to us all." He brushed back a tendril of hair from her forehead. "An angel of mercy. My own good girl." He kissed her cheek, and she looked at him through her tears.

"I tried, Papa, really I did. But afterward when—"

"That's all right, dear. I know."

"You know?" She looked at him, astonished.

"Of course. You forget that Emily was there, and Damon's parents."

"I'm not sure . . ."

"You were a heroine, Miranda. You took care of Damon until the end. It wasn't until his parents arrived that you collapsed. Emily told me all about it. She had her hands full

206

with her aunt—Mrs. McMasters fainted, too. But Cort was there, and he arranged everything—packed them all off to New York together. He even insisted that they take the baby and her nanny. And he was right. Little Polly was the one bright note in this whole miserable week." He smiled at her. "I know a grandfather is a little prejudiced, but that child is almost as beautiful as you were at her age."

"Oh, Papa." She had stopped crying and she made an effort to dry her eyes. "You say such extravagant things."

"True. Every word." He held up his hand solemnly, as if taking an oath. But then he sighed. "I must warn you, though, that there was a little gossip about you."

She clutched the arm of his chair and looked at him with alarm.

"Your Aunt Faith." He shook his head. "I don't know what gets into that woman. Here we were with two deaths in the family, and she wondered out loud if it was proper for you to be all alone in Washington in the same house with Cort."

"But I was sick, and the servants—"

"I know. Emily spoke to her quite sharply. I think Emily felt a little guilty, going off and leaving you, but she wasn't sure where her duty lay."

"But what happened?"

"Nothing happened. Richard was furious with his mother—and very worried about you. He wanted us to take the first train to Washington City, but then Cort's telegram arrived."

"And that explained everything?"

"We were still uneasy, of course, but Emily was sure that Cort would take care of you. He was so good about making all the arrangements, and I bless him for insisting that Polly come, too. But there, I'm repeating myself." He sighed and with an effort pulled himself upright. "Your old papa is feeling his years."

She shook her head, refusing to admit the possibility.

"It's true, though. Sometimes I think I have lost my touch. George and I went over the books last night, and he uncovered a fraud with the butcher that I should have noticed weeks ago."

"I thought Tom was doing the books now."

"Well, yes. But I should have caught it just the same. Tom is restless these days, and he never did have

George's head for figures. But let's not talk about that now." He dismissed the subject and summoned up a smile. "You're home again, and it's a joy to see you. Only . . ."

"Only?"

"The black dress."

She looked at him uneasily and retreated a step. "What about it?"

"It's just . . . Don't stay in mourning too long, Miranda. It makes you look so much older."

"But Jimmy—"

"Yes, we'll always mourn for him in our hearts, but wearing black . . . Oh, I know I'm wrong, and your Aunt Faith will think it's disrespectful, but please, as soon as you can, I want you looking bright and cheerful again."

"Yes, Papa."

There was doubt in her voice, and he heard it.

"Don't tell me you have dyed *all* your frocks already."

"Oh no," she reassured him hastily. "I haven't had the time. I wasn't feeling well, you know, so just this one . . ."

He was looking at her curiously, and she changed the subject abruptly. "Where is everyone, Papa? George and Emily and Polly?"

"They left this morning. George wanted to go yesterday, right after Damon's funeral, but Emily persuaded him to stay. Traveling with the baby, arriving in the middle of the night—it would have been too difficult."

"Too difficult," Miranda echoed, visualizing the horror of their midnight arrival. To be discovered . . . She shuddered and wondered again at her madness and at Cort's supreme arrogance in arranging all their lives to suit himself. Insisting that Polly go to New York—that was the master touch. His devotion to his godchild was what had finally cemented his relationship with George and Emily. It was one of the oddities of his character—he genuinely seemed to like babies and young children. "Before they grow up and lose their innocence," he had said to her once. And now she had lost her innocence, and the prospect of having a baby . . . No, she wouldn't think about that now. She had checked the calendar, and she had another ten days before she had to start to worry.

"You are so quiet," Will remarked. "I think the train journey has tired you. And perhaps you aren't completely recovered from your fever."

"Yes, you're right. I really should go to bed early. I'll just say a word to Tom. Where is he?"

Will frowned. "I'm not sure. He's been spending a lot of time at the Schuylers' lately."

She looked at him, surprised.

"I hope he's not really getting serious about Irene," he added, by way of explanation.

Miranda was stunned. "I can't believe he would . . ." She sighed. "Still, at least we'd keep him in New York. With George in Washington City and John in England and dear Jimmy . . ."

Will echoed her sigh. "They all grow up and go away. But Tom and Irene . . . No, I just don't like the idea of cousin marriages. But then," he got to his feet with an effort, "there's no need to borrow trouble. Besides," he smiled at her, "your Aunt Faith would certainly put a stop to it in any case. For once I would find myself in agreement with that woman."

Tom *had* been spending time at the Schuylers', but Irene was not the attraction. When Miranda cornered him in the office the next morning just before church, he was perfectly willing to explain. Indeed, he had been looking for the opportunity, and he closed the door with relief and perched on the edge of the desk, smiling at her hopefully.

"How would you like my job, Miranda?" He pointed at the account books and then, in a broad gesture, included the whole office.

Her eyes lighted up immediately, and then she went cold. "What do you mean, Tom? What are *you* going to do?"

"I'm going to enlist, of course. What do you think?"

"Oh, Tom. Not now. It's wonderful of you, of course, and I know you have been wanting to go for months now, but can't you wait a little while? Now that Jimmy . . ."

"I should never have let him go first." His eyes were bleak. "Papa . . . I had never seen Papa cry before."

"And don't you think he would cry for you, too? Tom, you can't do this to him. Jimmy not dead a week, and you want to rush off . . ."

He was surprised. "I thought you would be on *my* side. You have always been so hell-for-leather impatient to get on with the war. You never said anything directly to me, but I know you were disappointed when Richard talked me into joining the Seventh."

"Let's not talk about Richard. If he had any spirit, *he* would enlist."

"But he is!"

Astonishment made her speechless.

"Damn it, I wasn't supposed to tell you. He wanted to surprise you for some fool reason. Act surprised when you see him next time, will you?"

"I'm a terrible actress," she said and blushed suddenly, remembering Cort telling her that. Tom was too preoccupied to notice.

"Richard and I have been planning this for a month, Miranda, since before . . . before Fredericksburg." He gulped and was silent a moment before going on. "We wanted to have everything arranged and then sort of make a general announcement to the family."

"I don't understand what you are talking about."

"But now that Jimmy is dead," he went on, backing into his explanation, "I thought I had better tell you first, to help me convince Papa."

She looked at him, bewildered.

"It was really Richard who worked it all out."

"Worked *what* out?"

"Why, bringing John home to take over his job at Schuyler Shipping so that Richard could enlist with me. He was a little doubtful about whether *you* could be much help to Papa in the office here—"

"Oh, he was, was he?" She bristled automatically.

"But I managed to convince him. And now if you will help me convince Papa . . ."

She considered the idea. It was a golden opportunity, and Papa would *have* to let her help. And Mr. Dawson, too. It was a terrible time for Tom to be going off to war, of course, with Jimmy dead less than a week, but with John coming home . . . And John would be bringing Danielle. Of course they wouldn't be living at the Stratford indefinitely—they'd want a house of their own, uptown. Still, with John in New York, Papa would have one of the boys close at hand, and Tom would be under less pressure to stay home. And she *could* handle his job; she was sure of it, no matter what Richard thought. It was just like him to doubt her ability. She would show him. Why, after the hospital anything would be easy. She squared her shoulders and sat down at the desk. "You must show me everything, Tom."

He grinned at her. "I will. I certainly will. But don't you think you should get your bonnet and come to church with us now? It's going to be hard enough to convince Papa—we'd better get the Lord on our side first."

When they reached St. Paul's, Richard was waiting for them, much to Miranda's surprise. She wondered briefly what explanation he had given his mother for not accompanying the family to their regular services at Grace, but she forgot about that under his persistent, steady gaze.

"What's the matter?" she whispered to him finally as they stood for the processional hymn.

"Nothing." He smiled at her. "That is, I was trying to decide what was different about you, and I think I know."

She looked at him, alarmed, but he smiled again and joined confidently in the opening hymn. A little shakily, she followed his lead.

Afterward, even without any prompting from Tom, she invited Richard for midday dinner at the Stratford, and he accepted with alacrity. Will raised an eyebrow but said nothing, and he made the usual dutiful inquiries about the health of the family. Richard replied in kind, and the conversation stayed on this strictly conventional level on the brief walk back to the Stratford and all through the restless dinner in the family dining room. Will was drinking his third cup of coffee and still talking impersonally, soliciting Richard's opinion on the strength of the blockade of the Southern ports, and finally Miranda could stand it no longer.

"Papa, we have something important to say to you," she interrupted him.

He sighed heavily and put down his empty cup. "I'm not sure I want to hear." He looked at them all, finally fastening his gaze on Tom. "When are you going?"

"In three weeks. That is . . . How did you know?"

"Oh, my boy. I'm your father. You haven't had your mind on your job for two months now." Will's smile was rueful, and he shook his head. "At first I thought it was a girl." He looked at Richard. "I even suspected it was Irene."

Tom laughed, relieved to break the tension. "I know it's a bad time, Papa, with Jimmy . . ." He trailed off and looked at Miranda for support, but she was blinking back sudden tears, and that rattled him.

"I am enlisting, too, Uncle Will." Richard's emotions were under firm control, as usual, and his confident voice steadied them all. "We have been planning this for more than a month now, since before Fredericksburg."

He did not hesitate over that word, Miranda noticed. Fredericksburg. What was that? A little town in Virginia . . . and so much more. She remembered Jimmy's description: Pontoon bridges over the Rappahannock, the rutted frozen roads, the ranks of troops assembling under cover of night and fog, and, when the fog lifted, all Lee's armies lying in wait from Marye's Heights to Hamilton's Crossing. All the brave young men caught in that deadly fire. She blinked back her tears and listened to Richard's calm voice, explaining carefully about his commission, and Tom's, and the new regiment, and all the detailed plans about John and Danielle coming home.

"I finally convinced Papa," he was saying, "that I could be spared if John were here."

Will shook his head. "Spared? Don't talk nonsense. None of you can be spared."

It was Richard's turn to sigh. "I know this couldn't have come at a worse time, Uncle Will, but we worked it out the best way possible. We *are* bringing John home and that should be some comfort."

"And I am here, Papa." Miranda had found a grip on her emotions at last. "Tom will teach me his job, and I can be a big help to you. I know I can."

Will smiled at her. "And you won't run off and enlist?"

"No, Papa. I don't think they would take me."

"So." Will looked at them all. "Have you told me everything?" His gaze was searching.

"Wasn't that enough?" Tom laughed, completely unaware of any undercurrents.

Miranda was silent, conscious she was blushing under her father's watchful eyes. But he couldn't know. He couldn't suspect. A slight fever had kept her in Washington. She had nothing more to tell him at all.

Richard cleared his throat. "I have told you everything I can, Uncle Will. For now." He looked at Miranda, her eyes still downcast, the color high in her cheeks. "If Miranda . . ."

She glanced at him, startled, wondering if her guilt was that apparent.

Will studied them both, the rigidly proud young man, his strangely silent daughter, looking achingly vulnerable, not meeting his eyes, still blushing or still feverish—he wasn't sure. "I think I have had enough surprises for now," he told them. "I was wondering, Richard . . . What does your mother think of your decision to enlist?"

"She doesn't know yet. I am going to tell her today." He stood up, restless, and walked over to the windows. "She'll be furious, I know, but I had to do it. Papa agreed finally, but telling Mother . . . I know there will be an explosion."

"Good training for the real war," Tom observed, and he stretched lazily. "I'm not going to waste the rest of this beautiful day indoors. Do you want to go ice-skating?" He looked at Miranda, but she declined, as did Richard. Tom shrugged and departed, whistling, and Will looked after him and sighed. He stood up wearily, announced he was going to take a nap and suggested, rather pointedly, that Miranda was still recovering from her slight indisposition and should rest, too.

"In a little while, Papa," she agreed. "I thought I'd write a letter to George and Emily first."

"Give them my love," Will said, "and the baby, too." He touched her cheek and looked thoughtfully at Richard, still standing by the windows, sighed once more, and wished him good afternoon.

Miranda was surprised when Richard followed her into the library and closed the door.

"I thought you were going home to tell your mother." She sat down at the big desk and rummaged through the top drawer for her writing paper.

"I can do that later."

She looked up at him and smiled. "I'd like to be a fly on the wall."

He shrugged impatiently. "She'll get over it."

"I suppose so. But I know she will find a way to blame us, and somehow it will all be Tom's fault for persuading you. Or John's for agreeing to come home. Or even mine."

"How could it be yours?"

"I don't know. Because I was angry with you once for not enlisting at the beginning. I'm sorry I didn't understand, but you had to do what *you* thought best. It was all my fault about Damon, you know. I felt so guilty when he died."

"Don't be foolish, Miranda. He was perfectly capable of making decisions for himself. Just as I am."

She gazed at him, so confident, so assured, so busily managing his own life—and John's and Danielle's and Tom's. It occurred to her suddenly that in some ways he was very much like Cort, and she looked away from him and lost the thread of what he was saying. If only that romantic dream could have gone on . . ."

". . . and it changed you, Miranda." Richard's earnest voice drew her back to reality.

"Changed me?"

"I could tell as soon as I saw you this morning. All that responsibility in the hospital. And your very real grief. You aren't just a beautiful, willful girl any more. You have truly grown up." He paused, and there was new resolution in his voice when he spoke again, and she knew immediately that she didn't want to hear his next words, whatever they were going to be.

"I have been thinking about you for a long time, Miranda, and I—"

"Richard, don't say any more." She stood up quickly, as if to cut him off.

"No, hear me out. I have waited for so long, and perhaps I shouldn't burden you now when you are still mourning for Jimmy. Yes, and for Damon, too. But there isn't much time before we leave, and I can't let this day go by without telling you." He stopped short and looked at her searchingly. "I love you, and I have loved you for years, and I want to marry you."

Unbidden, she heard echoes of Cort's declaration. "How much I want you. How much I have always wanted you." He had never even said he loved her, but he had touched a chord that was still reverberating, drowning out Richard even as he spoke. Oh, life wasn't fair. It wasn't fair at all. Only three days. Tears welled in her eyes, and she had difficulty swallowing.

The silence stretched out.

"Say something, Miranda. I know you weren't prepared for— Why, darling, you're crying." His arms went around her tentatively, as if she were made of fragile glass. "I didn't want to upset you, my dear, dear girl." He groped for his handkerchief, and she accepted it gratefully and broke out of his embrace.

"Richard, I don't know what to say."

" 'Yes' would be a very good answer."

She managed a tremulous smile. "I don't think that would be fair to you. How can I give you an answer now, when I—"

"I know you don't love me the way I love you, Miranda. But . . . that will come. Once we are married. I would cherish you, darling, and honor you, and hold to you faithfully as long as we both shall live."

"You are too good for me." She blurted it out without thinking, and he stared at her for a moment and laughed uncertainly.

"I don't think I understand your joke. But if you can't say yes right now, at least don't say no."

"I won't say no," she agreed.

"Well, then." He reached for her hand. "I suppose there is hope."

"Hope," she echoed. And then she smiled a little crookedly. "Faith and hope and charity. How would you ever tell Aunt Faith? If she explodes when you tell her you are going to enlist, what will happen when you say you want to marry me?"

"I don't plan to say a word until I have an engagement ring firmly planted on your finger." He kissed her hand. "And then I could face the world."

She looked at him, tall and slim, more slightly built than Cort but with a whipcord strength that was enduring. And there was honor there, and trust, and a commanding sense of pride. And if he couldn't make her laugh or cry or love, send the blood pounding through her veins when he reached out to touch her . . . Well, she would try not to remember all that now. It was dangerous to let her feelings master her that way. Richard was her steady, reliable cousin, firm in his convictions, anchored to solid principles, unyielding in his sense of duty. He had standards, and he lived up to them. He would expect his wife to do no less.

"I admire you very much, Richard."

"Well," he smiled at her. "I suppose that is at least a start."

"I don't see why you love *me*, though." She said it seriously, and she was honestly bewildered when he laughed.

"Don't you ever see yourself in a mirror, Miranda?"

"Yes, of course." She knew she was blushing again. "But there has to be more to it than that."

"I could just stand here and look at you . . . But if you want me to give you the complete story of when and how I fell in love . . ." He led her to the window seat in the little alcove overlooking the park, and he did not release her hand, even after he sat down beside her.

"I have always liked you, Miranda. You were such a bright and lively little girl."

"You never paid any attention to me at all," she contradicted him, "except to tell me to go away and stop bothering you."

He denied that vigorously and dredged up his own version of the past in which he was always the benevolent older cousin, ready to defend her against any attack.

She eyed him skeptically. "I was a terrible tomboy, always tagging after my brothers, and your mother thought I was a bad influence on Irene. And you always had your nose in the air and hardly noticed I was alive."

"This is *my* story," he reminded her. "I will tell it my way, and *you* are here to supply the happy ending." He smiled at her, but she looked away, uneasy with his expectations.

"I remember so clearly the day I decided," he resumed. "It was just over three years ago. December 2, 1859. Do you know what happened then?"

"No. I don't think so."

"It was the day they hanged John Brown."

She stared at him, mystified.

"You had gone ice-skating with Irene, and she brought you back for tea. And you came in, laughing and radiant, and the melting snow sparkled in your hair, and you were so bright and glowing with good health and high spirits that it was as if you had just flashed into my life, like some new comet, from another world."

Miranda searched her memory in vain, but Richard continued, oblivious.

"That's when Mother was trying to pair me off with the Wickersham girl—Louise, I think her name was."

"Oh, yes. I think I remember."

"She was there, too, as pale and insipid as milk toast, and you came in, so dazzling. You were wearing a bright blue cloak and a little bonnet with wide ribbons."

Miranda nodded. At least she remembered the clothes.

"And the reason I remember it was the day John Brown was hanged is that you got into a fierce argument with Irene, and Mother was trying to quiet you both, and Louise just looked on, so embarrassed she wanted to fade into the wallpaper."

"And this was one of the celebrated times when you defended your little cousin against any attack?"

"You didn't need any help. Besides, I thought you were dead wrong."

"They why did you care?"

"Because *you* cared, so fervently. And I thought how wonderful it would be to have someone who could summon up such enthusiasm and excitement, who could add such color to what otherwise would be a very proper and conventional life."

"But *you* are very proper and conventional," Miranda objected.

"And very determined," he agreed. "And patient. I have been waiting for you to grow up."

"I might have married someone else. Damon kept asking me."

Richard brushed aside the thought. "I knew that wouldn't work out. And all the other young men trailing in your wake—I was close enough to see you weren't encouraging any of them."

"But I wasn't encouraging *you*, either."

"You didn't need to. I had already decided."

"*You* had already decided?" Why, he was every bit as arrogant as Cort and just as confident of ultimate victory. She found it chilling, and detached her hand from his and shook her head. "I am not ready to make any decisions now."

Richard accepted her answer calmly. "Think about it, Miranda. That is all I ask. I can offer you a good life, and I want to make you happy."

"Thank you, Richard, but I'm not ready to . . . say anything at all."

"That's better than saying no—and more than I could have hoped." He smiled at her and kissed her cheek. "I will come back tonight and tell you what Mother had to say about my enlistment."

"Oh, I don't think you should bother—"

"And I'll see if you have changed your mind yet."

She followed him to the door, still protesting, but he only

smiled. "I had better speak to your father, too, though I think he has already guessed."

Her eyes widened in surprise, and he laughed. "I don't believe he is very happy about the idea, but he knows he is going to lose you sooner or later. And at least you'll be right here in New York."

She closed the door after him and sat down at the desk again, but all thought of letter writing had vanished. How absolutely astonishing of Richard. She had told Cort she was going to marry a soldier and have a baby right away, but she hadn't really believed it. And she didn't believe it now. Besides, Richard wasn't just "a soldier," some faceless, anonymous figure going off to battle, perhaps never to return. Richard was forever, and she couldn't face that. Not now. Not so soon after Cort. So soon after Jimmy. Oh, why were all her problems such big ones now? She shivered suddenly, craving warmth and protection—and she knew it was Cort's arms she wanted around her.

She had tea with her father, and he was being determinedly cheerful about the future. He did not talk about Tom's enlistment—or Richard's—and he gave all his attention to the prospect of John's return, with Danielle. The sea voyage. The welcome home. The first days at the Stratford. "We must help them find a house," he was saying. "Not so far north as Gramercy, I think. There's no point in being too far uptown. Near Bond Street, perhaps, or Washington Square." The Schuyler Shipping offices were on Broad Street, and it could take an hour to get there through the clogged streets.

Miranda nodded, too distracted to worry about John's problems. Let Danielle handle all that.

"Or perhaps Brooklyn Heights," her father persisted. "Taking the ferry is really faster than the cars. Don't you think so?"

Miranda nodded, not really paying any attention, and her father sighed and gave up.

"You'd better tell me," he said. "Did he ask you to marry him?"

"What?" Miranda's teaspoon clattered to the floor, and she stared at her father, astonished.

"Richard. Did he ask you to marry him?"

"Papa, you're a mind reader. How did you ever know that?"

"It was so obvious. And you didn't really know?"

She shook her head.

"He's had his eye on you for years, and he came here today so full of determination that . . . So he *did* ask you. And what did you say?"

"Why, why I said I needed some time to think about it. I think that's what I said. I was so surprised that I hardly knew what answer to give him."

Will pushed aside his plate and contemplated her in silence for a long moment. "I don't want you to marry him, Miranda."

"Papa! Why not?"

"Let's just say it's because I disapprove of cousin marriages. I've already told you that."

"Well, yes. But I thought you meant Tom and Irene."

"*And* you and Richard. It's not as if you love him, surely."

"No," she acknowledged. "I don't love him. But he is solid and dependable and . . ." Her voice trailed off, and she thought of Damon and Jimmy.

"And?"

"He's going off to war, Papa."

"That's no reason for you to marry him. Damon went off to war, too, but—"

"And he died holding my hand, Papa. And Jimmy, too. They had never really lived at all, and then they were dead. Perhaps it was selfish of me, not marrying Damon. We could have had a child by now."

"Miranda, you can't go around accepting any brave young man who proposes to you, just out of some misplaced sense of duty."

"No. But I could marry Richard, and that would be very . . . safe."

"My dear innocent child. That's not good enough. Marriage is . . . You deserve more than that." He looked at her and then looked away, and when he spoke again his voice was so low that Miranda had to strain to hear.

"I . . . I loved your mother very much." He was groping for words, almost embarrassed, and he pulled out his pipe and made an elaborate business of tapping it out and tamping in a fresh supply of tobacco. "It is very difficult to talk about . . . about some aspects of married life." He was acutely

219

uncomfortable, and lighting his pipe didn't seem to help at all. "Do you understand what I am trying to say to you?"

"Yes, Papa. I think so. You loved Mama very much. I know that."

"Yes. But there was more than that. She loved me, too, you see. We were very happy together. All of you children—we wanted you. And we wanted each other. That isn't always true, you know. There are many marriages that aren't successful that way. A man can always . . . But I want *you* to be happy, Miranda. Happy the way Mary and I . . . I want you to be very sure before you surrender yourself in marriage."

It never occurred to him, she noted wryly, that she would surrender herself without marriage. Oh, Cort, why did we start something we could never finish? It was wicked of you to want me, to make me want you, when I *know* there is no future for us. If I could just stop thinking about you, remembering you, reliving every moment . . . And Richard is truly a good man. If I married him, I would be safe from you forever. Papa must be wrong. He doesn't understand that I . . . I don't deserve the kind of happiness he is talking about. And Richard will be going off to war, ready to sacrifice himself. Like Jimmy. Like Damon. If he wants to marry me, why should I refuse? If I can't have you, Cort . . .

She was conscious of her father's eyes on her, and she came to with a start. "I still don't know, Papa."

"Promise me something, Miranda."

She looked at him expectantly.

"Promise me that you will think about your *own* happiness. Not just this month or this year, but ten years from now, twenty years from now."

"But how can I do that, Papa? Everything changes every day. It's not the way it was when you were growing up, when everything was calm and peaceful and you knew it would always stay that way."

" 'Calm and peaceful.' What a child you are. And there are three graves in Greenwood Cemetery." He sighed. "But perhaps you are right after all. How can I ask you to think so far ahead? Just promise me you won't be hurried into making a decision. Take at least a month. Can you promise that?"

She nodded her agreement. A month. That was easy. She would know her own mind by then. Perhaps if the memory of Cort had started to fade a little. And she had begun to master Tom's job in the office. And John and Danielle were home. And Richard would take her in his arms and make her forget. And, most of all, if she knew positively that she was not pregnant.

And so the month passed, but it wasn't easy at all.

Richard and Tom left for Washington together. Miranda kissed them good-by, and she still had no answers. Richard gave her a locket with his picture, and she put it on immediately and promised to write to him every day, but she refused to acknowledge an engagement or even an understanding, and he repeated his proposal and said he would return soon and ask her again. And he would keep asking her until she said yes, because, and he smiled at her, he never gave up.

John and Danielle arrived and stayed at the Stratford while they looked for a house and waited for their furniture to arrive from England. Danielle had been seasick en route and was still not feeling well. Will looked at her questioningly, expectantly, but John shook his head, without comment, and Danielle confided in Miranda afterward.

"I don't know what the problem is. We've been married more than two years now, and we *want* children." She was in the fourth floor parlor suite of the Stratford, unpacking her trunks, and Miranda had offered to help.

"Well, now that you are back home," Miranda said, a little embarrassed that Danielle was confiding in her. It was strange—Danielle longing for a child, while she, Miranda, was lying awake nights worrying. She was only two weeks late, and surely there was no real cause for alarm yet, but every day wound the tension higher.

Danielle smiled wryly. "John and I joke about it. We say we are just waiting because we were afraid that if the first boy were born in England, he couldn't grow up to be President. But it's not a very good joke, and it gets worse because I always say I want him to be President of the Confederacy, and John insists he means President of the Union."

Miranda was appalled. "Do you truly mean that? If you are really with the Rebels—"

"Oh, I don't care who wins any more!" Danielle was impatient. "I just want it to end! All the fighting and dying. Your own dear brother. And I had two cousins who were killed last May at Williamsburg. And Stuart, my very first beau—he lost a leg at Sharpsburg; Antietam, you called it. I remember telling him once that he was the best dancer in all Georgia, and the first time we ever waltzed together I thought I was in love. And now he'll be on crutches the rest of his life. It's all so useless, and I want it to end. Don't you feel that way?"

"I want it to end, of course," Miranda said slowly, "but I want it to end in victory."

"It's not worth it," Danielle said. "None of it."

Miranda shook her head stubbornly. "I *have* to believe it's worth it. How could I accept all this death and destruction if I didn't believe . . ."

Danielle remained unconvinced. "Cort was right all along. We should never have let it come to war." But Dany could never stay with a general subject—she much preferred to talk about people instead. They were so much more interesting than abstract principles, and so much more fun to gossip about. "It's just plain stupid of Susanne to let the war separate her from Cort," Dany went on, changing the subject with a speed that Miranda found unsettling. "I think she's an idiot, staying in Savannah instead of being with him where she belongs."

Miranda made no comment. She had studiously avoided mentioning Cort's name, and she couldn't even bear to think about Susanne.

But Danielle needed no prompting. "And she's so smug about it, too. Just because she's pregnant again."

The room reeled suddenly, and Miranda grasped the wardrobe for support, but Danielle was rattling on, oblivious.

"He was there for a few days in September, you know, so of course the baby must be due in June. She wants another boy, but Cort said he'd rather have a girl this time. He's so fond of Polly—she's your godchild, too, isn't she? And Susanne says that . . ."

This can't be happening, Miranda was thinking. I am not standing in this room, worried sick about having a baby, and all the time Cort's wife in Savannah . . . And he must have known it all the time. How could he take me in his arms and . . . Dear God, I can't be pregnant. I just can't. And if I marry Richard . . . But that would be so unfair to him, even if he never knew. Cort would know. He would look at me and his eyes would gleam and I . . . I can't have his baby. I can't. There has to be some way . . . If *only* I'm not pregnant.

"And if it's a girl," Danielle was saying, "she might name

her after the two of us. Danielle Miranda Adams. What would you think of that?"

"I don't know," Miranda said, surprised to hear that she could keep her voice so steady. "Whatever they want, I suppose. I wonder," she was folding one of John's shirts with elaborate care, "I wonder when Cort found out he was going to be a father again. He . . . he hadn't mentioned it."

Danielle laughed. "Susanne said it was her Christmas present to him. She arranged for a courier to deliver a bottle of very old brandy to him on Christmas day and . . . But you were there, weren't you? It's strange that—"

"It was Christmas day that we got word Jimmy was arriving in Washington, and we went racing off to meet the ambulance wagon."

"Oh, yes, of course. That's why you didn't know." Danielle was all sympathy, and she sighed. "Life beginning and life ending. Birth and death. We have never lived with them so intimately before."

"No," Miranda agreed. "They can be uneasy companions."

Chapter 18

"**Y**OU'RE GETTING CIRCLES under your eyes, Pet," Will told Miranda two days later. "You mustn't lie awake nights worrying about the account books. You're doing a splendid job."

She smiled her thanks—and went right on lying awake worrying, though not about the accounts.

It was an unexpected conversation with the housekeeper that set her thoughts off in a new direction. Mrs. Darcy had come into the office to insist that one of the maids be discharged, and, since Will wasn't there, she told Miranda.

"But what has the girl *done*, Mrs. Darcy? And what did you say her name was?"

Mrs. Darcy pursed her lips, disapproving. "Flaherty is the name. Mary Kathleen Flaherty, and a disgrace she is."

"Oh, I know Kathy," Miranda said, smiling. "The pretty redhead on the third floor. Why, she's been with us at least three years. Whatever is the matter?"

"I don't really like to tell you, ma'am," Mrs. Darcy lowered her voice to a stage whisper. "She's got herself into the family way ... and her only seventeen years old and without a husband." Mrs. Darcy shook her head. "It's wicked, this new generation of immigrant girls. I have to keep a sharp eye on all of them. But little Flaherty—I thought she knew better."

"The poor girl." Miranda's sympathy was heartfelt. "But surely we can't discharge her without—"

"Without a character," Mrs. Darcy said grimly. "Yes, we can. It's hard enough to keep discipline over all these foolish girls, but if you start showing favoritism to any one of them, I ... I just won't be responsible, that's all."

"I see." Miranda picked up her pen and put it down again and looked up at the implacable Mrs. Darcy, standing so stiffly in her starched black gown. "Do you happen to know who the father is?"

Mrs. Darcy nodded. "Yes, I got it out of her finally. She didn't want to tell me, but I guessed. It's that young Kelly who works in the bar at the Astor House. And he fancies himself as a volunteer fireman, too. Told me once he was a hero. Him! A hero!" She sniffed. "Flaherty has been keeping company with him for months now, and him no better than he should be. Telling her wicked lies, I've no doubt. But that's no excuse. She should have known better."

"Yes, I'm sure you're right." Miranda sighed. "He's not married or anything, is he?"

"No, he's free as a bird. Free to go about seducing my girls, getting them into trouble—"

"*Girls*, Mrs. Darcy? Do you mean there is more than one?"

"Oh, no," she said hastily. "Not that I know of. It's just Flaherty so far, but I've no doubt that after she's discharged he'll turn his attention to the next foolish girl who takes her place and—"

"I think we should make him marry Kathy, and that will put an end to it." Miranda was decisive. "I want to talk to her."

Kathy Flaherty entered the office hesitantly and, following Miranda's directions, closed the door and sat down. The uniform was a little tight, Miranda noticed, and Kathy was pink with embarrassment; she could not meet Miranda's eyes.

Miranda was at a loss herself, and she blurted out the first question that came into her head. "Do you love him, Kathy?"

"I thought I did." She had a soft, whispery voice that somehow commanded attention. "Kevin said he loved me, and he said we'd get married. And now . . ."

"And now?" Miranda prompted her.

"Well . . . He says he still wants to marry me, but he doesn't have much money, and he wants to wait, and he thinks . . ." Her voice trailed off.

Miranda waited patiently.

"He thinks I should get rid of the baby." She risked a glance at Miranda. "He knows the name of this woman, and he says he'll pay for it, but . . . I don't know.

"I see. And what do *you* want to do?"

"Well." She gulped once, trying to hold back the tears. "He says it's not a sin. Not yet. Not until . . . not until I feel the baby move. But I don't know. I don't know what to do at all. We were going to be married, and now . . ." She gave way to tears, and Miranda was hard pressed to stay dry-eyed herself.

"Don't you have anyone to help you, Kathy? A father who could talk sense to your young man?"

She shook her head, sniffling. "He died three years ago, just before I came to work here. And I didn't want to tell Ma until . . . But I *thought* we'd be getting married."

Miranda sighed. "Well, then, I'll talk to *my* father. There's no help for it."

"But, I don't understand. What can he do?"

"Do? Why, he'll talk to Colonel Stetson at the Astor House. I think that if Kevin Kelly want to hold on to his job over there, he had better marry you; that's all. It's not fair for him to put you through all this and not come to your rescue."

Miranda attended the wedding a week later, wishing that her own problems were so easily resolved, but happy for Kathy and her unborn child. And happy for Kevin, too. Whatever doubts he may have had beforehand seemed to have disappeared, and he stood beside his bride, flushed and triumphant, as if the wedding had been his idea all along. Miranda shook hands with him afterward—he obviously had no idea why she was there or the part she had played—and he advised her blithely that every girl should be married and she should be sure to catch the bridal bouquet. Miranda gave him a wry smile and slipped away, eager to get back to the Stratford again.

She was in the office that afternoon going over the books with Mr. Dawson when she heard a familiar voice at the front desk, asking for her. There was a low murmur from the clerk, and a moment later he was standing in the doorway.

"There's a Mr. Cort Adams here, Miss Chase, asking to speak to you."

"Tell him I'm busy," Miranda said, glancing up from the ledger. "Tell him that Mr. Dawson and I—"

"Oh, that's all right." Guy Dawson could never learn to

take a hint. "He's your brother-in-law, isn't he? Of course you'll want to see him."

"Of course she does," Cort agreed. He brushed past the clerk, who shrugged and returned to the desk, and Cort came in and closed the door. He looked questioningly at Mr. Dawson, but she shook her head, and there was ice in her voice when she spoke.

"I'm very busy right now, Cort. Is there some special news you had to tell me?"

"I thought there was something you had to tell *me*." He looked her up and down, and she cringed.

"No, nothing at all." But she could not meet his eyes, and she colored under his steady gaze. In another minute he'd be telling her that she was a terrible actress, and even Guy Dawson would be aware that something was wrong.

Cort glanced at him again, ready to suggest that he leave them alone, but Miranda's silent plea was eloquent, and he yielded. "I just wanted you to know that I'll be in New York for a few days, Miranda. Your brother Tom and your cousin Richard came to see us in Washington yesterday, and I was going to tell you about their visit."

Miranda nodded. "So that was it. Richard would never have said anything about his proposal of marriage, but it was just the sort of thing that Tom would let slip. And here was Cort, coming to New York on the next train to see if it was true.

"When you have more time," he went on, "we'll have a long talk."

Miranda nodded again, not trusting her voice.

"And now I'll go over to the *Times* office for a while. And then I'll find Dany. Perhaps *she* is not too busy to see me."

Or too pregnant, Miranda was thinking. Or too furious with his calm arrogance. Had Cort really thought that she would want to see him again? What was it he had said once about a true and faithful woman, waiting for him? In how many cities of the world . . . She was even willing to believe that story about the marriage in England now. Damn him anyway. How could he come back into her life and make things even more difficult for her? She was conscious of Mr. Dawson's eyes on her, and she picked up the pen and looked, unseeing, at the column of figures before her.

"The bar receipts," she said, surprised that her voice was

under control. "Papa said we had a record trade last Saturday."

Cort dominated the conversation at the table that night, and Miranda withdrew immediately after supper was over, pleading a slight indisposition. "A headache," she corrected herself when Cort raised an eyebrow. But at least she had avoided an evening in his company with the family and the possibility that he would corner her in private somehow.

He was waiting for her in the office the next morning, and he closed the door behind her and locked it and pocketed the key.

"Damn it, Miranda, I have to talk to you."

"The clerk at the desk has a key," she said frostily. "All I have to do is call for him."

"You do that," Cort agreed. "By all means, call him if you get the least bit frightened. All I want to do is *talk* to you."

"Mr. Dawson will be here any minute."

"No, he won't," Cort contradicted her. "He's gone off with Dany to see about a shipment of furniture from England. She wanted to press me into that service, but I assured her that Mr. Dawson is much more knowledgeable about such things, and your father agreed with me."

She glared at him.

"Checkmate, Miranda. You *have* to talk to me."

She sighed and sat down behind the desk. At least she had a barrier between them. "What do we have to talk about? Can there possibly be one tiny bit of war news that you have been keeping back from us? After your monologue at the supper table last night, I would have thought there'd be nothing more to say."

"Dear God, Miranda, there is everything more to say." He sat down across from her, and she was conscius of his eyes on her, willing her to look at him. "Can you really hate me that much? I took the first train as soon as I heard. If you are truly pregnant—"

"And if I were, what would you do about it?" And how had he guessed? There was no way in the world he could have known, and no way she could hope to deceive him now. "So you came all the way to New York," she said, biting off the words. "What for? To marry me after you divorce Susanne? Yes, I know she's pregnant again. Dany told me." She looked at him, wondering if he ever knew remorse. "How could you, Cort? How could you deliberately set out to seduce me when you knew all along that Susanne—"

"She has nothing to do with this. Let's just leave her out of it completely."

"Oh, yes, I forgot." Her voice rose in anger. "She is your 'true and faithful'—"

"Stop it, Miranda." With obvious difficulty he was keeping himself under tight control, and his voice was deadly calm. "I am here to help you."

"What makes you think I need your help?" Deliberately she mimicked him, reflecting his cool control, but she was seething.

"Is it true you are going to marry Richard Schuyler?"

"I can't believe he told you that."

"No," Cort agreed. "Tom told us, and George is enormously pleased, and Emily just beamed. But I know you think Richard is pompous and stuffy and cold, and so the only conceivable reason you could be considering—"

"You aren't worthy to lace up his boots."

"I would never claim the privilege. Would you?" He looked at her searchingly. "Could you really marry him, Miranda?" He reached for her hand, but she pulled back, and he sighed.

"My dearest girl, you cannot possibly be sure yet that you are pregnant, and you must not panic and throw your life away by marrying the wrong man."

"Thank you very much for your advice, Mr. Adams, but now I have work to do, and surely—"

"Hear me out, Miranda. You must at least consider all the alternatives."

"Why, what an original idea, Cort! You came all the way from Washington City to tell me that? It would never have occurred to me. Just think! If I ever have a sleepless night again, I can lie awake and consider all the alternatives. That would be much less boring than counting sheep, wouldn't it?" She glared at him. "Just what do you think has been going through my head for five weeks? And just what *alternatives* did you have in mind?" She ticked them off on her fingers. "Suicide. Abortion. A long trip abroad. A secret marriage to Damon that I suddenly find it necessary to reveal. Or maybe you want to take us all to Utah where we can live in polygamous married bliss forever!" She sighed and picked up a pen.

"Go away, Cort. You can't do anything, and I have work to do."

"We aren't finished yet, Miranda, though I admit that you have made a strong case for condemning me as a complete idiot. We will rule out suicide. And the idea of moving to Utah hadn't occurred to me." She did not respond to his smile. "But let's consider the other possibilities. If you want to travel abroad, I will make arrangements, and I'll even join you there this summer and stay with you until the child is born."

"And then what? You'll rush back to Savannah and get Susanne pregnant again?"

"Now if you don't want to have the baby," Cort went on, disregarding her interruption, "I have the name of an excellent woman—"

"Yes, I am sure you do," she said acidly.

"It is quite safe, Miranda, safer than childbirth, and it could all be handled very discreetly. If at any time in the next month or two you decide . . ." He looked at her with compassion. "Oh, my dear girl, I did not ever want to bring you pain. When I think of you, and all the joy and beauty and passion—"

"Stop it, Cort." She gripped the edge of the desk and refused to look at him. "If you say one more word about that, I will scream. I promise you, I will scream."

He sighed, and the silence stretched out between them.

Miranda broke it at last. "If you have nothing more to say, then I suggest you leave."

"No, we aren't finished yet. I thought about the false marriage to Damon, too, and I am sure I could arrange some kind of documentation if you decide on that. I doubt if George and Emily would ever believe it—or your father, either—but they would never breathe a word against you. Those are some of the possibilities, Miranda, and I will help you, whatever you decide to do."

"And if I marry Richard?"

"Would you tell him, Miranda?"

"I . . . I don't know. He is so honorable and upright and—"

"Implacable."

"Perhaps." She thought about his character and wondered if he could possibly forgive her for something as monstrous as bearing another man's child. And she knew, absolutely, that she could never forgive herself if she deceived him. "I would have to tell him," she said, half to herself.

Cort nodded. "Yes," he agreed. "That is what I thought you would say." He looked at her with unmistakable longing, and then he stood up suddenly and walked away. At the door he paused for a moment before taking out the key. "I admire you enormously, my dear. Leaving you goes against all of my instincts—and against yours, too, I think, but I bow to your determination. It would be very unfair of me to take you in my arms and hold you again."

For a fleeting moment she longed for him to do just that, but she shook her head, and he sighed his compliance.

"And now I will surprise us both by being noble for a change."

Abruptly, he was gone, and she stared after him, unseeing.

I should marry Richard, she told herself. I should marry him and erase Cort from my life forever. Yes, and the baby, too. There is no way I can have his child and not have him haunting me, even in my dreams. I suppose I should have asked him for the name of that excellent woman he was talking about. But perhaps it is better that I didn't. I don't want him to know if I can help it. Not now. He might come back and see me cry.

But I'll have to confide in someone. Not Papa. Not Richard. A woman . . . She considered Kathy Flaherty. Kathy Kelly she was now. But Kathy had her information from Kevin, and how reliable would that be?

None of her giggling girl friends would know anything, and her relatives would be appalled. Aunt Sarah . . . Aunt Faith . . . She shuddered. And then she thought of Caroline's grandmother. Mrs. Cantrell might be shocked at first, but she was discreet and knowledgeable about all kinds of worldly things—surprising for a Quaker grandmother from Philadelphia—and certainly she would help.

Relieved to have made a decision, Miranda plunged into the morning mail.

And an hour later, the desk clerk brought her the next delivery. On top was a sealed envelope addressed to her in a bold hand that she recognized instantly.

Miranda dearest,

I long to take you in my arms and comfort you and protect you from all that is cruel and painful in this world, but I fear that my very presence is undermining your courage and making all your decisions more difficult.

If you need me for anything, anything at all, I will come at once, and I stand ready to help in whatever way I can. *Please* call on me.

I admire you, my darling—your honesty and your strength and your courage—and I deeply regret the pain I have caused you. But, Miranda, I can never regret the joy we have brought each other, and I will not let you shut me out of your life.

Always,
Cort

She burned the note immediately, but the words had seared themselves into her memory.

He had gone back to Washington on the noon train, Will told them at midday dinner. Dany was openly irritated that he hadn't stayed longer. She had wanted him to look at houses with her in Brooklyn Heights. And she was writing a letter to Susanne, and Cort would know how to get it delivered to Savannah. He could always get messages through the lines the fastest way and . . .

Miranda fled from her chatter and spent a dutiful afternoon at the Women's Central Association for Relief. Aunt Faith gave her a frosty smile—Miranda wondered if she had guessed about Richard's proposal—but Irene was unexpectedly cheerful. She joked about the approaching marriage of the Prince of Wales to Princess Alexandra of Denmark, and admitted freely that she had now given up all hope of being Queen of England one day. And now there was a wedding in New York that claimed all her attention. She had pored over the ladies' magazines giving every detail of the trousseau of little Lavinia Warren, who was about to marry General Tom Thumb in a ceremony that was being arranged, naturally enough, by P. T. Barnum himself.

"They are like doll clothes," Irene said, giggling, eager to share her knowledge. "Do you know she is only thirty-two inches high and she weighs just twenty-nine pounds? And her sister is even smaller!"

Miranda professed amazement. Irene could always be depended upon to talk about something absolutely frivolous.

For a blessed hour Miranda forgot to worry about anything at all, and she even agreed to accompany Irene to Barnum's Museum later in the week.

"Saturday is the last day we can see her before the wedding," Irene explained. " 'The Little Queen of Beauty,' Isn't that a wonderful title?"

Miranda laughed out loud, and Aunt Faith looked at her sharply.

"We were talking about Tom Thumb and his bride," Miranda explained, shaking out a wool shirt before folding it carefully to fit in the next box.

"I don't know what the world is coming to," Faith sighed. "Allowing that showman to take over our church for one of his exhibitions of freaks."

"It will be a proper wedding," Irene protested. "And what wonderful presents they're getting! Even President Lincoln is sending them a gift."

"That is hardly a certificate that admits them into the world of proper society, Irene. Birth and breeding—that's what counts. Just being elected President doesn't make you a gentleman. And as for midgets, or sailors from New Bedford . . ." She shook her head and wandered off to supervise the packing in the next room.

"What was all that about?" Miranda asked Irene. "Sailors from New Bedford. Are you still seeing Andy Dawson?"

Irene nodded. "I had a letter from him yesterday, and Mother has been lecturing me ever since. Now that Ann has finally gotten a proposal of marriage out of Madison Bradley, Mother is concentrating all her efforts on me. I might marry Andy just to get away from her."

"Oh, don't do anything foolish," Miranda cautioned.

"You sound exactly like Richard," Irene said. "Why don't you marry him and put him out of his misery?"

Miranda was startled. "How do you know about that?"

"Certainly not from him. Or from you, either. But everyone else is just waiting for the other shoe to drop. Even Mother knows, though she won't let herself believe it. What is taking you so long, Miranda? You know that Richard always gets exactly what he wants, and if he wants to marry you, he will. He's a bit of a stick, I know, but he can be reasonably jolly, too. And heaven knows you can count on him.

"That's the only thing I'm not sure about with Andy. He's always going to be sailing off to China or somewhere, and I don't know if I'd like that." She contemplated the future while she examined a mismatched pair of socks, and then she shrugged and rolled them together and tossed them into the box. "Still," she was arguing with herself, "he's always so exciting when he's here. What do you think? Is that kind of excitement in patches worth all the blank spaces in between?"

"I don't know," Miranda replied, honestly enough. "Why don't you ask Richard?"

"Oh, you're caught, Miranda. If you're already deferring to him, even when he isn't here, you're going to accept him next time. I just know you will."

"That's not what I meant at all," Miranda protested. "I just meant why don't you ask Richard about Andy's future. After the war he might be captain of his own ship. Maybe he could work for Schuyler Shipping—even be a partner someday. Then you could have the excitement *without* the blank spaces in between."

Irene paused to consider that possibility and then shook her head. "I can't see Andy behind a desk. But maybe he would take me to sea with him, all the way around the world. Wouldn't that be fun? You could come too, with Richard." She gave herself up to her fantasy, and Miranda joined willingly in the game, agreeing to wear a veil in Arabia and to don a grass skirt when they reached the Sandwich Islands. She tried to picture Richard in a loincloth, but imagination failed, and he remained, stiff and proper and disapproving, in his black frock coat. And when the fire on the beach burned low, and the tropical moon cut a silver path through the sea, it was Cort who came out of the shadows to claim her.

Deliberately, with conscious effort, she shattered that dream.

On Monday she would see Mrs. Cantrell, and she would confide in her then.

Chapter 19

It HAD BEEN more than a year since Miranda had started giving piano lessons to a dozen little girls and five little boys at the orphan asylum, and three of her pupils had shown so much promise that she wasn't sure how much longer they could profit from her limited knowledge and teaching ability. They needed a trained musician, she was sure, and that would cost money. She used that as an excuse to consult again with Mrs. Cantrell and suggest a private meeting.

"Of course, my dear," Mrs. Cantrell agreed. "You must come home with us for tea. Caroline's young man will be there."

"Which one?" Miranda asked, smiling, and Caroline laughed, still marveling at her own transformation.

"Jack Lorimer. Lieutenant Jack Lorimer." Just repeating his name seemed to give her pleasure. "You met him a year ago, Miranda. I saw him last week on his way home to Boston, and he is here again before he returns to Virginia. You remember him. You asked if he knew that reporter friend of yours in Washington City, Cort Adams."

Jack Lorimer was waiting for them in the front parlor when they arrived.

"The maid let me in," he explained, bowing to Mrs. Cantrell and Miranda, raising Caroline's gloved hand to his lips.

But afterward, when they were seated near the fireplace and the maid had served tea, his gaze returned repeatedly to Miranda, and he confessed his bewilderment that he hadn't remembered meeting her a year before. "I thought that bullet had passed only through my shoulder—it must have affected my brain, too." He smiled and edged closer to her on the sofa, and Miranda backed away, startled.

Caroline looked hurt. "I am s-surprised, too." It was the first time she had stuttered in months. "You have s-such a good memory, Jack. And you talked to her. Why, she even asked you about a friend from Boston, Cort Adams."

"Oh, do you know Cort?" Jack Lorimer seized the excuse to turn his full attention to Miranda. "I've been meaning to call on him in Washington City. He's married now, I think, but I haven't met his wife. Do you know her?"

"We've met," Miranda acknowledged. "But she's in Savannah."

"That's right—he married a Rebel. He always had remarkable taste in girls—remarkable success, too." He laughed with remembered delight. "I used to follow after him, picking up girls in his wake. I wonder what he's up to now."

Miranda was conspicuously silent, but she felt herself beginning to blush.

Jack Lorimer stared at her with open admiration. "Give me his address in Washington, and when I see him I'll tell him you are thinking about him."

"Oh, no! Don't bother to do that."

He looked at her hopefully, pencil stub poised to write on the back of an envelope—an envelope addressed to him in Caroline's writing.

She had to give him the address, but she wanted to divert him from Cort. "If you go there, you should greet my brother, George, and his wife, Emily, and their baby. She's my godchild," Miranda said, seizing on the first topic of conversation that came to mind—anything but Cort. "Such a dear little girl," she rambled on, talking about Polly at extensive length. It was a safe subject, she thought, and it should have been predictably boring to Jack Lorimer, but he was hanging on every word, smiling at her, watching the way her eyes lighted up when she described Polly in the bathtub, Polly reaching for a ribbon, Polly and her first taste of chocolate candy on Christmas morning.

She stopped abruptly and looked at the stricken Caroline. "I'm sorry," she said. "I shouldn't have run on like that. No one could possibly be interested."

Jack Lorimer was ready to object, but Miranda pushed aside her plate and stood up. "I really came today to talk about a problem at the orphanage."

Jack scrambled to his feet, protesting, but Mrs. Cantrell came to Miranda's rescue. And Caroline's. "We'll go up to my room, dear, for a nice quiet chat." She led the way to the stairs, and Miranda had a last glimpse of Jack Lorimer, reluctantly resuming his place at the tea table with Caroline.

"I'll just light the fire," Mrs. Cantrell said, reaching for the matches on the mantelpiece.

"Oh, I'll do that," Miranda insisted. She knelt by the hearth and built up the blaze and then looked around the cozy sitting room that had once been so dark and cheerless. There was no longer any trace of Aunt Josephine and her long years of gloomy suffering.

"I like it here," she said to Mrs. Cantrell. "And I like being able to come here to talk to you. But I am truly sorry about what happened downstairs just now. I had no idea he would be anything but bored by a lot of chatter about a baby he's never heard of and will probably never see."

"Oh, my dear, he's going to visit her the first chance he gets. He's no fool, and he can see she is an open door into your heart."

"Caroline—"

"Yes, dear Caroline. But Lieutenant Lorimer is not the only fish in the sea, and just because he is the first young man who ever paid attention to her, that doesn't mean she is bound to him. She should look at some of the others, too. She has led such a sheltered life, and she really needs a little more experience in the world. I would want to spare her a real heartbreak, but I don't think she is committed to Jack Lorimer forever."

"I hope you are right," Miranda sighed, but Mrs. Cantrell was determinedly cheerful.

"Now then, you must tell me about the piano lessons. I know the superintendent won't spend the money, but perhaps we can arrange a few special donations—we'll call them scholarships."

Miranda was willing to call them anything she liked, and she sat back, relieved that this small burden was being lifted from her shoulders. Sighing, she stared into the fire and tried to think of the right way to broach the subject that was really on her mind.

"Is it about Richard?" Mrs. Cantrell asked her finally. "Don't you want to marry him?"

"No, that's not it. Not exactly. That is . . ." Miranda looked at her, suddenly beseeching. "Oh, you must promise me you will never say a word. Not to Papa or Richard or anyone."

"I promise you faithfully."

"I don't know how to tell you. I don't know if I *should* tell you."

"My dear Miranda. You obviously must tell someone, whatever it is, and I am flattered, even moved, that you have chosen me."

"Well, then." She swallowed hard and felt Mrs. Cantrell's eyes on her, but she could not look up. She took a deep breath and made her confession in one desperate rush. "I think I am going to have a baby."

"Oh, my dear, that's not so terrible."

Miranda looked at her, astonished.

"So your first child is a few months 'premature.'" She smiled. "It's amazing how frequently that happens. I'm sure that if you told Richard he would—"

"It's not his child."

This time it was Mrs. Cantrell's turn to look astonished. "Oh, I see." But there was compassion in her voice, not outrage, and she reached for Miranda's hand. "And the child's father . . ."

"No. I can't marry him."

"Are you sure, Miranda? Often when a man knows that—"

"I am sure," she said. "He cannot possibly marry me."

"Oh, my dear child. Damon—the young man who was killed!"

"I don't want to talk about it."

"But Richard loves you, Miranda. If you took him into your confidence—"

"No. I couldn't do that. He would never understand. I can hardly understand myself. We could not go through life together that way."

Mrs. Cantrell sighed. "You may be right."

Miranda looked at her, hesitant about taking the next step, relieved when she didn't have to say the words.

"And you came to me, my dear, to help you find a way out of . . . of your difficulty."

Miranda nodded and blinked back sudden tears. Oh, Cort, I knew we would pay for our sins, but I didn't ever think it would be this hard.

"And you have thought about going away on a long trip . . . Yes, I can see you have. So, you have made a decision now, and I respect that. Now then, I will make some discreet inquiries and we will talk again. I don't know how much money . . ."

"I can pay whatever it costs. I . . . I have heard that it can be safe, safer than childbirth. And afterward . . . I will still be able to have children?"

"We will find you a safe way out," Mrs. Cantrell promised. "And no one need ever know."

"Thank you." The words seemed so inadequate, and when Mrs. Cantrell patted her shoulder, Miranda gave way to tears.

"You poor motherless child." She embraced her. "How cruelly the world has treated you. But this will pass, my dear. You will marry a fine man who loves you, as you love him—"

"But I don't." Miranda choked over the words.

"Well, then . . ." For a moment she was at a loss. "Sometimes love comes after marriage, if two young people are as well matched as you and Richard. The memory of Damon will fade."

"But it's not—" She stopped abruptly, aware that she was on the verge of betrayal—betrayal not just of Cort but of some basic part of herself. "It's not just Damon," she said, improvising, drying her eyes and trying to pull herself together. "It's the child, too."

"You will have other children, Miranda, children you can care for properly and bring up proudly, without shame or guilt." Mrs. Cantrell smiled at her. "Why, when you were telling us about Polly just now, you were glowing with pride and love. No wonder young Lieutenant Lorimer found you so bewitching."

Miranda looked at her doubtfully. "I didn't mean to have that effect."

Mrs. Cantrell laughed. "Of course not. That's why it worked. You always care so much, Miranda, and it all shows on your face, your very lovely face. Now, you will live through this bad time, however hard it is, and afterward, with God's help, you will make a good life for yourself and your husband and your family."

"I will try," Miranda said, but there wasn't much confidence in her voice.

"You will succeed," Mrs. Cantrell told her decisively. "And now I think we should go back downstairs and see how Caroline is getting along."

Over Miranda's protests, Jack Lorimer insisted on seeing her home.

"You should have stayed with Caroline," she accused him when he settled down beside her in a hackney carriage.

"I wanted to come with you," he said frankly. "Caroline is shy and sweet, but *you* are enchanting, and I want to know you better."

"I am practically engaged to be married," she told him.

"That's what Caroline said. But he's your cousin, and it's obviously been going on for years, so I don't think you're very enthusiastic about the match."

"You don't know me, and you don't know him, and I think you are too quick in making judgments."

"I have to be quick," he justified himself. "I am going back to Virginia tomorrow. My furlough is over and I'll be rejoining my regiment."

"It seems a strange time of year to be getting a furlough." She was relieved to be able to change the subject and not talk about herself.

"The army is in winter quarters—why not? And besides," his voice was suddenly grim, "I spent Christmas in the hospital, so I thought I deserved a little time off."

"Oh, I see. That makes a difference, of course." In the flare of the intermittent street lights, she was conscious of his eyes on her, admiring, hopeful. The Broadway traffic had thinned out, but they were still a few blocks from the Stratford. "Were you wounded?" she asked, mostly to break the silence.

"Concussion." He shrugged it off. "Nothing serious. They kept me on to nurse the others. The hospital was almost worse than Fredericksburg itself."

She sighed. "Yes, I believe you. My brother Jimmy, and a very good friend . . ."

"Wounded?" He was all sympathy.

"Yes. At Fredericksburg, too. They died a few days later."

"Tragic, all of it. And to lose a brother . . ." Was it just to comfort her that he took her hand? She wasn't quite sure how to get it back without seeming rude or precipitating a struggle.

"General Burnside," she said, pulling back a little to open up some space between them.

"General Burnside?" he sounded bewildered.

"Yes, Jimmy blamed it all on him. Did you think it was all his fault? Jimmy idolized General McClellan, but Cort said . . ." She trailed off. "I'm glad Lincoln has dismissed Burnside now, aren't you? What do you think of General Hooker?"

"I can't say that I've thought much about him at all," Jack said in all honesty. Clearly he wasn't interested in discussing army generals, not here, not now. "Miranda, you are by far the most beautiful—"

"Why, here we are at the Stratford!" She alighted from the carriage in a single bound, without waiting for help. "Thank you, Lieutenant Lorimer. Good night." She fled through the wide doors before he had finished paying the fare, but he followed her just the same and caught up with her in the lobby.

"Won't you even talk to me, Miranda? This is the last night of my furlough, and what harm would it do to spend an hour with me before I go back to the war again. Could you really send me off to battle, to fight and perhaps to die, without one kind word of farewell?"

She had the distinct impression that he had used those lines before, at other times, with other girls, and she sighed. "Lieutenant Lorimer—"

"Call me Jack," he insisted.

She refrained from calling him anything at all. "Thank you for seeing me home. Now, I am very tired and—"

"You don't look the least bit tired," he contradicted her. "You look as if you could go on for hours and hours, talking about your little godchild or General Burnside or those orphans or anything at all, and I would be absolutely fascinated from beginning to end." There was an echo of Cort in his voice that challenged her and put her on guard. She wavered for a moment and then shook her head. No, it would just add one more complication to her life if she allowed herself to pay any attention at all to Lieutenant Jack Lorimer.

"I really must say good night." But she had hesitated too long. Dany and John were crossing the lobby and they had seen her and there was no escape. Reluctantly she made the introductions, and Jack immediately commented on Dany's Southern accent and proceeded to trace the connection from Savannah to Susanne to Cort, so of course Dany insisted that they all have a late supper together, and Jack grinned at Miranda in triumph. She sighed and resolved to break away early.

Dany lingered at the breakfast table the next morning, talking about him. "If you weren't going to marry Richard, Miranda, you could certainly have Jack. He's charming. And he told us the funniest stories about Cort after you left. Did you know they were in school together, and there was this girl . . ." She rambled through a long complicated anecdote about a baker's daughter and some molasses cookies and cherry tarts, but it seemed rather pointless to Miranda, and she wondered if Jack had decided to censor the story halfway through. Whatever it was, she suspected the worst. Clearly, Jack Lorimer was trouble, and it was a good thing he had left New York and she wouldn't have to see him again. If she decided to marry Richard—and there seemed to be an increasing expectation that she would—then she would no longer have to bother with the Jack Lorimers of this world.

Mrs. Cantrell was as good as her word, and when she came to the Stratford the following Sunday, she had a supply of pills and, in case the pills should fail, the name and address of a woman doctor who had been trained in Paris and Vienna. At least the woman *said* she was a doctor, and she certainly had a foreign accent, and she claimed a medical education at the best schools and a long list of satisfied clients.

Miranda looked dubiously at the small bottle and read the label; Portuguese Female Pills, a Great and Sure Remedy for Married Ladies, Guaranteed to Bring Immediate Relief. She had seen the ads for such medicines in the daily papers, mixed in with the cures for baldness and cancer and loss of male vigor, but she had never really thought about the truth of the claims. A certain practical skepticism could not be submerged, but she desperately wanted to believe.

"Is it really safe?"

"My dear, I think it's safe, but I do not honestly know if it's effective in every case. The druggist assured me that his wife had used it and all was well, though she took to her bed for twenty-four hours."

"I see." Miranda tucked the small bottle into her reticule.

"I . . . I'll have to think about it." She wondered who might know about such things, and she shrank from asking Cort.

Mrs. Cantrell looked at her sympathetically. "It is all very difficult, I know. But everyone assures me that the one thing a woman must do is to make her decision early. The longer she waits for . . . relief, the harder it is."

"Yes." Miranda swallowed painfully. "I am sure that you are right."

"Now what I thought," Mrs. Cantrell went on briskly, "is that you should plan to stay overnight with us tomorrow. After our afternoon at the orphanage, you can come home with us—no, of course Caroline doesn't know—and you can take the pills then. I will be there to help if there are any problems, and no one else need ever be the wiser."

Miranda bowed to this practical advice, and she had no difficulty securing her father's consent for an overnight visit.

Monday night Caroline was still nursing bruised feelings because of Jack Lorimer's defection—Miranda had almost forgotten about him in light of more pressing problems—but Mrs. Cantrell bridged the recurring gaps in the conversation, rambling on and on about the difficulties in raising funds for the orphanage. And when that roused little interest, she talked endlessly about the war relief fund and the increasing competition between the Sanitary Commission and the various Christian charity organizations.

Caroline responded in monosyllables, and Miranda found it impossible to concentrate on anything but the small bottle in her reticule, and Mrs. Cantrell finally gave up any pretense that this was a normal social evening.

"I think we are all a little tired," she said, and both girls nodded their agreement, ready to escape to their own private miseries.

Miranda had been given Marty's bedroom, the one directly over Mrs. Cantrell's, and she was not altogether happy about that. Marty had been in the army for almost two years now, but something of his sullen anger still lingered.

"If you need me in the night," Mrs. Cantrell watched Miranda swallow the recommended dose, "just thump on the floor with this cane. I'm a light sleeper, and I'll be awake in an instant."

Miranda nodded, fighting back the sudden terror that had seized her. Oh, Cort, where are you tonight when I need you so desperately. Having a baby can't be any harder than this. I should have said I'd meet you in Europe. We could have had that time together, a month, two months, and then . . . and then . . . He would go away again. Back to Susanne. She blinked back her tears and managed a feeble smile for Mrs. Cantrell.

It was a long and restless night, and when she finally fell into a troubled sleep, she was tortured with dreams. Jimmy was dying again, and she couldn't find him anywhere. Her feet were like lead, and there was a fire, fire all around her. Cordelia had come to rescue her, and she hung back, looking for a lost doll. But it wasn't a doll; it was Polly, trying to grasp the ribbon in her hair and crying, her face turning red, red as blood. She woke up sobbing, and Mrs. Cantrell was there, reaching out to touch her.

"Wake up, child. I think you've been having a nightmare." Her voice was soothing, gentle. "I'm here now, Miranda, and you are all right." Caroline was standing in the doorway by then, hesitant, sleepy-eyed.

"I'm all right," Miranda echoed shakily, trying to believe it, wanting Caroline to go away and let her suffer in peace. "I'm all right," she tried again, but she was seized by sudden cramps, worse than anything she had ever known, and she broke out in a cold sweat and a wave of nausea swept over her. She sat up quickly, trying to choke back— But her stomach had already rebelled.

She felt better after she had vomited, a little weak and shaky, but better.

Mrs. Cantrell opened the windows wide to air out the room, and Caroline brought her a bottle of scent.

Miranda smiled feebly in thanks. "I must have . . . must have eaten something that disagreed with me," she said.

"I think it was the fish," Mrs. Cantrell declared briskly. "Mine had a slight off taste, so I had only a few bites. I'll tell cook to throw out the rest of it first thing in the morning."

"That must be it," Caroline agreed. "It's lucky I didn't have any. I hate fish. This just goes to show I'm right."

Miranda sighed and slid back under the covers. Grandmother and granddaughter conferred briefly, and after Caroline withdrew, Miranda drifted into quiet sleep. When she wakened again, Mrs. Cantrell was still sitting beside her, watching over her, hastening to apologize.

Miranda tried to reassure her. "I'll be all right. Truly. And after all, the druggist *did* say his wife had to stay in bed for twenty-four hours."

Mrs. Cantrell looked at her doubtfully. "I sent word to your father, and I told him it was just a slight case of food poisoning."

Miranda nodded and closed her eyes to conceal her tears. She had done nothing but deceive Papa ever since . . . And he trusted her and loved her so much. Oh, if she ever got out of this horrible situation, she would try so hard to be good. But while she was being punished, justly punished, why did Cort escape so completely? Nothing ever happened to him. He sailed through his life, getting his way in everything. Everything.

Strange—Irene had said that about Richard, too. He always got exactly what he wanted. That's why, if he decided to marry her, he would. Mrs. Richard Beekman Schuyler. Miranda Chase Schuyler. Well, why not? Everyone seemed to expect it, and she was too tired to fight against the tide that seemed to be sweeping them together. Richard would protect her from all this grief and misery, and he would give her a safe refuge. Perhaps she didn't deserve real happiness any more—oh, those lost days in Washington . . . Now she would learn to be grateful for simple peace.

A week went by, and whether it was the advertised effectiveness of the Portuguese Female Pills or a happy coincidence arranged by a forgiving Providence, Miranda could never be sure—but she gave thanks for her escape. She told Mrs. Cantrell to throw away the name and address of that woman who claimed a medical education in the best schools of Paris and Vienna—what a relief to avoid that misery!

And she willingly resumed her work at the hotel, a little pale and considerably subdued, but able to concentrate at last on the tasks before her.

And she had made up her mind to marry Richard.

Chapter 20

IT WAS ONLY a few days later, a Wednesday in early March, when the morning mail brought her four letters from Washington, all variations on the same theme, all written on Sunday.

Dutifully, she opened Richard's first.

Dear Miranda,

Tom and I spent this afternoon with George and his family, and they are all well and happy and send you their love.

We had barely risen from the dinner table when a certain Lieutenant Lorimer came to call, a brash and flippant young man, just the sort of person I would expect Cort Adams to number among his friends—although to give credit where it is due, Adams did not seem to be altogether happy to renew old acquaintance. What surprised and disturbed me, however, was that this Lorimer had recently met you and found you, in his words, "enchanting and bewitching."

Now I know, Miranda, that you would do nothing to lead him on, and I certainly understand why he finds you attractive, but I think you must be more cautious, my dear, and not allow a man like that to escort you home. And it is not like you to walk away with poor Caroline's first beau—though of course in the long run he would never be suitable for her at all.

This whole episode has convinced me, however, that we must not delay the announcement of our engagement any longer. I am coming to New York just as soon as I can—on Saturday, if I can arrange it—and I hope and

pray that you will give me the answer I am longing to
hear.

With all my love,
Your devoted Richard

The letter from Jack Lorimer was longer.

Dear Enchanting Miranda,

I think I have now met your entire family, and I must
agree with you that little Polly is the most beautiful and
delightful child it has ever been my pleasure to know.
Without a doubt she takes after you. But *she* climbed up
in my lap and put her arms around me, and I think Cort
was positively jealous. I didn't realize that Polly is *his*
godchild, too. She obviously helps to fill the void in his
life—I am sure that he feels keenly the absence of his
wife and child in Savannah. And I was amazed to hear
that he is going to be a father again, in the spring sometime. It takes more than a war to stop our Cort.

Your brothers George and Tom inquired most eagerly
about you, and Mrs. Chase—Emily—told me what a
heroine you had been in the hospital when your dear
brother Jimmy died. They all admire and love you so
much—a feeling I understand perfectly.

But oh, Miranda, I met your cousin Richard, too. He
is, perhaps, a very honorable and capable army officer,
but he is so rigid and cold and humorless. I know it is not
my place to advise you, but I cannot refrain. You must
not marry him, Miranda. You have never committed
yourself in all the years that he has been pursuing you,
and you must not make any sudden decisions now. If you
do not truly love him—and why else have you always refused?—then you must wait until the right man comes
along. I do not flatter myself that you could possibly consider me at this early stage in our friendship, but I long
to know you better, much better, and that will take time.

Please remember me to your father and to John and
Dany. Yes, and to Caroline and Mrs. Cantrell, too. I
hope to see all of you soon again, and you, Miranda,
most of all.

Write to me, please, please. I don't know where General Hooker is going to lead us, but someday this cruel

war will surely be over, and I am praying fervently that
we meet again.

Yours most sincerely,
Jack

Emily included a meaningless scrawl from Polly, together
with her own neatly penned letter.

Miranda dear,
I wish you had been here today to help me entertain
our quartet of handsome army officers, plus one equally
handsome newspaper correspondent. Polly assisted no-
bly—she is the most engaging flirt—but I longed to have
you here, enjoying all this barely submerged male ri-
valry. I have never thought that Richard and Cort got
along together very well, but they both have such excellent manners that we had a very pleasant dinner.

You know what a treasure Hattie is, and she positively excelled herself with a roast sirloin of beef and an
oyster sauce. And I had made the dessert myself, a
simple lemon cream, which turned out rather well. Cort
was most complimentary. George always likes to have
me prepare at least one dish every day, and it is true
that the only way you can properly supervise the work
of others is to know how to do it yourself. He says that
is what his father taught him, and dear George learned
his lesson faithfully. How lucky I am to have him with
me always . . .

But I was going to tell you about what happened
when your friend Lieutenant Lorimer arrived so unexpectedly. He and Cort had been in school together, as
you undoubtedly know, but they hadn't seen each other
in years, and I am not sure how eager Cort was to welcome him back into his life. But Lieutenant Lorimer—or
Jack as he insisted we call him (I deplore this hasty in-
formality and he realized that and respectfully addressed
me as Mrs. Chase)—Jack immediately turned his attention to Polly. He brought her three hair ribbons, of all
things, and you know what an affectionate little creature
she is. She crawled across the sofa right into his lap, and
Cort was distinctly jealous. He truly was. Well, that was
very entertaining and quite amusing, but when Jack Lorimer told us that he had fully expected Polly to be a

wonder child because he had met her godmother and *she* was so enchanting and bewitching, Richard withdrew into his shell; and if cold looks could kill, Lieutenant Lorimer would have frozen into an icicle on the spot. By then Polly had tired of her new friend and crawled back to Cort, but *he* remained almost as frosty as Richard, and it was up to Tom and George and me to salvage the rest of the afternoon.

We were actually relieved when Richard dragged Tom away before tea, and Lieutenant Lorimer left almost immediately afterward. I think he had determined to outwait Richard, no matter how long it took.

George says that Richard is planning a trip to New York at the first available opportunity—perhaps at the end of the week. He is so devoted to you, Miranda, and we admire him so much. I could never advise you in matters of the heart, my dear sister, but if you *should* decide to accept him, George and I would be enormously pleased. It is our dearest wish that you share a happiness like ours.

> Much love,
> Emily

She picked up Cort's letter last, not sure if she wanted to read it at all. The envelope was heavier than the others, and when she opened it, she discovered the reason: it contained three hundred dollars in greenbacks. Miranda was appalled.

My dearest girl,

I have been frantic with worry about you, and you *must* write and tell me what you have decided. If I don't hear from you by the end of the week, I will take the train to New York, beating out Richard Schuyler in a race to see you again. Don't be upset by the money, darling, but it occurred to me that I had made you fine promises to help but hadn't done anything practical at all. So—for travel arrangements or a consultation with a discreet doctor or even a train ticket to Utah (no, that's too far away), use freely what you need and call on me for more. I insist that you let me help you, Miranda, and you know you cannot deny me that.

Emily told me that she is writing to you about our afternoon visitors, and a mismatched trio they were. Your

249

brother Tom is a decent chap, of course, with a practical turn of mind that I find quite engaging. I hadn't realized that it was he who persuaded your father to renovate the Stratford and enlarge the bar and increase the number of bathrooms. Now he is sorry he didn't insist on an elevator, too, but that is surely an afterthought, a reaction to so much marching now that, by the time the war is over, he won't even want to climb stairs again.

I had very mixed feelings about seeing Jack Lorimer after all these years. We knew each other well as boys and got in and out of the usual scrapes together, but I find him shallow and superficial now, and certainly not worthy of you, darling. Even Polly saw through him after the briefest of flirtations and came back to me where she belongs. I could tell that you had given him short shrift, but the suspicious Captain Schuyler succumbed to jealousy and cold fury.

I find that man alarming, Miranda, and you surely cannot be thinking seriously of marrying him—you who are so warm and loving and giving. It would be a disaster, my dearest. I know I will never be able to bear the thought of you with *any* other man, no matter how worthy. But when I warn you about Richard Schuyler, I am thinking of you and *your* happiness. For me there could be no crueler retribution for the precious time we had together than the thought that I had driven you into a loveless marriage with that man. Better Jack Lorimer or any of a hundred others. But you must not commit yourself to your implacable cousin. Take time to think, my dearest, and you will know I am right.

I do not know what the future holds for us or how long this cruel war will disrupt all our lives, but I am convinced that there *must* be a way for us to be together again—if only you don't do something so irrevocable as marrying that man.

> With love, always,
> Cort

She refolded the letter, considerably shaken, and then immediately spread it out and read it all the way through again. It was the first time he had mentioned love, even in something as perfunctory as the closing line of a letter, and she wondered how carefully he had chosen the phrase: With love, always. If he had just dashed it off, it was meaningless, and she should ignore it. But if he had weighed every word, knowing how she would read his message, conscious that he had never made her any promises or commitments, then, then . . . It was still meaningless. He was still married to Susanne, and there wasn't the least suggestion he would change that. "A way for us to be together again." That wasn't marriage at all. That was nothing but a few stolen hours and a lasting sense of guilt, and surely she didn't need to learn that lesson twice. If Cort thought that accepting Richard was an irrevocable decision, forever separating them, that was the best argument in the world for the marriage.

She burned the letter, but she was too practical to destroy the money, too. She tucked it into her reticule, suddenly smiling to herself. And she dashed off a note to prevent him from coming to New York.

Dear Cort,

You will be relieved to know, as I was, that all reason for anxiety has disappeared. Please don't come to New York at present; it will just make things more difficult for me. I promise to think carefully about all your advice, and you should not worry.

I considered returning all those greenbacks to you but thought better of it. Mrs. Cantrell is setting up a special fund to cover the cost of piano lessons for colored orphans, and I think that is a more worthy use of the money than anything else you could do with it.

Miranda

Richard arrived Saturday evening. He had made a dutiful call at home first, to greet his parents and to make himself presentable again after the day-long journey. Standing ramrod straight in his meticulously tailored uniform, he paused at the entrance to the family parlor of the Stratford, drawn there by the sound of music. John and Dany looked up from their backgammon game and smiled, and Will sighed and put down his newspaper, but Miranda, unaware, facing away from him, continued to work her way through a Chopin mazurka. She was having trouble with the fingering, and she broke off to repeat one passage and was conscious suddenly of his presence. There was a pause, measurable in heartbeats, and then, as she had resolved, she ran to greet him with a kiss.

Within five minutes Dany and John and Will had all remembered urgent business elsewhere, and Richard closed the door after them, smiling at her.

"Miranda, I was hoping for this moment. I have brought you a ring, and it is my dearest wish that you will accept it—and accept me." He took her hand, but she pulled away, and he followed her, surprised at this evidence of capriciousness.

"Sit down, Richard, and let's talk about what we mean when we say engagement and marriage and all the rest of it."

"I would have thought that was quite clear. I love you, Miranda, and when you welcomed me just now, I allowed myself to believe that you . . ." He trailed off, seeming almost vulnerable, and Miranda had a moment of hope. Of *course* he had real feelings under that controlled surface. He loved her. He said he had loved her for years. How often did she need reassurance from this man who so prided himself on his honor?

"Richard, I have been thinking most earnestly about your proposal."

He looked at her hopefully, but she was glad he made no move to touch her. He had seated himself on the ottoman at her feet, and she could see the tension coiled within him.

"I admire you very much, and the fact that you have asked me to be your wife is a great honor. And if I were to marry you—"

"Miranda, my own dear love!" He grasped her hands, sure now of her answer.

"*If* I were to marry you, Richard. I haven't said yes."

"But you will. I know you will. You would never have let me come this close to happiness, only to deny me at the last moment. You could never be that cruel." He smiled at her—confident, expectant, triumphant—and she wondered how much he was really understanding her.

"Please, Richard, I am trying to be honest with you. I want you to know that I have doubts—"

"Oh, my darling, of course you do." He pulled her to her feet and embraced her. "I love you for your doubts, and your sweet innocence and reluctance, and all those dear feminine qualities that made you so desirable. You are trying to tell me that you aren't sure about this marriage, but trust me, darling, because *I* am sure. I think the best marriages begin like this, when a man has strength and confidence, and he longs to support his wife in her dependence and faith in him." His kiss was gentle, and she sighed, and he smiled at her. "Trust me," he repeated, and kissed her again. This time she willed herself to cling to him, and his rigid control slipped and his mouth on hers was hard and demanding. She broke away, surprised and breathing a little faster, but on the whole relieved—relieved to glimpse the latent passion he usually concealed so carefully.

He apologized immediately, profusely, for alarming her, but he pressed to set an early date for the wedding.

"Not so fast, darling." She sat down again, and reluctantly he resumed his place on the ottoman.

"You called me darling." He smiled with satisfaction and seized her hand and kissed it. "We could have the banns posted tomorrow, Miranda, and be married the first week in April. Ordinarily perhaps such a short engagement would be frowned on, but I have waited for you so long, and in this time of war . . ."

He was right, of course. If he were to go off to fight in the spring campaign, never to return, it would be like Damon and Jimmy all over again. But she had to make him understand her and something of the life she wanted.

"I would stay at the Stratford, Richard, helping Papa."

"Oh, Miranda, once we are married you would give up this foolishness about working." He dismissed her protest. "Now, of course, it would not be practical for us to buy a house immediately, since I won't be here to live in it with you—much as I would like to." He touched her cheek. "You would be lonesome, darling, and I would worry about your safety. I know it would be uncomfortable for you to move in with my parents," he was obviously trying to be considerate, "but I have thought of something else. When John and Dany move to Brooklyn Heights next month, I am sure they would be happy to have you live with them. You and Dany would be good companions, and I would know that John is looking after you. And of course when you come to Washington City—"

"No!" Her response was immediate and emphatic. She could never be with Richard under the same roof with Cort. It was unthinkable.

"Don't make hasty decisions, Miranda. Just because Washington has so many memories for you . . ."

253

She looked at him, astonished, but he was determined to be understanding.

"When Jimmy and Damon died there, it was a terrible shock to us all, but life goes on, my darling. You cannot forever let that sadness dominate your life, both our lives. Why Miranda, you are still looking pale, and Mother told me that you had been sick for almost a week. I could hardly believe it. You, always in such radiant good health, still allowing yourself to be prostrated by grief—"

"It was food poisoning," Miranda said flatly. But at least he had been diverted from talk about Washington. "Now, Richard, I haven't said yet that I would marry you, and I certainly will never agree if you are going to order me around like this. Papa needs me at the Stratford, and I am happy here, and I am going to stay. I am going to work in the office and learn just as much as I can. And I will continue to visit the orphan asylum every week and I will go right on working at the Sanitary Commission, and if that means you won't marry me, so be it."

She had shocked him, and for a moment he was speechless. But he controlled his anger and found an explanation for her behavior. "You are testing me, darling, trying to provoke me into some kind of lovers' quarrel, but that won't work. Of course we are going to be married. That's settled." He looked at the stubborn set of her jaw and made a tactical retreat. "If you are happy at the Stratford, I will allow you to stay here. And if your father really thinks that your work is useful," Richard obviously thought he could convince him otherwise, "then you can help in the office, too. But, my darling, you must understand that all this is temporary, only until the war is over."

She nodded doubtfully, surprised at his easy capitulation.

"That will give me an incentive to work for an early victory." He smiled at her.

She laughed, and he leaned forward to kiss her again, a formal kiss to seal a bargain.

"And now give me your hand, darling, and close your eyes." She complied with his wishes, and he placed the ring on her finger.

"It's beautiful, Richard." In the bright flare of the gaslight, the diamond sparkled, then shimmered and dissolved as her eyes filled with tears. They were going to be married. It was definite. She had freely given her pledge, and the diamond was lasting proof that she was his now forever.

Will expressed his misgivings later, after Richard had gone and John and Dany had bid them good night, their smiles reflecting their pleasure.

"Are you really sure, Pet? I know he loves you, and he wants to give you the world. He spent ten minutes just now outlining his financial prospects, and he really is extraordinarily ambitious. But I can't shake off the feeling that he is all wrong for you, and I don't want you rushing into something you'll regret for the rest of your life."

"I'm going to marry him, Papa. You asked me to wait for a month to make a decision, and I waited two. And Richard has loved me for years. That's not rushing at all."

"But if you have doubts, Miranda . . ."

"It is natural for me to have doubts—Richard said so, and I believe him. But *he* is sure, and when I think about it logically, I know it will be all right."

"Logically?" Will shook his head in wonder.

"He is so strong in his convictions and honorable and devoted, and he wants to give me a good life."

Will remained unconvinced.

"I don't know why you are making it hard for me, Papa. All the rest of the family have been urging me to marry him—John and Dany, George and Emily, Tom, even Irene. Only Aunt Faith is against us." She smiled at him. "You don't want to be all alone on the same side with her, do you?"

He sighed heavily and came over to sit beside her on the sofa. "If it is really what you want, Miranda, I will not stand in your way."

"Thank you, Papa." She kissed his cheek and he put his arm around her. She turned with relief to the simpler, practical matters. "Richard says we can have the banns posted tomorrow, and we'll get married next month. As soon as we can, he says. We thought we'd ask George and Emily . . ."

It was going to be a formal wedding, with a reception at the Stratford, and assembling her trousseau and working out the endless details kept her so occupied that she hardly had time to think about what it all meant.

She half expected Cort to arrive on the first train as soon as he heard, but she had a letter from him instead, mailed from Cincinnati. He was on his way to see the fighting in the west, he said, and he hoped to meet General Grant and perhaps get down to Mississippi to find out why Vicksburg hadn't fallen yet. He had received her reassuring note, and he made a wry reference to paying for piano lessons for orphans, but he was enormously relieved that she was all right. "And now there is certainly no reason for you to rush into marriage, darling. When I come back we will work out some way to be together again. You are always in my thoughts, and in my heart. Love, Cort."

Obviously he had left Washington before the news of her engagement could reach him, and perhaps that was just as well. If he would just stay away until after she was safely married, she would escape him completely.

On the night before the wedding, Will asked her once more if she was sure, and she burst into tears.

"We will call it off, Miranda. It is not too late, and I don't care what people say. If you are this upset—"

"No, Papa. You don't understand. I said I would marry him, and I will." The tears had surprised her—she had thought she was perfectly calm. "I've been rushing around so much this last month, and I'm just a little tired; that's all." She hoped she sounded convincing. After all, she had convinced herself.

Richard loved her, and he had offered her honorable marriage, a second chance after she had nearly ruined her life. She was grateful to him, she admired him, she would try to make him happy—and perhaps she would even learn to love him one day. And he was risking his life in this desperate war, like Jimmy, like Damon . . .

She blinked back her tears and gave her father a tremulous smile.

He patted her shoulder and looked at her doubtfully. "I wish your mother were here, Pet. She could have guided you where I . . . I will send in Sarah. I'm so glad she arrived early, and you need a woman's counsel now."

Miranda knew it was useless to protest, and she sat through a cloudy lecture on the submissiveness of women, with particular reference to the duties of wives, and it was all so full of euphemisms and mysterious warnings that it would have certainly shattered her had she been quite as naive as Aunt Sarah seemed to think.

"And a woman must bear these things," Sarah concluded, "even from a fine young man like Richard. Your reward will come from the children he will give you." She smiled and patted her encouragingly. "And that is the way of the world, my dear, and you will find life easier now that you are learning to accept it without rebellion." The monologue ended, Sarah kissed her good night and suggested she go to bed early to be well rested for tomorrow.

"Aunt Sarah, may I ask you something?"

"Of course, my dear."

"Well, then." Miranda looked at her curiously. "Are you happy? I mean, have you had a happy life?"

Sarah was surprised. "I think so, dear." She paused, as if considering her own emotions and feelings for the first time in years. "I have tried to do my duty, and there is satisfaction in that. Keeping busy—that's the secret. You'll find out that when you have two or three little ones climbing all over you and demanding attention, you won't have much time to think about yourself. And you certainly won't be fussing about abolition or women's suffrage or any of the rest of that nonsense."

"I see." Miranda looked troubled.

"Now don't worry about a thing," Sarah said briskly. "You will be a beautiful bride tomorrow. And within a year, if all goes well, you will be a beautiful mother, too. I will pray for you, dear, and for Richard. How long do you have together before he rejoins his regiment?"

"One week," Miranda said.

"One week," Sarah repeated. "Seven days. That's plenty of time."

Miranda did not bother to inquire for what.

Chapter 21

MIRANDA SPUN THROUGH her wedding day on a rising fever of forced gaiety, color high, voice breathless, poised on a tightrope between laughter and tears. And she was never more beautiful, more dazzling. Richard could not let her out of his sight. At the supper and reception, after the first dance, he dutifully relinquished her to her father, and then to his own father and to all three of her brothers, but that was enough. She was his, this blushing, radiant girl, a prize he had won, all his, to love and cherish and possess, this very day, this very night, now and forever.

Afterward neither of them had any memory of the wedding supper, what they had eaten, whether they had eaten at all, any of that grand collation the chefs had labored over for days. They had cut the wedding cake with Richard's sword—Miranda remembered that because she was so conscious of his arms around her, guiding her, the unexpectedly heavy pressure of his hands on hers, her new rings biting into her flesh, leaving angry red marks.

Later, when they were alone in the bridal suite of the Fifth Avenue Hotel and he had locked the door and turned to take her in his arms, all her feverish gaiety fled, and there was nothing left but a tense kind of fear. She knew he expected her to be nervous, but he also expected her to be inexperienced, and she was suddenly terrified that her body would betray her or that some unexpected, unexplainable guilty knowledge would make him doubt her.

Paradoxically, it was this very fear that preserved her innocence in his eyes—and turned the next hour into an agonizing trial for her. She was so tense that eventually he gave up all attempts to make her relax, and he simply forced her to submit, aware of her pain but convinced that he knew best and that he was completely justified in consummating the marriage, with or without her cooperation. He was her husband and he had his rights, and she was his wife and she must learn what that meant.

He consoled her afterward while she smoothed out her tangled nightgown and refused to look at him. "It will be all right, darling. You'll see. The next time will be easier, and the time after that." He smiled, assuring he was not displeased. "I am patient, Miranda, and you must be, too. We have all our lives ahead of us. I don't expect you to experience the same kind of . . . pleasure that is reserved to a man, and perhaps a few depraved women. You are too pure and innocent for that. But it will be easier for you in the future, darling, and when you make me happy, you will be happy, too. And you will know *your* joy when the children are born."

He fell asleep almost immediately, his arm heavy across her body, but she lay awake for hours, and his words echoed and reechoed: the next time, and the time after that. All our lives.

He was already gone when she woke up next morning, and she hurried to dress before he returned. He arrived simultaneously with the breakfast cart, and as soon as the waiters departed, he kissed her and pinned a new coral brooch to her dark green traveling costume, murmuring something about forgiveness. Miranda wasn't sure if she was to forgive him or if he was forgiving her, but she summoned a smile and kissed him, and he was satisfied.

When they were settled side by side on the train to Long Branch, she picked up the *Times*—he had bought all the morning papers as a matter of course—and she was surprised when he frowned at her.

"I haven't read that yet, Miranda."

"But you have the *Tribune,* dear. Of course if you would rather trade, I'll be glad to see what Mr. Greeley has to say."

"No, that's not what I meant. That is . . . Oh, never mind. Now that you've started, go ahead and read it." He looked uncomfortable, and she realized suddenly that he had bought all the papers for himself, that he wanted to read each one before relinquishing it to her, and that it had never occurred to him that she might find that objectionable or unreasonable. It was hardly worth making an issue of such a trivial thing, and since she had already started reading, she kept on, glad to be concentrating on something as impersonal as the news.

The war was not going well anywhere. The armies still faced each other in Virginia, the battle lines little changed since the defeat at Fredericksburg four months before. Why didn't Hooker fight? In the west Grant was still maneuvering his armies near Vicksburg, apparently with little success. And at sea the Confederate raider, the *Alabama*, was still attacking merchant ships at will. It was criminal that England had allowed a Rebel war vessel to be outfitted in her ports to prey on unarmed Union ships. John had raged about it only the week before, this piracy on the high seas, and when one of the merchantmen chartered by Schuyler Shipping was overdue five days, he had feared the worst. She looked up, ready to ask Richard about it, but she found his eyes on her, studying, her, smiling.

"What is it, darling?" She blushed a little under his continuing gaze.

"Nothing. That is, you are so lovely, and I just like to look at you."

"Oh, well, thank you."

"I bought you something else, Miranda."

She looked at him, surprised, expectant.

"This morning, when I decided to buy you the brooch, I had really gone to the bookstore first to see if I could find you some useful guide . . ."

"A guidebook? You mean a guide to Long Branch?"

"No, no, my sweet." He laughed. "It's just that last night you were so frightened, and I thought that perhaps if I could find you the right sort of book about marriage . . ."

"I see." She blushed, but she thanked him and turned to the title page, noting that the authors were a medical doctor and a learned clergyman. Their views on the submissiveness of women seemed to be remarkably similar to Aunt Sarah's—and to Richard's—though they phrased their advice somewhat differently.

Miranda read it all with fascination. She was particularly struck by one difficult case in which the doctor had been consulted by an embarrassed young man on his honeymoon. It seemed that his bride was so nervous that the only practical way for him to consummate the marriage was to have her anesthetized. On three successive nights the doctor arrived to administer ether, and he was pleased to report the bridegroom's complete success—and the birth of a child nine months later. It is true that the baby was a girl—there was some speculation as to whether anesthesia had been a factor but the doctor was frank to admit he didn't know. However, without benefit of ether, subsequently there had been born three healthy boys in the next five years, and the marriage now was obviously fruitful and therefore successful.

The lack of fruitfulness in marriage gave both doctor and clergyman considerable concern, and they thundered at length about the declining birth-rate of the old colonial stock that had built the country. Immigrants, by contrast, were having large families, which threatened the whole composition of society and could bring ruin by the next generation. This alarming vision of the future need not come to pass, however, and the nation could still be saved, but only if the basic social institutions were properly strengthened. This led the authors back to the problems of marriage, which meant, more specifically, the problems of women.

There appeared to be a fine line between the wife who was properly submissive (not requiring ether) and the small minority of deranged females who demanded more of their husbands than could be considered proper. Any demand from a woman was improper on the face of it, of course, since it was well known that women should make it their first duty to please their husbands; they could find their happiness in motherhood. A woman who didn't fulfill that ideal was obviously in peril and unless treated would be afflicted with hysteria and possibly even insanity.

Men were deemed to require little guidance, so the chapter devoted to their problems were considerably shorter. The only warning concerned the danger of overindulgence, which would lead to weakness. It was necessary to conserve one's vital powers for the daily hazards of the workaday world, and there followed a cautionary tale of a man who neglected his business, lost all his money, and became a drunkard—all because he had overindulged his conjugal rights, though it was probable that his wife had been responsible for this excess, of course. As to the proper frequency, the authors were deliberately vague. It might be possible as often as once a week, if a man felt vigorous and healthy, but there were definite dangers even then, and once a month was probably safer. The goal, after all, was healthy children.

Miranda looked speculatively at Richard, who had finished all the newspapers and was folding them into one neat stack. "Did you read this book before you gave it to me, darling?"

"I glanced at it in the shop, the chapter on advice to brides. I hope you are finding it helpful, Miranda."

"It's fascinating," she answered, truthfully enough. "I don't really believe all of it, but—"

"I thought there was a great deal of good common sense there, Miranda. And the authors are a doctor and a clergyman. What greater authorities do you need? You must not question everything, my dear. You are very young and impetuous, and I love you for it, but you must be guided by those who are older and wiser."

"Yes, darling, but this part about men, when they caution you about overindulging . . ."

"Let me see that." He scanned the chapter hastily, glowering, and she suppressed a smile.

"What do you think?" she asked innocently when he finally looked up.

"One must always view these things from the proper perspective."

"And what perspective is that?"

"In the first place, Miranda, the one author is a woman's doctor and clearly not an expert on men. And the other author is a clergyman, you see, and likely to be overly conservative. And you must remember, too," he was clearly improvising, "that both of them were being cautious, in case this book should fall into the wrong hands—the hands of a boy, perhaps, who is too young to be given all the information that a man requires."

"How is he going to acquire it then?"

"Miranda, I think this is a very inappropriate conversation. Now we have almost reached Long Branch, and I think you should make sure that you have all your belongings. I'll just call the porter . . ."

She noticed that he tucked the book under the stack of newspapers—and conveniently forgot to take it with him.

However, he was absolutely right about one thing: that night it was easier. He was really quite sweet, she decided, and if what he wanted was a submissive, virtually etherized wife, she could play that role, at least for the rest of the week. Perhaps she wasn't such a terrible actress after all.

The next four days went by pleasantly enough, and Miranda found it an entertaining game to ancitipate his wishes in little things. At breakfast in their suite she poured his coffee and added his two lumps of sugar, but he liked to stir in the cream himself. She stacked the New York papers (unread) at his place in the order he preferred them, and she encouraged him to read aloud the stories that most interested him and to comment on them at length. The first morning he complimented her on her thoughtfulness and kissed her. The second morning he smiled his thanks. And after that he considered it an established routine and something to be expected as a matter of course. From them on she thought twice before anticipating any of his little wishes.

As for the nights, they were bearable now that she understood what he expected of her: A willing compliance and nothing more.

But he loved her; there was no doubt about that. He was unfailingly courteous and protective, concerned about her comfort, thoughtful about the way he planned their days (he, of course, did all the planning), and completely generous with his time and money. He would always be generous with money, he told her, but the real luxury was time, these unbroken days and nights, with no duties to interfere with the sheer pleasure of being with her.

They went for long walks and drives the first three days; but then it rained and they stayed indoors and he decided she should learn to play billiards. He was an excellent player himself, and there was nothing he liked better than teaching her—teaching her anything. And in this game she was an apt pupil, eager to learn, and she glowed under his compliments. The afternoon was, she decided, the best thing about their honeymoon so far.

That evening they had coffee together in the hotel parlor and got into conversation with an older couple from Philadelphia. The man was limping, Miranda noticed, and it turned out that he was an army officer, convalescing from wounds received at Fredericksburg. Miranda told him about Jimmy and Damon and he was all sympathy, and they talked at great length about hospital care and how it could be improved. Richard was not silent, but he was clearly restless, and when the clock chimed ten, he looked at her significantly. But she had just launched into her speech about re-forming the ambulance system, and Major Dolman and his wife were an interested audience, and the fact that it was ten o'clock didn't concern her at all.

"It is late," Richard cut in at the first available pause, but she shook her head and went right on with her story about a wounded corporal who had almost died of hunger because no one had thought to feed him for three days.

By then Richard was standing beside her impatiently, and there was no way she could remain seated when he extended his hand in peremptory fashion and virtually pulled her to her feet. She excused herself as gracefully as she could under the circumstances, but Richard cut her off with a firm good night to the major and his wife. And the Dolmans viewed their departure with some amusement.

"You embarrassed me," Miranda said as soon as they had reached their suite.

"I am sorry, Miranda, but you deliberately ignored my wishes and went right on talking."

"And you ignored *my* wishes, Richard, when you could see I was interested in our conversation with Major Dolman and his wife."

"I could see your interest in *him*," he said pointedly. "I was unaware of any interest in her."

"Surely you aren't jealous."

"No, not of Major Dolman. But I am very jealous of my time with you, Miranda, and I see no reason at all to stay up late talking to strangers when we are on our honeymoon." He drew her into his arms and kissed her. "Oh, Miranda, why should I ever want to see strangers when you are here? Darling," his breath was warm in her ear, "we will go to bed now."

It was a command, and she obeyed him, but for the first time in weeks she gave her imagination free rein—and she wondered where Cort was and when he would be back and if he knew yet about her marriage.

In the morning Richard was slow to finish shaving, and when she arranged the newspapers at his place, she noticed the *Times* carried a dispatch about skirmishing near Vicksburg and she sat down to read it, sure she recognized Cort as the correspondent who had written it. She looked up to see Richard standing over her, obviously displeased.

"I was reading the news from Vicksburg, darling. Cort is there, and I think—"

"Miranda, you know very well that I like to read the papers first."

"Oh, darling, don't be silly. You weren't even here and I—"

"Miranda, I don't think you understand. The reason that I establish certain routines—"

"It's such a little thing, Richard. It's not worth making a fuss about."

"I agree, darling, that it is a little thing, but an important principle is at stake here, and I think we must reach an understanding about it now. I thought we had already. For the past four days you have—"

"I was just playing a game, Richard. I didn't think you would really care about something this insignificant."

"A game? Miranda, we are married. We are not playing games. Now you know how I like to begin my day, and I surely have a right to read the newspapers that I buy and pay for myself. I am not an ungenerous man, darling, and if you want me to order separate copies for you, I will do that gladly."

"That would be silly."

"I agree with you, dear. That would be silly. But if you should decide you really want them," his voice softened as he smiled down at her, and he touched her cheek, "I will indulge you in this admitted silliness. In the meantime, you will not displease me by doing this again."

She was absolutely astonished by his attitude and looked for a reason. "Does your father insist on reading the papers first, too?"

"I doubt if the question ever came up. Mother automatically defers to him in all things."

Miranda considered that and decided it was probably true. For the first time she experienced a feeling of sympathy for Aunt Faith, so confined at home by Uncle Paul and so bossy toward everyone else. "And you expect me to defer to you that way, too, don't you?"

"You are my wife, Miranda, my dearly beloved wife, and I want you to be happy. But we are called to different duties in this life." He rested a hand on her shoulder, dominating her, loving her, patiently instructing her in her proper role. "I am a fortunate man, darling, and prosperous, and if, God willing, we survive this terrible war, I expect to be very successful. And I will share my success with you, all of it. But while I am working hard for you, and the children we hope to have, I expect you to make life happy for me at home. And that means happy in all the small things—like reading the papers first or, last night, breaking away from strangers when I signal you."

"In all the small things," Miranda echoed. "And the large ones, too? You will make *all* the decisions?"

"I will always listen to you, darling, and take your wishes into account. But you must win my confidence in your judgment, Miranda, and remember to do what pleases me. Oh, my sweet, don't look so worried." He pulled her into his arms and smoothed the frown from her forehead and kissed her. "You *do* please me, you know. And I love you very much. You are so appealing and so beautiful and so open to this new world of marriage, and it is my greatest joy to teach you and guide you and to make you as happy as you have made me." He kissed her and led her to the breakfast table and, under his watchful eyes, she refolded the *Times* and placed it under the *Tribune* beside his empty cup and saucer.

She sighed and picked up the coffeepot, but he shook his head and touched it experimentally. "It's cold now, Miranda—all this unnecessary delay. Order a fresh pot, dear, and be sure to insist that they bring it quickly. I'll just see what Mr. Greeley has to say today." He settled down with the *Tribune,* and she dutifully coped with the vargaries of room service, all the time seething with rebellion. And she had thought he was sweet—so eagerly in love with her that he would indulge all her whims. When all along . . . Why, he was an absolute tyrant! He had confined her to her place, and for the moment she could see no way out. Thank God there were only two more days. She wouldn't spoil things for him now, before he went back to his regiment, but she did not consider this a final defeat.

That evening the hotel guests gathered around the piano, taking turns playing and singing. When Major Dolman turned to Miranda and asked if she would favor them with a selection, she glanced at Richard first to see if he approved, and when he nodded, she sat down and ran through her repertoire of patriotic songs, playing them all from memory, all the guests joining enthusiastically in the singing. Richard beamed at her, and she smiled uncertainly, and when the clock chimed ten, she looked at him again and he nodded emphatically. She finished the last chorus of "Tenting Tonight" and then excused herself, in spite of the objections of the major and two newly arrived lieutenants who wanted to start all over again with "John Brown's Body." But Richard came swiftly to her side, and they said their good nights.

"Newlyweds," she heard someone explain as they left, and she blushed, but Richard seemed oblivious. In their suite he had his arms around her even before the door closed behind them. "My darling, I have never been so proud of you."

"I didn't play *that* well."

"Oh, the music was fine, too. But when you looked to me for permission first . . . Miranda, my dear, dear wife, I would give you the world; but yours is the better gift—your own sweet self and my dearest treasure."

Afterward he told her again how much he loved her, and he hoped she had forgotten all that unpleasantness of this morning. He had forgiven her and wiped the slate clean, and tomorrow would be as perfect as this evening had been.

He possessed her physically, even in sleep, one arm across her body, his hand on her breast. And when she finally managed to slide away from his embrace, he stirred restlessly and moved closer and finally woke up.

"I was dreaming of you, darling," he murmured. "Such a lovely dream. And now that I am awake, I can see it has all come true." He smiled and reached for her again.

Richard had decided they would return to New York by steamer, and in the bright sunshine they stood by the ship's rail and watched the bluffs of Long Branch recede in the distance.

"It was a beautiful week, my treasure, and I hate to see it end." He pulled her closer. "And you will come to Washington next Saturday, won't you?"

"You don't know if you'll be able to get away, Richard, and I can't leave all my responsibilities in New York on the slight chance that you will be able to come to see me."

"But, Miranda, my darling, you know now that your greatest responsibility is to me."

"Richard, you promised me before we were married that I could go on with my life in New York, and I trusted you and I expect you to honor your pledge."

"But now that you are my wife, Miranda, I thought you would see things differently."

"I am still the same person that I was before, and you are still, surely, the same honorable man."

He sighed and released her from his embrace. "I will not go back on my word to you, but I am disappointed, Miranda, gravely disappointed." He looked at her reproachfully, but she turned away and focused on the distant horizon.

She thought it was about time for him to be disappointed in something—after his blind pleasure in their one-sided honeymoon. Was there really something wrong with her that she wanted more from him than he was prepared to give? But if she told him, she knew he would be shocked and think her depraved and wicked. And she lived with the guilty knowledge that she *had* been wicked, so perhaps he was right. Oh, Cort, I married Richard to escape you, and now I miss you more than ever. If only it were you beside me now, darling . . .

She blinked back her tears, and Richard moved closer to her and patted her shoulder. "Don't cry, darling. I didn't mean to upset you, but I *am* disappointed. I have been thinking that perhaps you are right, though, about making fruitless trips to Washington and tiring yourself. I wouldn't want anything to go wrong if it turns out that you are . . . that we have created a new life this past week. You must let me know immediately, darling, as soon as you have any indication of that.

"Now I should know by Friday if it will be possible for me to spend Saturday night in Washington, and I will send you a telegram; and you must respond immediately. Don't worry, my angel. I will be understanding if you have a good reason not to come." He patted her shoulder again. "Now I will tell you something that will probably seem strange to you, but you must trust my instincts on this matter."

She looked at him, puzzled.

"Of course I know that we have a standing invitation from George and Emily, and they would be quite hurt if we met in Washington and didn't let them know. But, Miranda, I could never stay under the same roof with Cort Adams, and if he is there, we will go to a hotel and not say a word to anyone."

She was astonished and curious and relieved, but Richard saw only the astonishment.

"I know, my sweet, that you would be disappointed if you made the long trip and then didn't see the family, but I could never put myself under obligation to Cort Adams by being his guest overnight."

"Why ever not?"

He laughed a little self-consciously. "I know you will think I am wrong—only women are supposed to have this kind of intuition—but I have always distrusted that man and his feelings toward you."

He saw her shock and moved to soothe her immediately. "Miranda, you are so innocent and trusting, but there have been times . . . I remember the night of the ball for the Prince of Wales—"

"He was flirting with Ann."

"Yes, but I realized afterward that he was just diverting me to reach you."

"Richard, that was all so long ago. And now he's married, and I'm married and—"

"All the same, Miranda, whenever he looked at you, he was the only man who ever gave me a moment's concern. I was never worried about Damon or Andy Dawson or any of the boys in the Seventh Regiment—I knew all along that in time you would turn to me." He took her hand, both her hands. "And I will never let you go."

"And Cort?"

"I think he is perfectly capable of forcing himself on any woman who takes his fancy. When you were stranded with him after Jimmy died, my first thought was to rescue you." He smiled at her. "Thank God it was all right and you were safe! I suppose he's found some actress in Washington by now." He sighed. "Susanne is very foolish to stay in Savannah and let him roam about at will."

"But Richard," Miranda paused to frame her question, "now that we are safely married, why are you still concerned about him?"

"I simply don't like the man; that's all. And I am sure that the feeling is mutual. Oh, we will be polite if we meet, and I know that George and Emily get along with him splendidly, but I prefer to avoid him as much as possible. You see,

Miranda, I, too, will sometimes let feeling triumph over rational judgment." He touched her cheek. "But you, beloved, you know that better than anyone in the world."

On the breeze-swept deck they were now the only passengers, and he drew her into his arms and kissed her. "My darling, how can I leave you and return to some cold and empty army cot, so far away from your warmth and gentleness?" He kissed her again and released her only when they were interrupted by a party of schoolboys intent on exploring the ship.

But when she turned to look at the horizon again, his arm was firm about her waist, binding her to him, locking her in.

BOOK TWO

Chapter 22

THERE WAS NO immediate summons to Washington. Richard had rejoined his regiment just in time to participate in preparations for General Hooker's first major campaign, a massive movement across the Rappahannock, designed to flank Fredericksburg.

But there was very little about the army in Richard's letters to her. It was part of his nature to be guarded in all matters of business—and war was his particular business now. He wrote to her almost every night, when he missed her the most, letters filled with yearning, letters of counsel and advice, letters of instructions about the kind of house they would build and how they would furnish it and the number of servants they would need. And he insisted that she call on his family regularly, and she was immediately trapped into spending every Sunday afternoon with them.

Marriage to Richard had made her acutely sensitive to the interplay between other husbands and wives, and she studied his parents with renewed interest. It was true that Aunt Faith deferred to Uncle Paul in everything, at least in Miranda's presence, and it was such an accepted part of their lives that it was obviously second nature to both of them.

Miranda's transformation from niece to daughter-in-law had been accepted indulgently by her uncle, unwillingly by her aunt. But now that it was an accomplished fact, Faith was making the best of it. This seemed to mean that she was freer than ever to give orders to Miranda, though she must have found that a frustrating occupation since Miranda stubbornly continued to cling to her former life. The Stratford was her anchor, the orphan asylum was her holiday, and the Sanitary Commission was her contribution to the war.

On some days, the fact that she was married hardly impinged on her consciousness at all. Except . . . except . . . she was beginning to wonder if she was pregnant. It was too early to know with certainty, too early to answer Richard's repeated questions, too early to acknowledge that her own life might change irrevocably. Her uncertainty was all mixed up with the superstitious dread that had overtaken her. The army was on the march toward Fredericksburg again, and she was terrified that Richard would be wounded, and her brother Tom, and she would be condemned to live that hospital nightmare all over again.

For days at a time she didn't think about Cort at all, and she had heard from him only once since he had followed Grant's armies to Vicksburg. It had been a curious letter, almost a love letter, and it puzzled her. But she had no plans to answer it, even if she would trust the mail to that distant battleground. In any case, she wasn't even sure if he was there any longer—there had been none of his dispatches in the *Times* for weeks now.

One morning in early May she was in the office alone when Cort strode in with no advance warning, closed the door, pulled her into his arms, and kissed her.

"We are going to be married, Miranda. Not immediately—not until after the war. But then, my darling, we'll be together for a lifetime, and—"

She broke away from him, stunned by his words, by his presence, and shocked into silence.

He looked at her, bewildered, reaching out to steady her, but she backed off hastily.

"What it it, darling? I *know* you love me, and now that I—"

Still speechless, she held up her hands so that he could see her rings, and all emotion drained from his face.

"Dear God. Not Richard?"

She nodded, swallowing hard, alarmed by the emotions he was stirring, trying to hold back her tears.

He moved to take her in his arms again, but she retreated and made the desk a barrier between them. Nothing he said was making any sense. He was talking about marriage and love and a lifetime together, and it was all impossible. She caught at individual words, trying to hold them in focus, but they blurred and vanished, and all she could see was his face and the way his eyes turned bleak when he saw her rings.

He still refused to believe it. "But why, darling? I asked you to wait, and I told you I'd work something out, and oh, my dearest, how could you throw your life away when we love each other so much?"

"But, Cort, you never said—"

"I wrote to you, darling. I said it explicitly. I said I loved you and I said I would work something out."

"You didn't say marriage."

"But I didn't know definitely about that. I could have been wrong, and I thought I owed Susanne a chance to explain."

"Explain?" The words were still fragments, and she stared at him, uncomprehending.

"You don't know yet? No, of course you couldn't know. The baby . . . When she acknowledged that the child wasn't mine—"

"What are you talking about?" She sat down heavily. If only her heart would stop pounding in her ears, maybe she could understand what he was saying.

He sighed and slumped into the chair across from her. "What is the point of it all now? I rushed to tell you, and all the time you . . . Oh, Miranda, how could you marry him? How could you?"

She flinched under his accusing eyes and fought to gain control of her emotions. "No answer would ever satisfy you, Cort. There is no point in talking about it. None at all." She looked at him and felt his tension and moved to change the subject, back to Susanne. "Tell me about her, Cort. And the baby."

He shrugged. "It hardly matters now, does it? But I suppose you should know. Why should I spare you the irony and the pain when you have deliberately ruined—"

"Cort, please. Every word hurts me, hurts you. You must not talk about all these . . . dreams that won't come true." She was trying to find an anchor in reality, in facts they must both face. "Tell me what happened with Susanne. Calmly."

"Calmly? You turned our world upside down and you want me to talk calmly? Dear God." He shook his head, but he took a deep breath, and the tension eased slightly. "Calmly," he echoed again in wonderment and sighed. "Very well. Calmly, then. About Susanne." He looked away, still trying to contain his emotions. "Susanne," he repeated. "I knew something was wrong when I saw her last September. For the first time she was not . . . She had changed. If she had just told me then . . . I don't know now. I think I would have forgiven her. God knows *I* hadn't been faithful either." He sighed again. "This hideous war. She should never have stayed in Savannah, and I should never have agreed."

"But the child, Cort. How do you know? When did you find out?"

"I suspected when I heard from her at Christmas. It was too pat somehow, the way she announced her pregnancy. Not like her at all. So I decided to make another trip to Savannah, and I timed it very well. I arrived a month ago, the day before she gave birth. I wasn't going to accept some story of a premature baby and have another man's bastard palmed off on me. It was a girl. Danielle Elizabeth. Seven pounds, twelve ounces."

"The poor child."

"Yes. She'll never know her father."

"How do you know? Who was he?"

"A Rebel officer . . . Susanne had nursed him in the hospital, and when he recovered . . . But he was killed at South Mountain last fall."

"Oh, Cort! How terrible for her. And what could you really expect her to do?"

"She was my wife, Miranda. I expected her to tell me the truth. She was still trying to lie to me, even after the baby was born."

"And now?"

"Does it really matter now? If only you had waited . . ." He shrugged. "I thought I had it all worked out. We could have been so happy."

The silence lengthened, and Miranda finally broke it. "What were you going to do?" She knew the answer would pain her, but she had to know.

"I told Susanne my terms, and she agreed. We'll be divorced as soon as the war is over. I won't charge her with adultery if she lets me take Bobby." He looked at Miranda, and there was a ghost of a smile that never reached his eyes. "I didn't think you would object to rearing my son with the other children we would have."

"Oh, Cort!" Her eyes welled with tears, and he reached for her hand, but she pulled back.

"At least take my handkerchief." He forced a smile. "I remember a time when you were reluctant even to do that."

"Oh, please, don't remind me of all that." She was trying

to choke back her tears, conscious of his eyes on her, conscious that unless she got rid of him quickly, she would somehow betray Richard. And he was her husband, she reminded herself, and he loved her, and at this very moment he was fighting for her on some distant battleground.

"I think you should go away, Cort."

"No, that was my mistake before."

She looked at him, puzzled.

"When I came to see you, when you thought you were pregnant, when I bowed to your determination to see it through yourself. All your courage and your strength and that crazy independence . . . Oh, my dearest, I think it was only then I realized how much I truly loved you. It wasn't just the passion we shared—"

"Stop it, Cort. You *must* stop. I am married to an honorable man who loves me and—"

"But do *you* love *him*, Miranda?" His eyes on her were searching, and when he spoke again, his voice was a deliberate caress. "When he takes you in his arms and holds you, when he kisses you—your lips, your eyes, that rapid pulse beating in your throat. It is beating now, and I—"

"Please, Cort. You must not say these things. You must not even think them." Her hands were in her lap, twisting his handkerchief, turning it into a rope that bound her—and made her conscious of the pressure of her rings. "All that is between us is past."

He shook his head, denying it, but she spoke rapidly, trying to convince him, to convince herself.

"It was wrong. It was sinful. It could have ruined my life forever." She took a deep breath to sustain her resolution. "And now I have been given a second chance, and I am not going to spoil it. I am not going to let you spoil it for me. I am sorry that you and Susanne . . . But Richard is blameless, and he should not be made to suffer for all that. He is a good man, and he wants to give me a good life, and—"

"He will make you miserable."

"I don't want to talk about it. I don't want to talk about it at all."

"Because Richard wouldn't approve? He will make you his prisoner, darling, bound in by rules and regulations."

"He didn't make the rules, Cort. And at least I am confident that *he* will abide by them honestly. He will not go away for weeks and months at a time, finding other women, breaking my heart, coming back to me at long intervals to see if I am still waiting faithfully."

"It would not be like that, Miranda; not with you. Even with Susanne, if she had come to Washington . . ." He sighed. "But that's too easy an explanation. You are right. It was all my fault from the beginning." He took refuge in a dream, rewriting the past. "I should have married you the first time I saw you, bearing that ridiculous stack of bundles from Stewart's, looking up at me from behind the front desk, all bright and shining and expectant, with the whole world ready to do you homage. I wanted you then, and I paid a terrible price for ignoring my feelings, and we have lost three precious years, but we will *not* lose the rest of our lives. There is no reason for us to lose another day, another night."

"Cort, I am married. I am Mrs. Richard Beekman Schuyler." She spoke the words clearly and decisively. "And I think I may be pregnant. Not even Richard knows that yet. I have promised to love and honor and obey," her voice cracked over that word, "and that is all there is to it. Now I think we should just try to forget this whole conversation— even the fact that Susanne's baby was not premature. Does Dany know that? Will you tell her?"

"I wasn't planning to. That was part of my arrangement with Susanne—she would agree to the divorce, and I would allow her to preserve her 'good name.' We made that bargain, and I will stand by it."

"Well, then, everyone will think you are a happy father again. Who knows, Cort? Maybe it will work out that way. After the war, when you see Susanne again—"

"You think I would go *back* to her?"

"Stranger things have happened. And you didn't give that marriage a chance, either of you. I will not make that mistake. And Richard would never let me. I will be going to see him in Washington," she made the resolution even as she spoke, "at the first possible moment."

"Tell me when you are coming and I'll leave. I couldn't bear to be under the same roof with him, knowing that you and he . . . I couldn't bear it."

"If you are there, we will go to a hotel. Richard has already decided that."

Cort raised an eyebrow. "What delicacy of feeling. On his part. Wouldn't it bother you at all? In my house, where we . . . Oh, Miranda, I can still see you on that first morning, the sunlight streaming in, the golden glow that touched you with a radiance—"

"Cort, I can't listen to another word. You must leave right now. Immediately. I will count to three, and if you aren't gone by then—"

"All right, darling. I will go. But I will be back." He paused at the door to look at her again. "You can't deceive me, you know. You still love me. You still want me. Nothing Richard has done has touched you yet. And I will not give you up. I will never give you up."

She had held back the tears until he left, but she could restrain them no longer. It's a test, she told herself, to see if I am strong enough to say no to him and mean it. A loving God who had forgiven her once would surely punish her wickedness if she should succumb again.

I must not see him again, she resolved, or think about him, or long for him. And when I am with Richard . . . I hope I am pregnant. If I have his baby, surely that will mean that everything will be all right. We will win this war and he will come home to me safely. Dear God, I will be a good wife to him. Truly I will. And Tom will be spared, and George, and everyone I love. I will not go through that agony with Jimmy again, or hold Damon in my arms and watch him die. And please, God, if I am truly pregnant, I will not do anything that would make me lose this child.

Dany joined her at the Cooper Institute the next afternoon to pack supplies for the Sanitary Commission.

"John asked me to come," she explained. "I am not comfortable with all these fervent advocates for the Union," her gesture specifically included Aunt Faith, "but I guess it's a good thing to help the wounded soldiers, whichever side they are on."

Miranda nodded her agreement.

"Besides," Dany went on, "I haven't seen you for five days, and I wanted to make sure you had heard the news."

"What news?"

"Why, about Susanne. She's had her baby already. I wasn't sure if Cort had told you. Danielle Elizabeth—two months premature, but I guess everything is all right. Cort seemed awfully subdued about it, but I think he is worried about her."

Miranda made no comment.

"He had a terrible time getting through the lines this time. Did he tell you?"

Miranda shook her head, and Dany dwelt at length on how a Union soldier had barely missed him when Cort clambered ashore from a rowboat on the federally held Tybee Island, controlling the approach to Savannah.

"He takes too many risks," Dany declared. "I sometimes wonder if he'll survive the war at all." She sighed. "I said as much to him—I thought he'd laugh. You know he's got more lives than a cat. But he said he thought he'd used up most of them by now, and he wasn't really sure if he cared much any more. He wasn't a bit like himself. Did you see him? Did you notice it?"

"I thought he was pretty much the same."

"I don't think so. Perhaps it's just that I know him better—after all, he's married to my sister—and I can see that something is troubling him."

Miranda did not contradict her.

"Oh well," Dany went on. "He was going back to Washington last night. I've never been there, you know, and I sort of hinted that I'd like to visit sometime—maybe travel with you when you go to see Richard, but he changed the subject and started talking about the war again." Dany was packing boxes methodically, her running commentary an accompaniment for her, a distraction for Miranda. "The war seems to be going on forever, doesn't it? We keep fighting and fighting over the same battlefields. Did you see the papers this morning?" She didn't wait for an answer. "It's been going on for days at Fredericksburg again. And that little town nearby. I never can remember it."

"Chancellorsville."

"Oh, yes, that's right. It's hard to tell exactly what is going on, but it sounds to me as if the Confederates are winning again. Lee is just the best general, that's all. And Stonewall Jackson and Jeb Stuart. Do you think Hooker is really any good? Isn't he just following in Burnside's footsteps?"

"Please God, Dany, I hope not. I think Richard is there, and Tom."

"Oh, Miranda, why didn't you tell me?" Dany looked at her with compassion. "Oh, I hope they are safe. Of *course* they are safe. But you should have stopped me. I would never have chattered on so foolishly. I don't know what's the matter with me. Please don't cry, darling. They'll be all right. You'll

280

see." She patted Miranda's arm helplessly and was almost grateful when Aunt Faith hurried over to see what the problem was.

"Are you feeling faint, Miranda? Richard warned me that I must not let you overdo."

"I'm all right, really. We were just talking about the war, and his regiment is at Fredericksburg, you know. It was mentioned in the *Tribune* this morning."

"Yes, I saw that. I know you're worried, dear. It brings back all the sad memories from last December. But you must have faith, Miranda, and get a grip on yourself. This kind of work is our contribution, you know."

"I know. I'll be all right. Truly." She changed the subject before Aunt Faith could inquire too closely into her physical condition. "Where is Irene today? I miss her—she's always such good company."

Faith glanced at the clock. "She's late. She was helping Ann shop for her trousseau, and they were going to stop at the Stratford, but she promised to be here by now. I have told that girl over and over again—"

Irene burst in, her face unnaturally pale, her voice not quite under control, and Miranda had a premonition of disaster.

"Who is it? Which one?"

"You must come at once, Miranda." Irene swallowed hard. "Uncle Will got a telegram from George, and Tom—"

"No!" She clutched at the table for support.

"He's wounded, Miranda, but he'll be all right. George *says* he'll be all right. But he thinks you and Uncle Will should come to Washington right away."

281

Chapter 23

"FIGHTING JOE" HOOKER they called him, the latest in the disastrous line of generals commanding the vast Army of the Potomac. In the spring of 1863, four months after Burnside had tried and failed, Hooker was aiming for Richmond again. He had moved his men across the Rappahannock, planning to flank Fredericksburg and trap the Confederate army before sweeping on to complete and final victory.

Badly outnumbered, Lee had nonetheless split his Army of Northern Virginia, leaving a small force in Fredericksburg to stave off the formidable threat that remained there, moving the bulk of his army to the Wilderness area near Chancellorsville, where the Federal forces had gathered in massive strength. And then Hooker's nerve failed him, and he pulled back his advance columns, returning to the defensive and surrendering the initiative to Lee.

Splitting his diminished forces once again, Lee sent Stonewall Jackson around the right flank of Hooker's army. It was a brilliant maneuver, a classic textbook study in military strategy—and a crushing defeat for the Union army. But it was an equally crushing victory for the Confederates, and their toll of casualties was alarmingly high. Among the wounded and soon to die was Jackson himself, the accidental victim of fire from his own soldiers.

But, once again, Richmond had been saved.

And, once again, the Army of the Potomac had been forced to retreat, bruised and bleeding, back across the Rappahannock, its losses greater even than at the battle of Fredericksburg in December.

It was two days after the defeat at Chancellorsville and late in the evening when Miranda and her father reached Washington. In the pouring rain the cobblestones were slick with mud, and the hapless horses picked their way slowly through the traffic clogging the streets around the train depot. George was nowhere in sight, but Will finally managed to hail a hackney carriage and have their trunks loaded on board.

They arrived at the big house on Massachusetts Avenue, and Emily greeted them, surprised that they had missed George but welcoming them with hugs and kisses—and the news that Tom was in the field hospital at Aquia Creek. He would be brought to Washington just as soon as more transport was available.

"He's going to live," she assured them. "And we think we'll be able to bring him here if the doctors decide that amputation isn't necessary."

Miranda clutched her father in an iron grip, but she said nothing.

"It's his left leg, below the knee," Emily explained. "He fought like a tiger when the surgeons wanted to take it off right after the battle, and I think now they'll be able to save it. We just don't know yet."

Will nodded and cleared his throat with some difficulty. "Can we visit him in the field hospital?"

"No, I don't think so. Only George has been there. But he says they'll bring him to Washington tomorrow or the next day. There's nothing we can do until then . . . So why don't you just get out of those wet clothes and we'll have a late supper. I'll help you unpack, Miranda." She led the way up the broad staircase. "You're in the green room this time, dear. I don't know what got into Cort, but he decided to take over the yellow bedroom as a study. He has already had the furniture moved out—insisted we give it to Hattie and Jeff for the carriage house. They were delighted, of course, but I liked that four-poster bed, and I thought one day Polly . . . However, he certainly deserves an upstairs study if he wants one—after the way we have spread out and taken over his house. Poor Cort. I think he's really upset about Susanne. It hasn't been much of a marriage for him, you know, and I do think she was foolish to stay in Savannah all this time. But that's enough about him. I know you'll want to see Polly—

she's changed so much in the past few months—but she's asleep now and I don't think we should wake her."

Miranda nodded her agreement, relieved by Emily's constant flow of conversation that spared her the necessity of comment. And thank God she had been moved from the yellow bedroom. She never wanted to see it again.

They were in the dining room when George came home, full of apologies for having missed them at the train.

"I was making arrangements about Tom," he explained. "I am going to the field hospital tomorrow with Cort, and the two of us will bring him here directly. That will be better than entrusting him to the ambulance service, and Cort says we can take better care of him at home than in a hospital—and I certainly agree with that."

Emily nodded. "And isn't it thoughtful of Cort, going out of his way to help Tom and insisting we bring him here."

"Where is he?" Will asked. "He passed through New York a few days ago, but he didn't even stay overnight, and I didn't see him at all. I haven't had a chance to congratulate him on his new daughter."

There was the briefest of pauses, and Miranda saw a look pass between George and Emily, making her wonder if they knew or suspected something. And then Emily moved to steer the conversation into safer channels.

"Both mother and daughter are doing well, I believe. But you haven't asked about your grandchild, yet." Emily made it an accusation, and then she smiled. "I'll begin to think you don't care."

Will hastened to make amends, and they were still talking about Polly when Cort arrived.

He was in rigid control of himself, Miranda noticed, shaking hands with her father, bowing formally to her until Emily laughed and said that she thought Polly's godparents ought to be on better terms than that. Miranda dutifully presented her cheek to be kissed, but they did not look at each other, and Miranda withdrew almost immediately, pleading exhaustion from the trip.

Emily was all sympathy—and feminine intuition. She was too discreet to ask direct questions, but she followed Miranda to her room to make sure she was all right, and she wondered out loud if it was only the trip that had tired her, or if perhaps there were other symptoms that a woman would recognize . . .

Miranda refused comment, and Emily apologized immediately for seeming to pry. "Of course if you have any news, darling, you would want to tell Richard first. It's very thoughtless of me. It must be terrible to be separated only a week after your wedding. I am so lucky to have George with me all the time, particularly through all the months we were waiting for Polly. I think of Susanne going through all that alone . . ."

Miranda looked at her sharply. "What do you mean? I saw that look you exchanged with George."

Emily sighed. "Yes, that was indiscreet of us. And we don't really know, of course. Why, I've never even *met* Susanne. But we couldn't help counting the months, and Cort has obviously changed since the baby was born. It is loyal of him to insist there is nothing the matter, but we know him too well. He is so grim and tense, ready to explode, and I am afraid he is going to be reckless, too. You must have noticed something, Miranda. He always used to make a game of flirting with you outrageously, and yet tonight he didn't even want to give you a welcoming kiss."

"Yes, but I'm married now, and that probably makes a difference."

Emily nodded, not entirely convinced. And after she left, Miranda locked the door. It was a silly precaution, she knew, and probably useless—undoubtedly he had a key. She felt safer when she propped a chair under the doorknob, and then she shook her head at her own foolishness. With her father next door and George and Emily across the hall, Cort would certainly not come sneaking into her room, even if she had given him any indication that he was welcome. And he wasn't. Never again.

They brought Tom home the next evening and settled him in the corner bedroom, next to Polly. He was pale and drawn from the rigors of the journey, but he was in determinedly high spirits—aided, George said, by the consumption of a whole bottle of brandy. Emily was shocked, but George assured her it was the best way to ease the pain of the trip.

"Besides," he added, "Cort and I took samples periodically, too, to make sure the brandy wasn't losing its effectiveness."

Emily shook her head, but Miranda laughed—a startling sound; she realized she hadn't laughed in days. Cort caught her eye and smiled, and she hastily turned her attention back to Tom.

The dressing on his leg had to be changed, and probably they should summon a doctor, but Miranda preferred to do it herself. The reason for packing a wound with lint remained obscure to her, and Tom winced while she picked out the last threads and looked at the slight accumulation of pus. Doctors always liked a wound to suppurate, so Miranda supposed that was a good sign. Nevertheless, she cleaned it all out—the smell bothered her—and rebandaged his leg. By then Hattie had brought him a tray, but he was too tired to eat very much, and he was asleep before Miranda had finished her ministrations.

"You are a girl of many talents," Cort said to her when the family had reassembled around the supper table.

Miranda eyed him warily, but his expression was bland, and everyone else seemed to take the comment at face value.

"Yes, she certainly is," Emily agreed. "And, Miranda, you must stay with us until Tom is completely recovered."

George echoed that invitation, and Will said he thought he could spare her. Cort was inscrutable, and Miranda had a moment of pure panic.

"I couldn't possibly," she said. "Just as soon as we see that his leg is healing properly, I must return to New York. I have responsibilities there."

"Something more important than taking care of Tom?" There was a silky quality to Cort's voice that put her on guard. "We were all aware of your devotion to Jimmy," he continued, in the same almost caressing tone, "and surely Tom deserves the same loving care."

Miranda looked at him, puzzled. There was something behind his words that bothered her.

"This time, of course," Cort continued, "we won't let you exhaust yourself by doing everything alone. If we all take turns sitting up with him and make a schedule . . . I'll volunteer for a few hours tonight, for instance, and then I'll call on you, Miranda, and we can always rely on Hattie and Jeff to cooperate."

To cover for them, he meant, and Miranda was horrified. Emily was right—Cort was reckless now, and if he thought that just by getting her alone . . . She wouldn't risk it. She would put a stop to all of this now.

"That's generous of you, Cort, but not really practical. You and George have other work to do. And I am sure that Papa and Emily and I can take care of Tom and make him well again. I'm going back to him right now, and I'll call you, Papa, when I get tired."

"Certainly, Pet. I'm a light sleeper, and I'll leave my door open. We can manage easily between us."

Tom slept soundly—all that brandy, perhaps—but Miranda had a restless night. Long after her father had dozed off in the chair beside Tom's bed, she lay awake behind her locked door. Deliberately, she avoided thinking about Cort. She concentrated on Richard, who was miles away in Virginia, while right down the hall Cort . . . The war. She would think about the war, and all the brave young men who had gone off to fight and die, like Jimmy . . . No, that was too painful. Would it never end? The victory that had seemed so tantalizingly close only a year ago when Polly was born and she had come to Washington and Cort . . . The orphan asylum. That was better. She made a mental list of all the children she knew there. And then she listed all the permanent guests at the Stratford. And all the members of the staff, too. She wondered when they could bring Tom home, and how soon after that he could rejoin his regiment. Thank God he wasn't in the hospital and she didn't have to relive that nightmare again, waking up afterward with Cort's arms around her . . . She punched her pillow viciously and tried again. Richard. He was her husband, and the next time she greeted him, she would run into his arms; and if Cort saw them, he would know how futile it was even to think about being together again.

She had breakfast with Tom in his room, hoping to avoid Cort that way, but he stopped off to make courteous inquiries about Tom's health. And then he turned his attention to her.

"You look tired, Miranda. Didn't you sleep well?" His voice sounded concerned, but there was a knowing gleam in his eye.

"I was worried about Tom," she said shortly.

"I'm going to be fine," Tom declared. "Why, this morning I can even wiggle my toes. Want to see me do that, Cort?"

Cort assured him he would like nothing better, and afterward he helped Miranda assist Tom in hobbling to the big chair by the window, propping up his injured leg on an ottoman he dragged in from his own room. Tom was properly appreciative, and after Cort left he commented again on what a good fellow he was.

Miranda said nothing. She was still conscious of the seemingly casual way Cort had rested his hand on her shoulder, a caress that had started the blood racing through her veins again. And when she shrugged it off, he smiled at her, looking her up and down, and she knew her color was rising. It was dangerous to be staying in this house with him again, and she had to do something. Anything. He had to be made to realize that all this must stop. Why of course! She had to bring Richard here! Surely his regiment was not far away, and George would be able to get a message through. George could do anything.

Miranda spent the next forty-eight hours taking care of Tom and avoiding Cort, two lines of action that were sometimes in conflict. But she managed to escape being alone with him, and he seemed content to let time and his hovering presence work their effect on her. She was conscious of the tension building between them, and she was increasingly worried that he would do something reckless—and so would she.

It was Saturday afternoon and they had just finished their midday dinner when Jeff appeared in the dining room to announce the arrival of Captain Schuyler. And there was Richard, hard on his heels, smiling at her. Miranda flung herself into his arms, determined to find refuge, and he kissed her warmly, possessively. His arm was firm around her waist while he greeted the rest of the family, and Cort was rigid with shock. From the protection of Richard's embrace, Miranda could sympathize with him and even know a moment's regret. But she knew she was safe now.

They trooped up to see Tom, and then Richard made dutiful inquiries about Polly, who was having her afternoon nap. But it was obvious that all he wanted was to be alone with Miranda.

"I have hired a carriage," he said, "and I thought we could take a ride. You look a little peaked, darling, and the fresh air will do you good. Surely Tom can spare you for a few hours?"

It was a rhetorical question, and Tom assured them he was

well on his way to recovery. "Take her away, Richard. Pretend you're still on your honeymoon."

"I don't have to pretend that," Richard said with conviction. "It's absolutely true." He touched her cheek and smiled at her. "We have twenty-four hours, darling. Time enough to forget all about the war. Just pack a satchel, and we'll take the carriage and simply disappear until tomorrow."

She nodded her agreement, and Emily beamed at them, unconsciously moving closer to George and the warmth of his embrace. Cort looked at both couples and then abruptly excused himself.

Will gazed after him and sighed. "The poor boy. He misses Susanne."

No one bothered to contradict him.

In the carriage Miranda welcomed Richard's arm around her, and she was content to let him take the reins and determine their destination—an inn in Georgetown that had been recommended by another officer in his regiment. She was eager to know about everything that touched his life, but Richard was reluctant to talk about the war or the defeat at Chancellorsville or what it was like to be in battle.

"But I was worried about you, darling," Miranda told him. "And if you don't tell me what it was like, I will imagine all sorts of terrible things, perhaps worse than the battle itself. Tom said you were very brave, and you were right in the thick of the fighting, and you rallied your men—"

"I am a soldier, Miranda, and of course I did my duty. It wasn't really so extraordinary, you know. The regiment was at full strength, and I have a good, well-disciplined company, and we carried the heights with the second charge."

"Then why did the Rebels win? Why do they always seem to win?"

Richard sighed. "We held our ground, but when the flank was turned . . . What we need is a greater will to win. We have the inherent strength, and the ultimate victory will be ours—I am more than ever convinced of that. It is just taking longer than it should. There are too many officers who worry more about casualty lists than about victory."

"But saving lives is important, isn't it?"

"The object is victory, Miranda. The Rebels are not going to surrender until they have been bled white. And they are not going to bleed alone. The sooner we face that fact, the sooner it will be over. And in the long run we will save more lives if we are willing to accept heavy losses now. It is not a pretty war. We have to shoot deserters, and we have to tear men away from their families and . . . Dear God, why are we talking about all this?"

"I was worried about you, darling, and all I did was ask a question."

"And I answered it, and now we are finished with the war. For the next twenty-four hours I don't want to hear another word about it."

"You are very autocratic, Richard. You say to the war, 'Begone,' and you expect it to vanish."

"I wish it would happen that way, darling, and that I were that powerful. But at least for these next hours I can control *our* lives, and I will."

"Always the commanding officer." She smiled, teasing him, but on a deeper level she knew it was true.

"You don't really object, darling." He pulled her closer, "You like to pretend to be modern and independent and different, but I know you better than that. A little while ago, when you rushed into my arms, I knew you were seeking protection from the world. Oh, Miranda, all I want to do is hold you and love you and keep you safe forever."

Later he returned again to the matter of her safety and her health and the whole way she was living in New York. "I think you are working too hard, darling, and that concerns me." They had finished a late tea in the hotel dining room, and he was holding her hands across the table. In the flickering candlelight, her engagement diamond gleamed and sparkled. He touched it, and the wedding ring that anchored it in place. "You are my wife now, darling, and you must promise to take better care of yourself. I think the carriage ride and our walk brought the color back to your cheeks, but you were looking pale and tired earlier today, and for your own sake, Miranda, you must cut down your activities."

"I am all right, Richard. It's just that taking care of Tom these past few days—"

"No, Miranda, it is more than that. I hear from Mother, too, you know, and she tells me that you never stop. Now of course your time at the Sanitary Commission is very valuable, and I certainly wouldn't ask you to give that up. And there are family visits and family duties that will always be a part of your life. But making that long trip every week to the orphan asylum is too much for you, I think. And you are obviously working too hard at the hotel, and I plan to speak quite firmly to Uncle Will about that."

"Richard, that's not a bit fair. You promised me before we were married—"

"Miranda, I worry about you."

"And, Richard, I worry about you—with considerably more cause. *You* are the one on the battlefield. I am perfectly safe, and if it makes me happy to fill up my days with useful work, I think you should be happy for me. I don't want to waste my time doing nothing."

"Taking care of your health is not a waste of time, darling. Not when we want children so much." He kissed her hand. "I had so hoped . . ."

Deliberately, she refrained from telling him she thought she was pregnant. It would be just like him to order her to stay home for the next seven and a half months. And a moment later he confirmed her in that judgment.

"Having a child is very important to me, darling. To us both," he amended. "And as soon as you know, or even suspect, that you . . . Then you must promise that you will give up all these other things and devote yourself to the new life you will be carrying."

"Richard, I would never do anything to jeopardize our child. But you must let me be the best judge of taking care of myself. After all, darling, I am nineteen years old now, and I have survived this long." She smiled at him, but he looked troubled.

"I did not want to talk about the war again, Miranda, but I think I must explain." He fell silent, brooding, and she looked at him expectantly, this taut, disciplined man, always so sure of himself, always so determined to reach his goals. She admired him and wished she were more worthy of him, and she felt her guilt as a terrible burden. If only she loved him and could confide in him and tell him what he was longing to hear. But if he tried to curb her independence, she knew they would quarrel, and he had only these few hours before he returned to his regiment . . .

He was explaining how deeply the war had affected him, the violence and destruction and death, and how this time together was an oasis of peace, a glimpse of another world. ". . . and I dream of you, darling, and long for you—every night. And in the midst of this cruel war, when all around me men are dying, the urge to create life is overwhelming. If I do not survive—"

"Oh, Richard, you must not say such things."

"I don't expect to die, darling, but we must face the possibility. And children are a kind of immortality. Don't look so worried, my sweet. I love you, and of course I will come back to you. I expect to take very good care of myself—and you must promise me that you will be equally careful. Promise me, Miranda."

She nodded, not trusting her voice, not sure what this agreement was, conscious only that Richard was talking about death—and she shivered in sudden fear.

He was immediately protective, and he worried aloud about a possible draft and the danger of a sudden chill. And then, smiling, he reminded her they had a fireplace in their bedroom, and perhaps it was time to retire now.

Cort was not at home when they returned Sunday afternoon. Richard lingered for an hour on the front porch with the family—Tom had hobbled downstairs for the first time and was now enthroned like a king surrounded by devoted subjects. Miranda sat next to Richard on the porch swing, holding Polly on her lap, and he smiled at the two of them and told her she looked like a madonna. Miranda acknowledged the compliment, but she was uneasy and a little worried. Richard had already drawn her father aside for a private conversation, and she had seen Papa looking serious and concerned and, finally, convinced, nodding in agreement. And then they had shaken hands, as if sealing a bargain.

Richard stayed until the last possible moment, and he was in the front hall kissing her good-by when Cort sauntered in. Miranda stiffened immediately, and Richard looked up, resentful.

"Didn't mean to interrupt," Cort said, with a half smile for Miranda, and he followed them back to the front porch. He scooped up Polly in his arms, and she laughed in delight. "My best girl," he said, kissing her, but he looked beyond the child to Miranda, and she blushed.

As if to make amends, she followed Richard to his waiting carriage and kissed him again. "Take care of yourself, darling. And come back to me soon."

He patted her shoulder. "Write to me, Miranda. Write to me with good news."

Cort reacted to that command, but the rest of the family had scrupulously avoided watching or hearing their farewells.

"How wonderful he looks," Emily said. "You are like a tonic to him, Miranda. You must stay with us as long as his regiment is stationed at Falmouth. Perhaps he'll be able to come next week, too."

"Of course you must stay," Cort agreed. He had taken Richard's place next to her on the swing, and, with Polly between them, his hand came to rest on hers on the child's shoulder.

She pulled back quickly, and his smile was lazy, knowing.

"I think we should return to New York, Papa, don't you?"

Will looked surprised. "You can stay, Pet. I think I'll go back tomorrow, but there's no reason you can't take care of Tom until he's well enough to travel. Then you can come home together."

"No, Papa. I'll come with you. I know the work has piled up with both of us gone, and—"

"Don't trouble yourself with all of that, Pet. Richard has decided that you have been working too hard, and he has convinced me. I should never have expected you to be able to take over for Tom, and if it is taxing your strength and putting an unnecessary burden on your shoulders, when you should be devoting yourself to—"

"Papa, I'm fine, and you said I was doing a good job, and it's not fair of—"

"Miranda, let's not talk about it now." Will closed the subject, and there was an awkward silence that Emily groped to fill.

Slowly the conversation resumed around her, but Miranda seethed in quiet fury. It wasn't until the sun disappeared behind a cloud and Polly sneezed twice that they all realized how cool it was and that it was time to go indoors again and assist Tom back to his room.

Miranda examined his leg, which seemed to be healing nicely, and she changed the dressing. Tom declared he would be fully recovered in no time at all.

"I don't expect you to stay here, Miranda," he assured her. "And if you want to go back to New York tomorrow with Papa, I'll understand." He patted her hand. "I don't know why he let Richard talk him into dismissing you from your job, but I'll help you change his mind." His smile was confident. "He can't say no to both of us."

"Tom, that is very dear of you, and I'll be enormously grateful. I *will* feel bad about deserting you, but—"

"It's not that I'm noble, Miranda." He grinned at her. "It's just that I think Papa is dead wrong, and Richard, too, and I'm all for a little rebellion in the ranks."

Miranda looked at him with frank curiosity. "Does Richard order you around?"

"What do you think? He's a captain and I'm a lieutenant, and that's the way the army works. Don't misunderstand me. I think he's a first-class officer, and I have complete confidence in his judgment, which is more than I can say for most of the colonels and generals. But he *is* a stickler for detail, and I wouldn't cross him when he thinks he's right—which is most of the time." He smiled and reassured her. "He's crazy about *you*, of course, and besides, he's not exactly your commanding officer."

"No, not exactly," she agreed.

"I know you won't let him push you too far." Tom grinned at her again. "No one ever has. But I expect loud fireworks the first time he tries."

She nodded doubtfully, and her smile was forced.

At breakfast the next morning Cort was not really surprised to learn that Miranda was leaving with her father after all. While she was packing he walked boldly into her bedroom for a few last words in private.

"Of course I would rather have had you stay, darling."

She flinched at the endearment but otherwise tried to ignore him.

"However, I could tell that the tyrannical Captain Schuyler had overplayed his hand. He might be able to order you around while he is here, but there is no way he can exact obedience when you are in New York and he is off leading his gallant troops into battle."

"He is an excellent officer," Miranda said shortly.

"I would never deny it. He's a terrible husband, though, and—"

"*You* are a fine one to judge."

"*Touché*. However, he is *still* a terrible husband, and I am fascinated to observe that you are deceiving him already."

She was outraged. "I would never—"

"Oh, not with your body, although I haven't given up hope there. But you are deceiving him just the same. You haven't told him about the baby, and now that he is being so stupidly autocratic, ordering you around, you aren't going to."

"None of this is any of your business."

"I see you aren't denying it."

"Go away, Cort. You aren't part of my life anymore."

"Nonsense. You are going to need me more than ever. If you persist in this deception—and I don't advise it, by the way—then you will need a confidant."

"Papa will—"

"He'll be shocked, Miranda. He may not have been pleased with your choice of husband, but he is certainly going to be appalled to find out that your marriage is on such shaky ground that you aren't even telling Richard about your . . . delicate condition."

"I . . . am . . . perfectly . . . all . . . right." She spaced out the words for added emphasis. "I'm just not going to disrupt my whole life until I am absolutely sure. After what happened before—"

"What *did* happen, Miranda?"

"That's enough, Cort. I am not going to talk about this any more. If you really have some feeling for me that goes beyond . . . If that is really so, then you must let me work out these problems by myself and not make things so difficult for me."

He sighed. "After I criticized Richard for being a tyrant, *I* can hardly start giving you orders, too. But please, darling, if there is any way I can help . . ."

Silently she finished packing, trying to ignore him.

He lounged in the doorway, determined to break through to her. "*Think* of the ways I could help, Miranda. Perhaps I could provide a few more piano lessons for colored orphans. Violin lessons?" His voice was gently teasing. "Art? Sculpture? Architecture?"

A smile tugged at her lips.

"For the sake of sweet charity, Miranda, don't you think you should at least invite me to the next piano recital?"

"I didn't know you were a music lover," she said, finally acknowledging his presence again.

"I didn't know I was a philanthropist, either, until you took me in hand. You see what a good influence you are on me, darling. Expanding my world. Showing me the finer things of life."

She laughed. "You really are outrageous, Cort. Here. If you insist on doing something useful, you can strap up my trunk."

Will and Miranda departed an hour later in a flurry of hugs and kisses. Cort's lips had barely brushed her cheek, but she was still conscious of the pressure of his hand on her shoulder, conscious of the rapid pulse beating in her throat, and the butterfly touch of his fingertips there. Thank God she was escaping back to New York.

Chapter 24

IN SPITE OF Richard's advice, Miranda resumed all her activities full force, but she took care to appear calm and rested, particularly when she was around Aunt Faith. And Faith was sufficiently distracted by the approaching marriage of her daughter to spare Miranda her usual intense scrutiny.

Ann Schuyler was to marry Madison Bradley, Emily's brother, in a formal wedding at the end of June, and by the end of May, Miranda was thoroughly bored by all the endless talk about it. She could not get out of being in the bridal party, even though she pointed out, honestly enough, that she wouldn't be a bit hurt just to be a spectator. This was particularly true now that it was unlikely that Richard could come home for the wedding—the army was still licking its wounds after Chancellorsville, and every man was needed.

Tom was impatient to return to his regiment, but he was still limping, and the doctor said he should wait at least another month. In the meantime, Tom paced the lobby of the Stratford impatiently, making rude comments to young men not in uniform, and Will found it necessary to reprimand him sharply.

Miranda had a more practical remedy for his restlessness. Her friend Lucy Blaine was equally restless and unhappy and impatient with civilians—her fiancé, Robert Devlin, had died in a Confederate prison three months earlier. Miranda insisted that Tom call on her to cheer her up. He went unwillingly the first time, grumbling about the distance to Gramercy Park. He remembered Lucy as a silly schoolgirl, but it was amazing how much she had changed. He commented on it every time he went to see her—which was almost daily—and he found her in full agreement with all his views. What a bright, intelligent young woman she was! *She* was still intent on crushing this rebellion.

That was not a universal sentiment in May and June of 1863. As the war dragged on and the casualty lists lengthened and hope of final victory seemed as remote as ever, in the North there was a rising clamor for negotiated peace. At mass meetings in New York's Cooper Institute and Brooklyn's Academy of Music, there were cheers for the Copperheads and General McClellan and boos for President Lincoln and the continuation of the war.

With the decline in patriotic fervor, voluntary enlistments in the army fell off, and the government moved to enforce the draft legislation already on the books. All men between the ages of twenty and forty-five were enrolled and subject to call, but anyone whose name was pulled out of the drum could escape by paying three hundred dollars or hiring a substitute.

This policy was widely perceived as unfair, "a rich man's war and a poor man's fight." All across the country there was a rising level of protest, with scattered acts of violence: destruction of enrollment lists, mob attacks on registration officials, night riders firing shots, the assassination of provost marshals.

All this unrest was disquieting enough, but the real shock was to come.

While the Federal Army of the Potomac was regrouping after Chancellorsville, General Lee had his Army of Northern Virginia on the march again, heading north through Maryland. Always mindful that Washington City must be protected, Hooker swung his troops into position on Lee's flank, and for a while it looked as if Antietam would be a battleground again. But Lee kept moving, and by mid-June the New York newspapers were shrieking invasion. Pennsylvania was open to the Confederate advance, but whether the target was the state capital of Harrisburg or any of the towns stretching as far west as Pittsburgh, no one knew.

The state militias were summoned again, and Ann Schuyler wept bitter tears as the Seventh Regiment marched off once more, taking Madison Bradley and all her plans for a June wedding with him.

Miranda, who was caught up in the excitement of the approaching battle, nevertheless spared a thought for her own role in the postponed wedding. Her pregnancy was still a secret, but if enough time went by, she would never fit into that pale green dimity bridesmaid's dress to march up the aisle with Irene and Emily and Caroline.

She had started countless letters to Richard, each time planning to tell him the news he was longing to hear, but always she held back, feeling selfish and guilty—and threatened by a loss of freedom. Finally, on the eve of battle, her guilt overwhelmed her, and she could deny him no longer.

Monday, June 29, 1863

Dear Richard,

I have delayed giving you my wonderful news, wanting to be absolutely sure before I raised your hopes, but now I can tell you: We are going to have a baby, darling—in January, if all goes well. And now you are counting the months and wondering why I didn't say something to you in Washington when we were together. But I thought it was too soon to be sure, Richard, and perhaps I was almost superstitious about telling you—as if the gods would be angry when mere mortals are so happy.

I am being very careful, darling, eating and sleeping well, enjoying this beautiful June weather, and *not* working too hard. Truly. I saw your mother yesterday, and she complimented me on how well I look. I haven't told her my happy news yet, since I wanted *you* to be the first to know.

[Miranda pondered that misleading statement and argued with herself that it wasn't really a lie. Accidentally, she had already told Cort, but she had really *wanted* Richard to know first.]

Ann is terribly disappointed that her wedding has been postponed. The last we heard, the Seventh Regiment was in Maryland, but was to be rerouted to Harrisburg. The newspapers are filled with the wildest speculation, and of course the news today that General Hooker has been replaced by General Meade, right on the eve of this most crucial battle, has come as a terrible shock.

Do take care of yourself, Richard. I know that if *you* were in charge, we would have an enormous victory at Chambersburg or Gettysburg or wherever the armies happen to meet. Just don't try to win it all by yourself.

The papers have been announcing the fall of Vicksburg every other day for two months now, but it still stands. My own theory is that we will have two enormous victories simultaneously, in the west and in the east, and then the Confederacy will collapse and you will come home to me. Home by Christmas, darling. Will you still love me when I am so big around that I won't need hoops or crinolines to make my skirts flare out?

Everyone else is well. John was worried about the strike on the docks, and I think there was some violence when free Negroes were hired to replace the discontented Irish workers, but the strike was broken and it all seems to be peaceful now. I couldn't help having sympathy for *both* sides. Prices have gone up a lot, and it is only fair that wages should be brought into line. But John told me I don't understand business and finance, and I suppose he is right.

Massachusetts has opened a recruiting office for Negro soldiers right here in New York, and you'll never guess who was there: Major Jack Lorimer! He stopped off at the Stratford to see me (he hadn't known about our marriage), and he tells me that his fellow officers (all white) think the Negro soldiers will give a good account of themselves in battle: They have more to lose if they are captured! And it is thought that we won't have to draft so many white men if these new recruits fight well. Jack was jumped in rank from lieutenant to major when he agreed to transfer to this new all-black regiment.

One of the Negro soldiers came to the orphanage last week, and you should have seen the hero worship of all the children. He taught the boys some new words to "John Brown's Body," beginning "Mine eyes have seen the glory of the coming of the Lord!" Very inspiring. I wrote it all out for you and I am enclosing a copy. It says so well what this war is all about, and why it has been worth the terrible sacrifices we have all made.

Take care of yourself, darling, and come home to me.

Your devoted wife,
Miranda

For the next week all eyes were focused on Gettysburg, and the New York papers poured out a torrent of news. But so often had first reports of overwhelming victory proved worthless later that Miranda could hardly credit the truth this time. Only when she read a dispatch in the *Times* signed "C. Adams" did she allow herself to believe it was a triumph. Cort would be the last person to proclaim a nonexistent victory. The one good thing General Hooker had done, she thought, was make correspondents identify themselves, and now, even after he was gone, editors were still frequently attaching the names of reporters to the stories they had written. What had started as a means of fixing responsibility for false rumors or betrayal of secret information was now becoming accepted newspaper practice.

The most moving account of Gettysburg was signed not by Cort but by another *Times* correspondent, Samuel Wilkeson, whose nineteen-year-old son, an army lieutenant, had been killed there. Miranda read it and wept.

Who can write the history of a battle whose eyes are immovably fastened upon a central figure of transcendingly absorbing interest—the dead body of an oldest born, crushed by a shell in a position where a battery should never have been sent, and abandoned to death in a building where surgeons dared not stay? . . .

My pen is heavy. Oh, you dead, who at Gettysburg have baptized with your blood the second birth of Freedom in America, how you are to be envied! I rise from a grave whose wet clay I have passionately kissed, and I look up and see Christ spanning this battlefield with his feet and reaching fraternally and lovingly up to heaven. His right hand opens the gate to Paradise—with his left he beckons to those mutilated, bloody swollen forms to ascend.

Miranda read the casualty lists with dread, and it wasn't until the following Sunday that she breathed a sigh of relief when she recognized Richard's handwriting on the letter Cort had delivered to her.

"It nearly killed him to accept a favor from me," Cort told her, "but he was so eager to make sure that you received this promptly that he overcame his scruples."

"He's all right, isn't he? Not hurt?"

"Not a scratch," Cort confirmed.

She tore open the envelope hastily, conscious he was watching her every move—and her face was a mirror as she read Richard's letter with increasing dismay.

Saturday, July 11, 1863

My dear wife,

What wonderful but disturbing news you write to me. Wonderful, darling, because of course I am delighted that we are to have a child as soon as January. And wonderful, too, that you have been in good health, in spite of your foolish disregard of all my instructions.

But, Miranda, you should have told me immediately. How could you keep such important news to yourself, secret from your husband who loves you so much and wants nothing but your health and happiness. I am shocked, Miranda, by your deception—a harsh word, darling, but a true one. How can I trust you now when *you* did not trust *me?*

I think of those golden hours in Georgetown when I opened my heart to you and told you how much the war has affected all my perceptions of life and death—and I realize now that all the time you knew and didn't tell me.

I am heartsick, Miranda, and no explanation will satisfy me. Could you really be so selfish that you put your daily activities in New York ahead of your duty and love and responsibility to me and to our unborn child? I reject that thought, darling. And yet the alternative is equally unbearable—that you are so foolish and so superstitious and you understand me so little that you want to surprise me with secrets that should never have been hidden at all. Miranda, how would you feel if I kept *my* most important news from *you?* Suppose I had been wounded and didn't tell you until two months later. How would you react? Wouldn't you wonder with every letter what I am holding back from you?

Perhaps the kindest explanation is that in your delicate condition you are irresponsible, as a child is irresponsible, and in my absence you did not know what to do. And so, if you are a child, darling, I will treat you that way. It is a great pity that your dear mother died so long ago and that you cannot turn to her in this time of need. I realize that you find it difficult to confide in my mother, but now, Miranda, you must go to her for advice and counsel. And you must let her take you to a good doctor, and then you must follow all his instructions completely. You must let nothing interfere with this precious life you are carrying, and I don't want you to stir outside the Stratford without his express permission.

I wish I could be with you now and during all these next months while you grow increasingly precious to me, but the end of the war is not yet in sight. We have won a great victory at Gettysburg, but I fear that General Meade has no will to follow it up ruthlessly, and the battered Confederate Army has been allowed to slink away once more. There is still a hard road ahead of us, though our victory is inevitable.

Until I see you again, Miranda, follow my instructions, and begin to earn my trust again.

> Your devoted husband,
> Richard

"Bad news?" Cort asked, eying her curiously.

She shook her head, not meeting his gaze.

"Orders you don't want to obey, then," he guessed. "Of course! You finally told him about the baby, and he's confining you to quarters until next January. Don't let him do it, Miranda. Hasn't he heard about all those healthy peasant women who work in the fields until the last minute, produce their children, and then go right back to the harvest the next day?"

"He doesn't think I'm a peasant." Miranda's expression was wry.

"He doesn't know you as well as I do," Cort said with satisfaction. "Imagine trying to transform that glowing, passionate girl I love into a submissive—"

"Cort, if you are going to talk that way again, I simply won't have anything more to do with you. Why can't you just be a friend—the confidant you said I needed?"

"I will be all things to you, darling, including friend and confidant. What is the problem? Isn't he happy to be the father of your child?"

"Of course he is. But he's very upset that I didn't tell him before, and now he isn't going to trust me about anything, and he wants his mother to rule my life until he comes home."

"I'm afraid you're going to have to battle that one out yourself, Miranda, the way most women do. The accepted technique is to pretend to go along on the surface but to maneuver the man into letting you do whatever you like anyway."

"I'm no good at those games, Cort. I don't like to be devious—and Richard says in his letter that I have to start all over again to earn his trust."

"Well, then, my dear, I am afraid that for the moment you are trapped."

"But he wants me to give up everything and just stay home. Oh, I wish you hadn't brought me that letter. I wish you had lost it and never delivered it at all. How did you happen to find Richard anyway?"

"I was looking for heroes, and someone suggested his name."

"Truly?"

"Word of honor. But in the aftermath of the battle, he was disciplining some poor corporal for getting drunk and oversleeping, and it all seemed so petty that I didn't really want to hear about the great Captain Schuyler on the field of battle. He wouldn't have wanted to tell me, in any case. He was barely civil when I interrupted him with the corporal. And even when I told him that I was leaving almost immediately for New York and would be glad to take a letter to you, it took him a moment to collect himself and accept my offer. I talked to the corporal while Richard was writing to you, and I got an enlisted man's reaction to the battle. Very enlightening, but hardly suitable for a newspaper directed at loyal and patriotic readers."

"But it was a great victory, wasn't it?"

Cort sighed. "Yes, and Lee lost men and supplies that he'll never be able to replace. But Meade is like all the other Union generals—he doesn't follow through. The Rebels are getting away again, and they'll be holding those lines in Virginia, and I suppose we'll be fighting over all the same ground again—at Fredericksburg and the Wilderness and Bull Run."

Miranda sighed, too, as much for herself as for Cort's pessimistic attitude toward the war. "It's so silly for Richard to worry about me when *he* is the one in danger. And he's already so angry with me that I don't see how it could be any worse if I went right on ignoring his advice." She was so absorbed in her own arguments, convincing herself, that she was completely unaware of Cort's half smile of encouragement. "I guess I should tell Aunt Faith—and Papa, of course—but as long as I feel this well, I'm not going to give up *anything*. And then when it turns out that I'm right . . ."

"The healthy peasant," Cort repeated.

"That's right." Miranda was willing to accept the title this time. "Just because he thinks I'm a child, that doesn't mean I am. He isn't *always* right."

"Are you going to tell him that? I'd like to be the courier on the letter. It might bring on a stroke of apoplexy—and then you would be an enchanting widow, Miranda. I hope you have saved that black dress I gave you."

"You are supposed to forget all that, Cort, or I won't talk to you any more."

"It's a memory I cherish and always will. Have you forgotten, Miranda? Have you really forgotten?" His voice was an insistent caress. "When you like awake at night, and sleep won't come, and you relive all—"

"Healthy peasants sleep very well at night. That's why they're healthy in the first place. Now why don't you just go away and let me finish the papers in peace."

"Don't bother," Cort advised her. "There's nothing in them today but the names of everybody who is going to be drafted. Probably no one you know. Surely all your former beaux have already enlisted. And the ones who haven't can buy their way out for three hundred dollars."

"You think that's unfair, don't you?"

Cort nodded.

"I do, too, but John says that if he is called, he won't go. His three hundred dollars would pay the bounty for some volunteer, and John says that men who can afford to pay are probably more valuable in their civilian jobs than they would be as soldiers. And maybe that is true for him, but I can see why a poor man would object."

"I would object mightily," Cort agreed. "And I find it

amazing that the beginning of the draft went so smoothly yesterday. I thought New York harbored a nest of Copperheads. It just proves once again that you can't believe everything you read in the papers."

Chapter 25

THE FIRST DAY of the draft in New York had gone peacefully enough. But the next day, Sunday, when the names of the men called were printed in the papers, there was time to reflect on what it all meant, and in the Irish saloons in the dock areas, where the immigrants settled in for some serious afternoon drinking, the grumbling and discontent and anger mounted rapidly.

Whether there was ever an actual conspiracy directed by Confederate sympathizers has never been documented. But the tinder for a spontaneous revolt was everywhere. The rising prices of food and clothing had far outpaced the immigrants' wages, and housing was in such short supply that rents had more than doubled. There had been a rash of strikes that spring—shipwrights, longshoremen, barbers, tailors, leatherworkers, journeymen coopers. A war to preserve the Union had little interest for these men—and a war to free the slaves even less. Indeed, there was outright antagonism toward free Negroes, and the vision of a million former slaves coming north to compete for jobs inspired real fear. Negro laborers had already been used to break the strike on the docks in June, and there had been isolated acts of violence even then.

The political leadership hadn't been helpful, either. At a Fourth of July rally in the Academy of Music, at the very time the Union was scoring its stunning victories at Gettysburg and Vicksburg, Governor Seymour gave a long speech in which he censured the draft and seemed to encourage resistance to the law.

But what really infuriated a poor man was the knowledge

that the draft had stamped him with a price tag—and three hundred dollars was the difference between life and death.

Violence crackled just beneath the surface, and with twelve regiments of the National Guard still away in Pennsylvania, there was very little military force in New York to keep the peace. The police force, mostly Irish, numbered less than two thousand.

Monday dawned, hot and sultry, a perfect day for a picnic, a holiday, a festive parade through the streets—a perfect day to assemble a crowd, lead a strike, incite a mob to fury, launch an assault on draft headquarters, and unleash a rabble to riot and pillage and destroy.

From the docks the longshoremen and day laborers marched north, gathering new adherents as they forced lofts and workshops to close in unexpected holiday. Horsecars and omnibuses could not move through the choked streets, and drivers abandoned their vehicles to join the swelling throngs. In a vacant lot just south of the Central Park, they listened to harangues by militants, and then they flowed in massive strength to draft headquarters at Third Avenue and Forty-sixth Street, smashing windows, grabbing bottles, cutting the telegraph wires along the way. They looted and burned the draft office, and one woman was crushed to death in the melee.

A small group of policemen, hastily summoned to restore order, fired into the crowd, killing three men, leaving a woman dying. The enraged rioters turned on them in fury, and they were forced to flee for their lives. The superintendent of police, arriving to see for himself what was happening, was recognized, mobbed, and so badly mauled that he was believed to be dying when his body was relinquished to a passing stranger.

The extent of the riot was still unknown when a platoon of Invalid Corps troops, all convalescent veterans, was summoned to action from the bivouac near City Hall Park. They marched north with fixed bayonets, encountered the fringes of the mob at Third Avenue and Fortieth Street, and were promptly overwhelmed.

By this time, the mob was a hydra-headed monster, moving off in many directions, spawning new violence, new looting, new burning, for any reason, for no reason. A soldier, a policeman, anyone who was well dressed—they were all fair game. And, at the other end of the social spectrum, all Negroes were attacked on sight. By mid-afternoon, Marston's Gun Factory at Twenty-first Street and Second Avenue had been looted and fired, the railroad tracks on Eleventh Avenue were torn up, the Bull's Head Hotel on East Forty-fourth Street was gutted, cattle were stampeding in the streets, and the whole block on Broadway from Twenty-eighth to Twenty-ninth Street was ablaze.

Armed with axes and pickhandles and brickbats, a menacing crowd had collected on Fifth Avenue, and about four o'clock in the afternoon they surrounded the Colored Orphans' Asylum between Forty-third and Forty-fourth streets.

Miranda had arrived there that morning, together with her cousin Caroline and Caroline's grandmother, Mrs. Cantrell. That early in the day, their carriage ride had been uneventful, and they were only vaguely aware of rumors of trouble elsewhere in the city. It would never have occurred to them to stay home, and they would have scoffed at the idea of danger.

Indeed, Miranda's spirits had never been higher. She had started a long letter to Richard, an even-tempered but absolutely firm declaration of independence, with only the lightest gloss of apology for not having confided in him before. She told him again how much she admired him, she reminded him of his promises before they were married, and she insisted that, since he had known her all her life, it wasn't fair of him to expect her to change so radically just because her name was Schuyler now, not Chase. Perhaps, as Tom has predicted, there would be fireworks, but that might be rather exciting, and she looked forward to it—just as she now looked forward to this hot summer day, surrounded by children who welcomed her with open arms and warm affection.

That afternoon one of the little girls confided that *she* wanted to grow up and give piano lessons to orphans, too. Miranda smiled and hugged her and sent her off with two gold stars instead of one.

By three o'clock, an unnatural hush had descended on the orphanage, and Miranda looked up, startled, when Mrs. Cantrell hurried into the front parlor and said that all lessons were over for the day. "We found out what happened to the matron in the infirmary," she explained.

"I didn't know anything had happened," Miranda was baffled.

"She didn't come to work today," Mrs. Cantrell said. "She was beaten by a mob on Second Avenue and barely got away. And her son, who brought us the message—he's very light skinned, and I suppose that's how he got through the crowd—he says he saw a Negro being lynched down on Horatio Street. I'm going to the nearest police station—I think we need some protection here—and you and Caroline should come with me."

"But nobody in his right mind would ever attack *children*," Miranda protested.

"Nobody in a mob even *has* a mind," Mrs. Cantrell contradicted her.

"Well, I think we'll be much safer staying right here and not going out to look for trouble in the streets."

"I pray you are right, Miranda, but I still think we should get some police protection—and fire protection, too—and I would feel safer with you and Caroline with me when I set out on this expedition."

"Take Caroline, then. I am staying here. If that crowd starts coming in this direction, just seeing a young white woman on the premises might help bring them to their senses. If I am here, and the superintendent, and all the other white members of the staff . . ."

Mrs. Cantrell nodded dubiously, adjusted her bonnet, and pulled on her gloves. Afterward, when she departed with Caroline, Miranda felt the first ripples of fear.

The minutes ticked by slowly.

Half hidden by the drapes, Miranda peered from the parlor window at the mob gathering on Fifth Avenue. As yet no one had ventured through the gate to the gravel carriage path, but already part of the wooden fence had buckled under the pressure of the crowd; and, even as she watched, a dozen men surged through, breaking off the pickets as makeshift weapons.

"Mrs. Schuyler! Why are you still here?" It was Mrs. Davis, the wife of the superintendent, and she had paused in the doorway, shocked to discover Miranda. "Come away from the window—they'll be throwing rocks at any minute!"

Miranda pulled the drapes shut hastily, restoring the room

to its usual gloom. "Can't anyone stop them? Where are the police?"

Mrs. Davis shook her head. "I don't know. They haven't come. But a few firemen got through, and one of them is trying to calm the crowd, at least until we get everyone out." She was systematically inspecting all the rooms, rounding up stray children and members of the staff, and Miranda followed her.

"I'll help," she volunteered. "I'll check the dormitories one last time."

"Tell the girls to go to the dining room," Mrs. Davis instructed her, "and send the boys to the back piazza. Most of them are there now."

Miranda nodded her understanding and raced to the top floor. At first glance it seemed to be completely deserted: The long line of neatly made little beds was empty, no one lurked behind the wardrobes, no one answered her call. She peered in every alcove and opened every door and was ready to abandon her search, but there was one last passage leading to an attic storage room. She flung open the door and was startled to find two little girls, paralyzed with fear, clutching each other. They had been cowering in the darkness, and they blinked in the sudden light and burst into tears. Miranda couldn't remember their names—they were sisters, she thought, and new to the orphanage—and they looked at Miranda as if she were some strange apparition from another world.

"It will be all right," Miranda said, trying to soothe them. "Don't be frightened. You must come with me to the dining room. All the little girls are there. You'll be safe there. We'll all be safe there."

They looked at her, uncomprehending, and the older girl screamed when Miranda reached out to touch her.

"I won't hurt you," Miranda said, surprised when the child cringed. "I want to help you. We must find the others . . ." Her voice trailed off, and she was conscious of the distant sound of glass shattering and the triumphant shriek of a woman's voice. They would be breaking in any minute, and there was no time for reasoned explanations.

"You *must* come," Miranda repeated, and she seized the younger child in her arms and determinedly pulled her away.

The little girl was wide-eyed with terror and unresisting,

but her older sister reacted with fury and hurled herself at Miranda, clawing at her arms.

"*I* take care of Reba," she screamed. "I *always* take care of Reba."

"Well, you're not doing a very good job of it," Miranda said. "Let me go."

The child was beside herself with rage, clutching at Miranda, who was finding it difficult to cross the room, carrying Reba, warding off the sister as best she could.

Reecee, Miranda remembered her name now. Mrs. Cantrell had said something about the girls when they were admitted in June. They were from the South, originally, and their mother had made a precarious living as a laundress; and when she died of tuberculosis, Reecee had fought desperately to stay on in their hovel near Five Points. She would kill herself, she had said dramatically, and her sister, too. They would *never* be sold into slavery. What strange ideas children had. This was the North, and they were free, and no one was going to hurt them. Surely no one was going to hurt any of them.

A brick crashed through the window on the landing, and Miranda clutched the child in her arms, and Reecee stopped dead in her tracks.

They had reached the second floor, and Miranda paused at the top of the broad staircase, conscious of the silence within the orphanage and the rising clamor outside. The rioters were on the porch now, she was sure, and any moment they would begin climbing through the shattered windows, breaking through the heavy oak door. Surely those thudding blows were the sound of an axe . . .

Beside her Reece shivered suddenly and cried out. "They lynch us?" She turned to Miranda, her voice rising in hysteria. "They catch us and they lynch us!"

"No, Reecee! No!"

"They lynch my Pa. I seen it. He run away and they catch him and I seen it. They pull off all his clothes and they take a knife and they cut him and the blood run down his leg . . ." She was babbling, crying, trailing off into incoherence and finally subsiding into a forlorn heap at the top of the stairs.

Miranda looked at her, horrified. "No, Reecee, please. It will be all right. You must come with me. In the dining room . . ." But that was definitely an axe breaking through at the front door. They could never go this way.

"The back stairs," Miranda said, pulling Reecee to her feet. "Hurry, hurry."

The child stared at her, unseeing, and immediately slumped to the floor again when Miranda released her. Reba was a deadweight in her arms, and she could never carry Reecee, too. "Please." Miranda was half crying. "We *have* to go, Reecee!"

The child was glazed with terror, unreachable.

Deliberately, crying with frustration, Miranda slapped her, twice, and Reecee gave her a look of pure hatred. But she was galvanized into action at last, and she reached the empty dining room two steps ahead of Miranda, who was still carrying Reba and panting from the exertion. The child was growing heavier by the minute, and Miranda moved on leaden feet through a nightmare of noise and confusion and fear.

"Nobody here," Reecee said accusingly.

"Through that door. I see them in the backyard. Hurry."

Under the protection of a dozen volunteer firemen, the children and staff were being led away from the orphanage, which was open now to the ravagers. Miranda could hear the sound of wood splintering and glass breaking as the mob thundered through the building. The first looters were already carrying off carpets, stools, chairs, dishes, iron bedsteads—anything they could get their hands on. What they couldn't carry off, they pitched from the windows or demolished in place. Fifth Avenue was strewn with books and papers. From the front parlor came a jangling discord as they attacked the grand piano with an axe, the repeated deliberate blows reducing it to kindling wood. Kindling . . .

And then, unmistakably, Miranda was aware of the smoke. Nothing terrified her more. From the deepest recesses of her memory, the panic clutched her again—the smell of smoke, the sight of flames, the sudden paralyzing fear.

The rioters had set the building on fire even before they could cart off all the furniture or throw it, in a rage of vindictiveness, to shatter on the ground. A heavy bureau crashed down, killing a white child on the fringes of the crowd, and a mother's shriek cut through the clamor. But the shock of sudden death had no effect, no effect at all.

Upstairs in the dormitories someone had found the children's clothes and was hurling them from the front window, festooning the trees with pinafores and drawers and socks and shirts. But the trees were not to escape the fury of the mob, either. Three men with axes were systematically attacking the elms and the maples, girdling the trunks, making sure they would all die. The shrubs had long since been trampled into the ground, and no trace remained of the neat picket fence, the lovingly tended flower beds. The infirmary was blazing now, and the workshops, and the superintendent's house. It was almost a miracle that the children had been spared, and Miranda watched numbly as Reecee and Reba joined the procession being led away to the nearest police station.

As if in a trance she gazed at the burning building, and she was ten years old again, and her whole world was on fire, and Cordelia was rushing toward her, pulling her to safety, half carrying her through the smoke-filled halls, turning back to see if Jimmy was safe. The same acrid smell, the same raging flames out of control, the harsh and jolting rumble as a floor collapsed, and the final devastation when the roof caved in and the flames shot up triumphantly, engulfing the ruins.

She wouldn't cry, she told herself. She would just take Papa's hand. Instinctively, she reached out . . . But that man wasn't Papa. That was some sweaty black-haired youth, gaping at the blazing ruins, and he turned now and looked at her and grasped her arm in an iron grip.

"Excites you now, does it?" He leered at her and drained the bottle he was holding in his other hand.

She recoiled in horror, but he wiped his mouth and pulled her into his arms. "Sure, you've come to the right man. Pat Corcoran knows just what to do with a girl like you." He kissed her, and she gagged at the taste of raw whiskey and fought desperately to escape his embrace.

"Sure, and it's a little wildcat you are."

She clawed at him and screamed, but the only person who even noticed was another youth, so much like Pat Corcoran that he could have been his younger brother—which, indeed, he was.

"You've got a beauty there, Pat," he said approvingly.

"Aye," Pat agreed, pinning Miranda's hands to her sides and holding her at arm's length to admire her. "A beauty. And a little tease, too. She came up to me, as bold as brass, and put her hand on my arm, just begging me."

"No, please," Miranda cried. "Let me go. You don't understand. I'm married and I—"

"The married ones are the best, Tim. She's just what we're looking for. There's trouble with the single girls. They come running after you, pointing to their bellies, but she's perfect. She's the one we'll take home."

"But if Ma is there, and the girls . . ."

"No. Not today. Nobody's home today. Just you and me and our little friend here."

"You mean you'll let me have her, too?"

"Sure, and why not? It's time you got started, and I'll show you. Why, she'll even like it, once I get her in the spirit of the thing. Came up to me as bold as brass—"

"No!" Miranda cried. "You can't. I'm going to have a baby and I—"

Swiftly, calmly, Pat Corcoran slapped her twice on the face, two quick blows that staggered her and left her speechless.

"That's enough," he commanded her. "Next time you'll feel my fist. You just be nice to us, and we won't hurt you— no more than a man ever hurt a woman."

"But I'm going to have a *baby!*" Miranda protested.

"Glad to hear it," Pat said approvingly. He looked at Tim and winked. "Now she can't ever blame us!" He roared with laughter, and Tim joined in.

Miranda seized her chance, twisted out of his grasp, and plunged into the crowd. They were after her immediately and caught up with her just as she lunged for safety to the only symbol of authority she could find—a man with the axe and helmet of a volunteer fireman. He had his back to her, watching the orphanage burn to the ground. After the children had been evacuated, the firemen had made no attempt to save the buildings, knowing they were powerless in this situation.

"Please," Miranda grasped his arm. "You must help me."

There was something familiar about him, but he looked at her blankly, and he saved his greeting for Pat and Tim, grinning at them. "I should have known you two would be here. Never a bit of a dust-up without the Corcoran boys. You held a torch here, did you?"

"I wish I had. A grand blaze it was, and now we're celebrating."

315

Miranda shook her head in disbelief and clutched at the fireman when Pat Corcoran tried to pull her away.

"So, Kevin," Pat was saying, "if you just hand over the little lady, we'll be off."

The young fireman grinned at them. "A bit of sport, is it?" He looked at Miranda, and she stared at him with sudden recognition.

"Kevin? Why, you're Kevin Kelly!"

"Aye, that's my name. Are you inviting me to come, too? I might just do that. I was never one to say no to—"

"Kevin Kelly, you have to protect me!"

He looked at her blankly.

"Don't you remember me? Miranda Chase. Miranda Chase Schuyler, it is now. I went to your wedding, and my father owns the Stratford, and if you don't save me from these two, these two . . ." Words failed her. "If Colonel Stetson ever found out that you didn't come to my rescue . . . And my father would—"

"Good Lord!" Kevin stared at her, and for a moment she was afraid he'd refuse. He hesitated, looking her up and down, weighing the odds, and then he sighed and shook his head regretfully. "She's off limits, boys. I know who she is, and I can't let you have her. Go find your fun somewhere else."

"But she came up to me, bold as brass," Pat Corcoran protested. "I don't give a damn who her father is. I found her, and she's mine." He grabbed her and tore her away from Kevin and pushed her, staggering and off balance, into Tim's arms. "Hold her," he commanded his brother, and he turned his attention back to Kevin.

Miranda lunged to escape, but Tim tripped her and they rolled on the ground, struggling. He was a slight, pimply-faced youth, no more than fifteen, surely, and he was awkward and excited and, as he fought with Miranda, clearly aroused. Pat Corcoran and Kevin Kelly had squared off and were going after each other with bare fists, but Tim was an alley fighter, and when Miranda hit him and her rings opened a gash along his cheek, he reacted with fury and pummeled her into submission, tearing at her clothes as she fought to get away from him. She was losing, and she knew it, and she was close to blacking out when someone threw half a bucket of water on both of them, calming Tim and bringing her back to full consciousness, coughing and sputtering.

"Here now, you two, this is no place for such carryings on."

Miranda clutched at her gaping bodice, bewildered, and she looked up at the disapproving man in clerical black. He was a priest, she realized, and the only symbol of authority likely to be heeded by this throng of people. Kevin Kelly was standing beside him, as wet and bedraggled as she was, but Pat Corcoran seemed to have disappeared.

"You're a disgrace," the priest said to her, to all of them. "Every one of you, a disgrace. Go home and pray to God for forgiveness for what you've done here. And you," he said to Miranda, "with this boy, on the ground, like animals!"

"No!" She was outraged. "I've never seen him before, and when he attacked me . . ."

The priest shook his head, clearly not believing her.

"I'll take care of her," Kevin said.

Miranda sighed gratefully.

"Is this man your husband? He was in a vicious fight— over you, I suppose. If you give him reason to be jealous—"

"No, please, you don't understand," Miranda began. "He's not—"

"That's all right, father," Kevin cut in. "Let's not bother him with long explanations, Miss Chase. Miranda," he amended hastily and grinned at her. "I'll take you home now."

She looked at him doubtfully.

"Home to the Stratford," he said.

"Oh, yes, please!" She turned and followed him eagerly, clutching her dress with one hand, trying to hold his arm with the other. She was limping and panting with the exertion of trying to keep up with him. Somewhere, she realized, she had lost her reticule as well as her bonnet, and she probably looked dreadful. Her hair was straggling, and she was bruised and dirty and wet and miserable, but with Kevin beside her she was safe. And surely if she looked completely disreputable, no one would attack her now.

He was half a step ahead of her, forcing his way through the crowd, and she struggled to stay at his heels.

"Please, wait. Stop a minute. I'm losing my shoe. And I'm going to have to rest. Isn't there any way we can get out of this crowd and find a carriage?"

"A carriage?" He laughed. "My dear Miss Chase, we're having a war in the streets and you think you can hail a carriage?"

"But, somewhere there must be . . . Is it like this all over New York?"

"Every part of it I've seen today," Kevin said. They had crossed Forty-second Street, and she was out of breath and feeling faint, and they paused before the Croton Reservoir. The crowd had thinned out here but there was no place to rest except on the ground.

"Can't you keep going?" he asked her. "It's a long hike to the Stratford, but I thought if I delivered you to your father myself . . ."

"But that's miles," Miranda protested. "I can't walk all that way." Somehow the heel on her shoe had broken off, and she realized that was why she had been limping.

Kevin stood glaring down at her, clearly impatient. "Well, I certainly can't carry you."

"You aren't going to leave me?" There was a note of panic in her voice, and she realized suddenly how dependent on him she was. He blurred and swayed, standing there, and she shook her head to clear her vision and to keep from fainting. It was hot, so terribly hot, and she felt queasy, as if she were going to be sick. The street shimmered with heat, and the sun was a blazing red fire in the west. In the west. It was afternoon then, late afternoon. Strange—she'd lost all sense of time. How many hours of daylight left? How many miles to the Stratford before it got dark? She could never make it.

She had used up her strength rescuing Reba and Reecee, and she had barely survived that encounter with the Corcorans. Tim had hit her repeatedly, and she was bruised and sore. All her body was sore. He had used his fists on her, and she was conscious again of those fierce blows below the waist, where there was pain now. The baby, she thought suddenly. Dear God, the baby. If I lose this child . . . And what would Richard say? She struggled to her feet.

"I can walk a few blocks," she said, "if you help me."

"A few blocks?. And then where would we be?"

That was a puzzle. Where? Somebody lived near. Somebody. Why, of course. Lucy Blaine. But could she really make it as far as Gramercy?

Kevin didn't think so. He continued to stare at her, and she could see he was sizing her up and reaching a decision. "I'll take you home," he said. "Maybe that's a better way to do it. Yes."

She looked at him uneasily. "What do you mean?"

318

"I live just a few blocks from here." He gestured vaguely toward the west, toward the river. "You come with me and I'll take you home. Kathy can take care of you, and then I'll go tell your father where you are. He ought to be very grateful to me."

There was something the matter with his offer, but she couldn't puzzle it out.

"Come on. What are you waiting for?"

"I want to go to Lucy's."

"Well, I'm not taking you there. We'll do this my way, or we won't do it at all."

She still hesitated, and he sighed.

"What's the matter? You think I'm going to rape you or something? I could have gone with the Corcoran boys if that's all I wanted from you."

"But you have to help," Miranda protested. "My father, and Colonel Stetson . . ."

"Yes, yes, yes," Kevin said. "I know all about your father and Colonel Stetson. Now are you coming with me or not?" He stared at her impatiently and then turned on his heel and started west on Forty-second Street.

I could go to Lucy's, Miranda was thinking. If I take it slowly and I don't have to fight my way through a crowd . . .

Two drunks were staggering toward her, and she retreated abruptly and looked around, hoping to see a policeman. There was no one to turn to, no one but Kevin, and he had paused a few yards away to see if she was following him. She sighed and acknowledged her defeat, and he came back to help her.

"Sure, you've made the right choice. I'm not going to hurt you, and Kathy will take care of you while I go find your father."

Miranda nodded, accepting his decision. She was feeling faint again, and she clutched his arm in sudden panic. "How far is it?"

"Not far. Not far." It seemed forever, and he half carried her the last two blocks. Miranda was conscious only of a mounting wave of nausea, and she knew she was going to be sick. Kevin held her head while she vomited into a gutter, and she clung to him, terrified. "The baby . . ."

Kevin looked at her, surprised. "Sure, the baby's all right. A fine little boy. He's a month old now, and Kathy—"

"No," Miranda protested. "*My* baby."

But he thought she was delirious, and he carried her across the street and up the stairs, and she fainted as soon as Kathy opened the door.

She came back to consciousness with Kathy washing her face and weeping over her. "Oh, Miss Miranda, please wake up. Please."

Miranda's eyelids fluttered and she struggled to hold on to reality, to escape the threatening darkness.

"I sent for Ma, and she knows about nursing, but you're bleeding, and I don't know what to do."

Miranda was seized by an agonizing cramping pain, terrifyingly familiar, and Kathy handed her a square of cotton—why, it was a baby's diaper! She tried to staunch the bleeding, but she knew it was too late. It was just like the last time. A relief it had been before, but now . . . Oh God, what was happening to her? Maybe she had done something to herself the first time, and now she would never be able to carry a child. The tears trickled down her cheeks, and Kathy stared at her, wide-eyed and frightened. And for Miranda, the world went black again.

Chapter 26

I N THE PALE dawn light, when Miranda emerged into consciousness again, a strange woman was hovering over her anxiously.

"Ah, you're awake at last. No, don't try to talk. Water? Here, I'll give you a sip of water. Sure, you're going to be all right. Yes, you will. It's a pity about the child, but I lost my first one that way, too. You'll be all right."

Miranda swallowed slowly, blinking back her tears. "Who are you?"

"Sure, I'm Mrs. Flaherty. Kathy's mother."

"Kathy's mother," Miranda echoed, trying to sort out what had happened.

"Kevin brought you here," Mrs. Flaherty explained. "He rescued you, he did, from that nigger asylum." She shook her head. "You shouldn't be mixing with the likes of them, child. Savages, all of them. Right out of the trees."

"No," Miranda protested. "It wasn't like that. There was a fire."

"Aye," Mrs. Flaherty agreed. "There was a fire, and then they attacked you, and Kevin saved you. He told us, and he's gone to tell your father. He rescued you, he did, and Kathy is so proud of him."

"The fire . . ." Miranda began again, but she trailed off. There was no use trying to explain. She didn't have the strength to contradict the story. Mrs. Flaherty disappeared, saying something about breakfast, and Miranda nodded. She stared curiously around the cramped little room, the whitewashed walls, the brightly painted crucifix, the double bed and the bureau crowding up against the washstand with the giant blue pitcher. Through the window she could see a courtyard strung with clotheslines, and already the morning sun was baking down, turning the enclosure into a blazing oven. She was hot, she realized, though she was wearing only a loose cotton wrapper—Kathy's, she supposed—and she was covered by an old muslin sheet. But she was clean and safe and being taken care of. Kevin was right in a way—he *had* rescued her. But where was he? And if he had gone to get Papa . . . Why, that was last night. Papa should have been here hours ago, even if he had had to walk every step of the way.

Kathy appeared in the doorway carrying her baby, and Miranda dissolved into tears. She had helped to save that child, and she couldn't save her own. And Richard! He would be so unhappy, so disappointed in her. Heartsick, he had said in his letter. He would think she had deliberately disobeyed him, and he would be so angry, Miranda turned away, trying to hide her tears.

Kathy put a timid hand on her arm. "Don't you want to see him? My little Kevin. He's such a beautiful little boy."

Miranda nodded, trying to smile. "Beautiful," she agreed, and her voice cracked.

"Oh, you poor darling." Kathy kissed her impulsively. "It's terrible about your baby. But *you* are safe. Wasn't Kevin wonderful? Saving you from all those savages!"

"Saving me," Miranda repeated and looked at Kathy, so full of pride and love. It would be foolish to try to explain. Miranda sighed. "Where is Kevin now, Kathy? And why hasn't my father come?"

"Kevin's at work," Kathy said. "And I don't know about your father. But we'll take care of you until he gets here. Don't worry. Ma doesn't think you should be moved for a while. If the bleeding should start again . . ."

Miranda nodded, but a small cloud of worry was starting to form. If Papa knew where she was, he'd be here by now, with Tom beside him. Yes, and Cort, too, if only they knew about her. Why, they'd be frantic with worry when she didn't get back yesterday. They would know about the orphanage burning to the ground—surely that was in the papers this morning. Or *were* there papers this morning? Had the whole city gone mad?

Slowly, dutifully, she ate the bowl of oatmeal Mrs. Flaherty brought to her, washing it down with a cup of milky tea. She asked them about the destruction in the city, about the mobs rioting in the streets, but they looked at her and shook their heads. It was bad, they knew, but nothing had happened in their few blocks, and Kevin had warned them to stay close to home. They weren't going to go looking for trouble.

"The newspapers," Miranda said tentatively, but they didn't usually bother with newspapers. Oh, two days ago they had bought one because Kevin's name was in it—he was on the list of men to be drafted. Kathy brought in a Sunday *Herald* to show to Miranda. Kevin was going to buy his way out, she said, if he could just get hold of some more money. They had forty dollars saved, and he hoped to borrow the rest.

And that explained it, Miranda realized. Kevin needed money, and in her rescue he had seen a way to get it. And Papa would pay—of course he would pay. But he should be here by now. If Kevin had reached the Stratford . . . She couldn't puzzle it out. Unless he hadn't gotten through. Suppose Kevin had tangled with the rioters or the police or the soldiers . . . She looked at Kathy, placidly nursing the baby, and she wondered if that thought had occurred to her.

"Didn't Kevin come home last night?" Miranda asked.

"No, he decided not to bother," Kathy explained. "He said it would take so long to get downtown—he had to walk, you know, because there are no cars or anything—and he thought he'd stay there. He starts work every morning at eight o'clock, and he said it would be foolish to walk home again and then turn right around and go back."

There was a kind of logic in that, Miranda supposed. Still, if he had gone right to Papa . . . There was something the matter; she just knew it. Maybe Papa had been caught in the riots!

As the day wore on and the sun glared down, the little room accumulated heat like an oven. Miranda turned and twisted uncomfortably, restless and worried and hot, so terribly hot. She was feverish, panting, the edges of reality blurring as she slipped into fitful sleep and haunted dreams and emerged again into a twilight of consciousness where there was only heat and misery and dimly perceived pain. Somewhere a baby was crying fretfully, and she reached out for him, confused. Was it her child? She should comfort him, save him, save him from all this heat. Hot as any fire it was. An inferno of fire. The orphanage was burning to the ground, and Cordelia had gone back to find Jimmy. But she was dead. No, Jimmy was dead. He was in the hospital and Damon . . . It was all so confusing, and the baby was fretting in this terrible heat. And where had everyone gone? Why had they all gone away and left her? It was dangerous to be alone. She had been alone in Washington, and Cort . . . . And now she was having his baby and he wasn't here, and she missed him so. She fell into another troubled sleep, haunted this time by Richard and some faceless child, a crying child who whimpered and hid from her. And Richard was angry, so angry with her and the crying baby, and he was accusing her of something dreadful. So dreadful she didn't even know what it was. She looked at him, bewildered, and then she saw the child clearly for the first time. A little boy, a dear little boy, and he had Cort's eyes. He smiled at her, and she was just reaching out to hold him when he disappeared, and she was roused to consciousness again. The baby was crying, Kathy's baby. And she was panting in the heat, and she had had a miscarriage, and Papa still wasn't here to rescue her.

The shadows were lengthening again, and Miranda stirred, half asleep and dreaming. Surely she was dreaming. That was Cort's voice coming from the next room, and Kathy was answering him, a puzzled Kathy, telling him Kevin wasn't here. Cort was disappointed, but he was thanking her and asking how to find him. Miranda listened, bewildered, and she cried out, but they didn't hear her. He would go away, and he wouldn't know she was here. He was so close, and he was leaving.

The baby whimpered again, and Kathy moved to soothe him, and Miranda gathered her strength and called out for Cort and staggered to her feet. She fell, and he heard her, and he was across the room in three strides, lifting her, holding her, turning on Kathy in cold fury.

"What have you done to her? Why is she here?"

Kathy clutched the baby in her arms, and she stared at Cort in blank amazement. Mrs. Flaherty rushed in from the kitchen, and she was furious with this stranger.

324

"Here, who are you? Put that poor girl back in bed where she belongs. She's had a miscarriage and—"

"Oh, my dearest." Cort cradled her in his arms. "We have been so worried about you. I didn't know until this morning that you were missing, but—"

"Here, now," Mrs. Flaherty protested. "Put her back in bed. She'll be bleeding again."

"Yes, darling, she's right." Miranda reached up to touch his cheek, to make sure he was really there. "But stay with me, Cort. Please stay with me. And tell me what's happened."

He tucked her into bed and sat down beside her, holding her hand. Kathy and Mrs. Flaherty looked on, surprised, perhaps even disapproving.

Miranda was beyond caring what they thought, what anyone thought. Cort was here, and he loved her, and he would save her. She looked up at him and smiled, and for a moment they locked out the world.

And then the baby cried, and Miranda was conscious again of why she was here, and her eyes glistened with tears. Cort sighed and touched her cheek in a caress as gentle as a kiss.

"How did Kevin find you, darling? I thought he was going to Papa."

Cort looked at her blankly. "I didn't see Kevin at all. I got his name from one of the volunteer firemen. I hardly knew where to start looking for you when you weren't with the children at the police station. And Mrs. Cantrell didn't even know you were missing. So I've been searching out all the firemen who were there, hoping one of them might have seen you, noticed you . . . Oh, my darling, are you going to be all right? I know how much you wanted this baby."

"Sure, and are you her husband?" Mrs. Flaherty looked at Cort, and her earlier disapproval melted into sympathy.

"But he's not her cousin," Kathy objected. "I've seen Richard Schuyler often enough to know—"

"He's a friend," Miranda cut in. "An old friend of the family."

Cort introduced himself, but Mrs. Flaherty looked from him to Miranda, doubting them both.

Kathy was simply bewildered. And then, suddenly, she was frightened. "But what has happened to Kevin? If he went straight to see your father . . ."

Cort looked at her, surprised, and Miranda explained that Kevin should have been at the Stratford last night. He could have covered the distance in less than two hours, surely, even with the crowds.

"There was a mob there last night," Cort said slowly, "packing City Hall Park and Printing House Square."

"The Stratford!" Miranda exclaimed. "Did they break in? Was anyone hurt?"

"No, not there," Cort soothed her. "They are all safe, Miranda. I saw your father this morning. No, the mob was after the newspapers, the *Tribune* particularly. They would have lynched Mr. Greeley if they had caught him, and he had to run for his life. Why, we had a regular battle in the streets. I was there. I even had a rifle in my hands." He shook his head, scarcely crediting it even now.

Miranda looked at him, wide-eyed, suddenly frightened for him. "You were in danger?"

"I don't think I had time to worry about it," Cort said. "I was caught up in the madness, along with everyone else. God, you should have seen Mr. Raymond and Leonard Jerome!" An echo of last night's excitement was in his voice, and he almost laughed. "Somehow they had procured a couple of mitrailleuses from the army. Breech-loading machine guns," he explained. "Experimental models, I think they are, and we set them up in the front windows of the *Times,* ready to shoot down anyone who came close. You'd have thought we were defending the Alamo, ready to die to the last man."

Miranda gazed at him in astonishment. This was New York. Her New York. Why, if she had been at home she could have seen the whole battle from her own bedroom.

"They didn't attack the *Times,*" Cort went on. "Mr. Raymond sent sixteen of us, armed with rifles, over to help protect the *Tribune.* The police were there—one hundred of them, maybe two hundred. Guns and billy clubs against a rabble of thousands. They broke into the *Tribune* offices, smashed all the windows, demolished all the furniture on the first floor . . . But they didn't get to the presses," he said with satisfaction. "The paper came out this morning, right on schedule."

"And all the people. What happened to them?"

"Luckily, the thunderstorm rather dampened their enthusiasm." He saw her puzzled look. "You didn't hear it?"

"I heard it," Mrs. Flaherty answered him. "Before midnight, it was. But this poor child was in no condition last night to hear anything that was going on in the world."

"Yes." Cort looked at Miranda again and touched her forehead to see if she were feverish.

"I'm better, Cort, truly, now that you are here."

"But Kevin," Kathy said again. "What can have happened to him? He was going straight to the Stratford. He thought, he thought . . ." She trailed off, sounding a little ashamed.

"What is it, Kathy?" Miranda looked at her with sympathy. "What did Kevin tell you?"

"He said . . . He wanted to . . . Oh, Miss Miranda, we *do* need the money, you know, and I don't know how we'll get along if Kevin has to go into the army. The men who are drafted can't even collect a bounty."

"Yes, Kathy, I understand. I guessed. He was hoping Papa would give him a reward. And Papa will. I know he will. I'll tell him myself."

"Oh, thank you! That's wonderful of you. This is the second time you've saved me."

"Well, you saved me, you know." Miranda smiled at her. "And Kevin, too," she acknowledged, and she explained to Cort what had happened to her yesterday.

He listened with growing horror, but one part of him was brooding on something else, and it wasn't until Kathy followed her mother into the kitchen that Cort voiced his suspicions aloud.

"It's extortion, Miranda, and maybe worse, and I want to get you out of here."

"What are you talking about? Oh, I know it's petty and nasty of him to rescue me just for the money he hopes to get from Papa. But he *did* get me away from those bullies, Cort, and Papa can afford to give him three hundred dollars to buy his way out of the draft. But if he didn't reach the Stratford at all . . ."

"I think he did, Miranda. I think that's where the note came from."

"What note? What do you mean?"

"This morning, when I got back to the Stratford . . . I hadn't known you were missing, darling, and I had been at the *Times* all night. It is not very comfortable trying to sleep half sprawled against a wooden desk." He smiled at her, pure mischief in his eyes. "I'm used to better beds than that."

327

She blushed, and it was a mark of her recovery that she could tease him, too. "You look terrible, Cort, with so little sleep, and you haven't shaved, and you have a streak of grease on your arm and a smudge on your cheek. And where did you ever get that terrible shirt! I've never seen you in anything so disreputable."

"But it's all part of my disguise," he said in an injured voice. "So I can blend in with the crowds. Of course if you'll only allow yourself to be rescued by a freshly scrubbed knight on a white charger, I suppose I could just go away."

"Don't you dare!" She clutched his hand in both of hers, and he smiled at her, and kissed her, and brought tears to her eyes.

"Oh, Cort, darling, please don't do that. Please don't. We can never—"

"My dearest, somehow we will work this out. I'll get you out of here, and then . . ."

And then? No, it was all wrong. There was Richard. And the baby. She shook her head, blinking back the tears.

Cort sighed, and after a long moment he cleared his throat and went on with his explanations, almost as if nothing had happened. Almost.

"I saw your father this morning, Miranda, and Tom. They had spent a sleepless night, and they were sick with worry. Darling, you really were foolish yesterday, going off to that orphanage again with the mobs in the streets and race warfare ready to break out."

"I didn't know, Cort. How could I know? *I* didn't do anything wrong. It was the rest of the world that went mad."

"Yes. Well, it's done now, and too late to change anything. But we have to get you out of here, before Kevin comes back."

"Why? And why isn't Papa *here?*"

"He didn't know where you were, Miranda. He still doesn't know. Sometime after midnight a note was delivered to the front desk—the night clerk didn't notice who brought it—and it just asked how much your life was worth—or your dead body."

Her eyes widened. "And you think that Kevin . . ."

"I don't know who else, and I don't want to take any chances."

"But Kathy would never agree to that. You saw her. And

her mother. They've been kindness itself, and they would never—"

"Yes, I think you are right. But if Kevin hasn't told them what he's doing, and if he shows up with a couple of his friends, pretending to take you to the Stratford, do you think they'll question him?"

"Oh, no! He wouldn't do that!" Miranda shook her head, refusing to believe it. "He wouldn't. Yesterday, with the Corcorans, he was fighting for me. He wouldn't bring them here, would he? Oh, Cort, they were going to rape me. And when Tim hit me, and the baby, too . . . And now I've lost this child, just like the last one . . ."

"Darling, you must get a grip on yourself. I'll get you out of here. There must be a way. Can you walk at all?"

"No, Cort, I don't think so."

"I could carry you down to the street, but we'll need a carriage. Or, better still, an ambulance. I wonder . . . I believe I noticed . . ." He crossed the room and went into the parlor, peering from the front window to survey the street. When he came back he was laughing. "I know how we'll do it. You're game, I'm sure. There's an undertaker in the next block, and I'll hire the hearse."

"Well, I don't think I'm ready to be laid out yet, but if you think you can manage . . ."

"Leave it all to me, darling. I'll have you home in an hour—if we can just manage to avoid the crowds and the barricades."

Mrs. Flaherty was dubious about moving Miranda, but Cort was insistent, and Kathy was an unexpected ally.

"I'll go with you," she declared. "I can help. You stay here and take care of the baby, Ma. Someone has to be here if there is any word from Kevin . . ." She trailed off into a half sob. "*Why* didn't he get there last night? I'm going with them to find out."

"It's dangerous in the streets," Mrs. Flaherty protested, but Kathy had made up her mind.

"I have to know what happened to him. If he's hurt, if he's . . . I have to know."

The driver was waiting downstairs with the hearse, and he looked on dubiously while Cort and Mrs. Flaherty deposited a mattress where the coffin was usually displayed in glassed-in splendor. But the undertaker had been well paid for this mission, and the driver had been promised a generous tip, and, when they were ready, he clucked to the horse and set off for the Stratford at a modified funereal pace.

It was a roundabout route they took, avoiding the streets with the barricades, once turning into an alleyway to escape being overwhelmed by a mob fleeing a contingent of policemen.

New York was an eerie city that day, a contrast of tumult and deadly silence, of exuberance and wild excitement and chilling fear. Some streets were completely deserted—not a carriage in sight, not a horsecar or an omnibus moving anywhere; all the frightened inhabitants had retreated behind locked doors and shuttered windows, trusting in prayers or loaded guns or both. And other streets were surging with life, the people glorying in their unexpected holiday, their freedom to smash and grab and drink and carouse and rebel against all authority. The looters had declared a Christmas in July, and they helped themselves to anything that took their fancy, and there was no one to deny them. The police had their hands full elsewhere, in the streets where the rabble had banded into an army, and there were pitched battles and barricades—and men and women and children dying.

With all the detours, it took two hours for the hearse to make its way downtown. Broadway was impassable, but the driver drew up to the kitchen entrance to the Stratford where Cort paid him off.

Miranda was the center of attention when Cort carried her inside, Kathy trailing after them both, on the verge of panic over Kevin. A waiter went tearing off to find Will Chase, and Tom met them in the lobby and pounced on Miranda. He insisted on carrying her upstairs himself, even if he *was* still limping.

"How did you get here so fast?" he asked Cort. They were in Miranda's room, hovering over her bed, and he still could hardly believe she was here, safe. "The second note said twenty-four hours. And Papa is still counting the money."

Miranda stretched out with a sigh of relief, and Kathy plumped up the pillows and smoothed the starched white linen sheets.

"What money?" Cort stared at Tom. "What are you talking about?"

Will burst into the room, and he was half crying as he embraced Miranda. "Are you all right, Pet? What have they done to you? Who was it? Ten thousand dollars they wanted, in cash, and I have it now, but . . ." He looked at all of them, bewildered. "I don't understand. They released her without the money? How did you bring her here?"

Cort rushed through his explanations, and Will sighed and held Miranda's hand. "I grieve for you, dear child, and for the baby. It happened once with Mary, too, and we were heartsick. And Richard will be so disappointed. But *you* are safe, and that's the important thing."

"And Kathy saved me, Papa. She and her mother took care of me when Kevin—"

Kathy burst into tears, and Miranda patted her hand.

"About that second note," Cort said. "Is it like the first?"

Will produced them both, printed on plain white paper, unsigned.

"Is it Kevin's writing, Kathy?" Cort turned on the girl suddenly. "Did you know about this?"

She shrank from him. "Dear God, I don't know anything. He would never . . . Oh, Miss Miranda, you must believe me. He thought . . . Well, maybe a reward. But not this. Never this. Oh, I can't believe it. He wouldn't be drafted to fight for niggers, he said, but he wouldn't do this."

Cort sighed. "I'll check out the Astor bar and see if he's there."

It was a sullen, defiant Kevin who appeared in Miranda's room half an hour later.

"I saved her," he insisted. "I don't know anything about any notes. I don't know anything at all." He turned on Kathy. "Tell them. Did I say anything to you about notes? A reward. That's all I hoped for."

"That's what he said." Kathy nodded her agreement, looking at them all pleadingly. "He didn't say anything to me about ten thousand dollars. He was going straight to the Stratford . . . Oh, Kevin, why didn't you?" She looked at him, and he looked away, and her trust in him dissolved in her tears.

"Well," Kevin said. "I was tired last night. I carried her home," he gestured vaguely at Miranda, "and then I walked all the way downtown, and I just didn't get around to coming over here right then." He looked at Will Chase, and there was still an echo of defiant swagger in his voice. "I was coming to see you right after I finished work. I was going to take you home with me, and you could see what a good job Kathy did taking care of your daughter for you. We deserve something, we do."

"Oh, Kevin." Kathy turned away from him, ashamed and weeping.

"And if you had just stayed home where you belong," he said, his voice rising in a threat.

"I wanted her to come with us," Cort cut in. "I found Miranda myself. Your wife didn't betray you, even unwittingly. She's a hell of a lot better than you deserve, and if you don't know that . . ." He shook his head. "Extortion is a crime, and when the police—"

"You can't prove a thing," Kevin said. "I saved her, I did." He turned to Miranda. "Didn't I carry you home myself? God knows what would have happened to you without me. Isn't that true?"

Miranda nodded weakly.

"Well, then." Kevin glared at Cort. "The government says I'm worth three hundred dollars, dead or alive. What's *she* worth?"

Cort looked at him with contempt. "So you seized your chance, and you took it. You would never have gotten away with it, you know. How were you going to arrange to pick up the money? Stupid . . . But the anguish you caused . . ."

Kathy was sobbing, but when Kevin put his arm around her, she pulled away. "Sure, now, darling, I wasn't going to hurt her. I wouldn't do that, Kathy. I just wanted to take care of you and the baby. Why, if we could just get a little money ahead, and I could open my own bar . . ."

Will sighed. "I'll give you three hundred dollars to get out of the draft, but I never want to see you again. Never!"

"You aren't fit to be in the army," Tom agreed. "We want *men*, not—"

"I want to talk to Kathy," Miranda interrupted. "I want to talk to her alone."

They all looked at her, startled, and Kevin was going to protest but thought better of it when Cort glared at him.

"Come, sit by me." Miranda patted the edge of the bed after the others had gone, and Kathy sat down reluctantly, still blinking back her tears.

"I didn't know, Miss Miranda. Please believe me. I didn't know."

"I believe you, Kathy."

"He's weak, my Kevin is. I don't think he set out to do anything wicked. Truly I don't. He was going straight to your father, he was."

"Yes, Kathy. But then on that long walk he started thinking, I suppose, and he just decided to see how much he could get."

"That's it." Kathy nodded her head vigorously. "That must be what happened. Oh, Miss Miranda, you won't let anything happen to him, will you? Mr. Adams talked about the police, but Kevin . . ." She looked at Miranda helplessly.

"And you still love him?" Miranda asked, surprised.

"Why, of course!" Kathy was astonished. "He's my husband."

"Yes, you're right." Miranda sighed. "He's your husband." And she was loyal to him, Miranda realized. Kevin Kelly, that weak, blustering, foolish man. And yet Kathy would stand by him. And I have Richard, she was thinking, and he is everything Kevin is not: strong and controlled and honorable. And he loves me, and I have lost our child . . . I won't cry now, not again, not while Kathy is looking at me so anxiously. What is it that is bothering her? Oh yes, Cort's threat about Kevin.

"I'm sure there won't be any trouble about the police, Kathy. Not unless Kevin does anything else. He won't hurt you, will he? He sounded so threatening just now."

"It will be all right," Kathy assured her.

"Well, if it isn't, you can always come here, Kathy. We'll take care of you, and the baby." She swallowed hard.

Kathy touched her cheek. "Sure now, we'll be all right. And we should be heading home now I think. The baby will be hungry and wanting me. I hope you'll get better soon, Miss Miranda. Ma says . . . Ma says . . ." Kathy blushed and couldn't look at her, but she was determined to get it out. "Ma says you have to wait at least three months before, before . . . She says it's like having a baby, only worse, and you have to wait and make sure you're all right, completely all right. But then you can try again." Kathy's embarrassment speeded her departure, and from the doorway she waved good-by.

Miranda waved back, and then she sighed and wondered what advice the doctor would give and how Richard would react.

It wouldn't have happened if she had stayed home, but how could she know there would be riots in the streets and hundreds killed . . .

Chapter 27

THE VIOLENCE PERSISTED for two more days. The children from the Colored Orphans' Asylum had found refuge in the nearest police station, but as soon as it could be managed, they were evacuated to temporary quarters on Blackwell's Island.

Sporadic rioting continued, and in one attempt to stem it, the city council, meeting in rump sessions, passed a resolution authorizing the use of tax funds to pay the three hundred dollars for any man who wanted to escape the draft. News of this action had little effect on the rioters, however, and a few days later the mayor quietly vetoed the whole idea. Looting continued—Brooks Brothers was stripped bare the second night—but the authorities were gradually gaining control of the situation. Governor Seymour returned hastily from his vacation on the Jersey shore and conferred with Mayor Opdyke, and they sent telegrams to Washington urging speedy return of the National Guard. By Thursday morning, when the Seventh Regiment debarked from the Cortlandt Street ferry, the city was staggering to its feet. Most of the horsecars and omnibuses were running again, merchants were unshuttering their shops, and workers were returning to their factories and lofts and shipyards.

It was time to take a reckoning of the loss of life and property, to clean up the destruction, and to raise money for the penniless and dispossessed. The riots had left five thousand Negroes homeless, and a special committee was organized to give them aid.

Slowly life returned to normal. When the draft resumed in

August—the offices well protected by the National Guard—there was no further violence.

Miranda was confined to her bed for three weeks, and she was still there when, with no advance notice, Richard came home to see her. Will had written to him immediately—and Miranda had added a shaky postscript—but it had taken more than two weeks for the letter to reach him. His regiment was back in Virginia, and there was skirmishing along the Rappahannock, and the mails had been delayed. Rather than trust his response to a letter, he came himself, spending a sleepless night en route to Washington and a long, tiring day on the trains and ferries to New York. He went directly to the Stratford, to Miranda's room, arriving just as the housekeeper emerged with a supper tray.

"Is she all right?" he asked anxiously.

"Getting better every day."

"Thank God."

"She may be asleep now," Mrs. Darcy warned him.

The room was dimly lit, and he closed the door quietly, set down his satchel, and tiptoed to her bedside.

She was still awake, but when she looked up at him and he smiled, she dissolved into tears. Whatever he had planned to say vanished before her grief.

"My darling!" He held her in his arms and kissed her, half kneeling by the bed, and then he sat down next to her, still holding her hand. "My sweet, foolish child. I love you so much, and I cannot bear the thought of your suffering." He leaned over her and brushed the tears from her eyes. "Are you still in pain, Miranda! Is there some medicine that—"

"No, Richard. There's no pain now. I'm just a little weak; that's all. I started crying because, because . . . Oh, darling, are you very angry with me?"

"Miranda, how can I look at you and see your tears and know your grief and be angry? When the letter came from your father, I felt . . . I can't express what I felt. I was shocked and disappointed, of course, but this . . . this is a punishment far greater than you deserve."

"Richard! A punishment?" She was appalled, and she clutched at his arm and sat up, staring at him in disbelief.

He arranged the pillows for her and made sure she was warm enough.

"It was foolish of you to disobey me, Miranda, but I am not angry now. I share your grief and I want to comfort you." He kissed her again. "But darling, you *did* distress me, made me heartsick with your deception, when you knew you were pregnant and you didn't tell me. I will never understand that. The miscarriage . . . That is a terrible blow, to both of us, but sometimes these things happen, and we do not always know the reason."

"But we *do* know the reason," she protested. "There was a riot, and I was nearly raped. I wasn't responsible for that."

"Darling, I know that. I know you weren't responsible for the riot. But if you had followed my advice, Miranda, you would not have been there. We would still be looking forward to the birth of our first child."

"Richard, then you do blame me."

He did not deny it. "But don't torture yourself, Miranda. We will have other children, darling, if only the war spares us."

"Oh, Richard, you make me feel so guilty."

"Foolish, Miranda. Not guilty. You will be careful now, darling, I know. And we won't let this happen again." He smiled at her. "I love you very much, and I always will. 'For richer, for poorer, in sickness and in health, in joy and in grief.' "

Miranda looked at him and sighed. And she had promised to love and honor and obey . . .

At his urging she told him exactly what had happened the day of the riot, taking him every step of the way, from the time she arrived at the orphanage that morning until Kevin delivered her, fainting, into Kathy's care. He was determined to know everything, and she relived the agony and cried again with the terror and shame of it all.

"Oh, my love, if only you hadn't been there!" He kissed her again, and this time she sighed and accepted his rebuke. He brushed away her tears, and she went on.

"And the next afternoon, when Cort found me and rescued me . . ."

Richard looked at her, surprised, and released her hand from his grasp.

"But you knew that, darling. You knew that it was Cort who found me."

"Yes, your father mentioned him in the letter, but I hadn't quite realized . . . What was he doing there? How did he get mixed up in this?"

"Well, he knew I was missing . . . and he was concerned . . ." She trailed off, and he stared at her, puzzled.

"Was he involved in the extortion attempt, do you think?"

"Of course not! He *saved* me."

"I wonder." He stood up and paced over to the windows and stood there, looking at the lights across the park. "He might need money. If the Robillard fortune is sinking along with the Confederacy . . ."

"No, you have it all wrong. Cort is wealthy now. He told me so himself."

He stared at her in amazement. "Why in the world were you discussing money with him? And how ill-bred of him to tell you such a thing!"

"Well, I think I asked him." She remembered the conversation vividly, and she blushed. It was in Washington, and the dressmakers had just left, and she was preening in front of the mirror, and Cort . . . She was miles away, in another world.

"Miranda, sometimes I don't understand you at all." Richard stood over her bed, looking down at her, and then he smiled. "You are so beautiful, even when your cheeks are flushed and streaked with tears and you are worrying that I might stop loving you. Oh, Miranda," he embraced her and kissed her and brushed back a stray curl, "I look at you now and I love you more than ever."

Purposefully, he crossed the room to lock the door, then turned back, unbuttoning the tunic of his uniform, smiling at her, wanting her.

"No, Richard." She shook her head. "You can't."

He couldn't have been more shocked if she had slapped him. "Darling, you must not refuse me! I rushed here to comfort you and forgive you and tell you how much I—"

"Richard, no! The doctor says . . . Darling, we must wait until I am well again. You know that. Surely you must know that."

"But, Miranda, I . . ." Protest died on his lips. "Of course, you are right. I didn't think." It took him a moment to regain control of himself. "But you will be all right?"

"Yes, darling. But we must wait. At least three months, he said. And even then, if I am not convinced that everything is normal . . ."

"Three months?" He kissed her hand and sighed, accepting the decision. "Three months. Of course, darling, we must make sure that you are well again. That is the most important thing. I will talk to the doctor tomorrow and make sure that you are doing all you can to recover from this . . . misfortune." He patted her shoulder. "I am sure of one thing, though. There will be no more expeditions to those orphans, Miranda, on Blackwell's Island or anywhere else. You've done more than enough for them."

She sighed, and he took that as agreement.

"And when I came in tonight," he added, decision in his voice, "I could see that the Stratford is functioning perfectly well without you, and so from now on—"

"Richard! You promised me!"

"Miranda, I am being very patient with you. You are not well, and you should not argue about this now. When you are fully recovered, we will talk about it again. Now I rushed here to see you, and I haven't had a proper night's sleep in thirty-six hours, and I am going to take a bath and go to bed."

She looked at him doubtfully.

"No, darling, not your bed." His hand rested on her shoulder. "That would be too much of a temptation. I'll have them bring in a cot."

"You could use Jimmy's room," she offered tentatively.

"No, I will stay with you. I have come all this way, and we will not be separated."

There was a knock at the door and he unlocked it, admitting her father and Tom.

"Mrs. Darcy said you were here." Will shook hands with Richard and briefly clasped his shoulder. "I'm glad you could come. Miranda needs some cheering up."

"I can't stay long," Richard said. "This is an emergency leave, and I'll have to start back the day after tomorrow."

"Why, then I can go with you!" Tom was obviously pleased at the thought. "I'm fully recovered now. Even the doctor admits that he can hardly see a sign of limp. And to think they wanted to amputate! Those army surgeons!"

"You must remember you had a good nurse," Will reminded him.

"Yes." Tom smiled at Miranda affectionately. "She's a wonderful girl, isn't she, Richard? Do you know that she saved two of those orphans from certain death? We're very proud of her."

Miranda looked at him with gratitude. Tom had been almost as upset that day as Cort, but he hadn't chided her once. And after Cort had gone back to Washington, it was Tom who did the most to restore her confidence and help her shed her guilt. She *had* saved those little girls, and then paid a terrible price for it.

"And Cort was wonderful, too," Tom went on. "Bringing her home in a hearse!" He laughed. "Who else would have thought of that?" He looked at Richard for confirmation.

"Very resourceful," Richard acknowledged. "If we have time in Washington, I suppose I should call and thank him formally for rescuing her."

He would force himself to do that, Miranda realized, recognizing his duty to good manners, if nothing more. But he hated to be under obligation to anyone, especially Cort, so this was one more burden she had placed on him. Why did he always make her feel so guilty?

Talk had turned to the war, as always, and they weighed the prospects for early victory. A new attack had been launched from the sea against Charleston and Fort Sumter, where it had all started. It would be fitting if it should end there, too, in the same place, with the capture and surrender of the city.

"But I doubt if that's the way to win," Richard contradicted Tom. "If we would just move on to Richmond . . ."

There was silence for a moment, and they all thought of how often they had used that phrase and what a price had been paid. And still the armies grappled in Virginia, no closer to Richmond than they had been two years ago at Bull Run. But the Union *was* winning, Miranda was sure. Even Cort, usually so pessimistic, had admitted that. With the fall of Vicksburg and Port Hudson, the entire Mississippi River was in Federal hands, and the South was effectively split in two. The blockade was an increasingly powerful stranglehold, and the European countries, always skittish about recognizing the Confederacy as an independent nation, had backed off completely now. The last hope for the South was the North itself—in draft riots and Copperheads and the intense, continuing pressure for peace at any price.

"But if we just fight," Tom was saying, "it could be over by Christmas. If Meade would only *move.*"

Will sighed. "Well, we aren't going to win it tonight. And Miranda is tired. And you, Richard, will you be going to visit your parents this evening or—"

"No, it's too late, Uncle Will. If you'll just have a cot brought in here . . ."

Will nodded his understanding, and Richard changed the subject hastily.

"Is the family all right? The mail has been so sporadic, and my last letter from mother was written the day before the riots broke out."

"They are all well," Will assured him.

"And we have been seeing a lot of Irene," Tom added. "She has come to visit Miranda every day this week. Of course I think that is because Andy Dawson is around, but Miranda provides a fine excuse."

Richard shook his head. "Mother isn't going to like that at all."

"Don't tell her then," Tom advised.

"Marty already has," Miranda cut in. "Irene told me this morning, and she is furious with him."

"Marty?" Richard looked at her, surprised. "So he finally came home on a furlough. I haven't seen him since . . . since the first Christmas of the war."

"He's just the same." Tom dismissed him with a shrug. "He's a bore and braggart when he's sober and a *nasty* bore and a braggart when he's drunk."

"He has a good side," Richard defended him, "although I admit that it's sometimes hard to find . . . So, you've told me about everyone except Ann."

"Ann? Nothing the matter with her." Tom laughed. "When the Seventh Regiment came back, Ann was in seventh heaven again."

"She hasn't set a new date for the wedding," Miranda said. "Early fall I think it will be."

"Perhaps I can arrange a furlough and come home," Richard said. And then he looked at Miranda and smiled. "October. From July, that's three months."

"I don't think Ann wants to wait that long." Tom laughed again. "But Aunt Faith wants to make sure that the war is going well and the city is calm so that this time the bridegroom will be sure to be here. They are still arguing about the date."

"They can compromise on September," Will said. "We'll all be back to normal next month. And you'll be up and about by then, Pet. And now I really think we should all say good night."

Richard closed the door after them and smiled at Miranda. "I'll make sure it's October, darling. And we'll have a second honeymoon."

The next afternoon, for the first time since her miscarriage, Miranda was up and dressed and in the family parlor. Richard had spent part of the morning with his mother and sisters at home and then had gone downtown to the shipping offices to have lunch with his father and John. When he returned to the Stratford, he was surprised and pleased to find Miranda looking so much better.

She was sitting on the sofa with an afghan draped over her, and Richard insisted on tucking her in carefully before he sat down beside her. He was in high spirits, not only because she seemed so well but also because the doctor had confirmed his hopes for her speedy recovery and Ann had agreed to a mid-October date for her wedding.

"After all, she wanted me there," he said, pleased with his success in convincing her. "Her only brother. And I told her that you would be well enough to be in the wedding party, too. And you will be, darling; I am sure of it. Fully recovered and eager to see me. I have decided," his arm circled her waist and he kissed her, "we'll go back to Long Branch. Won't that be wonderful?"

Miranda sighed, and he smiled at her tenderly. "It will all work out. You'll see. This was a sad loss, and I know the time seems long. You are young and impatient—and, I confess, I am impatient now, too. But October will come, and you will be well, and we will start all over again."

She nodded and was glad to bury her head in his shoulder where he couldn't study her expression and analyze her conflicting emotions. She was comfortable in his arms and drowsy, and he held her for a long time. She stirred only when she heard a discreet cough and a knock at the open door.

She looked up to greet Mrs. Cantrell and Caroline and, most surprisingly, Marty. He had been back five days, but this was the first time he had called on her. He was a captain now, with a promotion earned in battle, and he looked older with that sandy-red beard and mustache. She had never liked him, but after all he was her cousin and apparently even a hero of sorts. She smiled a welcome, and Richard rang for tea.

Caroline was embarrassed at disturbing them and apologetic, but Mrs. Cantrell cut through her confusion and kissed Miranda briskly and sat down to tell her all about their expedition to Blackwell's Island that morning.

"The children all asked about you," she said, "even that strange little child from the South. Reecee. Of course you remember *her*."

Miranda nodded. "I thought she hated me."

"You saved her life!" Mrs. Cantrell was astonished.

"Well, yes. But I slapped her. I had never struck a child before. And the way she glared at me . . ."

"That was when she was hysterical," Mrs. Cantrell said. "I don't think she even remembers it. Or, if she does, she understands why you did it. She's a very shrewd little girl, Reecee is. And so determined to be independent. Like you, my dear."

Miranda sighed, and Richard put his arm around her again.

"I am glad to see you looking so much better," Mrs. Cantrell went on. "You know, Richard, she had us very worried. I hadn't even known she was missing. Caroline and I were safe behind our locked doors at home when that distraught young *Times* reporter appeared on the doorstep. He said it was a matter of life and death, and when he mentioned your name, Miranda, I could see—"

Miranda looked at her, alarmed, and Mrs. Cantrell stopped short, and realization struck her. She knew. Miranda could see it in her eyes. Cort, so much in love with her. The reason for the pills and the "food poisoning."

Marty glanced at his grandmother curiously and then stared at Miranda. She could feel her color rising, and she moved closer to Richard and pulled his arm around her. He smiled at her, momentarily distracted. Caroline was unaware, as usual.

"So," Mrs. Cantrell made an effort and went on as if nothing had happened. "We were all much relieved when this man Adams tracked her down and rescued her." She changed the subject abruptly. "And now, dear, all the children are wondering when you'll be well enough to come back to us."

"I think that's out of the question." Richard was absolute.

Miranda did not flatly contradict him. "Perhaps when I am better I could come for a visit."

"Blackwell's Island is a very unhealthy place." As far as Richard was concerned, that settled it.

"Blackwell's Island is only temporary," Mrs. Cantrell said. "We are starting a subscription for a new building, and eventually we will move. And in the meantime we need money—"

"I will give you a generous contribution," Richard interrupted her. "But Miranda will not go back. Isn't that right, Miranda?"

She nodded reluctantly, and he smiled at her. "You name the amount of money, darling. Whatever you say, I'll give them gladly. I know this means a lot to you."

"Thank you, Richard. That is very generous of you." And it was, of course. He had no more interest in those orphans than Cort did, but to make her happy . . . But oh, she wanted to go back! The money was more important, of course. If she looked at it rationally, she knew that. Piano lessons were a frivolous luxury when the children needed food and clothing and a safe roof over their heads, and she ought to be sensible enough to understand that. It was silly to be close to tears, and she would *not* break down. Richard would be embarrassed. She swallowed hard and tried to smile and was glad to be distracted by the arrival of the maid with the tea tray.

"I'd like to know more about the riots," Marty was saying. "I understand from Grandmother that you got caught in the mob at the orphanage, and two of those dirty micks damn near—"

"Please, Marty, I don't want to talk about it." Miranda stirred her tea and refused to look at him.

"And then Uncle Will paid off the bartender who brought you home," Marty persisted.

"Cort brought me home," Miranda corrected him.

"Ah, yes." Marty stared at her. "He was so distraught, Grandmother said, and then he hired a hearse."

"That was very clever of him," Mrs. Cantrell intervened smoothly. "These are delicious scones, dear. Much lighter than last time. Have you hired someone new in the kitchen?"

"No." Miranda smiled at her gratefully. "It's the same man. But before I got sick, I was starting to consult more regularly with the chef." She spoke with increasing animation. "He had investigated some new ovens, and when I worked out the costs, I was able to prove to Papa what a good investment they'd be, and . . ." She was conscious of Richard's eyes on her, and she trailed off.

Marty returned to his original subject. "This Cort Adams,"

he said. "Why was he so interested in tracking you down, right in the middle of a riot? Did he know there was a price of ten thousand dollars on your head?"

"Oh, Marty, of course not!" Automatically she came to Cort's defense. "He *saved* me."

"I see." Marty contemplated her in silence for a moment. "Cort Adams saved you. And there was no money in it for him, you say. He took time out during a riot to go looking for you. Why? Don't tell me it was pure kindness and . . . brotherly love?"

"What are you insinuating, Marty?" Richard's voice was cold, and Miranda could feel the tension coiled within him; his arm around her waist had gone rigid.

"Nothing," Marty said. "Not a thing. I just think it's curious; that's all. This man Adams, a fortune hunter, married to a Rebel, a man with no principles at all where women are concerned, living on God knows what. And in the middle of a riot he goes out of his way to track down our beautiful cousin. *Your* beautiful wife," he amended. "What was in it for him?"

"Pure kindness and brotherly love," Mrs. Cantrell answered him firmly. "Marty, I'm ashamed of you." She turned to Miranda and Richard. "I apologize for my grandson's behavior. I would blame it on a concussion or a severe head wound if I could, but there really seems to be no excuse at all."

There was an awkward silence, and Miranda wished fervently that Marty would simply stand up and stalk away. But he was bearing up under Richard's glowers and his grandmother's disapproval, and Caroline groped to save the situation by changing the subject.

"Miranda dear, I think you remember Major Lorimer?"

Miranda nodded. It was obvious that Richard remembered him, too, from the way he grew tense again.

Caroline was completely oblivious. "I had a letter from him yesterday. He's coming to New York in a few weeks, and he wants to see me again. Isn't that wonderful?"

"Wonderful," Miranda echoed, without conviction.

"He asked about you," Caroline went on. "He knows you are married, of course, but he asked to be remembered to you, and he said he hoped to see you again when he's here."

Miranda smiled, and Richard stirred, restless.

Marty caught the movement. "Do you know him, Richard?

He seems to have bowled over Caroline, but I'm not sure that my little sister is any judge of men."

"I met him once," Richard acknowledged stiffly.

Marty waited for him to continue, and reluctantly Richard went on.

"Last March, I believe it was. He came to call in Washington when Tom and I were having Sunday dinner with George and Emily."

"That sounds all right then." Marty smiled at Caroline. "If he is a friend of George, then I suppose—"

"Actually, he is a friend of Cort Adams," Richard corrected him. "George hadn't known him before either."

"Oh, that puts a different face on the matter." Marty looked thoughtful. "Lorimer could be another fortune hunter."

"Oh, Marty, he is *not*." Caroline had finally lost patience with him. "His father owns property in Boston, and he has money, and Jack is an officer in the army, and he—"

"Are you sure about all this? If you have only his word, that's not enough. If he's another Adams, out for all he can get, I think it would be wise to investigate his reputation. And his financial standing. And while I'm at it," he looked at Miranda, "I think I'll check into Cort Adams again, too. There's something fishy about that man. He might be a spy, for all we know, trafficking in Confederate gold."

"Don't be ridiculous, Marty." Miranda was disgusted with him, but she couldn't quite keep the alarm out of her voice. What would he discover if he hired the Pinkertons again? That she had been alone with Cort in Washington. Well, the family knew that already. And that he had rescued her during the riots—but that was no secret, either. And he had held her in his arms and kissed her and she . . . She was married to Richard and she was faithful to him. That was all there was to it. If the Pinkertons wanted to go haring off after Cort, looking for mythical Confederate gold, they would just make fools of themselves.

Unexpectedly, Richard came to her rescue. "Marty, why don't you simply forget about Cort Adams? Whatever his motives, I owe the man a debt of gratitude for finding Miranda." He looked at her and smiled. "Darling, I think all this company has tired you. Perhaps you should lie down before dinner. Tom is leaving tomorrow, you know," he explained to Mrs. Cantrell, "and John and Dany are coming for dinner tonight. They had been invited even before anyone knew I would be here. Uncle Will suggested this morning that we expand the party to include the whole family, but I am sure that you understand that Miranda shouldn't have too much excitement now."

"Of course, Richard." Mrs. Cantrell stood up, pulling on her gloves. "We saw Tom yesterday when he stopped off on his way to call on Lucy. We said our good-bys then."

"But *I* didn't see him," Marty corrected her. "I might come by later tonight just to have a farewell drink with him. And with you, Richard. We haven't had a chance to talk about the war or the riots or those damned Confederate raiders or anything. John told me we have lost four ships to them, and the insurance rates are going sky high."

"Damned pirates," Richard agreed. "Our navy ought to give us more protection. But I looked at the books with Papa today, and the profits in the first quarter alone—" He stopped short. "We shouldn't bother the ladies with all this. Yes, do come by later, Marty. I'll be glad to see you."

Miranda had dinner with the family, but she was more tired than she had realized, and sleepy, smothering yawns, eyelids drooping. As soon as they rose from the table, she excused herself, and Richard followed to tuck her in bed and kiss her good night. And then he went off to join Tom and Marty in the bar.

It was well after midnight when he returned, and Miranda stirred sleepily and woke up when he barked his shin against the cot and stumbled against her bed. He sat down abruptly, unexpectedly, and Miranda looked up, still drowsy and a little surprised. The light was dim, and he loomed over her, a dark shadow.

"Sorry, darling." His speech was slurred, and she could tell he had been drinking brandy. "Didn't mean to wake you up." He leaned over to kiss her, but she turned her head and his lips brushed her cheek and touched her ear.

He looked at her, puzzled. "No, Miranda. You know better than that." He pinned her shoulders, and she stared up at him, startled, conscious of his strength, conscious, too, that his usual rigid control had slipped. "When I want you . . ." This time his lips found hers. He had never kissed her like

347

that, a sensual, lover's kiss, his tongue probing for hers. His hand slid under the covers, under her nightdress, and curved around her breast, and she was astonished to find herself starting to respond to him. "My darling," he murmured, "always so warm and willing. Always with the promise of more."

"No, Richard! Please." She tried to push him off and failed. "Darling, we have to wait. You know we must—"

He kissed her again, but she twisted away from him. "Richard, no!"

He stopped short, anger warring with desire, and she shook her head slowly. "Darling, you *know* I had a miscarriage. We have to wait. Please, Richard."

"A miscarriage," he repeated, and the word carried weight. "Those damned Irishmen, pawing my wife when she . . ." He stared at her and then shook his head, as if to clear it. "A miscarriage! Dear God, I . . . Forgive me, Miranda." He stood up abruptly and took several deep breaths. "I didn't hurt you, did I?"

She shook her head.

"I would never want to hurt you. You believe that, don't you?"

"Of course, darling."

"And you would never want to hurt *me*, either." He seemed to be pursuing some discussion from earlier in the evening, and she stared at him, mystified.

"No, Richard, I would never want to hurt you. I know you love me."

"Well, then." He sounded triumphant. "That's what I told Marty. I don't give a damn what he turns up. He can hire all the Pinkertons in the country. You know what I think?" He had a crafty look in his eye, and he didn't wait for an answer. "I think he's jealous. Yes, that's it. He'll never get a girl like you, and he's jealous. He's jealous of Cort Adams, and he's jealous of me. Of course," he smiled with self-satisfaction, "he has more reason to be jealous of *me*, because I have *you*." He leaned over to pat her, and for a moment she thought he was going to force himself on her again; but he recollected himself and squared his shoulders. "Not tonight. I can't have you tonight. I know that." He retreated to his cot and sat down to take off his boots. "I will wait for you, Miranda. I will wait for you to get well." He unbuttoned his tunic and tossed it on a chair, and he pulled off his trousers and left them on the floor. When he sprawled out on the cot, he was asleep almost immediately.

Miranda tiptoed across the room to hang up his uniform. She had never seen Richard drunk before, out of control, and she wondered if he would have any memory of this in the morning.

As for Marty, she dismissed him. Richard might be right about his jealousy—that would explain a lot. But the Pinkertons . . . They were worthless, Cort said. Always seeing things that weren't there. What could they possibly find out?

In the morning Richard apologized again, and then he complained of a headache.

But his condition was mild compared to Tom's. Even the prospect of Lucy's coming to see him off was not cheering. "Good Lord, what will she think of me?"

"She'll think you have no head for whiskey," Miranda told him.

"It was Papa's best brandy," Tom corrected her, "and we were trying to keep up with Marty, weren't we, Richard?"

"We drank him under the table," Richard confirmed. "And then *I* helped *you* to bed."

Tom grinned. "You thought you were stone-cold sober, but I knew better. You kept wanting to go upstairs to wake Miranda and bring her down to play the piano."

"Tom, I think you are exaggerating." Richard spoke with particular precision. He may have been tipsy the night before, but obviously he was determined to be in full control of himself this morning. And of Tom, too. "Now, we have only an hour to catch our train. Are you all packed? Are you ready to go?"

Tom gave him a mock salute. "Aye, aye, sir."

"You have been spending too much time with Andy Dawson," Miranda accused him, smiling. "That's not a *navy* uniform you have on."

Tom looked down at his blue tunic with feigned surprise. "Damn it, you are right. I *am* in the army. Well, at least I won't get seasick in all that Virginia mud." He kissed her good-by and, carrying his head carefully, he walked sedately down the stairs to greet Lucy.

Richard embraced Miranda one last time. "No, don't come

down with me, darling. I'd rather say good-by to you here, alone."

"Are you all right, Richard?" She touched his forehead, as if to smooth away his headache.

"I'll be fine, Miranda. I *am* sorry about last night. I promise you it will never happen again." He smiled at her. "Under normal circumstances, I would never be out drinking with the boys when you are home in bed, waiting for me." He kissed her, and she clung to him. "Until October, darling. I'll be counting the days."

"Oh, Richard, be careful."

"Don't worry, darling. No Confederate bullet would dare touch me. And *you* stay safe."

She nodded, and they kissed again. He picked up his satchel, touched her cheek one last time, and he was gone. She closed the door after him, and she waited at the window until he reappeared on the sidewalk with Tom and Lucy. They looked up and waved, and she followed their carriage until it was lost in the traffic of Broadway.

Richard will be in Washington this evening, she thought, and she wondered if he would take time to call on Cort. Immediately, she felt guilty again.

With both Tom and Richard gone, the prospect of the day stretched out before her, flat and featureless. There was nothing interesting in the papers, looking at the piano depressed her, and she wasn't really well enough to stir beyond the family quarters. She could catch up on her correspondence, perhaps, but she wasn't in the mood to write letters; she was only in the mood to receive them. And so, when she heard from Cort that morning, she tore open the envelope with more than her usual eagerness. He had lingered in New York only two days after he had rescued her, and she had not seen him alone during that time. Nor had she heard from him since, and she plunged into his letter with an enthusiasm that quickly turned to shock.

Dear Miranda,

According to your father's last letter, which George read aloud to us just an hour ago, you are making great strides toward full recovery. We are all very thankful for that, and I trust you will soon be completely well.

What I have to tell you now is very difficult to write;

and perhaps it is difficult to read, too, but I know it is necessary.

Darling, we must not see each other again.

Your father confronted me the night I brought you home, and he knows, Miranda. Not everything—not about our time together in Washington. But he knows I love you, and he doesn't want to face the possibility that perhaps you love me, too. He was and is warmly grateful to me for finding you, rescuing you, and he is not unsympathetic to my heartache. But he is adamant. And perhaps . . . perhaps he is right. You are, as he says, young and resilient—and you have a husband who loves you. Your father thinks that my presence could upset you, could tarnish your reputation, could make Richard jealous.

Divorce is not a word in your father's vocabulary, and I doubt if it exists as a possibility for you at all. Even if you could face the scandal—and I would hate to put you through that—I fear that Richard would never consent. If we cannot be together honestly and openly, I know now that there is no way for us to be together at all. It is better to face that fact now and make the painful adjustment to a life apart rather than to delude ourselves with cruel hopes that have no basis in fact.

You are wiser than I. You knew when I saw you in May, when I first learned of your marriage, that it was all over between us. Now that I agree with you, I hope it will be easier for you to have a happy life with Richard. And I want you to be happy, Miranda. I have never wanted anything but that.

You must feel free to come to Washington whenever you choose; I can always arrange to be away. I will not be staying at the Stratford when I visit New York in the future, and I will do my best to avoid you while I am there.

In a few years, perhaps, these precautions will no longer be necessary, and if we should see each other on the street, I will tip my hat and bow formally and pass on—and never once remember the way you looked up at me the first time I saw you at the Stratford, with all the world spread out before you; or the last day, in that dingy little bedroom when you had just lost your baby and you were in utter misery and you smiled at me, and

I knew I held your heart. And now, darling, I give it back to you.

For the last time:

All my love,
Cort

She finished the letter, her eyes blurring with tears, and she was still sobbing when her father found her half an hour later.

"You heard from Cort?"

She made no answer, but he could see the letter, still clutched in her hand.

He sat down beside her, and after a moment's hesitation she flung her arms around him.

"You forgive me, Pet? It's the only way, Miranda. Please, try to believe me. He's a married man, with two children, and there is no way it could ever work."

She had no answer for him, and he patted her arm and repeated all those meaningless platitudes about time and youth and resilience. And after a while, there were no more tears to shed.

"How did you know, Papa?"

"My little heroine who never cries . . ." He handed her his handkerchief and watched her dry her eyes. "How did I know? Cort gave himself away. When he came here that morning and discovered you were missing, that mask of cynicism disappeared, and there was only shock and fear and his love for you. He stormed out of the Stratford, and I wasn't sure if I was ever going to see him again. And when he brought you back, full of pride and love and tenderness . . . I am truly sorry for the boy. I can even understand how it happened—missing his wife, transferring his affection to you when you came to visit. It's a delusion for him, too, you know. If Susanne had been there, he would never have noticed you."

Miranda stared at him and swallowed hard and bit back her protests. If her father preferred this explanation, she would not contradict him.

"And it was only natural for you, Miranda," he went on, "to look on Cort as a kind of hero when he rescued you. And he *was* a hero. But hero worship isn't love, and you must not mistake these feelings now, when you are still upset and convalescing from your tragic loss—you must not confuse all this

352

with real love. If Richard had been here, *he* would have rescued you.

"Richard has behaved splendidly through all this, Miranda. I thought he would be angry with you. You know what grave misgivings I had when you married him, but he has proved to be understanding and truly loving. I think you will have a good marriage if you aren't distracted by someone like Cort. He is a likable chap with a great deal of easy charm, and if he fancied himself in love with you, he could cause you all kinds of unpleasantness and grief. I pointed that out to him, and he was wise enough to understand and to agree not to see you again.

"This will all fade quickly, Miranda. And then when the war is over, Cort will go back to Susanne. And you, Pet, you will be happy with Richard. This little infatuation will pass, has passed already. Isn't that so?" He didn't want an answer, not a real answer, and Miranda looked away.

"Tell me about Lucy," Will said, forcing the conversation into new channels. "Is she as serious about Tom as he seems to be about her?"

Miranda made an effort to join in his speculation, but she had no heart for it. Tom and Lucy could fall in love and get married and live happily ever after . . .

And she could never see Cort again.

Chapter 28

AUGUST DRAGGED on and became September, and some of those platitudes about time and youth and resilience turned out to be true. Miranda resolutely tried not to think about Cort at all—it was too painful. It was almost as if he had died, as Jimmy had died, and she sealed off that corner of her heart and waited for the scar tissue to form.

By early September she was well enough to spend one morning a week at the Cooper Institute with Aunt Faith, helping with the correspondence. Packing boxes required too much physical strength, Faith had decreed, and Miranda obediently did what she was told. Increasingly, she found herself dealing with the wives and children of sick and wounded soldiers, arranging transportation for them, listening to sad stories of absent husbands and rising prices and unscrupulous landlords, authorizing disbursements of children's clothing and emergency food supplies, writing endless letters to Washington in search of lost paychecks, unpaid bounty claims, and—hardest of all—information about soldiers missing in action. In the context of the real tragedies of this cruel war, her own problems shrank to insignificance. One morning a week immediately expanded to a whole day, and then two and three and four. Faith relied on her, and Miranda took pride in that and even began to develop an admiration and liking for her aunt that she had never had before.

In a curious kind of way the war had provided an outlet for Faith Schuyler, almost a vocation. In a society where the women of her class and background were thought unfit for the harsh world of commerce and industry, she had helped to carve out a volunteer organization that functioned with amazing efficiency and economy, free from graft and corruption. This was particularly noteworthy at a time when graft and corruption were endemic in the business world, and the war effort was plagued with waste and mismanagement and widespread thievery. There were all too many stories of fraud in the awarding of government contracts, of stock swindles and land grabs and outright bribery, of outrageous prices for moldy flour and adulterated beef and boots that fell apart in the first rain.

Shoddy.

Shoddy blankets, shoddy uniforms, shoddy guns and bullets.

And a new shoddy aristocracy.

There was money for the taking, enormous amounts of money. A flood of money from the government, a flood of money pouring into the railroads expanding to the west, a flood of money from the tide of immigrants still streaming into the country in spite of war and riots and exploitation. Land values in New York jumped every year, rents soared, and business had never been better for the merchants and tradesmen up and down Broadway. At a time when many a dockworker, many a soldier's widow, found it impossible to make ends meet, the display of new wealth reached ever gaudier levels.

There was no shame in that. If a man could afford diamond buttons on his waistcoat, diamond buttons he wore. And if his wife appeared at the opera in velvet and ostrich plumes and jeweled stomacher, that only proved he could afford such indulgences. After a multicourse dinner, he was likely to sleep through the opera himself, but that was no reason not to go, to see and be seen.

Old New York frowned at these shoddy upstarts, but they were making a place for themselves just the same. Their marble palaces were rising on Fifth Avenue, their children were seeking admittance to the best schools, and their financial contributions were helping to fuel the churches and the charities of established society. Aunt Faith might sniff disdainfully and refuse to admit these newcomers to the inner circles of the Women's Central Association for Relief, but she could hardly turn down their money and their gifts.

Miranda observed it all with interest and fascination, and at night she went home and wrote dutiful letters to Richard. She was working only two full days a week at the Stratford, she told him, and surely he couldn't object to that. And the rest of the time his mother was keeping an eye on her, and he certainly should not worry so much. And of course she was well, and she was looking forward to seeing him next week, and it was too bad that Tom couldn't get away, too (Lucy would be so disappointed), but George and Emily were coming after all, bringing Polly with them. Polly was going to have a little brother or sister in April, on her second birthday, perhaps, but Emily was still going to be in the wedding party. Only the immediate family knew, and no one else would be able to tell, and even Aunt Faith had reluctantly given her consent.

Richard came two days before the wedding, traveling with George and Emily and Polly, all of them arriving at the Stratford in the late afternoon. Richard was astonished that Miranda wasn't there to greet him—she rushed in twenty minutes later, full of apologies. There had been an emergency at the Cooper Institute, and a young woman had gone into hysterics, and Miranda had had to soothe her children and locate the woman's sister and—

Richard embraced her and kissed her, cutting off her explanations in midsentence, and George laughed.

"I think she's fully recovered," he said. "You ought to know by now, Richard, that she never does anything by halves."

Polly was tugging at her skirts, and Miranda stooped down to pick her up and hold her, and she listened to the conversation swirl around her and for the hundredth time decided that she loved them all and they loved her, and she should concentrate on all the good things she had in life and not go mooning over a lost dream. She kissed Polly—the child was falling alseep in her arms—and Emily carried her off to put her to bed. Miranda would have followed to help tuck her in, but Richard shook his head. She joined him on the sofa, and he put his arm around her, pulling her close so that only she could hear.

"What a loving mother you will be, Miranda."

"I hope so, darling."

"You are all right now, aren't you? The doctor has given you a clean bill of health, and tonight . . ."

"Yes, Richard, I am completely well."

He patted her arm and smiled. "I love you very much.

And if it wouldn't be rude, I'd skip dinner with the family and go off with you right now."

She shook her head, blushing a little, and he kissed her hand.

"It's that sweet innocence you have, darling. So appealing and dear to me. I have missed you so much and dreamed of you for so long . . ."

Will tapped out his pipe—he was talking to George and paying no attention to them—but the sound made Richard aware again of his surroundings, and, with an effort, he detached himself from Miranda to stand by the fireplace and join in the conversation about the war. Always, the war.

He agreed with George that it was unlikely there would be any more serious fighting in Virginia this fall. Lee had been repulsed in the latest skirmishing, and both armies would be going into winter quarters and saving their strength for the spring campaigns. The combined army and navy expedition against Charleston was a standoff, with Federal forces still trying to reduce Fort Sumter and reoccupy it. George had already written off that venture as costly and futile.

"It's a sideshow," he said. "What we really need is a fighting general for the Army of the Potomac. The war is still going to be decided once and for all in Virginia. If Lincoln would just bring in Grant . . ."

Richard nodded. "He's a butcher, but that's what we need. A butcher."

Miranda recoiled at the word. And Lincoln had just called for another three hundred thousand soldiers. More and more bloodshed. The wounded and the maimed and the dying. And all the widows and orphans. This cruel, cruel war.

Emily returned and sat down on the sofa beside Miranda while the men refought the summer campaigns.

"You are looking very well, Miranda. We had been so worried about you."

"And you, Emily, are positively glowing, and so happy."

"I *am* happy," Emily agreed. "And George is so pleased. We want a big family—lots of brothers and sisters for Polly. And cousins, too." She smiled at Miranda. "We had a head start, getting married first, but you could hurry and catch up. Have twins, why don't you?"

Miranda laughed. "I don't think I could manage more than one at a time."

"No," Emily agreed. "I couldn't either. But Cort just heard from his brother—you've met Warren, haven't you?"

Miranda shook her head.

"He's so much like Cort, and last month when he came to Washington . . ."

Of course Emily would talk about Cort. Why not? He lived in the same house with her and she got to see him every day. Miranda swallowed hard and tried to concentrate on what Emily was saying. Warren. Cort's brother. Warren and his wife, Abby, had just had twins. And yes, of course, that was wonderful.

"And Cort is going to Boston for Thanksgiving to see his mother and the whole family," Emily went on. "He hasn't been home for almost two years, and he realizes finally how much he has missed them. And then I think he wants to patch things up with Susanne again."

Miranda did not trust her voice to respond.

"He's worried about her and the children, and he's been trying to persuade them to leave Savannah. He thinks it's dangerous."

Miranda nodded, expressionless.

"I suppose he's right," Emily sighed. "If our forces try an all-out assault on Savannah, like the one at Charleston—"

"Charleston?" George caught the word and smiled at Emily. "So, you ladies are talking about the war, too. And just when we're ready to be diverted by some cheerful gossip. Tell us about the wedding plans, Miranda. What time is the rehearsal tomorrow? And is Madison going to be just as nervous as I was?"

Miranda smiled, grateful to George for not talking about the war, not talking about Cort, not talking about anything painful at all.

When she was alone with Richard later, and he had closed the door and turned to take her in his arms, she clung to him and kissed him and willed herself to respond. He drew back and looked at her, a little surprised, and she pulled his hand over her breast.

He broke away immediately, breathing heavily and clearly shocked. "What are you doing, Miranda? Why are you behaving like a . . . What is the matter with you?"

"Richard! Darling, you love me, and I thought you wanted . . ."

He grasped her hands in both of his and stared at her. "I am your husband, Miranda, and you are my wife, and such bold conduct . . . My poor darling, don't look so upset." He pulled her into his arms again and held her. "Just let me love you as you are, Miranda, warm and sweet and gentle."

"Yes, Richard. But I thought—"

He smiled at her indulgently and smoothed away her frown. "I know. You just meant to show me that you love me. But not that way, darling. It's not . . . becoming." He kissed her again, and she tried one last time.

"Richard, when you were here in August—"

"I came to comfort you, darling."

"Yes, but that night when you had a little too much to drink—"

"I apologized, Miranda. It will not happen again, and you should not continue to reproach me."

"I'm not reproaching you, darling. It's just . . . That night when you kissed me and held me, I felt . . . It was exciting, Richard, and I want you to make me feel that way again."

This time there was anger mixed with his shock. "Miranda, I will not have you sitting in judgment on me, making demands, telling me to do this or that because you find it 'exciting.' It is dangerous when a woman thinks she has . . . certain appetites. It leads to hysteria or depravity or God knows what kind of female problems!" With an effort, he calmed himself, searching for an explanation and finding one. "I think the trouble is that you had that miscarriage, but you are fully recovered now. I don't know what you imagined when you were in such a highly emotional state last summer, and I apologize again if I upset you that night. But you are my wife, and you have always made me very happy, and you should not fill your head with strange delusions." He studied her, obviously worried, and then the solution occurred to him. "If losing the baby is responsible for all this, then the cure is really very simple. When you are pregnant again," he smiled at her, "you will stop feeling guilty and confused." He kissed her gently, and his voice was a warm murmur in her ear. "It has been so long, Miranda. Not since last May in Georgetown. And I have dreamed of you and yearned for you, and now that I have you in my arms again . . ."

She heard the lines from that familiar script and suppressed a sigh, and she was Richard's dutiful, submissive wife, letter perfect in her role. To think that Cort had always told her she was a terrible actress!

She held back her tears, even after Richard had fallen asleep. She was not going to cry again. It was dangerous to give way to her emotions, and she should know better. She had known that when she was ten years old. Nothing that had happened to her this past year could be changed by tears, and she was not going to let herself be hurt or vulnerable again.

With Cort in Boston the last week in November, Will agreed to accompany Miranda to Washington for Thanksgiving. And at the last minute, Lucy Blaine decided to go with them. Both Tom and Richard had brief furloughs, and, unexpectedly, Marty arrived, too.

"We ran into him at Aquia Creek," Tom explained, "and he didn't have any special plans for tomorrow, and I was sure there would be enough turkey for him, too."

Marty nodded. "I thought it would be all right, once I knew Cort wouldn't be here."

Emily looked at him, a little surprised, and Marty volunteered an explanation."

"Never liked the chap. Not since the first time I saw him, when he was trying to lead Miranda astray."

"Watch yourself, Marty," Richard cut in swiftly. "I know you have had too much to drink, but if you start insulting my wife . . ."

"No insult," Marty said. "Little Joan of Arc held him off." He grinned at her, and Miranda could almost hear his unspoken words: *That time.* She stared at him, alarmed, and held fast to Richard.

"I think we should have an understanding, Marty." George looked at him coldly. "Cort Adams is a very dear friend, and I will not allow him to be insulted, by you or anyone else."

Marty shrugged. "Salt of the earth, Mr. Adams. Why, he has even made his money honestly. I thought sure we'd run into a little graft, but it's all real estate and part of a publishing company and a speculation in oil, of all things."

"You seem to be singularly well informed," George said, astonished.

Marty nodded, looking wise, and Emily changed the subject. "We will be having tea soon, but let me show you to your rooms first." Without waiting for a response, she led them up the stairs. "We weren't expecting you, Marty, but if you don't mind sharing with Tom . . ."

Richard dropped his satchel in Miranda's room, but he declined her offer to unpack for him. "There's not much more than my shaving gear and a change of clothes. We have to be back the day after tomorrow."

Miranda sighed, and he smiled at her. "I'll have ten days at Christmas, darling, and we'll spend the whole time in New York. Perhaps it was a mistake to go away in October. You really weren't fully recovered. I think that's why . . ."

She nodded. He had been disappointed to learn that she was definitely not pregnant, but he did not dwell on the subject. And neither of them had ever once referred to that conversation on his first night in New York before Ann's wedding, at the beginning of their own second honeymoon. She had moved like a sleepwalker through that week, and he had been puzzled and concerned and finally worried about her low spirits and her general state of health. And he felt guilty, too, for having been too demanding of her. He apologized again just before he was to leave. "I didn't realize, darling, that the miscarriage would have such a lasting effect on you. I should have known that someone with your sensitivity," he kissed her hand, "does not easily recover from such a tragedy. I remember you were the same way when Jimmy died. It's part of your sweet and gentle nature, and another reason I love you so much."

Miranda had only half heard him. She was concerned that if he didn't cut short this farewell speech, he'd miss his train, and then she'd miss her first morning back at the Cooper Institute. She was more than ready to put this week behind her, eager now to pick up her own life again.

". . . And I could tell you are taking care of yourself," Richard was saying, "because you are looking so much better now."

Miranda blinked and came back to the present, to Washington on the day before Thanksgiving."

"Mother writes that she doesn't know how she'd manage without you. That pleases me very much, darling, that you two are getting along so well."

"I admire her, Richard. She is so competent and well organized, and she really has a very good mind. I don't think she ever had a chance to use it before."

He was ready to protest that judgment, but Miranda was oblivious, caught up in the new project that interested her most. "She's on the committee for the Sanitary Fair, you know. And she's determined, we're all determined, that it will be the biggest and the best. Chicago may have been first, but we're going to contribute a lot more than their sixty thousand dollars. Aunt Faith went to the first meeting last week at the Union League Club, and Dr. Bellows was the speaker, and he said . . ."

Richard smiled at her indulgently, pleased with her animation and high spirits, confident again that she was the radiant, enthusiastic girl he had married.

Marty left early the next evening, after the roast turkey with oyster stuffing, after the ritual hour over the brandy and cigars with the men in the family, and after a few stormy words in private with Richard before they rejoined the ladies. Richard emerged from that conversation, having quelled his anger, looking thoughtful and wryly amused.

He explained it all to Miranda later. "Those damned Pinkertons. Marty is like a child with an expensive toy. It's his money, of course, but I warned him it was a stupid waste."

Miranda nodded, in full agreement. "Does Marty approve of Major Lorimer now?"

"Lorimer? That's right—he was a target, too. I almost forgot. Nothing the matter with him, Marty said. He's willing to welcome the fellow into the family, though I still think Caroline would be making a mistake. However, that's her problem. No, the most interesting information was about Cort. Gossip, really. Don't repeat this, Miranda. It could hurt too many people and perhaps reflect back on the family, on Dany particularly."

"Dany? But what has she done?"

"Nothing. Nothing at all. But she would be very upset to hear that Susanne . . . You must not breathe a word of this, Miranda, but it is quite probable that Cort is not the father of Susanne's little girl."

Miranda could think of nothing to say to that, and she was horrified that Marty was in possession of such a piece of knowledge.

"I know you are shocked," Richard went on. "I always knew it was a mistake for her to stay in Savannah, but I thought it was *Cort's* infidelity that would wreck that marriage. And to think that all along she . . ." He shook his head in disapproval, but he could not suppress a smile. "It's a terrible thing, of course, but I must say that it's almost a fitting punishment for him, after the way he has carried on."

Miranda did not respond, and Richard took her hand. "Perhaps I shouldn't have told you, darling. In an ideal world, you would be shielded from this kind of knowledge, but I thought you should know and be on guard against such scandals."

"On guard?" She looked at him apprehensively.

"Yes. After Marty dropped that little bombshell about Susanne, he hinted that the Pinkertons had found something incriminating about Cort and you."

"Richard!"

"No, no, my sweet." He took her in his arms and kissed her. "I could be jealous with cause, but *you* would never give me reason. It's just that Marty is an imbecile. *I* knew that you were here last New Year's. And I was frankly appalled to learn that the Pinkertons had asked the servants about you. No more appalled than Jeff and Hattie, though. They were scandalized."

"Oh, Richard, that's horrid. Having detectives snooping around, prying." (But thank God Jeff and Hattie were so loyal.) "It makes everything seem so . . . dirty."

"I'm sorry I had to tell you, darling, but I wasn't sure what Marty would say to you. I told him to call off the whole thing and forget about it, but he's unpredictable." Richard sighed. "I can almost feel sorry for Cort. Even if we kill this gossip about Susanne, he's bound to find out. Not that there will be much he can do about it."

"He could divorce her," Miranda said tentatively.

"Divorce? That would ruin all their lives! No gentleman would put his wife through such a thing, no matter what she had done."

"He could let her divorce him, then," Miranda tried again, curious to see Richard's reaction.

"That would still be scandalous, and it wouldn't be honest, either. And any divorce is so hard on the families. No, I am afraid they are all caught in this miserable situation."

"What would you do if I were unfaithful, Richard?" Miranda could not resist the question.

"You? Darling, don't be foolish!"

"No, really. What would you do?"

363

He laughed. "Put you on bread and water and then chain you to your bed until you recovered your sanity. My darling, how can I give you a sensible answer to such a foolish question?"

She forced a smile. "I suppose you are right. You always are. Doesn't it get to be a strain sometimes, Richard?" She was only half joking. "You and God? Both infallible?"

"I was only infallible when I chose you, my angel. That's what you are, you know." He touched her cheek. "I am only trying to live up to you."

It occurred to Miranda that perhaps *he* was only half joking, too.

Chapter 29

ALL THAT FALL and winter the Stratford was jammed to capacity, every room taken, and in mid-December Will reluctantly allowed cots to be set up in the ballroom for the overflow of soldiers en route to home or battlefront.

"I know they need beds, but when we can't give proper service . . . In the long run, it's very bad for the reputation of the Stratford."

"But, Papa," Miranda protested, "all the hotels are doing it. The Metropolitan takes in more than a hundred every night."

"I know, Pet. I've known that for months. And they are not alone. It's just that I hate to see our standards decline, even in a good cause. And Mrs. Darcy insists that the housekeeping staff is being run ragged, and finding reliable help these days is next to impossible. You know that."

"Yes, Papa. You are right."

She brooded about the problem, and late the next afternoon, after a full day at the Cooper Institute, she paused in the Stratford office to talk about it again. Will looked up from the ledgers and peered at her expectantly as she pulled off her gloves and cloak and sat down across from him.

"Papa, I think I have a solution for you."

"Solution?" He smiled at her, but she was being determinedly businesslike, and she pulled out a small notebook and checked a list.

"*I* know where we can find reliable help for the housekeeping staff." She was obviously very much pleased with herself.

"And where is that, Miranda?"

"At the Cooper Institute. It occurred to me that some of the poor women I see coming in for help might be glad to work here. They are certainly respectable and deserving, and if you and Mrs. Darcy approve, I could suggest— Why are you smiling at me like that. I think it's a *good* idea."

"Oh, Pet, of course it is. It's just that you are into everything these days, and now you are my employment scout, too. Talk to Mrs. Darcy and work it out between you. I give you a free hand. Come, give me a kiss." He hugged her and patted her shoulder and smiled. "I'm so pleased to see you cheerful and happy, Miranda. I *do* think you are rushing around too much, but since most of it seems to be at Faith's beck and call, I guess you have Richard's approval."

Miranda let that pass. "And one more thing about the hotel, Papa." She sat down again and studied the list in her notebook. "We definitely need more cuspidors. If we are going to have all those soldiers in the ballroom every night . . . Why do they *all* chew tobacco? I don't see how they ever get their girl friends to kiss them."

Will laughed. "I'll warn Richard not to take up the habit. This time, though, I'm ahead of you, Pet. I've already given instructions—a spittoon between every two beds." He looked at her notebook with interest. "What else do you have there?"

"Oh, that's all there is about the Stratford." She checked off the last item. "All the rest is about the Sanitary Fair. The Metropolitan Fair," she corrected herself. "Just think! Aunt Faith thinks we can raise three hundred thousand dollars! The men's committee is afraid we'll be in over our heads, but I *know* we can do it."

Will nodded solemnly. "How would they dare challenge you?"

"I know you are teasing me, but I don't care. It's going to be wonderful. We're writing to every single embassy and consulate abroad to organize and send us things. Can you imagine what we could charge for a shawl from Queen Victoria or a sword from the Prince of Wales? Even their autographs or signed pictures would be valuable. And if President Lincoln would give us a copy of his speech at Gettysburg in his own hand . . ."

"Are you going to write and ask him?"

"*I'm* not. But one of the women on the committee has met him, and she thinks he'd do it. He sent the original draft of the Emancipation Proclamation to the Great Northwestern

Fair in Chicago, and we are going to be bigger and better than that."

"I see. And the rest of your list?"

"These are letters I have to write tonight. Don't worry, Papa. I'll get it all done. And my letter to Richard, too."

"I am sure you will, Pet. You are becoming frighteningly efficient. Be careful or you'll be just like your Aunt Faith."

"Oh, Papa! She's really *nice* when you get to know her."

Will raised an eyebrow, but Miranda didn't notice.

"Dany," she said, half to herself. "Dany probably knows people in London who would be on the committee there." She wrote a note to herself about that, and she was so absorbed that she didn't notice the desk clerk standing in the doorway until he cleared his throat to speak.

"I'm sorry to interrupt you, sir. You know we are filled to capacity, but there is a Mr. Adams here who wants to speak to you."

The mention of that name pierced her self-control, and she dropped her notebook and pencil and then her gloves, too. She was still scrambling on the floor to pick them up when a half-familiar figure appeared on the threshold. She looked up, and Mr. Adams smiled at her—and it was Cort's smile, but he wasn't Cort. He helped her rise and retrieved her gloves and presented them with a flourish.

"You must be Miranda. Mrs. Schuyler," he corrected himself immediately. "I am Warren Adams," he introduced himself, "Cort's brother, from Boston."

"Oh, yes. That explains it." Miranda smiled uncertainly and knew she was blushing.

"It's good to see you, Warren." Will extended his hand. "How are you? And your wife? I understand you have twin daughters now, in addition to a son."

Warren nodded, smiling.

"And how is your dear mother?" Will went on. "I haven't seen you since . . . since Cort's wedding."

"That's right. We are all well, sir. The babies are quite a handful for Abby, but she is managing. And Mother is delighted with her new grandchildren."

"Splendid." Will motioned him to sit down. "And what can I do for you?"

"Well, I need a room, sir." Warren was clearly embarrassed. "Of course I should have written for a reservation, and I do apologize for that. But I had no idea that accommodations would be so hard to get. The clerk said something about a bed in the ballroom, and he seemed to think all the other hotels would be equally crowded."

"Very true," Will agreed. He paused a moment to look at Miranda, but she was calm now, and in any case he had a duty to be hospitable. "We are completely booked, I am afraid, but there is no reason you can't have Tom's room in the family quarters."

"That would be very good of you, sir, though I do hate to intrude."

"Nonsense. We'll be glad to have you. Miranda, why don't you take Warren upstairs and get acquainted. And ring for tea. I'll join you in the library in half an hour."

Warren Adams was older than Cort and, Miranda decided, more conventional. Carefully avoiding any mention of Cort, she inquired about Boston and the family and his trip to New York, and Warren was courteous and agreeable and just a shade reserved. He reminded her of someone—someone besides Cort—and it wasn't until he began talking with increasing animation about what he had been reading on the train that she placed him: He was just like Jimmy, most at home in the world of books. He had finished that vaguely scandalous work by an Englishman, Charles Darwin, and he had to share his enthusiasm with the first available listener.

It wasn't his field, he explained, but Mr. Darwin made it so clear, and when you stopped to consider the variations in nature and in domestication and the relationships between species and subspecies, then the whole theory of natural selection . . .

Miranda smiled at him, and he trailed off, apologizing for boring her.

"You weren't boring me," she assured him. "It was just that you reminded me so much of Jimmy. When he found the right book, he would light up like that, too."

Warren knew about Jimmy, his shattered arm at Fredericksburg, his death in Washington. It had been almost a year now, and Miranda discovered she could talk about him now, make him live again for this sympathetic new acquaintance who might become a friend.

"And Jimmy was a scholar," she summed up, "like you. You must have won all the prizes, too."

Warren looked at her, astonished. "I didn't know it showed. Or perhaps Cort told you?"

"No," Miranda contradicted him, "he didn't say a word about that." She tried to remember what he *had* said about his brother. Something about Warren having no head for business, and that was why the panic of '57 had such a disastrous effect on the family fortune.

"I was going to be a professor," Warren said, suddenly looking much younger, almost boyish. "I had studied in Berlin for two years and was planning to go back to work on my doctorate. But then Father needed me at home. After all, he was ill, and I was the older son, and I was expected to take over the management of the property." He shrugged. "That was a rather difficult apprenticeship, and it lasted far too long. However, I finally learned. I kept telling myself that if I could work my way through the German philosophers, I ought to be able to calculate interest on a business loan. And eventually I proved myself right." His smile was rueful, and for a moment he looked exactly like Cort. "Of course, in a paradoxical way, the war has helped a lot. It's almost impossible *not* to make money out of this tragedy." The thought depressed him, made him restless, and he stood up to poke the fire and wander around the room. "I don't know why I'm telling you all this. I hadn't expected to find you so easy to talk to."

She was startled and showed it, and he immediately apologized.

"That sounded rude, but I didn't mean it that way. It's just . . . Forgive me. Cort inherited all the charm in the family."

"Not all," Miranda assured him, and he inclined his head, acknowledging the compliment. "Why didn't you think I'd be easy to talk to?"

"It's my built-in prejudice against beautiful women, I suppose." He smiled at her. "They all used to head straight for Cort, and it wasn't until he went to England and I met Abby that I realized it was possible for a girl to be pretty and charming and intelligent all at the same time—and be interested in me, too, of course." He laughed. "You ought to meet her. Why, *she* will even pay attention when I tell her about Charles Darwin and the theory of evolution. And then she'll read the book, too."

Miranda smiled. "It sounds like a perfect marriage. And you have three children now?"

He nodded. "My hostages to fortune. I am afraid that it really *is* impossible to break away now."

"Break away?" Miranda was scandalized.

"I wanted to enlist, you see, and I still . . . But at the beginning there was a good deal of financial pressure on me to stay home, and now, with all the family responsibilities, I suppose it is impossible. The greatest adventure of my generation, and I am sitting at home, missing it all."

"Why, that's what Jimmy said!" Miranda looked at Warren in surprise. "He was so young when he enlisted, and he had his whole life before him."

"But if that was his choice . . . There are no easy answers." Warren sighed again. "I thought Cort had it all worked out, with marriage and a family and participation in the war, too—and without the guilt of killing, either. But I'm not so sure now. When he was in Boston . . . But perhaps that was just my imagination."

Miranda looked at him curiously.

He smiled. "The grass is always greener on the other side of the fence, I suppose. He told me *I* had made all the right decisions and that I should keep right on cultivating my garden."

Miranda didn't catch the literary allusion, but she knew what he meant just the same. All those duties and projects close at hand. Immediately she began to talk about the plans for the Metropolitan Fair, and when Warren told her his mother was working on the Sanitary Fair in Boston, scheduled for January, Miranda pulled out her notebook again. Perhaps they were doing something up there they hadn't thought of in New York yet, though, frankly, she doubted it. Still, she would write a letter.

Will came in just as Miranda glanced up from her list, and he smiled at her. "Are you drafting Warren to help, too? I must warn you, my boy, that if you have any free time at all, she will put you to work while you are here."

"That's right," Miranda agreed. "How long are you planning to stay?"

"Not more than three days, if that isn't too much of an abuse of your hospitality, sir. Cort wanted me to look at some property here. I saw him at Thanksgiving, you know, and we thought perhaps a joint investment . . . New York is growing so fast, and land values keep rising as the city moves north."

Will agreed. "Yes, I remember when I first moved here, when the Astor House opened, this was considered to be uptown. By the time I built the Stratford, we were right in the heart of it all. And now, I'm afraid the city is going to be passing us by."

"Papa!" Miranda was shocked. "The Stratford has *never* been so crowded."

"Because of the war, Pet. Who knows what will happen afterward? George and I were talking about it last month in Washington. I hate to face the possibility, but we may have to relocate eventually."

"No! You don't really mean that, Papa!" For Miranda it was an unthinkable idea. "I like it *here*."

"So do I, Pet. But George and Tom have to think about the future, and they will be the ones to make the decision."

"But this is home," she said stubbornly.

"Don't worry about it, Miranda. Nothing will change until after the war. And by then," he smiled at her, "you'll be moving into your own house, with Richard, and you'll be too busy to pay much attention to the Stratford any more."

"I'll always pay attention to it," she insisted, but he shook his head and started talking to Warren about the changes that had taken place in Boston.

Miranda sighed. They were all so sure that once she had children she'd never think about anything else at all. Richard was already making veiled references in his letters to any changes she might have noticed in her physical condition since Thanksgiving. And, as a matter of fact, she had. She was a few days late, but she saw no need for him to monitor her so closely. She'd tell him when she saw him at Christmas, if there was anything to tell.

It was two days later and the evening before Warren Adams was to return to Boston. Miranda had seen little of him since their conversation the first day, and she looked up, surprised, when he came into the Stratford office and closed the door. Cort had done that once—closed the door and pocketed the key . . .

Warren stood in front of the desk, obviously uncomfortable, and perhaps embarrassed, too. "I'm sorry to bother you, but there's a problem . . ."

For one fleeting moment, she thought he was going to ask her to lend him some money, but it was not that; it was much worse than that. At her urging, he sat down, but he still had trouble getting out the words.

"You said I was easy to talk to," she reminded him.

"Yes, but . . . perhaps I should just forget the whole thing." He stood up abruptly, almost knocking over the chair.

Why, he was as flustered—Miranda groped for a comparison—as she had been when she talked to Mrs. Cantrell about the possibility of an abortion.

"I am sorry," he said, speaking rapidly. "You must think I'm a fool, and perhaps I am, but when that Irish bartender at the Astor started talking about Pinkertons . . ."

Dear God. What was Marty up to now? And if he had dragged in Kevin Kelly . . .

"Sit down." Miranda was firm. "Start at the beginning. It may all be a mistake, but tell me."

"At the beginning," Warren repeated, reluctantly resuming his place. He still seemed doubtful, but he took a deep breath and began. "Well, then," he concentrated on a corner of the ceiling, not looking at her, "I was crossing City Hall Park an hour ago, and I ran into a friend from Boston, Chad Welles. He is staying at the Astor," Warren was obviously intent on remembering every detail, "and he suggested I join him for a drink, and we went into the bar. My voice . . . In New York, I am frequently told I have an accent. I don't hear it myself, but perhaps I do." He looked at her for confirmation, and she nodded. "And Cort and I have always known that our voices are much alike, so perhaps that explains it. And Welles called me Adams in the presence of the bartender, so that's how he knew my name. At any rate, Welles had an appointment and had to leave before I had quite finished my drink, and the bartender came back to see if I wanted anything else. An Irishman, with red hair. I had never seen him before in my life. And he stood staring at me with the most . . . malevolent expression. I couldn't imagine what was the matter with the man."

Warren darted a glance at Miranda, and she sighed, realizing that an explanation, at least a partial explanation, was necessary.

"You know that Cort rescued me during the riots?"

Warren nodded. "Yes. He didn't say anything about it to me, but when I was in Washington in September, George and Emily told me the whole story, called him a hero. He refused to talk about it—got up and left the room." Warren made an effort to smile. "Cort never used to have any trouble accepting praise."

Miranda made no comment on that. "This bartender that you met—it was Kevin Kelly?"

"That is the name he gave me. He expected me to recognize him."

"Yes. He had you confused with Cort, I suppose. You see, it was Kevin who helped me get away from the mob during the riots. And then he took me to his wife, and while she was taking care of me, he got this idea into his head that he would collect ten thousand dollars from Papa. But when Cort found me, that put a stop to Kevin's little scheme." Miranda looked to Warren for understanding, but he was still puzzled, and she went on. "I suppose Kevin is still nursing a grudge, even though Papa gave him three hundred dollars to escape the draft. But that was for Kathy's sake."

"I suppose that explains part of it," Warren said tentatively, but Miranda caught the doubt in his voice.

"What else did he say?" She realized she was clutching the arms of her chair, and she made a conscious effort to relax.

"He said, he said . . ." Warren's eyes were focused on the ceiling again, and he spoke rapidly. "He said that he thought it was worth something for a jealous husband not to be told that his wife was . . . attracted to me. And no doubt Mrs. Schuyler would be greatful for his silence, too."

"Dear God." But Kevin hadn't even been there. And it was five months since the riots, and why was he making these threats now? It must be because the Pinkertons had come asking him about Cort. And then Kevin had gone home and talked to Kathy and Mrs. Flaherty, and they had told him . . . What could they have said? What could they have known? There was no need to panic. Kevin couldn't do anything. If he went to Richard this very minute, what would happen? Richard would go storming over to the Astor and get Kevin fired. No, Kevin was making only empty threats. He thought he had recognized Cort, and he was willing to try a little blackmail, but Warren had said . . . What *had* he said? He was still trying not to look at her, still embarrassed at having wandered into this situation, whatever it was. Miranda collected her wits and made an effort to soothe him.

"I can't imagine where Kevin gets these crazy ideas. First extortion and now blackmail. Richard will be furious when I tell him. Kevin will be sorry he ever spoke to you. What did you say to him when he made that threat?"

"Why, I . . ." Warren was clearly embarrassed again. "I am afraid I lost my head. I said I didn't know what he was talking about, and then I threw what was left of my drink in his face and walked out." He risked looking at her again, and this time he smiled. "And it was really pretty fair brandy, too."

Miranda laughed, and that broke the tension.

"What do you think we should do about all this?" Warren asked her.

"Do? Why, I am not sure we should do anything. I'll tell Richard, of course." And he'll be furious with Marty, she was thinking, but there was no need to go into all that with Warren.

"I don't think that completely solves the problem," Warren said slowly. "As long as Kevin feels free to slander you and Cort, I think he's dangerous. We should stop him."

"What do you suggest?" Miranda was wary.

Warren looked at her and then looked away. "I think I must tell Cort. Or perhaps you should write to him, tell him that this Kelly is talking about blackmail. Of course there is no reason to submit to such threats, and I am sure that Cort would never pay, but this man should be warned off." Warren still could not meet her eyes. "Malicious gossip can be dangerous, even when there is no basis for it in fact."

Miranda studied him, and she knew he wanted to believe that—that there was no basis in fact for Kevin's story. But he knew Cort too well, and he hardly knew her at all, and he was uncomfortable with his doubts.

"I think you are right," Miranda told him. "I'll tell Richard, and I'll write to Cort and let him handle this." And Kevin would cave in before Cort. But that wouldn't solve it all. Damn Marty anyway. He was the one who needed to be shut up. He took a perverse pleasure in tormenting her, and he always had. And he could be as tenacious as Richard when he went after something.

Chapter 30

RICHARD AND TOM came home together for Christmas, and this time Miranda was waiting for them at the Stratford, with an unexpected visitor. Lucy Blaine just happened to be in the neighborhood, she said, and she thought she'd stop by. Miranda smiled at that transparent fiction, and Lucy giggled.

"I wanted to surprise Tom," she acknowledged. "And Mama said I could invite him to dinner tomorrow, and you and Richard, too."

"I'm sorry, but we can't come," Miranda apologized. "We'll be with Richard's parents."

Lucy looked startled, ready to protest, and Miranda hastily corrected herself.

"Just Richard and me," she amended. "I'm sure that Tom will be delighted to accept."

"Yes, he already has." Lucy's smile was broad. "He accepted even before I suggested to Mama that she invite him. Oh, Miranda!" Lucy could hardly contain herself, refusing to sit down, almost dancing around the room. "I don't know when I've been so happy. Tom is going to talk to Papa tomorrow after dinner." She swooped down on Miranda and kissed her. "We'll be sisters now. Isn't that wonderful? And all the time I was growing up I never even noticed him. I had a crush on George for a while . . ."

"I know. Everyone had a crush on George."

"And then there was Dev . . ." Lucy trailed off. She had been engaged to marry Robert Devlin, and he had died in the Libby Prison in Richmond.

"Do you still miss him?" Miranda asked, remembering how heartbroken she had been.

"It's not that I miss him exactly," Lucy said, trying to put her feelings into words. "But he was part of my life, the most important part of my life, for more than two years. And when he was captured . . . I'll always remember him, and he'll always be nineteen years old, the way I saw him last. Christmas, 1861. Do you know I'm already six months older than he was then?"

Miranda nodded, understanding. "And Damon and Jimmy will never grow old, either. But we go on living and changing."

"And learning to love again," Lucy added. "Tom is so wonderfully understanding. Dev was a dear boy, in my mind he always will be. But Tom is a man, and I think . . . I think I had to grow up a lot myself before I could really understand him and love him." She looked at Miranda for confirmation.

"I think he's very lucky to have found you, Lucy." And then she smiled, ready to claim a little of the credit for herself. "Of course, I whispered in his ear."

"Yes, I know." Lucy beamed at her. "I think you could hire out as a matchmaker."

"Not right away." Miranda brushed off the suggestion with a smile. "Not until the fair is over. You just *have* to volunteer, Lucy."

Lucy nodded absently, thinking only of Tom, but Miranda rushed on, fired with her own enthusiasm. "You know it's going to be in the armory on Fourteenth Street, and we're going to construct a whole new building right next door, too. It will be huge! The men's committee was afraid to invest the money at first, but when they saw how well organized we are and how many donations we are getting, they just had to agree. We've opened a special receiving depot on Great Jones Street, and the express companies are carrying all the gifts free of charge, and . . ." She was still talking, persuading, convincing, when the library door opened and she lost her audience. Tom was there, and Lucy hurled herself into his arms, and he kissed her. Miranda smiled at them fondly; and then, aware of Richard, she hurried into his embrace.

"How lovely you are, Miranda. More beautiful every time I see you." Richard held her at arm's length for a moment and looked her up and down, and his eyes held a question.

"I don't really know, darling." She felt herself blushing. "It's still too early to be sure."

"Darling!" He kissed her again. "It must be true. *I* say it's true, and you say I'm infallible, so that makes it official."

"Oh, Richard!" She laughed. "There's something the matter with your logic, but we'll wait and see."

He refused to entertain any doubts. "What a perfect Christmas present!" He embraced her again and then reluctantly broke away to greet Lucy and let Tom kiss Miranda.

"A perfect Christmas present?" Tom raised an eyebrow, and Miranda groped for an answer.

"Being together again," Richard cut in swiftly.

"Oh, yes, I agree with that." Tom smiled at Lucy and took her hand. "And what a wonderful surprise, to find you here, waiting for me."

"She just happened to be in the neighborhood," Miranda said with a straight face.

"Of course." Tom grinned. "Just the way I happen to be in the neighborhood of Gramercy Park whenever I get a chance."

"Mama said I should invite you to dinner tomorrow," Lucy said primly.

Tom gave her a formal bow. "Mr. Chase is pleased to accept. Mr. Chase would also be pleased to invite Miss Blaine to stay for tea this afternoon."

Richard stirred, restless, but Lucy needed no prompting.

"No, I wish I could, but they are expecting me at home, and I—"

"Then I will take you there." Tom was all agreement. "Just let me find Papa and tell him I'm here."

"I thought they would never leave." Richard closed the door after them and turned to Miranda, seated now on the couch near the fireplace. "Darling, let me look at you." He studied her, memorizing her, loving her. "I'd like a portrait painted of you, just as you are, in that very dress. Would you do that for me? Let me commission an artist, and you can sit for him, right here, exactly the way you are posed now. I've always liked you in blue. And when you look up at me like that . . . Why are you shaking your head, Miranda? What is it?"

"Nothing, except . . . Richard, I don't have time to pose for a portrait now. At least not until after the fair." She knew she had a perfect ally. "Your mother could never spare me now."

Richard sighed. "The fair! That's all the two of you ever talk about in your letters. I know it's important, but once it's over . . . When will that be?"

"I don't know yet. The original opening date was Washington's Birthday, but now that we are constructing a special building, it might be March or even April." She smiled at him. "And if I *am* pregnant, I certainly won't want to be sitting for my portrait in May or June. Of course if I'm not—"

"Unthinkable."

"Well, then, I'll just wait until I can pose with the baby."

"Darling!" He sat down to embrace her again. "You have made me so happy, Miranda. And now—you'll be happy, too, won't you?"

She looked at him, startled, and he saw her surprise.

"But of course I knew you were miserable, darling. It was only natural after you had the miscarriage."

"Yes, of course." Why did she immediately think he knew about Cort? Always that lingering sense of guilt. She repressed a sigh. Now was the time to tell him about Kevin and his threats. She should do it immediately and get it over with.

"Richard, I have some unpleasant news, but you must promise not to be angry or do anything rash."

"I won't do anything rash," he agreed, "but I can't promise not to be angry. What is it, darling? If you have gone on a shopping spree at Stewart's, I'll forgive you. I love to see you looking beautiful, and if you have exceeded your allowance this one time—"

"No, Richard. You are too generous, and that money is going into the bank. I never have any time for shopping these days, and I had to cancel my last three appointments with the dressmaker because . . . This isn't what I meant to talk about at all."

"No?" He touched her forehead to smooth away her puckered frown. "Don't worry about it, darling. Whatever is wrong, I'll make it right. Just tell me."

"I am trying to, Richard."

He smiled at her fondly. "You are so earnest. Like a bright little child who—"

"Richard, I am *not* a child. I am your wife, and I am trying to tell you about a threat of blackmail and malicious lies, and you won't *listen*."

He sobered immediately. "I am listening, Miranda." He

stood up abruptly, severing the physical connection between them, standing by the fireplace and looking down at her. "Is Marty involved in this?"

"Indirectly, yes." She was surprised by his perception. "But the threat came from Kevin Kelly." She explained, told him all about Kevin's conversation with Warren Adams in the Astor bar, but Richard looked at her, uncomprehending.

"I don't understand. If Kevin wasn't even there when Cort found you, what was he talking about? And why is he making threats now, five months after the fact?"

"Well, I suppose . . . I suppose that until the Pinkertons came around asking him about Cort and me, he didn't think about the possibility of blackmail. And then when he saw Warren, he just seized the opportunity and said whatever came into his head. He's not a very rational person."

"No, that is evident." Richard stood silent for a moment, not looking at her. "Still, when the Pinkertons asked him their stupid questions, something occurred to him, and he saw the possibility of blackmail. Why?" It was not a question addressed to Miranda, and she did not answer it. Richard chose to work it out in his own logical mind. "No, it wasn't *then* he saw the possibility—or at least he didn't tell the Pinkertons. If he had, there wouldn't exist the possibility of blackmail afterward. And anyway, a man like that would distrust detectives or investigators of any kind. He would stay silent, saying as little as possible. No, Kevin Kelly went home and talked to his wife, asked her what had happened when Cort found you. When Cort found you," he repeated. "After he went looking for you in the middle of a riot." He was very distraught that day, Mrs. Cantrell said." A small cloud of suspicion expanded into a towering thunderhead. Richard looked directly at Miranda.

"Why was he so distraught? Why did he come looking for you? What happened when he found you?" His voice had turned cold, hard, almost threatening. "What could Kevin Kelly have found out from his wife?"

Miranda reacted with anger. "Nothing!" she sprang to her feet, outraged at the accusation in his voice. "How can you look at me that way? I am your *wife*, and I have told you myself about these malicious . . . Oh, Richard, how can you be jealous? How can you say you love me when you have so little trust?"

Her question hung in the air, and he stared at her, clenching and unclenching his hands, his face flushed and his body rigid with tension.

The silence stretched out, and Miranda sighed and turned her back on him and walked away. She reached the door and paused there, hoping his anger would subside.

"No, Miranda. Don't go." He had mastered his temper, but it was an uneasy victory, and she hesitated, uncertain.

"I promised not to do anything rash." Richard's smile was forced. "I didn't promise not to be angry. I am sorry, Miranda. You are right. You are my good angel, and jealousy is my besetting sin." He crossed the room and grasped her hand and held it. "Will you forgive me, darling?"

It never occurred to him that she might say no, and she couldn't bring herself to answer him at all. He took her silence for consent, and he smiled at her.

"My good angel," he repeated. "I didn't mean to frighten you. I know you would not betray me. Whatever Kevin might say or do, he is obviously wrong." He led her back to the couch and waited until she was seated, but he remained standing, still agitated and tense. He took a deep breath, but he could not let go of the subject. "Now I know that you are innocent, but perhaps Cort said or did something that seemed strange that day."

"Oh, Richard, why must we talk about it? I had just had a miscarriage, and I was feeling utterly miserable, and suddenly Cort was there to rescue me. I was grateful to him. I thought *you* were grateful to him. You were going to stop in Washington to thank him."

"Yes, that's true." Richard looked uncomfortable. "I couldn't bring myself to do that. I wrote him a letter, but of course that wasn't the same thing. I am truly at fault. Perhaps if I had seen him, spoken to him directly, he would have told me himself why he was there and how he happened to be involved. Why *did* he take it on himself to search you out, Miranda? And what did he say when he found you?"

"Darling, *why* must you keep worrying the subject? He knew I was missing, and he looked for me. Papa said to me afterward that you would have done the same thing if you had been here. Isn't that true, Richard?"

"Yes, of course. But I happen to love you." It was not an answer calculated to allay his suspicion or his jealousy.

Miranda sighed and tried to reassure him. "Richard, you know you would have gone to the rescue of someone else—

Dany or Lucy or Cort's wife, if she had been here. And I wouldn't immediately have suspected *you* were in love with any of them. Why can't you give Cort credit for good motives, too?"

Richard kissed her hand. "I admire your sweet and trusting nature, darling. I don't think you are right about him, but you are clearly innocent, and I apologize for my temper. However, I think you should avoid him in the future. If he *does* harbor some special feelings for you, it would be simple wisdom not to see him again."

"Even though he saved me last summer?"

"For my sake, darling, because you love me and you don't want me to be troubled by jealously again. Now," his voice turned brisk as he changed the subject, "the first thing to do is put a stop to Kevin's silly talk of blackmail."

Miranda put a placating hand on his arm. "Richard, I think Cort will handle all that."

He looked surprised, and she tried to explain. "You see, when Warren told me what happened, he suggested that the best thing to do would be for me to write to Cort and let *him* take care of Kevin. After all, Cort was the one being asked for money."

"You told him before you told me?"

"I wrote to him last week, darling. After all, I knew I would be seeing you today, and I thought it would be easier to *tell* you. Isn't that so? Warren and I thought that this was the best way to handle it."

Richard shook his head. "You should have told me first. You must always tell me first, Miranda. This tendency of yours to keep things secret from me is your worst fault. You accused me a little while ago of not trusting you." He sat down beside her, taking her hand. "I *do* trust you, darling, but sometimes you make it very hard for me. I insist on knowing everything, and if something is troubling you, you must let *me* take care of it."

"But Richard, there are some things I'd rather do myself."

"Don't try to be independent, Miranda. It's not appropriate, and I don't like it. I am your husband, darling," he smiled at her, "and you must let me protect you. Now, is there anything else I should know about? If Cort is looking after Kevin, I suppose I should not interfere. I want to know what he is doing, though, and I will write and ask him. I don't want *you* to bother him again."

"No, Richard." She shivered suddenly, and he looked at her, alarmed.

"A chill, Miranda? Do you need a shawl?"

"No, I am all right."

He put his arm around her and pulled her closer to him. "That's better, isn't it, darling? I will always take care of you and keep you safe. I love you very much, and you make me very happy. And now, when we share the hope that you are carrying our first child . . ."

She relaxed in his arms, more tired than she had realized, and his voice, murmuring endearments, was soothing as a lullaby. All those familiar words, reprised again and again. She was drowsy, and she allowed herself to drift into sleep, having heard it all before.

In spite of Richard's presence, Miranda was able to accomplish most of her set tasks during the week between Christmas and New Year's. On the two days that he looked in at the shipping office, she hurried off to the Cooper Institute, and during their protracted visits with his family, she spent most of the time closeted with Aunt Faith, working out a classification system for the extraordinary volume of salable merchandise pouring in for the Metropolitan Fair.

She was so busy that she didn't even realize that Cort had come and gone until Dany told her on New Year's Eve. The Blaines were giving a lavish party that night to celebrate Lucy's engagement to Tom, and all the family and an astonishing number of friends and acquaintances were there. Dany was doing some last-minute primping in the upstairs room reserved for that purpose, and she peered at herself in the mirror and caught Miranda's eye, noting her surprise.

"Cort wasn't at the Stratford," Dany explained, "because he stayed with that friend of Mr. Raymond, Leonard Jerome. He has a truly scandalous reputation, that man, but he is *so* wealthy. And Cort says his house is a real palace. Even the stables are built of brick and marble."

"I've heard about it," Miranda said. "Mr. Jerome owns part of the *Times*; I think that's his connection to Mr. Raymond." She studiously avoided talking about Cort, but that didn't stop Dany.

"Cort was here only overnight, but Richard spent Tuesday morning with him—I'm surprised he didn't mention it to you.

382

John and I met them for lunch that day; they had just come from the Astor."

Dany chattered on, oblivious, and Miranda seethed quietly. She was supposed to tell Richard everything, but he could go off with Cort and solve the problem of Kevin and never mention it at all. It wasn't fair, and she would tell him that, and she didn't care if he *did* get angry. Besides, she didn't like the idea of Richard making friends with Cort when she was completely cut off from him.

"And then Cort will go to Savannah to see Susanne and the children." Dany was full of news. "I think he might persuade her to leave Georgia at last. Times are so hard there now. It's one thing to do without coffee or tea or new dresses, but Cort says there are real shortages of food now, and it could get dangerous, and they might even have riots. And there isn't enough medicine, and if there should be an epidemic . . . He's always such a pessimist, but perhaps he is right. And in any case, I've said right along that Susanne should be with him." Dany looked at Miranda for confirmation. "And I do want to see her again. It's been more than three years. The summer before the war, in Saratoga. You remember. We were all there, and John and I were falling in love, and Richard helped us elope. That was so kind and wonderful of him, and he managed everything so well. He and John are very much alike. I suppose that's one of the reasons you love him, isn't it?" Dany needed no answers to keep her monologue going. "They are both so capable and so thoughtful and so sure of themselves. It means that we never have to worry about anything at all."

Miranda made no comment. Dany seemed to have wrapped her whole life around John and was content. If only she could feel that way about Richard . . . She glanced down at her new sapphire pendant, Richard's Christmas present to her, and its hard brilliance caught the light and sparkled. Just an hour ago he had fastened the thin chain around her neck, bending to kiss the shadow between her breasts where the sapphire came to rest.

"I will look at you at the party tonight, darling, and I will see this jewel, my gift to you, touching you, kissing you, claiming you—until I can hold you again when we return."

Richard was waiting at the foot of the stairs when she and

Dany came down, and he looked at the sapphire and smiled. Her response was a blush, and that delighted him.

He led her into the connecting parlors, converted for this evening into a ballroom, and he swept her into his arms for the first waltz. "You are the most beautiful girl here, Miranda. The most beautiful wife." He smiled at her. "The most beautiful mother-to-be. And my pride in you is enormous."

Her lips curved in an automatic smile, but her voice was cool. "Sometimes, darling, I think you see me as some kind of fashionable ornament to display to the world, as if I were *your* sapphire pendant, your proof of discriminating taste and good judgment."

"And so you are," he agreed. "More precious to me than any jewel. 'Who can find a virtuous woman? For her price is above rubies.' You see, I have Biblical authority."

"Yes, you have an answer for everything, Richard." She was glad when the dance ended, and she welcomed his suggestion of a glass of punch. Abruptly, she challenged him with a question. "Why didn't you tell me that Cort was in New York? Dany said you all had lunch together day before yesterday."

"And so we did."

"But you should have told me."

"I would have if I had had an opportunity. But by the time I saw you that night, you had spent an exhausting day working on the fair with Mother, and the two of you hardly seemed to notice Papa and me at all. If Irene hadn't been there, full of her usual giddy gossip, Papa and I would have felt quite abandoned."

Miranda refused to acknowledge his complaint. "But you should have told me," she repeated. "Did you see Kevin Kelly? What did he say?"

"Nothing. That is, he said he might have made a mistake, but he still didn't think it was right that a total stranger should throw a glass of brandy in his face. He managed to work up quite a feeling of injury about the whole episode. He was so blatant about it that Cort actually laughed. Kevin Kelly could squirm out of anything. I was glad to have a look at him—the man is such an obvious and unscrupulous liar."

Miranda nodded, relieved that Richard was satisfied,

tempted to ask about Cort but holding back. It was futile to think about him any more.

But Richard operated under no such constraint. "Perhaps I have judged Cort too harshly." He had finished his punch, and he contemplated the empty glass. "The man seems to be genuinely concerned about his family in Savannah—not just Susanne and the children but her parents, too. Mr. Robillard is not well, you know."

"Dany didn't seem worried about him."

"No, I don't believe she realizes how serious it is. Apparently her mother doesn't want to alarm her. But Cort says that Mr. Robillard has had a stroke and is partially paralyzed. Susanne can't bring herself to leave now, although I think she had agreed to come before this happened."

"I see. She was really going to move to Washington?"

"Cort was making arrangements to get her a pass through the lines with the children. He still hopes she'll be able to come if her father improves." He left unsaid the alternative.

"Of if he dies . . ." Miranda spoke the words aloud.

"That may be more complicated," Richard said. "I don't know if Susanne will want to leave her mother all alone. And I doubt if a fire-eating Rebel like Mrs. Robillard will consent to come North."

Miranda sighed.

"Poor Cort," Richard echoed her thought. "Just when he was willing to forgive and forget and start all over again."

"Forgive?" Miranda looked at Richard in surprise. "Did you talk to him about . . . about the real father of Susanne's little girl?"

"He knew," Richard said. "I had to tell him about Marty and those damned Pinkertons before we went to see Kevin Kelly. And I started to say something about some other malicious gossip, probably equally untrue, concerning Susanne, but he interrupted me and said he knew about it. He said he would thank me not to repeat it, and of course I assured him of my silence. He didn't admit that the gossip was true, but I think he knows it is. I rather admire the man, willing to shoulder these responsibilities, willing to try again. It shows a true Christian spirit."

Miranda made no comment, but inwardly she was raging. Could he really go back to her? Love her again? Be happy with her? Take her in his arms and caress her, send the blood pounding through her veins . . . It was just a year ago tonight, and I was giddy with champagne and tears and laughter and desire. Oh, Cort, will I ever get over you? Will I ever *feel* that much again? When I have a child, not your child, will all that make me truly happy?

She finished her glass of punch, but it was mild, too mild. "I think I will have some champagne, Richard. Lots of champagne. A magnum, a jeroboam, a rehoboam. How much is a rehoboam, Richard? Could I drink that much, do you think? Would it make me tipsy? Let's split a whole rehoboam, darling, and see what happens. Wouldn't that be a wonderful way to welcome in the new year?"

He smiled at her. "I think you are giddy on one glass of punch, and that's enough." He reached for her hand and held it. "Darling, I have already decided how we are going to welcome in the new year. I will kiss you at midnight, and we will be the first guests to leave to go home."

"But, Richard, the party will last for hours, and I want to dance with every man here and be the belle of the ball. Won't that make you proud?"

"Very proud, Miranda. But we'll leave early just the same." He relieved her of her empty glass and stood up. "I should dance with Lucy, I suppose, and wish her well. Where is she?"

"With Tom." Miranda peered at the couples circling the floor. "No, John is dancing with her now. Let them finish this polka, Richard, and then we'll change partners."

She danced with John and Tom and Papa and Richard again and his father and Mr. Blaine and Major Lorimer, who had arrived with Caroline but seemed to be spending most of his time with Irene. Caroline was clearly upset, but Irene was unrepentant. Andy Dawson was away at sea, back on that picket ship near Savannah, and Irene had to dance with *somebody*, she defended herself. And if Major Lorimer found her more attractive than Caroline, what could she do about it? Miranda sighed and moved back to the dance floor with Lucy's younger brother, Larry. She had always thought of him as such a little boy, but he was eighteen now, and he towered over her. He was a student at Columbia and, as he told her, determined to enlist as soon as the spring term was over. Miranda nodded and then, with sudden inspiration, she suggested he meet Caroline, who was just eighteen, too. Caroline was usually interested only in older men, she said, like Major Lorimer, but since Larry was so mature for his age

. . . He swallowed the flattery whole, and Miranda grinned as he squared his shoulders and moved decisively to Caroline's side. Major Lorimer rose to the bait, following after him, and Miranda was so engrossed in watching that she hardly knew she was dancing with Madison Bradley. But then she had always found Madison very easy to overlook. He might be Emily's brother and Ann's husband, but he never seemed to have an identity of his own. The orchestra took a break, and Madison escorted her to the row of little gilt chairs edging the room.

She sat down next to Mrs. Cantrell, who smiled a welcome and immediately started to talk about the oprhanage.

". . . And we still miss you, my dear, but I understand why you couldn't come back."

Miranda nodded wistfully. "I wouldn't have time for it now, with all the preparations for the fair. We will be having a special children's section, you know. Perhaps . . ." Her face lit up. "I have a wonderful idea. Caroline could have the little girls sew a complete wardrobe of doll clothes that we could sell in the toy section. Wouldn't the children like to do that? I just know they would want to help the soldiers."

"They certainly would!" Mrs. Cantrell echoed her enthusiasm, smiling at her. "I am glad to find you so cheerful again, Miranda. And you are looking so well." She patted her arm. "Is it all working out for you, my dear?"

Miranda hesitated. "Yes, I think so. As well as I could expect."

Mrs. Cantrell looked at her with understanding. "A pity. I can see why you . . . He's a good man, I think, caught in an unhappy situation."

Miranda showed her surprise. "But Richard is not unhappy."

"No, dear, of course not. I meant Cort, with his difficult marriage."

"You mean you know about . . ."

"About the daughter who isn't his. Yes. Marty can't keep a secret like that. Surely you know him that well."

"Then everyone will know." Miranda sighed. "Dany, too."

"Eventually, I suppose." Mrs. Cantrell shook her head. "It will be hard for Cort—and for Susanne—but living with that secret wouldn't be easy, either. So, they will be together again when the war is over?"

Miranda nodded. "Perhaps even sooner than that . . . And he's never going to see me again."

"A wise decision. A clean break is the only way, Miranda." Mrs. Cantell paused before she went on. "And there is another factor to be considered, too. I think that Marty has confused feelings about you. Perhaps he once fancied himself in love and you rejected him?"

"Was that supposed to be love?" Her voice rose in astonishment. "He makes me shudder."

"Well, whatever it was, or is, I think he is a little unbalanced on the subject. That's the only explanation I can find for those detectives. Unfortunately, though, Marty seems to have a certain native shrewdness in judging your reactions to other men. He is convinced, for instance, that there is something between you and Cort, and he would like to be able to prove it."

"So that he can tell Richard?"

"Not necessarily. Perhaps he simply wants to tell himself that you aren't the perfect girl he had imagined you to be, and therefore he can forget you. Or perhaps he thinks if he had some kind of hold over you, you would . . . respond to him."

Miranda looked at her, shocked.

"I could be wrong, dear, but I think you should be wary of him. It's another reason that your decision not to see Cort again is wise. And surely even Marty will give up eventually; perhaps when he knows you are pregnant again."

Miranda was startled. "How did you know? I'm not even sure myself."

Mrs. Cantrell smiled. "Perhaps *you* aren't convinced, but Richard exudes such a sense of pride and confidence and well-being that there could be no other explanation. He loves you very much, doesn't he?"

Miranda nodded, not meeting her eyes.

"It can still work out, dear. Be patient."

Miranda had nothing to say to that, and she changed the subject. "Have you noticed that Caroline has made a new conquest? Larry Blaine has hardly let her out of his sight."

Mrs. Cantrell was willing to be diverted, and Miranda took refuge in talking about someone else, chattering on about Caroline and Larry, summoning up a cheerful, surface animation. That is how Richard found her, and she smiled at him automatically and moved into his arms for the waltz that ended at midnight with his kiss.

Larry Blaine had rushed to throw open the windows to let in the sound of church bells and cannon and firecrackers, and, with a pang too sharp to conceal, Miranda remembered New Year's Eve a year ago, Cort's arms around her, his lazy smile. "The whole world is celebrating, darling."

"What is it, Miranda?" Richard looked at her, alarmed. "Is the draft too much? It was very hot in here, you know, but I'll have Larry close the windows again."

"No, it's all right. Thank you for being so concerned."

His arm circled her waist protectively. "I am always concerned."

"I know." She forced a smile to cover her emotions. "It's a wonderful party, isn't it?"

"Yes, darling. Happy 1864. I wish we could spend the whole year together." He kissed her again. "And since you are having such a good time here tonight, we'll stay at the party as long as you like."

It was a major concession, but she didn't really want to prolong the evening. They toasted the New Year with champagne and hopes for early victory, and Richard drank to her good health and to the safe delivery of their first child.

And then they went home together.

Chapter 31

IN FEBRUARY MIRANDA's work on the fair brought her an introduction to Leonard Jerome, the Wall Street millionaire with the scandalous reputation. She was curious to see his extravagant mansion, which was famous not only for its lavish stables but also for its luxurious private theater. A perfect little jewel box, everyone said, ideal for the display of Mr. Jerome's latest "protégées." The celebrated young opera star Adelina Patti, who drew ovations at the Academy of Music, was privileged to try out her new roles in these sumptuous surroundings. And when she departed for even greater triumphs at Covent Garden, a succession of other stars glittered on his private stage.

Mrs. Jerome, charming, elegant, discreetly blind to her husband's affairs, devoted herself to their young daughters and longed for the day when she could take them back to Europe. In the meantime, she fulfilled her role as perfect hostess and ignored the gossip.

But gossip or no, Leonard Jerome was a power to be reckoned with. A fervent patriot, he was determined to show his devotion to the Union cause, and to that end he was organizing benefit performances in his private theater, all the proceeds going to the Metropolitan Fair for the Sanitary Commission.

Aunt Faith, with Miranda beside her, called at his Madison Square mansion to work out the schedule of performances in coordination with other fair activities. They found Mr. Jerome most cooperative, even leading them on a private tour of the theater. They politely admired the tasteful gold and white décor, the enormous crystal chandeliers, the statuary in every niche, and the ingenious lighting effects that bathed the stage in every color of the rainbow. Mr. Jerome was obviously proud of his elaborate toy, and Faith hastened to agree that she had never seen anything like it. Surely, invited guests would clamor to come, cheerfully contributing as much as five dollars a ticket.

Amateur theatricals were so entertaining, Mr. Jerome assured them, and he would hire Mr. Wallack himself to direct the plays and perhaps to stage a brief act from an opera, too. One of his dear friends was an accomplished soprano, and he so loved to hear her sing. If she were surrounded by other attractive young ladies, what a beautiful scene that would be.

"You, my dear," he smiled roguishly at Miranda, "will certainly dazzle us from the stage."

"Oh, no! I couldn't possibly." For protection she moved closer to Aunt Faith.

"You will find it great fun." He brushed aside her objection. "We are recruiting a very select group of ladies and gentlemen, all of them most eager to take part. And of course we'll have a supper party for the performers and special guests afterward. Mrs. Jerome will send out formal invitations to both of you, and to your husbands."

Miranda looked doubtfully at her aunt.

"It's not that we don't appreciate the honor, Mr. Jerome." Faith could rise to any occasion. "The treasurer of the fair, Mrs. Strong, was telling me only this morning how much she looked forward to 'treading the boards' in such a good cause. And in other circumstances, I am sure that Miranda would be delighted to appear, but I hardly think it would be suitable for her . . . at this time."

Leonard Jerome looked mystified for a moment, but Miranda's blushes and cast-down eyes gave him a clue, and he was suddenly understanding. "But you will at least come to a performance and to a party. When you have been working so hard for the fair, you deserve some of the rewards."

To celebrate the opening of the Metropolitan Fair, Mayor Gunther declared the first Monday in April a holiday. Flags and bunting draped the buildings from the Battery to Fourteenth Street, and there was a huge parade with brass bands and ten thousand soldiers. Wild cheers greeted them all, black and white alike, from the celebrated Seventh to the newest

Negro regiment. New Yorkers seemed determined to put the summer riots behind them, to celebrate together on this festive occasion, and it was the greatest turnout since the demonstrations for the Prince of Wales before the war.

Miranda had spent a frantic last day, supervising the final arrangements at the Old Curiosity Shop in the armory. And she was present that night with her father when the fair opened with formal ceremonies, speeches, and a massed choir singing the "Hallelujah Chorus."

The invitations had been strictly limited to six thousand paying guests, but Will found the buildings too crowded for comfort. He quickly retreated to the Wigwam near the entrance where eighteen Iroquois braves were performing ritual dances for a delighted audience. The Indians were somewhat less delighted. They had been recruited from upstate for the first weeks of the fair, expecting to begin their engagement in March. Now they had launched a fight over their contract, insisting that the time they had spent waiting (and, in some cases, getting drunk) should count toward fulfilling the terms of their agreement. It wasn't *their* fault that the opening had been delayed until April.

But that was a minor problem. Overall, the fair was going to be a smashing success. Boston had raised one hundred forty thousand dollars, and Cincinnati had proudly topped that with two hundred forty thousand, sending a broom to the organizers of the fair in Brooklyn in a challenge to do better. The Brooklyn fair, which had opened on Washington's Birthday and had continued into March, made four hundred thousand dollars, and now the Brooklyn ladies had forwarded the broom and the challenge to New York.

It was possible to spend days visiting the booths and buying merchandise from every state in the Union and from virtually every country in the world. The letter-writing campaign to consulates abroad had brought in gifts from as far afield as St. Petersburg and Smyrna, Hamburg and Rio de Janeiro. There was coffee from Costa Rica and scrimshaw from the Esquimaux, and even coal from Newcastle.

The fair committee had made a point of announcing that no gift would be refused, and the very first offering had come from a poor family who contributed a tin pan—a widow's mite duly acknowledged with appropriate fanfare.

Churches had booths, states had booths, and Harlem and Staten Island and Westchester and Buffalo. The city police had elected to contribute a day's pay, but the firemen were participating directly with a huge exhibit of equipment and regular demonstrations of rescue techniques. The florists sent daily offerings to the elaborate Floral Temple, where fashionable young ladies sold boutonnieres at extravagant prices to gentlemen of all ages. Merchants contributed clothing and furniture and china and kitchenware. There were groceries for sale and needles and thread and sewing machines and india rubber goods and saddles and boots and cloaks and mantillas and fancywork of all descriptions.

There was a machinery department, a boat-building exhibit, and a whole separate building with farm implements and animals for sale.

The Picture Gallery, displaying such notable paintings as *Washington Crossing the Delaware*, was enormously popular, and the newspapers began to editorialize at great length about the need for the city to organize a metropolitan museum of art. Mathew Brady contributed a selection of his famous photographs, and publishers stocked a library and a bookstore. The collection of autographs on display came from all the crowned heads of Europe, as well as from artists, writers, scientists, and musicians. Every President of the United States was represented, starting with George Washington. Of special interest was the copy of the Gettysburg Address that Abraham Lincoln had written out in his own hand.

In the Knickerbocker Kitchen the specialties of old New Amsterdam were recreated for modern New Yorkers, and the waitresses, clad in Dutch costumes, included such leaders of society as Mrs. Stuyvesant, Mrs. Schuyler, and Mrs. Roosevelt.

There were benefit performances at all the theaters, and Mr. Barnum gave a week's proceeds from his Museum. There were children's concerts and recitals and new programs every day in the special exhibition rooms. Particularly popular were the *tableaux vivants* in the children's department. Irene and Ann and Caroline took turns appearing in the final scene, swathed in red, white, and blue, representing "Liberty Triumphant on the Battlefield." Miranda harbored a secret envy of her cousins but, even though her pregnancy was invisible to the world, it would have been shocking for her to appear in such a public display. Aunt Faith even cautioned her about donning the official costume of the fair—a red, white, and blue sash over a black silk dress—but she relented when

Miranda promised to stay behind the counter at the Old Curiosity Shop whenever she was on duty there.

With Richard away in Virginia, Miranda had expressed doubt about attending a theatrical evening at the Jeromes', but Aunt Faith was firm in her insistence that she go.

"It would be rude to send regrets now, Miranda, when we are expected. Mrs. Jerome assured me that there will be many family groups there, and the fact that Richard can't come is no reason for you to stay home. Uncle Paul can escort you into supper, if that is what you are worried about. But we'll know a great many of the guests, and I am sure you won't feel out of place. I don't understand your reluctance, dear."

Miranda did not enlighten her. Perhaps it was foolish to assume that Cort would be there, just because he had stayed with the Jeromes twice since Christmas. Dany had told her that, expressing surprise on each occasion that Miranda hadn't seen him. And until the Army of the Potomac broke out of its winter quarters, Cort might very well find time to come to New York again.

He was the first person she saw as soon as they entered the reception hall. Her breath caught, and she hesitated, wondering if she could still escape, but there was no way out. Of course Aunt Faith noticed him, too, and beckoned imperiously. She turned to Miranda with a happy smile. "Cort will be your supper partner, dear. He can tell us all about Emily's baby and Richard's last visit in Washington."

Cort bowed to them both and shook hands with Uncle Paul, but Miranda could not meet his eyes. Faith chatted with him easily, asking polite questions about the family in Savannah, and Cort was responsive, keyed up, his energy reaching out to envelop her.

Mr. Robillard was still partially paralyzed, Cort said, though he was able to speak again. And Susanne was well, and the children, too, though now she didn't know when she could come to Washington; she didn't see how she could leave her parents under the circumstances. The food riots in Savannah hadn't touched them directly—only the poor were really suffering. Confederate money didn't go very far, but Cort had supplied the family with Yankee dollars, and he didn't think they would go hungry.

Paul Schuyler shook his head. "Jeff Davis is a damn fool as well as a traitor. Why doesn't he give up now and spare them all this misery? As soon as the spring campaign starts . . ." He laid down his views on military strategy, and Cort listened gravely, not saying a word in contradiction.

Congress had created the rank of lieutenant general for Ulysses Grant, who was now in command of the Union forces; and surely the war would be over as soon as he moved the Army of the Potomac toward Richmond once again.

Miranda sighed and thought of Richard and the inevitable battles to come. She touched her sapphire pendant and was aware again of Cort's eyes on her.

"Richard is well," he said. "He was in Washington last week, but he declined to stay overnight. I think he felt that he should spare Emily any extra effort as hostess, though of course she was delighted to see him. Still, perhaps he was right. The baby was born three days later. George Washington Chase, Jr."

"We got the telegram, but the name seemed to be in doubt." Miranda smiled for the first time, still not looking at him. "I knew Emily would win. She insisted all along the first boy had to be George. How does Polly like having a little brother?"

"She is a little bewildered, I think." Cort smiled. "She seemed to believe he was a new toy for *her*, and she didn't see why her mother was playing with him so much."

"Dear Polly. I would like to have been there for her birthday."

"I missed it, too. But I'll give her my present when I go back at the end of the week."

Miranda caught an odd note in his voice, and when she glanced up, his eyes locked on hers.

"At the fair yesterday," he said, "I bought her a complete wardrobe of doll clothes, made by the little girls at the Colored Orphans' Asylum."

Miranda made no response, but he had touched her, and he knew it.

"Caroline will be so pleased." Faith was completely unaware of any undercurrents. "I don't know if you have met my niece, Caroline Schuyler, but the doll clothes were a special project of hers. Miranda, dear, I think you gave her the idea."

Miranda nodded, not trusting her voice.

Faith plunged into a detailed account of the fair, with much praise for Miranda, and Cort listened attentively and smiled and said all the right things. And they greeted other guests and exchanged compliments with the Jeromes, and Miranda smiled automatically and tried to tell herself that it was just another party, just another social evening, and there was no need to be conscious of her heart hammering for attention. She fingered her sapphire pendant and tried to think of Richard, but with Cort standing there . . .

And at last it was time to enter the theater for the presentation of two brief scenes from Verdi's *Ernani* and a comic play called *The Ladies Battle*. Miranda found it impossible to concentrate on the performance, and afterward she remembered nothing of what she had seen. When the lights dimmed, she was conscious only of Cort beside her. He didn't touch her. He didn't say a word. But a current of emotion flowed between them too intense to be ignored.

It was a mistake to have come tonight. A terrible mistake. All that feeling of longing and desire belonged to Richard, but she felt powerless to divert it. She was pregnant, she reminded herself, in her fifth month. At a time like this, how could Cort still dominate her life? And then, astonishingly, she felt the child quicken within her, Richard's child, their child, their future.

The applause and curtain calls broke through her shell of self-absorption, and Aunt Faith was looking at her, worried.

"What is it, dear? Are you feeling faint?"

"No, I'm all right. I think," she leaned forward to whisper, "I think I felt the baby move for the first time."

Faith beamed at her. "How happy you must be, dear. Paul, Miranda says—"

"Oh, don't tell him now." Her color was rising, and Cort looked at her with surprise.

"It's all right, Miranda," Faith said. "He's the baby's grandfather, after all." She whispered in his ear, but Paul simply looked embarrassed.

"Are you all right, child?" His voice was a little gruff, and he was clearly uncomfortable. "Shall we take you home now?"

"No, I'm fine. Truly."

"We'll leave immediately after the supper," Faith declared.

"You must not get overtired, dear, and I'm sure the Jeromes will understand. And Cort, too."

He nodded, his smile a little puzzled, and he took Miranda's arm to escort her into the dining room. "I wish you could stay, darling."

The endearment startled her, and she looked around guiltily, but no one else had heard.

"There is nothing wrong, is there? I know about the baby, of course, from George and Emily. You are looking so well ... But just now, in the theater, did something happen?"

She was silent, and with her free hand she fingered her sapphire again.

He sighed. "I know you can't forget Richard. But you can't forget me, either. Can you, Miranda?"

She refused to look at him, but she was very conscious of his hand on her arm; and even when he released her and she was sitting beside him, she still felt the pressure of his touch. Determinedly, she tried to concentrate on the conversation at the table—the talk about the performances tonight, about the fair, and then the war, always the war.

Virginia was still relatively quiet, but the first news had trickled in of a massacre at Fort Pillow in western Tennessee, and they were all agreed that it was shocking, outrageous. General Nathan Bedford Forrest had led a detachment of Confederate cavalry against the sparsely defended outpost, and after the surrender many of the Federal troops, both black and white, had been cruelly murdered by the victorious Rebels. Negro women had been killed, and several children, too. Bayoneted, shot, sabered—even the dead were mutilated. And then the bodies were rolled down the bank to the river or piled in heaps to be burned, a jumbled pyre of the dying and the dead.

"Rebel savages," Paul Schuyler proclaimed. "Hanging is too good for them. To massacre prisoners in cold blood, wounded and defenseless, women and children alike."

Cort shook his head.

"Surely you aren't defending those butchers?" Paul stared at him, amazed.

"No, I could never defend a massacre." Cort spoke slowly, almost unwillingly. "Perhaps it happened—this whole war is filled with such senseless killing. But these first reports are fragmentary, perhaps exaggerated. We'll have to wait for a full inquiry."

"The reports sounded convincing to me," Paul contradicted him. "And we have a full record of their savagery. Andersonville should be proof enough of that. Our men are dying there, twenty-five a day at last report. Do you deny that? And the ones still alive are living skeletons. Skeletons in rags. I was in Annapolis last week when the first prisoners in the exchange arrived. Seventy pounds, one man weighed. That's torture, right out of the Middle Ages. I'd hang the lot of them, starting with Jeff Davis himself." Paul made his pronouncement, and no one disagreed.

Faith sighed and put her hand on his arm. "I think perhaps this is too harsh a conversation, dear. Remember that Miranda . . . When you men are alone, you can be as bloodthirsty as you like."

Mrs. Jerome gave the signal for the ladies to withdraw, and Miranda stood up too quickly, bent on making her escape. For a moment she felt dizzy and had to grasp the back of her chair for support.

Cort reached out to her instinctively. "I will take you home."

"Oh, no, please. I am fine."

"Cort is right." Faith was in firm agreement. "We'll say good night to the Jeromes and—"

"Now, Faith," Paul Schuyler protested. Clearly, he did not want to leave before the best part of the evening. He had sat through that silly performance in the theater and made polite conversation all through supper, and now that it was time for brandy and cigars, he refused to be dragged away. "Cort can take Miranda home."

"Nonsense," Faith hissed in his ear. "How would that look?"

Paul was impatient with such niceties, and Faith groped for a compromise.

"I could leave with them." She looked at her husband questioningly. "You didn't want to stay for the dancing?"

"Fine, fine. You be champerone. I'll follow along as soon as we are finished here." He sat down again, eager to resume his war on the Confederacy. Even from the hall they could hear his voice booming in outrage. "Those damned pirates, attacking our ships . . ."

Once settled in the carriage, Faith decided it wasn't necessary for her to make the long trip to the Stratford and back when Cort and Miranda could easily take her directly to Washington Square before proceeding downtown. She had observed the proprieties by leaving with them, and that was sufficient.

Miranda did not protest, feeling caught up in a chain of events that led inevitably to this moment, alone with Cort. They rode in silence the rest of the way, not touching, and she felt the tension building between them. He dismissed the carriage when they reached the Stratford and followed her inside, up the stairs to the library.

When he closed the door, she moved into his arms as if she had never been away, and when he kissed her, she came alive again, aware, acutely sensitive to his touch, conscious of her drumming heart, conscious of the rising tide of passion ready to engulf them both. He was unfastening the row of tiny buttons on the front of her dress, easing down the ruffled bertha, his lips finding the hollow between her breasts, pushing aside the sapphire that Richard—

Abruptly she broke away, breathing hard, fighting to regain control of herself. Cort made no move to stop her, but she felt his eyes on her, willing her to come back. She clutched the sapphire like a talisman, and she stood in the little alcove overlooking the park, waiting for the roaring in her ears to subside, waiting for her heart to beat normally again. Richard, she reminded herself. And the baby. She looked down at her gaping bodice and automatically refastened the buttons.

"We weren't going to see each other again," she said aloud, her voice still a little shaky.

"We tried, Miranda. We both tried. I stayed away. Even at the fair yesterday when I saw you from a distance and you didn't see me, I left immediately. But now that we are together again, and I know you want me as much as I want you . . . Just sitting next to you in the theater tonight—"

"I didn't want to go. I was afraid you'd be there. I knew it was too soon. Please, Cort, I have been trying so hard to forget you, to bury all these emotions forever. It's dangerous to feel this way."

"Dangerous," he agreed. "But exciting, darling, poised on this knife-edge between joy and pain, awake to all your emotions, opening yourself again to all the passion and wonder and astonishment of being alive."

She shook her head. "I can't. I won't. It's a moment, and it ends, and what happens afterward hurts too much. I don't want to cry again. Ever. I haven't cried since . . . since I read your letter last August. I don't want to see you again, Cort. I want all these feelings to shrivel up and die. You must feel that way, too. Why else are you going back to Susanne?"

"Are you jealous, Miranda?"

"How can I be jealous? I have a husband. Why shouldn't you have a wife?"

"You didn't answer my question. I know you have a husband, and the very thought of him . . . You are carrying his child, and I wish it were mine. With all my heart, I wish it were mine."

"But if you go back to Susanne and live with her in Washington . . ."

"Will it hurt you, Miranda? Will you think about us? Will you wish you were there in her place? When the fire burns low on the hearth and I hold her in my arms—"

"Stop it, Cort. I don't want to think about it. I don't want to think about it ever again. You want me to say I'm jealous. All right. I'm jealous. But there's nothing I can do about it. And if you are going back to her to be cruel to me or to her or to yourself, then—"

"No, darling. I am going back to her because I can't have you, and I want to make some decent effort to reconstruct my life. That's what you hope to do with Richard. It isn't working, I'm afraid, but you will break your heart trying. Dear God, I could wring his neck. He is systematically robbing you of all your joy and passion and spirit, forcing you into some preconceived role of dutiful, submissive wife. And you are such a terrible actress, Miranda. He must be blind."

"He loves me. Or at least he loves his vision of me. It would be so much easier if I could be what he wanted, and I am trying. Perhaps it will be better when our child is born. I felt the baby move tonight, Cort, for the first time. I was sitting next to you and—"

"Cause and effect, Miranda?" He could not keep the sarcasm from his voice, or the pain in what followed. "Emily said the child is due at the end of August. I couldn't help counting. Thanksgiving, in Washington, in my house. Couldn't you spare me that?"

"Oh, Cort, *you* started all this. New Year's Eve, a year ago, and I am still trying to get over you. You make it so hard for me, darling. For us both." She turned away from him and stared, unseeing, at the lights across the park.

He reached out, as if to touch her, and then dropped his arm. "I'm sorry. I shouldn't have come. I won't bother you again, Miranda." A worldly cynicism entered his voice and then faded. "What a pity we can't all be more like the Jeromes. Susanne would turn a blind eye in my direction and never fuss. And if I chose to spend my happiest hours with you, I would know I would not be breaking your heart—or mine. Or even Richard's." He sighed. "I suppose that twenty years from now, when I am nursing my gout and Susanne is plump and matronly, you will still be my far-off princess, the dearest part of my life. I only hope to God you aren't dead inside."

"I will be plump and matronly, too," Miranda said firmly, "with half a dozen children. And all the girls will be suffragettes," she said, turning back to him, forcing a smile, "and all the boys will be reformers."

"Hold on to that much of your dream, Miranda." He looked at her with longing. "But, my dearest, we could have had so much more. At least let me hold you one last time."

She shook her head.

"A farewell kiss? I promise to stop there."

"No." She clutched her sapphire pendant. "*You* might promise that, but how can *I*? How often can I find the strength to say no to you when I—"

He kissed her again, and she clung to him and buried her face in his shoulder. He was murmuring endearments, parting endearments, pledging not to see her again, and she swallowed hard, forcing back the tears, finding no words for her emotions. And then she felt the sudden tension in his embrace before he dropped his arms and stepped back, away from her.

She looked at him, bewildered, and was finally aware that the door had opened and her father was standing there, shocked and angry, more angry than she had ever seen him.

"You will leave immediately, Cort, and never come back."

Miranda looked at him pleadingly. "But, Papa, you don't understand. We were just saying good-by."

"Miranda is right, sir. We were saying good-by."

"You were never to see her again. I had your word of honor as a gentleman. How dare you take advantage of her, and now, of all times, in her delicate condition."

"I am sorry. It was all my fault." His eyes were bleak, and he shook his head when Miranda tried to protest.

"But, Papa—"

"Go to your room."

"Oh, Cort." She reached out to touch him. "I didn't want it to end like this."

"Miranda!" Her father raised his hand as if to strike her, and she looked at him, appalled. And then she swallowed her tears and her anger and lifted her head.

"Good-by, darling." She tried to smile, but she couldn't force her muscles to cooperate. "Don't blame yourself." Abruptly, she gathered up her skirts and fled.

She did not cry, and she was composed and waiting when her father entered her room.

"I have never in my life been so disappointed in you, Miranda."

"We were saying good-by," she repeated stubbornly.

"He should not have been here. Why in the world did you leave the party alone with him?"

"We weren't alone. We were with Aunt Faith."

"And then he came sneaking back?"

"No. Both of us took Aunt Faith home. She knew we were together. *She* trusted us."

"I trusted you, too, before tonight."

"Oh, Papa, *nothing* happened."

"It is fortunate that I discovered you in time."

"Why did you come into the library at all?"

"I was restless, waiting for you, and I thought I had heard your step half an hour ago. How long were you with him?"

"I don't know. Not long. We were saying good-by," she insisted.

"This time I hope you both mean it. Dear God, Miranda, how can you even think of another man when you have a loving husband and a child on the way? I remember when your dear mother—"

"Don't, Papa. Don't tell me again how happy you were. I don't want to hear. I am trying so hard, and I want this baby so much, and perhaps then . . ."

He sighed. "All right, Miranda. But I must have your word that you won't see Cort again."

"I won't, Papa."

"Then that ends it, and we won't talk of this again. My poor child . . . It's probably my fault, too. Sarah always said

I would spoil you. I should have heeded her advice years ago and sent you to Litchfield."

"Papa! No! How can I stand it if you stop loving me, too?"

"Oh, Pet, how can you say such a thing? Of course I love you, and I can't bear to see you so unhappy. How *can* Cort mean so much to you? How can he trifle with your affections when he has a family of his own?"

Miranda looked away and clutched again at her sapphire pendant. "Let's not talk about it any more. It's over. How many times must I tell you that?" And how many times would she have to repeat it to herself before she was truly convinced? The war would end, and Richard would come home, and they would build their house and fill it with children. She would concentrate on them, live for them. The first boy would be named Richard, of course. And the first girl . . . The children would have all the happiness she had missed, with the whole world to choose from. A little girl like Polly. Why, of course! She'd call her Cordelia! And she would grow up and marry for *love*. Why, if Cort's son, Bobby, was anything like him . . . Oh, what a traitor her mind was, drawn to Cort on any pretext.

She wrenched her thoughts back to the present and kissed Papa good night. She should go to bed and try to sleep. In the morning Aunt Faith would be expecting her at the depot on Great Jones Street. If she could just concentrate on that, on all the duties at hand, all the work on the fair. They would ticket the next selection of merchandise and supervise the delivery . . .

Oh, Cort, will I ever see you again?

Chapter 32

THE FAIR ENTERED its final week, still drawing huge crowds, but the center of attention had shifted to the Department of Arms and Trophies. It had been a popular exhibit right from the beginning, with its display of weapons and banners and uniforms honoring the heroes of the past and present. So educational, everyone agreed. And patriotic, too. Who could not be stirred by the roll call of battles and heroes from this cruel war, the torn and bloodstained regimental flags, the spent bullets scavenged from the peach orchard of Shiloh, the cornfield at Antietam, Cemetery Ridge at Gettysburg. And then there were the heartbreaking personal souvenirs—a farewell letter, a lock of hair, a pocket Bible, a cherished photograph of a boy who would never grow old.

But what made the Arms and Trophies Department so newsworthy in the waning days of the fair was the hotly contested election to choose the most popular general of the war. Tiffany's had donated two elegant swords, encrusted with silver and gold and gems, one to be awarded to an army general, the other to a naval officer. It cost a dollar to vote for your favorite, no limit to the number of dollars and ballots you could buy; and this was one election in which ladies were given the right of suffrage, too. The contest for naval officer excited little interest (Commander S. C. Rowan of the *New Ironsides* won over Admiral Farragut, 462 to 332). But the voting for the most popular general developed into a fierce political struggle, with the lead seesawing daily between General Grant and General McClellan, between unconditional surrender and negotiated peace. Toward the end, there were remarkable surges in the vote totals, each side pouring in its

404

contributions at the end of the evening, expecting to overwhelm the opposition. On the closing day, the Grant supporters came from behind with a massive outpouring of votes and dollars (the Union League had been canvassed), and the final score gave their man 30,291 votes, swamping Little Mac's 14,509.

Miranda read the final results with enormous satisfaction—another $44,800 for the Sanitary Commission.

By the time they closed the books on the fair, they had grossed $1,340,000 and netted $1,176,000, more than all the other cities' fairs combined.

What remained unsold when the doors closed for the last time was auctioned off or packed up and given to the fairs in St. Louis and Philadelphia, and it was early June before the committees disbanded and life returned to normal, normal for wartime.

By then the spring campaigns were under way, with battle casualties mounting to record levels. Grant, as promised, was a fighter, and he hurled the Army of the Potomac across the Rapidan, aiming at Richmond once again. There were savage battles in the Wilderness, at Spotsylvania Court House, at the North Anna, and at Cold Harbor, the powerful Federal forces moving relentlessly as the Confederates yielded inch by inch, exacting their payment in blood. Farther west, General Sherman was marching his troops into Georgia, making such rapid progress that his army was menacing Atlanta by early June. That was good news for the Republicans, meeting in convention to renominate Abraham Lincoln and to choose Andrew Johnson for Vice President. Their hopes for victory in November would be heavily dependent on the progress of the war.

As spring turned into summer, in Virginia the visions of triumph on the battlefield shimmered like a mirage on the desert, beckoning the troops forward, only to dissolve once again in the realities of blood and mangled bodies and casualty lists that seemed to have no end. In mid-June Grant's armies crossed the James River for a back-door approach to Richmond through Petersburg, and they almost seized the victory then and there. It was so close, so heartbreakingly close. But Lee executed his usual miracle, and the Confederate forces held. Grant settled in for a costly siege operation, and the casualties continued to mount alarmingly.

In the North the movement for peace, always strong,

gained new adherents. Surely there ought to be some way out of this terrible war, some way to end the death and destruction and the rivers of blood. Horace Greeley took the lead, and when two Confederate emissaries arrived in Canada, he urged President Lincoln to sound them out.

In the meantime, Rebel troops under Jubal Early mounted a daring attack on Washington, swooping in as close as Silver Spring. It was a diversionary raid that caused considerable excitement—the Lincolns left their summer residence at the Soldiers' Home for the comparative safety of the White House—but there was little real danger. And Early withdrew hastily when the Federals organized a pursuit force—that didn't quite manage to catch him.

The flurry of peace overtures continued, and Mr. Greeley, with naively high hopes, met the self-proclaimed Confederate diplomats at Niagara Falls. He carried a document from Lincoln that said peace would mean a restoration of the Union and the end of slavery, but the Confederates still demanded complete independence. With no room for compromise on either side, there could be no negotiations, no settlement, no peace. The irrepressible conflict would be fought through to the end.

As if to emphasize that fact, Lincoln called for another five hundred thousand volunteers to fill the ranks of the decimated armies. Five hundred thousand men, to be enticed to join by Federal, state, and local bounties—or to be prodded, if necessary, by the fear of conscription.

At the end of July the Confederate cavalry made another spectacular raid, this one reaching as far as Chambersburg, Pennsylvania. The Rebels demanded a ransom of five hundred thousand dollars in currency or a hundred thousand dollars in gold, and when the money couldn't be raised, the troops set fire to the town.

The burning of Chambersburg startled the North, but the raid had no lasting effect on the course of the war. Much more devastating to Union hopes that day was the failure to seize Petersburg. For a month a regiment of Pennsylvania troops, most of them miners, had been tunneling more than five hundred feet toward the Confederate lines. Early in the morning they set off their explosion, blasting out a huge crater that at first seemed to have shattered the Revel defenses. The Yankee troops surged forward, but the Confederates rallied, finding easy targets in the thousands of attacking soldiers vainly trying to scramble up the sides of the vast excavation. By the time the Federal forces had been ordered back, their casualties numbered in the thousands.

Among the wounded was Lieutenant Thomas Jefferson Chase.

When the telegram arrived, Miranda opened it with shaking hands, but it was Lucy Blaine who made the decision to go to Washington to see him. She was determined to be there when Tom's hospital ship docked at the landing station in Aquia Creek. And she was, with Will and George beside her. Tom revived when he saw them all, holding fast to the ship's rail and waving a crutch in the air to signal his exuberance.

"It's the other leg this time." He grinned at them all. "The Rebs are trying, but they still can't shoot straight." He put his free arm around Lucy and kissed her, and then he showed off his dexterity with the crutches. "I'm an old hand at this, and I'll be as good as new in another three months. Two, with a devoted nurse." His arm circled Lucy's waist. "That means you. Let's get married right away. Think what a nice long honeymoon we could have. You wouldn't really care if I had to hobble around at the beginning, would you?"

"Oh, Tom, I'm just so glad to see you *alive!* I didn't bring my trousseau, darling, but if you don't mind a bride in a slightly dusty traveling dress, I'll marry you today."

George smiled at them both. "Surely you can wait until the end of the week. It will take at least that long to make arrangements—to wire your parents, Lucy, and see about a minister, a ring, a wedding supper, whatever you want."

They were married three days later, plenty of time for her parents to arrive, and even her brother, Larry. It wasn't the lavish affair she had once planned, but Lucy said it was the most wonderful wedding she had ever been to, and the most romantic, because it was hers.

Miranda heard all about it afterward, first from her father and then, two weeks later, from Lucy's mother. Mrs. Blaine had been disappointed at first that Lucy hadn't taken time even to be fitted for a new wedding dress (all those yards of white organza still in the box from Lord and Taylor). But Lucy looked lovely in her borrowed finery, the antique ivory satin gown that had been Emily's wedding dress. Mrs. Blaine pulled out a picture to show Miranda. "That was Cort

Adams' wedding gift to them—he wasn't able to be there, but he insisted on arranging for a visit to the photographer's studio. Wasn't that thoughtful of him?"

Miranda nodded and asked the question she had not dared to ask her father. "Why wasn't Cort there?"

Mrs. Blaine looked puzzled for a moment. "It wasn't clear to me why he didn't stay. I thought at first he had gone back to Grant's headquarters in Virginia, but afterward Emily said something that made me think he had crossed the lines and was trying to reach Susanne and her family. Sherman is sure to capture Atlanta any day now, and if the army moves farther into Georgia, they will certainly march toward Savannah."

Miranda made no comment, and Mrs. Blaine turned back to the subject of Lucy's wedding. "And Larry was there, you know. I still think of him as my baby, even in an army uniform. He's so glad to be in the same regiment with Tom and Richard, and I must say that I feel better, knowing some of his officers. Larry likes Tom so much, and of course he admires Richard enormously."

Miranda basked in reflected glory. "Yes, I know he's a good officer, but very strict and demanding. Tom says that's a good thing—Richard created such a storm on the one occasion when the food wagons didn't get through that his company hasn't gone hungry since."

"I didn't know about that, dear, but Larry told me he deserves a medal for his heroism after the crater collapsed at Petersburg."

Miranda looked surprised.

"He didn't tell you? But he went plunging in before the smoke cleared and helped drag out three wounded soldiers. Tom told us about it. It's a miracle any of them got out alive—the barrage of gunfire was so fierce."

"I didn't know. No one said a word to me. They all think I'm too fragile to be told anything at all." She rested a hand on her bulging stomach and felt the baby move again. He (or she) was protesting this confinement, too.

Mrs. Blaine smiled sympathetically. "The last days are the hardest, dear. Next week, is it?"

"I hope so."

"And are you all ready? Still sewing and knitting and crocheting?"

Miranda laughed. "I didn't ever master those arts. But the

layette is huge just the same. Aunt Faith keeps bringing me wrappers and booties and dresses, and I think I could outfit quadruplets. And three of the children at the orphanage made an afghan—it was a little grubby by the time they finished it, but Caroline washed and steamed it for me, and it shrank only a little. I promised to wrap the baby in it the very first day. And Caroline crocheted the most delicate little bonnet; it exactly matches Richard's christening dress. Aunt Faith had saved that, of course, and we'll use it next month for young Richard Beekman Schuyler, Jr. Dickon, I'm going to call him."

Mrs. Blaine smiled. "Are you so sure it will be a boy?"

"Positive. He is so demanding."

Mrs. Blaine laughed. "Miranda, my dear, you'll learn that little girls can create just as much fuss. I am glad you are looking so well, and I hope I am not tiring you."

"Not at all. Will you stay for tea? Mrs. Cantrell and Caroline are coming, and I'm sure they'll be glad to see you."

Mrs. Blaine hesitated before accepting. "I'd like that, dear, if you don't think it would embarrass your cousin."

"Embarrass her? Caroline is shy, of course, but I hardly think—"

"Larry is quite infatuated with her, you know, but I think she is very unsure about her feelings for him. And the last time I saw her, just before Lucy's wedding, she turned beet red when I invited her to come with us. Larry would have been so happy to see her, and since she is Tom's cousin, I knew she would be welcome. But she actually stammered when she said she didn't see how she could arrange to go on such short notice, and she thanked me profusely for inviting her, but she was obviously very much upset."

Miranda nodded. "I see. I didn't know you had asked her to the wedding, but I know why she would have been upset. It was three weeks ago that she heard Major Lorimer was missing in action."

"I didn't know. I didn't realize . . ." Mrs. Blaine looked puzzled. "I remember Jack Lorimer from Lucy's engagement party, but I thought he was Irene's beau."

Miranda sighed. "I'm not sure if he's anyone's beau, but Caroline has been half in love with him for years. If only he would make up his mind one way or the other. That is—if he's still alive. Poor Jack. And poor Caroline. Not knowing—that must be the worst of all."

Mrs. Blaine agreed, and in the silence that followed, Miranda rang for tea.

When Caroline and Mrs. Cantrell arrived, they brought Marty with them. Miranda had had no idea that he was in New York, and she was astonished to see him. But she introduced him to Mrs. Blaine and was relieved to see that he was on his best behavior. And Caroline was glowing with happiness for the first time in weeks."

"He's alive!" she said, hugging Miranda. "Jack is alive!"

"Why, that's wonderful, Caroline! When did you find out? Where is he, and is he all right?"

"Marty brought the news this morning. He was all night on the trains and ferries from Washington, but he said he wanted to tell me himself. Wasn't that dear of him?" Caroline beamed at her brother, but Marty was willing enough to share the credit.

"I saw George yesterday," he explained. "I knew that if anybody could find out what happened, he was the one. And sure enough, he checked through all the latest reports, and Jack is listed as missing, believed captured."

"Oh, I thought you meant he was safe. That is . . ." Miranda trailed off. "Still, it he's a prisoner, at least he's alive."

"It's not so bad in the officers' camps," Caroline said, trying to convince herself. "They aren't all like Andersonville."

"And anyway, the war will be over soon," Marty assured her. "Another month or two and we'll free them all."

"We'll free them all," Caroline echoed, and she looked to Miranda for confirmation. But Miranda had busied herself pouring the tea, and she missed Caroline's plea for reassurance.

"Let me tell you about the wedding," Mrs. Blaine said, seizing a topic to divert them from the war. She brought out Lucy's photograph again, and Mrs. Cantrell and Caroline made all the appropriate comments.

"I learned something else from George," Marty moved closer to Miranda, paying no attention to the others.

Miranda eyed him uneasily and stirred her tea.

"Cort Adams is missing."

The words didn't penetrate immediately. She had time to set down her cup and saucer and grip the arm of the sofa, but her voice betrayed her emotion. "What . . . what do you mean?"

Beside her, Mrs. Cantrell was suddenly alert and broke off the conversation about the wedding.

"Cort Adams is missing," Marty repeated, measuring Miranda's reactions with undisguised interest. "He had slipped through the lines almost three weeks ago on his way to Savannah, and no one has heard from him since."

Mrs. Blaine looked bewildered. "But how *could* anyone expect to hear from him?" She was conscious of the tension and tried to break it with a joke. "It's not as if we have telegraph service to the Confederacy."

Marty gave her an impatient glance. "George should have had a message a week ago. It was all arranged. Cort didn't even get as far as his first stop in Virginia."

"Does George know what happened?" Mrs. Cantrell spoke calmly, but she had a protective arm around Miranda, and she was furious with Marty for upsetting her.

Marty shrugged. "Maybe his luck ran out. Or maybe he was just careless. He isn't the first Yankee reporter to disappear without a trace."

"But that's terrible!" Caroline was all sympathy. "He was such a good friend of Jack's."

"And of the whole family," Marty said, still staring at Miranda.

"Yes," Mrs. Blaine agreed, "such a good friend. He made Lucy and Tom so welcome in Washington, said they could stay there until Tom is well enough to travel to New York. I hadn't realized it was Cort's house until Emily told me. Will she and George be able to stay on there, do you think?" And then, realizing the implications of her question, she backed off hurriedly. "But naturally we don't know yet what has happened to him. He might be perfectly all right."

"Captured," Caroline agreed. "Like Jack. Do they treat reporters like prisoners of war? I've never thought about it before." She looked questioningly at Miranda, who did not answer her.

"Are you all right, Miranda?" Caroline always asked the wrong questions. "You look so pale. Is it the baby?"

Miranda summoned a shaky smile. "I'm not sure. I think . . . I think perhaps I'm just a little tired, and it would be better if you would leave now. I don't mean to be rude, but . . ."

Mrs. Blaine stood up hastily, pulling on her gloves. "All

this talk of war. Very upsetting for you, dear. At a time like this, you should be thinking only happy thoughts."

That made no sense to Miranda. Her mind was in turmoil, and she needed all her concentration just to look calm during the flurry of leave-taking. She would have asked Mrs. Cantrell to stay, but that would have required some explanation for Marty, and she wanted him out, immediately.

They were gone at last, but her heart was still racing, beating erratically, and she stood by the open window, clutching the heavy drapes, trying to breathe deeply. It was hot; it was always hot in New York in August. She seized the irrelevant thought. That's why she used to leave the city in the summertime. Why didn't she do that any more? She hadn't been away on a real vacation since before the war, that summer in Saratoga with Richard and his family and the Robillards and Cort . . . Oh, what could have happened to him? Where was he now?

If he had been captured, he probably wouldn't be exchanged. Yankee reporters were treated like prisoners of war, like officer prisoners of war for the most part. There had been two of them from the *Tribune* in Richmond, in the Libby Prison, and then they were transferred to North Carolina somewhere. If Cort were there, he'd be able to get word out. He could bribe a guard, send a message somehow. He could always do things like that. Nothing could stop him . . .

But something had. Gone three weeks and no word. If George was worried, then there was real cause for alarm.

But he couldn't be dead. She refused to admit the possibility. He might be lying wounded in some isolated slave cabin, out of touch with the world, with no one to care for him properly, no one to feed him and love him and nurse him back to health. So that he could return to Susanne.

She dragged through the next week, blaming her depression on the war news, the political news, the long hot summer, the endless wait for the baby, anything but Cort's disappearance. She read the casualty lists with dread, and for the first time allowed herself to question whether the war was worth all this sacrifice.

The Democrats, meeting in convention in Chicago, adopted a peace platform that had been heavily influenced by the

Copperheads. And then, in partial contradiction, they nominated General McClellan for President.

Divided as they were on the question of peace and war, they faced a Republican party that had its own factions to contend with. Lincoln had been nominated on a Union party label, but the Radical Republicans had split off with their own candidate, General Frémont, who promised a harsh Reconstruction once the war was over.

There was considerable pessimism among supporters of Lincoln. Political experts noted that no President since Andrew Jackson had successfully sought a second term, and Lincoln had been only a minority winner in 1860. In late August, accepting the possibility of McClellan's election, Lincoln secretly asked his Cabinet members to sign, without reading, a memo pledging cooperation with the new President. If the war news continued to be bleak, no one doubted the prospects of a Democratic victory in November.

The South clung to the hope that McClellan would be elected. If they could hold out that long, then perhaps the Democrats would sue for peace.

And so, even though Admiral Farragut damned the torpedoes and sealed off Mobile, and even though Sherman was investing Atlanta, as long as Lee held firm at Richmond and Petersburg, the country faced another gloomy fall and winter of bitter conflict.

Miranda pored over the newspapers and tried to put Cort out of her mind. And she dutifully read and reread the barrage of letters from Richard. He was still in the lines near Petersburg, worrying more about her than he was about himself, worrying about the baby most of all. And he was still doubtful about the nurse Miranda had hired for the child. What exactly were the woman's references? Just because she was a poor widow who had been working at the Sanitary Commission, that didn't necessarily mean that she measured up to his exacting standards. The choice of someone to care for his infant son (or daughter) was too important to be left to some whim of Miranda's, to some object of charity she had found at the Cooper Institute. The fact that this Megan Kennedy had a ten-year-old daughter of her own would distract her from her single-minded devotion to their baby, and surely there was some more likely candidate that his mother could find for them.

Miranda was exasperated. Why, in the middle of a war, was Richard worrying about a domestic problem? And it wasn't even a problem. Megan was capable and experienced (if you counted raising her own daughter), and Miranda liked her enormously. If Richard was going to fret, Aunt Faith would simply have to write to reassure him again. Faith had expressed some reservations: Megan seemed to be an intelligent woman, still young enough at thirty to deal with the demands of a baby but mature enough not to be foolish or irresponsible, but she had never worked as a servant before. However, since Miranda was so determined, Faith gave her reluctant endorsement. Megan, with daughter, Maureen, moved into the Stratford, occupying what had been Jimmy's room. Will was somewhat bemused by these additions to the family—or to the staff; there seemed to be some question about their role. But he gave in to Miranda, as he usually did, to be rewarded with a spark of her old enthusiasm. And the little girl turned out to be quiet and well behaved, in stark contrast to Miranda when she had first been turned loose in the Stratford at that age. But then Maureen wasn't turned loose. She never ventured into the public rooms or into the family quarters, and she scuttled up and down the backstairs as if determined to remain invisible. Much of her time was spent in the kitchen, where she stared wide-eyed at the inexhaustible supplies of food. In the six months since her father had been drafted and gone off to war to be killed, the family had gone from working-class poverty to dire want. For Maureen it was a simple miracle not to be hungry all the time.

Showing none of his father's brisk attention to punctuality, Richard Beekman Schuyler, Jr., made his appearance in the world a week late. Glowing with pride, Miranda held him in her arms at last, exhausted but triumphant. She had known all along the baby would be a boy. Richard would be so pleased. Such a strong, healthy child, smiling at her. Of course he was smiling, she insisted—he was safe and warm and very much loved. The baby yawned and settled into sleep, and Miranda yielded him to Megan and followed his sensible example.

In less than a week she was up and dressed, rapidly regaining her strenth and eager to get back to the Cooper Institute. Faith looked at her doubtfully and suggested she wait for at least a month. She was nursing the baby, of course, so she couldn't be away from him too long.

"But Dickon will come with me," Miranda said. "Megan can take care of him, and I'll be there whenever he needs me."

Faith was shocked at the suggestion. "It would not be suitable. Not suitable at all. We can't turn our offices into a nursery, and I am surprised at you, Miranda, for even suggesting such a thing. You may come in for a few hours in the afternoon, dear, but Dickon stays at home. Why, it wouldn't be healthy for him to be there, even if it was proper."

Miranda knew better than to press the point. It was a great concession that she was to be allowed to come back at all. Only the unrelenting demands of the war made it possible for her to venture out so soon after the baby was born.

In far-off Virginia, Richard was still advising her to stay at home and rest and eat properly—the baby must be well nourished. If she gained a little weight, that was to be expected. He longed to see her again, but it was unlikely that he would be able to get to New York before November. They should not put off the christening on his account—it was important that the baby be baptized, and he agreed that George and Emily should be the godparents. He loved her very much, and he didn't see how the Rebels could hold out much longer, and he would certainly be home before Christmas, whether the war was still going on or not.

From Cort there was no word at all. Warren Adams passed through New York on his way back to Boston, acknowledging that his expedition to Washington had been fruitless. George had pulled all the strings he knew, Mr. Raymond of the *Times* had exerted his influence, the war department had made inquiries, but Cort Adams had disappeared from the face of the earth. There were many nameless graves in Virginia, and it was unlikely that he would ever be traced. The disposition of his estate would have to wait until the war was over, but in the meantime George and Emily could continue to live in his house in Washington, and Warren would handle his investments and send support to Susanne and the family in Savannah.

Miranda listened with an attempt at calm control that her father tried to reinforce later.

"It's a sad loss to his family, of course. We have all made such heavy sacrifices—I think of Jimmy every day. But all our lives go on. How lucky we are that George and Tom and Richard have survived. And now you have Dickon, too. Such a good, happy baby. And you were right, Pet, to choose Megan to take care of him."

Will rambled on, talking about the future, life after the war, Richard coming home, the families together again. George and Tom had already narrowed their search for a new site for the Stratford, far north on Fifth Avenue, near the Croton Reservoir. They would take out a mortgage on the present hotel . . .

Miranda nodded, still reluctant to accept the changes in her world. She should be grateful that she had so much, that the war news was better again, that victory was inevitable, no matter which Presidential candidate won.

General McClellan had repudiated the peace plank in the Democratic platform, and then General Frémont had withdrawn from the campaign, throwing his support, albeit reluctantly, to President Lincoln. With Sherman's army cutting a wide swath through Georgia, no one doubted that the war was finally grinding on toward victory. Lincoln's reelection was assured at last, even though New York City voted two to one against him.

A week after the election Miranda was in the library writing a letter to Richard when Dany burst in on her.

"He's dead, Miranda." Dany's eyes were brimming with tears, and she threw herself on the couch and gave way to her grief. "I just found out. After all these months . . ."

"After all these months," Miranda repeated, and her heart lurched. She had refused to believe it until now. The dream had died months ago. It should never have been born at all. He had been married from the beginning, and then there was Richard, and now there was Dickon, too, and there had never been any room in her life for Cort at all. Gone forever. That pulse of excitement and danger, his eyes gleaming when he looked at her, his knowing smile, the cool intelligence that penetrated any sham. All the strength and charm and passion . . . Richard, she reminded herself. I am married to Richard.

"The letter came from Susanne." Dany was struggling to get control of herself. "It took two months to get here. He died September 6."

"Five days after Dickon was born," Miranda said, trying to hold fast to her realities.

Dany wasn't even conscious of the interruption. "They were all with him—Susanne and the children and Mama. She was holding his hand, and he opened his eyes and looked at them all with so much love . . ." Dany broke into sobs again.

Miranda swallowed hard and tried to think of something comforting. "It was good they were there," she said finally.

Dany nodded and wiped her eyes. "I knew about his stroke, of course, but he was getting better and—"

"Stroke?" Miranda retreated a step and gripped the back of a chair. "What are you talking about?"

"Why Papa, of course. What did you think? He died, and I just found out, and there was no one to talk to who knew him at all. I went to the office to see John, but Uncle Paul said he'd gone to the docks, and I couldn't follow him there, and I just had to tell someone. And you knew him, a little. Oh, Miranda, I haven't seen him or Mama or Susanne since before the war. Not for four long years, and I miss them so." She renewed her weeping, and Miranda reached out to hold her.

"Dany, I'm so sorry." And she was, but one part of her mind was rejoicing. Not Cort. This time, not Cort. Poor Dany, to lose a father, an anchor to the past. But it wasn't Cort. And at least Dany had John, and she loved him.

"All my childhood," Dany sobbed. "I'm losing it all. Home will never be the same again, and even if I can go back someday to Savannah—" Her voice cracked on the word, and she took a deep breath before she went on. "Even when the war is finally over, it will all be different. Susanne sounded so frightened in her letter. Cort was on his way to rescue her, but if he is dead now, too . . . And they are all waiting there, right in the path of Sherman's army. Oh, Miranda, what if I never see any of them again?"

"Dany, it can't be that bad. And the war will end soon. It just has to. And your mother is all right, isn't she? And Susanne and the children? You'll see them all one day."

"I hope so. Susanne says that they are all right. There's a lot of sickness in the city, but so far they have been well. Just Papa—" Her voice cracked again. "And I wasn't even there for the funeral." She looked down and smoothed her dress, a royal blue silk with dark braid. "I should have put on mourning. I didn't think. I got Susanne's letter and I just ran out of the house and jumped on the ferry. It's a wonder I remembered to reach for my hat and cloak."

"You poor dear. But I'm glad you aren't home by yourself. You must stay for dinner. We'll send word to John to come here, and he can comfort you better than I."

Dany nodded, and Miranda tried to divert her. "Dickon should be waking up now. He's growing so fast. Don't you want to see him?" Miranda didn't wait for an answer, and Dany reluctantly followed her to the nursery.

Megan had just finished changing him, assisted by Maureen, who was rocking him now and crooning a lullaby that seemed to have no effect whatever. The baby was bright-eyed and wakeful and hungry, demanding to be fed, and when Miranda took him in her arms, opening her dress, he reached for her greedily. She took enormous pleasure in satisfying his needs, more pleasure than she had ever had from Richard, and her emotions were so tangled that she didn't know whether she should feel guilty about that or not. All she knew was that Dickon was the most completely satisfying part of her life, and he was hers, to love without restraint or caution or fear of discovery.

Dany looked at her wistfully, and then she turned abruptly and bolted from the room.

Miranda was startled for a moment, but she made no effort to follow. Dickon came first. He would always come first. But she roused herself enough to send Megan off to comfort Dany before settling back in the rocking chair, cradling the baby. She was content to burrow more deeply into her cocoon with Dickon, shutting out the world.

Chapter 33

O N A SUMMER day in August, Cort had crossed through the lines in Virginia and made his way to Charlottesville. Standing in line to buy a train ticket, he was rudely accosted by a Confederate soldier on crutches.

"Why aren't you in the army, healthy man like you?"

"I'm a newspaper correspondent," Cort said mildly, "from England."

"A likely story!" the soldier sneered. "There's no news here. The battlefield is miles away, back there." He gestured vaguely toward the north. "You're a deserter. I can smell one out every time."

"My good man—"

"A deserter," the soldier repeated, hobbling to the door. "Sergeant Jackson," he shouted, "I've found another one."

The sergeant looked at Cort dubiously and examined his identification, but when a routine search yielded a hundred dollars in Yankee greenbacks, the sergeant decided he had different game. "A speculator!" He spit out the word. "They'll know you in Wilmington, I'll be bound."

Wilmington, North Carolina, was the last of the Southern ports where the blockade-runners made even an attempt to land; and it was also where the speculators gathered to bid up the prices on the few luxuries that trickled in from abroad. Who but a speculator would be carrying Yankee dollars? An exchange of telegrams with the authorities in Wilmington yielded a vague description of a murderer who might be this man Adams, now passing himself off as a journalist.

Cort's protests were futile, and three days later he was dumped, unceremoniously, in the Wilmington jail.

They held him for two weeks before finally admitting there was no reason to charge him with anything. They were still suspicious, but, as the warden explained to him, the fact that he had been willing to stand trial worked in his favor. If he had made even one attempt to bribe the guard, he would not be walking away now, a free man.

Cort did not quite trust the warden or his reasons for letting him go. He suspected they were still keeping an eye on him, and it seemed wise to leave Wilmington as soon as possible, particularly since he wasn't feeling at all well. He blamed that on the terrible food in jail, but now even a reasonably good meal at the local hotel didn't seem to help. He felt feverish, too, and was worse in the morning. Nevertheless, he boarded the first train out of the city.

Three hours later the conductor found him slumped in his seat, eyes glazed and skin clammy, and he was bundled off the train at the next stop, an unidentified crossroads in South Carolina. There wasn't even a proper depot—this was a flag stop, and the train had paused only long enough to discharge Cort and one other passenger, an elderly gentleman who looked at Cort with some surprise.

"Are you sure you have the right place? This is Caine's Crossing."

Cort heard the words without comprehension and, for the first time in his life, fainted dead away.

When he revived he was in a carriage, propped up against his satchel, the elderly gentleman peering at him anxiously.

"I am taking you home," he explained. "I couldn't leave you there. Who are you? Where are you going? What's the matter with you?"

"Sick," Cort whispered. "Very sick." Somehow he had lost his hat, and the sun was glaring down unmercifully. He raised his hand to shield his eyes and tried to focus on his rescuer, but in the shimmering heat he could barely distinguish outlines. It was a relief when they turned into a shaded private drive, but when they stopped in front of a white-columned house, he didn't have the strength to move.

The carriage was immediately surrounded, a blur of faces, black and white, and there was a babble of welcoming voices. Cort couldn't sort them out, and he made no effort to try. Strong arms lifted him down and carried him to a cool bedroom on the second floor, and the last thing he remembered before passing out was a pretty young woman holding his head while he sipped a glass of water.

She was there again when he swam back to consciousness late in the day, and she smiled at him and laid down her knitting and came to his bedside.

"So, you are reviving at last." She rested a cool hand on his feverish forehead. "A little water?" He nodded, and she poured a glass from a frosted pitcher. "My name is Dorothy Caine, Miss Caine." She was staring at him with frank interest. "My father brought you home, said he found you at the flag stop. Who are you? Where are you going? What happened?"

Cort hesitated, realized they must have checked his belongings—though they probably hadn't found the concealed pocket in his satchel where the money was hidden. He told her part of the truth—his name, his destination, the fact that he was a newspaper correspondent. But he identified himself as an Englishman, and he neglected to say that he had a wife and family in Savannah.

"I wasn't feeling well when I left Wilmington, and I don't know what's the matter with me." He looked at her questioningly, but she shook her head.

"The nearest doctor is miles away. We used to have Dr. Andrews, but he's with the army in Virginia now. I do most of the nursing on the plantation, but I don't know what kind of fever you have. We have herbs, but no real medicines."

Cort nodded and tried to smile. "I thank God I fell into such good hands."

She took him literally, looked at her hands, looked at him, and then blushed.

"Eddy put you to bed," she told him primly.

"Eddy?"

"He drives the carriage. He picked up Papa at the flag stop and brought you home and then carried you up here."

"All by himself?" Cort couldn't credit it.

"He's a big man, too. And once he got here, his son Trevor helped."

"I see." Cort nodded. "And where is 'here'?"

"Why, Cainewood, our home, near Florence." She went on to explain that she was one of five children, three daughters and two sons. The boys were in Virginia with the army, the older sister was married and living in Florence, and the younger one, the baby of the family at fifteen, arrived with the supper tray just as her name was mentioned.

"And this is Rosemary," Dorothy said.

Rosemary blushed at the introduction, and Cort smiled at her and made an immediate conquest. That, as it turned out, was a terrible mistake on his part.

The sisters were in and out of the sickroom for the next three weeks, and they looked on it as a positive triumph when Cort finally declared himself well enough to totter down to the dining room to have supper with the family.

He had written to the Robillards almost immediately to explain where he was and to instruct Susanne to get in touch with his brother, Warren, so that the family would not worry. And he also asked if Susanne could come to Cainewood with one of the servants to help him continue his journey to Savannah. He wrote twice more, and there was still no response. It was true that mail service in the Confederacy had deteriorated, but by the first week in October, Cort still had no word. He had no explanation for the delay, and he fretted about it with all the restless energy of a convalescent, wondered if Susanne were ill and her parents, too, and he could think of no reason at all for their continued silence.

Mr. and Mrs. Caine, so obliging and hospitable all through the month of September, were clearly beginning to have doubts about him now. Rosemary had obviously developed a crush on him, and he could not tease her out of it. Even Dorothy, Miss Dorothy, as he called her respectfully, was looking at him with troubled eyes.

"Papa doesn't believe you," she told him frankly. It was a Sunday night in early October, and he was restlessly pacing the front porch, virtually recovered from his illness. Typhoid fever, he had decided it was—that jail in Wilmington was a very unhealthy place.

Dorothy continued to gaze at him, but Cort was silent.

"Your friends in Savannah should have come by now, should have written to you at least," she said. "Papa doesn't believe they exist. He thinks you are a Yankee spy."

"And you, Miss Dorothy, what do you think?"

"I . . . I don't know. I don't think you are here to betray us. But I don't think you have told us the whole truth." She was sitting, very still, on the porch swing, and he stopped his restless pacing to study her.

"You are right," he said finally. "It has been an abuse of

your hospitality not to explain myself, but at the beginning I didn't know you."

"And now?"

"Now, I think I can trust you."

"Yes, Mr. Adams, you can trust me."

He smiled and sat down beside her. "Well, then, to begin, I am *not* a spy, though I must confess to being a Yankee. I'm a newspaper correspondent for *The New York Times*."

"I see." But she was clearly puzzled and didn't see at all. "But you were in Wilmington . . ."

"Yes. A case of mistaken identity. They had thrown me in jail, and when they released me, I was already coming down with typhoid. I owe my recovery, I owe my life to you. To your family," he amended hastily when he saw her emotional response. "You have *all* been so good to me, Miss Dorothy, and I can never fully—"

"We have loved having you here, Cort."

It was the first time she had called him that, and he was conscious of the light pressure of her hand on his arm.

"Miss Dorothy, I know you have a fiancé with the army in Virginia, and—"

"Cort, I haven't seen Blake for two years. I haven't heard from him in six weeks. I don't know if he is alive or dead, if I still love him, if I ever loved him, if he'll ever come back to me." She took a deep breath, but she plunged on. "What is important is that *you* are here, Cort. You are here now, as if fate had sent you, and I . . ."

He kissed her. He saw no graceful way not to, and she was soft and yielding, and there was a sweet fragrance in her hair that reminded him, reminded him . . . An afternoon in Washington, with the lilac and dogwood and magnolia, how many springs ago? Miranda, so very young and appealing, looking up at him.

With an effort he pulled back, smiled at Dorothy, touched her cheek. "How very dear you are. If I were to stay here, I'm afraid I would lose my head completely."

"There is another girl, isn't there?"

He nodded. "And with you, there is another man."

She looked doubtful, but he was insistent. "Yes, there is, And he will come back to you. Any man would come back to you—when this cruel war is over. It can't be long now."

"No, it can't be long," she echoed him. "And we will lose,"

she went on her voice bleak. "And nothing will ever be the same."

He did not deny it, and he let the silence lengthen.

At last she sighed. "Will you leave tomorrow, Cort?"

"I think that would be wise. I'm strong enough to travel alone now." He smiled at her suddenly. "I'm even strong enough to resist you. You have no idea how astonishing that is."

She laughed. "What a charmer you are, Cort. You make even a rejection seem like an enormous compliment. What will you do? Where will you go?"

"Savannah. I have to find my friends. I can't imagine what has happened that I haven't heard yet."

"*I* know." The voice came from the shadows, and Rosemary emerged from her hiding place by the steps. "I know all about it. I just wanted to keep you here, Cort." She was half crying. "It's not fair. Dorothy has a beau. It's not fair for you to kiss her when you knew all along that I loved you."

"Rosemary!" Dorothy was shocked. "You should know better than to skulk about in the bushes. And where is your pride? To tell this man that you love him when you have just heard his declaration for someone else."

"I don't care." She was blubbering. "He kissed you. You practically asked him to. I could tell. It's not fair to Blake. And it's not fair to me, either. I helped him. I helped nurse him just as much as you did. He should have kissed *me*. He should have loved *me*. And I'm not engaged or anything." She began to cry in earnest, and Cort looked at her helplessly.

"Rosemary, I think you are a very attractive little girl. Young lady," he corrected himself quickly. "And someday the right man will come along and—"

"No he won't," she wailed. "You are the only one. All the boys in the county are gone, all the ones I ever liked at all. And I'll grow up and be an old maid, and it will all be your fault."

"My dear girl, you can hardly blame me for—"

"Yes I can. You came here and you were sick and we took care of you and you were so nice and it's all your fault. You were supposed to fall in love with your nurse. It's in all the stories that way. It's so romantic. And I love you, and I don't see why—"

"Rosemary!" Dorothy was exasperated. "You are behaving like a silly schoolgirl. What will Mr. Adams think of us all?"

"I don't care what he thinks. I wish he'd never come at all. I wish I hadn't taken the letters. I just did it so he'd stay."

"You took the letters?" Cort looked at her, astonished. "You took the letters I wrote to Savannah?"

She nodded. "I didn't throw them away or anything. And I didn't read them, either," she added virtuously. "They are all upstairs in my bureau drawer. You can have them back. I don't want them any more. And I don't want to see you again. Ever again. And I'm glad you're leaving tomorrow. And I'll love you forever." She burst into tears again and fled into the house.

Cort stared after her and shook his head.

"Don't worry." Dorothy touched his hand. "She'll get over it. She is just at the age to fall in love with the first stranger who smiles at her. And you *do* have an irresistible smile, Cort."

"Not half so irresistible—" He choked off the automatic compliment. There were some habits that were hard to break.

Dorothy smiled at him with complete understanding. "Yes, you are right. We are both pledged to other people. When Blake comes back . . . I wish you well, Cort. It was cruel of Rosemary to keep the letters. Your girl friend in Savannah must be desperately worried about you."

"My girl friend in Savannah?"

"Of course. Why else would you be risking your life this way?"

He did not respond. He had never thought of it in terms of risking his life. He had simply felt an obligation to take care of Susanne and her family, and his own life didn't really matter very much to him any more. He was doing this for Bobby. That was all he had now. His son. And the boy had a mother and a half sister and grandparents, all of them somehow dependent on him. He could not save Bobby and leave the others behind.

"Now about the trains," Dorothy said, glad to turn to a practical subject. "There really aren't any schedules any more. Eddy can take you to the flag stop, but you'll just have to be prepared to wait for hours. Are you well enough for that, do you think?"

"Very well, thank you." he said it formally, and she smiled.

"I'll come with you. And Rosemary, too, if she's recovered. We'll have a picnic while we wait."

He was changing trains in Charleston when he was recognized as a Yankee again.

"No," he said in a voice of tired protest. "I am not a spy."
They took him into custody just the same.

Chapter 34

RICHARD CAME HOME at Thanksgiving, his first long furlough in almost a year and his first opportunity to see his son. Arriving earlier than expected, he found Miranda and the baby posing for the portrait he had commissioned months before. She was surprised to see him so soon, but she made no attempt to rise, reluctant to disturb the sleeping child in her arms. Richard paused to memorize the scene, and then he rushed to embrace her.

"Be careful, darling." Miranda presented her cheek to be kissed. "Don't wake him."

Richard looked at her in surprise, blamed her restraint on the presence of an outsider, and brusquely ordered the man to leave for the day.

"It was to be a two-hour sitting," the artist protested, "and I've hardly been here half that time."

"That's all right," Richard assured him. "I'll make it up to you." He packed him off immediately and turned to Miranda again. "Motherhood agrees with you, darling. Let me kiss you now and—"

"Richard, look at him. He's waking up. Isn't he beautiful?"

"Beautiful," Richard agreed, smiling at her, touching the baby lightly. "My son. You have given me a son, and I love you more than ever."

"Take him, darling," Miranda insisted. "You can't really know how wonderful he is until you hold him, feel his warmth, his flesh pressing against you, demanding all your love."

"Not quite all," Richard corrected her, but he took the

427

baby willingly enough, holding him in one arm while he embraced Miranda with the other.

"Be careful, darling," she protested. "You're awkward with him, and he's going to cry."

"Worse than that!" Richard handed him back hastily. "He's wet. Where is that nurse you insisted on hiring? Let *her* take care of him. That's what I'm paying her for."

"It's her afternoon off," Miranda said. "I can change him. I'm very good with him. Just you come with me and see."

He followed her to the nursery, half protesting, half amused, and afterward at her insistence Richard took him again. But he immediately deposited the baby in his crib, over Dickon's vociferous objections.

"He wants to be held Richard," Miranda protested.

"And so do I." He embraced her and kissed her, but the baby continued to wail, and Richard sighed and released her. "You knew I was coming. Why of all days did you give the nurse this afternoon off? Very poor planning, Miranda."

"You weren't coming until tonight, Richard. Don't always blame me for everything." She brushed by him to pick up the baby, then sat down in the rocker to nurse him.

Richard observed her total concentration with some surprise and then shook his head. "Damned if I ever thought I'd be jealous of my own son."

Miranda only half heard him.

"You look so complete," Richard went on, "as if you didn't need me at all."

Miranda nodded, the words barely registering.

"But you *do* need me, Miranda. No matter how many children we have. I love you, and once this damned war is over and I can come home, I insist on being the center of your life again."

"The center of my life," she echoed, smiling at the baby in her arms.

"Look at *me* when you say that, Miranda."

She glanced at him, surprised, and he smiled at her ruefully.

"Did you hear a word I said?"

"Of course, darling. You said that when the war is over, you'll come home to us again. And you said you love me. You always say that."

"And I always mean it. You are what keeps me sane, Miranda, all through this miserable war. At the end of the day, when I can write to you and think about you and dream of you, then I can forget the horror of it all."

"In your letters, you never talk about the war at all, Richard. I'd like to hear about it. I wish you would share your thoughts with me, darling. It seems so silly for you to be worrying about me and the baby when *you* are the one in so much danger."

"I don't want you to be troubled with all of that, Miranda. And it's such a pleasure for me to think about you and plan our life together. At least that is one thing I can control. Now I have decided that this week we—"

"We are going to your parents for Thanksgiving dinner tomorrow," Miranda interrupted him. "Papa, and John and Dany, and you and I and the baby. And Caroline and Mrs. Cantrell. And Ann and Madison, of course, and his parents. Irene wanted your mother to invite Andy Dawson, but he had to leave yesterday. He has his own ship now. Did you know that?" She did not wait for his reply. "It was being re-fitted at the navy yard in Brooklyn, and that's why he was here. Irene thinks he's going back to Savannah, and he'll be there by the time Sherman and the army arrive. Dany is worried sick, but she's talked to Andy, and he said he'd look up her family as soon as the city surrenders."

"Did anyone ever find out what had happened to Cort?"

"No. There has been no word at all." Her voice was calm, but she shivered suddenly, and the baby reacted by whimpering.

"Is he all right?" Richard looked at him anxiously. "Should I build up the fire?"

"No, everything's fine, darling. It's time for tea in the family parlor, and I'll take him with us. It's the one hour of the day when Papa breaks away to be with the baby. Even if I'm not here—"

"Where would you be?" Richard looked at her, clearly disturbed.

"At the Cooper Institute, working with your mother. You know that."

"And you leave the baby?"

"Megan takes care of him, Richard. When she can get him away from Maureen or Papa."

Richard seemed doubtful.

"Make up your mind, darling. You don't really want me

with him twenty-four hours a day. He has to get used to other people. And I have to have a little time for myself."

"And this week, even *more* time for me," Richard insisted.

She smiled at him vaguely and adjusted Dickon's bonnet and led the way to the parlor.

"We'll be with the family all day tomorrow," Richard said, "but Friday is mine. I'll want to spend some time at the shipping office with Papa, of course, but you and I will go out together that night. There must be something special at the theater, darling, or at the Academy of Music." He headed for the stack of newspapers by Will's chair and consulted the amusements column. "Edwin Booth," he said with delight. "I remember when you and Lucy were crazy about him. You both went around declaiming speeches from *Richard III*. 'Your beauty was the cause . . .' How does it go? 'So I might live one hour in your sweet bosom.' "

"Don't, Richard. Don't quote those lines."

He looked at her, surprised, and then he smiled. "Women are so changeable. And you, darling, can be very flighty. But Booth isn't playing the wicked Gloucester this time. It's *Julius Caesar* with his brothers Junius and John Wilkes. That sounds wonderful. I'll get tickets." He consulted the newspaper again. "A benefit performance to raise money for a Shakespeare statue in the Central Park."

Miranda nodded. "That's right. I remember now. They dedicated a pedestal in April on Shakespeare's birthday. The tricentenary or tercentenary or something like that."

"Tercentenary," Richard said, pleased to be able to set her straight. "He was born in 1564, and so it's three centuries—"

He was interrupted by a maid, bringing tea, followed immediately by Will, who picked up Dickon before he realized Richard was there."

"So glad to see you, my boy. And what do you think of my grandson?"

Richard smiled. "I think he should have his father here to exert a little stern discipline. And then he'll need a great many little brothers and sisters or he'll be insufferably spoiled."

"He's perfect," Will insisted, "just as he is. But of course if you and Miranda want more . . . Just think, I have three beautiful grandchildren, and a fourth on the way. Did you know that Lucy is expecting?"

"Tom got her letter last week. He let out such a whoop

430

that for a moment I thought the war was over. And even the Rebels called out to see what had happened."

"Are the lines that close?" Miranda looked at him in alarm.

"Quite close," Richard acknowledged. "Our men have talked to them. When we call a truce to collect the wounded or bury the dead, then newspapers change hands, and perhaps a little of our coffee for their tobacco. And ten minutes later we're sniping at each other again. I don't know why they don't surrender and get it over with."

"I wish Tom could have come home, too," Miranda said wistfully.

"We flipped a coin. Thanksgiving or Christmas, and I came first."

"But I wanted you both," Miranda protested.

"Not this year, darling. But just as soon as they surrender, we'll all be home forever. After the war . . ." It was a fantasy he had dreamed so often that it was already as familiar as a twice-told tale. Miranda listened with a half smile and finished her tea and reached for Dickon again. He was more real to her than Richard had ever been. Richard always arrived as a stranger, interrupting her life, insistent and demanding for a week or two, then disappearing for months at a time while she reverted to her normal world, still her father's dearly loved daughter, reigning over the Stratford. It was hard to imagine that that would ever change. Other people changed. Went away, got married, had children, died, disappeared without a trace . . . But she and Papa went right on at the Stratford just the same. She could picture Dickon growing up here, running through the halls, sliding down the bannisters, getting into mischief. Papa would spoil him, as he had spoiled her . . .

And where was Richard in all of this? Why, it wouldn't be like that at all. Richard would be strict with his son, with all his children. He would want them to be quiet and dutiful and rigidly contained, replicas of himself, and he would never understand them at all. Miranda clasped the child in her arms and vowed she wouldn't let him be dominated that way. She shouldn't let herself be dominated that way, either, but it was so hard to strike out for herself when Richard was here so briefly. When he had only a week and he would be going back to war so soon, surely she owed him happy days and nights, memories to take back to the cheerless trenches near

Petersburg. After all, she had Dickon now, and he was worth all of Richard's autocratic demands on her. Only a week, she reminded herself.

While she was nursing the baby, it wasn't likely she would get pregnant again. That's what Emily had told her, but Miranda remained doubtful. Look at all those women who had a baby every year, and not bottle-fed babies, either. Well, there was no help for it. Richard hadn't been with her since last January, and he certainly would not be denied this week. His eyes on her were already hungry, and he would reach for her as greedily as Dickon ever did. What an odd man he was. He had invented a dream wife and blindly cast her in the role. She had known him all her life, she had married him and shared his bed and borne him a son, but he still didn't understand her at all.

It was Thanksgiving, and all the family had gathered at Washington Square with Richard's parents. Uncle Paul carved the turkey with his usual precision, all the while discoursing on the conduct of the war and the importance of demanding unconditional surrender. Dany sighed and wondered aloud how her mother and sister were faring this day, but Paul assured her that just as soon as the South gave up, they'd have something to be thankful for in Savannah, too. Faith made an effort to change the subject, but Paul was intractable, and the war and the sins of the Rebels were foremost in his mind. Last month a Confederate lieutenant had led twenty-five soldiers on a raid from Canada into Vermont, swooping down on the little town of St. Albans and robbing three banks of two hundred thousand dollars. The lieutenant and half his command were seized and seventy-five thousand dollars recovered, but there was much speculation about what those men were really up to and what the rest of them were planning to do with the money they had taken.

"They were going to outfit a ship," John said. "That's what I heard. They would bring it into the harbor here and set fire to the whole dock area. Then if the Irish longshoremen would riot again, or at least go on strike, the Rebels would have enough Copperhead support to take over City Hall. Once they had control of the police—"

"That's foolish talk," Will interrupted. "The police are loyal. Even in the middle of the riots last year, they stood firm. And now, with the war nearly over, there's no reason to doubt them at all."

"I didn't say it would happen," John said. "I just said that was the rumor I had heard. There are a dozen rumors every day about Rebel plots and spies. On Election Day they were supposed to set fire to all the hotels. A lot of nonsense. They ought to know that the only place for fighting is on the front lines. Virginia—that's where the war will be won. Isn't that so, Richard?"

Even Paul deferred to Richard as the family authority on war, the army captain who had lived through Burnside and Hooker and Meade and Grant and was now with the forces inching their way toward Richmond, extending the lines at Petersburg, paying dearly for every yard of advance.

Richard didn't want to talk about it. "We are winning," he said, looking up from his well-filled plate. "The Rebels are still too stubborn to admit it, but they are being crushed, and they can't last more than a few months." He spoke with finality, hoping to end the discussion, but he had not reckoned with Caroline.

"That's what Jack says, too. I've heard from him at last." Her smile was beatific. "He had received the package we sent to him, and most of the things in it got through, though apparently the guards helped themselves to the food. But he must have found the money—he said that he had never cherished the contents of a Bible so much, and he particularly admired the binding. That's where we hid the greenbacks."

Irene was fascinated. "What a clever idea. How did you ever think of that?"

"Miranda told me." Caroline was more than willing to share the credit. "After she asked Mr. Raymond about Cort to find out if newspaper reporters were always treated like prisoners of war, he told her all the best ways to get packages delivered and what to put in and everything."

Dany looked up, startled. "Does that mean he's found Cort? Why didn't anyone tell me?"

"No, no, not at all," Miranda said hastily. Her father was staring at her disapprovingly, and she felt her color rising. Richard glanced at her, puzzled, but Caroline sailed on, blissfully unaware.

"I wrote to Jack about Cort, but he doesn't know what happened to him, either. Jack is in the prison in Columbia. I wonder if Sherman will get there."

Dany sighed. "I was so hoping we would have some word from Cort by now. If only he were alive and he could get through to Susanne and Mama."

John reached out and clasped her hand. "Don't worry, dear. Andy assured us he'll look after them. It can't be much longer."

"Andy has his own ship now," Irene said proudly. "If the United States navy trusts him that much, Papa, then after the war you should—"

"Irene," her mother warned, "don't start that all over again."

Dinner was nearly over and Paul Schuyler was feeling expansive. He smiled at his younger daughter, not heeding his wife's signals of disapproval. "Certainly the boy has proved himself over and over. I think we might look on him with some favor, perhaps find an opportunity for him at Schuyler Shipping."

"Oh, Papa!" Irene sprang from her chair and rushed to kiss him.

Faith shook her head, but Paul ignored her, looking to Richard and John for approval.

Richard steered a diplomatic course. "He's certainly worthy of his own ship. I'm not sure yet if he deserves Irene, too."

She stuck out her tongue at him, as if she were still only six years old, and he laughed. "Maybe *you* don't deserve *him*," he amended.

"I think he's a fine young man," John observed. "And Dany and I appreciate his offer to help Susanne and her mother. I'd certainly welcome him into the company."

"And into the family?" Irene challenged him.

"That's not my decision." John smiled at her.

"All this is quite premature," Faith said firmly. "We must wait until the war is over." Deliberately, she changed the subject. "Did you get tickets for the benefit tomorrow, Richard?"

He nodded. "Excellent seats. This is the first time the three Booths have ever performed together. It's an event, something to tell our grandchildren." He reached for Miranda's hand, but she was alert to Dickon's imperious wail and excused herself abruptly.

They were dressing for the theater the next night, Richard insisting that she look her most beautiful. "It's an occasion, darling, and I'll take you to Delmonico's afterward and show you off to the world." He looked at the satin dress spread out on the bed, pale blue with scalloped flounces outlined in darker shades. "That's pretty, Miranda, but I remember it from last New Year's. Don't you have something new?"

"What an incredible memory you have, Richard. But I've hardly worn that dress at all, and I'm just so pleased that at last I'm able to get into it again—though I admit I feel as if my lacings will pop at any minute."

"That's not good for you, Miranda. And if we're going to Delmonico's afterward, how will you be able to eat anything at all?" He opened the door of the huge armoire in her dressing room and fingered the gowns there. "Here's something I like." He pulled out the white and gold taffeta she had worn to the theatrical evening at the Jeromes. "I don't remember this. When did you have it made?"

"Last April. I haven't worn it since."

"April. Well, you were four or five months pregnant then; it's bound to be a little bigger than that blue gown. Try it on." He loosened her stays, and she had to admit that she felt more comfortable. But the dress reminded her of Cort, and she fastened the little buttons and smoothed the ruffled bertha, and she could feel his arms around her again.

Richard smiled at her, pleased she had complied with his wishes, and around her neck he fastened the thin chain of her sapphire pendant. She reached for her earrings, but he shook his head. "No, not those, Miranda." With a flourish worthy of a magician, he produced a small package from his pocket. "To celebrate, darling. This time together. Our son. A true Thanksgiving." He opened the velvet jewel box, which contained earrings that exactly matched her pendant. They sparkled against the white satin lining, and she looked at them, astonished.

"Darling." She grasped his hand in both of hers. "I wish you wouldn't be so extravagant. I don't feel . . . worthy of so much."

He pulled her into his arms and kissed her. "You have given me a son. And you have given me yourself. I have no gifts that can equal that." He kissed her again. "Now if you'll just put these on . . . I have a carriage waiting, darling, and I don't want to be late. This is an evening we'll always remember."

They arrived at the Winter Garden early, with plenty of time to see and be seen. It was a glittering audience that had been attracted to this benefit. Never before had the three sons of the late great Junius Brutus Booth appeared on the stage together. Edwin, the most celebrated of the brothers, was the driving force behind the production, and he had cast himself as Brutus. His older brother Junius was playing Cassius, and his younger brother, John Wilkes, was the rabble-rousing Marc Antony.

Miranda had hastily read a synopsis of the play that afternoon, but she need not have bothered; Richard was intent on explaining it all to her in minute detail, between greetings to friends in the audience. She recognized the Jeromes and nodded to them, and at the first intermission she introduced them to Richard.

"Captain Schuyler," Leonard Jerome shook hands with him briskly. "It's a pleasure to make your acquaintance, sir. We missed you last April when we were giving our own benefits."

"I'm sorry I couldn't be there, but the army doesn't always cooperate in matters like that." Conscious of Mr. Jerome's appraising eyes on Miranda, Richard took her hand possessively.

"But at least your beautiful wife could be with us," Mr. Jerome went on. "I wanted her to take a bow from our stage, but she wasn't prepared to make her debut then. Perhaps some time in the future . . ."

Richard was ready to object, but Mrs. Jerome cut in smoothly. "I heard about the birth of your son. Richard, Jr., is it?"

Miranda nodded, smiling. "Dickon, we call him. Richard saw him this week for the first time."

"I congratulate you, sir." Leonard Jerome clapped Richard on the back. "How long will you be in New York? Perhaps you could both join us in December at our next gala."

"I'm sorry, sir, but I'll be back in Virginia by then. The war goes on, you know."

Mr. Jerome sighed. "Yes, I'm afraid it does. But surely it's in the final stages now. Just take care of yourself, young man. The casualty lists are still terrifying. We have lost so many brave young soldiers."

"So many losses," Mrs. Jerome agreed. "Tell me, dear," she turned to Miranda, "have you had any word from Cort

Adams? I hadn't realized what special friends you were until I saw you together last April."

Richard looked at Miranda, surprised, and she felt her color rising. "No, we haven't heard anything. His wife is in Savannah, you know, and she is frantic with worry about him—and about the approach of Sherman, too."

"How dreadful for her." Mrs. Jerome was all sympathy. "And Cort is such a charming man."

"A real lady-killer," Leonard Jerome agreed. "I can't believe he's dead. He'll be back, young lady, to flirt with you again. Don't give up on him too soon."

The Jeromes moved on, greeting more friends, and Richard stared after them, shaking his head. "I'm not sure I approve of him, Miranda. And I don't think you should accept any more of his invitations."

"Of course not, Richard. I was there in April only at the insistence of your mother."

"Yes, I realize that. Now about Cort—"

"Isn't it time to return to our seats now, darling? I don't want to miss anything, and you were going to tell me what happens next."

Richard smiled, delighted to be cast in the role of teacher once again, and he led the way back.

The curtain rose on the second act, and applause greeted the appearance of all three Booths. Miranda glanced at Richard, who was intent on the unfolding action, but she was suddenly restless. There was something not quite right somewhere. She shifted in her seat, uncomfortable, and then realized what the problem was. A trace of smoke. She sniffed again, had a moment's doubt, and then was sure. Smoke. Definitely, smoke. There was fire somewhere, very near. She clutched at Richard's arm, willing herself to be calm. A crowded theater, narrow aisles, the horrifying vision of being trapped as the flames shot higher . . .

She was not the only one showing signs of fear. Around her there was a rising murmur as the audience edged toward panic. Edwin Booth, who had disappeared from the stage, returned abruptly and rushed to the footlights and raised both arms to command attention.

"There is no reason to be alarmed, ladies and gentlemen." His voice rang with authority. "We have put out the fire. It is completely extinguished. It was just a small blaze, ladies and gentlemen, very small, near the stairs. A few buckets of water killed it completely. I think we should have a round of applause for the very alert stagehand who acted so promptly, so efficaciously." Edwin Booth led the applause himself, his brothers joining in, while a nervous handyman emerged from the wings for an embarrassed bow, then retreated immediately with a severe case of stagefright.

Laughter mingled with applause from the audience, and Booth, a master at controlling any crowd, held up his hand for silence. "We will lower the curtain, ladies and gentlemen, and start at the beginning of the act. I wouldn't want any of you to miss anything. We owe a complete production to all of you—and to Mr. William Shakespeare, too."

Keyed up by the excitement, the audience alert and responsive, the Booths tore up the stage, and when the final curtain fell, the clamor of applause was deafening. Richard turned to Miranda with his pronouncement on the evening: "There will never be a *Caesar* to equal this one. Never."

Edwin Booth was taking a solo curtain call, and the audience rose for a standing ovation. Booth bowed again and beckoned his brothers to join him, Junius as the lean and hungry Cassius, John Wilkes, dark and saturnine as Marc Antony.

"They were wonderful," Miranda agreed, "all of them. But I still like Edwin best. He is opening in *Hamlet* tomorrow—"

"And I already have tickets for next week," Richard interrupted her. "A surprise, darling. And we'll take your father and John and Dany, too. She needs some diversion."

"Richard, how very kind of you." She reached out to take his hand. How could she deny him anything when he was so unfailingly thoughtful.

"And now we'll go to Delmonico's, where I can show you off."

They were waiting in the lobby for their carriage when they heard the first rumors of other fires that evening.

"Right here in the Lafarge House," a man was saying excitedly. "The bedclothes had been soaked in turpentine, and by the time they discovered it, the whole room was ablaze."

"Arson? Is that what you mean? The fire was set deliberately?"

"That's it," the first voice proclaimed. "Arson. It was arson here, too, if you ask me. Right here at this theater."

"Oh, no!"

"Surely not."

"Who would do such a thing?"

"Why the Rebels, of course. Damned sneaking cowards."

"A Confederate plot?"

"It must be. They can't win on the battlefield, so they're attacking women and children behind the lines."

Miranda looked at Richard for confirmation, but he was openly skeptical.

"This is the way rumors start. Don't worry about it, Miranda. I know you have an exaggerated fear of fire, but stay calm, darling. You behaved very well at the theater tonight." He patted her arm. "Ah, I see our carriage."

At Delmonico's there were more rumors of fires.

"Barnum's Museum," someone said.

And then a woman's voice, high-pitched, carrying. "Did they rescue the animals? Can you imagine? Wild animals in the City Hall Park?"

"Utter nonsense," Richard scoffed.

The waiter looked at him doubtfully. "I don't know, sir. We've heard about fires in two theaters, the Winter Garden and Niblo's Garden, and so I'm not surprised that there was arson at Barnum's Museum. And of course at so many hotels, too."

"Hotels?" Miranda was startled. "What do you mean, so many hotels?"

"Why, there have been fires all over New York. The St. James, the St. Nicholas, the Metropolitan, Lovejoy's . . . Probably more. These are just the ones we've heard about so far. Arson, everywhere. It's obviously a Rebel plot."

"The Stratford?" Miranda asked him anxiously. "Have you heard about the Stratford?"

"No, not yet. Was it set on fire, too? I'll add it to our list."

"Miranda," Richard spoke to her firmly, "can't you see that these are simply overblown rumors? And you," he fixed his cold eyes on the waiter, "should know better than to disturb a lady with such wild stories."

"I'm sorry, sir. I'm just repeating what we keep hearing from our guests. But don't worry, ma'am. We're keeping a sharp eye out here at Delmonico's. No Rebels will get a chance to spread their turpentine and phosphorous around here." He smiled at Miranda and handed the menus to Richard, bowing slightly as he departed.

"Richard, I'm worried. I think we should go home right now. The baby—"

"Miranda, Megan is taking care of the baby. Now if you don't trust her—"

"Of course I trust her, Richard, but if there was a fire at the Stratford, I want to be there to make sure everything is all right."

"Miranda, that hotel functions perfectly well without you. Uncle Will was running it before you could walk, and I have great confidence in his ability to go right on running it until George takes over. Now I don't want to hear another word about it." He picked up a menu and studied it with interest. " 'Squab with oyster dressing, *poulet á là Marengo,* roasted pheasant with truffles.' These aren't army rations! Of course the prices are a scandal, but you have to expect that. What would you like, darling? Aren't you glad now that I loosened your stays and made you change your dress? Wasn't I right?"

"Richard, I still think we should go home. If there is an arson plot—"

"I seriously doubt that there is a plot to burn down the Stratford, and I will not go rushing down there on a wild-goose chase. I'm surprised at you, Miranda. Didn't you understand me? I said I didn't want to hear another word about it. Now, have you decided what you want to order?"

She shook her head.

"In that case, I'll consult with the waiter and order for both of us. Where is that man?"

She excused herself to retire to the ladies' parlor, and when she returned she picked up her cloak. "We have to leave, Richard. I heard about a fire at the Astor House, too, and that's so close to the Stratford that—"

"Miranda, I have already ordered supper, and I expect you—"

"Richard, if you won't take me, I'll go myself."

He glared at her, but she stood firm.

"I couldn't eat a bite, worrying about Dickon and Papa and everyone."

It was obviously true, and glowering at her wouldn't change anything. "Damn it, Miranda, why must you ruin our evening? I have looked forward to this feast at Delmonico's for months, and now when I see the waiters bringing the first course . . ." He settled the bill and stalked out of the restaurant, and the carriage ride back to the Stratford was ominously silent.

Chapter 35

THERE WERE NO wild animals running about in City Hall Park, and Barnum's Museum appeared silent and deserted, normal for a midnight in late November. Lights were blazing, as usual, at both the Astor and the Stratford, and Miranda was conscious of the presence of a small contingent of firemen and policemen.

Her father was in the lobby, and she rushed to him, not waiting for Richard.

"I'm glad you're all right, Pet. I was worried about you. We heard about the Winter Garden—" He broke off to soothe another guest, who came in babbling about fires all over the city.

"It's all right. We're patrolling the halls constantly, and there hasn't been a sign of smoke here. Yes, I know about the fire at the Everett House, too. That makes eleven hotels so far, and two theaters, and Barnum's Museum. But there's been no major damage anywhere, and no loss of life." He paused to cough and clear his throat. "Yes, it must be a Rebel plot. Please don't worry. We're patrolling the halls . . ."

"Is there anything I can do to help, Papa? I'll look in on Dickon, but then I'll stay up with you. If some of the women guests are frightened—"

"Miranda!" It was the first time Richard had spoken to her since they had left the restaurant. "I think your father is managing the situation very competently without your assistance. There is no need for you to lose sleep over all this."

"Richard, I couldn't possibly go to sleep. Now I know you were hungry, so why don't you order something here?" She didn't wait for his reply. Just as soon as she checked on Dickon, she would get out of this elaborate dress and stay up with Papa to look after the Stratford. Imagine! A Confederate plot, right here in New York! Why, except for Dickon, it was the most exciting thing that had happened since . . . since Cort rescued her in the riots.

Dickon was sleeping peacefully, and she didn't disturb him. Hastily, she stripped off her taffeta dress and donned a sober gray merino, and she didn't even check the mirror to smooth her hair—or notice that she was still wearing her new sapphire earrings.

At the top of the stairs she hesitated, then veered off to make a complete tour of the hotel. She noted with approval that buckets filled with sand or water had already been set out in all the corridors—of course her father would have taken those precautions immediately.

On the fourth floor she encountered Guy Dawson, who was pacing slowly down the hall, taking deep breaths and looking for telltale wisps of smoke.

"Why, Mr. Dawson, I didn't expect to find *you* here. It's after midnight."

"Of course I'm here." He looked at her with surprise and indignation. "In a moment of crisis, would I desert the ship?"

She smiled. He was so proud of Andy these days that he even tried to talk like him. At that moment he sneezed, and she looked at him in alarm.

He blew his nose vigorously and assured her he was all right, but she shook her head.

"How can you smell anything if you are coming down with a cold?"

"I can still keep watch," he told her, but she insisted on joining his patrol.

On the third floor Miranda caught the first trace of smoke and clutched his arm. He looked doubtful, but he followed her dutifully, and when they turned a corner, she was convinced the smell was stronger. It was Guy Dawson who spotted the faint wisp at the end of the corridor, and he sprinted to the last door, pulling out his pass key. He knocked first, but when there was no answer, he flung open the door. The bed was ablaze, and the fire jumped to the drapes as soon as the draft from the open door reached them. They went up in a sheet of flame. He sprang to the windows, but it was too late to prevent the fire from spreading to the wooden sills and frame. Miranda threw a bucket of water over him—he hadn't realized he had singed his hair—and then she turned and ran for help while he alerted the sleeping guests in the adjoining suite.

With firemen already on the premises, they were able to confine the damage to one room. Afterward they stripped off the shreds of drapes and the sodden mattress and rolled up the damaged carpet. Will coughed as he poked at the wreckage and was thankful they had caught it in time.

"It's all part of the same plot," a police sergeant assured them when they were back in the lobby. "I could still smell the turpentine. That's what they do: douse the bedclothes with turpentine and add the phosphorous and then go out and lock the door. Eventually it smolders into a fire."

"Who was in that room, Papa? Can we have him arrested?"

"I'll check the guest book," Will said, and he scanned the pages rapidly.

The police sergeant shook his head. "It will be a false name, and you'll never see him again."

" 'David Jackson, Baltimore,' " Will read from the register. "I didn't notice him. Did you, Guy? Who was on the desk?"

"I didn't see him, either." Guy Dawson studied the page with the signature. "Peters was on duty then. Maybe he'll remember."

"I think *we* saw him, Richard." Miranda looked at him eagerly. "Remember? Just as we were leaving for the theater there was a pale, thin man with a dark mustache. He was peering at my jewelry, and I just knew he was up to no good."

"Miranda," Richard had been in a foul mood for three hours now, as he always was when he lost complete control of a situation. "Don't mix in with something you know nothing about. You have no reason to believe that that man was 'Jackson.' You are getting overly excited, and it's not good for you."

"I saw him," she insisted. "Mr. Peters called out after him—he'd left his gloves on the desk. He was probably nervous, don't you think? I remember it distinctly. 'Mr. Jackson, aren't these your gloves?' Don't you remember he said that?"

Richard had no recollection of the man, and he turned away impatiently.

The police sergeant was all attention, though, and Miranda

repeated her story for him and elaborated on it. 'Jackson' was about her father's height, she thought, but very slim, like Richard. And young, too. Certainly under thirty. No beard, no sideburns, but a mustache like . . . rather like the sergeant's.

"If you trimmed it a little here," she said, reaching out to show what she meant. The sergeant grinned at her, and Richard glowered again at Miranda. She ignored him and went on with her description of the man's clothes, which were conventional and anonymous. The sergeant thanked her profusely, and Miranda beamed. And then she had a sudden inspiration. "Do you know where you should start to look for him? For all of them?" She didn't wait for an answer. "In a hotel that *didn't* have a fire. It was sheer luck that their plot didn't work, and they certainly wouldn't want to stay in a place that was going to burn down while they slept! Don't you think I'm right?"

"Possibly," the sergeant said, grinning at her again. "You're certainly eager to help. Would you like to join the detective force, ma'am? If we ever recruit ladies, I think you might be a real asset."

"Why, thank you, sergeant. That's a possibility that never occurred to me." She darted a glance at Richard, but no trace of a smile marred his grim expression.

The sergeant went off to transmit his report and, Miranda hoped, to discover which hotels had escaped the arson plot.

"It shows how desperate the Rebels are," Guy Dawson asserted, "trying to burn down New York while we sleep. I think I'll make one last round to make sure we're all right."

"I'll go with you," Miranda said, eager to participate.

"No, Miranda." Richard grasped her arm and would not release her. "You have done enough. Mr. Dawson and your father can take care of everything. Good Lord, what more do we need? With a volunteer fireman posted on every floor, you ought to feel completely safe." He sought confirmation from her father. "Isn't that true, Uncle Will?"

"There's no danger now," Will agreed, coughing again. He cleared his throat and smiled at her. "You've been a big help, Pet, but you probably should get some sleep now."

"I'm too excited to sleep," Miranda contradicted him. "You're staying up all night, aren't you, Papa? I will, too."

"Miranda!" Richard would brook no further opposition. "It

445

is three o'clock in the morning." He tightened his grasp on her arm, and she winced with sudden pain.

She glanced at him, not sure if he knew that he was hurting her, or if he cared. But how could she argue with him in front of Papa and Mr. Dawson and the three policemen who still lingered in the lobby? The only graceful way out was surrender.

In their bedroom, Richard released her, and she massaged her arm where he had held her in such an iron grip. She was always astonished by his physical strength. He was tall and deceptively slim, but he was lean and hard and disciplined; it occurred to her that there was something rather frightening in his rigidly controlled power. She smiled at him tentatively, but he ignored her and swiftly made his preparations for bed. He glanced at the gold and white taffeta dress, still draped carelessly over the chaise where she had tossed it, and then he looked at her for the first time.

"And this was going to be such a perfect evening!"

"*I* wasn't part of the Rebel plot to burn down New York, Richard."

"You certainly managed to let it ruin everything. We could have stayed at Delmonico's and had our celebration and let your father worry about this damned hotel."

"Richard! How can you say such a thing!"

"Good God, Miranda! Sometimes I think you love this place more than you love me."

She made no response to that and withdrew to her dressing room. He paced the bedroom impatiently, and when she finally emerged, she was wearing a robe over her nightgown.

"Just where do you think you are going?"

"Next door to the nursery, to see if Dickon is all right."

"You'll hear him if there is any trouble."

"He might have breathed in some smoke. Or maybe he kicked off his covers and is getting cold."

Richard gave an exaggerated sigh, but he followed her and watched as she hovered over the sleeping baby, tucking him in once again. Richard's anger melted then, and he smiled at her. "What a beautiful mother you are, darling." He pulled her into his arms and embraced her possessively, and his mouth sought hers.

A spark of rebellion flared, and Miranda turned her head away. "It's so late, Richard, and I'm tired."

"You were going to stay up all night," he reminded her.

"But now I just want—"

"Don't resist me, Miranda." There was command in his voice, and sudden tension in the strength of his embrace. "You succeeded in spoiling our evening, but now you will make it up to me." He cupped her chin and held it firmly. "Of course you will." He kissed her. "You want me to forgive you, darling. I know you do. And how can I deny you anything when you make me so happy."

She sighed, and he kissed her again, and there was no way out. Only a week, she reminded herself. Only a week.

He was whispering all those familiar endearments, how much he loved her, yearned for her, dreamed of her, but then he broke off with a murmur of exasperation. "Take off your earrings, Miranda. I don't want you to lose them in bed."

She reached up to touch them, surprised. "I forgot completely."

"So that's what my presents mean to you." He shook his head in mock reproach. "You don't care about jewelry, or supper at Delmonico's, or any of the luxuries I give you. But never mind. We'll forget all that. I see you here with Dickon, and I know where your heart is. Miranda, precious." He smiled at her. "A little girl next time? As beautiful as you are, darling, but more tractable. Come to bed now."

The Rebel arson plot to burn down New York had been ambitious, but it came to nothing. Six Confederate agents had registered at nineteen hotels, and the plan was to set them all on fire almost simultaneously. Then, with so many blazes all over town, the fire brigades would lose control and the whole city would go up in flames. In addition to the arson at the hotels, fires were set in two theaters, at Barnum's Museum, a lumberyard, and two barges in the river. But the incendiary materials—turpentine and phosphorous—were not very effective, and in every case the fires were contained without loss of life and with a minimum amount of damage.

Some weeks earlier Canadian officials had notified Secretary of State Seward of a Confederate arson plot scheduled for Election Day, and he had relayed that information to the local authorities. Nothing had happened then, but rumors continued to circulate. And so, when the first fires broke out the day after Thanksgiving, the police knew what they were dealing with, and they moved quickly to take special precautions.

Afterward the Hotel-Keepers Association posted rewards, and the police eventually rounded up the agents responsible. Their leader was hanged.

At the Stratford, Will gave orders for repairs in the burned-out room, and then he took to his bed, exhausted. He was nursing a persistent cough, but he made light of it. "All that smoke," he said, by way of explanation. "There's nothing the matter with me that a good sleep and a little brandy won't cure."

Miranda looked at him doubtfully, but she certainly understood the need for sleep. It had been a short night for her, and she had dragged herself out of bed before seven to nurse Dickon again.

Richard slumbered on, and by the time he had breakfast, it was almost noon. He looked at the circles under her eyes and canceled their afternoon carriage ride. She must take a long nap to be fresh for this evening—he had rescheduled dinner at Delmonico's, and afterward they would come home and go to bed early.

She sighed, and he smiled.

"Yes, darling." He was happy with her, happy with the world, and last night's half-joking suggestion had hardened into a resolution. "A little girl next year. I'd love that. Why, by the time she is born, the war will be over, and I'll be home to stay."

"Yes, Richard."

"You might sound a little more cheerful about it. But then, I see how tired you are. How is your father this morning? He didn't get any sleep at all, did he?"

"No, but he's in bed now. He didn't look a bit well, and he's started coughing again."

Richard sympathized, and then plunged into the morning papers. He was studying the real estate advertisements with particular interest, and when Miranda returned to the parlor, carrying Dickon, he smiled at them both and told her his decision.

"I'm going to look at property this afternoon, darling. There's no point in delaying any longer. If I can find a suitable site for our house, I think I'll go ahead and buy it. We might as well choose a builder and get started now. And then when the war is over, we can move in right away." His mood was expansive. "A house of our own. No more of this hotel existence, but a proper house. And every day I'll come back to you and the children."

"It will all be so different." Miranda kissed the baby in her arms and tried to visualize the future, but her mind rejected the picture.

"Yes, so different," Richard agreed with satisfaction. "I'd like to be near Washington Square or one of the streets just off Fifth Avenue. Do you have any preferences, darling?"

"I'll have to think about it. I don't know yet where George and Tom will be. And if they open a new Stratford, way uptown . . ." Her eyes filled with tears, and she blinked them back. There was no point in crying. She couldn't hold on to her childhood forever. There was a new generation to think about now.

"Well, then, leave it all to me." Richard put down the newspapers and stretched luxuriously. "I'm glad you want me to make these decisions, darling, and I'll do what's best. It might be wiser to buy a brownstone and remodel it. Add an extra story and a mansard roof. That would make it very modern."

"It all sounds so expensive, Richard. Can we afford it?"

"Papa will sign a note for me, and I'll pay him back. He's already agreed to that. He and Mother would like to have us live near them, and I think that would be a splendid idea. It pleases me, darling, that you get along with her so well these days."

"Yes, Richard. I wonder what she will do, though, afterward."

He was puzzled. "Afterward?"

"Yes, after the war is over and there's no more Ladies Central Association for Relief, no more Sanitary Commission. Irene will get married, too, and then there will be no one at home, and what will she do?"

"Do? She doesn't need to do anything. How funny you are, Miranda, worrying about something like that. When *you* are forty-nine years old, darling, you won't need to do anything either—just run our house properly and always be there to welcome me home." He smiled at her. "Put down the baby now, precious, and come kiss me."

Will remained in bed for two days, and then insisted on

going back to work. He was still coughing, though, and he went into such a paroxysm the first time he lit his pipe that Miranda was thoroughly frightened.

"I'm all right, Pet." But tears had started in his eyes, and he wiped them away hastily. "Perhaps, perhaps the smoke doesn't agree with me." Regretfully, he tapped out the tobacco and put his pipe away.

"A little brandy?" Richard suggested, and Will nodded gratefully.

"I'll be right as rain tomorrow," he assured them. "I wouldn't miss Edwin Booth as Hamlet for anything."

John and Dany joined them at the theater, and if Will wasn't fully recovered, he refused to admit it. But he sat on the aisle, and twice he took refuge in the lobby where his coughs would not disturb anyone else. Only Miranda, straining to hear him, showed any sign of worry. John was intent on making Dany forget, for once, her fears about her family in Georgia. And Richard, who had planned this last evening of his furlough, was determined that they should all enjoy themselves. Will was in firm agreement on that, and he insisted that he was well enough to go with them afterward to Taylor's Saloon. Miranda noticed, though, that he ate only half his serving of oysters, and he didn't even order an entree.

"Tell us about your house, Miranda," Dany said, making polite conversation.

"It's not ours yet," Richard answered for her. "We're still dickering over the price, and Papa will have to settle the transaction after I go back to Virginia. But I think we'll come to terms."

"But tell us about it," Dany repeated. "I know it's a brownstone on West Tenth Street, but I want to know all about it."

"Well," Miranda looked at her doubtfully, "I've seen it only once, and Richard is going to have it completely remodeled, so I don't know exactly."

"I have to find an architect," Richard explained. "It's a sound building, and I'm sure we can add another story, but until we see some plans . . ."

"How you must look forward to it," Dany said. "Having a house of your own."

Miranda made no comment, but Richard smiled in satisfaction. "My castle," he said. "Just as soon as the war is over . . .

"The war," Dany echoed, and a shadow touched her.

"You heard from your mother," John reminded her, "and she said they were getting along all right."

"Another letter?" Miranda looked at Dany, hoping for a miracle. Perhaps Cort . . . But if there had been a miracle, Dany would have told them right away.

"It took seven weeks to get here," Dany said. "Anything could have happened since the beginning of October. And Uncle Toby was sick."

"Uncle Toby?" Miranda had never heard of him.

"He was Papa's . . . valet and butler and everything. From the time they were boys." Dany flushed a little under Miranda's questioning eyes. "Yes, he's a slave," she admitted, "but he's part of the family just the same. Oh, I know you think that's wrong, and I suppose it is—I just don't know any more. But Mama said Uncle Toby was so broken up over Papa's death that that's why he's ill in bed himself. And he dotes on Bobby, and Mama says they are inseparable, even in the sickroom. Imagine! Bobby is three years old, and he's already decided he'll be a doctor when he grows up, so he can make people well." Dany pulled out her handkerchief and dabbed at her eyes. "Cort would have been so proud of him."

Miranda sighed, and Will looked at her sharply. He cleared his throat, preparing to change the subject, but he was seized by another fit of coughing. This time John was alarmed, too, and he agreed with Miranda that it was time to end the evening.

"Has Papa seen a doctor?" he asked her while they were waiting for a carriage.

"He doesn't want one," Miranda answered. "And I've been so distracted this week . . . But after Richard leaves tomorrow, I'll insist that Papa do something."

"I know he'll be reluctant," John said, "but you can get around him." He smiled at her. "You always do."

It wasn't easy. Not until Miranda expressed alarm about Dickon being exposed to something contagious in all that coughing did her father finally consent to be examined.

Dr. Simpson tapped Will's chest and put his ear over his heart and looked grave. He used a stethoscope, too, but he didn't really hold with some of these modern medical ideas. Direct auscultation was best, he said. Now the problem was that Mr. Chase had a weakness in his lungs, brought on, no doubt, by breathing in too much smoke on the night of the fire. Pure mountain air or a sea voyage would help, and Mr. Chase must stay on guard against colds and catarrh. The use of tobacco was perfectly all right if he enjoyed it, but if he began to cough, he should stop immediately. In the meantime, a prescription for a soothing syrup would help.

Will listened impatiently and got out of bed as soon as the doctor left.

"A sea voyage," he scoffed. "I can't think of anything worse than the ocean on a cold day in December. I'd never get my breath at all."

"But you have to take care of yourself, Papa." Miranda had been alarmed when Dr. Simpson made his examination. In his nightshirt her father looked so thin. Now that she peered at him closely, she was sure he had lost weight. And when he insisted on getting dressed and taking his place at the dinner table, she noticed that his shirt collar gaped. She pointed that out, and Will sighed.

"Yes, Miranda, I think I have lost a little weight. But it's not serious. I just haven't had much appetite lately. But I'll be all right."

Under her observant eyes, he filled his plate and doggedly began to eat. He smiled at her, and she tried to convince herself there was nothing to worry about.

And then he coughed again.

Chapter 36

WHEN CORT ADAMS was arrested in Charleston, he told the complete truth: he was a correspondent for *The New York Times*, going to Savannah to see his wife and family. The authorities checked only the first part of that statement, and Cort was immediately hustled off to the temporary jail for Yankee officers. His protests went unheeded, and two days later he was shipped off to Salisbury, North Carolina.

In the prison there, the first person he saw was Albert Richardson, a correspondent for Mr. Greeley's *Tribune*.

"Welcome to Salisbury, my friend." Richardson's greeting was sardonic. "It's the garden spot of the Confederacy."

Cort looked at him, astonished. "Good Lord! Al Richardson. Is it really you behind that beard? I haven't seen you . . . for a year and a half. We were on our way to Vicksburg."

Al nodded.

"But I thought you were in Richmond, in the Libby Prison."

"They brought us here in February."

"Us?"

"My colleague, Junius Browne. I don't think you know him. He's with the *Tribune*, too. And we have since been joined by William Davis from the Cincinnati *Gazette*. And now you. The cream of the newspaper world, you might say."

Cort shrugged off that comment. "But why won't they release us, exchange us, let us out of here?"

"God knows. God and the Confederate Secretary of War. He has turned down all our appeals. It's not that we haven't made inquiries, I assure you. But it's like talking to a brick wall. In my case, I think it's because they don't like the politics of Mr. Greeley, but that's not much justification."

"Not much," Cort agreed. "And I didn't even know you were here."

"News travels slowly," Al said. "We didn't get our first letters from home until three weeks ago, seven months after we arrived. And I've had only one package, missing half the food by the time it reached me. You wouldn't be carrying a slab of roast beef in that satchel, by any chance?"

Cort shook his head. "I was rather hoping to be fed a square meal once I got here. The food was rather sketchy on the train."

Al laughed. "It's rather sketchy here, too. You haven't come to Delmonico's, Cort, or even to Willard's. But it's not Andersonville, either. Not yet." Al clapped him on the back. "Come with me. I'll show you our section of the floor. Our home—probably until the war is over. And you can tell me how you wound up in this godforsaken place."

The principal prison at Salisbury was a four-story brick building, formerly used as a cotton factory. Also within the stockade were six smaller brick tenement houses and a new frame hospital with hay mattresses for forty patients. The hospital was always filled, and there was a waiting list to get in, but turnover was rapid. Some patients recovered, of course—from scurvy, dysentery, pneumonia, or vaguely diagnosed fevers. But for the others—the mule cart appeared daily to haul the bodies from the dead house to the expanding cemetery across the road.

Originally, Salisbury was not intended for prisoners of war. The six hundred men confined there were Confederate convicts, Yankee deserters, Southern Unionists, and a scattering of others—civilian newspaper correspondents, sailors, three United States officers held as hostages. But a few days after Cort arrived, everything changed drastically.

With Sherman in Atlanta, preparing to march south, Andersonville was no longer the most convenient dumping ground for captured prisoners. And Salisbury was. By the end of October, ten thousand men had poured through the gates of the stockade. Ten thousand men. There was no room for them in the buildings, no room at all; and, like animals, they were forced to scratch out burrows in the ground, the lucky ones with a piece of tent flap for shelter, most of them with nothing at all. Ten thousand men. Scantily clad, always hungry, lacking shelter, sanitary facilities, and an adequate supply of clean water. The makeshift hospital had room only for the dying, and the mules dragging out the dead carts staggered under their increasing burdens.

And still the prisoners poured out of the railroad cars, into the stockade.

Cort Adams, who had been pressed into service in the hospital, quietly began to copy the official list of the dead, the ever lengthening list of the dead.

With mounting outrage he calculated the numbers. "They are dying, *we* are dying at a rate of thirteen percent a month. Three hundred twenty last week alone!" He looked at his fellow correspondents, and they were equally appalled. Junius Browne was working in the hospital with him, sharing the horror.

"We have to get out of here," Cort said. "We have to get out and tell the world what's happening." They were finishing their evening meal of corn bread, salt pork, and what passed as coffee, and Junius was dividing the last of the dried apples.

"We've been through this discussion before," Al Richardson reminded him. "It's not as if we haven't *wanted* to escape."

"But now we must. I don't care what the odds are." Cort was somber. "In any case, how much longer can we expect to survive if we stay here? We're lucky to have a roof over our heads, but we aren't exactly flourishing on *our* rations, either. And winter is coming, and who knows what diseases and epidemics."

"Yesterday," Junius gazed at them all, "one of the new prisoners exchanged his tin cup for a potato."

"My God." Cort shuddered. "Why, that's his death warrant."

Junius nodded. "Yes. Today he didn't even bother to line up for the rice soup."

"They ran out of that soup before half the men got any at all." Al shook his head.

Davis, usually so reserved, uttered a quiet curse. "God damn all Rebel bastards. God damn them all to hell, now and forever, life everlasting, world without end."

"Amen," Al agreed.

"In the meantime," Cort went back to the business at hand, "how do we escape?"

"There are always tunnels," Junius offered with a wry smile. "I know of seven being dug right now."

"But not one is halfway to the line yet," Al objected. "And you can't tunnel more than fifty feet without getting air into the shaft somehow. I don't see how any of them can work."

"We don't have that much time." Cort dismissed the tunnels. "We have to escape while we're still strong enough to get over the mountains."

Junius agreed. "If we can reach the hills, we'll find friends. There's a lot of Union sentiment up there, and on into eastern Tennessee."

"Knoxville," Cort said. "That's the place to go."

"It's as good a place as any," Davis agreed. "I approve of the destination, gentlemen, and also the route over the mountains. But you're leaving out something. How do we go through the main gate here, and just how far do you think we can get before anyone notices and sends out search parties? We aren't exactly unknown to the authorities. I have a feeling they'll miss us."

"Cort and I have our hospital passes," Junius began tentatively.

"The hospital is within the stockade, too," Al pointed out.

"Yes, but it's close to the gate, and there's a certain amount of traffic. If the guards were temporarily distracted . . ."

Davis scoffed at the idea. "So the four of us would just walk through?"

"Audacity," Cort said. "'De l'audace, et encore de l'audace, et toujours de l'audace.'"

"No doubt that would fool a French guard any time." Davis remained skeptical. "I think our cracker friends would be more wide awake than that."

"We wouldn't all go at once," Al said, warming to the idea. "The plan would be to slip through one or two at a time and then rendezvous that night. Hole up for a couple of days in a barn or slave cabin until the hunt is called off, and then strike out for the hills."

"We ought to lay in a few days' supply of rations," Junius said thoughtfully.

"I'd need something better for my feet." Davis stretched out his legs to display the soles of his shoes, inadequately pieced out with cardboard. "I wouldn't feel the least bit audacious in these."

Cort laughed. "I'm glad you see fit to join us."

"I could help out with the shoes," Al said, and the mood immediately darkened. Al had taken charge of distributing the tattered garments of the dead to the living. There was no need for shoes in the expanding row of common graves just outside the stockade.

"We should think about clothes," Cort said, intent on working out the problems. "It's going to be cold in the mountains at night."

"It gets pretty damned cold right here," Junius agreed.

"Those poor devils outside in the mud." Davis shivered in sympathy.

"We *have* to get through," Cort said with conviction. "God knows what they're thinking in Washington. To know what it's like and not make an exchange—it's barbarous."

They were silent, and Cort carefully tucked away his list of the dead. How many columns of long gray type were there now? And how many would he added before they escaped? *If* they escaped.

"The hospital passes," Davis said, obviously pursuing Junius Browne's idea. "Do you and Cort really need them? They know you belong there anyway. If Al and I took yours, and you used a little of that audacity . . ."

"Perhaps we could forge something good enough for the two of us," Junius looked at Cort, "while Davis and Al used ours."

"It's a possibility." Cort thought about it. "It shouldn't be too hard to lift a little of that official paper from the office."

"Now about the rendezvous the first night." Al scratched his head absentmindedly and dislodged a few lice. He had been a prisoner for a year and a half, but there were some things he would never get used to, and he looked at the lice with distaste before crushing them.

"The rendezvous," Junius prompted him.

"Yes. I think we should go no farther than that big barn you can see from the front gate. It's not more than a fifteen-minute walk, and no one will look for us so close to home. We can slip away later, after the search parties are called off."

Junius disputed that, and Davis thought they should cover as much distance as possible the first night.

Cort was doubtful. "I wish we could get hold of a map. I'd feel happier if one of us knew this section of the country."

"Higbee," Davis said thoughtfully. "Hank Higbee. He's that Unionist on the top floor. He's from these parts, and he used to be a surveyor. I think he'd draw us a map. God, for a chew of real tobacco, he'd come with us as a guide."

"No!" Cort was emphatic. "We can't expand this group, and particularly not with someone like Higbee. They'd know we were heading for the hills, and we'd never get away. Four newspaper correspondents, three of us from New York—they'll expect us to go straight to Virginia on the railroad. If we can get a map out of Higbee, fine. But don't invite him to come."

"I think he's working on one of the tunnels anyway," Junius said.

"So much the better." Cort looked at the muddy sediment in his empty cup. "Is there any more of that foul stuff you call coffee?"

Junius looked injured. "I burned that corn and ground it myself. If you can't treat my handiwork any more respectfully than that . . ." But he threw another handful of the charred grain in their one battered pan and brought the water to a boil.

Cort proposed a toast. "This is Thanksgiving Day, in case any of you needed to be reminded. Let's hope we soon have something to be thankful for. Gentlemen." He motioned for them to stand up. "To freedom!"

They raised their tin cups in mock salute, but they echoed his toast with an emotion that surprised them all.

"To freedom!"

Chapter 37

TOM CAME HOME to New York for Christmas, not to the Stratford but to Gramercy Park. The next afternoon he brought Lucy to the hotel for tea, and Miranda met them with Dickon in her arms. Tom was full of admiration for his young nephew, but he was frankly alarmed when he saw his father.

"You look like a refugee from Andersonville," he said bluntly. "What's the matter? Aren't you eating enough?"

"You sound like Miranda." Will forced a smile. "I'll be all right. I just haven't had much appetite lately. But you, my boy, are looking very fit. And Lucy is just blooming."

"Thank you, Papa Chase. That's because I'm so happy to have Tom home again."

"Nothing the matter with *her* appetite," Tom said, grinning, "now that she has the excuse of eating for two."

"Tom, please." She looked embarrassed, but he refused to stop.

"We're all family, sweetheart. Papa and Miranda understand. This girl," he put his arm around Lucy, "is determined that our child will be a young giant. Why, she had more for dinner today than *I* did, and I'm fresh from army rations in Virginia."

Miranda looked at her critically. "I don't think you've put on very much weight, Lucy. I think you look fine."

"I agree with that." Tom was irrepressible. "A nice, comfortable armful. Just a little more of her to love."

Lucy blushed, and Tom pulled her close. Will smiled at them benignly, and Miranda had a stab of pure envy. They obviously loved each other so much.

459

"How is Richard?" she asked, thinking how desolate Christmas must be in the dangerous trenches near Petersburg.

"He's fine. He sends you his love, and he misses you." Tom paused, struggling with himself, but he had never been any good at keeping secrets. "Very soon, I think, he'll be sending you some good news."

She looked at him inquiringly.

"I'm not supposed to tell, because it won't be official for a few more days."

"But, Tom, if you have gone this far, you can't stop now."

"No, Richard wanted to surprise you. He'd be furious with me—"

"Never mind all that. Just *tell* me."

"I don't know . . . You're sure you won't let on that you knew it all along?"

"Tom, don't tease me." She threw a pillow at him, and he caught it before it did any damage to the tea tray.

"Sometimes I think you aren't a day over five."

"Sometimes I think you aren't, either. For heaven's sake, if you have a secret burning a hole in your pocket, let it out."

"That's a decidedly mixed metaphor. I remember a class in rhetoric—"

"Lucy," Miranda appealed to her, "how can you stand him?"

"Darling," she smiled at Tom, "I want to know, too."

"In that case," he kissed her, "I'll tell all. Richard is getting a promotion. He'll be a major, a staff officer attached to regimental headquarters."

"Oh, that's wonderful!" Miranda exclaimed. "And it sounds so much safer, too. Is it?"

Tom shrugged. "On a day-to-day basis, I suppose so. He won't be in the forward lines. But in an attack, I wouldn't predict anything. If a bullet has your name on it . . . However, we have all survived this long, and it's just a few more months now."

She had been hearing that for years, but this time it seemed to be really so. Now that Sherman had marched all through Georgia to the sea . . . His army, cut off from all communication for so long, had finally surfaced again near Savannah, had taken Fort McAllister, and had made contact with the Union fleet. The troops were investing the city, and it was expected to fall any day now. How much longer could the South possibly hold out?

On the day after Christmas, John and Dany had invited the immediate family—Tom and Lucy and Will and Miranda and the baby—to have dinner with them in Brooklyn Heights.

That morning the newspapers had carried Sherman's telegram to President Lincoln: I beg to present you, as a Christmas gift, the city of Savannah, with 150 heavy guns and plenty of ammunition and also about 25,000 bales of cotton.

The city had actually fallen December 21, but the message had had to be taken first by ship to Fort Monroe, Virginia, and the telegram dispatched from there, arriving on Lincoln's desk just in time for the holiday itself.

Will and Miranda had been doubtful about Dany's reaction, but she greeted them with a happy smile.

"Good news! Andy Dawson sent me a telegram. He's seen Mama and Susanne, and they're all right! They're all right, Miranda! Isn't that wonderful? The telegram says 'letter follows.' But they've survived. Thank God!"

"Thank God!" Will echoed, and for once his words weren't punctuated by a cough.

"And I had good news, too," Miranda said. "I always dread telegrams, but this one came from Richard. It's official: He's Major Schuyler now."

John smiled with satisfaction. "I'd make him a general, but this is a step in the right direction. Think how much we have to celebrate."

Miranda nodded. "Richard is going to be in Washington in mid-January for a few days, and he wants me to come."

"And are you going?" John looked at her expectantly.

"I don't know. I'd like to see George and Emily and the children, and show them how much Dickon has grown. But Papa doesn't feel like making the trip, and I hate to leave him alone."

"Don't worry so much, Pet. Megan can help you with the baby, and you won't be gone all that long. I'll be fine. I'll even have Maureen for company."

"Megan is afraid you'll spoil her, Papa."

"Would that be so bad? It didn't do you any harm." Will put his arm around her, and Miranda smiled at him, but she could not conceal her worry. He still coughed too much, and he was noticeably thinner. He had taken to lying down for a nap every afternoon, like Dickon, and he was always short of breath when he climbed stairs. She would have pressed him to consider installing an elevator, but he was reluctant to make any major investments in the Stratford if George and Tom were really going to build a new hotel . . . Miranda emerged from her cloud of worry when Tom and Lucy arrived, and then Dickon demanded her attention, and by the time they were ready to sit down to dinner, Tom was telling them stories about a pompous general and his insufferable wife, and he had both Lucy and Dany in gales of laughter. Will smiled, and John opened another bottle of wine, and Miranda stilled her nagging doubts and allowed her glass to be refilled.

George met the train when Miranda arrived in Washington in January, and she marveled at how much the city had grown. In the four years since the war had started, the resident population had more than doubled, mushrooming from sixty thousand to one hundred forty thousand. The civilians who had flocked there in search of government jobs and war contracts had been joined by thousands of soldiers stationed in a ring of camps and forts surrounding the city. The contrabands had come by the thousands, spreading their festering slums in the low-lying marshes. And after every battle the wounded flooded the hospitals, as many as fifty thousand in the bloody aftermath of Grant's campaigns. In increasing numbers the relatives of hospitalized soldiers arrived to seek them out and nurse them back to health. The hotels and boardinghouses had never been more crowded, and there was an unending demand for more housing, more workers, more shops, more tailors and dressmakers and blacksmiths and saddlers, more saloons, more brothels, more everything. Even the animal population had multiplied. Foggy Bottom was filled with wagon sheds and corrals for thirty thousand horses and mules.

Washington's sewer system was still virtually nonexistent, but the aqueduct had finally been completed, assuring a plentiful supply of water at last.

Miranda, who had observed the changes in the city over the years, was more impressed than Megan, who was seeing it all for the first time.

"But it's not nearly as grand as New York," Megan protested. "Where are the great hotels and the shops and the theaters and the parks?" Only the Capitol building, with the dome rebuilt at last, gave her any satisfaction at all. She was surprised at the sight of so many black faces on the streets, and she was amazed to see that all the draymen and hackmen and carriage drivers were Negroes. In New York the Irish had all those jobs.

Miranda had a moment's panic about how Megan would react to Jeff and Hattie and the rest of the staff, but all went smoothly. Megan admired the house on Massachusetts Avenue and breathed a sigh of relief when she discovered that Hattie could brew a proper cup of tea.

Richard had not yet arrived, and Miranda had time to exclaim over Polly and baby George and to bask in the compliments for Dickon. And she had time to ask about Cort, too.

"No trace of him," George said. "Of course the South is in such chaos that they don't have records in Richmond of half their prisoners. But I know damn well that if Cort were alive, he'd have managed to get a message through. I'm afraid I don't have much hope."

Miranda nodded, preserving a surface calm, but Emily was sensitive to her distress and gave her a thoughtful look.

"And we've had such sad news from Savannah," George went on.

"But Dany had a telegram," Miranda contradicted him. "Her mother and Susanne are all right."

"Yes, they are," George agreed. "But the little boy, Bobby . . ."

"What happened?" Miranda clutched convulsively at Dickon in her arms.

"Diphtheria," George said, shaking his head. "One of the servants, Toby, was sick with it, and by the time they discovered what it was, Bobby had been exposed. The two of them died a week apart. Susanne barely recovered herself."

"Dear God." Miranda blinked back her tears. To lose a child . . . Poor Cort. Was there nothing left? He had loved that boy so much, had been willing to go back to Susanne . . . Oh, darling, if *I* could have had our baby . . . But then there wouldn't be Dickon, and life without him was as unthinkable as . . . life without Cort. And today Richard would be arriving, possessive, demanding, intent on shaping her to

463

his desires, convinced she was his loving wife and the perfect mother of their children. And if he ever thought otherwise . . . But no, he was too determined in his vision, forcing reality to bend to his will, and for her there was no way out. She swallowed hard and was aware of Polly tugging at her skirts.

"See baby," the child demanded.

"Yes, of course," Miranda agreed. "This is your little cousin, Dickon."

"No." Polly had no interest in him at all. "Come, see my baby. Baby Peggy."

Miranda was bewildered, but Emily came to her rescue. "She means you should come look at her dolly. Cort went wild last year for her birthday and gave her a whole wardrobe of doll clothes. Polly changes Peggy oftener than I change the baby."

"I see." Miranda yielded to Polly's demands and followed her to the nursery, where Georgie was asleep. "I don't suppose she still remembers Cort."

Emily shook her head. "It's been six months. An eternity at that age."

"Yes, an eternity." Miranda sat down in the rocking chair to nurse Dickon, and Polly looked at him jealously and then climbed into her mother's lap with her doll.

"The letter about Bobby." Miranda could not let the subject go. "Did Susanne write to you?"

Emily seemed to be embarrassed. "No. The letter was addressed to Cort. We weren't quite sure what to do when it arrived last week, but his brother, Warren, had told us to open *all* the mail and send on anything important to Boston. So that's what we have been doing."

"I see. But if she wrote to him, she must think Cort is still alive."

"She doesn't know either. But on the chance that he might be, she had to tell him about Bobby. She had met Andy Dawson, and he arranged for her to get a letter through to Washington. And to Dany in New York, too. Susanne is simply crushed by all that has happened—the little boy, her father, the war. And she doesn't know whether Cort is alive or dead." Emily paused before going on. "And she isn't sure if he will ever want her back, now that the boy . . ."

"Then you know," Miranda said, not thinking.

"That the little girl isn't his? Yes, we had speculated about it, you remember, but Susanne's letter makes it clear. Did you know all along, Miranda?" Emily gazed at her with dawning comprehension. "If Cort told you himself, then——"

"Richard told me." It was technically true, but she felt her color rising just the same. "Marty found out, but Richard asked me not to say anything, to protect Dany and the family."

"I see." Emily was still puzzled, but she let the subject drop. "I don't know what Warren will make of the letter. Or of her. He is so very straitlaced."

"He'll be understanding," Miranda said, with conviction. "Discreet and understanding. Like Cort." She had said too much again, and Emily was looking at her with compassion.

"Dear Miranda. I wondered, but . . . When you took such elaborate precautions to avoid each other, when he didn't see you when he went to New York, and you stopped coming here . . ."

"I am married," Miranda said firmly. "I have Dickon. And it was impossible——" Her voice cracked and she stopped abruptly.

"Yes, of course, dear, and I won't say a word. Not even to George. I think he wondered, too, why you were avoiding each other, but he just made a joke about Richard being jealous and then forgot about it. George has so many worries since Cort's disappearance. When Warren was here, the two of them had some harebrained idea about going south to search him out. They were saner the next morning, but George has been restless ever since, and he's started talking again about getting a transfer to the front lines to see some real fighting."

"Oh, Emily, don't let him. Tom is there, and Richard, and we've lost Jimmy and Damon, and I'm worried about Papa . . ."

"Papa?" Is it really that serious?"

"Find Papa," Polly said, sliding off her mother's lap and trudging to the door. "I find Papa."

"Yes, that's a good idea," Emily agreed. "Is Dickon asleep? Call Megan to put him to bed, Miranda, and we'll find George. He'll want to hear what you have to say about his father."

465

George sighed at the news and shook his head. "John mentioned it in his last letter, and Tom is worried, too. I don't know what to say. I'll try to get to New York this month, and perhaps we can persuade Papa at least to take a rest. Can you and Guy Dawson run the Stratford together for a while?"

Miranda looked doubtful.

"Come now," George teased her. "Where's all that eager confidence? I expected you to be insulted that I even asked. You know you can do it. You understand the books?"

She nodded.

"And of course you know all the staff, and there have been no major problems since the arson plot. You can call on John if something worries you, and if he has doubts—"

"John never has doubts," Miranda contradicted George, smiling for the first time.

"Then there's no problem at all," George insisted. "But what I was going to say was that you can always send me a telegram, and if it's urgent I'll come right away."

"Not if you are in the front lines," Emily cut in, seizing her opportunity to argue against his transfer.

He looked at her, and then he bent down to pick up Polly. "No, not if I am in the front lines," he agreed. He was silent for a long moment, and then he kissed the child. "How can I go off and leave you all? I'm afraid you're right, Emily. It was a foolish idea. But I did want just one chance to prove to myself that I could be a real soldier." He sighed, and his smile was rueful. "Do you realize that at every family gathering for the next forty years I'm going to have to listen to Marty brag about being a hero and never be able to say a word?"

"A heavy penance, darling." Emily took his hand. "But worth it, to keep you safe and whole."

"So it's settled," George said. "I give up my dreams of glory, and you, Miranda, take over the Stratford and give Papa a rest."

"I don't know if Richard will agree."

George was astonished. "But he'll be in Virginia. Why would he object?"

"He's difficult about things like that."

"Nonsense, Miranda. You could always get around Papa. I can't believe you don't manage Richard the same way. He's crazy about you, and he'd give you the world. I know about that house he's bought. Why, it's as grand as this one. In New York Emily and I won't be moving into anything like this for years."

"That's all right," Emily assured him. "I wouldn't even mind living in the hotel for a while if we need to save some money."

George smiled at her, and Miranda retreated before their solid wall of devotion and settled into Cort's chair. So Emily wouldn't *mind* living at the Stratford. I only wish . . . I just know I'll have a major battle with Richard over managing the hotel and, yes, perhaps I'll get around him, but he won't like it, and somehow he'll make me feel guilty, stepping out of my role, not living up to his standards. George expects Emily to argue with him. She even wins sometimes, when she's right. It would be crazy of him to go off to war now and perhaps be wounded or killed. Dear God, let him survive. Let all of them survive. And please let Cort come home. Even if I can't see him again, even if he goes back to Susanne and forgets all about me, let him be safe.

Richard arrived just as she was tucking Dickon into bed for the night. He stood in the doorway, smiling at them, and when Miranda said she'd never been kissed by a major before, Richard laughed and quickly remedied that situation.

"I couldn't tell any difference at all," she teased him. "Emily, if George is promoted, it will be the same as ever."

"I'm glad to hear that." Emily moved closer to George, and he put his arm around her.

"Miranda," George looked at her fondly, "you said you couldn't manage Richard. Why, he's putty in your hands."

She felt the sudden tension in Richard's arm, but he forced a smile. "What do you mean? What have you been saying about me?"

George answered for her. "All compliments, my dear major, I assure you. But Miranda was worried that you . . . You see, we have decided that Papa needs a rest, and so Miranda and Guy Dawson will manage the Stratford for a few months on their own. She was a little doubtful about your reaction, but of course you'll be proud that she—"

"Proud?" He was stunned. "I can't believe that . . . Of course if Uncle Will is seriously ill and needs help in running

467

the hotel, we must make arrangements, but I don't think it would be suitable for Miranda to be concerned with all that. You might go off with him on a brief holiday, darling, but—"

"I think George is right," Miranda said. "Mr. Dawson and I will manage the hotel, and I can call on John if I need him, or send word to George if we have a serious problem."

"Miranda, you can't possibly—"

"Of course she can, Richard," George contradicted him. "She grew up there. She knows it like the back of her hand. And Papa would feel much better leaving it all to her, keeping it in the family."

"May I remind you, George, that Miranda is *my* family now, and her name is Schuyler, not Chase. I think this whole idea is completely preposterous. In any case, this is something I will resolve with Miranda later, without your assistance."

George looked at him, amazed. "What a stuffed shirt you are, Richard!"

"Darling," Emily tried to soothe him. "I think that perhaps Richard needs a little time to get used to the idea, that's all. Now I'll just check to see how Hattie is getting along with dinner, and we should be sitting down soon."

There was an awkward silence after she left the room, and Miranda groped for a safe and uncontroversial topic of conversation. "The House of Representatives," she said, seizing on the day's headlines. "I think they'll finally pass the anti-slavery amendment, don't you?" There was no response, but she pushed on, nonetheless. "The Senate voted for it last year, and I think it was a disgrace that the House didn't manage a two-thirds majority then. But according to the newspapers today . . ." By the time Emily returned, Miranda had settled the slavery issue to her complete satisfaction, and George was being cooperative with his comments, though Richard was still a thundercloud.

Emily presided with her usual calm at the dinner table, and when she began to talk about Susanne and Mrs. Robillard in Savannah, she finally aroused Richard from his brooding silence. He was shocked to learn of Bobby's death, and he expressed sympathy for the family.

"Andy Dawson is going to see that they get transportation to New York," he told them.

"I didn't know that!" Miranda was astonished. "Dany didn't say a word to me about it."

"Dany doesn't know. John worked it all out with Andy in November, but at that time we didn't know what he would find in Savannah—the family might not have survived a siege. Until we had good news, John didn't want to get Dany's hopes up. The plan was to bring Mrs. Robillard and Susanne and the children to Brooklyn until the war is over."

"Do you think they will come?" Miranda was still surprised.

"They'll have to," Richard said. "Sherman's army has been living off the country all through Georgia, and God knows what there is left for the civilian population. In any case, the transportation is completely disrupted, and what food is available might not get to the cities. I know we're sending relief shipments—Papa helped organize the committee—but that's a stopgap measure. It's better to get them out of there until the war is over, and it will do Dany a world of good to be reunited with her family."

"How thoughtful of John," Emily said.

Richard agreed. "And Andy Dawson has been very cooperative. I think Mother is going to have to relent and let him marry Irene."

Emily beamed. "Another wedding! I'd like to meet Andy. What's he like, Miranda?"

"Well, he's very direct. And very open."

"And he was once a beau of yours," George teased her.

She colored. "Not for long. That was mostly his father's idea, I think."

"In any case," Richard said comfortably, "I put a stop to it."

"*You* did?" Emily was surprised.

"Of course." Richard settled back in his chair. "I had decided years ago to marry Miranda. And while I was waiting for her to grow up and agree with me, I had to make sure that no one else came along to distract her." He smiled at her fondly. "You never had a chance, darling. I was here all along."

"And I thought marriages were made in heaven," George said.

"Mine was," Richard agreed. "But God helps those who help themselves."

George laughed. "Richard, I don't think you need any help at all, even from God. But I think you might unbend a little.

Now about the problem with the Stratford . . . Emily, why don't you and Miranda let me thrash this out with Richard over brandy and cigars?"

Emily rose at once, but Miranda hesitated. She was glad to have George on her side, but perhaps she should fight her own battles. "But it concerns *me*," she began.

"It concerns Papa and the hotel first of all," George corrected her. "I want to explain all that to Richard before anyone gets emotional."

"I will be very calm," Miranda said, gripping the edge of the table.

"But if you stay," George objected, "will Richard be calm?"

Miranda studied them both. Richard's temper was building again, and perhaps George was right. Reluctantly, she got to her feet and left them alone.

In the music room she sat down at the piano beside Emily, and they had worked their way through three duets before the men rejoined them, George with a half smile of victory, Richard still tense and obviously uncomfortable.

"Until Uncle Will recovers," he addressed Miranda formally, "you will be in charge. With the assistance of Guy Dawson, of course, and with the advice of John and George, if you need them."

"Yes, Richard." She was subdued in her triumph, George's triumph, and this was not the time or the place to ask questions.

"Well, then," Emily said briskly. "Miranda and I have been practicing. Do you think we can get through even one of these duets without breaking down in the middle?"

"Probably not," Miranda said, smiling, "but let's try."

Alone in their bedroom, Miranda waited for an explanation.

"I preferred not to quarrel with George," Richard said. "You should not have allowed him to interfere with our lives, Miranda, but it's done now. As soon as the war is over and we are in our own house and I am home to stay, there will be no necessity for you to be mixed up in things that shouldn't concern you. I am trying to be understanding, darling, and I know that you are not completely to blame. I like Uncle Will, but he did bring you up in a most peculiar way.

470

It's no wonder that sometimes . . . Still, it will all work out when I am home again. I'd rather think about that." He embraced her and kissed her again. "Reunions are so sweet, darling, and soon we'll be together always."

Chapter 38

THEY WERE EATING breakfast the next morning when the telegram arrived, triggering sudden fear. George tore open the envelope and read the astonishing message, his face lighting up with joy.

"It's Cort! He's escaped—he'll be here as soon as he can get transportation from Tennessee."

"Coming home!" Emily could hardly believe it.

"Dear God, thank you." Miranda's voice trembled with emotion.

"An answer to a prayer," Emily agreed.

"So he has come to life again." Richard added cream to his coffee and stirred it in. "Where has he been?"

"The telegram is from Knoxville," George said. "I'll read it to you. 'Escaped from prison, Salisbury, North Carolina. Terrible ordeal. Story in *Times*. Arriving Washington, earliest train.'" George looked up at a beaming Jeff. "Yes, it's true. Tell Hattie and everyone."

"Yes," Emily agreed. "We must tell them all. Do you suppose Cort sent telegrams to Warren and Dany and Mir— everyone?"

"Probably, but let's telegraph them anyway, in case any of his messages went astray. Wonderful news!" George pushed back his chair and stood up. "The New York papers don't come in until later, but—"

"George," Richard remonstrated. "It can't possibly be in today's *Times*. Sit down and finish your breakfast."

"I hardly feel like eating. I haven't been this happy since . . . since Georgie was born."

He reread the telegram, commenting on it, wondering

472

about Cort, where he had been and how he was now, deciding to check the train schedules to discover when he might arrive. Emily joined in his happy speculation, while Richard went right on eating breakfast and Miranda sat absolutely still, in a daze, in a dream, scarcely hearing a word.

He's coming home. The words reverberated again and again. He's alive and he's coming home. To Washington. And I'll be here to see him and welcome him and tell him . . . Oh, if only Richard weren't here. Just Cort with me—and no one else. A few days together, and I'd live on it the rest of my life.

She was conscious of Richard's eyes on her, and she studiously buttered a muffin and made a pretense of eating. Chewed, swallowed, washed it down with coffee. She didn't taste a thing. He's coming home. Alive and coming home.

It was two days before the dispatches began to appear in the *Times:* CAPTURE AND IMPRISONMENT. DEPLORABLE CONDITIONS IN SALISBURY. OUR MEN DYING. DESPERATE ESCAPE THROUGH THE SNOW. AIDED BY NEGROES AND LOYALISTS. BUSHWHACKERS IN THE MOUNTAINS.

In addition to the story of escape, there was a signed article on the urgency of a prompt exchange of prisoners. The *Tribune* carried similar appeals from Albert Richardson, and both newspapers raised again the whole question of the shifting policies on prisoners of war.

At the beginning of the conflict, prisoners usually had been exchanged or simply released if they gave their parole not to fight again. Such trust soon broke down, but some exchanges continued, particularly of the sick and wounded.

In the North there was an ongoing debate about whether such a policy actually prolonged the war. The prisoners returned to the South went right back into the Confederate army, but many of the Yankees, weakened by their subsistence on scant rations, their terms of enlistment expiring, were thankful to return to civilian life. Those who had given their parole not to fight again had effectively escaped from battle—and if parole and exchange were made almost automatic, that made capture a definite temptation.

Another major stumbling block came up midway in the war when Negroes were recruited for the Union armies and the South adamantly refused to treat these soldiers as prisoners of war, to be exchanged on the same basis as whites.

When, at gunpoint, captured Negroes were pressed into service building fortifications, Yankee commanders in the field, without waiting for permission from Washington, promptly forced captured Confederate soldiers into similar work. After that, the lot of Negro prisoners improved somewhat, but for more than a year there were virtually no exchanges.

In the North, the reports of prison conditions in the South precipitated heated debate, and many of those who still argued against a policy of exchange had their own solution to the horrors of Andersonville: Make the northern prisons just as grim.

The correspondents who escaped from Salisbury had no patience with debating points. They wanted the prisoners freed before they all died—or enlisted in the Confederate army. When faced with starvation, an appreciable number of Yankee soldiers, particularly the foreign conscripts, had no difficulty in changing flags: They expected to desert at the first opportunity, and they did.

Miranda pored over the newspaper reports, waiting impatiently for Cort's return, racked with guilt whenever Richard looked at her with love in his eyes. He was leaving tomorrow to return to Petersburg, and she knew she should take the first train back to New York. She had promised not to see Cort again, but how could she tear herself away when he would be here so soon? His mother was coming, too, and his brother, Warren. Emily had received the telegram from Boston that morning.

It was early afternoon when Richard returned, having completed his business with the war department.

"We'll move into a hotel for tonight," Richard said to Emily as soon as he heard about the expected guests. "You won't have room for all of us, and we won't want to spoil the hero's return."

"Nonsense," Emily protested. "I've worked it all out. We'll just move Dickon into the nursery, and Megan, too. Mrs. Adams can have that room. And we'll put a bed in the upstairs study for Warren. That used to be your room, Miranda, before Cort took it over."

Miranda nodded, not saying a word. She cradled Dickon in her arms and looked up to see Richard smiling at her fondly.

"It gets harder to leave you each time," he said simply.

She swallowed over the lump in her throat and held out

her hand to him. Swiftly, he crossed the room to sit beside her, and Emily, displaying her usual tact, murmured something about moving that extra bed from the attic and disappeared.

Richard embraced her, and she kissed him, her husband, the father of her child, so devoted to her. It would all work out. Surely it would all work out. She just had to be patient. The baby stirred, and she settled him more comfortably in her lap, Richard's arm still around her.

That is how Cort found them when he paused in the doorway, dropping his satchel, handing his cape to Jeff who had rushed from the pantry to greet him.

"Yes." He smiled at them all. "I'm glad to be home."

He had lost weight in prison, and he was tired and drawn from his exhausting journey, but when he smiled at Miranda, the sun shone for her again.

The clothes he had worn on his month-long trek through the mountains had been reduced to tatters, to be burned as soon as he reached Knoxville. But the badly fitted suit he was wearing now only emphasized how gaunt he was. He had shaved off his prison-grown beard, and he looked oddly vulnerable, open to too many emotions.

Emily ran down the stairs for a welcoming kiss, Hattie emerged from the kitchen and hugged him impulsively, and Miranda looked up at him with her whole heart in her eyes. Richard crossed the room to shake hands while she struggled to her feet with the baby still in her arms.

"Miranda." Cort smiled again, but there was pain in his eyes. "What an unexpected pleasure to see you, too." His lips brushed her cheek, and then he touched the baby. Dickon promptly curled a plump fist around Cort's finger. "And so you have a son."

She nodded, not trusting her voice.

"What a fine young boy. I'm something of an expert when it comes to children, you know. What are you calling him?"

She was still too overcome to speak.

"Dickon," Emily answered for her. "But of course he is really Richard, Jr."

"Of course." Cort nodded and detached himself from the baby's firm grasp. "And where is my godchild? I missed six months of her life."

Polly ran in, eager to see what all the excitement was about, and she was astonished to be swooped up in the arms of this tall dark stranger. Not sure whether she liked it, she looked uncertainly at her mother. Emily smiled, and Polly laughed then, and the stranger grinned at her. She kissed him, as if she had done that before.

"Dear God, I'm glad to be home." Cort settled into his favorite leather chair with Polly in his lap, and he looked at all of them expectantly. "Tell me the news," he said. "I never did get to Savannah. But you must have heard from them by now. How are they all? Did Mr. Robillard recover from his stroke? I thought I would be there in September for Bobby's third birthday but," he allowed himself the ghost of a smile, "I was unavoidably detained."

"You don't know?" Emily looked at him with compassion, and there were sudden tears in her eyes. "No, of course you don't."

"Know what?"

She was too overcome to answer, and Miranda looked grief-stricken, too.

Richard shook his head and cleared his throat, unhappy to be the bearer of bad tidings. "In the letter from—"

"They are all dead," Cort said bleakly. "I can tell just by looking at you. They are all dead. How did it happen?"

"No, no, not all. But your little boy . . ." Richard paused, but there was no way to soften the blow. "Bobby died of diphtheria. My deepest sympathy, Cort. To lose a son . . ." He couldn't go on, and he reached instinctively for Miranda, who was holding Dickon so tightly that the baby wailed his protest.

With an effort of will she relaxed her grip and soothed him, and Richard put his arm around her and touched the baby again, as if for reassurance.

Cort looked at the three of them, and there was misery in his eyes. "So I have lost Bobby, too. I'd have given up if I had known. At Salisbury, that ordeal in the mountains, earlier when I had typhoid . . ."

"Oh, no, Cort!" Emily brushed away her tears. "You wouldn't give up." She tried to rally him. "There are too many people who love you. And it's important what you did, bringing us a firsthand report of that miserable prison."

"I'm not the first," Cort said with a tired shrug.

"No," Emily agreed. "But you and Mr. Richardson can make yourselves heard. George says the policy will be different now. There's just too much pressure on Mr. Stanton to speed up the exchanges. You helped to save lives, Cort."

"But not Bobby's. I botched it all up from the beginning. From the very first time I saw—"

Miranda shrank from his gaze, and he stopped abruptly.

"I go right on ruining things, don't I?" He shifted his attention to Polly, who had been exploring the contents of his coat pocket. She had found the stub of a pencil and was scrawling on his notepad. "Are you going to be a writer, too?" He forced a smile. "I hope you will always tell happier stories than mine.

Polly smiled, uncomprehending, and her laughter bubbled up again. Cort brushed a lock of hair from her forehead and looked again at Miranda, and she sighed and kissed Dickon.

"So, Richard," Cort had his voice under control, "you were saying there was a letter about Bobby."

Emily cut in to explain, and Richard added the latest news from John—Mrs. Robillard and Susanne and the little girl would be arriving in New York at the end of the week.

"Will you want to bring them here, Cort?" Emily was briskly efficient. "It's your house, after all, and George and I always knew that our stay here would be temporary. I can take the children to my parents in Brooklyn, and the war will be over soon, and—"

"No, no," Cort protested. "You must stay. I don't know what I'll be doing." He was silent, thinking about the future. "I suppose I should go to New York and see them all. Susanne must be grief-stricken, too. Poor girl. We'll have to sort it out somehow." He sighed and shook his head. "I don't want to think about it now. God, what a homecoming! And I thought all I would do was soak in a hot tub and devour one of Hattie's dinners and go to sleep for a week."

"You can still do that." Emily smiled at him. "But don't sleep for a week. Your mother and Warren will be here tonight. They want to welcome the hero home from the wars."

"Hero!" Cort scoffed. "I'm glad they are coming, of course, but it would have been nice to have one day of peace and quiet. To come home to a house bulging at the seams . . ."

"Quite right," Richard agreed. "I've already suggested to Emily that I should move my family to a hotel for the night. I go back to Petersburg tomorrow, and then Miranda will be returning to New York with Dickon and the nurse."

"So soon?" Cort's eyes locked on hers for a moment, and she nodded.

"Richard," Emily protested, "it's all arranged for you to stay here."

"Of course," Cort agreed. "I didn't mean to sound inhospitable." He let Polly slither to the floor, and she wandered back to her mother. "But I think I'll have that bath now. And put on some decent clothes, if any of them still fit." His eyes caught Miranda's and he tried to smile. "In spite of everything, I'm glad to be home."

"I don't know." Emily lowered her voice, though Cort could hardly hear her from his room upstairs. "He has lost so much weight. Did he say he'd had typhoid fever? How did he ever survive! And then to come home to such tragic news. I could never have told him. Richard, I am glad you are here."

Richard was doubtful. "Perhaps we shouldn't stay. Poor Cort—I can understand his grief. But seeing us, Miranda, so happy—the contrast is too great. When I look at you and our own dear son, and soon, we hope, another child—"

"Richard," Miranda protested, "we don't know that yet. There is no way to know that, and while I am nursing Dickon, it's very unlikely—"

"Yes, darling, you keep telling me that. But there is a special glow about you these past few days. I'll make you a small wager that I'm right. Say . . . a diamond brooch for a kiss."

"Richard, don't be so wildly extravagant."

"Why not? I like to give you presents." He smiled at her and appealed to Emily. "Don't you think I'm right? Can't I give her anything in the world if I want to?"

Emily was clearly uncomfortable. "Perhaps she just wants a little independence, Richard."

It was not the response he expected, and he raised an eyebrow. "Don't tell me *you* want to manage a hotel, too."

Emily considered it with mock seriousness. "It might be rather interesting at that. If I could learn enough from George to help, it would be wonderful to be able to work with him." She winked at Miranda. "Wouldn't you like it, Richard, if Miranda could give you advice on how to run Schuyler Shipping after the war?"

"Preposterous! You can't seriously believe—"

Emily shook her head, smiling, and Richard broke off self-consciously.

"You are teasing me. I am just a little slow-witted today. For a minute there I thought you meant it." He forced a laugh. "It's just one more problem to blame on the Rebels: Women have gotten so used to organizing to help fight this damned war that they don't know their place any more."

Miranda sighed, and the baby yawned, and she went upstairs to let Megan put him down for his nap.

The visitors from Boston arrived in time for dinner, and Miranda immediately felt herself drawn to Cort's mother.

"I would recognize you anywhere," Mrs. Adams said confidently. "You look so much like your mother, even to the way you hold the baby in your arms. I can still see Mary with little George, and Cordelia hiding behind her skirts, peeking out at us just the way Polly is now."

Polly retreated shyly, and "little" George picked up his daughter and displayed her proudly for Mrs. Adams' closer inspection.

"I want to hear all about George as a baby," Emily said with anticipation. "Maybe I'll learn something useful."

"To avoid the same mistakes," George cut in.

"To make Georgie turn out exactly the same," Emily contradicted him. "Let me show you to your rooms. I think Cort is still asleep—he just got in this afternoon—but he said to wake him as soon as you arrived."

"How is he?" Warren asked.

"And how did he take the news about Bobby?" Mrs. Adams could not keep the emotion from her voice. "When we read Susanne's letter, we knew it would be a terrible blow. The poor little boy. And Cort . . ."

"What a wretched homecoming for him," Warren said.

Emily agreed. "And I don't think he's a bit well. He's lost so much weight. And didn't he say he had had typhoid fever?" Emily looked at Miranda for confirmation.

Miranda nodded, wordless, not trusting her voice again, turning away from Mrs. Adams' penetrating gaze.

Cort took his place at the head of the table at dinner, determinedly playing the role of host and raconteur, even making his deprivations at Salisbury sound amusing. And he had polished the story of his escape while writing about it for the newspaper, and he told it with relish—three hundred forty miles through the snow, from barns to slave cabins to the isolated farmhouses of Union sympathizers. The correspondents had finally joined a larger group being led over the mountains by an organization called Sons of America—refugees from the Confederate draft, bushwhackers, deserters from both armies, independent mountain men who wanted no truck with distant governments in either Washington or Richmond.

"You ought to write a book," Warren told him.

"I've already started one," Cort acknowledged. "And so have Al Richardson and Junius Browne. I don't know about Davis. It will be a race to see which of us gets to the book shops first."

"Don't drive yourself too hard." Mrs. Adams had been shocked by Cort's appearance, and she reached out now to put her hand on his arm. Still a hard, muscular arm, though he had obviously lost a great deal of weight. His cheeks were almost hollow, and he had cut himself shaving, as if the new contours of his face were unfamiliar. His elegantly tailored frock coat gaped at the neck, and the watered silk waistcoat appeared to be a size too large, though it had been a snug fit the last time she had seen him wearing it.

"I'll be fine, Mother," he assured her, but she was not convinced.

"Did you really have typhoid fever? How could you survive that in a prison hospital?"

"Ah," Cort said, smiling, signaling Jeff to open another bottle of wine. "That's another story."

They looked at him expectantly, and he described his five weeks at Cainewood and the two pretty girls who had nursed him there.

"I should have thought of that," George said. "All that time we were worried about you, I should have known you'd be too busy breaking hearts to get a message through. The next time I won't give you a second anxious thought."

"There won't be a next time." It was a firm commitment. "I'm through with all that."

"Through with newspapers?" Warren couldn't believe it.

"Through with taking reckless chances," Cort said. "And perhaps through with breaking hearts, too. That has its own risks." He avoided looking at Miranda and deliberately changed the subject. "I've talked enough, and it's your turn

480

now. You must tell me everything that has happened since I've been away. In Boston, New York, Washington, the war . . ."

They responded to his questions, only Miranda holding back, smiling vaguely at all of them, intent on preserving a mask of calm tranquillity. Her eyes were drawn to Cort again and again, no matter how often she forced herself to look away. It was only when she became aware that Mrs. Adams was watching her with puzzled interest that Miranda made a conscious effort to join in the conversation. George was telling them about Papa and the importance of making him rest, and Miranda echoed his concern and, before she quite realized it, she was talking about how she would manage the Stratford while he was away. She spoke with increasing animation, and Cort and Warren rewarded her with identical smiles, but she was conscious that Richard was growing tense again, and she backed off hurriedly. "Of course Mr. Dawson will really be doing most of it," she said, "and I can always call on John."

"Nonsense." Warren didn't believe that for a minute. "I'd back you against the world. Isn't that right, Richard? Miranda can do anything she sets her mind to."

Richard did not answer him, but George responded with enthusiasm. "I've never known her to do anything by halves."

Richard acknowledged that. "When you commit yourself, darling, I know it's forever. We just have to make sure that you choose wisely in the first place."

Miranda nodded, suddenly self-conscious with everyone watching her. Emily chose that moment to rise from the table, and Miranda followed gratefully, glad to escape to the music room. She sat down at the piano, partly to avoid conversation with Cort's mother, who seemed to be all too observant. She listened eagerly, though, as Emily asked questions about George's childhood—and Cort's.

When the men rejoined them, Miranda was still at the piano, silent, absorbed. Richard smiled at her fondly. "Let's have a little music, darling. Something to welcome Cort home."

"Like 'Dixie,' " Warren suggested with a laugh. "We'll serenade the hero's return."

Obediently, Miranda accompanied them in a high-spirited chorus, which took on somewhat ironic overtones. It was true

481

that his old times there were not forgotten, but he certainly didn't wish to be in the land of cotton any time again soon.

She moved on to "Battle Hymn of the Republic" and "Tenting Tonight" and "When Johnny Comes Marching Home" and was ready to stop when, inevitably, someone asked for "When This Cruel War Is Over." Conscious of Cort's eyes on her, she played it through faultlessly, dry-eyed, though she did not join in the singing. Nor, she noticed, did he.

She had had enough, and she stood up, looking at Richard, who nodded, smiling.

"It's been a long day," she said, taking her cue, "a long, eventful day, and I think perhaps it's time to say good night."

"Yes," Richard agreed. "And since we'll both be leaving tomorrow . . ." His arm locked around her waist.

"Of course." Emily was understanding. "And after your travels," she looked at Mrs. Adams, "you probably want to get a good night's sleep, too. And certainly, Cort, you—"

"I had a nap this afternoon," he contradicted her. "I think I'll linger here, work on a bottle of brandy." He avoided looking at Miranda and Richard, though he was acutely aware of their departure, their footsteps on the stairs, the closing door of their bedroom.

"I'll stay with you," Warren said. "We can't have you drinking alone on your first night at home." He made a joke of it, but there was real concern behind his words.

In their bedroom, Miranda sat down in front of the mirrored vanity and shook her hair loose from its confining chignon. She brushed it out slowly, and Richard's eyes caught hers in the mirror.

"I love to watch you do that, darling. I'll miss it tomorrow night. I'll miss *you* tomorrow night." He moved efficiently through his preparations for bed and then methodically packed his satchel. "I'm glad we stayed. That was a fascinating story of escape. I really have to admire Cort, don't you? To have gone through all that and survived. And then to come home to the heartbreaking news about his son, to be willing to shoulder the problems of his troubled marriage."

Miranda stopped brushing her hair.

"Of course he'll go back to her." Richard answered her unspoken question. "That's been inevitable all along. Perhaps when they have another child . . . But I don't blame him for getting drunk tonight. God knows how *I* would react if I had lost so much. No, darling, don't plait your hair. At least, not until afterward. I want to see it spread out on the pillow, framing your lovely face." He pulled her into his arms and kissed her. "My own beautiful madonna."

Richard left early the next morning, without waiting for breakfast. Miranda would be leaving later, and Warren volunteered to take her to the train depot. He was nursing a headache, trying to cure it with additional cups of coffee. Cort had not come to breakfast at all, and Mrs. Adams expressed concern.

Warren offered soothing words. "I think he'll be all right, Mother. He has his work. And he and that other correspondent, Richardson, have an appointment to see the Secretary of War today. If the prisoner exchange can be resolved, I think that Cort will be convinced there is some point to all his efforts."

Mrs. Adams nodded, and she looked at Miranda again. "Do you really have to leave today, dear? We have had so little opportunity to talk, and I would like to know you better."

"Thank you." She acknowledged the compliment. "But we have made our plans, and Papa expects me. I promised him not . . . It would really be better to go home immediately." She would not subject herself to another sad parting from Cort. Richard and Dickon were her realities. And Cort would go back to Susanne. And have another child.

"Are you very worried about him?" Mrs. Adams showed obvious concern.

Miranda was silent and felt herself beginning to blush. Had Cort's mother guessed, too? First Emily and now . . .

"What exactly is it?" Mrs. Adams continued. "George said he was coughing, but Will always had a persistent cough. It never gave him any trouble before."

"Oh, you mean Papa!" Miranda said, and immediately felt foolish, but she rushed on, trying to cover her embarrassment. "Yes, I am very much concerned about him. I know he has always had a slight cough, but ever since the arson plot when he stayed up all night and exhausted himself, it seems to have become much worse. We have to persuade him to take a long rest."

"I'll come at the end of the week," George assured her. "He can't say no to both of us."

"The end of the week," Mrs. Adams echoed thoughtfully. "Do you think we might travel together, George? Warren has to be back in Boston before then, but I would like to stop off in New York."

"Of course." George welcomed the idea. "You can help us persuade Papa, too."

"And I'll come with you." Cort was an apparition in the doorway, and they looked up at him, startled. He had cut himself shaving again, and his eyes were bloodshot, but he had dressed meticulously, and he was carrying himself rigidly straight, his head too fragile to be moved easily.

"You'll come with us?" George was surprised.

Cort sat down carefully, and Jeff hurried to fill his coffee cup. Cort nodded his thanks and regretted the motion. "Nothing else, Jeff." His smile was pained.

"I have to go to New York," Cort resumed. "I want to prove to Mr. Raymond that I'm still alive. Barely. And now that I know Susanne will be there in Brooklyn . . ." He trailed off and looked at Miranda again.

"So, the three of us will make the trip together," George said briskly. "I'm glad it works out that way. But now," he pushed back his chair, "it's time for me to get to work."

"And I want to make sure that Megan has finished packing." Miranda excused herself, too, and fled from the room.

She saw Cort again before they left. He handed her into the carriage beside Warren, and he deposited Dickon carefully in her arms.

"A beautiful child," he said aloud. And then, breathing the words in her ear, "More than ever, I wish he were ours. Yours and mine."

Chapter 39

WITH MIRANDA AND George and John solidly arrayed against him, Will yielded to the demand that he take some time off, go away for a complete rest. And after he thought a moment, he supplied the destination himself. "I'll go to Litchfield," he said, "and stay with Sarah. God knows there's nothing to do there, but Sarah will be happy to coddle me, and she does know how to set a good table. And now that Henry's getting a bit deaf, I won't be subjected to those long, boring theological arguments."

Miranda was doubtful, but if Papa was willing to rest for a month or two, she would agree to anything. John promised to accompany him on the train trip, but not for another week. He wanted to make sure that Mrs. Robillard and Susanne and the little girl—Deedee, they were calling her—were properly settled in. They had arrived yesterday, and Dany had been overjoyed to greet them all.

"Just seeing her happy," John said, "makes it all worthwhile. It's quite an undertaking for Dany, you know, suddenly expanding our household to five, but she glories in it." He looked wistfully at Dickon, asleep in Miranda's arms, and abruptly changed the subject. "You said Cort came with you today, George?"

"And his mother. For some reason he seemed reluctant to stay with us at the Stratford, but of course I insisted."

Neither Will nor Miranda volunteered the reason for Cort's reluctance.

There was an awkward pause, and then John spoke again. "You are probably wondering why we don't invite him to Brooklyn to be with Susanne."

Will looked puzzled, Miranda concentrated on Dickon, and George sighed.

"I think we know," George said. "The little girl . . ."

John looked embarrassed.

"We all know," Miranda agreed. "Except for Papa."

"Know what?" Will looked at his three children, grown now, all of them, even Miranda, in uneasy possession of a secret that troubled them.

"It's very awkward," John said, "and I didn't realize . . . When Dany suggested that Cort stay with us, Susanne burst into tears. And then the story came out. So you know?"

"Yes," George said. "And Cort's mother and brother, too."

"And Marty and Mrs. Cantrell," Miranda added.

"Good Lord. Susanne can never keep it secret then."

"Since everyone else knows," Will observed mildly, "whatever it is, you might as well confide in me, too."

Reluctantly, John told him the circumstances of Deedee's birth, and Will sighed and looked at Miranda, who was studiously occupying herself with Dickon. "That explains a great deal." He turned to George. "And what is Cort planning to do now?"

"I don't know. I don't think he knows. I think that when he set out for Savannah with the idea of rescuing Bobby and the family, he had half persuaded himself to go back to Susanne. But he has been through so much, and so has she . . . He is in New York to see her, though, and perhaps they will decide to try again."

John was doubtful. "Perhaps. But Susanne seems very frail to me, and not ready to make major decisions. She had diphtheria, too, you know, and barely pulled through. It was such a terrible year—taking care of her father, watching him die, losing Bobby . . ." John trailed off, his voice husky, and he looked again at Dickon. He had to clear his throat before going on. "So then in December when Sherman marched in, I think they believed it was going to be the end of the world. They had a Yankee colonel quartered with them, but that proved something of a blessing in disguise. Not that you would ever get Mrs. Robillard to admit to that." John managed a half smile. "She's an unreconstructed Rebel if there ever was one." He paused again, but there was no way to avoid telling them. "I must warn you that all this has affected her mind, and she has become . . . strange. Dany thinks it is only a temporary condition, and I fervently hope she is right.

But you will see for yourselves when you come for tea to-morrow."

Miranda was reluctant to accompany George and her father to Brooklyn the next afternoon. She was curious to see Susanne again, but one brief glance would have satisfied her. And to see Cort with her, husband and wife . . .

Dany greeted them at the door, and John was right: She was glowingly happy, reveling in all the activity, obviously capable of managing a much expanded family, in her element with all of them turning to her for direction—her mother, her sister, her little niece. And John, smiling at her benignly, had waved the wand that made it all happen. Her love for him, for all her family, was a radiant force that starkly illuminated the uneasy distance between Cort and Susanne.

Cort had made an immediate conquest of Deedee, a darting little pixie of a girl with an elfin look much closer to Dany's gamin features than to Susanne's more conventional pale prettiness.

Miranda was shocked by the change in Susanne. She had always been a slight girl, tiny waist, delicate features, but she was thin now and unnaturally pale. A hard year she had had, and she had spent her strength. Spent her emotions, too, and Cort was a stranger who looked at her with compassion—and she had nothing for him but tears.

Mrs. Robillard had aged, and she leaned on her daughters both physically and emotionally. The war had broken her life in two, and all was sunlight and promise before the guns had fired, but now the darkness was closing in on her family and her country. And on her mind, too. She had total recall for everything that happened before, and she could be witty and entertaining—and sometimes endlessly boring—on all the complicated family relationships that had been her life and her recreation. But the recent past was such a confusion of bleak events that she could not reconcile it with life the way it should be, and she simply chose to overlook or forget what didn't please her. It was all a bad dream. If only she ignored it long enough, the Yankees would go away and Susanne's secret shame would disappear and Mr. Robillard and Bobby and Toby and the whole lost way of life would still be there. Surely soon she would wake up from this confusing nightmare.

Deedee was confused, too, but it was the confusion of a

child suddenly overwhelmed with unimaginable numbers of new relatives, all making a fuss over her. Susanne had been too embarrassed to introduce Cort to Deedee as her father, and so the child was on a first name basis with him.

"Bye-bye, Co't," she said, slithering out of his lap and making a beeline for Miranda, who was holding Dickon in her arms. "Bobby?" she asked, pointing to the baby.

Miranda shook her head, shocked into silence, looking to Susanne for an explanation.

Deedee crawled into her mother's lap, and Susanne sighed. "She asks that about every child under the age of five. I don't think she even remembers Bobby—it's been three months. But Mother talks about him as if he were still alive, and Deedee looks for him everywhere."

"How very hard for you, my dear." Mrs. Adams patted her shoulder.

"It will be better now," Dany said confidently. "She's such a dear little girl, and so bright and quick."

"And you should see Bobby!" Mrs. Robillard said. "He's going to be a doctor, you know, and take care of his Grandpa and his Uncle Toby and everyone. Did you leave him at home, dear? Why isn't he here?"

"Please, Mama." Dany put a soothing hand on her arm. "You *are* home. You're home with John and me."

John agreed. "You'll be all right. It just takes a little time to get used to new surroundings."

Miranda looked at him, mystified, but he sounded as if he meant it. Could he really think that Mrs. Robillard would recover? And as for Susanne . . . Well, perhaps Cort could nurture her back to health, but it would be a labor of love, or a labor of penance. And she really looked too delicate to have another baby. Miranda cradled Dickon in her arms, such a strong and healthy child. And for the hundredth time she wondered if Richard were right, if she possibly could be pregnant again so soon. She had mixed feelings about that, but she was very conscious of her own strength and vitality, and of course she wanted more children, their animal warmth pressing against her, flesh of her flesh. It helped to satisfy a physical need that Richard— She broke off that chain of thought. He had given her so much, he was so devoted to her, so concerned about her health and well-being. And she was here in New York, safe and comfortable, while he was still fighting in this cruel war. So much crueler for Cort and Susanne than it had ever been for her.

"I would like to have my shawl," Mrs. Robillard said to Susanne. "Northern winters are always so cold."

Miranda thought the house was uncomfortably overheated, but Dany rose immediately to comply with her mother's request.

"The blue one, Mama?"

"No, no, Dany. The one with embroidered roses. Susanne, you know what I mean. Bring it to me, darling, please."

Dany sighed and took Deedee from her sister's arms while Susanne went to look for the shawl.

"It's in my bedroom," Mrs. Robillard called after her. "On the third floor."

"Yes, Mama, she knows," Dany said. "But I wish you'd let me or John or the servants fetch and carry for you. Susanne really shouldn't be exhausting herself going up and down stairs all day."

"But Susanne always knows what I want, dear. And this is my treasured shawl that was embroidered by your great aunt Louise as a wedding present for her sister—your grandmother, dear. It's been in the family since—"

"Yes, Mama, I know, but I could have sent Bridget for it and spared Susanne."

"I don't know, dear. I'll just never get used to white servants. It seems unnatural somehow. I don't trust them."

Will cleared his throat and coughed, and Mrs. Robillard looked at him sharply.

"Catarrh," she said. "Now for catarrh, my second cousin, Dr. Marshall Meriwether . . . But first I must tell you about Marshall. He was descended from the same Meriwethers . . ."

Dany sighed and hugged Deedee and looked at Miranda. "I really think Susanne should get away for a rest, a complete rest. She has carried the whole burden for so long. I could take care of Deedee and Mama. And I think I could help Mama face reality again. She does have total recall, you know." Dany paused to hear how far her mother had traced the Meriwether genealogy, and Miranda noted Papa's bemused expression. All this had been launched when he cleared his throat.

She caught George's eye, and he winked and then crossed the room to join her. "I think Papa is sorry he coughed."

Dany agreed. "But he looks a little better now, don't you

think? I'm glad he'll be getting away for a rest. I was just telling Miranda that Susanne needs to go away, too. I thought that coming here would do it, but both Mama and Deedee are so demanding."

George looked thoughtful. "Yes. And I know Cort agrees with you. I told him he should bring Susanne back to Washington, by herself. We'll take care of her. And perhaps she and Cort . . ." He left the rest of the sentence unspoken.

Dany agreed. "Yes, just seeing him again, last night and today, has helped her enormously. He is so kind and compassionate, and I think that all they need is some time to themselves."

Miranda suppressed a sigh and concentrated on Dickon. The afternoon seemed endless, and she insisted on leaving as soon as they finished their tea. Mrs. Adams came with them, but Cort had decided to stay for supper.

They walked to the ferry in the chill twilight, George carrying Dickon, Miranda slowing her pace when Papa took her arm, Mrs. Adams strangely silent.

Miranda looked at her inquiringly.

"Susanne—such a frail little girl," Mrs. Adams said, thinking aloud.

"She'll perk up once we get her to Washington," George said confidently. "With a few good meals and real rest, she'll get her health back and wake up from the nightmare of this last year. And then she and Cort . . . The war was very hard on both of them, but I think they can put all that in the past and go on together."

"Of course," Will agreed, clasping his arm around Miranda.

She was silent, and Mrs. Adams looked at her with complete understanding.

By the end of the week they were all gone—Mrs. Adams in Boston, Papa in Litchfield, and George and Cort and Susanne in Washington.

Miranda turned her attention to the hotel, glad to let it absorb all her available time.

Chapter 40

T HE WAR WAS surely drawing to a close, even though one last attempt at peace negotiations had failed. President Lincoln himself had gone to the Hampton Roads Conference with Secretary of State Seward to meet the Vice President of the Confederacy, Alexander Stephens, and his delegation. But the two sides were as far apart as ever, the South still seeking independence, the North still insisting on union. There was no way to compromise, and more blood would flow.

Sherman turned north into the Carolinas, and his troops cut a wide swath through the virtually defenseless countryside—the battered Confederate armies simply melted away. General Lee still held on at Richmond and Petersburg, but he, too, noted the "alarming frequency of desertion from this army," and he protested the "ration too small for men who have to undergo so much exposure and labor as ours."

In Washington on March 4 President Lincoln took the oath of office for a second term: "Fondly do we hope—fervently do we pray—that this mighty scourge of war may speedily pass away. . . . With malice toward none, with charity for all, with firmness in the right as God gives us to see the right, let us strive on to finish the work we are in; to bind up the nation's wounds; to care for him who shall have borne the battle, and for his widow and his orphan—to do all which may achieve and cherish a just and lasting peace among ourselves, and with all nations."

Two days after the Inauguration New York celebrated the coming victory with a giant parade—a "Triumph," as the newspapers hailed it. Schools and businesses shut down for the holiday, guns fired in military salute, the church bells rang in joyous clamor, and flags and bunting draped every public building. The parade route stretched south on Broadway from Fourteenth Street as far as the Stratford, the Astor, City Hall Park, then wound north again to merge into a mass meeting in Union Square. The soldiers marched, ten thousand strong, the craftsmen of two hundred trades joined in, and the bands blasted out their triumphant music, echoed by the roaring crowds, cheering in one continuous ovation.

Somewhere on the distant battlefields the war was grinding on, but here in full display were all the elements of victory: Armed force, industrial strength, and the overwhelming confidence that comes with success.

Miranda had ordered the Stratford swathed in bunting, taking care that it not cover the windows or block the view from her favorite vantage point in the library. All the family had been invited. Dany and John brought Deedee with them to share in the excitement, but Mrs. Robillard had declined the opportunity to view this Yankee celebration. Mrs. Cantrell came with Caroline and her unexpected guest, Major Jack Lorimer, home from the war. He had lost twenty pounds as a prisoner, but he was recovering, and in Caroline's eyes he was handsomer than ever.

"Miranda!" Jack kissed her warmly. "You are just as pretty as I remembered. And Lucy. You are blooming, too. I'm sorry I missed your wedding, but perhaps you'll invite me to the christening."

Lucy blushed. The baby was due in two months, but she had raised the top hoop of her skirt, and she had hoped that her pregnancy was not so immediately obvious. But perhaps Caroline had whispered in his ear and that was the only reason he knew. Caroline seemed to have told him everything— he asked when Mr. Chase would be back from the country, and he inquired about Dickon, and he even introduced himself to Megan's little girl, Maureen, who was shyly passing around a plate of cookies and darting quick glances up Broadway, impatient for her first glimpse of the parade.

Irene arrived with Ann, who had brought a telescope. "I want to see if I can pick out Madison," she explained, "and I don't care if you *do* laugh." He would be marching with the Seventh Regiment, and Ann was convinced she would be able to recognize him from ten blocks away. She adjusted the eyepiece and accepted a cookie from Maureen, who was staring with frank envy at the telescope.

Irene smiled at the little girl. "Ann, let her look, too."

Ann glanced at the child, noticing her for the first time, irritated that a servant's daughter was being treated like a member of the family. Too many social barriers were breaking down, and Ann disapproved. Maureen might be a well-behaved little girl, but Ann had been shocked when she discovered that Miranda had enrolled her in Miss Benson's Female Seminary and was paying the tuition from her own clothing allowance. "What did Richard say?" Ann had asked when she found out.

"Richard?" Miranda had been astonished at the question. "I don't think I mentioned it to him. He has enough to worry about with the war. Or our new house. All his letters are filled with instructions about that. I wouldn't trouble him about Maureen. He just wants to hear about the new roof and the central heating system." It was a good thing his parents lived so close and could check the workmen every day—she hadn't been there for a week. Richard wouldn't like that, but the hotel still came first. If only there were more time. She promised herself she would start to look at wallpaper and furniture and all those household things, just as soon as Papa came back. He had quickly become bored in Litchfield, and Miranda expected his return almost daily, perhaps in time for the Triumph. The whole family was here, but she wanted him most of all.

Lucy's parents were deep in conversation with the Bradleys, who had just returned from a visit in Washington with Emily and George. Miranda caught a reference to Cort and his wife, and Dany was all attention, immediately asking about Susanne.

"I thought she seemed frail," Mrs. Bradley said, "though Emily assured me she has gained a few pounds and is much better. She misses Deedee, of course, and Cort says he wants the child with them just as soon as possible."

"I know," Dany said. "John and I will hate to give her up, but we'll take her with us to Washington next week. And if Susanne is so much better, we'll leave Deedee there."

"And your mother?" Mrs. Bradley inquired.

"Mrs. Robillard will stay with us for a while," John answered for Dany. "I think she is adjusting now, though she is still a little . . . confused."

Dany swallowed painfully, unwilling to talk about it, and her eyes followed Deedee, who had run to the window.

"They're coming!" Maureen exclaimed. "I see them." She fumbled with the telescope and then handed it to Deedee, who promptly dropped it. Ann snatched it back and shook her head. It was bad enough to be dealing with a servant's child, but she drew the line at Susanne's illegitimate daughter. Ann still had not recovered from her shock at this scandal, and she fervently wished that Susanne would take her disgrace back to Savannah. After all, she wasn't really a blood relative, and if only she would disappear, perhaps the gossip would, too. Sometimes Ann felt like the last defender of the family honor. Even her mother was wavering, about to surrender to Irene's demands to marry out of her class. Andy Dawson might be commanding his own ship, but Ann still saw him as a jumped-up cabin boy from New Bedford, lacking family, money, connections. The fact that he had rescued Susanne and her crazy mother and bastard child was just another mark against him.

The first of the bands was passing, almost drowned out by the rising clamor from the crowds, and then the Seventh Regiment paraded by. Ann drew their attention to Madison, well back in the ranks, marching as proudly as if he had won the whole war by himself.

Miranda refrained from comment. There had been a time when she thought the Seventh was the ultimate symbol of military glory, but the bravest and the best had long since gone on to the real war. She wondered if Richard and Tom and George would ever choose to rejoin, and she yearned for them to be here, marching with the real heroes, the veterans of Shiloh and Chancellorsville, Antietam and Gettysburg, Vicksburg and Chickamauga and the Wilderness and Cold Harbor. And Fredericksburg. Dear Jimmy. Gone with Damon and all the thousands of brave young men, never to return.

Rank after rank the soldiers marched, and then came the omnibuses and ambulances with the maimed and wounded—the one-eyed and one-armed and one-legged men, forever bearing the scars of this cruel war. Ann had put down her telescope, and Dany made an effort to distract Deedee until there was something more cheerful to see. More bands, a huge model of the *Monitor*, firemen and fire engines, cannons firing salutes, and dozens of floats with tradesmen demonstrating their skills: blacksmiths at their forge, operators at their sewing machines, cigar-makers rolling fine Havanas, carpenters and plumbers and winemakers and bakers and butchers and shipbuilders, and even the craftsmen from Mr. Steinway's company working on a grand piano. P. T. Barnum was in the parade, too, together with two floats with curiosities from his museum—a stuffed giraffe, a walrus, an elephant. Deedee crowed with delight, and John held her high to get a better view. She waved at the Arabian camels, led by a native Bedouin in flowing robes, but Maureen much preferred the war elephant, Hannibal, and she seriously suggested to Miranda that it be sent at once to Virginia to take part in the final battles of the war.

Miranda listened gravely but pointed out that Hannibal would be a very large and tempting target; and besides, he would probably frighten the horses. Reluctantly, Maureen allowed herself to be persuaded.

Another band was passing, blaring out the jubilant "Battle Cry of Freedom," and Uncle Paul turned to Faith, echoing the triumph of the music. "One more battle. That's all it will take." The might of the Union was passing in review, and victory was sure.

"One more battle," Faith agreed, adding her own coda, "and then Richard will be home." She put her arm around Miranda, who shivered suddenly.

"Are you all right?" Faith looked at her, concerned. "You have been working too hard again, dear, and I wish your father—"

"I'm fine," Miranda assured her, "and Papa is coming back soon. It's just that when Uncle Paul said 'one more battle,' I thought of all those other battles, all the wounded and dying, and I wondered how much more we can stand."

Dany looked at her with sympathy. "You just want it to end. I know. That's what I pray for every day. No more bloodshed. No more widows and orphans, burned out and homeless. No more of Sherman's army—"

"Now see here," Paul bristled. "An army on the march—"

"Please," Miranda tried to calm him, "let's not refight the war. It's nearly over, and we've won." Why didn't it feel more like a victory? The cheers and ovations were still reverberating from Broadway, but the ghosts of the dead rose up to haunt her. Still, the Union had been preserved, and slavery had been abolished, and that's what she had wanted. "We've won," she repeated, convincing herself, "and it *must* be worth it all."

But when her father appeared in the doorway, a chill gripped her heart, even before she noticed the telegram in his hand.

"Papa!" She flung herself into his arms, and he kissed her.

"My dear child." His eyes were wet with tears, and his voice was choked.

She looked at him in alarm, dreading his news.

"I'm sorry to be bringing you such terrible—" He broke off, coughing, and Faith turned ashen and groped for her husband's arm.

Will cleared his throat, the unwilling center of attention. "Richard has been gravely wounded." He held out the telegram. "George says you must come at once."

Miranda stood silent, immobile, willing herself to be calm.

Faith burst into tears, and Paul patted her helplessly, looking stricken. Irene clutched at them both and began to sob, and Ann, reacting more slowly, quietly fainted. Dany revived her with smelling salts, and Will, still clasping his arm around Miranda, tried to control his emotions. He had forgotten about the parade, he said, and when he arrived in New York it took him forever to make his way through the crowds from the train depot to the hotel. In the front office he paused to greet Guy Dawson, who was standing there in a state of shock, holding a telegram addressed to Mrs. Richard Schuyler. Poor Guy. He had been invited to join the celebration upstairs, but how could he present himself as the bearer of tragic news. And of course he knew it was tragic. Why else send a telegram? Will looked at Miranda for a response, but she remained speechless, concentrating on nothingness— not crying, not fainting, not thinking at all.

It was John who took charge, speeding the departure of the guests, deciding that Uncle Paul and Aunt Faith should accompany Miranda to Washington, handling all the arrangements himself and seeing them off three hours later, Miranda carrying Dickon and still looking dazed.

"I'll send a telegram to George," John assured her, "and he'll be waiting for you." He turned to his uncle and gave him the train tickets. "And I think you have everything you need."

Paul cleared his throat. "Thank you, my boy. I don't know what we'd do without you."

John looked a little embarrassed, as if trying to ward off compliments. "About Deedee," he said. "We certainly won't be making the trip to Washington with her while all of you are there. It will just add to the confusion. Perhaps Cort will bring Susanne to Brooklyn for a while. We'll welcome them, of course." He kissed Miranda, and she clung to him for strength.

John smiled at her. "You'll take good care of Richard, I know. And just seeing you will make all the difference."

It was the middle of the night when they arrived, and Cort was there to meet them. "George has gone to bring him home," he explained. "Richard is on a hospital ship, and we expect it tomorrow."

Miranda nodded her understanding.

Cort was calm and efficient, ushering them to a waiting carriage, looking after the trunks, treating them all with a formal courtesy that allowed no room for emotion.

"Do you know how it happened?" Paul asked.

"We aren't sure. There was no major attack, but of course there are always minor skirmishes, patrols, sharpshooters . . ."

"He is still alive?" Faith looked at Cort beseechingly.

"As far as we know. George sent off a barrage of telegrams as soon as he received the first report. I'm sure the doctors are doing everything possible."

Paul coughed to cover the emotion in his voice. "We were watching the victory parade," he said. "It's a damned outrage, to have this happen so close to the end."

"A damned outrage," Cort agreed, "all of it, from beginning to end."

Miranda thought of Jimmy and Damon and prayed fervently for Richard. It wasn't fair of God to demand so many sacrifices. Surely He could spare Richard. I will love him, she pledged in a silent bargain with God. Truly I will. He has so many admirable qualities, and he wants our life together so much. It wouldn't be fair to him to be taken now. And it wouldn't be fair to Dickon, either, to be deprived of a father.

Emily greeted them when they arrived, and a sleepy Susanne emerged from Cort's room to add her welcome. She had put on Cort's robe by mistake, and she looked like a child playacting in a grown-up's world. Her blond hair was still tousled, and she turned pink with embarrassment when she realized how she was dressed.

Cort smiled at her indulgently and did not look at Miranda.

"We saw Deedee today," Miranda said, conscientiously relaying her brother's message. "John said to tell you that he and Dany will put off their trip to Washington while Richard . . . But if you and Cort want to come to Brooklyn, you'll be welcome."

Susanne thanked her and turned to Cort for his decision.

"We'll wait and see," he said. "The most important thing is to take care of Richard."

"Of course, darling," Susanne agreed promptly. "Whatever you say."

Richard arrived the next afternoon, accompanied by both Tom and George. They had commandeered an ambulance at the Sixth Street Wharf, and somehow Richard had survived the jolting two-mile trip from the landing stage. He was unconscious when he was carried into the house, up to the corner bedroom where Tom had twice been a patient.

"He saved my life," Tom said, his voice breaking with emotion.

Miranda glanced up at him briefly, but she turned her full attention to Richard, carefully pulling off the blood-soaked bandage at his shoulder. Someone had packed the wound with lint, and there were already signs of pus. Susanne quietly fainted, and Cort carried her away. Uncle Paul was looking queasy, too, but Aunt Faith came to Miranda's aid, and they cleaned out the gaping hole and applied a new bandage.

"A minié ball," Tom said. "The surgeon dug it out, but he explained that Richard had lost so much blood . . . He dusted the wound with morphine, though, and said there was a chance. I don't know . . ." His voice was husky again. "We must pray for him."

Miranda looked at Uncle Paul, but he was too overcome to speak, and he simply bowed his head and closed his eyes. They joined him in silent prayer, and the minutes ticked by slowly. Polly appeared in the doorway and stared at them curiously.

"Are you playing church?" She was obviously puzzled. "Can I play, too?"

"Not now, darling," Emily smiled at her. "Why don't you go and look for Uncle Cort?"

Polly hesitated, but then wandered off obediently, ready to find someone more entertaining.

Paul coughed to cover his emotion and turned to Tom. "You said Richard saved your life?"

Tom nodded, clearing his throat. "I'll tell you from the beginning." He glanced at Richard and swallowed hard. "It was late in the afternoon, three days ago. He had just come from headquarters, and we went down to our forward trenches to inspect . . . to inspect the Rebel fortifications." Tom paused again, and it was an effort for him to continue. "Something caught his eye—perhaps the sun shining on a rifle barrel; I don't know. But he jumped at me, sent me crashing to the ground, and I heard the shot, and he fell immediately, bleeding so much that I was sure he was dying." Tom's eyes welled with tears, and Miranda reached out to touch him. He clasped her hand like a lifeline, and he went on with difficulty. "I just know that bullet was meant for me. The Rebels wounded me twice, and the third time . . . Dear God, he can't die. He has as much to live for as I do. I see you, Miranda, and I think of Lucy . . ." He could restrain his tears no longer, and Miranda held him in her arms while he wept unashamedly. One part of her mind had closed off, and she was dry-eyed, soothing him, moving like a sleepwalker, afraid to wake up.

She saw Cort through the open doorway. He was holding Polly, and he looked tired and worn, as if he had never recovered from that prison ordeal. No, worse. As if he had never escaped, and the future held no promise at all. He didn't even glance at her, but he paused for a moment to wait for Susanne, and he shifted Polly to his other arm. He squared his shoulders, then, and summoned up a smile, and Susanne took his hand. Miranda heard their footsteps on the stairs, going away. Together.

Miranda barely stirred from Richard's side for the next twenty-four hours. Aunt Faith observed the vigil, too, but Paul was restless, moving in and out of the sickroom, pacing about with such nervous energy that Miranda finally ordered him out. He was welcome as long as he remained seated, she told him, but as soon as he stood up, he had to leave. Miranda was implacable, and Paul retreated, abashed. He had never met such steely determination in a woman before, and it baffled him.

"I wouldn't argue with her," George advised. He settled back on the sofa and watched Paul resume his restless pacing in the music room.

Tom agreed. "Miranda is committed to saving Richard's life, and with God's help, she will. Don't cross her."

Cort remained silent, and he looked across the room at Susanne, who was holding Georgie in her lap. She kissed the baby, and her eyes filled with sudden tears.

Emily was understanding. "You always see Bobby, don't you? And now you miss Deedee, too."

Susanne nodded. "I was so looking forward to her visit with Dany. But now . . ."

Emily sighed. "Perhaps you want to go back to Brooklyn."

"I don't know." Susanne looked at Cort, incapable of making the decision herself.

"I think that might be best," Cort agreed. "I should be going back to the front lines, to be with the army in its final victory. But I could take you to New York first."

Her face lighted up. "Would you, darling? I'm just in the way here. You have been so good to me, all of you, and I know I am better. But I miss Deedee and Mama, and I need them with me to feel truly at home."

"We'll work it out," Cort promised, "just as soon as the war is over."

Susanne smiled, content to let him take over completely.

Miranda was only distantly aware of their departure the next day. Richard was conscious at last, and when he opened his eyes and recognized her, she felt that her prayers had been answered. Never had she loved him so much as now, when he needed her desperately for life itself.

"I'll take care of you, darling." She leaned forward to kiss him. "You are going to live."

He was too weak even to reach for her hand, but his eyes held understanding. Faith kissed him, too, and then she hurried off to summon Paul and the rest of the family.

Miranda held his head while he sipped a little water, and she strained to understand what he was trying to say. "Tom," she finally deciphered his faint whisper. "Tom is fine, darling. He's here. You saved his life, and he's here."

His lips moved again, but there was no sound. "For you," he was trying to say. "All for you."

Her eyes filled with tears, and she kissed him again. "Darling, how can I ever love you enough?"

Faith returned with Paul, followed by Tom and George and Emily. It was too much for Richard, and he turned his head away, and his eyes fastened on Miranda again.

"Do you want to sleep now, darling?" She smoothed back the hair from his forehead. "Shall we all go away and leave you in peace?"

"You." His lips formed the word, and she leaned forward to hear. "You stay."

"Of course, darling. I'll be right here." She settled back in the chair, but he looked troubled, and she moved nearer to him again.

"Closer," he insisted. "So I can touch you."

She held his hand until he fell asleep again, and when he woke up he was hungry and thirsty, as dependent on her as Dickon and just as demanding. He would allow no one else to take care of him, and for three days she was his willing slave. It wasn't until she quietly fainted, slumping forward on the bed, that Faith exerted her authority and ordered her to get some rest. By then Richard seemed to be out of danger, and he was aware enough to be overcome by remorse.

He apologized profusely, and when Miranda came back, refreshed by her nap, carrying the baby, he tried to make amends.

"I'm sorry, darling, to put you through all this. You'll think me just as much a child as Dickon." He couldn't bear the thought. "I hate to be dependent—it isn't natural. Always, I want to take care of *you*."

"Not now, Richard, when you're wounded. Let me have my turn, too."

He looked doubtful, but he let it pass. Propped up against the pillows, he was breathing more easily. And when his supper tray arrived, he insisted on feeding himself. Faith considered that a sign of progress, and she departed, smiling. Miranda nursed the baby, conscious of Richard's eyes on her, his desire stirring though he was still as weak as a newborn child.

For a moment his eyes held hers, and she blushed.

"How very precious you are." He had finished his meal, and so had Dickon, and she rebuttoned her dress and gently patted the baby.

"You are pregnant again, aren't you, darling?"

"I don't know, Richard. While I'm nursing the baby, it's very unlikely."

He shook his head, smiling at her. "I say you are pregnant, and you say I'm infallible. That makes it true."

"Oh, darling, what has happened to your logic?"

"Wasn't I right about Dickon?" He reached for her hand. "I think I promised you a diamond brooch. And you owe me a kiss."

She laughed. "What a silly bargain that was."

"I will hold you to it," he said. "Right now. Come, kiss me."

"You do sound better," she teased him. "The voice of command again." She leaned forward, but the baby was a partial barrier between them.

Richard smiled at his son. "I'll kiss you, too, Dickon, but isn't it your bedtime?" The child looked at him curiously and shook his head, almost as if he understood. Richard laughed and prodded the baby gently. Dickon reacted by clamping his whole fist around his father's finger, and he would not let go.

"You win," Richard acknowledged. "Six months old and you can already beat your father in a wrestling match. Take him away, Miranda; he's exhausting me." There were beads of perspiration on his forehead, and she wiped them away with a towel. "My angel of mercy." He touched her hand. "Put him to bed, darling, and hurry back to me. You still owe me that kiss."

His parents were there when she returned, and Paul was relieved to find the patient so much improved. "You gave us a scare, Richard. Don't do that again."

Faith smiled. "He's going to be all right. And the war will be over before anything else can happen to him."

"Quite right," Paul agreed. "Our prayers have been answered, and I've been thinking how we can celebrate." He had resumed his restless pacing, but he stopped short and smiled at Miranda, remembering her earlier orders. "What would you like, dear? I thought about giving you and Richard a trip abroad, a proper honeymoon. How would that be?"

"I don't know." Miranda was startled. She sat down on the bed next to Richard and took his hand. "What do you think, darling?"

He smiled at her. "I could always go on a honeymoon with you."

"But with Dickon, and if you are right about . . ." She trailed off, blushing.

"We'll wait until the baby is born," Richard assured her. "After all, I may need a few months to get back on my feet, too."

"I didn't realize . . ." Paul looked embarrassed. "You didn't tell me," he accused his wife.

"I haven't told anyone," Miranda said hastily. "I'm not at all sure." She changed the subject. "This is very generous of you, Uncle Paul, but we'll have to wait for a while. And I don't know about traveling with a small child—or children."

"Take Megan with you," Paul offered. "Take her little girl, too." He was feeling expansive, euphoric. Richard was recovering, the war was nearly over, and all was right with the world again. God could be depended on after all.

"We could go in Andy's ship," Miranda said, testing her uncle's reaction.

Paul nodded, smiling. "If that is what you want."

"It's not what *I* want," Richard objected. "It's going to be a crowded enough honeymoon, with three children and a nursemaid. I draw the line at my future brother-in-law."

Faith sighed. She had agreed to Irene's engagement under protest, but she was still praying for a miracle. Her hopes had soared when Major Jack Lorimer came to call, but Irene had shown no interest at all. Faith was acutely disappointed, and Jack had resumed his desultory courtship of Caroline.

"You decide whatever you want," Paul addressed his son. "And whatever Miranda wants, too, of course." He looked at her and smiled. "So much like your dear mother. I remember when Mary . . ." And then his face clouded over. "You take care of her," he warned his son, his voice suddenly hoarse. "There's such a thing as *too* many children, you know."

Richard reacted with anger, and Miranda was startled.

Faith tried to mollify them both. "I am sure it will all work out for the best. You always look so well, Miranda, and I am so grateful that Richard is recovering."

Paul backed off and made an awkward effort to apologize. "It's just that I don't want to go through this again. Worrying about you, Richard, and then worrying about Miranda, too. I like things to be calm and orderly. Too much emotion—it's unsettling."

Richard understood completely.

"Well, then," Paul was glad to move on to something completely practical. "I don't really think you need us here any longer. Faith, we'll go back to New York where we can be useful. John is overworked at the office, and without me . . . And you should get back to supervising Richard's house."

Tom knocked at the open door. "It looks like a family conference."

"Yes," Miranda agreed, "but you're part of the family, too."

He smiled at all of them and came over to the bedside. "You are looking so much better, Richard. I can go back to the regiment with good news."

"You are going back?" Miranda was surprised and disappointed, and she tried to suppress her alarm.

"Of course." Tom was matter-of-fact. "What did you think? That I had leave until the war was over?"

"Oh, Tom, I wish you did." Miranda looked up at him, and he put a comforting hand on her shoulder.

"I'll be all right now. Richard stopped the one minié ball that had my name on it." His voice was confident. "I'm safe now. And, thank God, he is, too. With any luck the war will be over in another month, and I'll be home in time for the birth of my first son."

"Or daughter," Richard said. "Our little girl will need a playmate her own age."

Tom looked at him, surprised, and then he grinned at Miranda. "You weren't going to tell me?"

"I wasn't going to tell anyone because I'm not sure, but Richard . . . Darling," she smiled at him, "I've never known you to be such a gossip."

"We'll tell only the immediate family," Richard decided. "No need to make things harder for Susanne when she—"

"But she's not here," Tom said. "I guess you were too sick to realize . . . Cort took her to Brooklyn three days ago, and then he's going back to Virginia."

"I missed seeing her then." Richard was disappointed. "I thought she and Cort were reconciled."

"They are," his mother assured him. "But while you are here and Cort is away, it seemed more sensible for her to be in Brooklyn with the family. She misses Deedee and her mother."

"I see. But they *are* together again." Richard smiled at Miranda. "I told you it would all work out, didn't I?"

504

"Yes, Richard. You were right." There was nothing else to say.

"Well, then," he leaned back against the pillows, satisfied with his world but clearly tired. "I'll say good night to all of you. Except you, Miranda. Stay with me."

When the others had gone, he smiled at her again. "You still owe me that kiss."

"Yes, darling." She leaned over to brush her lips against his, but he was not satisfied.

"Sleep here tonight." He patted the bed. "I want you beside me, just to be able to touch you—so warm and sweet and gentle."

She looked at him doubtfully, but he was insistent, and she had never learned how to deny him anything. Physically he might be weaker than his own infant son, but he could still dominate her completely. She tried to puzzle it out after he fell asleep. He was always so convinced he was right. Perhaps that was it. His strong convictions simply overrode her doubts, and it was easier to give in than to protest. And when he was convalescing, as he was now, or when he was home briefly on a furlough and his time was so limited, so precious, he made her feel selfish when she raised any objections at all. Would it ever be different? They had been married almost two years now, and she still didn't know.

Cort came home later that night. She heard the stir of his arrival, but she turned over in bed and tried to go back to sleep.

Beside her Richard was restless, murmuring her name, and he woke up, reaching out to make sure she was still there.

"Yes, darling, I'm here." She kissed his cheek, and he sighed his content. "Everything is going to be all right."

In the morning Cort came in with Tom to say good-by. They were going back to Petersburg together, and Miranda had a sudden pang of fear. Would she ever see either of them again? If Tom had almost been killed only last week, and if Cort felt so trapped by his life that death held no terrors for him anymore . . .

Tom was oblivious to her anxiety, and Cort had put on his mask of formal courtesy, inquiring politely about Richard, expressing the proper wishes for his speedy recovery. Tom kissed her good-by, but Cort allowed himself to be distracted

505

when Polly ran in, and he made such a fuss over the child that he barely shook hands with Miranda.

Emily saw them off only moments later. George had already left, taking Uncle Paul and Aunt Faith to the train depot, and the house seemed strangely empty and quiet. Richard was asleep again, and Miranda tiptoed from the room to join Emily at the breakfast table for one more cup of coffee.

"A little peace, at last," Emily said, helping herself to sugar. "We have had an unending stream of company ever since Christmas. First Mrs. Adams and Warren and then my parents and Susanne and Uncle Paul and Aunt Faith and Tom . . ."

"And Richard and me," Miranda added, echoing Emily's weary tone.

Emily laughed. "You don't count as company," she said. "I never have to fuss over you. You don't keep telling me I'm spoiling the children, the way my mother does. And you don't sit looking at them with tears brimming in your eyes, like Susanne. The sooner she gets pregnant again, the better."

Miranda made no comment, and Emily looked at her shrewdly. "In the long run, that will be best, you know. I'm so glad you're going to have another baby, Miranda. I know you'll fall in love with Richard all over again. And Susanne is really devoted to Cort, and this time she's determined to stay with him."

Miranda stirred her coffee, still silent.

"George thinks she's too frail." Emily leaned forward, her voice confidential. "He thinks they should wait. But then," Emily smiled at her, "George is very cautious. He isn't sure *you* should be having another baby again so soon."

Miranda blushed. It had never occurred to her that George might discuss such things with Emily, and she didn't know how to respond.

"I told him that he should let you and Richard plan your own family," Emily went on, "but he was unconvinced. He can't understand why you always let Richard dominate—"

"Please, Emily. I don't want to talk about it."

"I'm sorry, dear. I said too much. It's just that we love you, and we want you to be happy."

Miranda finished her coffee hastily, glad to escape upstairs again. Dickon was demanding her attention, and she knew that Richard would be waking up, a fretful convalescent when she wasn't by his side.

The next three weeks were an unending strain.

Richard was restless, impatient with his slow progress, frequently impatient with her, though he was always apologetic at the end of the day.

"I'm not used to being taken care of," he explained for the twentieth time. "It's not natural for a man to be this dependent."

"But, Richard," she protested, "when you aren't well—"

"Don't argue with me, Miranda. I don't like it under any circumstances, and especially now, when I need all my strength to recover."

She bit back her response. It was futile to pursue this conversation over and over again, and she gave up.

"That's better." Richard smiled and patted the place next to him on the chaise longue. "Come sit down beside me, darling, and let's talk about pleasant things. I want to get back to New York and inspect our house, don't you? Mother says the painters will start work next week . . ."

On the first Sunday in April, Marty Schuyler stopped off to see them en route to New York, and Richard debated whether he was well enough to make the trip, too.

Marty encouraged him. "I'll be glad for the company, and I can look after you all."

Miranda was ready to object, but Marty went right on.

"The reason I'm going to New York," he explained, "is that Jack Lorimer still hasn't formally proposed to Caroline. If he can't make up his mind, I'll simply tell him to go away and stop bothering her."

This time Miranda voiced her protest. "Marty, you can't do that. Let Caroline decide for herself."

"I'm not stopping her," Marty said. "She wants to marry him. I'm just giving him a push."

"You might just push him away."

Marty shrugged. "If he is so easily dissuaded, good riddance. Even my grandmother is tired of this shilly-shallying."

Miranda remained doubtful. "I don't think your tactics are right. But in any case, we can't possibly go with you. Richard still tires too easily, and the doctor is worried about pneumonia at this stage."

"Doctors always worry too much," Richard said. "And *you* are the one who is tired."

Miranda could not deny that. The strain of the past month had caught up with her. And now that Dickon was teething, he had kept her up half the night. She was exhausted, completely exhausted, and that afternoon Richard insisted she lie down for a nap. When she woke up an hour later, still tired but alert to Dickon's wails, she was astonished to discover that Richard had made an abrupt decision: They would leave for New York that night.

Miranda renewed her objections. After all, he was still too weak to walk without assistance, and she would be carrying the baby, and—

He overrode all her protests, and Marty backed him up. George and Emily looked troubled, but they were strangely silent.

Chapter 41

THE CARRIAGE RIDE to the depot tired Richard, and he was glad that George had had the foresight to arrange for a stretcher on the train. Miranda made a pillow of her shawl, and she sat down beside him, still carrying Dickon. Marty saw to the trunks and returned to take his seat across from Miranda. He had bought all the available newspapers, and he offered a choice.

Richard shook his head. "I couldn't possibly concentrate once the train starts moving. Miranda, you read to me, darling. And you can put the baby down here. There's room next to me."

She worked her way through the war news, with emphasis on the dispatches from Virginia. Near Petersburg, Grant's armies were on the move at last, according to a story from C. Adams in the *Times*. Heavy rains had bogged down the advance, but the troops had made progress at Dinwoodie Court House, and they were turning the Confederate right flank at Five Forks.

"I wish I were there," Richard said. "This is the end. We'll be in Richmond by the end of the week. All these years and years . . ."

"So many dead and buried." Miranda thought again of Jimmy and Damon.

"They are paying for it," Marty said.

Miranda looked at him blankly.

"The South," Marty explained. "They are paying for starting the war. Sherman's troops are teaching them a lesson they'll never forget, and I'm glad."

Miranda was horrified. "You can't be *glad* about what's happening there. Why the destruction—"

"That's what war is." Marty was matter-of-fact. "It's all death and destruction—not flags and bands and parades. Destroy enough and make sure it doesn't happen again."

"You can't mean that," Miranda protested. "That's not war. That's revenge. It's not war when you deliberately burn down a whole city, leave women and children homeless. Why, Dany had friends in Columbia, and they are refugees now. They barely escaped with the clothes on their backs."

Marty shrugged. "Sounds exaggerated to me. Wade Hampton's cavalry set fire to a few bales of cotton, and it got out of hand. And I suppose some of our soldiers got liquored up that night and held a few torches here and there. I'll lay odds that Sherman didn't issue orders."

"The city burned down just the same."

Marty didn't care. "It's not the first city to be destroyed in this war. Look what the Rebels did to Chambersburg. And what about the Confederate arson plot in New York? How would you have felt if you had seen your precious hotel go up in flames?"

"Just the way those people in South Carolina feel today."

"Precisely," Marty agreed. "I don't blame them for hating us, but they're a conquered province, and they got what they deserve."

"A conquered province?" Her voice rose in astonishment, and she found a forgotten reservoir of emotional commitment. "But we fought the war to abolish slavery and preserve the Union." She warmed to her argument, latent anger rising to the surface. "We don't want conquest and—"

"Miranda," Richard interrupted her. "Calm down, darling. Marty fought on *our* side, remember? He's a soldier, and he understands all this better than you do."

"As I remember it," Marty said, "*you* were the fire-eating abolitionist when the rest of us were all at peace. Now that we've won your war for you, you might be a little more grateful."

"I am," she protested. "But you have it all wrong. I believe what Lincoln said: 'With malice toward none, with charity for all . . .'"

"Poetic words." Marty shrugged them off. "He's weak, like a woman, and not realistic at all. The Congress will be tougher. Isn't that right, Richard?"

"Perhaps. But don't get her all upset, Marty. In her condition, she shouldn't be worrying about things like that. Help me sit up, darling, and then take the baby; he's getting restless. And I'm feeling a little faint, and I want some water. And then let's see what Emily and Hattie packed for us in the lunch basket."

She followed his instructions to the letter, conscious of Marty's all-too-observant eyes on her.

Richard sampled the chicken, but he wasn't really hungry, and he complained of a headache and tightness in his chest. He sought refuge in sleep, and she tucked him in carefully and rested a cool hand on his forehead. Was it her imagination, or was he really a little feverish?

"The faithful, loving wife," Marty said, but there was an edge to his voice, and she glanced at him, uneasy. Richard had fallen into a restless sleep, his breathing heavy.

"I can't believe he makes you happy," Marty said, "particularly when the gallant Mr. Adams is still in the picture."

"Marty, don't you ever give up?"

"You don't even deny it."

"There's nothing to deny. Why don't you find a nice girl and get married and settle down?"

"Nice girls are boring," he said frankly. "They're all like Caroline. And bad girls are too easy. It's the ones teetering on the edge who are interesting."

"I'm so far from the edge that *nothing* will move me. Dear God, Marty, Richard and I have been married for two years. We have a child we love dearly, and perhaps—" She stopped abruptly and felt her color rising.

"You still blush like a shy little girl. It's very becoming, even enchanting, and I know it disarms Richard; but it doesn't fool me at all. You're too grown up for this kind of playacting, and you still have a mind and a spirit struggling to get out. You can't possibly allow yourself to be forced into that rigid little mold Richard has waiting for you."

"I don't want to hear any more."

"Not now, perhaps, but there will come a time . . . I give you six months in that house, just you and Richard, you obedient to his every whim, and you will be screaming to get out."

She shook her head in disbelief, and she reached for Dickon. She wasn't going to listen to another word.

"I'm not going back to the shipping business," Marty went

on conversationally. "I was fed up with it," he smiled wryly, "even before the war gave me a patriotic excuse to leave. Uncle Paul can buy me out, and I'll have money to live as I please, anywhere in the world."

"I hope you'll be very happy." She cradled the baby, feeling safe with him in her arms.

Marty shook his head. "Dickon isn't enough. A dozen children won't be enough. You'll find out, and better soon than late. There will be less heartbreak that way. But if you invest your whole life in an unhappy marriage, never having lived at all . . . You'll regret it, Miranda. I know you better than you think. I don't have Richard's patience, but I have my own kind of persistence, and I expect to get back to New York often enough to see how you are faring. It will just be a matter of timing."

"Never."

"Timing," Marty repeated. "It worked with Cort Adams, and it will work with me, too."

She glared at him and automatically turned to Richard for protection. "Darling." She leaned over to smooth back the hair from his forehead, and she was startled to discover he was burning with fever. Alarmed, she transferred the baby to the seat beside her, but Dickon immediately protested vigorously.

Richard stirred, blinking his eyes and coming slowly back to consciousness, then pushed back his blanket. "Hot," he said fretfully. "I'm so hot. And thirsty." Miranda held his head while he drank a cup of water, but Dickon was crying in earnest by now, and she knew it would be a long and exhausting night.

"Is it very hot in here?" Richard struggled to sit up, but the swaying motion of the train was too much for him. "I think I am going to be sick." He clutched at Miranda, and she promptly reached for the pile of discarded newspapers.

Afterward, Marty helped her clean up.

"Still hours to Jersey City," he said, consulting his pocket watch. "We'll have to carry him to the ferry."

"But with the baby . . ."

"Don't worry," Marty said. "I'll find a couple of porters. Is it just the train ride, do you think? Or is there something more serious."

"I don't know." She was suddenly conscious of how tired she was, bone weary, the month of strain catching up with her. If Richard were seriously ill, with the influenza, pneumonia . . . "I don't know at all." All night on the train. It was too much to bear, and they should never have come. She was worn out, exhausted, and Dickon was heavy in her arms, and when Richard looked at her with glazed eyes . . . "Oh, I wish I were home. Papa will be there, and he'll take care of everything."

"But Uncle Will is sick, too, and—" Marty stopped abruptly.

"He's better," Miranda said. "I had a letter from him last week, and . . ." She read contradiction in Marty's eyes, and a chilling fear seized her. "What do you know, Marty? What are you keeping from me?"

"Nothing. That is . . ." He sighed and shook his head. "You might as well be told now. George had a telegram from John this afternoon, but it's not serious. Really, it isn't," he assured her. "If it had been truly serious, George would have come, too. Uncle Will was asking for you. That's all."

"Oh, why do people keep these things from me?"

"Richard didn't want to worry you. He insisted he was well enough to travel. Emily was doubtful, but he was adamant. You know how he is."

"George told *him*, but he didn't tell *me*?"

"You were finally taking a nap, getting a rest from the baby, and Richard didn't want to waken you. He said you would hesitate to move him back to New York, and you would worry about whether you were doing the right thing. So he made the decision for you. To spare you, he said."

Richard stirred and began to shiver, and Marty looked at him uneasily. "That was when he was feeling so much better, of course."

"Of course," Miranda echoed wearily. Richard's forehead was clammy now, and the flush had left his cheeks. He was pale and shaking with cold, even under the blanket, and Marty draped a coat over him, but that didn't seem to help. Nothing helped, and the night stretched out, the hours endless.

It was an interminable journey, the train creaking and swaying, Dickon increasingly fretful and crying out his frustrations, Richard moving restlessly on his narrow stretcher, and Miranda trying to soothe them both, her nerves fraying with exhaustion and worry.

By daybreak Richard had fallen into a troubled sleep, and

when they took him off the train at last, he was unconscious, a dead weight. It was a nightmare transferring him to the crowded ferry, and they reached New York just in time to be caught up in the din of morning traffic. Morning traffic? She had never seen—or heard—anything like it. People were pouring into the streets, shouting and cheering, waving flags and setting off firecrackers. The whole city seemed to have gone berserk.

"What is it?" Miranda could barely make herself heard. Church bells added to the clamor, and the distant guns in the harbor forts were booming a salute.

A jubilant soldier seized her, baby and all, and she had to fight him off.

"Richmond!" he shouted at the top of his lungs, and he hugged her again. "Richmond has fallen!"

"Dear God!" She stopped short and tried to soothe Dickon, who had started to cry again. Marty was struggling through the crowd, directing the two porters who carried Richard's stretcher.

"Bedlam," Marty yelled at her. "But it's wonderful! Richmond is ours!" He found a place for the stretcher just outside the terminal. "Stand guard, Miranda, while I try to find a carriage—and a driver who hasn't gone mad."

They were an hour traversing the eight blocks to the Stratford, and Miranda held Dickon on her lap and clasped Richard's hand. She looked numbly at the crowds clogging the streets, but their jubilation was sealed off from her, and she felt nothing at all.

Home, she thought. I want to be home. I want to see Papa at the door to welcome me. And George, tall beside him, and the other boys crowding close, John and Tom and Jimmy. Richmond has fallen at last, and I hardly care at all. I just want to be home, a little girl again, with Papa to take care of me, the way I take care of Dickon. She fought back her tears and her dread, and time stopped. They were stalled within sight of the hotel, engulfed in the cheering crowds, and she was an alien in a foreign land.

Marty finally jumped from the carriage and guided the horses himself, forcing a passage to the kitchen entrance of the Stratford. They could never get through to Broadway.

Guy Dawson greeted them in the deserted lobby. "Thank God you are here." His face was unnaturally haggard and gaunt, as if he hadn't slept for a week.

"Papa?" Miranda choked over the word.

"He's been asking for you, but I think he's out of danger now."

"Danger," she echoed numbly. Dickon was crying again, and she patted him automatically. "What happened? I have to see him." She headed for the stairs, and Guy hurried to catch up with her.

"We have had the doctors, and Megan has stayed up to nurse him, and your brother John has been here the past two nights."

"Dear God!" Why hadn't they sent for her at once? But Richard was sick, too. She clutched the newel post on the first landing, feeling faint, and she watched as Marty directed the stretcher-bearers upstairs.

"I'll send for a doctor," Marty assured her.

"And for Aunt Faith and Uncle Paul," she called after him.

It couldn't be happening again. Not Papa and Richard both. Like Jimmy and Damon . . . The clamor from the streets penetrated her consciousness again, and she saw that the door to the library was open, and the windows, too, and Maureen was curled up on the alcove window seat, looking lost and frightened.

So much like me . . . But I am grown up, Miranda reminded herself, and I don't cry any more. She squared her shoulders and took a deep breath. "I'm home, Maureen, and everything is going to be all right."

The little girl blinked back her tears and ran to be comforted. "Is he better? Please say he's better. I want to stay here with all of you and be a family again."

Miranda hugged her. "That's what I want, too. That's why I'm here. Now, why don't you take Dickon to the nursery. He's been on the train all night, and I think he needs a bath."

"Oh, yes!" She was eager to help. "Give him to me. Nobody has let me do anything for three days. Not even Mama." She went off happily, crooning over the baby in her arms, glad to have a mission at last.

The door to Papa's room was ajar, and Miranda pushed it open and tiptoed in. She was barely conscious of John and Megan and their silent greetings. Papa seemed to be asleep, his breathing a rasp, but when she leaned over to kiss him, he opened his eyes.

"I dreamt you were here." He smiled and gripped her hand. "Stay with me. Stay as long as I need you."

The words familiar, an echo from the past, and she groped to remember. "As long as I need you." Damon had said that then they brought him to the hospital. And then he had died. It was a nightmare, happening all over again. Damon and Jimmy. Richard and Papa. No, she wouldn't let it happen again; *God* wouldn't let it happen again.

She choked back her fears, but her voice trembled with emotion.

"I'm here, Papa, and I love you."

He closed his eyes, and his breathing was quieter, more regular.

In whispers John and Megan told her what had happened. Papa had seemed quite well the first week after he came back, but then the weather had changed, become cold and rainy, and the dark smoke from a hundred thousand chimneys added to the gloom and mixed with a lingering fog. His spells of coughing became more prolonged, and the doctors disagreed about the cause—catarrh, inflammation of the bronchial passages, emphysema . . . His lungs were weak, they all agreed, and there was no remedy for that but rest.

Rest, Miranda said, that's what they all needed. She sent Megan off to bed, but John refused to go home. This was no time to fight his way through the crowds to go back to Brooklyn, he said. Perhaps if he shaved—Miranda had been surprised to see him with a two-day growth of stubble—and got cleaned up, borrowed some fresh clothes from Papa, he'd feel like a new man.

But first they should see how Richard was faring.

Not well.

Mrs. Darcy was with him, having taken over from Marty, but she couldn't begin to handle such a recalcitrant patient. Richard was conscious again, and even though he was weak and exhausted, he was adamant in refusing her ministrations.

"That woman," he paused for breath and pointed an accusing finger at the housekeeper. "She wanted to undress me." He was still panting with the exertion of fighting her off. "Send her away, Miranda. *You* take care of me."

"Yes, darling. Of course."

"I'm glad you are here." Mrs. Darcy was eager to escape. "And to think I complained that your father was difficult!

Why, compared to your husband, Mr. Chase is a perfect lamb."

"I'll tell him that," Miranda said, summoning the ghost of a smile. "I can see we're going to have our work cut out for us, with both of them sick at the same time."

With John's help, she put Richard to bed, his complaints mingled with complete exasperation when he found he didn't have the strength to sit up without assistance. "Help me, Miranda. I can't seem to breathe properly lying down. And open the windows, John. It's stuffy in here."

The cheers from the crowds, the din of firecrackers and cannon and church bells, poured in with the sunlight, and Richard was puzzled.

"A celebration," Miranda explained. "Richmond has fallen."

"Then we've won at last." He lay back against the pillows and listened to the clamor from outside.

"It sounds like it," Miranda agreed. She looked up to see Guy Dawson hesitating at the door.

"I hate to bother you with hotel business." He was unsure which of them to address, but it was Miranda who answered, claiming responsibility.

"What is it, Guy?"

He blinked at this use of his first name, hearing a new authority in her voice. "The celebration for Richmond," he said. "Shall we bring out the bunting and the flags? Mr. Chase had ordered illuminations for the final victory."

"Is it final?" Miranda was puzzled. "Did Lee surrender?"

"Not yet. But it has to happen soon. And the Astor is being decorated now, and if you'll look across the park," he gestured to the windows, "you'll see that Printing House Square is already draped with flags."

"Well, then, the Stratford can't lag behind."

"Rockets and fireworks tonight, too?"

"Let's not add to the noise." Miranda was decisive about that. She looked at Richard, who seemed to be utterly exhausted. "Just the illuminations tonight, Guy. And free meals to soldiers in uniform."

"And free drinks?"

"No!" She was emphatic. "Never again!" They had tried that once before with disastrous effect.

Guy gave her a mock salute and disappeared to carry out orders.

John had listened to this exchange with some surprise, possibly even disapproval. "Now I see what Uncle Paul meant. In Washington he said you ordered him around like a drill sergeant, and he was too astonished to protest. He said you probably ordered God to save Richard's life, and even *He* had to obey."

"Miranda," Richard interrupted, impatient, needing her. "My head hurts. Make it stop. Make the noise stop, and the light . . ."

John closed the windows and drew the blinds, and she laid a cold compress on Richard's forehead and waited for the doctor to come, bearing stronger remedies.

Richard fell asleep, having taken the prescribed dose of laudanum, and Faith stayed with him. Paul departed, uneasy, and Miranda returned to her father, who was awake now and coughing again. But when he saw the dark circles under her eyes, he insisted that she go to bed.

"Not now," Miranda protested. "Not when I've just arrived. I think if I took a bath . . ." She was conscious of the accumulated grime of the long train journey, and she remembered that she hadn't eaten since last night. And Dickon would be hungry for her again, and then Richard . . .

The bath helped, and Maureen brought her a lunch tray, and Dickon seemed to have calmed down at last. Her body cried out for sleep, but she kept a vigil by her father's bedside until Megan came to spell her again. By then the crowds had thinned out, and John decided it was time to return to Brooklyn. Dany had her hands full, he explained, with Susanne and Mrs. Robillard and Deedee, all of them needing her care. He had been doubtful about leaving her, but with Papa so sick . . .

"I'm better," Will declared, but his voice was still weak, and John hesitated.

"Go home," Miranda insisted. "We can manage."

"I'll be back tomorrow," John promised. "Megan, make her get some rest. If she doesn't think about herself, at least she ought to have some consideration for the baby."

So the news of her possible pregnancy had reached John, too. Then Dany must know. And Susanne. And Cort. She must be very tired. She had managed not to think about Cort for weeks now. She had simply turned off her mind whenever he entered her consciousness. Now he was a looming presence, haunting her again. Surely life didn't repeat itself over and over, going around in endless circles. Jimmy and Damon dying; Cort's arms around her. Papa and Richard . . . No, not again. The warmth of Cort's embrace. It couldn't happen. She was married. Nothing could happen. And Cort was reconciled with his wife, and perhaps Susanne was pregnant again. With Cort's child this time.

"I must rest," Miranda said aloud, echoing John's instructions. But Richard was asleep in her bed, and she sought refuge in Tom's room.

When she woke up, Mrs. Darcy was hovering over her, uncertain about whether to rouse her. It was dark outside, and Miranda was conscious of a noise like thunder. It couldn't be New Year's Eve . . .

"What is it?" She gripped the covers, shaken.

"Don't worry, dear." Mrs. Darcy was soothing. "It's the celebration for Richmond. The cannons are still firing salutes. And they are setting off rockets on the roof of the Astor."

"And Papa? And Richard?"

"Asking for you. Major Schuyler is asking for you."

She scrambled out of bed, feeling dizzy, and she had to grasp the bedpost to maintain her balance. For a moment she stood by the open window, taking deep breaths, surprised when the night sky was suddenly illuminated, rockets bursting bright as daybreak. The crowds massed in the City Hall Park cheered, and Miranda turned to Mrs. Darcy, asking for more news.

"I don't know. The papers have put out extras all day, but I haven't had a chance to read them."

She found Richard feverish again, and Faith relinquished her place at his side.

Paul had abruptly stopped pacing when he saw her, and he stood by the windows, staring at the illuminations in every window of every newspaper office on Printing House Square. Another rocket lit up the sky, and the crowds cheered again.

"They are all so damned happy." Paul turned his back on the celebration and sought an outlet for his pent-up emotions. "You, Miranda. What in God's name possessed you? He should never have been moved. Why did you bring him home?"

"Now, Paul." Faith took his arm. "You know Marty said it was all Richard's idea."

"And a damn fool idea it was." He glared at his son and transferred his rage. "Bullheaded. He's always been that way. I don't know where he gets it."

In other circumstances Miranda and Faith would have exchanged knowing glances, but they had no heart for that now. Faith made an oblique reference to the late Judge Schuyler, and Paul allowed himself to be diverted.

Richard stirred, restless and uncomfortable, and Miranda called for ice and wrung out another cold compress. She studied his profile against the pillow, the sharp, aquiline features, the wide brow and deep-set eyes, the strong line of his jaw, stamped in the same mold as his father and his grandfather. And his son, too. Stubborn and willful, all of them, and blindly self-confident, overriding all obstacles in their path. It was admirable in some respects, and certainly Richard was just as demanding of himself as he had ever been of her. He might hold a narrow vision of the world, but he would always live up to it, at whatever cost. He had saved Tom's life, she reminded herself, and he had insisted on this trip to New York just so that she could be with her father . . . She swallowed hard and excused herself to run across the hall to see how Papa was faring. Sleeping peacefully, Mrs. Darcy told her, and Miranda returned to resume her vigil with Richard.

Ann arrived with Irene, both of them upset.

"But he was better," Irene kept insisting. "Papa said you made him well."

"Is it pneumonia?" Ann asked, standing at the foot of the bed. She was frightened of sickness in any form, and she couldn't force herself to come any closer.

"Can you hear me, Richard?" Irene took his hand, and his eyelids fluttered. "Why, that's wonderful. You're awake." She beamed at him and assured him he would soon be fine. "I want you at the wedding," she said confidently. "Just as soon as the war is over and Andy comes home. It won't be long now. You know Richmond has fallen?"

He had closed his eyes again, but she rattled on, happy to give him so much good news. "We captured twelve thousand soldiers and fifty guns, the papers said today. And now Grant is chasing Lee, and just as soon as he catches him, it will be all over. Over at last! Isn't that wonderful?"

Another rocket burst echoed her enthusiasm, but Richard only sighed.

"Don't tire him," Ann said, withdrawing toward the door. "I don't think we should stay long."

"But we've only just arrived," Irene protested. "And I want to talk to you, Miranda, and see Dickon. And how is Uncle Will? And Mama says you are expecting again. When? I want you to be in the wedding, but of course if you are too far along by June——"

"Irene," her mother cut her off. "This isn't a social visit. You are tiring Richard, and Miranda doesn't have time to——"

"Time," Miranda said, and she picked up Richard's gold watch, peering at it in the dim light. "I must check Dickon."

Irene followed her to the nursery, and Ann trailed along, glad to escape the sickroom.

The baby was asleep, at peace with the world, his hand resting possessively on a stuffed tiger. The toy was already showing the ravages of his affection, one paw partly chewed off, but Dickon was single-minded in his devotion. Miranda smiled at him, his Schuyler heritage solidly displayed even in his sleep. And why not? She was the Judge's grandchild herself, and Dickon had a double concentration of willfulness.

She leaned over to tuck him in more carefully, and he stirred and temporarily lost contact with his toy. Miranda restored it to him hastily, before he could wake up, demanding attention again. So much like his father, refusing to be denied anything.

"Such a perfect child!" Irene exclaimed. "What is your secret, Miranda?"

She smiled. "I give him whatever he wants."

Caroline and Mrs. Cantrell called the next afternoon, Caroline glowing with new-found happiness. Major Jack Lorimer had made his declaration at last and had gone to Boston to inform his parents. He would be returning with an engagement ring, she said, an heirloom that had been willed to him by his grandmother.

Miranda listened with half an ear, pleased that Papa was better, that he seemed to be paying attention to Caroline's unaccustomed stream of conversation.

If only Richard were as far along. His mother was with him now, and she would call when he woke up, but Miranda couldn't really concentrate on Caroline and her happy chatter.

Marty deserved some of the credit, Caroline admitted

freely. Wasn't she lucky to have a brother who could step in and resolve all her problems? If only he could find the right girl and settle down, too. But Marty was so restless, she went on. He was thinking about going to Georgia now that the war was nearly over. There would be all sorts of opportunities in the coming Reconstruction, he said. Like investment property. He could buy the Robillard house in Savannah to start with. Dany and Susanne wouldn't want it, and he understood that it faced one of the squares. Caroline rambled on, and Mrs. Cantrell smiled at her affectionately and then turned her attention to Miranda.

"For once in his life Marty seems to have done something right. Or perhaps his timing happened to be good. Whatever it was, he certainly galvanized Major Lorimer into a decision."

"I'm glad for her," Miranda said. "For them both," she amended. "And I hope that Marty . . ." She was conscious of a slight stir across the hall, and she excused herself abruptly.

Richard was awake, wanting her by his side, close enough to touch. The boundaries of his world had shrunk to this one room, and he needed her there to stave off the darkness.

The week passed in a blur of emotion and repeated crises and fretful demands from Richard, followed by the frightening moments when he gasped for breath. It was pneumonia, the doctors agreed, and his lungs were filling up with fluid and there was little they could do.

Mr. Chase seemed to be resting more easily, but if he should contract pneumonia, too . . . Certainly the two patients should be kept apart, and Dr. Simpson was reluctant to allow Miranda to nurse them both.

"You are looking run down," he warned her. "We can't have you getting sick, too, and the baby not getting enough nourishment."

"I'm fine," she said automatically, "and so is Dickon."

"Now, if you think you are pregnant—"

"I'm not," she said bluntly. "I was never sure, but now I know. Just yesterday . . ." She trailed off, a little embarrassed. "I'm not pregnant," she repeated firmly. Richard would be disappointed, but she would wait until he recovered before telling him. She wasn't sure of her own reactions. Relief? Regret? Right now she was too preoccupied with Richard and Papa to think about anything else.

"I suggest a spring tonic," Dr. Simpson said, writing out a prescription. "And if you would drink a pint of stout or porter every day——"

"I'm fine," she reiterated. "It's my husband, Major Schuyler, who is sick. Why can't you do something for *him?*"

Dr. Simpson shook his head. "His fate is in God's hands now, and yours."

Palm Sunday dawned, bright and sunny, and Miranda roused herself from the cot near Richard's bed. He had lapsed into a fitful sleep, and his mother was nodding, too.

"You should get some rest," Miranda said, but Faith refused. Like Richard she drew on an inner discipline that had carried her through this nightmare week, but her taut strength was near the breaking point now.

"You must take care of Dickon, Miranda." Faith managed a fleeting smile. "And make sure that your father is all right. I'll order breakfast."

Papa was awake, still having trouble with his breathing but convinced he was better. "It's been a terrible siege for you, Pet." He tried to muffle his cough and failed. "Don't worry about me so much." He smiled at her. "I've had a good life, and it would be no tragedy if I were taken now."

"Don't say that, Papa." Her voice cracked, but she refused to cry.

"My little heroine." He stroked her hand. "I don't mean to upset you. It's Richard I worry about. Megan says it was his decision to come back to New York, just so that you could be with me."

She nodded, not trusting her voice.

"He loves you very much."

"Yes, Papa."

He waited, expectant, and she gave him the answer he wanted to hear.

"And of course I love him, too."

He smiled at her. "I know. I just wanted to hear you say it. I hope you tell him often, just in case he has any doubts."

"Richard never has any doubts."

"He is human. He likes to be reassured. *I* like to be reassured."

523

"But, Papa, you *know* I love you." She kissed him, and he patted her hand.

"Of course I know. But I always like to be told. I can't believe that he is any different."

After breakfast Faith declared she wasn't tired at all, and when Paul arrived she suggested they leave Richard in Miranda's care and go to church. She felt the need for that kind of strength, and Paul was prompt to agree. He was useless in a sickroom, and any reason to escape was welcome.

Miranda plumped up the pillows for Richard and helped him to sit up. He was gasping for breath again, and when she held him in her arms, she was conscious of his frailty. For the first time she acknowledged to herself that he was dying. The thought had been unreal before, something from a nightmare, the past doomed to repeat itself. But this wasn't Damon, a wispy ghost from her past. This was Richard, her husband, the father of her child. This was happening now. He was dying—before he ever knew her at all, before she ever broke through to find the real person under that rigid and disciplined exterior he showed to the world.

He made a feeble gesture toward the windows, and she pulled back the heavy drapes and let the light stream in.

"It's Palm Sunday, darling. April 9."

"I missed," his voice was a low rasp, "I missed our anniversary."

"I did, too, darling." She kissed him, twice.

"It wasn't two years," he said.

She looked at him questioningly.

"I've been lying here, counting our days together. It's not two years."

"I don't understand."

"I was gone so much." He looked at her wistfully. "We had only six weeks all together, before I was wounded. And five weeks since then, but that doesn't count."

"If you say so, darling."

"Six weeks," he repeated. "I count the days—at Long Branch, in Washington, New York." He paused, gathering his strength. "I loved them all—all the days, all the nights. It wasn't enough. I wanted a lifetime. To love you and cherish you, to know at last that you loved me—"

"Oh, Richard!" She was overcome with guilt and blinked back her tears.

"Miranda, precious, you have always made me so happy."

She kissed him and swallowed over the lump in her throat. "I love you, Richard." She wished it so fervently that for the moment it was true.

He smiled at her. "I know. You are so stubborn, Miranda. You wait until now to tell me that, to tell yourself that, when I have known for so long. And now that I am dying—"

"No, Richard."

"I *am* dying, Miranda. Let's not pretend. And don't argue with me, darling." There was still a trace of authority in his fading voice. "Let's not waste our precious time that way."

"Whatever you say, Richard."

"That's better. Now, I have been thinking about your future without me."

"No, Richard, I—".

"Miranda, please. Just listen." He was having difficulty breathing again, and he lay back against the pillows, his eyes still fastened on her.

"Darling, you are exhausting yourself."

"About your future," he repeated stubbornly. "And our children. I want you to marry again."

She drew back, astonished.

"They will need a father," Richard said. "You would spoil them, darling. You know you would. And I will *not* have them brought up in a hotel."

She bit back her protests, and he managed a smile.

"Yes, I know. *You* survived. But it wasn't good for you, darling. And staying on here, without me—that would be worse. You would insist on being part of it, and Uncle Will would let you. You are too strong-minded, Miranda, and you always have been. It's not suitable for a woman. It's not right. I don't want my wife—"

"Darling, don't worry about these things. I would devote myself to Dickon, and I would always—"

"Miranda, it's not just the children. It's *you*. You will need a husband, darling, and someone very strong."

"Like you, Richard?" She was teasing him gently, but he wasn't aware.

"Exactly."

"Do you have someone in mind?"

This time he was conscious that she was smiling, and he smiled, too. "I haven't had time to draw up a list, but I will give it some thought." He lay back, looking at her with love, and she forced back her tears. "Just be sure to choose wisely, Miranda. Stop and think whether I would approve."

"Oh, darling." She shook her head. "I don't know whether to laugh or cry. Someday, when you are better, when you have fully recovered and are barking out orders again, I will remind you of this day. And I'll ask you then for your list of possible husbands. Who knows? Perhaps there will be someone I'll like better than you. We'll run off together and shock the world."

"Never." He reached for her hand. "There is one thing I have always known, even before I was sure that you loved me . . . There has never been anyone else, and there never could be. You are my beautiful madonna, faithful and true to me, and I wanted to spend the rest of my life living up to you."

"Richard, darling." She could restrain her tears no longer. "I have never been good enough for you."

"You said that once before."

She looked at him, puzzled, her eyes still blurred with tears.

"When I first proposed to you . . . I remember every detail." He closed his eyes and saw it all again. "When we were separated so often, so long, I used to relive all our time together, right from the beginning. And when I asked you to marry me, you didn't even know I loved you. You were so sweet, so unprepared and innocent. And you said you weren't good enough for me. It was preposterous then, and it's even more preposterous now. Oh, Miranda," he reached out to brush a tear from her cheek, "you have always been my dearest dream come true."

It was an illusion he had cherished from the very beginning and it would be impossibly cruel to shatter it now. She kissed him again and held his hand in both of hers.

"I could never be that perfect, darling, but I tried."

"I know." He relaxed against the pillows and seemed to breathe more easily. "You always gave more than I could ever ask. That's how I know you loved me, darling. Actions speak so much louder than words. You were always there, so responsive and loving and dear to me. If I had invented and shaped you myself, I couldn't have made you more perfect."

"Darling, you are so extravagant. I couldn't possibly live up to all that."

"You did," he insisted stubbornly. "You always did. Sometimes, of course," he smiled at her again, "I had to remind you."

"Sometimes," she agreed, with a wry smile.

"Promise me, Miranda."

"Anything, darling."

"You will bring up the children to love me."

"Richard, please, don't make me cry."

"I have never been very good with children, you know." He lapsed into silence and closed his eyes. His breathing was shallow and irregular, and she watched his struggles with growing alarm.

Megan appeared in the doorway, carrying Dickon, but she did not cross the threshold. Miranda hesitated. Until now she had been so careful about keeping the baby out of the sickroom, but she couldn't tear herself away from Richard now.

"It's all right," she said to Megan. "I'll nurse him here."

The child looked up at her with his father's dark eyes, and she held him in her arms and her eyes swam with tears again.

"Miranda." Richard's voice was a faint whisper, and she had to strain to hear. "Our unborn child."

"Yes, darling."

"If she is a girl, I want to call her Miranda."

She nodded, clutching at Dickon for support.

"As beautiful as you are, darling, and as loving."

"Richard, please. Don't use your strength."

"And a boy." He was as determined as ever. "Name him for Jimmy, and for Damon, too."

She choked, and Dickon looked at her with wonder and reached up as if to pat her cheek.

Richard smiled at them both. "I would have liked to see him grow up."

Richard was still conscious when his parents returned, though he couldn't rouse himself to speak.

In the late afternoon when the shadows were lengthening again, he plucked feebly at the bedclothes, and Miranda took his hand and kissed him.

He focused on her with obvious difficulty, and he strained to whisper her name. "Miranda, I promised you . . ." He couldn't find the words.

"Yes, darling?"

"I promised . . ."

"You promised me the world, darling, and you always gave me everything."

"No . . . I wanted . . ." He looked at her helplessly. "Diamonds . . ."

She stared at him, bewildered, but Uncle Paul understood.

"He wrote to me from Washington, when he thought he was recovering." Paul's voice was unnaturally hoarse. "He wanted me to have Tiffany's design a brooch for you. They are working on it now, but . . ." He shook his head helplessly.

"Richard," Miranda brushed back a lock of hair from his forehead. "Don't worry about that now. I don't want diamonds, darling. I never wanted—"

"I promised you," he repeated.

"I'll take care of it," Paul assured him, reaching out to pat him awkwardly. "And we'll always take care of her, and the children."

Richard sighed his understanding. He had discharged his last obligation. His eyes fastened on Miranda once again. "Just to see you, darling, looking beautiful . . ."

He didn't speak again, and he died that night, unaware that he was surrounded by all the members of his family.

Unaware, too, that the church bells were ringing again. The telegraph wires were still humming with the joyous news from Appomattox Court House: Lee had surrendered the Army of Northern Virginia to General Grant.

Chapter 42

RICHARD'S FUNERAL was Wednesday, Wednesday of Holy Week.

The fasting and solemn dedication of Lent, the blossoming renewal of spring. The family mourning for the dead, the country celebrating in victory. Private sorrows felt all the more keenly in the midst of public rejoicing.

The war wasn't over yet—Jefferson Davis and the Confederate government were in flight from Richmond, and General Joe Johnston still had a shrinking army in North Carolina, but there would be no more major battles.

For the fourth anniversary of the firing on Fort Sumter, Major Anderson was returning to Charleston for a formal ceremony to raise the Stars and Stripes again. The cannon roared for victory, and for peace, and the Union was preserved.

The *United* States of America, in fact as well as in name, united by force of arms, one nation, indivisible. The irrepressible conflict that had shattered so many lives was history now, and in Washington President Lincoln turned his attention to binding up the nation's wounds.

After Richard was buried in Greenwood Cemetery, the family returned to the Stratford.

Miranda had insisted that her father stay at home. That morning he had convinced himself he was strong enough to sit through the funeral, even if he couldn't make the trip to Brooklyn for the burial service, and dissuading him was difficult. His coughing had subsided, but he was weak, and he leaned on George for support. Tom was still with the army in

Virginia, but George had brought Emily and the children to New York, and Miranda found them a source of strength and practical help. George agreed that Papa must stay home, and Emily concurred, offering an inducement.

"The children can stay with you," she said. "You can have them all to yourself, with just Maureen to help, to make sure they don't wear you out."

Will allowed himself to be persuaded, sitting down again, one arm around Miranda. "I wanted to help you, Pet. This has been such a terrible month for you."

"Just get better, Papa. That would be the most help of all."

He was gaunt, and his hacking cough filled her with alarm, but he seemed to be out of danger, and if he would only rest . . . She was pale herself, showing signs of strain, and in her black moiré dress she looked older, the light of eager expectation gone from her eyes.

Will looked at her and sighed. "I remember you in black before, when Jimmy died. But you weren't so pale then. You were still flushed from fever and—"

"Please, Papa. Don't remind me." She hadn't planned to wear this dress, the one that Cort had given her. It only reinforced her sense of guilt. Why hadn't she loved Richard more? If only there had been more time, time to know him truly, time for him to know her as she really was. But then perhaps he would never have loved her at all. She had never been good enough for him, and if he had realized that . . . And here was this dress, reminding her of her guilt.

Megan had pulled it out of her wardrobe, searching for something suitable, so pleased with her find. And Miranda had recoiled immediately.

"No. It reminds me of the past, and I—"

"Try it on. The material is beautiful, and the style is perfect for you."

In the end, it was simpler to wear it. She didn't have time for something new, and it wasn't as if Cort would be in New York to see her. After Appomattox he had returned to Washington, George said, and now he was to have an interview with the Secretary of War about Reconstruction policies, and he was hoping to see the President himself . . .

Susanne was at the funeral, a pale wraith beside Dany and John, but she had not come with them to the Stratford.

"All my sympathy, Miranda." Susanne had kissed her after the graveside service. "I know what it is to mourn. You'll forgive me, though, if I go home to Mama and Deedee now. I'm not feeling very well."

Miranda nodded.

"I wish there were something I could do. Perhaps next week, when Cort comes for me . . . At least," Susanne patted her arm, "at least you have Dickon." She looked over at Lucy, so obviously pregnant, requiring the assistance of both her father and her brother to clamber into a waiting carriage.

"Is she going to be all right?" Susanne asked. "Do you think she should have come?"

"She insisted," Miranda said. "Richard saved Tom's life. They have decided to name the first boy after him."

Lucy came to the Stratford, too, and from across the library John eyed her uneasily.

"It looks as if she could have that child any minute," he whispered to Dany. And Miranda overheard him.

Dany smiled. "You always worry too much. Why, yesterday when Susanne was so happy about the baby, the first thing *you* said . . ."

Miranda moved away abruptly. Susanne had said she wasn't feeling very well, and that explained it: She was pregnant, of course. Cort was tied to her irrevocably now.

She bumped into Andy Dawson, who put a protective arm around her and kissed her cheek.

"Miranda, my dear, you are looking faint. Why don't you sit down and let me bring you something. A cup of tea? That's what I'm getting for Irene. She's over there on the sofa with your father. Why don't you join them, and then I can talk to all of you."

She allowed herself to be steered in that direction, and Irene moved over to make a place for her. Irene had been crying at the funeral, and she was still in an emotional state, but her grief for Richard could not blot out her joy now that Andy was here.

"Isn't he wonderful, Miranda? Everything about him is wonderful. And do you remember? It was Richard who introduced us. It was Christmas, the first year of the war, and you were giving a party for Jimmy."

Miranda nodded and forced a smile and accepted the tea from Andy. She remembered it very well. Richard had made a point of diverting Andy's attention away from her, and

Irene had been enchanted. She still was. And Andy was obviously devoted to her.

"We have waited three years," he said to Will. "Don't you think that is long enough?"

Will agreed that it was, and Andy clasped Irene's hand. She was not yet wearing a ring—the formal announcement of their engagement had been delayed when Richard was wounded and now her mother refused even to talk about it. While the family was in mourning, there was to be no discussion of wedding plans at all.

"It doesn't have to be a big wedding," Irene said. "Just the family. Would it really be disrespectful to Richard, Miranda? If *you* would talk to Mama . . ."

"We are going to be married in June," Andy said. "That's two months."

"And I want the family there," Irene said. "I told Andy we could always elope, but I'd rather have all of you with us. Surely Richard would have wanted that, too."

"Of course, Irene." Miranda swallowed over the lump in her throat. "I'll talk to Aunt Faith. I'm sure I can persuade her. What does Uncle Paul say?"

"Papa says whatever we agree to do, it's all right with him. But he doesn't want Mama upset. He worries about her, and he hasn't the faintest idea how to help. Richard's death has been such a terrible blow . . . I think Papa is going to ask you to move in with them, just to give Mama a real interest in life."

Miranda was aware of her father's startled reaction.

"I don't think that would be a good idea, Irene." Miranda knew it was impossible.

"I know," Irene agreed. "That's what Mama said, too. She doesn't like the idea of Dickon growing up in the hotel, the way you did, but she knows you will never want to live in that brownstone without Richard."

Miranda sighed. Uncle Paul had already asked her what she wanted to do about the house, and she didn't know. Perhaps Irene and Andy . . .

Andy was doubtful. He didn't want to start married life by plunging so deeply into debt.

"First we are going to take a trip around the world," Irene said, her eyes shining with anticipation. "I've always wanted to do that. Remember, Miranda? We talked about it once. I wanted you and Richard to come with us." She looked questioningly at Andy. "Could we bring her along, do you think?"

Miranda smiled. "I don't recommend a third person on a honeymoon. Besides, I wouldn't want to leave Papa." When he got better, perhaps she could go away with him, to the seashore or the mountains. Saratoga again. Just as soon as Tom and George were out of the army and back in New York, ready to take over the hotel. If they mortgaged the Stratford to build a new hotel uptown . . . A wonderful idea occurred to her. The boys could manage the new hotel, and she and Papa could stay on at the Stratford. Two hotels. Why not? With the money she inherited from Richard . . . No, he would be appalled. He didn't want Dickon growing up that way. To think that on the very day of his funeral she was rebelling against his dying wishes. He wanted her to remarry, but she wouldn't want that life again, ever. There was no one in the world she would ever want to love. No one who was free.

She looked at the few single men in the room and rejected them one by one. Larry Blaine, Lucy's younger brother, gazing sadly at Caroline. Major Jack Lorimer, strangely uncomfortable with Caroline clinging to his arm. And Marty Schuyler, bored and restless, eager to get away. He was going to Georgia, was already dickering with John to buy the Robillard house, and he was looking forward to reaping the fruits of victory in the coming Reconstruction. With Caroline and Mrs. Cantrell he had called yesterday to express sympathy and, curiously enough, he seemed to mean it. But he could not resist an oblique comment about the prisoner set free when the jailer died. And he promised to return when she was ready to put aside mourning. That was as good a reason as any to stay in black for the rest of her life.

She sighed, and Will put his arm around her and whispered a suggestion. "Why don't you see if Dickon is awake, Pet? I'm sure everyone will want to make a fuss over him, and then they'll all leave." He gave her a conspiratorial wink, and she withdrew, to return minutes later carrying the baby.

On the threshold she paused, unconsciously making an entrance—the bereaved young widow clasping her infant son. Framed by the doorway, she was a striking portrait in black and white, the pale oval of her face in dramatic contrast to her dark mourning, her arms around the baby a frail shield for him against the world.

The emotional response was immediate.

Paul blinked back unexpected tears, and Faith groped for his hand and held fast. Lucy wept again, and John looked over at her in alarm, fearing the effect on her of so much emotion. And Major Jack Lorimer abruptly detached himself from Caroline to rush to Miranda's side. Mrs. Cantrell observed his defection and sighed, and Marty shrugged and wrote him off as his future brother-in-law. Emily looked thoughtful and whispered something to George, who was immediately shocked. Emily smiled, and George stared at Jack Lorimer, refusing to credit the idea that this man was showing such obvious interest in Miranda on the very day of her husband's funeral. John was disapproving, too, but Dany exchanged knowing glances with Emily, and they nodded their agreement: Miranda needed someone, and why not Jack Lorimer?

Later that evening Emily drew Miranda aside to give her some sisterly advice. They had looked in on the sleeping children and then lingered in the nursery, reluctant to leave.

"Dickon will need a father," Emily said. "I know it's too soon for you even to think of such a thing, but I want to plant the idea now, and you should not reject it out of hand."

"No!" Miranda was emphatic. "I will never go through this again. I will make my own life, not tied to anyone."

"A child, particularly a boy, needs—"

"I can take care of him myself. And Papa," she swallowed over the lump in her throat. "Papa will help." He will live a long time, she assured herself, and everything would be the same as it used to be, except she had Dickon now.

"Miranda, dear, that's no life for you. Now I know that this is premature, but when Major Lorimer calls on you—"

"What are you talking about?" Miranda looked at her, uncomprehending. "Jack Lorimer is engaged to Caroline."

"I don't think so, dear. Not yet. Not formally. And when he rushed to your side today—"

"Emily!" Miranda was astonished. "I have no interest in Jack Lorimer, and Caroline loves him. She told me herself that they were engaged. It was just last week before Richard . . . before Richard died. Jack was going to Boston to bring back a ring, a family heirloom."

"She wasn't wearing it today," Emily said. "And when he deserted her for you, I knew that—"

"You're imagining things."

"No, dear, I saw it very clearly. And so did Dany. And Caroline, too, I'm afraid."

Miranda shook her head. "It doesn't matter in any case. If you are right, I'll just send him packing."

"Yes, dear, I know it's too soon. And of course he has always been too forward, but he has known you and admired you for a very long time, and I think he would be understanding. Of course no one could ever replace Richard, and you will mourn for him and always remember him. But after time passes, you will think of the future, and you will need to make a new life for yourself."

Miranda turned away, unwilling to listen, and Emily tactfully changed the subject—but not her matchmaking determination.

And the next afternoon Major Lorimer called.

George was disapproving, Emily concealed a knowing smile, Miranda was cool and distant and concentrated on Polly, and Will, after his first surprise, extended a cordial invitation to stay for tea.

"How is Caroline?" Miranda asked pointedly. "I didn't expect you to call without her."

Jack Lorimer refused to be abashed. "I believe she was planning to visit Blackwell's Island today," he said calmly. "Yes, two lumps of sugar, please."

Emily smiled and handed him his cup of tea. "Are you planning to stay in New York for Easter, Major Lorimer?"

"I have been looking forward to it," he said. "Will you be here, Mrs. Chase? Perhaps in the afternoon you could all join me in a carriage ride through the Central Park. I understand the new plantings are very beautiful." He looked first at Emily and then, more hopefully, at Miranda. "Very beautiful," he repeated.

She sighed, and Polly gazed at her curiously and climbed into her lap. "Please, may I have a ginger cookie?"

Miranda looked at Emily for approval and then agreed, smiling.

"Thank you, auntie."

Jack Lorimer reached out to touch the little girl. "What pretty manners she has. I remember the first time I saw her—it must be two years ago—and she came right to me and crawled into my lap. I get along very well with children," he said to all of them, but again he looked directly at Miranda.

"Yes," Emily agreed. "You are very much like Cort in that way."

"How is he?" Jack asked. "I saw his wife at the funeral, but I didn't have an opportunity to speak to her. She didn't come back to the hotel."

"No," Emily said. "She wasn't feeling well."

There was an awkward silence while everyone considered the probable reason for Susanne's indisposition.

"But *you* are looking well," Jack said to Miranda. "In spite of your sad loss. Major Schuyler was a fine man, I know, and no one could ever replace him in your heart. But he has left you a precious legacy in your son, and in the child . . ." He trailed off, embarrassed for the first time.

Miranda blushed. Caroline must have told him, but the fact that she wasn't pregnant had not yet caught up with Richard's premature announcement.

"Yes," Emily said briskly. "Miranda must think about the future. We all mourn for Richard, but we know that life goes on."

"Please excuse me," Miranda said abruptly. Her eyes were filling with tears again, and she fled to the nursery to hold Dickon in her arms. They were all crowding in on her too fast. She hadn't been able to come to terms with Richard's death, and already they were surrounding her, advising her, asking her to make decisions.

Irene and Andy wanted her to smooth the way for their wedding, Aunt Faith expected her to fill the void created by Richard's death, Emily insisted on playing matchmaker, Caroline needed help to get Jack Lorimer back, and Jack . . . He was going to be a problem. And then she worried about Papa, and Dickon, and the Stratford, and the plans for the new hotel.

The new hotel.

It was always easier to think about things than to worry about people. Now if Papa took out a mortgage on the Stratford . . . Uncle Paul had said something about Richard's will, and he was coming the next day to tell her about it. Richard had never talked to her about money at all, and she had no idea of his income or his wealth. But she fastened on the dream of managing the Stratford with Papa while George and Tom opened a new hotel uptown. What better way to invest her inheritance?

It was not to be. Richard had set up a trust for her, Uncle Paul explained, and she would have a generous income—contingent on the continuing profits of Schuyler Shipping—but no access at all to the principal.

"A wise provision," Uncle Paul said, looking at her benignly over his spectacles. "This way you will always be well provided for, and you can't go out and squander the money foolishly."

"But for an investment," Miranda protested, "to build a new hotel." She explained her ideas, but Paul cut her off with a wave of the hand.

"No, Miranda, don't even think about it. My dear child, I know you want to help your brothers, and it is sweet and generous of you, but you must not mortgage your future or Dickon's. I have every confidence that George and Tom will be able to finance the new hotel, and with the sale of the Stratford—"

"But I don't *want* to sell the Stratford. It's *home*."

He looked at her in surprise. "Miranda, my dear, we can give you a home. Faith and I would be delighted to have you move in with us."

"No. Papa needs me, and—"

"Yes, I know. But Will's health is so frail, and you must be prepared . . ." He trailed off, aware of her shock. "That is, I just wanted you to know, Miranda, that you could always have a home with us."

She sighed. He didn't understand. He thought he was being helpful, and he didn't understand at all. "Thank you, Uncle Paul. I know you want to take care of me, but I just want to take care of myself."

"Richard has done that already," Paul said with satisfaction. "He thought of everything. He always did. And when Dickon grows up, you may be sure there will be a place for him in the company. John will see to that, if I am not here. John and Andy."

Miranda nodded. It would have been so easy if she had the money, but perhaps there was another way. She would have to learn more about mortgages and interest rates and taxes and building costs. Papa would teach her, if he were well enough. She heard his cough, and he came into the family parlor with Faith, who was carrying Dickon.

"Miranda, dear." Faith sat down in the rocking chair, still holding the baby. "When I went into the nursery, that little girl, Maureen, was taking care of our precious boy. She's too young to be trusted with that kind of responsibility. Where is Megan?"

"At mass, I think. It's Good Friday, and I told her she could take as much time as she wanted."

Faith was disapproving. "Well, wherever she is, she should not pass off her responsibilities to a child. And you must not allow it, Miranda. Richard's only son deserves better than that."

Miranda bit back her protests and tried to be understanding. Aunt Faith was still in an emotional state over Richard's death, and it wouldn't do any good to argue with her. She had transferred all her worry and concern to Dickon, and she expected perfection from all those around him. And if she began harping on the perils of growing up in a hotel . . .

To forestall that conversation again, Miranda inquired about Andy and Irene and expressed her hope that the period of mourning for Richard would not interfere with their wedding in June. "Richard would not have wanted to delay their happiness," she said firmly.

Paul sighed and looked at his wife, and her eyes filled with tears again.

"I simply can't go through with all that," Faith said. "With Ann we had all the preparations twice, and when I think of sending out all the invitations and assembling the trousseau and planning the dresses for the bridesmaids and—"

"A very small wedding," Miranda said. "Just the family. No one else."

Faith looked doubtful.

"Irene doesn't want a lot of fuss, and certainly Andy doesn't. And they don't want to elope" (Faith looked shocked), "but they *do* want us there. Richard would have wanted that. I know he would. All the family together."

Faith began to cry, and Miranda took Dickon from her when he began to whimper his distress.

Paul looked on, helpless, and he muttered something about leaving. He had to repeat the suggestion before Faith heard him and automatically accepted his decision. And when he helped her to her feet, she sagged against him.

"I had always thought she was so strong," Will said, after they had left.

"She is," Miranda assured him. "But she devoted herself to bringing up her children, and now that they are gone, and the war is over, she doesn't have anything to do with her life. And I think that frightens her. It frightens *me*. I won't live my life that way, sacrificing everything . . ." She squared her shoulders, and there was determination in every line of her body.

Will gazed at her, obviously troubled. "I hate to see you change so much, Pet, putting youth and joy behind you. Just because you have lost Richard, you must not seal yourself away from the rest of the world. I don't mean that you have to marry again. I never did. I just mean that you shouldn't turn yourself into the sort of person who doesn't care or feel because it hurts too much."

She was stubborn in her denial. "No, I have Dickon. I have the family. I care about them. And you had the hotel, Papa. *I* will have the hotel, too." With growing conviction, she outlined her plans for the future.

Will shook his head. "It's too risky. If I were a young man again . . . But to think about mortgages on two hotels, with the war over and the possibility of another panic and hard times . . . We could lose everything. No, I'll mortgage the Stratford to give George and Tom a start, but then I'll sell it and retire."

She was still arguing with him when George and Emily returned from Brooklyn. George was willing to consider the idea, but Emily sided with Will. It was too risky; risky for all of them. Emily didn't offer her second objection: Miranda would certainly remarry.

Major Lorimer had already broken off his engagement to Caroline.

Chapter 43

Miranda had been sleeping poorly for weeks, one part of her mind always half alert to Richard, to Dickon, to her father, and tonight was no exception. But what wakened her past midnight was the sound of rapid footsteps and an unfamiliar stir in the lobby. And then she heard her father's muffled cough. Hastily she pulled on a robe and smoothed back her hair. Across the park there seemed to be some commotion in Printing House Square. Some new excitement about the war?

She opened her door and was surprised to see George at the end of the hall, talking in whispers to her father, both of them looking shocked.

"What is it?" A cold chill seized her. "Tom? Is it Tom?" Her voice rose, charged with emotion. "What happened?"

"No, Pet." Will reached out to soothe her. "It's not Tom. But the tragedy . . ." He choked over the words. It's President Lincoln."

George nodded his confirmation, looking grief-stricken. "He's been shot. He's dying. And the Secretary of State, Mr. Seward. He's been assassinated, too."

"Dear God!"

"Not so loud, Pet. You'll wake up the entire hotel."

"They've gone mad," George said. "If it's a Rebel plot, they've all gone mad. Lincoln, Seward, half the Cabinet . . ."

"What happened?" Miranda clutched at George, and her voice was rising again. "How did you find out?"

Another door opened, and Emily joined them.

"I heard something," Will explained. "I was awake, and I

540

knew there was something the matter. That kind of stir—I can always tell. I went down to the lobby to see."

"And I heard you," George said. "I was afraid you'd fall."

Will ignored that. "A man had just rushed in from across the park. It's on the telegraph from Washington—President Lincoln has been mortally wounded. He was at the theater tonight, and an actor shot him. Booth. Wilkes Booth, they think it was."

"Oh, no!" Emily was shocked. "How can that be? We met him once, didn't we, George? Cort knew him—Booth was one of those actors he knew in Washington."

George was doubtful.

Megan emerged from her room, looking anxious, and a sleepy Maureen trailed in her wake.

"But they can't have shot him," Maureen protested. "I thought the war was over."

"Yes," Miranda said heavily. "So did I. What more can they do to us?"

"What more can we do to *them*?" George said ominously. "Traitors. Even after they lay down their arms to surrender, they turn around to stab us again."

"We'll hang them," Maureen said, with the easy practicality of a child. "Just the way the song says: 'We'll hang Jeff Davis on a sour-apple tree!'"

"An eye for an eye, a tooth for a tooth." Will sighed. "I had hoped we were past all that."

"And that's not what Lincoln wanted," Miranda objected. "I remember what he said: 'With malice toward none, with charity—'"

"It's too late for that," George interrupted. "The country will never stand for that now. By God, *I* won't stand for it, either. Marty was right after all. They took up arms against us, and they deserve to perish by the sword now."

"His terrible swift sword," Maureen said, pleased with her knowledge. "That's from a song, too."

"Yes," Megan agreed, and she put an arm around her. "Too many songs. Too many easy phrases. 'When this cruel war is over . . .'" She looked at Miranda, and her eyes filled with tears. "Both of us, widowed, losing half our lives, and now the country . . ."

"Yes," Miranda completed her thought. "And now the country is in mourning, too."

They pounced on the first editions of all the New York newspapers, devouring the few paragraphs hastily added to an inside page. The news of the assassination had arrived too late to remake page one, but not too late to turn the column rules, those wide vertical bands of mourning that heralded tragedy.

Lincoln was still alive, but the wound was mortal. The dying President had been carried to a house across the street, where he was quickly surrounded by grieving members of the Cabinet. In an adjoining room Mrs. Lincoln wept with her son, Robert, hastily summoned from the Executive Mansion. Secretary of State Seward, attacked in his sickbed at home, his throat slashed, was believed to be dying, too. And so was his son, Frederick, who had rushed to his father's defense. Washington City was in an uproar, tension growing as rumors of conspiracy spread. A crowd gathered outside the rooming house where the mortally wounded President breathed his last, never recovering consciousness.

The news of his death set off shock waves of grief—and cries for vengeance.

It was too much to be borne. After four years of civil war, after all the burdens of the long years of sacrifice, after crushing defeats and hopes deferred and victory purchased at such a fearful cost, this final tragedy was incomprehensible.

Later editions of the newspapers made it clear that the assassin, an actor identified as John Wilkes Booth, had successfully made his escape, presumably with the aid of Southern sympathizers and traitors. It was obviously a vast conspiracy—the attack on Secretary Seward made that clear—and the Secretary of War, Mr. Stanton, organized a hunt for the murderers. There would be no mercy for any of them—and no mercy for the defeated Rebels suspected of offering aid and encouragement.

Throughout the North the people went into mourning, the week of rejoicing turned into bitter grief. Black streamers, black crepe, and flags at half staff, pictures of the martyred President, dense crowds in the street at spontaneous mass meetings, weeping, praying, singing hymns—one vast outpouring of emotion.

Easter Sunday. Never had there been such an Easter. The symbolism of the victory at Appomattox on Palm Sunday, the leader slain on Good Friday, the harrowing emotions of triumph and defeat, of death linked to lasting victory and slavery abolished forever. The fervor with which the Easter hymns were sung, all the words taking on new meaning.

> The strife is o'er, the battle done,
> The victory of life is won . . .

> Lord! by the stripes which wounded thee,
> From death's dread sting thy servants free . . .

> Loosed from Pharaoh's bitter yoke
> Jacob's sons and daughters . . .

> Love's redeeming work is done,
> Fought the fight, the battle won . . .

For the martyred President, instant deification. For the traitors who struck him down, eternal damnation. In the wave of hysteria that swept the country, the voices of moderation were drowned out, and passion overwhelmed all reason.

In New York, where all the buildings were draped in black, where the theaters closed and the churches filled, the giant pictures of the slain President stared out at signs that made a mockery of all he stood for:

> No More Compromise
> Death to the Rebels
> He Will Be Avenged

There were no signs at the Stratford, but the Lincoln portrait was draped in black, and mourning streamers replaced all the festive bunting. Private grief and public mourning merged into one.

Too much had happened too fast, and Miranda was still in a state of shock. George and Emily accompanied her to church on Easter Sunday, but she could not concentrate. Her mind wandered, back into the past, in this church, with Richard. Only four days ago his flag-draped coffin had rested here. Only two years ago she had walked down this aisle to become his bride. In this very pew, when she had first donned mourning for Jimmy, Richard had looked at her and smiled and told her she had changed, grown up . . . She tried to make sense of it all—the war, the victory, the death, Richard gone, and Jimmy and Damon . . . It was too much.

The sermon was incomprehensible, Christ and Lincoln fused as mysteriously as victory and sacrifice.

In the confusion of the present, Miranda caught an echo from the past. Once before there had been this emotional reaction—when the guns fired at Fort Sumter and all the world rallied around the flag, leaving her bewildered. The war had nothing to do with abolition, Richard assured her; they were fighting to preserve the Union. But somehow abolition had come out of it. Richard had been wrong. Everyone had been wrong. And now, when the President had been killed and the country was caught up in a new emotional frenzy, she was isolated again. Surely Abraham Lincoln would not have wanted this passion, this vindictiveness. It was all wrong. Everyone was wrong. Of course Marty would go off like a skyrocket, crying vengeance. And perhaps it was understandable that Uncle Paul, looking for some scapegoat after Richard's death, should thunder for reprisals. But to hear the same call for revenge from George and Emily, from John and Major Lorimer and Mr. Dawson and Lucy . . . Everyone but Papa, who had sighed and put his arm around her and said there had been too many deaths and he didn't want to mourn again. And she looked at him, gaunt and sad-eyed, and she blinked back her tears and prayed fervently that he be spared, that she would not soon be mourning him, too. She had been rocked by too many emotional storms, and Papa was her only solid anchor now.

That afternoon Major Lorimer called, but Miranda refused to see him.

He was understanding, Emily told her later, and he would return when she was no longer prostrated with grief. In the meantime, since he had hired a carriage and the day was balmy, perhaps George and Mrs. Chase and Polly and Georgie would accompany him on a drive . . .

Polly came back, chattering happily about Uncle Jack and the ride through the park and the two black horses who trotted so fast she could feel the wind in her hair. Emily smiled at her enthusiasm and couldn't refrain from commenting on the rare qualities of a man who was so devoted to little children.

Miranda only sighed, and she was frankly relieved when George and Emily returned to Washington two days later. Major Lorimer, perhaps taking their hint, left for Boston the same day. He had called once more, but only to deliver a note of sympathy and understanding—and a promise that he would come again.

In Washington the funeral for President Lincoln was scheduled for Wednesday, in the East Room of the White House. Afterward the body lay in state in the rotunda of the Capitol, and a vast throng filed past the catafalque, a steady stream of mourners for the rest of the day and the night and another day. And then the coffin was taken to the funeral train that was to bear the martyred President by a long, circuitous route to his final resting place in Springfield.

In New York there were elaborate preparations for the funeral procession and a great clamor to take part.

In the published order of march there would be a place for the Seventh Regiment, for city, county, state, and Federal officials, for clergy and the Chamber of Commerce, for Masonic and other orders, for temperance organizations, for trades, societies, and avocations, for the civic societies of Brooklyn, and for delegations from Washington. But oh, irony of ironies, the organizers of the procession refused to allow Negro groups any participation at all. It would be controversial, they said, and perhaps some of the others would withdraw. Better for the sake of peace and harmony that the dark-skinned race be understanding and still their objections. It would be unseemly to bring discord into this day of solemn mourning and dedication.

The wisdom of this exclusion was debated in the newspapers, and a few editorial voices were raised in protest. Behind the scenes the organizers were pressed to reconsider, but they were adamant: No Negroes.

Chapter·44

On the sunday after Easter, the day before the funeral train was scheduled to arrive in New York, Caroline and Mrs. Cantrell came to the Stratford to call on Miranda. Mrs. Cantrell was brisk and talkative, as always, but Caroline was silent and woebegone, and her eyes welled with tears whenever she looked at Miranda. The fact that she was mourning the loss of Major Lorimer rather than Major Schuyler hardly lessened her grief, and Miranda found herself cast in the role of comforter.

"I'm sorry, Caroline." Miranda was completely sincere. "I don't know what came over Jack. Perhaps just the emotion of the funeral that day . . ." She trailed off and looked to Mrs. Cantrell for support, but there was no agreement there.

"No, Miranda, I don't think we should spin such illusions for her. If Major Lorimer is so easily attracted to other girls, there is no reason to expect him to change, even if he does come back to Caroline one day. A man so unstable . . . A man like that will bring only heartbreak."

Miranda acknowledged the truth of that. "Perhaps you are right. It's better to know now, Caroline, not after you are married and there is no way out."

"I love him," Caroline said stubbornly. "I've loved him for three years. And I still wish . . ." Her voice trembled, and she couldn't go on.

"I don't know what to say." Miranda looked at her helplessly. "You may be sure, Caroline, that I'm not giving him any encouragement. I refused to see him twice before he went back to Boston, and I certainly won't answer his letters."

Caroline brushed away tears and didn't respond.

"There's Larry Blaine," Miranda said, trying to cheer her up, but Caroline continued to droop.

"I remember," Miranda went on, "the engagement party for Tom and Lucy. After Larry was so attentive to you, Jack seemed to be almost jealous. Didn't you think so?"

She appealed to Mrs. Cantrell, who smiled in agreement.

"Yes, dear. I noticed that, too."

Caroline looked doubtfully at her grandmother.

"You can't just sit home and cry." Miranda was decisive. "If I were you, I'd pay a little attention to Larry."

"And then Jack might come back?" Caroline clutched at the straw, then thought better of it. "But if I am not really interested in Larry," she looked puzzled, "is it even fair to see him?"

"I think he'd see you on any terms," Miranda assured her. "Besides, how do you know you're not interested if you won't even talk to him?"

"*You* won't talk to Jack," Caroline pointed out, reasonably enough.

"That's different," Miranda said. She wasn't quite sure how it was different, but it was. Perhaps because she didn't want a husband, and Caroline did.

"I don't know." Caroline's resistance faltered, leaving her vulnerable to persuasion.

"We'll call on Lucy," Mrs. Cantrell said firmly. "That is certainly proper, and if Larry should happen to be there . . . Well, we'll just see what happens. And now, Miranda, you must tell us about your father. I was hoping that he would be better, up and about by now."

"Yes," Miranda agreed. "I was hoping that, too. He takes a long nap every afternoon, just like Dickon, but they should both be waking up soon. I'll get the baby now, and I'm sure that by the time tea is served . . ."

After the visitors had left, Will smiled at Miranda as she settled down across from him on the sofa.

"Do you realize, Pet, that Mrs. Cantrell was here for more than two hours and didn't once ask me for a contribution to anything?"

"You sound disappointed."

His laughter was cut short by another spasm of coughing.

Miranda looked at him in alarm, but he reassured her and then changed the subject. "I was hoping to see John today."

"He'll be here for the funeral procession. And I think he has persuaded the whole family to come. Even Mrs. Robillard. After all, it's a historic occasion."

"Yes." Will sighed heavily. "We have had so many historic occasions, crowding in each other, overwhelming us." He studied his daughter, and the silence lengthened between them.

"Are you going to be all right, Pet? Truly all right? I've been thinking . . . You didn't ever have a real life with Richard at all. Just a few days now and then, hardly time to know each other."

She nodded sadly and turned away, refusing to cry again. This was the worst of it—they had never known each other. He had idolized her, tried to turn her into his dream. And the lost love she had wanted to give him was now so charged with regret that she was in danger of transforming him into the same kind of idol he had made of her. It was too hard to think about things like that. Dickon, she reminded herself. Papa. The new hotel. Mortgages and interest and bank loans.

Will sighed. Miranda was pushing him away again, refusing to let her heartbreak show, talking about money, stubbornly insistng on this wild idea of two hotels.

"I don't want to hear another word about it," he said with decision. "It's too risky, and I will not gamble away what I have spent a lifetime building. That is all there is to it."

"What would it take?" she persisted. "If I could raise a hundred thousand dollars . . ."

"Not enough." Will shook his head. "The furnishings in the public rooms alone . . . Oh, Miranda, don't worry about such things. Now," he smiled at her, "if you could raise a *million* dollars, you can come talk to me about hotels. But I have had enough for this evening, and if you won't talk about something else, I'll go back to my reading. All these tributes to Lincoln . . ."

"Yes, Papa." She sighed. A million dollars was clearly out of reach, even if she could find some way to borrow against her inheritance.

"And when the funeral train stopped in Baltimore," Will was saying, "the whole city was in tears. Did you read the *Times*, Miranda? Cort had a very moving account of what happened there. And in Philadelphia and Harrisburg, too. In

548

his letter, George said that Cort was going all the way to Springfield, all that long sad journey."

"Yes, I read the account in the *Times*," Miranda said, but she was off on another tangent. Cort had money. Lots of money. And property in New York. He and Warren had invested heavily in building lots on Fifth Avenue. And he knew and trusted George and Tom. Why couldn't he back the new hotel, while she and Papa kept the Stratford, free and clear? If Cort arrived with the funeral train, he might bring Susanne here to be with the family to see the procession, and she could talk to him . . .

It didn't happen quite like that. Cort was already in New York that Sunday evening, and he came directly to the Stratford. Will had retired early, and Miranda had gone down to the lobby, to the little office next to the reception desk. She was poring over the books, totaling the weekly receipts, making rapid calculations of future profits, drawing up optimistic balance sheets, covering the lined paper with long columns of figures.

A knock at the door interrupted her, and she was surprised to see Cort standing there, his face unreadable.

He had caught her unaware, and she said the first thing that popped into her head.

"Cort! I was just thinking about you . . . and your money."

She missed his startled reaction, her mind still focused on dollars and cents. She remembered enough of her manners to stand up to shake hands, but she rushed right on. "Now that you are so rich, how would you like to invest in a new hotel?"

He smiled and took her outstretched hand in both of his. "Miranda, my dear girl, you never cease to amaze me. Here I have come to call on you, searching for the proper words of sympathy, and the first thing you do is ask me for money."

She blushed and retreated behind the desk and motioned him to sit down. "I didn't mean to shock you, but—"

"You could never shock me."

She refused to acknowledge the interruption. "It's just that I have been going over these figures," she tapped the paper on the desk, "and I know that a new hotel would be a very good investment. And if someone has the capital, he can take advantage of a real opportunity. Don't you think so, Cort?"

She barely glanced at him, concentrating on the balance sheet in front of her. She had put a clamp on her emotions, and all she was interested in was business.

"I usually believe in taking advantage of opportunities," he said, and his voice was edged.

"Well, then," Miranda was brisk, deliberately ignoring any double meaning in his words, "are you interested? What can I say to convince you? You know that George will be an excellent manager, and with Tom to help him, it's sure to be a success. The city is growing so fast, and in a good location—"

"What about the Stratford? What would happen to it?"

"But that's the whole point, you see. Papa and I could manage it together. We wouldn't have to mortgage it or anything. And then life could go on just the way it always used to, and I wouldn't have to worry about anything. Just help Papa get better."

"And that would be enough for you?"

"Yes, it would." She was completely sincere, and for the first time she looked at him directly. She had convinced herself, and she was sure.

He held her eyes, probing for some emotional response. "You would not marry again?"

"Never!"

"It was as bad as all that?"

She colored under his searching gaze. "No, that's not what I mean. It's just . . ." She looked away, uncomfortable. "I don't want to go through all that again. Richard . . . He was such a good man, and he loved me so much, and it has been so hard since . . . I don't want to talk about it, Cort." She could never explain it to him. When she herself couldn't understand, how could she make him see? He had never liked Richard or admired all the fine self-sacrificing qualities that made him so noble. If only she had been more worthy . . .

Cort sighed. "Richard would have made you miserable, and you still don't see that, darling."

She flinched at the endearment and stared, unseeing, at the papers on the desk. "Don't talk about it, Cort. Don't talk about anything like that. It's too hard." And he had no right to press her for answers. She swallowed over the lump in her throat and went on with determination. "Now about the new hotel. Are you interested? Do you want to see some figures?"

"Why don't you invest yourself? Surely Richard left you well provided for."

"Yes, but it's all in trust. I can't touch the money. Unless . . . Is there some way I can borrow against the trust, do you think? Against my future income?"

"I'm no lawyer, but I doubt it. Richard certainly would have foreseen that possibility and guarded against it. He wouldn't have wanted your second husband to get his hands on your inheritance. But then he wouldn't have wanted you to marry again."

"Oh, but you're wrong!" Miranda sprang to Richard's defense. "It was his dying wish that I remarry and give Dickon a father, and the child he thought—" She broke off hastily, blushing again. "He was very unselfish, thinking only of me and the children. He didn't want them growing up here, at the Stratford. That is . . ." She trailed off, aware of what she had said.

"That is, you are now hell-bent to disobey his deathbed commands."

She sighed and twisted her rings and looked away. It wasn't fair of Cort to upset her this way.

"Ah, well. Let the honored dead rest in peace. 'The good is oft interred with their bones.' So, the noble Richard wanted you to remarry, and I understand there is an immediate candidate for your hand."

So Cort knew that already. She made a wry face and acknowledged he was right. "On the very day of the funeral. I didn't even realize . . ."

"Poor Jack Lorimer." Cort shook his head in mock pity. "I thought Emily had misread the situation, but I see she was right."

Naturally Emily would have told him. And had he come to see her just to discover whether the story was true? He had done that once before, in this very room, after Richard had proposed marriage. That's when she thought she was pregnant . . . She slammed the door on that scene and tried to think about the hotel, but Cort was gazing at her, stirring the memory of all those forbidden emotions that she had put away forever. He was married, she reminded herself, and Susanne was pregnant . . . The new hotel, she repeated silently, and the Stratford. She clung to the hope of a calm and peaceful life with no tears, no regrets.

"And Jack is buzzing around already," Cort went on. "His timing was always terrible. I used to tell him that. On the very day of the funeral . . . However," he smiled at her, "if

551

Jack had not been so precipitous, I would have waited much longer myself. A decent interval, as they say. But it is probably better to talk about it now, darling, to make plans for the future, our future, together."

She flinched as if he had struck her. "No! How can you say such things? How can you even think them when Susanne—"

"Poor Susanne. But I think she is beginning to realize . . . She has already told me that she wants the child—"

"The child. Yes. Oh, Cort, when you know she is pregnant, how can you even think—"

"Pregnant!" He stared at her in amazement. "What the hell are you talking about? Susanne isn't pregnant! It's impossible!"

"But Dany said . . . That is . . . When Susanne wasn't feeling well, and I heard Dany . . . It was the day of Richard's funeral, and I heard her say that Susanne was so happy about the baby, and I just assumed . . ."

"Dear God, what must you think of me? That I would force another child on her when the poor girl is dying?"

Miranda looked at him, uncomprehending. "Dying?"

Cort nodded. "Surely you must know how frail she is."

"Frail," Miranda agreed, "but won't she get better?"

"No." Cort was somber. "She is dying. Her heart . . . It could happen any time." He stood up, restless, and paced the office. "The doctors, the best doctors here and in Washington all agree. They say her heart was affected by the diphtheria." He cleared his throat before going on, and when he spoke again his voice was remote, filtered through a layer of recently acquired medical knowledge. "The disease often has that effect, I understand. They even have an imposing medical name for it: Toxic diphtheric myocarditis."

"But what does that mean? How do they know?"

He sighed. "They can tell when the hearbeat is irregular. Arrythmia. Everything has a name. Not a cure, but a name. She has fainted several times, too. The Adams-Stokes syndrome—loss of consciousness, with irregular pulse. Cerebral anemia. You see, I'm becoming quite the medical expert."

"But can't the doctors *do* something?"

"No. They're only good at terminology, preferably Latin or Greek. And each doctor has a different theory about what drugs she should take: calomel, Dover's powder, belladonna, iodide of mercury, chloride of lime . . . I don't believe any

552

of it. Except the call for absolute rest. And no excitement, of course." He paused and looked directly at Miranda. "Certainly she could never carry a child, even though she longs . . . It's impossible." He spoke with finality.

Miranda was still bewildered. "But, Cort, you said . . . Earlier you said that Susanne wants the child . . ."

He looked at her, puzzled for a moment, then remembered. "Deedee," he explained. "I was talking about Deedee. Susanne has already told me that she wants the child to be brought up by Dany and John. They love her and want her, and of course I will have no claim . . ." He trailed off. "I have no claim on anyone." He fastened his eyes on her and reached for her hand. "Only you, darling, and I would not have spoken so soon, but I don't want to lose you again."

"Please, Cort, don't say that." She turned away from him. "I don't want to hear you say that. Too much has happened, and the world has turned upside down, and I just want a little peace in my life. Now that the war is over . . ." Yes, much better to talk about the war, not all these painful emotions that made her feel so guilty. "You were right all along about the war, Cort. The very first day I met you, you were so sure it would be the worst of all possible solutions, and you were right."

He shrugged. "I take no pride in that. And in any case, you were right, too. Quoting Seward at me. The 'irrepressible conflict.' Those words that haunt us still." He sat down and looked away from her, seeing again the bodies and the battlefields, the crowded hospitals, the horrors of Salisbury. "Still, as wars go," he managed a wry smile, "this one had more reason than most. It restored the Union and abolished slavery. You can't say that much for most of the bloody battles of history. Though God knows what is going to happen now. Lincoln dead and all those vengeful little men with an excuse to ride triumphant."

"It's all wrong, isn't it, Cort?" It was such a satisfaction to know that he agreed. "President Lincoln would not have wanted all this thirst for revenge."

"I don't know if he could have stopped it, but the dear Lord knows he would have tried." Absently, he touched the mourning band on his coat sleeve. "The first time I heard him, when he gave the speech at Cooper Union—"

"I remember," Miranda said. "I even remember that I wasn't very much impressed."

"Five years ago you were very young," Cort smiled at her, "and you have changed. We have all changed. Lincoln, too. But the speech . . . It was reprinted last week, and I read it again. 'Let us have faith that right makes might . . .' That's the kind of faith that's going to be in short supply in Washington, I'm afraid. I don't think I could stay there to witness what will happen next. And in any case, I should be here, with Susanne. You do understand that, Miranda? I . . . I think I owe her something. Some kind of comfort in these last months."

"You don't owe me any explanations, Cort. She is your wife, and I have no right—"

"Don't talk nonsense. I love you, and you love me, and we belong together. Don't deny it, Miranda. Don't keep denying it to yourself. We will have to wait, and wait in silence, and that will be terribly hard. But you must know that I will come for you, and I want you to understand . . . It's the same kind of loyalty you had to Richard, darling, even when you didn't love him."

"But I—"

"No, hear me out. You didn't love him. How could you? He didn't even know you. Not the real you. And he would have broken your heart, and your spirit, if you had let him. I don't know if I could have stood by to watch it happen."

"He loved me," Miranda said stubbornly. "He was brave and honorable and self-sacrificing, and I was never good enough for him."

"Rubbish! Did he tell you that?"

"No, of course not. He thought I was some kind of angel who—"

"And that's ridiculous, too. Wake up, darling. I know you better than that. You know yourself better than that. You have a mind and a body and a spirit, a whole life to live, a joy to share. You would never have been happy with him. And now that he is gone, you will not hide yourself away, living on shriveled dreams and old memories, a willing prisoner of the past. Not while I am here to stop it."

"But Susanne—"

"I will do what I can for her. I think she will be happier staying on with the family—Deedee, her mother, her sister. And it will be better for the little girl, too, not to have her life disrupted again. John and Dany already treat her like their own child, and now that Dany . . . It's still a secret, I think, but Susanne wrote to me. Dany wants to be absolutely sure before she tells anyone else—she and John have been disappointed before."

"So that's what she meant! Dany is going to have a baby!" It made sense now, that fragment of conversation overheard at the funeral. "And she said John was worried. Of course! Oh, I'm glad you told me, Cort."

"Don't breathe a word to anyone else."

"I won't. Not even to Papa."

"And not a word about us, either."

"But I haven't said yes, Cort. And you and Susanne . . ."

"We will work it out when I come back from Springfield. I'm resigning from the *Times*, and I'll finish my book, and then we'll just have to see what the future holds." His eyes locked on hers again. "We will be together, darling. You know we will."

"But the hotel, Cort, and Papa, and Dickon . . ."

He smiled at her. "You insist on holding me up for an investment in that new hotel. All right, darling, if that is your price. No, don't show me the figures now—I trust you. And I trust George and Tom to make a go of it. We'll all have to sit down together and see what it will cost, how best to raise the money, what kind of mortgage . . . And if you want to hang on to the Stratford . . . Perhaps that would be a good idea. You treasure your independence, and I don't know how long we will have to wait. What else? Your father. Surely. he wants to see you happy. That's the best medicine in the world for anyone. Darling . . ." He pulled her into his arms to kiss her, but she resisted him. "Now what?" He drew back to look at her. "I can't answer *every* question, but I try."

"Please, Cort. It's all too fast. There's Dickon."

"He needs a father. Richard said so himself. And the fact that you are pregnant—"

"But I—"

"All my wives have children by other men." He grinned at her. "I think it must be some great cosmic joke, as if the Almighty had chosen to make an example of me." He smoothed her puckered frown and kissed her forehead. "Just don't make a habit of it, darling. The *next* child will look like me."

She forced a smile. "But I'm *not* pregnant, Cort. Richard believed that I was, but . . . And when he was dying, I couldn't bring myself to tell him the truth." Her eyes filled with tears, remembering. "Even at the end I was deceiving him."

"Even at the end you were making him happy," Cort corrected her. "At whatever cost to yourself."

She shook her head, unconvinced. "You are always so sure of yourself, Cort. But I need time to think things through, and if I choose to stay at the Stratford without you—"

He cut off her protests, tracing the outline of her lips, touching her throat to feel the pulse throbbing there.

She looked at him, startled, and tried to break away. "That's not fair, Cort. I am trying to think clearly, and you know you can always mix me up when you . . . If you are going back to Susanne, and if you think we must be silent about . . . about any future plans, then I don't want you to touch me or hold me or kiss me. And we must not see each other alone, or—"

"Darling, I don't want to make it hard for you. I just want you to say yes and kiss me and tell me you will wait."

She still looked troubled.

"We'll take it in simple stages," he assured her solemnly. "Promise me you won't marry Jack Lorimer or anyone else."

"That's easy, Cort." She smiled at him. "I promise. But that doesn't mean—"

"And you will wait for me."

"Well, I suppose if I am not marrying anyone else, you could say that I am waiting, but I—"

"And you will marry me, Miranda." He dropped his arms and stepped away from her, but his eyes held hers. "You love me. The color is rising in your cheeks, and there is a roaring in your ears, and that pulse is beating in your throat, and I'm not even touching you. You want me, darling. You know you want me—as much as I want you. All your joy and passion and spirit." His voice was an insistent caress, breaking down all her defenses. "All of you. Not some idealized dream. Alive and astonished and always a little too independent. And stubborn and determined and honest. And loving me, Miranda, always loving me."

It was true. It would be foolish to deny it. He had always been able to see right through her, right through to her heart. Of course she would wait for him and marry him and love him and fight with him and laugh and cry and work and dream and make a life together.

But she needed time. Richard, she thought, and she groped

for some way to reconcile the pain of his death with the future Cort was opening for her. Richard . . . If only she had really known him. He had wanted her love, and the love of their children. And there was only Dickon now. She blinked back her tears.

The boy would grow up loving his father, she resolved. Surely she could do that much for Richard now. All those shining qualities: honor, courage, strength, devotion. That was his real legacy. That's how she would remember him.

She swallowed hard, choking down the emotions of the past.

Cort was waiting, supremely confident of her decision, eager to welcome her into the warmth of his embrace.

Perversely, she retreated a step and picked up the sheet of figures she had been working on. It was important to assert herself now, at the beginning. This was going to be a different kind of marriage.

"About the hotel, Cort." She cocked her head, ready for the challenge. "Just how much money would you like to invest?"

Epilogue

MONDAY DAWNED, CLEAR and balmy, and all New York prepared for the farewell tribute to President Lincoln.

The funeral train, heavy with a nation's grief, was progressing slowly through the countryside, cutting a path through the crowds of sorrowing men and women and children who lined the tracks.

Mrs. Lincoln was not on board. She had remained in seclusion in Washington while the train carried its sad burden on the slow and painful journey all the way to Springfield. A delegation of government officials, secretaries, staff, friends made the long pilgrimage, retracing the route of Abraham Lincoln on the way to his first inauguration.

In Jersey City the train ground to a halt, and with due formality the President's coffin was transferred to the ferry. Across the river in New York the Seventh Regiment provided an honor guard as the coffin was transferred to a waiting hearse. And then, to the dull beat of the dead march, the body was borne to City Hall to lie in state.

Crowds lined the streets and the park, and it was just before noon when six soldiers carried the heavy mahogany coffin in the catafalque and placed on it a floral cross, all to the swelling music of the Pilgrim's Chorus from *Tannhauser*. An honor guard stood by as the upper third of the coffin was opened to reveal the face of the martyred President. Photographs were taken and sketches made, and it was noted that the face was much sunken and there was marked discoloration.

Long lines formed to view the body, all that day and night and into the following morning, an endless procession of mourners, weeping and praying, wanting one last glimpse of the fallen leader. About five o'clock in the morning the embalmer came again to repair some of the ravages effected by time and exposure to the dust and grime of the city. With a handkerchief he brushed the face, which had progressively darkened, arranged the slackening jaw, cleaned the collar and coat, dusted the neckcloth.

And still the mourners came, in lines that stretched ever longer as the morning wore on. There was no way to admit them all, and the timetable was rigid. A city was waiting. A nation was waiting. The embalmer and the undertaker returned to close the coffin, and promptly at noon the ceremony began.

From the library windows of the Stratford, the family watched as the troops presented arms and the drums rolled. Every head was bared as the pallbearers, with slow and careful steps, transferred the coffin to the special funeral car.

Miranda wiped tears from her eyes and accepted the field glasses from Papa. The coffin rested on a large platform covered in black broadcloth, trimmed with silver lace and fringe. Above it was a pavilion, a temple of liberty with a golden dome, flags draping the pillars, mourning plumes nodding in the breeze. The car was drawn by sixteen gray horses, shrouded in black, each horse led by a Negro groom.

Irene Schuyler was peering at them through the telescope. "So they *are* allowing Negroes," she said, puzzled. "I thought the city council wouldn't permit it."

"They're only servants." Ann dismissed them and reclaimed the telescope. "That doesn't count."

"No," Susanne corrected her. "There will be others marching, too. Cort told me. The Secretary of War, Mr. Stanton, sent a telegram. Negroes marched in Washington, and he said they must be allowed in the procession in New York, too."

"Quite right," Paul Schuyler agreed. "The organizers here had to back down. The problem is that they stirred up so much fuss in the first place that now the crowd is likely to get out of hand when they see that colored groups are participating, too."

Mrs. Cantrell shook her head. "I pray you are wrong. The children at the orphanage would never understand."

The orphanage, Miranda repeated to herself. Why, I can go back there now! I gave it up only because Richard was so insistent. He never wanted to allow . . . He loved me, she reminded herself, and he thought he was protecting me. But now that he is dead . . . She sighed. It would take a long time to come to terms with the past.

Beside her, Susanne sat down abruptly. "I am just feeling a little faint," she apologized, "but I'll be all right." She accepted Dany's smelling salts and forced a smile. "Cort didn't think I should come today, but I insisted. Why, by the time he returns from Springfield, I'll be *much* better." Deedee crawled into her lap, and Susanne hugged the child for reassurance. "Such a big girl you are getting to be."

Dany looked at her sister doubtfully. "If you think that Deedee is too heavy to hold . . ."

"Don't treat me like an invalid," Susanne protested. "I'm getting well. That's why I'm here today—to prove that to Cort. This morning he said he'd stay in Brooklyn, not make the trip to Springfield at all, just because he was worried about me. I couldn't let him do that, miss his last assignment."

"Of course not, dear." Dany swallowed hard, and John moved close enough to put his arm around her.

They know, Miranda realized. They both know. And Susanne, too. Why, she has the same kind of courage that a soldier has. Just like Jimmy. And Damon. And Richard. Of course Cort would want to stand by her, comfort her . . . In joy and in sorrow, in sickness and in health . . .

Through a blur of tears Miranda looked again across the park, and faintly she could hear the music from the Seventh Regiment band. The funeral cortege was beginning its slow progress through the densely packed streets.

The whole city had turned out for this final farewell, and photographs show the throngs that packed the streets and sidewalks, the windows and balconies and fire escapes and rooftops, even the trees and the lampposts. At Union Square, a six-year-old child witnessed history passing by, and a strangely prescient photograph shows the young Theodore Roosevelt solemnly watching the end of an era.

The long, slow procession extended for miles—soldiers, sailors, marines, bands; the dignitaries and officials and clergy; all the scheduled participants who had clamored for a place of honor in this last tribute to the martyred President.

At the very end, cordoned off by a protective line of police, a small contingent of Negroes marched together. After the controversy surrounding their taking part, it was almost a surprise that the crowds were warm in welcoming them.

The liberal newspapers expressed satisfaction—surely it showed that hatred had been put aside and reason had triumphed. The hasty compromise that permitted this segregated participation was a curiously flawed victory, but few seemed to be aware of that.

The procession ended at the Hudson River Railroad Depot, where the funeral train, its muffled bell tolling, was waiting to depart. New York had said good-by. With a final ruffle of drums, the pomp and ceremony had been completed.

Abraham Lincoln was going home.

ABOUT THE AUTHOR

MARIE R. RENO, who came to New York
by way of Pennsylvania and Illinois, has
been a magazine, book-club, and paper-
back editor. Her first novel, FINAL
PROOF, was published in 1976 and was
nominated for an "Edgar" Award by the
Mystery Writers of America. She is working on her next novel.